MW01140280

REBELLION

THE COMPLETE TRILOGY

M.R. FORBES

Published by Quirky Algorithms
Seattle, Washington

This novel is a work of fiction and a product of the author's imagination.
Any resemblance to actual persons or events is purely coincidental.

Cover illustration by Tom Edwards

1. MAN OF WAR

[1]

"SLIPSTREAM RETURN PATH IS SET AND LOCKED. REACTOR online. Realspace engines online. QPG primed and ready."

Captain Gabriel St. Martin leaned back in the seat of his starfighter, closing his eyes and putting his hand around the crucifix his father had given him when he was three years old. He remembered his mother at that moment, the same way he did every time he prepared for a recon mission to Earth.

A mission that would take him sideways into the jaws of the enemy, with the odds of making it through somewhere around fifty-fifty.

Gabriel had never met his biological mother. She had been dead for nearly fifty years. She was dead twenty years before he had even been born. A casualty of the invasion of Earth, when the aliens they called the Dread had arrived in their terrible black ships, overpowering all of humankind's defenses, slaughtering billions, and swiftly seizing absolute control.

He remembered her now in pictures and videos, a limited history of a woman both young and beautiful, happy and carefree with the love of her life, then Captain Theodore St. Martin, a pilot in the

United States Space Force. Things had been so simple then. So easy. The United States was only one of the countries reaching for the stars with the help of new technological breakthroughs and shared initiatives.

At the time, it had seemed unfortunate that the only way to get funding for that reach was to funnel it through the military. To build machines of war in a limitless expanse where there was enough territory for anyone who wanted it. According to his father, there had been numerous arguments across the House and Congress about how and where to fund the new space race; the race that would determine the future of every nation involved.

Nobody had known how all of those arguments would be wasted.

Nobody had expected there was something else out there.

Nobody had guessed they wouldn't be friendly.

Once, it had been fun to create stories about hostile aliens. They were exciting and adventurous, and made for heroes that children could look up to. Besides, most philosophers, scientists, and think-tankers had tended to believe that any race that managed to reach the level of technological achievement needed to make a starship and access the slipstream would have evolved beyond such uncivilized, wanton destruction.

Gabriel wished the smartest men in the room had been right. If they had, he wouldn't be about to take a ride through Hell.

"Everything checks out," he said through the ship's comm. "Wish me luck, 'Randa." He lifted the crucifix to his lips, kissed it, and then dropped it back under his flight suit.

Senior Spaceman Miranda Locke laughed, the soft tone of it crackling in his ears. She was nowhere near as pretty as her voice suggested. It didn't matter. She was a good person and an even better friend. "Like you've ever needed luck. Firing launcher in five, four, three..."

Gabriel reached out and took hold of the main control stick of the small starfighter. The station's rail launcher would accelerate him out into space at over 5,000 meters per second, hurling the ship into the calculated inception point of the slipstream without any manual intervention.

There was usually no need for a starfighter pilot to get themselves into slipspace.

The pilot was for after the vehicle came out.

"Two, one... Go!"

Gabriel was pressed back in his seat, the station's artificial gravity extending its reach into the launch tube. His teeth clenched as the inertial dampeners fought against the sudden and intense g-forces. He could feel the crucifix pressing into his chest, reminding him of his mother and her lost dreams even as he hurtled toward space. He could see the metal walls and lights passing him as an increasing blur, along with the rapidly approaching darkness of the universe beyond.

He always asked for luck when he made a run. As the most successful recon pilot in the New Earth Alliance Space Force, he always wondered if the next time out would be his last.

He had seen so many pilots come and go. More than a few had never returned from their first mission. This would be number sixty-seven for him. He had earned the right to retire and spend the rest of his days on Alpha Settlement seventeen missions ago. He could meet someone, start a family, and be given all of the comforts the closest thing humankind had to a war hero could want.

The thought had never crossed his mind. Retirement wasn't in his family's lexicon. Neither was the concept of quitting. Like his father, General Theodore St. Martin, the Old Gator, was fond of saying: "Your mother gave her last breath to save the lives of thousands, including you and me. We ain't never going to let that be for nothing. We'll find a way to beat those couillons off our planet. They think we ain't good for nothing? Heh. I'll tell you what, son, I ain't never gonna die until they're gone, and you can't either."

Of course, that had been before the accident. Before his father had lost the use of his legs. Before he had become addicted to medicine that sucked away both his pain and his mind.

General St. Martin's days as a productive member of society were done, and the Dread continued to hold the Earth. His old man was still alive, though. Still as good as his word.

It was up to Gabriel to do his part, and that meant making run after run until his luck ran out.

[2]

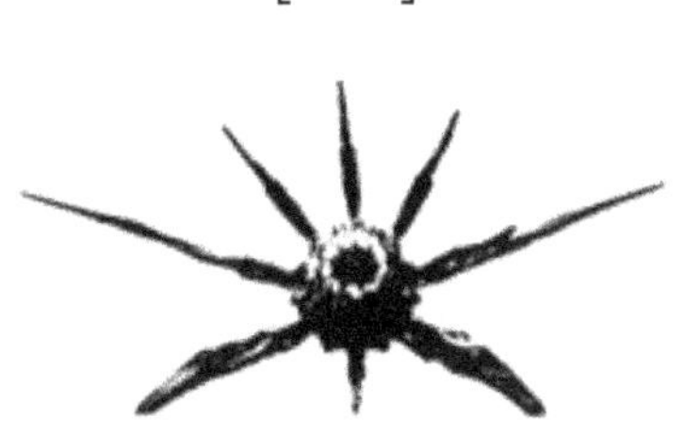

Gabriel's starfighter shuddered as the onboard computer triggered the quantum phase generator. Gabriel looked to the left when it did, watching as the pock-marked, triangular wings of his craft began to blur.

The QPG was the most advanced piece of tech on the ship. It was also something he barely understood. Even after ten years as a recon pilot, it still seemed more like black magic than actual science.

From what he understood, the QPG worked by creating a shift in the quantum properties of the spacecraft's specially engineered and painted surface, a process called phasing. This process enabled the vehicle access to the strange and barely understood currents of time and space that ran both above and below what was now called real-space. These currents, known as slipstreams, weren't controllable, but they were measurable. The measurements allowed calculations, which in turn allowed humankind to take advantage of them. By phasing into a slipstream, a starship could be carried from one part of the universe to another at faster than light speeds without any of the unwanted time dilation side effects, without having to worry about crashing into some other celestial body, and without the possibility of being attacked.

In other words, the slipstream was a free ride from one part of the universe to another, at speeds that averaged out to between forty and sixty thousand times the speed of light. For Gabriel, it meant that the trip from the New Earth Alliance orbital station in the Calawan system back to Earth would take somewhere in the range of five to ten hours.

That was one of the biggest downsides to slipstreams. The currents were just that, rippling waves of time and space distortions whose relative strength or weakness had a very real effect on travel. At the distance between Calawan and Earth, this variance wasn't a problem. It was; however, a remaining limit on humankind's ability to explore more of the universe. There was always talk within the Alliance of abandoning the planet and finding a new, more suitable home further out amidst the stars. In fact, it was what the colony ship they had escaped on had been designed to do. One problem with that idea was that trying to ride a slipstream in distances greater than a few hundred light years made logistics a challenge.

The other problem was the simple fact that not everyone on Earth was dead, and not everyone who had escaped was of a mind to leave them behind. Theodore St. Martin had been one of the most vocal supporters for remaining in Calawan, and his position as the man who had piloted the only ship to escape during the evacuation gave everyone cause to listen to him.

A tone from the cockpit dashboard signaled to Gabriel that the phase was complete, and the slipstream had been successfully joined. Not that he needed the computer to tell him that. The entire universe changed once a craft entered slipspace, the myriad stars fading away and leaving the view as a gigantic, blank, black canvas just waiting for God to come along and start painting again.

Gabriel tapped a few commands out on the touchscreen beneath his right hand. Then he reached up and lowered the secondary visor on his flight helmet, covering his view with an already running virtual reality simulation, lest he risk succumbing to what doctors had termed 'the slips,' caused by staring out into the void for an extended period of time. It was one of his favorite sims. A lifestream recording he had made seven years ago of himself and his fiancee, Jessica, having dinner. She had been a pilot, too. Everyone had told him not to get involved with another soldier like him. Everyone had warned him about the dangers of getting attached.

He had been young and stubborn. He had already survived twelve missions by then, and at the time he had believed that only the fools died young.

He knew better now. Jessica was anything but a fool, and it hadn't saved her in the end. She had gone on a run the day after the recording was made.

She had never come back.

He didn't watch the lifestream to depress himself, or to ruminate, or to fill himself with regret. He watched it when he was feeling weak. When he was losing hope. When he had the sinking notion that he wasn't coming back this time. He watched it to remember the sacrifices that had been made and to reinforce his belief in the value of what he was doing.

After all, if he went on the mission and survived, it meant that someone else wasn't taking his place. It meant that someone else wasn't dying.

Of course, the part where they danced against the backdrop of an Ursae Majoris solar flare always brought him to tears. She had been so beautiful, so talented, so filled with joy and life and hope for the future. They had been a perfect match. Maybe too perfect in a time as dangerous as theirs.

Hope for the future. That was what being a recon pilot was all about. It was the reason Gabriel risked his life to go back there again and again, making daring runs across the atmosphere for the smallest possibility of picking up any little bit of intel the planet-side resistance could provide, even when most of the time they didn't transmit at all.

And how could he ever give up that hope when there were still people alive on Earth doing their damnedest to fight back?

[3]

"Move it, move it. Let's go people. We don't want to be the last squad on Earth to be gunned down by those alien bastards."

Major Donovan Peters waved his arm in a furious windmill, motivating the rest of the men and women behind him, twenty in all, to surge forward across a dangerous chasm of twisted steel, cracked concrete, and shattered glass.

It was a warm evening. Too warm, as far as Donovan was concerned. And too dry. The ash and dust were hanging heavy in the evening air, picked up and left there by heavy winds earlier in the morning.

It was lousy weather for a transmission mission, or t-vault, as it was more commonly known. Green cadets liked to have fun saying "transmission mission" as many times as they could as fast as they could before they tripped up.

They stopped right after going on their first one.

Donovan wasn't really sure why they even bothered anymore. There had been nothing new to transmit in months.

Major Donovan Peters. He had been promoted two months earlier, rising to Major not because he was especially suited to the position but because he had managed to survive. Rank these days didn't mean anything close to what it had when the countries that sprinkled the Earth maintained standing militaries. It was chain-of-command, sure, based on the United States structure since it originated with General Alan Parker, the man who had first organized the survivors into a unified resistance. Back then, they had tried to follow the military guidelines, and for a while they had even managed to make something they liked to call progress in their guerrilla war against the alien invaders.

Back then. This was now, and now the promotions came as people died. There was no other system left to it.

And people had died. Nearly half of their forces in the last year alone. Donovan had no idea why, but the Dread had come to the decision that they were finished playing games with the remaining free humans, and they were going to end the resistance once and for all. He had heard the reports from the other militias around the globe, and they were all the same. The Dread were intent on wiping them out and ending the war once and for all.

"Sweep left," Donovan said, keeping his voice low and tight and guiding the squad with his hands.

They ran together out amidst the shattered buildings of what had once been Mexico City, Mexico, turning left and heading through a break in the debris. They were clothed in simple uniforms, dark green and roughly woven by hand, damp after a quick dump of water. Their faces were coated with a light orange clay, as were the back of their hands and bare feet, whose hardened soles beat down on the broken remains without being pierced. Boots were hard to come by and hard to maintain, and runners needed to be nimble without the distraction of a shoelace coming untied, or an old sole coming loose.

Donovan scanned the field ahead of them, his eyes picking over the charred city. He was only twenty-three years old. He had been born to this life, as had his mother. His grandfather had been in Los Angeles when they had come, only a child himself at the time. He had told the story in more personal detail than any video could show.

Not that he hadn't seen the videos of the first attack as well. All of them had. It was an important part of their upbringing, a remembrance of why they lived the way they did, and why they fought.

As he searched for a break that would lead them north to the building he had picked out for the needle, he could picture the massive plasma flume pouring from the sky, superheating the air around it, vaporizing millions and turning Mexico City into this. He shuddered slightly before regaining himself and motioning the team ahead.

He was the oldest of the group of twenty charging through the wreckage. Other than worn rifles, they were carrying only the equipment that would enable the needle to make the transmission. He didn't know what the message they carried was. He never did. General Rodriguez never briefed the t-vault team on the contents.

Donovan waved the team to the right, around an old barricade of burned out cars that had probably been constructed thirty years earlier. He had once thought it strange that the surrounding jungle had never encroached on the abandoned urban center and that everything stayed so well preserved despite the passage of years. Their Chief Science Officer, Carlson, had told him it was because of the nature of the Dread's plasma weapons. They had rendered the earth infertile, unable to sustain plant life wherever the flumes had scorched.

They were getting closer to the old skyscraper, once fifty or sixty stories tall but reduced in the attacks to fifteen or so. They needed to get the needle up over the terrain to ensure it would transmit with a good spread, making it easier for the passing starfighter to capture the message.

His Lieutenant, Renata Diaz, suddenly raised a closed fist. Within a heartbeat, Donovan and the rest of the squad were down behind whatever cover they could find.

Donovan crouched behind the barricade, pressing his body close against it and forcing his breathing to slow. The ability to control fear and panic was one of the most important for a t-vaulter, as the alien's scanners were able to not only sense heat, but to pick up the rhythm of a rapid heartbeat. It took a lot of practice to become adept at staying calm in such dire circumstances.

His eyes stayed forward, focused on Diaz. She had been the first to put eyes on the enemy scout, so it was her job to track it. It was a dangerous role, as the scout would notice all but the smallest of motions. It was hard to watch something without moving. Her head turned slowly, deliberately, her eyes locked onto the craft.

Donovan didn't need to see it. He had seen too many of them already. The scouts were relatively small and oblong, their undersides bristling with sensor needles. They were one of the few things the aliens used that wasn't covered in the black, ridged armor that protected them so well.

He counted the seconds in his head. By the time he reached sixty, the scout had passed over them and continued, sweeping through the empty city. The Dread knew that they were out here somewhere. They had been searching for the fifth iteration of the Mexico rebel home base for nearly fifteen years without success.

Diaz reached the second sixty at the same time he did. She lowered her raised fist, and the team got back on their feet and into formation.

"Damn close," Donovan said. "Let's try to open our eyes next time."

"Screw you, Major," Diaz said, glancing back at him with a smile.

"Is that an invitation?"

"In your dreams."

He put his finger to his lips. She gave him a different finger.

"In my dreams, or yours?" he asked, smiling. He knew where he stood with Diaz. She was pretty, but she was also his best friend's sister. The banter was a tension release. Nothing more.

Donovan scanned the sky, double-checking for any more of the scouts. When he didn't spot any, he waved his team forward again.

"Let's keep it going, soldiers. Who wants to live forever, anyway?"

[4]

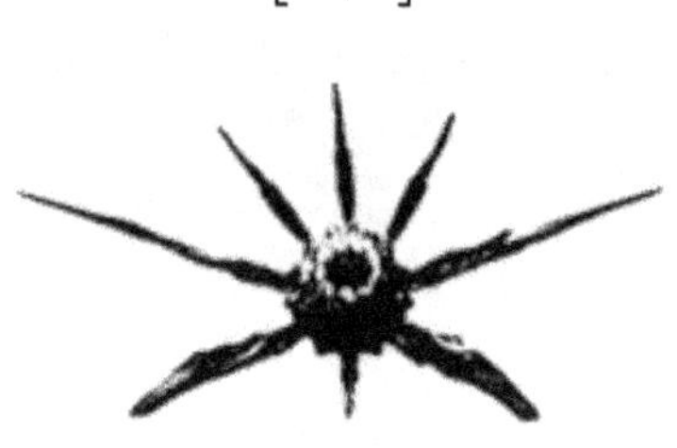

The squad reached the top of the building, picking their way up an emergency stairwell and then over a pile of rubble to get there. As soon as they had moved into position, each member of the t-vault team unloaded their cargo and hooked it up with practiced precision. Their only light came from the nearly vanished sun and the rising stars, giving them the barest illumination. They quickly snapped together battery packs, signal amplifiers, trackers, and finally the twenty-foot tall transmission needle that would send the message out.

Donovan crouched next to the needle, pulling a dark green home-spun bag from his back and untying the top. A small box sat inside, and he lifted it out and placed it next to the needle. Then he went back into the bag to remove a wire, which he connected to both the box and the whip.

"How long until the flyby?" Corporal George Cameron asked. He was the youngest of the group, fourteen years old. This was only his second time out.

Donovan put his hand on his wrist, feeling the time on a braille watch. They didn't dare risk using anything that emitted light out here. Once the needle was up, the only things they had to protect themselves were darkness, dampness, and stillness.

"Not too long now if the slipstream calculations were right," Donovan said.

He didn't know exactly how the ground force managed to coordinate with the space force. He knew there was something to slipstream patterns that made certain days and times more likely than others. That wasn't to say they hadn't crossed signals in the years since they started the information dumps, and he knew there were plenty of times that the space forces had passed by the Earth and his team had nothing to send. In fact, this was the first message he had delivered in nearly six months.

"Everything is online," Diaz said, running her fingers along a flat board on the ground in front of her.

"Ears are open?" Donovan asked, looking over to Private Gabriella Sanchez.

She was wearing a pair of headphones, and would be listening for the signal from the passing ship that it was receiving. It came in as a minor blip, a tiny anomaly in the normal static of celestial noise that took keen attention and hearing to catch.

She put her thumbs up to signal she was monitoring.

Donovan tapped the ground with his hand, signaling the rest of the team to spread out and watch for the enemy. It was the other reason t-vaulters went barefoot. Once the light was completely gone they would use vibration to communicate.

Donovan took a seat next to Sanchez, putting his back against the remains of a wall and tucking in his legs. There wasn't much to do once the needle was up and active, at least not until the package had been picked up and it was time to go home, or until they were spotted and they had to run.

Except they wouldn't be running this time. The squad didn't know it, but he had been ordered to hold position and get the transmission off no matter what. According to the Colonel, this was the most important message they had sent in nearly a dozen years. It was a message that was deemed worth the lives of the twenty men and women gathered in the burned out husk of a skyscraper, sitting in darkness and listening to the sky.

Donovan wasn't afraid of those orders. He was honored to be the one to take on the mission, and he knew his squad would be honored, too. Why hadn't he told them? Honor or not, knowing they had no options would get into their heads and change their approach. He needed them in top shape, as precise as always.

He was sitting in the same spot for close to an hour when Diaz slid down next to him, careful not to make any sounds that would distract Sanchez. She pushed her shoulder against him, smiling when he looked at her.

"Nice night," she mouthed.

"It's too hot," he replied.

Mexico had always been too hot for him, even though he had spent his entire adult life with the resistance here. He still had nightmares about the days spent on the run, when the Dread had discovered the Los Angeles base. He remembered holding his mother's hand, the look of fear in her eyes, along with the anger that burned there. He remembered the heat of the explosions behind them and the screams of the dying. He remembered his fear of the monsters that hunted them, large and black and spitting fury. That fear had transformed into anger as he had aged and learned that they weren't monsters at all. They breathed, they bled. They lived and died.

He wanted nothing more than to kill them. All of them.

"Are you okay?" Diaz asked.

Donovan hadn't realized he'd sank into those memories again. He blinked a few times to clear his head before nodding.

"Memories," he said.

Everyone had them. There wasn't a free human alive that couldn't relate to loss or death or destruction. It didn't matter that the invasion had happened three generations earlier. The stories lived on; the videos and images lived on, the resistance lived on. In a lot of ways, humankind had grown strong in their failure and their weakness. That they were still fighting was a testament to that.

"Matteo's birthday is next week," Diaz said. "Did you get him anything?"

Donovan shook his head. "I tried to carve a baseball bat from an old tree branch. I spent three weeks on it. Maybe I'll tell him it's a wizard's staff instead."

Diaz shook, laughing silently. "He hates that fantasy stuff."

"I know."

"Hey, do you think Gibbons likes me?"

Donovan glanced over at her, and then looked out across the darkness for the Corporal. He was crouched at the edge of the wall, peering out into the night and watching for the enemy. He was one of the biggest men in the squad, over six feet tall and heavy with muscle even though he was only eighteen. The same age as Diaz.

"You like Gibbons?" he said.

She shrugged. "He's kind of cute, in a brutish way."

"It's not like there's a lot to choose from, is there?" Donovan asked.

She stuck her tongue out at him. "He's not that bad."

"He's a good soldier. And yes, I think he likes you."

Sanchez reached out and tapped Donovan on the arm, giving him a thumbs up.

The messenger had arrived.

He tapped a code into the ground to alert the others. They tapped their feet back in return, acknowledging the message. Diaz worked the control board, sending more power from the fuel cell to the needle to increase the signal output.

Donovan felt his watch. The pilot was later than expected but within the calculated time. He had no idea how the scientists were able to track the slipstreams so well, but he was glad they were. The less time they had to sit out here-

The thought was interrupted as a flash lit the sky and Gibbons fell backward, a smoking hole in his chest that cast an eerie light on the rest of the squad.

They had been spotted.

[5]

A soft vibration against Gabriel's arm woke him from his sleep. He evacuated into the tube connected to his flight suit, and then opened his mouth and found the smaller tube that would allow him to drink. His throat was always parched after sleeping in the cockpit, his limbs always stiff. He tapped his control pad a few times, and the vibrations spread to the rest of his appendages, getting the blood flowing again.

He checked his mission clock. The currents were slow today. Eleven hours.

He was almost there.

He tapped the control pad again while clearing his throat.

"Captain Gabriel St. Martin mission recording sixty-eight. Successful join with the slipstream. Time to arrival, eleven hours fourteen minutes. Preparing for departure. Engines online. Weapons system-" He paused to turn it on. Not that it mattered. Everyone knew they had nothing that could pierce the armor of the Dread defenses. "Weapons system active. All systems nominal."

The recording was standard operating procedure. From now until he re-entered the slipstream, everything he did would be saved for review upon his return to Calawan.

He leaned forward and flipped a few switches on the dashboard. A small screen lit up in front of him, giving him a map of the solar system. The stream would drop him near Earth's moon. It was dangerously close, but they were under orders to conserve fuel whenever possible. While the stations had hydrogen converters, the growing population and expansion of the colony required that more and more of it be diverted to keeping people alive. Gabriel could only imagine if Theodore were still lucid. He could picture his father storming into a council meeting and cursing up a storm about chopping the dicks off the resistance so that Joe and Mary Scientist could make another mouth to feed.

Not that they didn't want mouths to feed. The remains of free human civilization was in a constant, delicate balance. Too few heads and their life support systems wouldn't have enough hands to maintain them, the excavation equipment that fueled their expansion would have no one to drive it, and the military wouldn't have enough soldiers to prepare to fight a war that might never come. Too many heads and they would starve.

Children had been and still were a priority, though there was less desperation now than there was thirty years ago. Not all of the eggs that had been carried off Earth with the fleeing colony ship had ever been fertilized and implanted into a surrogate. Gabriel had been lucky because of who his father was, and even then he had been left to wait his turn. Theodore St. Martin hadn't wanted a son until he was older so that he could stretch his family's involvement in the resistance for as long as it took.

Gabriel drew in a breath. Held. Released. He took in another. He was nearing the end of his slipstream route, and in less than a minute the QPG would deactivate and the ion thrusters would kick on. He would have eight minutes to blast across the upper Earth atmosphere and listen for a transmission from the freedom fighters on the ground before rejoining the slipstream on the other side.

All he had to do was avoid the Dread defenses.

As long as it took. Gabriel often wondered how long that would be. Fifty years had passed. They had been sending ships back to

Earth for the last twenty-seven of those. At first, they had done little more than take pictures and record video which was used to monitor the enemy's build-up on the planet. It hadn't been as dangerous then because the Dread didn't care that much about the initial sorties. They weren't worried about the one that got away, not when they had defeated everything the governments of the world had to throw at them without losing a single ship.

Then the first transmission had come. Until then, the resistance in space had no idea there was a resistance on the ground. Somehow, small pockets of people around the world had managed to stay hidden from the aliens and to find shelter and food. The initial communications had been simple and straightforward messages about who they were and what they were doing. Later transmissions had described the situation on Earth.

It wasn't good, and time hadn't made it any better. The ground-based resistance was shrinking. The messages were fewer and further between, as the forces either had nothing new to report or were unable to find a safe place to set up a transmit needle.

As long as it took. Gabriel wanted to believe he would live that long. He wanted to believe his father would live that long, and fulfill the promise he had made all of those years ago.

The truth was, they had lost everything in the initial attack. It was only stubborn determination that kept them going despite every bit of evidence and logic pointing to their eventual demise.

Gabriel held onto hope because hope was the only thing he had.

It was the only thing any of them had.

[6]

"Departing slipstream," Gabriel said for the sake of the recording. "Firing ion thrusters."

The starfighter shook like it was entering the atmosphere as the QPG brought him back in phase with realspace and his main control thrusters began to fire. Gabriel held the stick steady, lifting the secondary visor from his helmet and putting his attention forward.

The craft shuddered one last time and he was back out into space, the moon a large mass ahead of him and the Earth barely visible beyond.

"Here we go," he said, shifting his free hand from the control pad to a smaller stick that would handle the vectoring thrusters. One eye landed on the fuel monitor. Every move he made would have to be measured against his power supply.

He increased the thrust, angling the fighter to swing around the moon, using its limited gravity to help boost his acceleration.

It had taken him almost a dozen sorties before he had grown accustomed to what humankind's home planet looked like now, compared to what he had been shown in videos and pictures salvaged in the colony ship's datacenter. While the general size and shape and color remained the same blue marble as it had always been, it was the change in the surface features that was the most striking.

There was a time before the Dread had come when the dark side of the planet would be lit with the glow of cities, lines of illumination that spread through small areas and left the rest of the land in darkness. The light side would reveal itself in spreads of green or brown or gray, where sister cities rose into the atmosphere, the tallest being almost six kilometers in height.

The wasted remains of those cities were still visible. On the light side, their majestic silver forms had been reduced to dark black splotches that on closer inspection revealed heaps of slag and broken concrete and glass. The surrounding countryside was also obliterated, transformed from forest or grassland to barren stone and dust.

On the dark side, there was nothing. No light, and no indication that a civilization had ever existed there at all. There was so much emptiness. So much death and destruction hidden yet hinted at in that space. Even now, it caused Gabriel to feel a chill.

The alien construction was more centralized, though there were smaller outposts positioned in strategic locations around the globe. An endless array of networked tunnels, towers, and spires occupied the bulk of the land within the planet's tropical zone, between the Tropic of Cancer and the Tropic of Capricorn. The structures were dark, no more than black spots in the day that made it seem as if a colony of giant ants had settled itself across most of Africa and the northern part of South America. At night, they too were lit with a glow, though it took on a more blueish hue and was dimmer than anything humans had created.

The aliens' orbital defenses were a blockade that hung between Gabriel and the ruined Earth. They hadn't always been there. They had started to appear only after the resistance had made their first successful broadcast, and the NEA's flyby had been rewarded with a choppy recording of a man known only as David revealing the first of the aliens' secrets.

The reason why they had come.

Those defenses materialized as small satellites that surrounded the planet, numbering in the hundreds of thousands. They were round and ridged, coated in the same dark carapace as everything the aliens made, the damned armor that none of humankind's weapons were able to pierce. Not even nuclear warheads had broken through the material, detonating directly against it and leaving nothing but a minor wound. It was the one and only reason they had lost the planet. How do you defeat something that you can't hurt?

It would never stop them from trying.

Those satellites came to life as Gabriel drew closer, their sensor arrays picking up the arrival of his starfighter. Small thrusters hidden beneath the carapace began to fire, turning the satellites toward him, while their plasma cannons extended from cover like a turtle poking its head out of its shell.

"I have been targeted by the enemy," Gabriel said calmly. Every mission started with the satellites firing at him. His skill and experience would get him past this first line of defense. "Taking evasive maneuvers."

His hands worked the two sticks with practiced ease. Gabriel kept an eye on his power reserves while adjusting to take a more chaotic path. The satellites changed their position to line up the plasma cannons and opened fire on him.

Gabriel switched up his vectors, bouncing and dancing as he drew ever closer to the defenses. The fighter was armed with a heavy ion pulse cannon, but there was no point in trying to use it. The beam weapon would strike the armor without a hint of damage made, and it would use up too much of his precious fuel.

Instead, Gabriel scanned the field of satellites for an opening. He found it a moment later, a gap in the defenses that would allow him through. He spun the fighter in a tight rotation while creating a bit of wobble in the flight path with the vectoring thrusters. It was enough to keep the enemy's targeting computers from getting a solid lock, and their shots scattered around him.

He was centimeters from death with every blast yet he remained completely calm. He had done this so many times. He had survived so many times. Luck was important, sure, but so was skill.

The starfighter slipped silently into the open lane, racing past the satellites within seconds. Gabriel eased up on the throttle then, changing course and heading further down toward the thermosphere. The satellites ceased operation behind him, their instructions limited to monitoring space outside of the ring.

He dove quickly, keeping his eyes open and scanning the field ahead of him. The satellites were dangerous, but they were the least of his concerns.

"Entering the thermosphere," he said, using the two sticks to maneuver the fighter. He flattened out some, running a horizontal arc along the upper atmosphere. All of the debris from the initial attack had long ago burned up or had drifted unencumbered out into deeper space, yet somehow a few non-functional human satellites had managed to remain in their orbit, unaware of what had become of the people who had put them there.

He took his hand off the thruster control and moved it to the touchpad. He tapped in a rapid sequence, opening up the onboard receivers. He wouldn't know if he had gotten anything until he returned to Delta Station, but it was better that way. To pause or hesitate for even a moment would be the difference between life and death.

"Activating receivers. Let's hope we get something this time."

He kept his head moving side to side, while at the same time watching the HUD for any hint of motion from his sensors. He knew this was the calm before the storm, even if he wouldn't see the storm coming until it was almost too late.

He swept along the atmosphere, racing over the northern hemisphere, not too far from the Tropic of Cancer. It had been so long since they had captured anything, Gabriel wondered if there was anyone left down there to transmit, and if not, how they would ever know it.

It was a wayward thought that almost cost him his life.

[7]

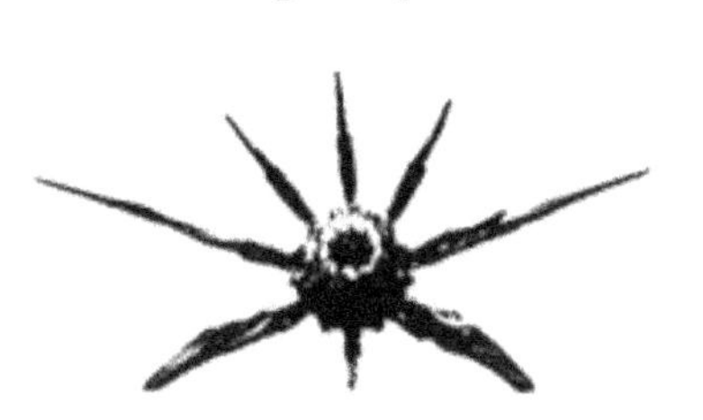

DONOVAN DIDN'T HESITATE AS HE TAPPED OUT ORDERS WITH HIS foot, getting the team moving. Three to try to draw the enemy away, five to keep a tight defense on the needle, and the rest to hold the perimeter. He didn't need to be quiet, but some directions were more efficient to issue by feel.

"Diaz, go," Donovan said, choosing her as one of the decoys. Not because they were usually able to escape alive. She was their fastest runner.

Diaz looked like she was about to argue, but then she hopped to her feet and ran, sliding down a fallen girder with acrobatic ease. Plasma rifle fire blasted into the space behind her as the enemy soldiers tried to get a bead.

"Fox, cover her," Donovan shouted.

Private Fox aimed his rifle, opening fire with conventional bullets. The weapons were vastly inferior to the alien plasma rifles, but they were all the resistance owned, taken years earlier from gun shops and homes from as far south as Acapulco and north into the southwestern United States. It didn't matter that much, anyway. There was nothing the humans had that could pierce a Dread soldier's carapace armor.

The slightly better news was that the Dread rarely sent their real soldiers after t-vaulters.

Donovan felt his watch again. The flyby would take about eight minutes, but only twenty seconds or so would put the pilot in range of the transmission. There was a small switch on the computer that would pop out when a connection had been made, and the signal sent. Sanchez had her hand on the box, waiting to feel it happen.

Thirty seconds passed. Mexico City was a nightmare, lit by the flashes of plasma as the bolts poured into the surrounding concrete and steel, burning into it where it hit. Donovan heard a thud, turned and saw Amallo was down. He unslung his rifle and rushed to the Corporal's position, looking down toward the street.

A half-dozen enemy combatants had gathered behind the charred wreckage of a car. They were the typical Dread response to a transmission, what the resistance called HSCs or human simulacrum combatants. Clones. They were all identical in appearance: six and a half feet tall, bald, muscular, and wearing simple cotton shirts and pants.

From what Donovan had heard, the clones were easier for the Dread to make than the impenetrable armor they used to build pretty much everything else, and so they would grow them out, program them, and send them to find the resistance. Once in awhile, after an HSC put eyes on a t-vault, a real Dread soldier piloting one of their mechanized armor would show up. It would then blow the hell out of everyone and everything nearby, ending the transmission and the t-vault team in a hurry.

At least, that was the rumor. Donovan was still alive, which meant he had never seen it happen.

The clones stared back at him, finding him with alarming ease, genetically modified to see in the dark. Donovan barely slipped behind the wall before a gout of plasma fire spewed up at him.

"What have you got, soldiers?" he shouted.

"Counting twenty-four, Major," Rollins replied. "They aren't going easy on us today."

Twenty-four? Not going easy was an understatement. That was twice the normal number of clones scouting for a t-vault squad.

"Sanchez?"

He looked back at the Private. She shook her head. The transmission hadn't been sent yet. Damn.

He peeked around the corner of the building, taking a quick shot at the clones below. His bullets hit the car in front of them, and they returned fire, sending him back to cover again.

A shout and Rollins was down.

"Come on," Donovan whispered, glancing up at the sky.

He could see the dark splotch of the Dread's orbital defenses blotting out a pattern ahead of the stars. He knew it wasn't easy for the pilots to get through that mess.

It wasn't exactly a cakewalk on the ground, either.

A groan and Mendoza fell off the side of the building, her head torn in half by plasma. Davids went to cover her position, firing a steady stream down at the clones. His gun clicked empty, and he ducked to the ground, grabbing a magazine from his pocket and slapping it in. They had been traveling light and fast, and only had two reloads.

"Sanchez?" Donovan asked again. Only a dozen seconds had passed, and he was getting a bad feeling about this one.

She shook her head again.

He glanced down at the HSCs. They were gone.

What?

They wouldn't have retreated. It meant they were either making their way up through the building or the decoys had managed to pull them away. Except the decoys rarely worked anymore.

"Stay on it," he said to Sanchez, putting a hand on her shoulder. "I'm going to intercept."

Sanchez's eyes opened wide. He might as well have told her he was going to kill himself.

Donovan reached the steps and started down, leading with his rifle. He could hear the plasma sizzling against the walls above him and the echo of the return fire from his squad outside. It was nearly pitch black in the stairwell, good for the clones and bad for him. He dug a small wrist light from his pocket, slapping it on. It gave him just enough illumination to see the stairs before he tripped down them.

A plasma bolt lit the area, and Donovan threw himself to the ground, barely avoiding being hit. He rolled down the steps, feeling the edges of the concrete digging into him, leaving cuts and bruises as he fell. He hit a landing and rolled to his feet, directing his rifle down while he tried to get his bearings. That had been too close.

He kept his back to the wall while he listened for the footsteps of the clones climbing the stairs. When he picked them up, he started to descend again, his bare feet silent as he went down. In the glow of the wrist light, he noticed he had lost a lot of the clay that would hide his heat signature. It didn't matter much in here, but if he survived long enough to run?

He would worry about surviving that long first. He hadn't made it to Major by being stupid.

He stood still again. The clones were getting closer. He pulled the wrist light off and turned it over. There was a small switch on the bottom, and in one motion he flicked it over and threw it down the steps.

The light flared from it, a bright flash that revealed the enemy position and blinded their sensitive eyes. Donovan charged at them, weapon firing, cutting them down in a hail of bullets. He didn't stop shooting until his magazine was empty, reaching them as the last one hit the floor and stopped moving.

He knelt down and grabbed one of the plasma rifles. It was rounded and slender, designed to rest on the forearm of one arm and stabilized with the opposite hand. It deactivated as it left the clone's grip, and he tossed it aside. It was a foolish hope to think they might forget to pair the weapon.

He slapped a new magazine into his gun and continued the descent, feeling his watch as he did. Four minutes had passed, and the fire from both sides had calmed somewhat. The transmission had to have been sent by now.

He reached a pile of rubble, stepping carefully out onto it and surveying the area. Gomez's body lay at a crude angle across the lower portion of the debris, his arm blown off by a plasma bolt. A dead clone lay nearby.

"Sanchez," he shouted, his voice echoing. He looked back and up. Her face appeared over the edge a moment later, illuminated by her wrist light, and she gave him a thumbs up. The transmission was sent. "Where are the clones?"

She put her arms out to the side and shook her head. She didn't know.

"Grab whoever's still alive up there and let's get the hell out of here. The stairwell is clear."

A heavy vibration shook the ruins, sending small bits of debris rolling down and a cloud of dust into the air. A second rumble followed. Then a third. He heard the soft whine of moving parts. What was that? He crouched low, scanning the buildings around them. The vibrations were steady, and getting stronger. He caught a bit of motion in the corner of his eye and turned to aim his rifle.

"Donovan," Diaz said. Sweat had washed the clay away from half her face and left her hair a damp mess. "Run."

[8]

THE ENEMY STARFIGHTERS CAME OUT OF NOWHERE, DARTING through the cover of lower clouds and taking a direct vector toward him. His sensors beeped in a panic as they picked up the burn from the thermosphere, and he cursed himself for letting his focus slip for even an instant. He put his hands on the controls and added thrust, shooting ahead of the enemy ships and forcing them to tail behind.

He kept an eye on them on his HUD. They appeared as red triangles there, but he knew what they looked like. Wide and slender, the wings rounded and sharp at the fore and aft, with a cockpit that swept up from an inverted center. They were made of the same ridged black carapace as the satellites and the alien buildings. Some pilots called them Bats. Others called them Rays. To Gabriel, they were nothing but trouble.

There was still some debate about whether the alien craft were piloted manually, remotely, or autonomously. Since no one had ever shot one down, it remained a point of contention. Unlike a human starfighter, the cockpit had no obvious viewport, but that didn't mean the aliens weren't using some advanced tech, or even something as simple as camera feeds, to see out of the ship. They certainly didn't fly like they couldn't see, and they hugged Gabriel's aft as he juked and jived across the sky, doing everything he could to prevent them from getting a lock.

His heart was racing while his head remained calm. If he panicked, if he lost concentration now, he would die. No matter how the enemy ships were flown, they were extraordinarily skilled and impossible to defeat. The only option was to keep going, to keep trying to avoid their efforts to bring him down.

Gabriel threw the stick hard to the right, and the starfighter tipped over and turned. He threw it to the left, and it rolled back the other way. His computer complained as it registered the enemy fire, and Gabriel felt his first pang of true fear as a shot from a plasma cannon nearly tore a wing from the fuselage. As it was, it left a long, trailing scorch mark on the back of the fighter.

"Come on, come on, come on," Gabriel said, forgetting about the recording. "Is that all you've got?"

His hands worked the sticks, keeping the fighter from ever flying a straight vector that the enemy ships could target. He checked his mission clock. Two minutes to egress. The run was almost complete.

The sensors cried out again as a second pair of enemy ships were detected, coming at him from the front.

"Damn," Gabriel said, throwing both sticks forward. The fighter dipped and headed down toward the surface as the four enemy ships blew past one another before circling back to follow.

Gabriel's eyes jumped from the mission clock to his power reserves. He had gotten closer to the surface, and deeper into Earth's gravity than he had wanted. It was going to cost him. He couldn't shake the enemy fighters and make it back to the slipstream in time.

A million calculations darted through his head. A million options for how to make his next move and try to get back to Delta Station. He had outmaneuvered four enemy ships before, and he could do it again. The one place the aliens didn't have human starfighters beat was in overall thrust.

He slowed down, easing off on the throttle once more. The

enemy fighters were wedges on his display, sliding into position behind him and gaining.

Good. He wanted them close.

He was more cautious with his maneuvers now, making short, tight jumps and turns that were just enough to keep the alien fire from scoring a direct hit. Plasma cannons sent bolts scattering around him, close enough to scorch the frame and raise more warnings from the computer. He ignored it, keeping his focus on the result.

He slowed even more. The alien ships continued to close in, their shots drawing dangerously near as he dangled the bait. What he was doing was insane, and he hoped he would never have to do it again.

The four alien fighters were only a few hundred meters behind him. At their current velocity, if he had cut his thrust they would slam into him and tear him apart without taking a hint of damage themselves. In fact, one of the ships began to accelerate harder, inverting the idea.

That was Gabriel's cue. He pulled back hard on the left stick while pushing the right stick forward. The fighter changed direction as the thrusters went to full burn, and he shot up and away from the enemy. They were too close to change direction easily and too slow to catch up.

They were smart enough not to try.

Gabriel kept going, watching his power levels sinking further and further. He could see the orbital defense ring up ahead, and he narrowed his eyes and gritted his teeth. He couldn't risk slowing down or he might not have the power or the velocity to get back into the slipstream.

His eyes scanned the ring, picking a path through the round devices. He wasn't worried about their fire on the way back out, especially not at this velocity. He would blow past and be gone before they could touch him.

He was only seconds away from the ring when he saw the wedge enter his display, coming on from his left faster than anything he had ever seen before. He turned his head to watch one of the alien starfighters bearing down, using constant heavy thrust to gain a velocity that would be unmanageable for maneuvering.

Except it didn't need to maneuver. It was headed right for him.

Gabriel couldn't believe it. After sixty-seven missions, had his luck had finally run out?

Not yet.

"Pic kee toi, asshole," he said, using one of his father's favorite cajun cusses. He flipped a switch next to the thrust stick, engaging the emergency overdrive. It would nearly drain his fuel cell but it was either that or die.

The fighter's velocity jumped, throwing him into the midst of the satellites at high speed. He deftly shifted the vectoring thrusters, whipping the craft this way and that, somehow managing to avoid the satellites, in some cases by a meter or less.

The incoming enemy fighter tried to follow. Gabriel looked back over his shoulder, watching as its plasma cannon loosed a stream of bolts into the satellites to clear a path, his eyes opening in wonder as the satellites blew apart beneath it. There had been rumors forever that the aliens' weapons could overcome their shields, but there had never been any definitive proof.

Until now.

Gabriel put his eyes back forward. The enemy fighter was still behind him, but the obstacles had forced it to slow, its design not able to maneuver quite as well as he could. He angled the fighter to the inception point, checking his velocity. Then he hit the touchpad to activate the quantum phase generator.

The wings began to blur, the ship shaking heavily as the unharmed phased surfaces compensated for the damaged ones. The computer continued to beep warnings; a new one added as his fuel cell reached critical levels. There would be just enough juice to keep the QPG powered and to run life support.

Gabriel found the enemy ship still racing toward him. He had never seen one so intent on stopping a sortie before, and he wondered if he had picked anything up from the resistance on the ground, and if so what it was. The intel he had just gathered on his own was more than enough to have made the trip worthwhile.

Watching the enemy's plasma beam pass harmlessly through the fighter as he joined the slipstream was even more rewarding.

"This is Captain Gabriel St. Martin," he said, a little less calmly than before. "Mission complete."

He switched off the recorder and leaned back in the seat.

It was going to be a nice, quiet ride home.

[9]

DONOVAN DIDN'T QUESTION WHY DIAZ HAD COME BACK. HE spun around again, looking for his team. The vibrations were getting stronger and closer, the whine louder with each passing breath.

"Damn," he said, returning to the mouth of the stairwell. He found the remainder of the t-vault squad almost down. Sanchez and Cameron. Were they the only ones left?

They had abandoned the needle and the equipment, carrying only their rifles. Donovan waited until they caught up to him, putting his hand on their shoulders to guide them out the door. He heard Sanchez gasp as she exited.

"Dios Mío," she said, her face pale and afraid.

Donovan followed her eyes out to the corner of a distant building. A dark shape had emerged from behind it.

It was easily twenty meters tall, a wide, squat body resting on massive mechanical legs that ended in three claw-like toes that dug deep into the broken pavement. A massive plasma cannon rested on either side of the torso, serving as arms, while smaller weapons jutted out on either side of a rounded bulge in the center that had to be a cockpit or remote control unit of some kind. The whole thing was a rippled black, covered in the protective carapace.

Donovan had been a child the last time he had seen the Dread's mechanized armor, when they had been laying waste to the ruins of Los Angeles in an effort to root out the resistance. In his nightmares, he remembered them only as black monsters.

The real thing wasn't much different.

Its presence only confirmed what he had already guessed. The aliens were done being patient with the resistance and had every intention of ending it now.

"Come on," he said, running ahead of them, letting himself slide down the pile of rubble to where Diaz was still waiting.

She had her rifle against her shoulder, facing the armor. There was nothing their guns could do to hurt that thing, but maybe it made her feel better to act like there was.

"What are you doing here?" he asked as he reached her.

The armor was closing in fast, and before she could answer a massive flume of plasma launched from the left cannon. He could feel the static and heat of it as it passed overhead and struck the top floor of the building where they had set up the needle. The entire thing vanished in pulverized rock and superheated slag that rained down on them as ash. It burned where it touched the skin.

"No time," she replied. "Follow me."

The remaining members of the t-vault team followed Diaz as she sprinted away. They had only gone a few meters when a spray of pulsed plasma tore into the rubble behind them, lighting up the sky in a red hue and leaving a burning heat at their backs.

"This way," Diaz said, reaching a building and turning left down a tight alley.

Donovan could feel the vibrations on his bare feet. The Dread armor was following them.

"It knows we're out here," he said. "It can see us."

"You lost all of your clay," Sanchez said.

Donovan looked at the others. Sanchez and Cameron were still coated.

"Diaz, wait," he said, bringing his Lieutenant to a sudden stop. "Sanchez, Cameron, go that way and find a place to hide."

"We're not splitting up, sir," Cameron said.

"Yes, we are. They won't be able to track you, and we can't afford to lose any more soldiers. Do it. Now."

They hesitated for a heartbeat before bolting. The Dread machine was catching up with them.

"You just wanted to get me alone, didn't you, D?" Diaz said, smiling.

"I want them to survive this," he replied, not in the mood for jokes.

"Come on," Diaz said. She started running again.

Donovan followed. It was a challenge to keep up with her as she made tight angles through the wasteland of a city, vaulting wreckage and squeezing through small gaps. Donovan could feel his lungs burning from the dust, smoke, and effort. He could hear the armor behind them, gaining ground with every passing second.

A whine, and projectiles chewed through the buildings behind them, sending shards of concrete into the area. One hit Donovan in the shoulder, burying itself in his back. He stopped himself from crying out, desperate to keep moving.

Diaz looked back, seeing he was hit. A concerned look flashed across her face, but she didn't slow. They reached another alley, and she pointed to an open door. They ducked inside, finding themselves in what had once been the lobby of a hotel. There was debris everywhere, along with a few old corpses and some rats that scurried away at their approach.

"Where are we going?" Donovan asked. He held his left arm across his chest to ease some of the pain.

"Here," Diaz said, leading him to the back of the space and ducking under a partially collapsed ceiling.

He followed her through to a bank of elevators. One of the doors was open, and Diaz brought him up to it. He looked into the shaft. There was nothing but darkness below. The vibrations of the armor were growing stronger behind them, so close that Donovan was surprised it hadn't turned them to ash already. The rats had to be confusing its thermal sensors.

"Now what?" Donovan asked.

Diaz kicked some of the debris into the shaft. A few seconds passed until he heard the distinct sound of it hitting water. He didn't need a verbal answer to his question.

He grabbed her hand and jumped.

[10]

GABRIEL LEANED FORWARD AND HIT THE SWITCH TO DEACTIVATE the QPG. The fighter shook slightly as it disengaged from the slipstream and reentered realspace. Warning tones immediately began ringing out in the cockpit, and the power indicator flashed red.

His main battery was dry. He had two hours of reserve power to keep his life support going.

It was more than enough.

Delta Station floated ahead of him, a few thousand kilometers distant. It was brightly lit from here, its large, saucer-like head spinning slowly while the narrow docks and launch cannons remained stationary below, trailing downward into a near spike where the sensor array and communications antennas poked out from the bottom. It was a simple design and looked a lot more impressive from the outside than it was on the inside. Every part of it was function over form. Every ounce of material that had gone into its making was calculated and planned. Their printers could only manage so much per day, and everything that was constructed was essential to someone.

"This is Captain Gabriel St. Martin. Miranda, are you back on duty?"

"Gabriel. Welcome home."

Miranda's voice made him smile. He hadn't been worried about making it back once he'd joined the slipstream. It still wasn't the same as actually being home.

"I could use a lift back," Gabriel said. "My cell is empty."

There was a pause at the other end. She knew what that meant. How close he had come to not making it back at all.

"I guess you needed my luck after all," she said.

"For sure," Gabriel replied.

"I'm sending Captain Sturges out to bring you home. ETA, ten minutes."

"Sounds wonderful. Did I miss anything while I was gone?"

"Around here? In one day? Not much. One of the compressors broke on Alpha. All of the build jobs had to be reorganized to emergency print a replacement. Oh, and Shawna had her baby."

Gabriel tried to remember who Shawna was. With a total population of around twenty-thousand, there were some people who were able to keep track of nearly everyone else. Gabriel wasn't one of them. He wasn't interested in entertainment through gossip.

"Boy or girl?" he asked.

"Boy. Bradley Williams. Twelve pounds, four ounces."

"Big boy."

"Yup."

"Did they assign him yet?"

"Not yet. Space Force is arguing with Engineering over him."

"He sounds like he might get too big for Space Force."

"He's the right size for infantry. They're projecting him at over two meters."

"Just what we need. Another mouth to feed and body to train for a ground war that will never happen."

"You sound like your father."

"Good."

His father was right on that account. Twenty-thousand people and a quarter of them were infantry. Ground soldiers with guns that couldn't pierce Dread armor and no protection of their own. They weren't going to get the aliens off of Earth like that. Their only chance at victory would come from space. They needed to blast the Dread like the Dread had blasted them.

The existence of the infantry division was an asinine waste. It was also proof that despite his father's stature in the government of the New Earth Alliance, it hadn't been enough to guide every military decision. The council thought the infantry was good for morale, and General Cave loved having the resources and the control.

Just because humankind had nearly been wiped out of the universe, it didn't mean the survivors would give up on their politics.

Sometimes he wondered if things would be different if one of the colony ships launched from India or Japan had survived the exodus.

"Do you know if the resistance sent a message?" Miranda asked.

"You know I don't," he replied. "But that was a good nonsequitur."

"I don't want to bring any more of your father out of you. I'll be listening to you rant for the next thirty minutes."

"He ranted because he was passionate."

"I know. And so are you. That's not always a bad thing."

"Not always?"

"Sturges is approaching. I'm going to leave you in his capable hands now. Locke out."

Gabriel laughed at the abruptness of her disengagement. She really was afraid to get him going. He turned his attention to the ship that was vectoring toward him. It was a simple supply transport, also known as a BIS, or box in space. As the name suggested, it was nearly square, with a large front viewport and a couple of small thrusters breaking the shape on either side. He could see Captain Sturges through the transparency, his wrinkled face wrinkling even more when he smiled.

"Captain St. Martin," Sturges said, his voice gruff and aged. "I heard you needed a ride home."

"Yes, sir," Gabriel said. They may have been the same rank, but Sturges was forty years his senior and a survivor from Earth. The last part alone meant he deserved respect.

"Close call?"

"Too close."

"I can see the burn marks on the frame. You're lucky you didn't lose integrity or shake apart when you joined the slipstream."

"How lucky?" Gabriel asked.

The BIS was getting closer, slowing and turning so that Sturges could collect the fighter in the rear cargo hold.

"Son, you don't want to know. You might not go back out there."

"As long as I'm not dead I'll go back out there. How lucky?"

"I'd say a few extra prayers tonight if I were you. You'll have to divert some of your backup power to thrusters to get in line."

"Yes, sir," Gabriel said. He worked his touchpad to shift power, ignoring the warnings from the computer.

He took hold of the secondary stick and gently fired the vectoring thrusters until the fighter was lined up with the back of the BIS. The transport's cargo hold was easily big enough to swallow him, and Captain Sturges directed the ship expertly, taking the fighter inside and then closing the bay door. A light on the front of the bay turned green once the space had been filled with air and the suppressor was reactivated. At that point, Gabriel opened the cockpit and got to his feet, feeling the blood rushing back to his legs.

He shook them out for a few seconds before climbing onto the wing. He took a moment to survey the damage, surprised to see how much of the frame had been burned away, leaving the inner skeleton and wiring of the craft exposed. He clutched the crucifix in his hand again, quickly thanking his mother for her intervention.

Then he jumped down to the floor and made his way to the front of the BIS, opening the cockpit door and entering.

"Captain Sturges," Gabriel said.

The older man glanced back at him. "Gabriel. Have a seat."

Gabriel sat down in the open co-pilot's seat. The BIS had been designed before the Dread had come, back when they had the manpower to use two people to fly a transport.

"I'm going to haul you back to Alpha," Sturges said. "That fighter of yours is going to need some reconditioning."

"I'm supposed to deliver the recorder to Colonel Graham on Delta," Gabriel said.

He laughed. "I know the procedure. I already spoke to Graham. He's on Alpha, too. You can drop it with him there."

"Why is he on Alpha?" Gabriel asked. He knew Graham. The man didn't like leaving Delta. He didn't trust that his subordinates could run the station without his constant oversight.

"General Cave ordered him there. Before you ask me why, I don't know. I get more intel because I'm old and people think I'm special for riding the Old Gator's ship away from the Dread, but they don't tell me everything."

Gabriel was silent. General Cave wouldn't have called in his officers if he weren't thinking big thoughts.

"Anyway," Sturges said, breaking the silence. "I'm sure your father wouldn't mind seeing you."

"He doesn't even know who I am anymore."

"Maybe not outwardly. Deep down, I think he knows. When was the last time you visited him?"

Gabriel thought about it. "I don't know. Six months?"

"He's getting up there, Gabe. You don't want to regret not spending more time with him when he's gone."

Gabriel stared out through the viewport. They had taken a wide angle around Delta Station, and now he could see Alpha Settlement up ahead. It was a long, low network of domed buildings that spread from a large central hub, all of which was resting at the bottom of a deep crater in the largest of Taphao Kaew's three moons. The original settlers had named the moon Manhattan after the famous Earth city.

Behind Alpha Settlement, sitting at the far edge of the crater was a starship. The U.S.S.S Magellan, a nearly three-kilometer long dagger of scarred and dirty metal that had transported the escaping humans from Earth to Calawan over fifty years ago. She was sitting abandoned and empty, a half-century restoration project still underway, working to convert humankind's only large space-faring vessel from a passenger ship to a military one. Over the years, she had been bolstered with extra layers of armor and newer damage control systems, while the inner configuration had been re-imagined to add fighter launch tubes and landing bays and provide for the needs of both the flying and ground units of the NEASF. It was an incredible amount of work for a population as small as theirs and a testament to what they could all achieve when they worked together.

It was also a constant and sad reminder of the cold hard truth of their existence. The restoration was unfinished, and who knew how long it would remain that way? The Magellan had no weapons systems or offensive punch of any kind. She was sitting dormant, waiting for the day when a means to defeat the enemy's defenses would be discovered.

A day that might never come.

To Gabriel, the sight of the ship was a strong reminder of his father. It had been a while since he had paid the man a visit. It was hard for him to bring himself to do it. He preferred to remember his old man as the spitfire he had been, not the invalid he was today. Still, he knew Sturges was right. He didn't want any more regrets.

"I know. Okay, I'll stop by."

"Good man."

[11]

Gabriel waited for the loop transport to come to a stop and the entry hatch to swing open. He stepped into the small cylindrical vehicle, taking the first of two seats at the front. The loop system would carry him quickly from the hangar at the western edge of the settlement to the central hub where the Star Force Headquarters were located. He had changed from his flight suit to a standard issue pair of dress blues, grabbing a pair from the general commissary after showering off his hours inside the cockpit. A satchel was slung over his shoulder containing his fighter's data recorder.

Captain Paul Sturges sat down beside him. The older man had also showered and changed though he was wearing more casual utilities. A few other NEASF members filed in behind them, filling the small pod in no time. The hatch closed and the pod rushed ahead through the connecting tubes, a trip to that would take less than thirty seconds to complete.

"I know that you don't know why Colonel Graham is on Alpha," Gabriel said. "Do you know anything else that isn't common knowledge that I might be interested in?"

Sturges glanced over at him, flashing a wry smile. "I should have known you would ask me that when I sat here."

"You have about fifteen seconds to answer."

Sturges shrugged. "Nothing more than rumors and hearsay."

Gabriel watched the man's face. He didn't like Sturges' expression. "Anything credible? And please don't lie to me, Captain. We've known each other a long time."

"Heh. I've known you since you were still crapping your diapers. I know something, but you aren't going to like it, and I don't want that news to come from me."

Gabriel hadn't been expecting that answer. He felt his heart start to thump. "Paul-"

The loop slowed.

"Nothing definite, Gabe," Sturges said. "Just some things the military leadership and the Council have been talking about."

The pod came to a stop, and the hatch opened. The passengers disembarking in the central hub stood to depart. Sturges wasn't one of them.

"What kind of things?" Gabriel said, leaning over the man as he crossed the pod.

"I shouldn't say."

"Come on. Spill it."

Sturges looked back to check on the other soldiers. Then he leaned up and forward to whisper.

"Some members of the Council think we should start preparing the Magellan to take everyone into deep space. The science team believes they've discovered an Earth-type planet a year out."

Gabriel felt the heat rush to his face, his anger rising. "They want to abandon Earth?"

It wasn't the first time the subject had come up. Every time the scientists claimed they had found an E-type, someone on the Council decided to start pushing to take the colony there, even if it meant leaving the resistance behind.

"You know Siddhu is on the council," Sturges said. "She said the team presented a very compelling case. They believe they've really found one this time."

Gabriel barely heard him. He stood straight and stepped out of the pod, turning his head back over his shoulder. "Thanks for the tip."

He stormed away from the station, his mind a sudden blur of anger and frustration. Captain Sturges' wife was a strong woman, and she was usually on the side of the military. The rest of the Council wasn't nearly as accommodating. If the case were strong enough, they would vote to leave Calawan and their home world behind.

And there was nothing he could do about it except be angry and follow orders.

Sturges didn't want to tell him about it. He shouldn't have pushed. They said ignorance was bliss, but it was a lesson he still hadn't managed to master.

Gabriel made his way into the central dome. It was a massive structure, hundreds of meters high and wide and the home to all of the New Earth Alliance's government facilities, twenty-five floors worth in all. It was the place where every decision concerning the remains of free humankind was made, and a place where Gabriel always preferred to avoid. As soon as he stepped foot on it, he couldn't wait to catch a transport back to Delta Station.

He headed directly to the middle of the structure, where a centralized administrative station sat ahead of the elevator tube that carried people up to the offices. It was early morning, and the area was relatively quiet. He was thankful for that. In the middle of the day, there would be hundreds of people crowding the floor, either waiting for a scheduled appointment, transferring from one loop to another to cross the settlement, or enjoying a work break by socializing.

"Captain St. Martin," the receptionist said when he reached the station. She was dark-skinned and chubby, with a big, welcoming smile and bright eyes. "Welcome back. How was the mission?"

Gabriel tried to remember her name. "Good morning." He paused. "I'm sorry. It must be the slipspace fatigue. I can't remember your name."

"Danai," she said.

Gabriel shook his head. "Danai. I can't believe I forgot a pretty name like that. I came back; that's about as good as I ever hope for. I heard Colonel Graham is here on Alpha?"

"Yes, sir," she replied. "He's in one of the visitor offices upstairs."

Gabriel smiled. He had been worried the Colonel would still be asleep. He slipped the satchel from his shoulder and handed it out toward Danai. "Can you do me a favor and make sure that he gets this."

"You can deliver it to him yourself," someone behind him said.

Gabriel turned slowly. He knew that voice.

"Captain," Major Vivian Choi said.

Gabriel stood at attention. "Major," he said, saluting.

"Relax, Captain," Choi said with a warm smile. She was a handsome woman in her fifties, her graying hair suited to her matronly face. She was wearing similar dress blues to his, though her jacket had a lot more decorations on it. "We've been waiting for you to get back."

"You have?" Gabriel asked, releasing his stance.

"You sound surprised. Why wouldn't we be relieved to get our best pilot back from his sixty-fifth mission?"

"Sixty-eighth," Gabriel said. He was sure she was happy that he had returned. He wasn't convinced the reason was purely personal. "I almost didn't make it back at all."

"Thank heavens you did. Is the data recorder in that satchel?"

"Yes, ma'am. Like I said, I was going to send it up to Colonel Graham."

"I think he'd prefer if you delivered it yourself. Come with me, Captain."

"Yes, ma'am," Gabriel said, following her as she headed for the elevator.

He waved to Danai on the way past, who gave him a quick wave back. He would have rather left the recorder with her and made his way over to see his father. The less time he had to spend on Alpha, the better.

They stepped into the elevator, the doors closing behind them.

Major Choi turned to face him, her mouth open to speak. Gabriel decided to beat her to the punch.

"Forgive me for being blunt, Major, but does your impatience over my return, and Colonel Graham's presence on Alpha have anything to do with the rumors that we're going to be leaving this system and abandoning the resistance on Earth?"

[12]

"WHERE DID YOU HEAR THAT?" CHOI SAID, HER FACE TURNING to stone.

"I'm not going to rat out my sources," Gabriel replied. "Is there any truth to the rumor?"

"There is always some truth in rumor," Choi said.

"Playing coy, Major? Whatever is going on, you can fill me in. I don't have the power to change any of it anyway."

"Not directly, no. But you have the respect of your superiors, and that still counts for something."

"Did you just compliment me?" Gabriel asked.

"I did. I'm not only interested in that data recorder, Captain. Your presence here is important to me on a personal and a professional level."

"Why?"

"Personally? You should know why. Beyond that, because your father saved my life when I was only a little girl, along with the lives of my brother and my parents. Professionally? Because I need all of the support, I can get."

Gabriel didn't like the sound of that. "What do you mean?"

Her eyes fell on the data recorder. "If you got the information from Captain Sturges, then yes, what he said is true. I'm trying to stop it."

Gabriel was silent. He couldn't believe that this argument was going to come up again. "Does it have legs?"

"Strong ones, unfortunately. A lot of the population is tired of living this way."

"A lot of the population has only lived this way."

Choi smiled. "Funny, isn't it? Most of the New Earth Alliance has never set foot on Earth. Hell, most of the NEA has never even seen Earth. They're in love with the fairytales their parents tell them about how wonderful it was. I'm not saying it wasn't wonderful, especially compared to this, but isn't that the reason we keep fighting for it instead of packing up and heading out? The grass isn't greener in another system. Life is going to be harder than we want wherever we go."

"You're preaching to the choir, Major. I don't keep risking my life because I was drafted. I care about what happens to the people on Earth."

"I know you do. That's why I need your support."

The elevator stopped at the top floor, the doors sliding open.

"What about Colonel Graham?" Gabriel asked. "Is he on our side?"

Choi didn't have to speak to answer. Her face wrinkled, and she shook her head lightly. Gabriel felt a slight chill at the response. Graham was one of the last people he could ever imagine giving up the fight.

"Mind your words, Captain," Choi said as they crossed from the elevator to the outer corridor at the edge of the dome. Small viewports in the side gave him an impressive view of the Magellan, sitting vacant and lonely at the edge of the chasm. "Graham is going to be on the offensive. I know you have your father's temper sometimes. Don't let him bait you."

"I'll try."

They rounded the dome, reaching a pair of wide doors guarded by an infantryman in dark fatigues and carrying a rifle. His presence was purely symbolic. There had never been a violent incident in the NEA settlement.

"Major. Captain." The soldier saluted as they approached.

"Spaceman," Choi said, returning the salute. "Is Colonel Graham still in the visitor's office?"

"Yes, ma'am."

"Thank you."

Like everything else in the settlement, the offices of the New Earth Alliance Space Force were spartan, designed with a bare minimalism where every piece of equipment existed because it had a specific value and purpose. The main reception area was nothing more than a flat table affixed to a central support pillar, with a small hinged panel to allow the receptionist to get into a lightweight chair behind it. A small tablet sat on the table in front of him, while a second chair occupied the corner for people to sit in while they waited.

"Spaceman Owens," Major Choi said, approaching the desk. A smaller man with a bald head and glasses sat behind it.

He stood and saluted. "Major Choi." He saw Gabriel behind her and saluted him as well. "Captain St. Martin. Congratulations on your mission."

"Thank you, Gene," Gabriel said. He had known Owens since childhood. "How are you feeling?"

"I have good days and bad days," Owens replied, in reference to his heart condition. It was the reason he had been relegated to desk work. "Today is pretty good so far."

"We'll take what we can get, eh Gene?"

Owens smiled. "Absolutely."

"Spaceman, we're here to see Colonel Graham," Major Choi said.

"Of course, Major. He's been expecting you. Are you bringing Captain St. Martin in with you?"

"Yes."

"I should go and inform him, ma'am. He doesn't like surprises."

Choi chuckled. "There's no need to warn him that I'm coming. I'll take full responsibility for his bluster."

Owens didn't look happy about the idea. He motioned towards the hallway behind him. "Second office on the right, ma'am."

"Thank you."

Gabriel followed Choi past the desk. They didn't have to go far to reach the visitor's office. The door was closed, but he could hear Graham tapping furiously on his tablet behind it.

"Mind my words?" Gabriel whispered. "You're going to get him riled up before I say anything."

"That's the idea," Choi replied. "That way he won't blame you."

She knocked on the door. The tapping stopped.

"Come in," Colonel Graham said. His voice was rough and hoarse, as though he had been born screaming at people and had never stopped for a breath of air. Gabriel knew the Colonel well enough to know that probably wasn't far from the truth.

Major Choi opened the door. She entered first, with Gabriel right behind her. Graham's eyes narrowed at the sight of him.

"Colonel," Choi said, as both she and Gabriel saluted him.

Graham got to his feet. He was a large man. Over two meters tall, with broad shoulders and a thick frame. He had a long forehead with a wisp of black hair laid flat on his scalp, brown eyes, a flat nose that had been broken a few times, and a crooked smile. He was an imposing figure who had driven cadets to tears on more than one occasion.

"Major Choi, you're early. And Gabriel, I heard you got into a bit of a scrape on your run. I'm glad to see you here in one piece."

"Thank you, Colonel," Gabriel said. He stepped forward, opening his satchel and pulling out the data recorder. "Mission complete."

Graham smiled. Gabriel knew those were the Colonel's two favorite words. He didn't reach for the recorder, instead putting up his hand. "Normally I would take this from you and arrange to have it transported back to Alpha. Seeing as we're already on Alpha, you might as well bring it down to the lab yourself."

"Yes, sir," Gabriel said, tucking it back into the satchel.

"Thank you. Dismissed, Captain. Major, please, have a seat."

Gabriel didn't move right away. Major Choi had obviously come early to time her arrival with his. She wanted him to be there.

"Do you need something, Captain?" Graham asked.

"Colonel," Choi said. "I'd prefer if Captain St. Martin participates in our discussion."

Any sense of lightness that the Colonel had managed to project vanished from him in an instant. He clenched his jaw, his eyes burning a hole into Choi.

"I see," he said, pausing.

"Permission to speak freely, Colonel?" Choi said, not backing down.

"Sure, why not, Vivian? I don't want to be accused of running away from a fight."

"I didn't come here to fight, James," Choi said. "But I think Teddy's son has a right to be a part of this in his father's place."

Gabriel took that as his cue. "If you don't mind, Colonel?"

Graham looked at him, and then back at Choi. Then he sat down. "Fine. Speak your mind, Gabriel. We've known each other too long, and I respect you and your father too much not to let you."

"The Major told me about the Council and the Earth-type planet. She said you support the option to leave Calawan."

"I do. It may come as a surprise to you, Gabe, but not all of us want to spend our entire lives committed to a war we can't win. Let me rephrase that. A war we can't even fight."

"I thought you believed in the cause."

"I believe in the future of humankind. I believe that our civilization deserves to carry on beyond this." He waved his hand at the sparse office. "We've been living on borrowed time since we came to Ursae Majoris. We were never supposed to live this way. The Magellan was intended to carry us thousands of light-years away, not a handful. Yes, we have the printers and the compositors, and they've kept us up and running, but every year we spend more and more man-hours maintaining what we've got and fewer and fewer able to construct anything new. We can't let the technical debt keep piling up forever. Eventually, something is going to give, and we're all going to wind up dead."

It was a good speech. A good argument. Gabriel could feel his opinion losing strength as he absorbed it.

"There was a reason we decided to stop here instead," Choi said. "A reason we didn't keep going into deeper space."

"Because we weren't ready," Graham said. "The astronomers hadn't come up with a viable system they were confident contained an Earth."

"That isn't the only reason," Gabriel said. "And you know it."

"You mean your father? Yes, he convinced the others to stop here so we could send back one of the scout ships. The goal was to see if there was any way to get anyone else out, not to start plotting some magical rebellion that was going to liberate Earth. I've supported your father in that for years. You know I have, Gabriel. I've been in charge of Delta Station since it was built, and I've dedicated all of my adult life to the mission."

"Then how can you just turn your back on it?"

It was the wrong thing to say, and Gabriel knew it as soon as the words left his mouth. Every remaining member of the Magellan's original population had some degree of survivor's guilt.

"Turn my back on it?" Graham said, rising to his feet again. "Don't make the mistake of thinking this is an easy decision, Captain. Or that I haven't spent sleepless nights wondering if I'm doing the right thing. There is no good decision here. Whatever we do, we lose something important. I've been trying to ignore the facts for years. I sided with your father the last time the Council was considering moving on. We can't win this fight. We never have, not once, managed to so much as scratch an enemy ship. It's been fifty years, and we still have nothing that can hurt them. How do we fight that, Gabe? How do we sit here and ask all of these people who have never breathed real air, who have never walked around without a dome over their head, who have never seen daylight just to hang in there while we figure something out? We've had fifty years to figure something out. The scientists have found us a new home, and it's time to go and claim it."

Gabriel stood in stiff silence, working to control his anger. He could feel his fingers digging hard into his leg, trying to relieve some of the sudden tension he felt. It wouldn't do him any good to yell back at the Colonel, even if he did have permission. No. He had to push back with facts.

"We have a home, Colonel," he said, at last, his voice somehow managing to come out flat and calm. "We still have people there. We know that the enemy used the healthiest and most intelligent as templates to update their genetics because centuries of cloning and modification drained away their diversity. It's the same reason the Magellan carried the frozen eggs and sperm of over a million people. It's the same reason I'm standing in front of you right now.

"We also know they took others as slaves to do menial work that they believe is too demeaning or too dangerous to waste their kind or risk damaging their machines on. Finally, we know that the war on Earth isn't over. We've received this information from the remaining free humans that have continued to fight back against the Dread since they arrived, in spite of the fact that as you say, they never have so much as scratched the enemy.

"You think our people are tired of their life? Imagine spending every day in hiding, afraid that you won't survive to see the sunset one more time. Imagine having to claw and scrape for everything you have, knowing it might be taken away at any moment. Imagine the effort it takes to reach out to the only people in the universe who might be able to help you. To the military that abandoned you. That gathered up their personnel, loaded them in a starship and escaped to the stars, lucky as hell they had a hero at the helm.

"Daylight? Fresh air? What do those things mean in the absence of security? Those are our people down there, Colonel. People we swore to protect, and a war we promised to fight. Not win. Fight. Humankind may survive by fleeing further out into the universe. But what kind of legacy will we leave? And do we deserve to carry on with a history like that?"

Gabriel drew in a deep, calming breath, unclenching his fists. His father's passion was more volatile and animated. He tended to stay more introverted.

Both Major Choi and Colonel Graham stared at him. Choi had a big smile on her face. Graham was stoic though it appeared to Gabriel that his words had at least been heard.

"Thank you, Captain," Graham said in a flat monotone. "I'll take your comments into consideration. Dismissed."

Gabriel came to attention, saluting and then spinning to head out the door. Major Choi's hand ran gently over his own in support as he passed.

He paused as the door slid open, turning back to Colonel Graham. "By the way, Colonel, I watched a Dread fighter blast one of their own orbital defense satellites to dust. The technology to defeat their armor exists. They have it. We need to discover it."

He exited the room then, satisfied with the surprised looks on both Graham and Choi's faces.

"He reminds me so damn much of his father," he heard Graham say as he headed away. "You knew he'd be able to push me."

"I didn't know for sure," Choi said. "I had a feeling he could bring you to your senses."

"I'm not quite there yet. Anyway, even if you can change my mind, it won't be enough to convince the Council."

"That's the trouble with history and legacy. Time forgives all sins."

[13]

Gabriel stood at the edge of the platform, waiting for the pod that would carry him along the western loop, beneath the chasm to residential. He still had the satchel with the data recorder slung over his shoulder, having decided he would deliver it after he talked to his father.

Well, tried to talk to his father, anyway. The last time he had stopped by to see him, his old man had remembered who he was but thought Gabriel was four years old and kept asking him for his mother. Gabriel had walked out when Theodore had started to cry.

He couldn't stand to see a man like his father bawl like a baby.

The pod arrived, and Gabriel climbed in, taking a seat next to a younger man he didn't recognize. The man smiled politely before turning his attention to his tablet, where a page full of gray numbers swam against a black background. The hatch closed, and the pod raced off, reaching the western loop before the man could finish looking over his page.

Gabriel climbed out, joining the handful of passengers on their way into residential. The younger man was one of them, and he stared at the tablet as he walked, nearly knocking into a woman with a child. His face turned red, and he apologized as he shuffled past them.

An engineer or an astronomer, Gabriel guessed. They were the ones who tended to have their faces pointed down instead of out, more interested in calculations than other people. He moved with the line, through the archway, and onto a long, wide concourse.

Residential was carved into the rock beneath the chasm, and so it was more open and natural than the central hub and one of the few places to trade gray, metallic walls for multi-colored stone. The bottom level of the concourse was designed for socializing and shopping, with some storefronts, restaurants, and pubs in simple stalls along the floor. In the early days, the NEA had tried to bypass the token economy for more of a communist-style arrangement. It had failed miserably. The Magellan was a United States colony ship, and despite the fact that most of its passengers had been part of the military, they had adjusted more easily to a new life that was as close to their old as possible.

Gabriel crossed the lower level, taking in the smell of cooking meats and the colors of fresh vegetables laid enticingly out along the thoroughfare. It was all transported in fresh from Beta Settlement on Taphao Thong daily. The meats were grown in vats of nutrients, the vegetables on hydroponic farms. All of it was made possible by the water and chemical rich atmosphere of the planet. He had to admit that as much as he hated the more chaotic and busy nature of life in Alpha Settlement, he did miss the food.

He paused at a stall and picked up an apple. "How much?" he asked, holding out his thumb to transfer the money from his account.

"For you, Captain? It's free," the merchant responded, giving him her best smile. She was young and pretty, and might have elicited more interest from him if he were in a better mood.

As it was, he barely noticed her flirtation. "Thanks. Enjoy your day."

He savored the taste as he walked. The NEA didn't have the resources to waste on printing kitchen equipment for Delta Station, leaving his regular diet as ninety-percent nutrient packs: a dark, foul-tasting liquid that contained everything a healthy soldier needed. They would also get occasional shipments of things like cocoa and coffee, but it never lasted long.

He climbed the steps near the center of the concourse up to the second level. Residential was composed of cutouts in the rock, with most of the spaces consisting of three or four small rooms and assigned based on need. As the population had grown they had continued building up to the five levels they had today, though the signs of further excavation were obvious in the corner of the area. The population was still growing, which meant residential had to grow with it.

Gabriel made his way to the back, eating the entire apple, core and all, as he did. Gabriel had spent his childhood in the same, simple two-room space near the front of the concourse where Theodore had been living since it had first been excavated. Gabriel approached it with a growing sense of anxious trepidation. He never knew who he was going to get when he came to see his old man.

He was surprised when the door to the home slid open before he reached it. He was even more surprised when General Alan Cave ducked through it.

"General," Gabriel said, coming to attention and saluting.

"Relax, Gabriel," Cave said. "I'm not here in any official capacity. I just stopped by to pay an old friend a visit."

Gabriel relaxed his posture. Alan Cave hadn't even been a member of the military when he had boarded the Magellan back on Earth. He was a government contractor at the time, who happened to be in the right place when the order to launch was given. It was Gabriel's mother who had gotten him allowed past the barricades, eager to save every person she could. The act of sacrifice had made General Cave and Theodore fast friends, and over time the man had joined the military and used his intelligence and charisma to rise through the ranks and eventually become their CO.

He was a tall, lanky, gentle man, with a tight crop of curly gray hair, dark skin, blue eyes, and a soft but powerful voice. He wasn't a soldier, not in the traditional sense, but he was an exceptional motivator and leader of men. He was well into his eighties and still as fit and hearty as ever.

"How is he?" Gabriel asked.

"Pretty good, today," Cave replied. "He remembered my name. It's been a few weeks since that happened."

"Do you come to see him often?"

"At least twice a week. It's tough to see him like this. I imagine it's a lot tougher for you. Even so, I owe him a debt I can never repay. This is the least I can do."

Gabriel wasn't sure how to take the second part of the General's answer. It was Theodore's influence that had gotten him pulled from the freezer and inserted into a surrogate in the first place. He owed his father for his life, even more so than a child of a traditional pairing.

He suddenly felt guilty for making such infrequent visits that he had never run into the General before now.

"I was over in the hub earlier," Gabriel said, shifting the topic away from his father. "I joined a meeting with Major Choi and Colonel Graham."

"Oh?" Cave said. "So you know about the plans to remodel the Magellan again?"

General Cave's choice of words didn't go unnoticed.

"I do," Gabriel replied. "I assume you're opposed to the idea?"

General Cave hesitated before answering. "The Council is concerned with the level of resources being dedicated toward militaristic ends while the population continues to expand. You know that we can only grow so far before we reach a maintenance level. We're getting close to it now. We're exploring every option."

"That isn't a no," Gabriel said.

"It isn't," Cave agreed. He put up a hand before Gabriel could speak. "Look, I know how you feel. And I certainly know how your father feels, even if he can't say so himself. The fact is we have to consider everyone in the settlements. We can't barter the future of the human race on the promises made by dead men."

"Not all of the men are dead. You're one of them."

Cave laughed. "So is the Old Gator. Who else is left? Sturges. Siddhu. Patel. Maybe a dozen others who were adults when we arrived in this system. The past is dying. The future still has hope if we're brave enough to see it. Even if that means breaking those promises. We can refit the Magellan, take the civilians to a new planet, and then come back and continue our fight. It won't take more than ten, twenty years."

"Twenty years? There may not be a resistance in twenty years."

"I know. Believe me, I do. The messages have been fewer and farther between with each passing year. It was getting harder to ignore the truth before the reports on the E-type. Even I can't ignore it anymore. I don't want to betray the trust your father had in me, but there's more at stake here."

Gabriel couldn't believe what he was hearing. First Colonel Graham, and now General Cave? It was as if all of their leaders were losing their faith and courage at once. After fifty years they were ready to let the aliens have their home, and everyone left on it.

"I can see you're disappointed by my answer," Cave said. "I understand why, Captain, and I wouldn't expect anything less from you. You're your father's son, and you should be damn proud of that." He reached out, putting his hand on Gabriel's shoulder. "I'm sorry it has to be this way."

Gabriel looked up at the General and nodded, fighting to keep the disappointment from showing. Cave released Gabriel's shoulder, straightened his jacket, and started walking away.

"I'm sorry, too," Gabriel whispered, too low for Cave to hear. If only he had spared a few seconds worth of power for thrust, he could have brought his fighter back to Delta and stayed oblivious to everything that was happening down on Manhattan.

He would rather be ignorant than feel disappointed and betrayed by the people he had spent his entire life looking up to.

He took a moment to gather himself before approaching the door to his father's home. If only he could tell his father about any of this. If only his mother had made it to the starship on time, or Jessica hadn't died.

The door slid open, and the smell of fresh urine wafted out.

Gabriel had never felt more alone.

[14]

GABRIEL ENTERED THE SMALL HOME, EVERY STEP HE TOOK tempting him to turn his heel and walk back out. He could hear motion in the back of the living quarters, where the heavy smell of sick piss was making the air in the space hard to breathe.

"Come on now, General," he heard his father's nurse, Sabine, saying. "We need to change your pants. You've wet yourself again. It's a good thing General Cave left before you did."

Gabriel remained in the front of the quarters to wait. There were two bedrooms at the back of the excavation. His father's door was on the left and open, though he couldn't see his father or Sabine through it. His eyes shifted to the one on the right. That had been his room once, long ago. He was sure it was in the same condition as he had left it when he had headed off to NEASF Officer Training fifteen years earlier. He doubted his father had ever even opened the door after Gabriel had closed it on the way out. Theodore St. Martin believed in a person's right to privacy, almost to a detrimental degree.

If he hadn't, he would have known of his wife's plan to stay behind and guide the others to the Magellan when the Dread came. As it was, he had only learned of her betrayal once they were well underway. A betrayal that had only led him to love her more.

Gabriel blinked a few times, trying to wipe the stories of the past from his thoughts. He was almost successful, until his traveling gaze fell on the far wall. It was smooth, solid stone, painted white. A projector affixed to the ceiling directly above the wall was beaming a near life-size photo of his mother against it.

He had seen the image a million times before. He had grown up with the vision of her timelessly placed against the wall whenever they weren't using the system to watch a video, or communicate with someone else in the settlements. For some reason, maybe because of what he knew was happening with the Council, the sight of her face nearly brought tears to his eyes.

She was standing in a field of marigolds, wearing a simple blue dress that hung loosely from her athletic frame. Her red-gold hair lay in a braid over her right shoulder, and her blue eyes squinted involuntarily in conjunction with a wide, white smile. Her face was heart-shaped and filled with life, and just looking at it made her selfless compassion obvious. His father had always called her an angel, and Gabriel had never had reason to doubt it.

He clutched at her crucifix without thinking, gripping it beneath his shirt. The necklace had been delivered by one of the families she had saved, dropped into his father's hand with a simple, painful message.

"I love you. I'm sorry. Get these people to safety."

Theodore St. Martin always did what his angel asked.

Gabriel clenched his fists. As far as he was concerned, his mother had meant all of the people on Earth. And now they were considering abandoning them. It was bullshit. Plain and simple.

"Oh, Captain St. Martin. I didn't know you were here."

Sabine's voice pulled Gabriel out of his anger. He looked at the nurse, forcing a smile. She was only fifteen years old, still in training to become a full member of the medical staff. She was rail thin, her face innocent. Gabriel could barely remember being innocent anymore.

"How is he?" he asked, his voice a whisper that made Sabine shrink away from him.

"He voided in his pants again," she said. "It's been happening more often the last few days. I was going to get Doctor Hall to come and look at him."

"Is he lucid?"

"I just gave him his medicine. It always steals some of his strength, but he screams in pain without it. If you want to talk to him, your timing is pretty good."

Gabriel nodded, looking back at the bedroom. He wasn't sure he wanted to go in there. Especially not with the way he was feeling.

"Are you okay, Captain?" Sabine asked.

"Yeah, I'm okay. Thanks for asking. I just got back from a mission, and I think I'm still a little shaken."

"Do you want to take anything? I have a benzodiazepine that might help."

"No. Thank you. You're going to get Doctor Hall?"

"Yes, sir."

"Can you give me ten minutes?"

"Of course, sir."

"Thank you, Sabine." Gabriel took a couple of steps toward the bedroom before pausing. "Sabine?"

"Yes, Captain?" the girl asked, stopping at the front door.

"Did you give my father the benzo?"

"Yes, sir. A pretty high dose, in addition to the painkillers. General Cave's visit made him pretty upset. I think that's why he wet himself."

Gabriel turned the rest of the way around. "What do you mean?" he asked. "What did he say to him?"

"Oh, I don't know, Captain. He made me stay up front, and he spoke softly so I couldn't hear."

Gabriel wondered what Cave might have said. Had he told Theodore of their plans to convert the Magellan back into a transport and give up the fight for Earth? Why would he do that?

"Thank you, Sabine," he said again, spinning around and moving more purposefully into his father's bedroom. He had a sudden need to speak to his father before the meds took full effect.

[15]

"There isn't anything going to bust that armor of theirs, sir," Theodore St. Martin said in his signature Cajun drawl, his eyes flicking back and forth as he sat at the edge of his bed. "That nuke was a direct hit. I swear it hit that coullion dead on."

He was silent for a moment while the other person in his waking dream spoke.

"No, sir," Theodore replied. "I ain't saying we should give up, but we need to get these people out of here. If Command is going to call an evac, now's the time to do it." Another pause. "Already called? Yes, sir. I'm on my way."

"Dad," Gabriel said, entering the room and approaching his father.

Theodore was clothed in his dress blues, his wrinkled shirt tucked neatly into a crisp pair of pants, his suit jacket slightly askew. His chair sat at a right angle to him, within easy reach should he decide he wanted to move.

He wasn't moving right now. He was reliving a moment Gabriel had seen him relive before.

"Dad," Gabriel said again. He wanted to pull him out of it before it got painful for both of them.

"Reactor is online," Theodore said. "Thrusters are warming up, QPG nacelles set and locked. What's our load look like?"

Theodore paused again, waiting for the answer.

"General," Gabriel said, still trying to get his father's attention.

"I can see them all coming in. You sure that many are going to fit? Look at the heifer down there. I don't recognize her. She got clearance to board?" A pause. "My wife? Where is she? Not on board? You kidding me, Sergeant? Well damn, boy. Don't just sit there, go and get her. This litter ain't leaving without its Queen."

Gabriel felt his heart begin pounding harder. He didn't want to hear this. Not again. He knew what came after. The bawling. The tears. Why did he have to show up now? It would have been better to come once his old man was already sleeping. Sit with the corpse for a few minutes and take his leave. His conscience would be salved, but he wouldn't have to deal with the memories.

"Damn it all," Theodore said. "We need to get these people loaded double-time. Sergeant, why are you still standing here? Orders? I don't give a damn about your orders. You find my wife, you hear me boy, or we're all going to die."

He rocked side to side, as though he were feeling an explosion.

"Took some flak to the armor. This ain't looking good. Who the hell is letting all these people through? Those are civvies out there, and this boat is for VIPs only. Two by two onto the damn Ark. All the right kinds to keep civilization going, just like we drilled. Can't you people get anything right?" A pause and his face reddened. "Where in the name of all things holy is my wife?"

"General St. Martin, atten-shun," Gabriel shouted.

His father froze. Gabriel knew it wasn't because of him. He stepped forward, throwing out his palm to slap his old man.

Theodore caught his wrist, squeezing the nerve and making his whole hand go limp and numb.

"Who the hell you think you're striking, boy?" Theodore said, his eyes suddenly alive and looking up at him. "Don't even think of telling me it's me."

Gabriel shook his hand, trying to rid it of the sudden pins and needles. "Dad," he said, feeling a sense of relief. "It's Gabriel. Do you know me?"

"Why in the world wouldn't I know my own son?" Theodore asked. "Of course, I know you."

"How are you feeling?" Gabriel asked.

"My legs are itching like crazy," Theodore said, reaching out to scratch limbs that weren't there. "Feel like I'm buried up to my balls in bullet ants. Hurts like a son of a bitch."

"You need your stimulators," Gabriel said, looking around the room. He found the small pads on the nightstand and grabbed them. "I'm going to roll up your pant legs."

"Whatever for?"

"To help the itching."

"I don't need you to nurse me, boy. I can take care of myself."

"I know you can," Gabriel said, rolling up the left leg to reveal the scarred stump. He put the stimulator on it, and could see the relief in his father's eyes.

"What kind of voodoo is this?" his father said, reaching out to roll up his other pants leg so Gabriel could attach the stimulator.

"Do you know where you are?" Gabriel asked.

"I'm old, Gabe. I'm not senile. Alpha Settlement, Calawan system."

He was better than usual, but not completely straight. He didn't seem to know he had lost his legs. Gabriel put the stimulator on the right stump.

"Don't know why they hurt so much," Theodore said. "Too much running, I suppose."

"General Cave was here to see you," Gabriel said.

"Alan? He left a few minutes ago."

"What did you two talk about?"

"Just shooting the breeze, son. He stops by a few times every week. Talked about all the bullshit he has to deal with. Bullshit I for one am glad to be out from under."

"Did he mention the Magellan?"

Theodore's face changed to hear the name of the ship. "They want to take her," he said, his voice suddenly distant.

"You know?"

"I do now." He lowered his head. "It's wrong, son."

"I know."

"They're pissing on her grave. I told Alan that. He thinks sorry means jack to me. So what we haven't found a weapon to break them yet. So damn what? Nothing is invincible. You know that, boy, don't you?"

"I do, Dad."

"I told him I was going to stop this garbage. That I'm going to go before the Council and tell them what I think of what they want to do. I won't let it happen. They ain't going to do that to me. You hear me, son?"

The words were strong. The man behind them looked weak and frail. Tears were rolling into his eyes.

"I hear you, Dad. I'm with you."

Gabriel knew his father would never make it in front of the Council. He could see him fading away with each passing heartbeat, his eyes losing their sudden burst of soul.

"You're a good boy, Gabe. A good son. I'm proud of you. Your mom would be, too." Theodore shook his head. "So damn tired, son. Think I'm going to rest a while. You're late to school again anyway, ain't you?"

Gabriel reached out, helping his father shift so he could lay back in the bed. He was grateful he had gotten thirty seconds of the real Theodore St. Martin before the meds had hit him again.

"Can you get your mom for me, son?" Theodore asked. "I just want to see her face one more time before I go to sleep. I want her to sing to me like she used to."

"I'll get her, Dad," Gabriel said, fighting to keep himself from tearing up. "Just wait here, okay?"

"I will. You're a good boy, Gabriel."

Gabriel positioned his father's head on the pillow, turning away and heading out of the bedroom, wiping at his eyes as he did. He slipped out of the home, walking right past Sabine and Doctor Hall without saying a word.

In his head, all he could hear was his father's voice.

"They're pissing on her grave."

Not if there was anything he could do about it.

[16]

They were lucky that when they hit the water, it was deep enough to break their fall and not their limbs.

It didn't mean they hit the surface softly, or that there was no pain involved. Loose cabling in the narrow shaft got caught on Donovan's arm as he fell, wrenching it back and causing an agonizing throb from the shrapnel wound while turning him over and putting him in an awkward position.

Seconds later, he hit the water almost flat on his back, the force pushing his shoulder forward, snapping it back and sending another shiver of pain through his limb. He swallowed water as he sank a few feet below the surface, feeling a panic at the idea of escaping the Dread machine only to drown. He kicked his legs, pushing himself back up, breaking the plane a moment later. He used his good hand to cover his mouth and help silence his coughs.

"Donovan?" he heard Diaz whisper. It was dark down here, and she had the only light.

It appeared next to her face a moment later, providing just enough illumination for him to start swimming slowly toward her.

"I'm here," he whispered in reply. "Coming to you."

He could still hear the Dread above them, the earth shaking and bits of debris being knocked loose with every heavy step. They would have disappeared from its sensors the moment the water doused them. There was nothing it could use to track them where they had gone. The only question was whether or not it would decide to obliterate the area in an effort to kill them.

He reached Diaz a moment later. Her head was poking out of the water; her wrist held up next to it to provide the light. She smiled as he reached out and put his hand on her shoulder.

She opened her mouth to speak, but he put his finger to her lips and shook his head. There was no sense risking being picked up. They had to stay quiet until the enemy left.

They were still for a few moments. The water was too deep to stand in, and now Donovan saw that the top of a subterranean garage was only a few inches over their heads. They tread water as quietly as they could, leaving soft splashes and a faint bubbling in the distance as the only sounds, which echoed in the small space.

They kept their eyes locked on one another, not wanting to be separated down here. The wound on his back stung sharply, and he wondered how clean this water was, and where it had come from. Not to mention, how had Diaz known it was down here? It was a question for later.

Later came soon enough. A few more minutes passed, followed by the sound of the mechanized armor trudging away through the city above.

"You're bleeding," Diaz said before Donovan could say anything.

"I've got some shrapnel in the back of my shoulder," Donovan replied, still whispering.

"Does it hurt?"

"You better believe it. It isn't serious unless it gets infected or I bleed to death. Either way, we need to get out of here and get back to the base. Doc Iwu can patch me up."

Diaz didn't answer right away. She had a concerned expression on her face.

"What is it?" Donovan asked.

"I found this place during one of the scouting missions before we made our run. The shaft, I mean. I saw it had water in it, and I remembered it in the case of an emergency. Better safe than sorry, right?" She smiled, the water dripping from her lips as she did. "I don't know how to get out of here. I don't even know if there is a way out of here."

Donovan pointed up. "There's one way out if we can climb it."

"With one arm?" Diaz asked.

Donovan tried to flex his other shoulder, stopping halfway because of the pain. There was no way he was going to be doing any kind of climbing, and Diaz wasn't strong enough to carry him out. If it had been the other way around, and she was the one with the shrapnel, it might have been different.

"You can climb out," he said. "Go back to base and get me some help. If you can't make it, leave me here. I'll see if there's a way out."

"Are you loco? I'm not leaving you here."

She swam over to the shaft, the doors just visible above the water. She lifted her arm as high as she could to shine the light on it.

"It doesn't matter anyway, Major," she said. "The walls are smooth metal, and the cables are at least twenty feet over our heads. We're both stuck down here."

[17]

"I hope Sanchez and Cameron made it out. Someone needs to report back that the package was delivered," Donovan said.

"I'm sure they'll be fine. Sanchez isn't a rookie. She knows how to hide, and she'll take care of Cameron."

"And we'll take care of each other. That's how it goes, right?"

"No way, amigo. You're wounded. I'll take care of you. My brother would kill me if I didn't get his best friend home alive."

"Your brother would kill me if I didn't get his sister home alive," Donovan said, smiling. At least he had gotten trapped down here with someone he knew and trusted. "Let's see if we can find a way out."

"Not yet. We need to pull the shrapnel out of your shoulder and get it wrapped. You're turning the water a nice shade of pink."

She lowered the light to the surface so he could see. He hadn't realized how much blood he was losing, and the sight of it made him feel a little queasy.

"Don't pass out on me," Diaz said.

"How are we going to bandage this submerged?"

"We'll have to figure something out, won't we? Give me your shirt."

"What?"

"Your shirt. We need something to wrap it with, and I'm not giving you mine."

Donovan laughed and reached for the buttons of his shirt, undoing them with his good hand. "You'll have to help me pull it off."

Diaz swam behind him, whistling softly when she saw the wound. "Hang on, D. Let me get a closer look."

He could feel her moving behind him, getting her face closer to the injury.

"Okay, it looks like it isn't too deep, but it can't clot with the shrapnel in there."

"It isn't going to clot very well wet either."

"No, but it has to help. I'm going to pull it out on three, okay?"

"Yeah, o-"

Donovan grunted as Diaz pulled the shrapnel from his back. One hand put pressure on the wound while the other worked to get his shirt off.

"That wasn't three," Donovan said.

"It would have hurt more if you were expecting it. Don't be such a baby."

"I'm still your CO," Donovan said.

"Sorry. Don't be such a baby, sir."

He helped her get his shirt off. She used a utility knife tucked under the waist of her pants to cut it into a long strip that she then wrapped around his upper back and shoulder. It took a bit of an effort since they also had to tread water the entire time, but once it was done, he found the pain had subsided substantially.

"There's some good news," Diaz said, circling back in front of him and putting her light against the water.

There was no sign of blood.

"The water's flowing somewhere," he said. "Hopefully, if we follow it, we get the hell out of here."

"Oh, come on, D, it's not so bad. It's like a vacation down here."

"Maybe compared to ten minutes ago. I don't like the whole not knowing how to get out thing."

"We've been through worse."

"We all have, which is why I'm not afraid. I am eager, though."

"Me, too."

"Then there's nothing to do but swim." He reached out. "Take my hand. I don't want to lose you."

She grabbed his hand in hers, using the other to shine the light ahead of them. Donovan flattened out, and they both began kicking.

They reached the edge of the garage a minute later. A solid wall above the water remained solid below it, blocking off their escape from that side.

"There are two more," Diaz said.

Donovan nodded.

They traced the perimeter. They were fortunate the water was temperate, but even so being submerged in it was starting to make Donovan cold. Or maybe it was the loss of blood? Either way, he was shivering by the time they finished moving along the western wall.

"South," Diaz said. "It has to be South." Her eyes fell on his lips. "We need to get you out of here. You're getting a chill."

"Yeah. I'm just about ready to leave. It's a nice place to visit, but I don't want to stay."

They continued swimming, moving around to the southern end of the garage. The entire surface was more solid stone.

"This isn't the outcome I was hoping for," Donovan said.

"I hear bubbling," Diaz replied. "Do you hear it?"

He listened for a minute before nodding. "Yeah."

"Bubbles mean air. Air means an exit, right?"

"I hope so."

They swam across the center of the garage until they found the source of the noise. Large air bubbles were hitting the surface of the water in a steady rhythm.

"I'm going to check it out," Diaz said, letting go of his hand. "Wait here?"

He laughed. "Careful. I might run off with a feisty mamacita while you're gone."

"As if," she said, rolling her eyes. Then she drew in and expelled a few breaths, expanding and gathering air into her lungs. She gave him a thumbs up before vanishing beneath the water.

He could see the light on her wrist fade as she dove, disappearing after a few seconds. He sat in complete darkness, the bubbling the only sound as he counted the time and waited for her to come back up.

He saw the light return as he reached the thirty-second mark. Her head broke the surface a moment later, and she breathed heavily as she spoke.

"I think I found where the air is coming from. The collapse left an exposed pipe. It's six feet wide, at least. A drainage pipe or something. It has a hole in it, and it's venting. It looks big enough for you to squeeze in."

"You want me to squeeze into a submerged pipe? How is that going to help?"

"The pipe is damaged, and if we can cover it and keep some of the air from escaping, we can use it to breathe."

"What happens if the pipe gets smaller further down?"

"We die. Do you have a better option?"

He didn't. "I can't swim down there like this."

"I've got you covered. There's lots of crap on the floor down there. I'll bring something heavy up. Just hold onto me and let yourself sink."

"I never knew you were so resourceful."

"You've barely ever noticed me at all, D. Not as anything more than Matteo's sister."

"That's not true, or you wouldn't be my Lieutenant."

She rolled her eyes again. "You know that isn't how promotions work these days. I just happen to be the second best t-vaulter in Mexico."

"You're number one to me right now," Donovan said.

"Don't get all sappy on me, Major. I'll be right back."

She took in more air and vanished beneath the surface again. Donovan watched the light fade away once more. He'd never realized she had felt excluded from his attention. Maybe because he never wanted Matteo to get the wrong idea about his intentions. He liked Diaz. She was smart, witty, funny, and she had a warm heart. But how do you be friends with your best friend's sister without them thinking you're looking for something else?

Then again, if he had gotten closer to her, could he be certain he wouldn't be?

He couldn't believe he was even thinking about it. It had to be the loss of blood clouding his mind.

The light returned a handful of seconds later, with Diaz swimming hard to reach the surface holding a metal plate that might have come from the bottom of a car. She clutched it tight against her chest, her legs pumping to keep her on the surface.

"Are you ready for this?" she asked, beginning to fill her lungs once more.

He followed her lead, taking quick gulps in and out. Then he reached out and wrapped his arm around her shoulders, putting them so close their foreheads were touching. They kept their eyes on one another as they began to sink.

[18]

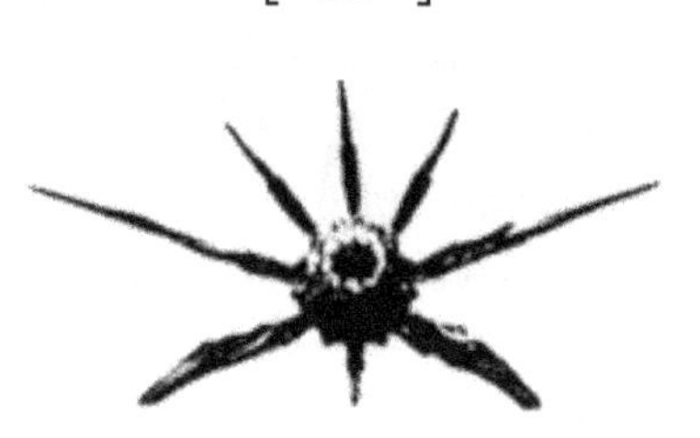

DONOVAN'S LUNGS WERE BURNING BY THE TIME THE WEIGHT OF the metal Diaz was holding carried them the seven meters down to the pipe below. From what he could tell in the dim light and murky water, the plasma fire that had caused the garage's collapse had also made a crater on the ground, which had exposed the pipe. He doubted it had always been damaged and leaking. As his feet touched the ground alongside the pipe, he could tell the wound was fairly fresh, and he wondered what could have caused it.

The Dread, of course. The question was, why? And was the damage intentional?

He didn't have time or air to examine it further. Diaz handed him the weight, turning herself over and swimming down into the pipe. She kept her wrist up so he could find her, taking two steps to the lip of the cut and looking in. He wasn't as sure as she had been that he would fit.

He kept his grip on the metal and stepped over the edge, feeling the air bubbles slipping against him as they made their escape. His feet made it in without issue, as did his legs. He clenched his teeth as the jagged edges of the hole approached his upper body and shoulders, closing his eyes and saying a silent prayer.

He felt a scratching along his arm, a piece of the metal digging into his flesh. It was all he could do to stay still instead of panicking and trying to swim, letting the metal slide through and release him. He looked over at his left arm. It was cut and bleeding, but it was nothing compared to his shoulder.

Diaz grabbed at the piece of metal he was holding, pointing at the hole. They lifted it together, laying it across the opening and holding on. The venting air tried to pull it aside, but the added weight helped keep it in place. Donovan was ready to pass out. They had no idea if this plan would work.

It did, well enough. Some of the air escaped, but some of it remained in the pipe, continuing with the flow of water. Diaz nodded, and they both let go of the metal, pushing off the side of the pipe with their feet. He was out of breath, his body begging for him to take in the water. He held his mouth closed, growing desperate for air and imagining Diaz felt the same.

They traveled twenty meters or so, with Diaz holding her hand up to the top of the pipe. She gripped a seam suddenly, tilting her head up and back. Donovan did the same, bringing his face up next to hers in no more than a few centimeters of air.

They both breathed in harshly, taking massive swallows of oxygen. Donovan's stomach muscles were contracting and cramping, sending waves of pain throughout his body. By the look on Diaz's face, she was suffering something similar.

"That sucked," Donovan said, the words coming out in a broken whisper.

"We made it," Diaz replied. "That's all that matters now."

They continued along the pipe with the air bubble, keeping their heads down and coming up every fifteen seconds or so to take a breath, hoping that the pocket was large enough to sustain them. Neither one of them had any idea how long the pipe was, or where it was going.

Or if it went anywhere at all.

An hour passed. Then another. They stopped stroking, letting the flow of the water carry them for a while, floating on their backs with their heads in the air pocket as best they could, holding one another's hands so they wouldn't be separated. Time seemed to fade away with the constant, soft whoosh of the flowing water and the sounds of their light breathing. Each heartbeat began to bleed into the next and Donovan found his thoughts wandering. They settled on the mission, and on the men and women who would never be returning home.

He remembered Diaz's question about Gibbons, and in his mind he saw the man fall dead again, burned by a plasma rifle. She was a good Lieutenant, a skilled t-vaulter. That she had mentioned an interest in anyone meant she was considering giving up the rifle to bear children. She wanted warriors, he realized. Children that would be strong and healthy, like Gibbons had been. Like she was. Offspring were the best way the free females could help the cause. At the same time, no one had ever presumed to stop them from fighting. It was still a choice to be made, not an expectation to be followed.

He turned his head slightly so he could see her, on her back with her head only inches from his. She had her eyes closed, thinking her own thoughts while they floated. Was she thinking about Gibbons, too? About children? He had known her since she had been born. He was seven at the time, and already best friends with Matteo. It seemed strange to him that she would be a mother. He felt too young to be a father, and she was so much younger than him. Was it what she wanted, or what she felt she needed to do? The resistance was slowly dwindling, their numbers dropping every year. If they could clone people like the Dread did, instead of having to reproduce them the old fashioned way, maybe they would stand a chance.

"Do you want to bring a child into this world?" he said out loud without thinking.

Diaz's eyes opened, and she turned her head enough to see him. "What?"

"I was thinking about Gibbons and you. Do you really think it will change anything?"

She positioned her head straight up again. "I want to believe it would," she said. "But I don't know. You're projecting my offhand chatter pretty far."

"I'm tired, and I lost a lot of blood," he said. "I couldn't help but start thinking about everything. I don't know if it's my mind that's tricking me, or if I'm more sane than usual. You've seen what's been happening here in Mexico; I know you have. I've heard it's worse in other places. That the resistance has been wiped out. Japan, Nigeria, Florida. We lose another base every week."

"Those are only rumors."

"Are they? We lost sixteen people today, Renata. How many soldiers does that leave us with?"

She was silent while she listed the names in her head. Just the fact that she could name them all was enough of an answer. "Twenty-six."

"We can't keep going like this. It would take you the rest of your reproductive life to replace what we lost in five minutes."

"So what do you think we should do?" Diaz asked, annoyed. "Give up? Kill ourselves and save the Dread the trouble."

"No. I'm not saying we should ever give up. I think we need to change our tactics or something. Maybe forget about the messengers and focus on fighting our own war. How many people have we lost getting these transmissions out?"

"A lot. We need the space forces. We can't do anything about orbital bombardment without them, and that's exactly what the Dread will do if we start gathering in large numbers again. You remember Charlotte, don't you?"

It was one of the stories that was told around the mess. A free human force of nearly ten-thousand had managed to assemble there. They even swarmed a Dread armor and almost got it to topple. Then the enemy had sent a plasma flume down on them, bathing the armor and the city both. The city was slagged a second time.

The armor wasn't even scratched. In fact, as the legend went, the excited energy had cleaned it up real nice.

"I don't know if we have ten-thousand left in the world," Donovan said.

"Can you try not to sound so dour?" Diaz said. "The last thing we need is to beat ourselves."

Donovan was silent.

"Anyway," Diaz said, "I don't think you're completely wrong. What we've been doing hasn't been working well. I think we've gotten too predictable. The Dread know when we're going to be transmitting. They're waiting for us. We need to take them by surprise."

"How?"

"If I knew that, I'd be the General. Everything we can think of would be easier to say than do."

"How I'd love to get a bullet through that armor of theirs just once," Donovan said. "How I'd love to see the look on one of their faces."

"Fifty years, and nobody even knows what they look like," Diaz said. "To be honest, it is hard to stay upbeat when everything seems so hopeless. But what else can we do? No, I don't think having kids will help the overall fight, but it's still important. We have to keep our hope, or we might as well let ourselves die right here and now."

Donovan locked eyes with Diaz. "Well, I'm not going to let you die, so I guess that means I can't let myself die either."

"I think you've got that reversed, amigo. I'm the one saving you."

"Oh? I'm the man here, Lieutenant. And the CO. I'm saving-"

He didn't get to finish his comment. Without warning, the water, and the pipe they had been traveling in vanished beneath them.

[19]

THEY WENT OVER THE EDGE TOGETHER, LOSING THEIR GRIP ON one another as the pipe opened up and spilled out into a deep well.

Donovan made a better landing this time, keeping his body knife straight and cutting through the pool below, sinking deep enough that his feet scraped the bottom. There hadn't been time to hold his breath, and he kicked furiously to get himself to the surface once more.

His head broke the water, and he took in air while he looked around, suddenly fearful. They appeared to be in a collection area of some kind, with pipes trailing into the large underground space from every direction. He found a small ledge on the south side, where a small control room sat unoccupied, a glowing screen visible through a window; a computer awaiting instructions from handlers that would never return.

Diaz was already at the ledge, pulling herself onto it. He swam more slowly now, letting the apparent safety of the place allow him to relax a little bit.

She was in the control room by the time he dragged himself onto the platform.

"I thought you were taking care of me," he said, struggling to get up with one arm.

"You're the man and the CO. I figured you could handle it."

He regretted starting the macho humor, peering past her at the control screen. "What is this place?"

"Flood control. We were luckier than I realized."

"That pipe only fills when it's been raining a lot?" Donovan said.

"Si. The pipes lead from smaller drainage areas throughout the city, collecting the rainwater and bringing it through here before sending it on to be purified. All that rain the last couple of weeks left the tank nearly full, which is a good thing for us. It would have been a painful landing."

"I can't believe that thing is still working," he said, motioning to the control pad.

"It isn't. The last line says 'critical error.' I think it can cut off the flow to this tank and divert to another one in case it starts to overfill. We're lucky that didn't happen or we would have drowned for sure."

"Lucky us," Donovan deadpanned, shifting his arm. It was starting to throb again, the wound disturbed by the fall.

"We aren't dead yet. That has to be good for something."

"Only if there's a way out."

Diaz pointed behind him. He turned around, smiling when he saw the open doorway and the sign that read "Salida." Exit.

"Perfect," he said. Something had gone right today.

They moved to the door, passing through and following it to the left. There was a second door, there, also open, which lead to a narrow set of iron stairs that smelled of dampness and decay. Donovan grabbed the railing and started to ascend.

"Try to keep quiet," Diaz said. "We don't know where we are, or what might be out here."

"Yes, sir," Donovan replied, saluting her and causing a sharp jolt of pain in his arm.

"Was it worth it?" Diaz asked.

Donovan shrugged and kept climbing, lifting his head so he could see the top of the stairwell. It was a good thirty meters up. The door at the top was closed.

It didn't take long to ascend. They stopped in front of the closed door, and Donovan put his ear to it to listen. He didn't hear anything on the other side, and so he tried the manual handle. It was an old door to an old system. The door clicked as it came free of the latch, and he pulled it open slowly, peering out into the darkness beyond. The area was deserted.

"Come on," he whispered, moving out into the open.

They cleared the doorway, finding themselves inside a small concrete bunker. It was the outer entrance to the system below. A final door rested between them and the outside world.

"When we go through the door, I'll get our bearings, and then we run back to base," he said. "We don't slow down for anything."

"Can you make it?" Diaz asked. "You lost a lot of blood."

"As long as my adrenaline holds out. I'm sure I'll pay for it tomorrow."

"Okay. I'm ready."

Donovan approached the door, listening against it one more time. He could hear a faint noise in the background, a soft hum that could have been anything. It was probably the pump that ran the purification system.

He grabbed the manual handle again and started to turn it. The door was unlocked, and he let it click softly before starting to push it open.

He had only moved it six inches when the sight of what lay beyond made his heart begin to race, and he pulled it quickly and quietly back closed.

"Dios Mio," he said, turning to face Diaz.

"What is it?" Diaz asked.

"I don't believe it," Donovan said, stunned by what he had seen. "We're in. We're inside."

"Inside what?" Diaz's face took on a look of excited curiosity.

"The city. The Dread city."

[20]

GABRIEL COULDN'T HELP BUT SMILE AS CAPTAIN STURGES guided the transport into Delta Station's waiting hangar. After everything he had learned during his hours on Alpha Settlement, he was glad to be home.

The BIS touched down on the floor of the hangar, magnetic clamps catching the tiny skids at the bottom of the box and holding it in place while the smaller bay doors were slowly closed. Once they had sealed and locked, the compressed air that was sucked from the chamber was released back in, pressurizing the area. The suppressors were re-activated, returning gravity to the space as well.

The red light in the BIS's cockpit turned green. Sturges turned in his seat to face Gabriel.

"I'm sorry about all of this garbage with the Council," he said, absently tapping the control pad to open the rear cargo door. The transport had been loaded up with foodstuffs and laundered uniforms, among other things. "If there's anything Siddhu or I can do to help, you just let me know."

"Thank you, Paul," Gabriel said. "I don't know if there's anything that anyone can do. It seems the people with the most pull have made up their minds. That doesn't mean I'm not going to try."

"I'm with you, Gabriel. Whatever you need."

Gabriel nodded, squeezing the older man's shoulder on his way to the back. He angled around the cargo and past the crew that was waiting to unload it.

"Captain," the Logistics Officer, Second Lieutenant Daphne O'Dea said, saluting him as he departed.

"Lieutenant," Gabriel said, returning the salute. "Let me know if there are any treats in the resupply, will you?"

"For you or Wallace?" she asked.

Gabriel spread his hands innocently. "Does it matter?"

"Only one of you is cute enough to over-ration. By the way, it's good to have you back."

"Thanks, Daphne. How's Soon?"

She shook her head. "Don't get me started. He's been trying to fix that old inverter again. He nearly blew a hole in our quarters and vented us into space."

Gabriel smiled. Captain Soon Kim considered himself a tinkerer, but he rarely got the things he tinkered with working again. He and Daphne had only been married a few months, and the honeymoon was close to being over. Captain Kim was next up on the mission detail.

"Well, tell him I said hello if I don't see him first," Gabriel said. It had been almost thirty hours since he had slept, and he was planning to head directly to his quarters to drop.

"Will do. See you later, Gabriel."

Gabriel passed across the hangar towards the exit. His eyes wandered to the starfighter bays on his left. They only had five left. Six if he counted the one that had been left on Manhattan. Engineering could probably print more if they were given clearance, but considering current events he doubted that would happen.

He moved from the hangar into the network of corridors that ran across Delta Station. Everything was a mixture of gray metal and small viewports here, a spiderweb of identical hallways that were hard to navigate for cadets fresh out of training. When Gabriel had first arrived, he had made it a point to learn the layout of the station within his first twenty-four hours. Even then, it had taken him forty-eight.

He had no trouble finding his way around now. He had seen every corridor so many times he could point out all of the scratches, dents, and smudges that identified one against another, and he could get anywhere in the base faster than many of the others. Some only bothered to learn their routes and didn't care about the rest. He wasn't like that.

He passed by the gym, waving at the few soldiers inside who were keeping their strength up with basic weights and cardio. It was simple throwback tech that was easy to produce and maintain and just as effective as programmed muscle stimulation and bio-electric conditioning, even if it took more overall effort. From there, he dropped four levels down, further into the spike where berthing was located. As a Captain, he had his own living space on the second level, a fifty square meter apartment complete with a bedroom, bathroom, and den. It was as sparsely produced and decorated as everything else on the station, but it had a full-sized transparency with a nice view of Manhattan, and it was a place to call home.

He finally reached his quarters, having grown more tired with each step he took. It was more than the lack of sleep. He couldn't get his father's words out of his head. Or his tears. Half of the people on the Council wouldn't have been alive if it hadn't been for Juliet St. Martin. He would have hoped they would have more respect for her sacrifice.

He tapped his palm against the door, and it slid aside. Wallace was waiting behind it, as expected. Gabriel could feel his depressed mood turning slightly as the Golden Retriever started whining and wagging his tail, sitting obediently and waiting for him to pour on the attention.

"Hey, Wallace," Gabriel said, stepping over the threshold and reaching down to pet the dog's head. "How are you doing, buddy?"

There weren't a lot of pets in the colony, but there were some, incubated and born in the laboratories in Charlie Settlement from the frozen sperm and eggs that had been loaded onto the Magellan.

The colony had access to over ten-thousand species, though only three dog breeds and one cat had been born so far. Wallace had half the genes of Theodore's pet Golden, Po'boy, who had died during the invasion.

Wallace's tail continued to swish back and forth as Gabriel moved further into his quarters, petting him as he did. Wallace had been a gift from his father after Jessica had died. It was a misguided but otherwise meaningful effort to help him adjust to her loss, and to be honest, to an extent it had.

"Yeah, it's been a rough day at work," Gabriel said. "I missed you, too. Remind me to thank Miranda for taking care of you while I was gone."

Wallace looked up at him, mouth open and tongue hanging out.

"Scientists," Gabriel said, shaking his head. "They don't care about people. They care about proving themselves right. Earth is our planet. Right, buddy?"

Wallace nuzzled Gabriel's hand.

"I saw one of their satellites get blown apart. I know it's possible. Maybe if they put as much energy into figuring that out as they have bent over blurry images of sensor readings."

Gabriel pulled off his jacket and unbuttoned his shirt, taking everything off until he was in a white t-shirt and underwear. He looked out the one-way transparency to Manhattan below, the outline of the Magellan visible beneath a light dust storm. He stared at it for a moment, remembering the look in his father's eyes again before crossing to his bedroom and laying down. Wallace jumped on the bed next to him, immediately curling up on the free side.

They were both asleep within minutes.

[21]

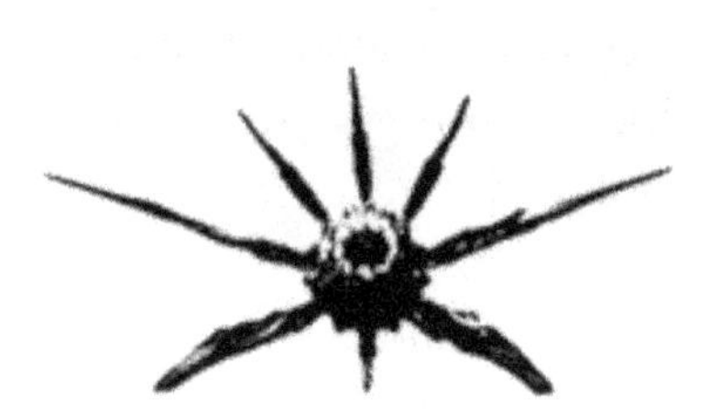

Gabriel woke six hours later. Wallace was still laying beside him though he had changed position to stretch his body across the bed and lay his head on a pillow.

"Lazy mutt," Gabriel said, reaching over and patting the side of the dog.

Wallace turned his head for a moment and then rolled onto his back so Gabriel could reach his stomach.

"Spoiled, lazy mutt," Gabriel said.

He slid off the bed and onto his feet, crossing to the bathroom. He pulled off the rest of his clothes and stepped into the shower, tapping the regulator that would give him three minutes of hot water every twenty-four hours. No more. No less.

He let the infused water clean off the grime, taking the full minutes before toweling off and throwing on a pair of utilities. He was off-duty for the next three days, and he was hungry.

"Come on, buddy," he said to Wallace, crossing the front of his quarters. "Let's see what's for breakfast."

Wallace's ears perked up at the word, and he rushed ahead to the door. He started whining a moment before a tone signaled someone was at the door.

Gabriel tapped the panel to open it, finding Miranda on the other side.

"Gabriel," she said, surprised. "I didn't know you were back."

"Yup. I hitched a ride with Captain Sturges. I couldn't take being in Alpha any longer than I had to."

Miranda kneeled to pet Wallace, looking up at him while she spoke. "Is it your father?"

"Believe it or not, he was the best part of the trip. It's everything else that's going to hell."

"Oh? What do you mean?"

"You haven't heard the rumors about leaving Calawan?"

"I've heard them. I didn't think they were very serious. You know how we NEA types like to gossip."

"Well, they're serious. Not only that, but General Cave is backing the idea."

Miranda stood, clearly shocked. "General Cave?"

"Even worse, he told my father what they plan to do. I got a few minutes with him before the meds knocked him out again. You should have seen the look in his eyes. I can't forget it."

"They're only trying to do what's best for everyone."

"That's what General Cave and Colonel Graham said. And maybe they are trying to do the best for the people in Calawan. The humans here don't count as everyone."

"You mean Earth? I get where you're coming from, Gabe. I do. I swear. But we've never even been able to hurt the Dread. How are we supposed to help the people on Earth?"

"I've heard that argument before," Gabriel said, suddenly tired of talking about it. "We were headed down to the mess. Do you want to join us?"

"Maybe you've heard the argument, but I don't think you're listening to it. You're as stubborn as your old man." She smiled as though she was giving him a compliment. "Personally, I don't think either choice is that great. Unfortunately, they're the only choices we have."

"So which one do you prefer?"

"Fight or flight? I don't know. My heart says fight. My head says flight."

"You always like to take both sides."

"Because every story has two sides. You should be open to the one you don't agree with some time. You want others to be open to you."

"Only when I'm right."

Miranda laughed. "You're impossible. Come on, I'll grab something with you."

"Let's go, Wally, " Gabriel said. "Time to eat."

Gabriel walked side-by-side with Miranda down the corridor, while Wallace ranged ahead, pausing at the doors to sniff the food behind them. They took the central elevator up to the base of the main saucer, diverting to Delta Park. The park was the station's main recreational area, a one thousand square meter expanse of artificial greenery that did its best to substitute for the real thing.

"Other than the business with the Council, how is your father these days?" Miranda asked as they left the park. "How long had it been since you saw him last?"

"Six months," Gabriel said. "He's, I don't know, well enough? It's hard to say. He spends most of every day medicated and lost in his head. For all intents, he might as well be dead already."

"That's a terrible thing to say."

"The only reason he isn't yet is because he's still waiting for us to win this war. It's all he has to keep him going. My mother believed in God and Heaven, and I know he wants to join her there. The only thing he cares more about is the promise he made to see this through."

Miranda was silent for a few seconds. "It's kind of sad, isn't it? Everything that's happened to him?"

"Yes. You can understand why I'm so against giving up the fight. I also don't believe in giving up on the people that we abandoned."

"Abandoned? That's not fair, is it?"

"My father said he abandoned them. They ran away in the Magellan instead of helping fight back. He's always said it was the one order he regretted following."

"Fight how?"

"Any way they could. Or, in the words of my father, 'wrasslin' with their bare hands until they sank into the bayou.'"

"Your father always had a colorful way with words."

"He still does when he's himself."

They reached the entrance to the mess. Captain Kim was coming out as they were going in, and he paused ahead of Gabriel, smiling and saluting.

"Captain St. Martin. Daphne told me you were back."

"Soon," Gabriel said, dropping the salute and taking his friend's hand. "I heard you almost blew up the station again."

Soon laughed in his deep voice that belied his petite frame. He was just over five feet of fast-twitch muscle, though his spiked hair gave him another few inches. "Lies. Nothing but lies. I almost blew up our quarters. The emergency seals would have closed us off before we could take anyone with us."

"Well, I'm glad I had a station to come back to."

"Yeah, I heard you were on Alpha. I'm sorry, man. At least you made it back here alive. Sturges said you took some nasty damage on that last run."

"It was close. It wasn't the first time. You know how it is."

"I sure do." Soon clapped him on the shoulder. "I've got to run. I'm due for a slipstream drill in thirty. I don't get to skip another rotation to fool around with my wife."

Soon's smile disappeared as he realized the meaning behind what he said. Gabriel felt the twinge of old sadness creeping up, and he forced it back down.

"It's okay," he said instead. "If it were up to me you'd be retiring to keep the population going. We could use some more good pilots."

"Thanks, Gabriel. I only need about sixty more runs to catch up with you."

Gabriel was sure they wouldn't have sixty more runs. If they were going to be leaving Calawan, they would pour every available resource into refitting the Magellan. With the weight of the entire colony behind the effort, he imagined it wouldn't take more than a few months.

"See you soon," Miranda said. Soon rolled his eyes at the old joke and walked away, pausing to pet Wallace's head before continuing.

Wallace wandered over to Gabriel's side, his eyes fixed on the inside of the mess. There were nearly one hundred soldiers inside, seated at the simple tables with a bland stew in front of them. At least they had some real food today.

"That's one of the people we're saving if we leave," Miranda said. "You know if we stay he's more likely than not to die skimming Earth's atmosphere."

"I know," Gabriel replied.

If he could change things, he would. He didn't want anyone else to have to go through what he had, or what his father had.

Some things were bigger than a single person.

Some promises couldn't be broken.

[22]

"You asked to see me, sir?" Gabriel said, standing in the open doorway of Colonel Graham's office on Delta Station.

Graham looked up from his tablet. His office was an out-of-place aberration compared to the rest of Delta Station. His desk was custom printed and painted, meant to resemble wood as closely as possible. His chair was cushioned. He had three paintings hanging on his walls, carried from Earth in the Magellan. The artist had never been famous before. They were all priceless now.

A second cushioned chair sat opposite him. He waved Gabriel over to it.

"Have a seat, Captain," he said. "I want to talk to you."

Gabriel tried to judge the topic by the Colonel's tone. Graham could be a gruff man, but he could also be very kind. He was somewhere in between.

"Yes, sir," he said, taking the seat, keeping his posture rigid.

"Relax, Gabriel," Graham said, closing the door with a tap on his pad. "This is off the record."

Gabriel let his limbs slouch slightly. "Is my father okay?"

Graham smiled. "He's fine. This is about the other day when you stopped by with Major Choi to see me."

"I apologize if I was out of line, sir," Gabriel said. "You know my emotions get the better of me sometimes."

"First, I said this is off the record. No 'sirs' required. Second, you weren't out of line. You spoke from your heart, and I respect the hell out of that. It's one of the best traits you inherited from your father."

"What's the worst?" Gabriel asked. He already had a feeling he knew the answer.

"Your stubborn determination. Which can be a good quality, too. If I had to pick another one, it would be that you don't shave as often as you should."

Gabriel ran his hand along his chin, feeling the prickliness of it. He had been in the gym when he received the Colonel's summons and rushed to get himself together.

"In any case, after you left my office I had a long conversation with Major Choi. I'm not saying I agree with you. Not yet. I do want to hear more about your experience."

"You have the data recorder," Gabriel said.

"We do, but I haven't heard the contents yet. I wanted to get your perspective first-hand."

Gabriel told Colonel Graham about the mission, starting from the moment he left the slipstream, and ending when he re-entered it. Graham leaned forward when he related the part about the enemy starfighter destroying its own satellites, interested in every detail Gabriel could give him.

"Was there anything about the weapon that seemed strange to you?" Graham asked.

"No. It seemed like a standard plasma cannon to me. Except when the bolts hit the satellites, they blew as if they had no armor at all."

"Incredible. Fifty years, and it's the first time anyone has seen anything like it. Is it coincidence or providence that you witnessed it right before the Council is set to meet about what to do with the colony?"

"I don't believe in fate," Gabriel said.

"Neither do I," Graham replied. "But I do believe in God, and that's the question that's keeping me up at night. I thought I had made up my mind about leaving, but then you dropped that bomb on me, and now I'm not so sure."

"If there is a God, why would He let the Dread kill billions of innocent people?" Gabriel asked. That was the question that had often kept him up at night. It was the reason he asked for luck and kept the crucifix as a charm instead of a religious symbol. His mother had faith, and look where it had gotten her. "And don't say He works in mysterious ways."

"Freedom of all His creations. Including the Dread. That doesn't mean He's happy with what they've done, or that they won't pay for it when they die. I had thought maybe He had other things in mind for us, that this new planet would be an Eden. I'm not the only one. That's what the Council is calling it. Did you know that?"

"No."

"It is. Anyway, my heart says we should stay. My head says we should go."

"Spaceman Locke said the same thing. If you're spiritual, what does your spirit say?"

Graham was silent. He stared at Gabriel as if he could find answers there.

"The Council is convening tomorrow. I'm going to be taking a transport down to Alpha to attend. I want you to come with me."

"Why?"

"Faith. I want you to talk to the Council."

"So I can get myself court-martialed?" Gabriel asked.

"If God wants us to stay and fight, He'll send His message through you."

Gabriel wasn't about to attribute his passion to someone else's will. "Do you really believe that?"

"I do."

"Then I guess I'll see you tomorrow," Gabriel said. "Is there anything else, sir?"

"No, thank you. You're dismissed."

Gabriel got to his feet and saluted before turning on his heel and heading out the door. Colonel Graham could call it providence if he wanted to. He could claim it was the work of an all-powerful being, and who knew? Maybe it was. He'd been having that argument with himself for years, and it always ended with his mother and his home world lost. How did Graham, or his father for that matter, manage to stay with God when God hadn't stayed with them?

He was sure he would never know.

[23]

"Are you serious?" Diaz asked, pushing past Donovan and opening the door to a hairline crack.

She pulled it closed a few heartbeats later, turning to look at him.

He knew what she had just seen. The small control room for the drainage system was sitting in the corner of an expansive area beneath the Dread's impenetrable cocoon. Looking up, he had seen the dark carapace made visible by an organic light that seemed to run in jagged lines along it, a bluish-white illumination that accented ridges and dips and extrusions on the material that he had never witnessed before.

Ahead of them, he had seen what he assumed was a machine of some kind. It was large and dark and made of a compound he didn't recognize. It was as though they had taken liquid oil and molded it into parts, and then assembled those parts and connected them with more of the dark material in tubes and channels that gave the entire thing a menacing and lifelike appearance.

He had heard it humming while the door was open, and had seen how the ground seemed to vibrate below it. That was all he had taken the time to absorb before his fear had made him close the door again. He had no idea if there were any Dread in the area, and now that they had managed to get into the city, he found himself scared of the idea of seeing one of the aliens. If they did, they would be the first free humans to lay eyes on them.

"I don't know what to say," Diaz whispered. "Or if we should be scared or excited."

"Excited?" Donovan asked.

"This is a pretty incredible opportunity. No one has ever been inside before."

"You don't know that. It could be no one has ever been inside and made it back out."

"Well, we're inside, and whether we choose to be scared or not, there's only going to be one way out." She pointed at the door.

"I'm trying not to be afraid. It isn't working that well."

"I'm with you on that, amigo."

They stared at each other in silence. Donovan tried to get his nerves and his breathing under control. They were going to have to go out there. It wasn't like they had a choice unless they wanted to stay in the control room and starve. Except he doubted that would happen either. The Dread hadn't destroyed the building or the drainage system. In fact, it was possible they were using it for something, which meant they were no safer here than out there.

"You still have your knife?" he asked.

Diaz laughed. "What good is that going to do against them?"

"None if they're armored. We know they use clones for at least part of their army, and the clones are just like us."

"Actually, they're just like each other. Literally. And better armed."

Donovan forced a smile. The trauma they had already been through was making them giddy. He could feel himself shaking, his frayed nerves begging for release. He struggled to get them under control. He was still the CO of this unit, even if it only consisted of one other soldier. It was his duty to lead.

"Then we'll have to be sneaky. We're t-vaulters. We're good at that. How's my shoulder?"

Diaz circled behind him to check it. "It looks like it stopped bleeding. How does it feel?"

"It hurts. I'll live. Come on."

Donovan returned to the door, slowly pushing it open a third time. This time, he opened it enough to stick his head out and take in more of the area.

The machine right in front of him was only one of a dozen identical devices, arranged in a circle around the center of the massive space. What looked like thick cables ran from each of them to the middle, where a large platform rose to the top of the structure in an hourglass shape of bundled cord. As before, he could see the ground vibrating beneath and around each of the machines. The cords leading to the ceiling were shifting as well though the effect wasn't as noticeable in the air.

What he didn't see were any other life forms, alien or otherwise. They were safe for now.

"What do you think it is?" Diaz asked, following him out of the room.

They stayed close to the small, cement building, tracing its walls to the rear. The side of the alien structure was only a dozen meters away at the back and gave off a faint odor that Donovan had never experienced before. It was sweet and rich; a pleasant smell.

"It may be their power source," he said. "Or one of them, anyway."

"What do you think would happen if we destroyed it?"

"Probably nothing good for them, but considering we only have a utility knife? I don't like our odds."

Diaz nodded, and they moved toward the wall. When they got close enough, they both reached out to touch it at almost the same time.

The material was cool to the touch, smooth and solid as steel or iron. Leaning in for a closer inspection, he could see tiny veins of various shades of gray moving through it and along it. He didn't know if they were intentional or simply the coloration of whatever it was made from. The other thing he noticed was that the shape of it was uneven. Not only were there sharp ridges in seemingly random places in the material, but there were also gentle slopes and valleys that he would never have noticed without running his hand along it.

"It's amazing," he said.

"It's also the death of humanity," Diaz replied.

Donovan removed his hand. "Do you see a way out?"

"There," she said, pointing to a break in the material a short distance away. "It looks like a corridor."

"Let's try to stay in the shadows as much as possible, and hope they don't have an alarm."

Diaz smiled. "I bet they don't expect anything to get in here. If we had a little bit of C-4, we could blow this entire area, no problem."

"We'll be sure to come back with some."

They made their way across to the adjoining corridor. It was much smaller in scale, ten meters high and wide. It was also darker and more foreboding, with the bluish light filtering from the ceiling in regular intervals and casting the chitinous material in an eerie light. The hallway ended a few hundred meters back, forking into a pair of adjoining corridors.

There was still no sign of life. The only noise to be heard was the soft humming from the machines behind them.

"I feel like this is a good time to say something witty and inspiring," Donovan said. "Nothing's coming to me."

"Let's try not to die," Diaz said.

"Good enough."

[24]

DONOVAN AND DIAZ NAVIGATED THROUGH CORRIDOR AFTER corridor, taking random turns to the right or left fork based on educated guesses of which direction they were facing and which direction might lead them out of the Dread city, careful not to move in a way that would bring them back to where they had started.

An hour passed with no sign of anything beyond the dim hallways, which all began to look identical after a while. The only sound was the light slapping of their bare feet on the cold floor. The only comfort was the fact that they weren't alone.

They had spent years in the shadow of the massive alien base. They had spent years in hiding, fearful of what lay behind the black walls. Only now they were behind the black walls.

And there was nothing.

For Donovan, it defied expectation or explanation. Where were the Dread? From the outside he had assumed the aliens were thriving beneath their protective cocoon, taking advantage of the humans they had enslaved. It was common knowledge that they had come to harvest humanity's genome, to splice humankind's DNA into their own as centuries of scientific rather than sexual reproduction had destroyed their diversity and left them weak and riddled with illness.

It was understood that they had rounded up people by the thousands, testing them for compatibility and quality and using those who matched their criteria for specific applications like the identical bald soldiers.

That information had led him to think the enemy numbered in the millions or at least had millions of slaves. Maybe they had stumbled into a low traffic area, but millions of anything would be sure to make some kind of noise or be some level of obvious.

"Maybe they don't use this area anymore," Diaz whispered, apparently thinking along the same lines.

"Whatever that is back there is up and running," Donovan replied. "Which doesn't suggest it's been abandoned."

"Then where is everybody?"

"Your guess is as good as mine."

They had given up slinking along the sides of the hallways twenty minutes earlier, moving at a faster pace by walking right down the middle. It was so quiet Donovan was sure he'd hear something coming before it was able to sneak up on them.

"We know the perimeter of the city is over one hundred kilometers long," Donovan said. "If the density is low enough it would make sense there would be nobody here."

"Who maintains everything, then? Unless they have a central monitoring system."

Donovan stopped walking, his eyes scanning the walls, ceiling, and floor around them. "Let's say that they do. Do you think they know we're here, and they're just watching us? Waiting to see what we'll do next?"

Diaz bit her bottom lip, considering. "No. Why would they need to monitor inside their walls?"

"We don't know where they came from. Just because human technology is inferior to theirs, how do we know theirs isn't inferior to someone else's? If there are two intelligent life forms in the universe, it stands to reason there are three or more."

"You're reaching, D," Diaz said. "Besides, if they're watching us there isn't anything we can do about it. We have to find a way out."

They started walking again, though Donovan paid more attention to the structure around them now, looking for anything that might resemble a sensor or a camera. Diaz was right. If they were being watched, so be it. The Dread had chosen not to intervene, at least not yet.

Ten more minutes found them at another intersection. Donovan was about to ask Diaz which way she thought they should go when he realized the structure of the corridor had changed. The hallways on both sides of them were no longer completely straight, instead curving gently until they vanished into the distance.

"I bet this corridor makes a ring," Diaz said. "Now we're getting somewhere."

"Stay alert," Donovan said, moving to the inside of the curve. It wouldn't hide them for long, but it was better than nothing.

They turned to the left and began following the curve. As they moved further in, new corridors began to appear on the outer side of the ring, while indents began lining the inner.

"Doorways," Donovan said, feeling a sense of fear rising with his heart rate.

"Somebody has to be here, don't they?" Diaz asked, taking her knife from her waist and holding it up defensively. Any of the doors could open at any time.

They kept going. Eventually, the inner curve revealed a corridor that dove deeper into the center of the circle. Donovan could see what appeared to be a green laser stabbing through the middle of that hallway, signaling the center of the ring. He had no idea what it was, and he wasn't eager to find out.

"Which way is north?" he asked. His sense of direction was fine outside when he could check the sky.

"This way, I think," Diaz said, pointing toward the corridor across from them. It led away from the circle, down another long, straight passage.

"Let's keep going north until we can't anymore. Otherwise, we'll be lost in here forever."

"Agreed."

They started heading for the northern corridor.

A soft swishing noise sounded to their right.

One of the doors was opening.

There was no time to think. No time to consider. It was fight or flight.

Donovan threw himself at the figure coming out of the doorway, hitting it hard with his injured shoulder, acting so quickly he never got a look at what he was attacking. He felt his arm smack against a rough frame, and he bit his tongue to keep from crying out at the pain his assault caused him.

Then he was falling, tangled up with the enemy and landing on top as they both crashed on the floor inside the room.

Donovan squirmed and scrambled, trying to get his feet under him and put a few inches of distance between himself and whatever he had hit. He could smell the same sweet odor again, and see a small patch of stark white flesh and silver hair layered over a bony ridge.

The alien hissed beneath him, trying to shake itself loose. Donovan lifted himself slightly, getting a good look at an orange, humanoid eye. Then Diaz was in the room beside him. She fell to her knees, her knife coming down hard, burying it in that orange eye. Cranberry colored blood began to run out, and the body went limp below him.

"Take that you son of a bitch," Diaz whispered angrily, releasing a sharp breath.

The door slid closed behind them.

[25]

DONOVAN ROLLED OFF THE CORPSE BELOW HIM, HIS SHOULDER throbbing. He came to his knees on the opposite side, his eyes only the second pair to ever take in the sight of the enemy.

"I never knew what to expect," Diaz said, her body trembling.

The pierced orange eye was matched with a second, anchored to a face that was decidedly humanoid. Between them was a tiny, flat nose, a small arc with a pair of nostrils that led down to very human-looking pink lips and white teeth, the mouth hanging slightly open in a forever silent scream. Tracing the outline, he saw the ears were also small and pressed tight against the head, while some small, bony ridges created an almost reptilian shape to the upper portion of the skull. Short, fine, silver hair grew from the scalp behind the ridges, giving the alien a near-demonic appearance.

Except nothing about it suggested it was demonic. In fact, the white skin made it look more like an angel. Donovan's eyes trailed down a milky neck to narrow shoulders and a small frame, dressed in simple black cloth that appeared to be composed of a similar material to the unbreakable armor. A pair of slippers covered the feet while four-fingered hands lay exposed at the alien's sides.

Diaz reached down, pulling at the cloth and lifting it away from the Dread's waist. The dead alien was clearly a male.

"So much like us," Donovan said, barely able to breathe.

"Maybe now," Diaz said. "We don't know what they looked like before. They've been using human genes to fix themselves."

"I can't believe you killed one." He realized he was shaking, too.

"Me neither." She pulled the knife from its eye. "I can't say I feel sorry for it."

Donovan finally pulled his eyes away from it, quickly scanning the room. It appeared to be living quarters of some kind. A transparent enclosure sat in the center of the space; alien symbols illuminated in a grid against the surface and what appeared to be a mask dangling from the top of it. Behind the enclosure was a more traditional human mattress, complete with white sheets tucked into the frame it sat on, which blended in with, or was protruding from the wall behind it. A seam that suggested a storage area sat on the left of the enclosure, while an archway was on the right.

They got to their feet. Donovan approached the enclosure, making as good of a mental image of it all as he could. He peered through the open archway into what had to be a bathroom. A small tube protruded from the wall at the right height for urinating into, while a second tube extended from the wall in a position that was clearly intended for defecation. It was both familiar and completely alien at the same time, a conjunction of advanced technology and crude adjustments in response to the form the Dread had taken.

He couldn't help but wonder what they had looked like before.

"I wish I could read this," Diaz said, stopped in front of the enclosure and staring at the symbols. They were simple lines in even, measured strokes that bore a very vague resemblance to the Roman alphabet.

"I wish I had a way to record all of this," Donovan said.

He returned to the body on the floor, patting it down. He felt an odd protrusion over the chest, and he pushed aside the alien's clothing until he found a round, flat, black pin the size of a fingernail.

"I wonder what this does," he said, unclipping it and holding it up.

"I wonder what any of this stuff does," Diaz said. She was trying to figure out how to open the seam in the wall. She ran her hands along it until it split in two, sliding apart to reveal its contents.

"Their wardrobe is pretty boring," Donovan said, looking into the storage area. Shelves of black cloth lay inside.

"No hobbies, either," Diaz said. "The room has nothing else in it. What do you think they do for fun?"

"Destroy civilizations," Donovan said. "It's too bad none of its clothes are even close to fitting me. I could use a shirt."

Diaz grabbed a piece of the cloth and unfolded it. It looked way too small for the alien. She pulled at it, finding that it stretched well. "I think it'll work," she said. She tossed it to him, along with a pair of the pants. Then she started unbuttoning her shirt.

"What are you doing?" Donovan asked, catching the cloth. It was incredibly light and soft.

"Changing," she replied, undoing the last button and holding the shirt open just enough that Donovan could see the center of her bare chest between her breasts. "You could try being a gentleman."

Donovan had forgotten his manners, and he felt his face heating up as he turned the other way. "You could have warned me first."

"You saw me unbuttoning. Don't turn around, I'm changing my pants. You should change yours, too. Leave the shirt. I'll tear some new bandages for you with this."

Donovan did as she suggested, slipping out of his torn and filthy pants.

He pulled the pants up, a little uncomfortable over the way it hugged against his groin, and then turned around. The black material had stretched around Diaz's form, pulling tight against her body in a way that likely revealed a little more than she wanted.

"Try not to stare," she said, reaching into the closet and grabbing another shirt. She put the knife to it, intending to cut it into strips for his shoulder.

It bent and shifted beneath the knife, but it didn't break. She tried stabbing it instead. It seemed to solidify against the force, not allowing the point through.

"The compression should keep enough pressure on it," Donovan said. "Help me get the old bandages off."

Diaz nodded and reached for the disgusting shirt. It was torn and soaked with water, sweat, and blood, and smelled awful.

"When did you grow up?" Donovan asked as she dropped the soggy wrap on the floor. He knew Matteo's kid sister had held a crush on him for years, but she had always been Matteo's kid sister. It was the first time he had noticed she wasn't a little girl anymore.

"Puberty was six years ago," Diaz replied. "Like I said, you've never paid me much attention before." She stepped away from him. "Maybe you see me now?"

[26]

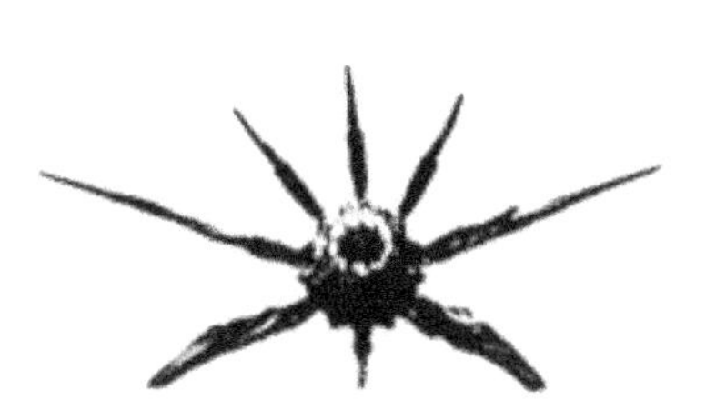

DONOVAN TUGGED AT THE ALIEN MATERIAL THAT COVERED HIS arms. It stretched so easily, and yet when he tried to jam the knife into it, it became as hard as stone or steel.

"I wonder if this stuff can stop a plasma bolt, too," he said. The material was incredibly comfortable though the nature of it did leave him feeling a little exposed. At least he wasn't alone in that.

"What do we do now?" Diaz asked.

"We can't stay here," he replied. "That thing was going somewhere, which means it's probably going to be missed."

"First things first, then." Diaz pointed to the door. "How do we get out?"

Donovan smiled. "Good question."

He stepped over the dead alien, examining the hatch and the frame around it. Human doors had manual knobs or levers or a touchpad control. He didn't see either of those. He couldn't believe they were going to get stuck here, discovered and killed because they couldn't open it.

"Maybe it's voice activated?" Diaz said.

"I hope not. We don't speak alien."

"Next time you tackle an alien, make sure you stay out in public."

"Yeah, I'll try that."

Diaz laughed softly, coming over to help him, running her hands along the wall near the hatch. "There could be a control hidden in the wall, like the symbols on whatever that enclosure thing is."

"It looks like a breathing apparatus of some kind. Look at its face. That nose seems too small and improperly formed to breathe easily."

Diaz glared down at it for a second. "It's disgusting."

They spent another minute trying to work the door. Donovan slammed his head back against the wall, angry with himself for his ineptitude. "This is ridiculous."

"What about sensors? Maybe it works by detecting that he's leaving?"

"Only him?"

Diaz shrugged. Donovan backed up and then walked toward the door as if assuming it would open ahead of him.

It didn't, leaving him with his nose right against the metal.

"Damn it," he cursed, tempted to slam his fist against it.

"You can say that again," Diaz said. He could tell she was getting uncomfortable with the situation, and the earlier stress relieving light-heartedness was wearing off. "What if it only works when one of them does it?"

"That would be good security, but I wouldn't think they need it."

"You wouldn't want someone just walking into your room on you."

Some of the humor returned to her eyes, and Donovan dropped his eyes to the floor. He had been fourteen when eight-year-old Renata had walked in on him unannounced and caught him masturbating.

"I can't believe you remember that."

"It was another two years before I knew what you were even doing," she said. "It's nothing to be ashamed of. Lots of people do it."

"Do you?" he asked.

"I don't think that matters, does it?"

He wasn't sure if she was being dodgy because she was ashamed, too, or because she didn't want to make him more uncomfortable.

"It might."

She stared at him for a moment.

A tone sounded in the room. It seemed like it came from everywhere.

They both froze, their eyes darting around the space in search of somewhere to hide.

There wasn't anywhere.

"Mierda," Diaz whispered.

Donovan looked at the dead alien, still sprawled on the floor. "There's only one thing to do," he said, moving closer to the door and crouching down, ready to attack.

The tone sounded again. Diaz joined him, handing him her knife. "I'm with you."

A muffled voice followed the second tone, more localized this time. Donovan returned his attention to the Dread until he remembered the pin. He unclipped it from his top. Someone was speaking through it. The voice was female, the words in a language he didn't know.

"I think someone missed him," Diaz whispered.

Donovan passed the knife back to her.

"What are you doing?" she asked.

"Change of plan if the door opens."

"Yes, sir."

They stood and waited. The tone sounded a third time, and the voice through the pin grew more concerned.

A short hiss was the only warning they had before the hatch snapped open. Donovan didn't waste any time, stepping forward and grabbing the newcomer, yanking them inside and wrapping his arms around them from behind, his hand falling over the mouth.

The alien struggled in his grip, making noises beneath his hand and trying to get away. The hatch closed behind them as he held on, her struggle causing his hand to slip.

Teeth came down on his hand, biting through his skin and drawing blood. An elbow hit him hard in the gut, and he lost his grip. The woman pulled herself away, waving her hand toward the hatch.

It slid open, but Diaz tackled her again before she could get out. It closed a second time.

Donovan recovered, moving to help Diaz. She had the alien on the floor, her knees digging into its legs and her hands holding its arms down.

"Stop moving," Diaz hissed.

It wasn't a Dread beneath her.

It was a woman. A human woman.

[27]

SHE STARED BACK UP AT THEM, HER LARGE BLUE EYES WIDE with fear, her body trembling in kind. She had fair skin and reddish-blonde hair that spilled out around her shoulders. She was wearing the same black outfit as they were though hers was more in the style of a dress and hung more loosely from her frame. She wore the same black pin as the Dread. She also had a second one next to it. It was the same shape and size, but a luminescent blue in color.

"A clone," Diaz said to Donovan.

"I saw how it opened the door," he replied.

"Then we don't need it."

She motioned her head toward her knife, which she had dropped on the floor.

Donovan picked it up and approached them. It was obvious to him that the clone was terrified. It knew what he was going to do.

"Donovan, do it," Diaz said.

Donovan knelt down, putting the knife to the clone's throat. A tear rolled down the side of its face. They were trained from an early age to recognize that enemy humans weren't human. That they were made, not born and raised. There were stories of the early resistance, from before the Dread built their cities and the alien operations were more out in the open. People had seen the factories where the first clones were created, even if they had never seen the Dread outside of their armor before today. It was the scientists who had guessed what they were using them for.

They had been taught that clones were as good as robots. They didn't think. They didn't feel. They followed instructions programmed into them. Organic machines that looked like you and me. To mess with our heads and make them harder to kill? Or because it was simply easier to make a person given the resources available on the planet?

"Major," Diaz said, using his rank to appeal to the soldier in him.

He was hesitating, and he knew it. The clone was crying. He had been raised to be a soldier. To do battle and fight a war. He had no problem killing the enemy when it was trying to kill him.

This was different.

"Give me the knife. I'll do it."

Diaz lifted her right hand to take the knife. Donovan pulled it away. The clone could have used the chance to try to escape, but she didn't. She continued to lay beneath Diaz, sobbing.

"No," Donovan said. "She might be useful. Yeah, great, we can open a door. We might need a little more than that to get out of here."

"D-"

"No. It's my decision. Look at her."

"It."

"Her. Genetically, she's a human just like us."

"No, she isn't. She's a machine. The enemy."

"She isn't trying to get away, and she's terrified."

"Oh, please. They're probably programmed to cry crocodile tears in self-defense. Please give me the knife."

"No. Get off her. That's an order, Lieutenant."

Diaz and Donovan stared at one another. Then Diaz reluctantly rolled off the clone.

Donovan held the knife over her. "If you scream, you die." He pointed it at her and then pantomimed cutting his throat.

"I understand," she said.

Donovan felt a chill at the shock of her words. "You speak English?"

"I speak seven human languages. English, Spanish, German, Japanese, Chinese, and Arabic." She stared up at him. "I've never met a human before. Your interaction with one another is intriguing."

"Who are you?" Diaz said, clearly confused.

The clone sat up, moving slowly and wiping the tears from her eyes. She seemed much less frightened now that she knew they weren't going to kill her.

"My name is Ehri," she said, her voice putting an odd emphasis on the 'eh' that sounded more like a growl. "That was Tuhrik. He was my Dahm."

"Dahm?" Diaz said.

"It is difficult to describe in your tongues. Not a master because that would suggest I am a slave. Not a partner because he did hold dominion over me." Her face wrinkled slightly. "More like a commanding officer." She looked at Diaz. "You called your husband Major. Is he also your commanding officer?"

"Husband?" Diaz said.

"I have read many teachings on the topic of human culture. It was my duty as second-" she paused, trying to think of a suitable word. "Scientist. Tuhrik was a scientist. I was his most senior assistant."

"I'm not her husband," Donovan said. "What kind of science do you do?"

"Alien sociology and genetics."

It took Donovan a second to realize when she said alien, she was talking about them.

"Why does a geneticist need to read about human culture?"

"It is one thing to emulate the biology of a thing. It is something else to understand the individuality. By understanding a culture, we can better assimilate it."

"Individuality?" Diaz said. "You're a clone. One of thousands. All exactly the same."

"You are wrong in that, Lieutenant," Ehri said. "Yes, there are hundreds who share my identical sequence of DNA, sampled many years earlier from a human that the Domo'dahm - that is something akin to a King, or Prime Minister, or President - found very compelling. However, there is only one Ehri who is second to Tuhrik. I have earned that distinction through the value of my work under him. If we were all the same, there would be no distinction made between us."

"What about the soldiers?" Donovan asked. "The clones sent out to hunt us?"

"They are simpler creations, yes. Even they have an individuality. It is only less defined."

"You said assimilate. Is that what the Dread do? Invade planets, kill billions, and steal their culture?"

"You have long called us the Dread. We are known as bek'hai. That was not always our way, but like humans, we have evolved to suit our need for self-preservation. Our home planet became uninhabitable. We were forced into scientific reproduction to cover our losses, which were many. These clones of ourselves were flawed, unable to reproduce naturally, and so we continued to make copies. Our genetic diversity was lost, and we needed to find an intelligent species to help us restore it. We found Earth."

"You could have asked for help," Donovan said. "Instead of destroying our civilization to save your own."

"It was the Domo'dahm's decision to take it. He rationalized that humankind would not allow such use of its own. Despite your petty differences, you are a species that is very loyal to one another."

"We are, aren't we? You say that like it's a bad thing."

"Not at all. Perhaps if we were more alike, our situation would have been avoided."

"So you screwed up, and we have to pay for it?" Diaz asked.

"Yes."

She said it simply and without emotion. Donovan had to move in front of Diaz to keep her back.

"You bitch," Diaz said.

"Lieutenant," Donovan said, grabbing her. "Get a grip on yourself."

It was the perfect opportunity for Ehri to steal his knife and stab him in the back of the neck. She didn't. Instead, she waited while Diaz backed up.

"You aren't afraid of us," Donovan said. "Why?"

"You've already expressed your desire to keep me alive, and I have never met humans before. The original collection was completed before I was made. We know much about humankind before we arrived, but little of how you have adapted to our occupation, other than that you have continued to resist it despite your obvious technological inferiority. The Domo'dahm does not find such intellectual endeavors worthwhile, but Tuhrik believed they were invaluable. He might have even spoken with you, had you not killed him."

"You don't seem too upset that we did," Donovan said.

"Our future depends on replacing the drumhr, the intermediate genetic splicing of bek'hai and human, with a new, more robust iteration. We are closer than ever to achieving natural reproductive capabilities once more. Tuhrik would be satisfied to know that this conversation occurred as a result of the end of his life."

Donovan could barely believe it. There was no human alive that would be so willing, no, almost happy to be captured by the enemy. Yet here was this clone telling him that she thought to be here with them was a good thing, and that her CO would have approved. The concept was more alien to him than the corpse on the floor a meter away.

"You are fortunate that you attacked Tuhrik," Ehri said. "Most of the bek'hai do not share his opinion of humans. They resent that they required you to survive. They resent the physical weaknesses that you have burdened them with, such as the need for oxygen. We had to construct the regeneration chambers to restore them to health on a daily basis."

Donovan looked back at the clear enclosure. He had been right about its purpose. "Burdened them with?' he said. "They could have picked a different planet."

"There was no other planet. Intelligent life is not rife throughout the universe. There is one other that we know of, and they would have defended themselves easily against our assault."

Donovan wasn't that surprised to hear there were other aliens out there. He was surprised to hear that they were even more powerful than these aliens.

"I don't suppose they'll be dropping by Earth anytime soon?" Diaz asked.

"No."

"You aren't worried about telling us all of this?" Donovan asked. "We've been fighting for years to get even the smallest shred of intel, and you've just spilled it all like it's no big deal."

"We have never sought to hide our nature from humankind, or you would know nothing about us at all. We did what we had to do, as you have done what you must. I don't know what brought you here, or how you got through our walls, and I don't care. That is a question for the military to worry about. I am a scientist, Major. I seek knowledge and understanding that will better the goals of my species. That is what I was made to do. That is my motivation for being. Considering that, how might I best understand you if you have no platform from which to understand me?"

"Fair enough, I guess," Donovan said, feeling every bit as inferior as Ehri claimed they were.

Her motives didn't align with the human way of thinking. She was talking to them, the enemy, for no other reason than to use the experience as some kind of scientific study. It was crazy.

"Besides, Major, this may be my one and only chance to further my studies and come to a true understanding of current human culture before you are eliminated. The Domo'dahm has decided that the remnants of humankind are to be exterminated within the year. Even if you manage to escape, you will not survive for long."

[28]

GABRIEL'S EYES SWEPT ACROSS THE CHAMBER, TAKING A QUICK inventory of everyone present. It had been two years since he had last been to a Council meeting.

That was the time when his father was awarded the Medal of Honor and honorably discharged from active service.

He could still see the scene in his mind. His father was newly injured, grimacing in pain and cursing up a storm while the Council tried to tell him why it was a good idea for him to retire.

"I have no intention of retiring until the day my chest stops rising and falling for good," Theodore had said. "Pain ain't nothing but a reminder, and I've been reminded of what those alien bastards did every day since we left Earth."

The last time, Gabriel had sided with the Council. His father was seventy-eight years old, and to be honest, the accident had been his fault. He didn't have the vision he once did or the mental acuity. He was a danger to himself and those around him. It was sad but true.

He winced involuntarily as he recalled the way his father had chewed him out for taking the Council's side. Theodore had called him every bit of Cajun slang he had ever heard, and when he was done with that he had switched to English. Gabriel had taken it, sitting and letting his father dump all of his anger and hurt and frustration on his shoulders. He had stayed while the General had bawled into his hands. He had left only once his father was out of energy and asleep.

It had taken four months for him to work up the nerve to go back.

Most of the Council was already assembled. He hadn't been in front of them since the last round of elections, and he only recognized half of the faces. The council was always made up of twelve people. Six men. Six women. Two pairs each from Alpha, Beta, and Gamma settlements. Ten of them were present, along with General Cave, Colonel Graham, Major Choi, Captain Sturges, and three people Gabriel didn't know. Well, two. He recognized the younger man as the one from the pod. The scientist. He guessed the other two were scientists as well. A man and woman, young enough to have been born in the Calawan system and old enough to be one of the first.

"Captain St. Martin," Major Choi said, noticing him at the back of the room. She went back to meet him.

"Major Choi," Gabriel said, saluting.

"We're in the Council Chambers," Choi said. "We're all civilians in here. People of the NEA."

Gabriel smiled. "Right. How have you been, Vivian?"

"Not bad. I'll be better once this business is done. Are you ready to hit them where it hurts?"

Gabriel had spent the last three days trying to work out everything he would say. He had written the beginning of a speech and erased it over one hundred times. In the end, he decided he would wing it and just say whatever came to mind.

"As ready as I'll ever be."

"I went to see your father before I came here," Choi said. "He isn't looking too good these days. Sabine said they had to increase his dosage to keep him calm."

"I saw him a few days ago. It's this bull that's killing him. He and General Cave used to be best friends. Now he sees him as a traitor."

"It's a shame when people wind up on opposite sides of something like this. I have a lot of respect for General Cave, but he's wrong. Plain and simple."

Gabriel noticed General Cave looking his way at the same time Major Choi said it. He smiled and nodded politely to the General, not making the mistake of saluting him as he had Choi. He would never lose respect for the man, but that didn't mean he was on his side in this particular battle.

He felt a soft breeze behind him, turning to find the two missing Council members at his back. They were easy to identify by the simple medallions they wore around their necks. He knew them both. Charles Ashford and Lucille Guttmann. They had both been part of the Magellan's maiden flight, and advanced age had left Charles overweight and Lucille walking with a cane, which was the reason for their late arrival.

"Gabriel," Lucille said, smiling. "I didn't expect to see you here."

"Hi, Gabe," Charles said.

"I didn't know you two had been voted onto the Council," Gabriel replied. "It's good to see you both. How long has it been?"

Charles laughed. "I think you were still in diapers, the last time I saw you."

"Come on, it can't have been that long."

"No, but you were Second Lieutenant St. Martin at the time."

"I didn't realize it had been so long."

"If you'll excuse us, Gabriel," Lucille said. "We're already running late, thanks to my useless old rear end."

Gabriel smiled and moved out of their way, taking a seat next to Major Choi. Colonel Graham joined them a few seconds later.

"Colonel," Gabriel said, giving him a larger nod than he had General Cave. They had taken the BIS down together earlier in the day.

"Gabriel." Graham's face was grim.

"Is everything okay, Colonel?" Gabriel asked.

"I hope so."

Gabriel didn't like that kind of reaction from someone who was supposed to be his ally in this. "What's going on?"

"God gave me the answer I was looking for," Graham said. "It wasn't the answer that I wanted."

Gabriel was about to ask him what he meant when the echoing bang of one of the medallions on the table at the front of the room called the meeting to order.

[29]

The Speaker's name was Angela Rouse. She was the youngest person on the Council, the same age as Gabriel and one of the biggest critics of the NEA's military arm. Gabriel knew that no matter what he said, she would never vote in favor of remaining behind. He was okay with that. She wasn't the only person whose vote mattered.

Of course, Colonel Graham's attitude beside him was leaving him lacking in confidence about their chances. Something had changed since Captain Sturges had dropped them off earlier. Some new information had come to light. What?

"I am hereby opening the fifth meeting of the twenty-third New Earth Alliance Council," Angela said. "Are all Council members present and in sound mind and body?"

"We are," they all responded.

Angela reached down and tapped a key to start recording the meeting. "This is an out of cycle meeting to discuss certain information that has come to light in recent days regarding both the activity of the NEA Space Force and the future of the civilian population of the NEA. The goal of this meeting is to hear from relevant parties and arrive at a decision. Either remain in the Calawan system and continue our surveillance of Earth or recondition the starship Magellan once more to carry all surviving members of the NEA to a newly discovered Earth-type planet, which will be referred to as Eden. Are there any questions before we begin the discussion?"

There weren't.

"Okay. I understand we will be hearing from Chief Astronomer Guy Larone, as well as Colonel James Graham to present both sides of the current argument. I'm sure I don't need to remind the Council that your decision should be made from your perspective of what is best for every member of the New Earth Alliance, and not from any past loyalties, friendships, or nostalgia."

"Angela," Captain Sturge's wife, Siddhu, snapped. "We're well aware of our responsibilities."

The two women made sour faces at one another, giving Gabriel a feeling this meeting was going to be more contentious than he had expected. It seemed the Council was already well divided on the issue.

"Colonel Graham, would you like to make your case first?" Angela asked.

Gabriel glanced over at the Colonel, whose eyes shifted to avoid his. He turned his attention back to Angel as Graham stood and straightened his uniform. She had a pleasant look on her face.

Something was definitely wrong.

Major Choi could see it too. She put her hand on his arm, and they looked at one another.

"What's going on?" she mouthed.

He shook his head. He didn't know, and he didn't like it.

Colonel Graham reached the front of the room.

"Thank you, Angela," he said. "Members of the Council, assembled guests." He turned to acknowledge them all, his eyes passing over Gabriel again. "I came here today to present an argument about the importance of the work the Space Force is doing, both in continuing the reconnaissance of Earth and in maintaining the status of the Magellan as a starship preparing for war. I came here today to present Captain Gabriel St. Martin. He is the son of Retired General

Theodore St. Martin, the man who saved the lives of everyone in this system, past, present, and future. He came here to present his compelling and impassioned perspective of our responsibilities to those we were forced to leave behind." He paused, his eyes finally finding Gabriel a dozen meters away. "Unfortunately, I can't do that."

A tense silence followed, with every member of the Council appearing confused except for Angela. Gabriel sought out General Cave. His face was stone. Whatever was happening, he knew about it already. Of course, he did.

"As you know," Colonel Graham continued, "Captain St. Martin returned from a reconnaissance mission three days ago. While our missions as of late have consistently resulted in an empty data recorder, we did finally receive another transmission from our brothers and sisters on the ground. It contained a recorded message from the Mexico based resistance, created by General Rodriguez based on a transcript he received from General Alan Parker in New York. I'd like to play that message for you now."

Colonel Graham reached into his pocket and removed his tablet. He tapped it a few times and then placed it on the desk in front of the Council.

A holographic image rose a foot above the device, spreading into a small but realistic visual of a man in a simple green uniform with a battered, tarnished pin on the chest.

"My comrades beyond Earth," he said, his face tight. "My name is Colonel Christian Rodriguez. You have seen my face before, in transmissions dating back almost a dozen years. Since the Dread arrived over fifty years ago, we have been fighting the good fight, gathering as much information as we can and passing it on to you in hopes of one day finding a way to defeat their technology."

The hologram bowed its head for a moment before continuing.

"The Dread have recently begun to step up their military presence throughout the resistance inhabited regions of the planet. Already, we have confirmed the destruction of bases in Jakarta, Indonesia, Cairo, Egypt, Osaka, Japan, and Kenya, South Africa. Our base here in Mexico is under constant threat, having lost over a third of our fighting forces in the prior three months. Our analysts are convinced that the Dread have tired of our pecking at them for the last half-century, and of passing intel along to you. It may be that we are drawing nearer to discovering their secrets. Or it may be that they have other plans that require ending the resistance once and for all. I don't know, and I don't think I ever will."

He paused again, looking off to the side. He bit his lower lip, clearly uncomfortable with what came next.

"My comrades beyond Earth. I don't know what your situation is. I know that fifty years have passed, and you have been unable to help us. I know that you have been trying your best. I know that some of your pilots and ships have been lost. I'm sorry, my friends. This is a fight that we cannot win. We have tried, but we have failed. The resistance is on the verge of collapse and will be disbanded soon, our larger groups breaking into smaller ones in an effort to evade detection. All of us here are grateful that you did not abandon us to our fate. Your presence has given us a strength that has allowed us to continue for all of these years.

"Even so, the day has come where I must ask that you move on. I know the ship you escaped on was designed to travel much greater distances than you have. If you have the chance to find a better life somewhere else, I beg you to please take it. Please carry on our civilization and our legacy. Maybe one day you will discover the technology to defeat the Dread armor. Maybe one day, you will avenge us.

"This will be the last transmission sent. Good luck, and Godspeed."

[30]

The recording ended. The hologram vanished.

The room was still. Silent.

The only sound Gabriel heard was the thumping of his pulse in his ears. The only thing he felt was the heat of his anger and anguish rising into his face, at the same time the skin along his arms prickled from a sudden, intense chill.

What the hell had just happened?

Everyone in the room was in shock, except for Angela, Colonel Graham, and General Cave. They had known. They had heard it earlier.

It was over.

Just like that.

He felt sick. He felt weak. He wanted to cry. To punch something. To close his eyes and not wake up. What was his father going to think when he heard about this? Would he even survive the news?

Colonel Graham picked up the tablet and made the long walk back to his seat. The room remained silent.

Gabriel looked at him as he sat. Graham's eyes were apologetic. He had decided he wanted to keep fighting as much as Gabriel did. It seemed God had other plans.

"Do we even need to hear Guy's report?" Charles asked. "I think the way forward is looking pretty clear."

"Is the Council ready to vote?" Angela asked.

"Aye," they all responded. Even Captain Sturge's wife, Siddhu.

Gabriel had come to argue, but there was no argument left. Even the people on Earth didn't want the New Earth Alliance to help them anymore.

"Okay. All in favor of retrofitting the Magellan and preparing for the trip to Eden, please raise your hand."

Every hand in the Council went up without hesitation like a dozen knives through Gabriel's heart. He felt each one individually, stabbing into his soul and stealing everything he had ever believed in.

Beside him, Major Choi gripped his arm tighter. "It will be okay," she said softly, trying to help him through it.

"Very well," Angel said. "The Council moves to-"

"Um. One minute, Councilwoman Rouse," a voice said from her right.

Gabriel's head felt like it was about to explode, but he still managed to turn it, finding that one of the scientists, the one from the pod, had stepped forward.

"Is there a problem, Reza?" Angela asked.

"Hmm... Well, it's not a problem per se," the scientist replied. "I mean, it is a problem, but it isn't completely- well, it is kind of related to this."

"Reza, we talked about this," the other male scientist said. He had to be Guy. "Your numbers are off."

"Hmm... No. I don't think so. In any case, I think the Council needs to know about this before they make any decisions."

"That's why you wanted to come here? To question our work?"

"I wanted to come to make sure everyone here is informed."

"Informed about what?" Angela said.

Guy moved ahead of Reza. "My apologies, Angela. I-"

"Informed about what?" she repeated.

The man stepped ahead of Guy. "The slipstream calculations to Eden. They're wrong."

"They are not wrong," Guy said.

"They are," Reza insisted.

"Guy, be quiet," Angel said. Guy closed his mouth, his face turning red. "Reza, tell us."

"There was an error made in the slipstream equations. Eden is too far away for the Magellan to reach it. To be precise, Guy's calculations assume a one-year retrofit and project out the slipstream currents to that date, making an estimate of plus or minus three months based on the wave power. I've checked every number three times, and that's just wrong. The travel time is going to be six months at a minimum, and the slipstream variation may be double that based on the planet's location."

"English, please," Lucille said.

"The Magellan was only designed to carry ten-thousand. There are twenty-thousand of us, give or take. If we try to make it to Eden, we'll starve to death," Reza said.

Angela didn't look happy with the news. "Guy?"

Guy made a face at Reza before turning to Angela. "Sarah and I both did the calculations, Angela. We are one hundred percent confident that they're correct. And, unlike Reza here, neither one of us flunked advanced calculus the first time we took it."

"That was a bullshit grade," Reza said, angry at the comment. "Mrs. Ramini hated me."

"Really, Reza?" the female scientist said, finally speaking up.

"Enough," Angela said. "Reza, can you prove the calculations are off?"

"I can show you my work."

"And we can show you ours," Guy said. "Angela, we've known each other for years. You know my work is solid. I'm not the Chief Astronomer because of my good looks."

Reza laughed at the comment, causing Guy to turn on him.

"One more time, Reza, and you'll be staying on Alpha for re-training. Maybe the military wants you."

Reza made a point of clamping his mouth closed before backing up a few steps.

"You can decide who you want to believe," Guy said to the Council. "Sarah and I have fifty years of experience between us. Reza has only been in Astronomy for three years."

Angela looked over the rest of the Council, checking their expressions.

"I trust you, Guy," she said. "I think the rest of the Council does as well."

Reza didn't say anything at that comment. Instead, he stormed from the meeting room.

"General Cave," Angela said. "I expect a full report on the current configuration of the Magellan on my desk in two days, along with an estimate of how long it will take crews working double shifts to refit her. It's clear the Dread have tired of the humans on Earth. What if they get tired of us being out here, so close to them, as well?"

"Of course, Angela," Cave said. "I would like to point out that we have no reason to believe the Dread know we're out here. There has never been any sign of them anywhere near this system."

"There's a first time for everything, General. I don't want us to be here when that happens."

General Cave spread his hands in submission.

"Thank you all for coming," Angela said, turning to address both the Council and the assembled guests. "I hereby call this meeting adjourned." She tapped her touchpad, stopping the recording. Then she tapped her medallion against the table, ending the meeting.

Gabriel remained motionless in his seat as the Council members got up and began to file from the room. Graham exited without trying to say anything while Major Choi continued to squeeze his arm.

General Cave approached him a moment later, kneeling down to get to eye level. "I'm sorry, Gabriel," he said. "I never intended for things to go like this."

Gabriel stared at him, still unable to find any words. It was over because he had made it out with the message. It was over because he had survived.

"Do you want me to tell your father, or do you want to do it?" Cave asked.

Gabriel was silent. If only he had died, this wouldn't be happening. There would still be an argument left to be had.

"You should do it, Gabriel," Major Choi said.

Gabriel looked at her. He wasn't going to cry in front of them. He pulled his arm away from her, glaring at General Cave as he got to his feet.

He left the chamber without a word.

[31]

"So, what do you intend to do?" Donovan asked, staring at Ehri. Her statement had chilled him to the core. Not because she intended it that way. Because it was true.

"I will observe," she replied.

"You won't call the guards or give us away?" Diaz asked.

"No. I wish to study your critical thinking patterns, threat processing capabilities, and problem-solving skills."

"Even if that means we kill some of your kind?"

"Yes."

"I guess that's why you said you would be better off if we were more alike. No human would ever agree to watch their own kind die in the name of science."

"I have studied Earth history. That may be true more recently, but it was not always so. Do you know of Nazi Germany, and what you called World War Two?"

"I've heard of it," Donovan said. "I don't know the details."

"It was not one of humankind's finest moments," Ehri said. "Though I have been able to draw some parallels between the leaders of that time and the Domo'dahm."

"How do you become the Domo'dahm?" Donovan asked. "Inheritance? Election?"

"Neither. Genetic testing. We look for markers that highly correlate with strong leadership. We call them the pur'dahm. These bek'hai are raised to become Domo'dahm. Of course, only one will, and only if the current Domo'dahm dies. It is extremely competitive. Even so, simply being one of the chosen elevates a bek'hai to what you might call a prince."

"Are they all as violent as the current ruler?"

"Just like I am different from my clones, the Domo'dahm are all quite different. Tuhrik was once a pur'dahm. He abandoned the cell to pursue his desire to study humans."

"So you're saying if we can kill this Domo'dahm of yours, we might be able to get a replacement that will stop trying to destroy us?" Diaz asked.

"It is not that simple. No. My suggestion to you is to find your way out of here. To take what you have learned to your people."

"I thought you were just an observer?"

"It is only a suggestion."

"Thanks for the idea," Donovan said, turning to Diaz. "I'm starting to think; this is a one time opportunity. There's no point in going back to base with nothing but a few alien vocabulary words."

"I agree. We should try to find something more substantial. Something that can help us survive, and maybe even fight back."

Donovan turned back to Ehri. "The other bek'hai in here. Are they armed?"

"Do you mean bek'hai, or clones?"

"Both."

"The soldiers are. Most others will raise an alarm if they see you."

"They won't attack us?"

"Only if they are armed."

Donovan stared at the clone. She had a pretty face. A sweet, compassionate face. She was biologically human. He had to remind himself she was still the enemy. All of her talk of observing could be nothing but talk. They had no way to know if she would raise the alarm as soon as they left this room.

"You're wondering if you can trust me," she said.

"Yes."

She stood up. He held the knife, following her across the room to a blank space on the wall.

"Put your knife to my back." She reached back and lowered her dress enough to expose her skin. "Here. A heavy stab will sever my spine."

"What are you doing?" Donovan asked.

"Earning your trust. Duck down. You don't want to be seen."

Donovan did as she said, pressing the knife to her porcelain flesh. She waved her hand, and the wall turned into a video screen.

"Surhm, Aval, Trinia, your attention," she said in English.

Three identical versions of her stopped what they were doing, turned, and stood at attention before her. The hand holding the knife tensed, as Donovan prepared to stop her from giving them away.

"Dahm Tuhrik has chosen to remain in his chamber for today. Please continue your work as assigned."

"Yes, Si-Dahm," they replied together.

"Also, remember to practice your human languages. Understanding is the key to assimilation, and the future of the bek'hai."

"Yes, Si-Dahm."

She waved her hand, and the screen vanished.

"You can remove the knife now," she said.

Donovan pulled the knife away. Ehri turned to face them. "I have now had the opportunity to steal your weapon and use it against you. I have had the opportunity to signal an alert that would guarantee your capture. I have also shown you that I have not lied to you about Tuhrik's studies. Is there something else you would like me to do to prove that I will not betray you to the others?"

Donovan glanced over to Diaz. She was thoughtful for a few moments and then shrugged.

"I can't think of anything," she said. "It's your decision, D. Trust her or kill her?"

Donovan handed the knife back to Diaz. He trusted Ehri with a certainty that surprised him. That fact gave him an idea.

"I'm going to trust you, but I also have a proposal."

"A proposal?"

"If you want to study humankind, you need a bit more exposure than just the two of us trapped in a maze. The sample size is too small, and you won't learn anything about who we are when we aren't under the gun."

She smiled softly. "What do you suggest?"

"Do a little bit more than observe. Help us get out of here, and then come with us." He figured she would say no, but there was no harm in trying.

The offer seemed to catch her off-guard. She took an involuntary step back. "You want me to help you? You want me to come with you? Why would I do that?"

"You're a scientist. You want to study humans. The best way to do that is to spend time with us."

"Donovan, you can't," Diaz said. "We don't know-"

"I can," Donovan interrupted. "It's my decision, remember? Look, you said it yourself. There's no way we can win in the end. So what's the harm in helping us get out of here, and getting to spend some time in our world? You clearly don't care if some of your kind die in the process, and that's the worst that can happen."

She stared at him in silence. He began to wonder if he was wrong about her. Would she change her mind and raise an alarm instead?

"I admit, I am intrigued by the idea," she said at last. "More than intrigued. I am excited by the potential. But also concerned. The Domo'dahm will send an army to destroy your base once it is located. There is a high probability I will die with you, and all of my learnings will be lost. It is one thing to sacrifice a few bek'hai in the name of science. It is another to sacrifice them for nothing."

"There isn't much I can do about that other than to promise to do my best to keep you alive," Donovan said. "It's high risk, high reward all around."

She was silent again, considering. Finally, she held up her right hand with her index and pinkie finger extended, and the rest of her hand closed.

"Put up your hand like this," she said.

Donovan copied the posture.

"This is how the bek'hai make deals with one another. Press your fingertips to mine."

Donovan did. The skin on her fingers was softer than anything he had touched before, and he could swear he felt a cool electricity pass between them as they made contact.

"We have a deal, Major. This touch is my bond."

"This touch is my bond," Donovan repeated.

He wasn't sure if that was part of the routine. It just felt right.

[32]

"Follow behind me," Ehri said. "Stay close."

She approached the door to Tuhrik's room, waving her hand and opening it. She took a step out into the corridor, checked both directions, and then continued moving. Donovan and Diaz filed out behind her. Donovan spared a glance back into the room, at Tuhrik's dead body, before the door slid closed. Whatever twist of fate had brought them here and guided them to that room, that Dread, and finally to Ehri, he was thankful for it. He had no idea how they would escape without her.

Even with her, it was no guarantee.

Ehri swept down the corridor, moving to the inner portion of the circular hub. The green light was visible ahead of them, growing in intensity as they drew nearer.

"Where are we going?" Donovan asked.

"The light is a transport mechanism," she said. "It will carry us to another part of the ship."

"That's the second time you said ship," Diaz said. "You mean this city is really a starship?"

"Yes. I suppose you are too young to have seen the bek'hai invasion."

"My grandfather always said the alien ships were massive," Donovan said. "I always figured he was exaggerating."

"All of the bek'hai live within a starship, each one connected to the other through constructed tunnels."

"We arrived through a drainage pipe. We came out in a huge room with a bunch of machines arranged around a central spire."

"A power generator. The energy is sent to the ships around it so that they don't need to cycle their reactors. This allows us to reduce maintenance and keep the ships ready for departure."

"Why do you need to be ready to leave?"

"We do not. It is an artifact of our past. When our planet collapsed, we were nearly destroyed for good."

"Collapsed?" Donovan asked.

"Yes. We mined it for every precious metal and resource it could provide. We didn't realize that by removing so much material we were weakening the very soul of the world. Small earthquakes turned into larger and more frequent earthquakes until the planet became unstable. Shortly after, it shook itself to death."

They moved past hatches on either side of the corridor. Ehri didn't seem concerned that they would open, and Donovan guessed she knew for certain that they wouldn't. The green light was right on top of them now, and Donovan could see it wasn't a normal light. There was a near-transparent platform at ground level, and shimmering motes flowed within the luminescence.

"We must step in together, or we will be separated," Ehri said.

"How does it work?" Diaz said, looking uncertain about it.

"Are you familiar with quantum entanglement?" Ehri asked.

"No."

"It is something like that. This one teleports vertically."

"How do you control direction?"

"With your hands. You will see."

They reached the lip of the light. Ehri reached out and took Donovan's right hand with her left, and Diaz's left hand with her right. As before, he marveled at how soft her skin was, and how alive it felt beneath his palm. Judging by Diaz's expression, she was experiencing something similar.

"Here we go."

Ehri stepped onto the platform with them. Donovan felt a moment of panic, afraid they were going to plummet straight down, where only more of the light awaited them. Instead, Ehri lifted his hand, and he could feel he was rising. He could see the floors slipping past his eyes too fast to count.

Seconds later, she lowered her hand, and they came to a stop.

"This level is equal to the ground level outside," she said. "The exit is not far, but there are more bek'hai soldiers up here than there are below. Below is for the passive."

"Exit?" Donovan said. "Wait a minute. I thought you were going to help us?"

"I am helping you to escape."

"We aren't ready to escape," Diaz said. "It doesn't do us any good to get out of here if we have nothing to bring back."

"You have me," Ehri said. "I have a large quantity of information about the bek'hai that I am willing to share."

"Do you know how the armor works?" Donovan asked.

"Armor?"

"The black carapace that covers everything. We've never been able to defeat it, not even with our best weapons."

"Your weapons are inferior."

"I know. Until we can overcome it, we have no chance of winning."

"I told you that you will lose."

"Yeah, well, I'm not ready to lose yet. If you don't know how to defeat it, is there someone here who does?"

"I'm certain there is," Ehri said.

Donovan came to a stop. "Why the sudden freeze?" he said. "Are you having second thoughts?"

"I made a promise, Major. I will not break it. I don't know much about the carapace, as you put it. It is not my area of study. If you want me to bring you to someone who might, we will have to go back down. The longer we linger here, the more likely it is you will be killed, and I am not eager to see that happen. I do not want to lose my opportunity to witness human interaction."

"We can't leave without something," Diaz said.

Ehri was about to answer when her eyes narrowed, and she motioned them off to the side of the hallway. A moment later, what Donovan assumed was a bek'hai soldier walked past.

It was taller than Tuhrik. Taller even than Gibbons. At least seven feet, maybe more, with thick, heavy limbs and a much larger head than the scientist had possessed. The same white skin, silver hair, and ridges were partially obscured by black cloth beneath a chestplate of the dark armor. It glanced their way as it passed, not registering alarm when its eyes fell on Ehri, and she raised her hand, three middle fingers extended out in what looked like a form of salute.

It continued past. Donovan could feel Ehri's tension ease.

"We are fortunate," she said. "Klurik is a pur'dahm. He barely sees other bek'hai; I doubt he noticed you at all. Still, we must be more careful."

"We need to go back down," Donovan said. "We may never get another chance like this, and I'm sorry, but the only way us humans survive is for us to come out of here with useful intel. If that means taking another scientist by force, then that's what we have to do. Ehri, if you don't want to be part of this, we can go on our own."

She shook her head. "I told you, Major. I wish to observe how you think and act. Every decision you make is part of that, regardless of my hopes for what I will learn. If you are going back down, then I am going back down."

They turned back toward the transport, only a few meters away. As they stepped toward it, a figure stepped out. A clone soldier. Its eyes grew large as it took in the sight of them.

Diaz didn't give it time to recover from the surprise. She was on it in an instant, her knife slicing cleanly across its neck while her hand covered a mouth that barely had a chance to scream.

"Druk," Ehri whispered beside Donovan. "We cannot go back. Not now."

"Diaz took it out, it's fine," Donovan said, moving toward the transport.

Ehri grabbed his arm. "No. All soldiers are tracked and monitored. They will know he is dead, and they will send a team to discover how."

Donovan looked back at the green light and Diaz kneeling over the dead clone in front of it. Was Ehri lying to get them to leave?

"Major, please trust me," Ehri said.

Again, Donovan decided he would. "Diaz, let's go."

"What?" Diaz said. "D, we can't."

"No choice. Our cover is blown. Come on."

She hesitated.

"That's an order, Lieutenant."

Diaz ran back to them. They ran together to the end of the hallway. Ehri brought them to a stop when they arrived, cautiously peering around the corner.

"The barracks are that way," she said, pointing to the right. "There is an exit this way."

They went to the left. They hadn't gone far when somebody shouted something in the alien tongue behind them.

"Run faster," Ehri said.

They did. Donovan felt the heat of plasma bolts on his back a moment later, striking the area around them. There was another corner up ahead. All they had to do was reach it.

They did, moving so fast that it made turning the corner difficult. Donovan slammed his injured shoulder into the wall, absorbing the intense pain, momentarily blinded by a plasma bolt that hit the wall in front of him. The wall sizzled for a moment but remained unharmed by the blast.

"Donovan," Diaz said, urging him forward. He was too slow compared to her and Ehri. He fought off the pain and surged ahead.

"How far?" he heard Diaz ask.

"A few more corridors," Ehri replied.

"We aren't going to make it."

It was his fault. He wasn't a fast runner to begin with, and his injury was only making it worse.

"Go. Leave me here, I'll hold them off."

He shouldn't have said it. Diaz came to an abrupt stop, forcing Ehri to stop a moment later.

"Not going to happen, amigo," Diaz said. "Keep moving or we all die."

"There's no time," Ehri said. "We'll have to try to lose them and come back. This way."

She waved her hand in front of a hatch Donovan hadn't even seen. It slid open to reveal another corridor. It was smaller than the one they were in and barely lit at all.

"Do not slow down," Ehri said, running ahead of them.

She moved through the passage like she had done it a thousand times, navigating from one corridor to another, one door to the next. Diaz and Donovan struggled to stay behind her, following her through the bowels of the alien starship. Donovan wished he had more time to admire the technology and to make sense of what each piece of equipment did. Earth had been in its space-faring infancy when the Dread had arrived, and his only experience with it was climbing through part of the wreckage of the Chinese colony ship Wèilái.

He lost track of how long they were running for. Ten minutes? Twenty? What he did know was that they didn't see another living thing the entire time. For all the systems buried beyond the main livable space of the starship, it seemed that little needed to be done to maintain it.

Finally, Ehri came to a stop in front of a hatch. She waved her hand, and it slid open. "In here."

Donovan's chest was pounding, his breathing heavy from the exertion. Diaz was in better shape, but still breathing hard. He looked at Ehri. She wasn't winded at all. "Where are we?" he asked.

She smiled. "Go inside."

She was silently asking him to trust her again. He didn't hesitate this time, nodding and stepping through the doorway.

"Dios Mio," he heard Diaz whisper behind him.

"Why would you do this?" Donovan asked.

[33]

"You wanted me to help you," Ehri said. "This was all I could think of."

Donovan's eyes darted around the room. It was a small space, no bigger than a supply closet. It was the contents that made it count.

He reached out, putting his hand to one of a hundred plasma rifles that rested in racks on the floor while his eyes fell on a suit of the black armor near a second hatch in the front of the room. It was way too big, even for him, but just seeing it left him in awe.

"An armory?" Diaz said. "You brought us to an armory?"

"You deserve a chance to fight your way out," Ehri said. "The odds are still against you, but if you escape you will have earned it."

Donovan lifted the rifle from the rack. Of course, he had held the same kind of weapon before. When they were taken from fallen clones, they were always inactive and unable to be used. This one made a soft humming noise as he wrapped his hand around the grip. A small display of alien symbols appeared on the side of it.

"It isn't secured," he said, feeling a sense of awe to be holding an active version of the weapon.

"No. The coding process occurs when it is lifted by a soldier. You do not have the genetic markers for the process to occur."

"You're saying we can walk out of here with this?" Diaz said, lifting a rifle of her own.

"If you survive, yes."

Diaz looked at Ehri as though she wanted to hug the clone. "We'll survive. Won't we, amigo?"

Donovan nodded. "Can we go back the way we came?"

"Yes." She lifted her head slightly. "They are still tracking us. We won't get back out without a fight. Come on." She motioned toward the door.

"Aren't you taking one?" he asked.

"I will not harm my own," Ehri said.

Donovan couldn't argue with that. They followed Ehri back out into the depths of the ship, retracing their steps. They hadn't gone far when Ehri waved them into a small niche in the wall. The soldiers appeared a moment later, moving efficiently through the space while scanning it for signs of their passing.

Donovan lifted the rifle, sighting down the barrel. "Diaz," he whispered, using his other hand to direct her. She raised her rifle, taking aim.

"Make it painless for them if you can," Ehri said.

Donovan pulled the trigger. There was no kick from the weapon, only a gentle wave of heat as the plasma bolt launched across the area and hit its target in the chest. The clone crumpled to the ground.

Diaz fired at almost the same time, catching her target in the chest as well. The other clone soldiers scrambled to find cover and at the same time figure out where the attack was coming from. Donovan hit another as it moved toward a pipe that ran from floor to ceiling.

"We can't afford to get bogged down here," Donovan said. "Ehri, which way?"

He looked back at her. The alien scientist's face was completely pale. She had to be wondering if she had made a mistake.

"Ehri?" he asked again.

"That way," she replied, regaining herself. "Down the corridor to the third crossing, turn right."

"Did you get that, Diaz?"

"Yes, sir."

Donovan took point as the return fire began coming in. He crouched low, checking on Ehri to make sure she was staying down as well. They had the high ground, giving them a strong advantage in the fight. He fired down at targets as they moved away from their cover to shoot back.

"Be careful of your rate of fire," Ehri said. "If the symbols turn yellow, it is a warning that the weapon is overheating. If they turn red, you are running out of power and the weapon will need to be recharged."

"Recharged?" Donovan said, suddenly aware of how many shots he was taking. He was stupid for thinking the alien weapon would have unlimited ammunition.

"It takes approximately one thousand bolts," Ehri said.

He was glad to know he wouldn't be running out of power soon. He fired more slowly, taking better aim as they finished crossing the space and reached the corridor. They started running again as soon as they did, heading back the way they had come.

"Where is everyone?" Donovan asked a short time later. They were nearly back where they had started and had yet to encounter any other soldiers.

"They'll be waiting for you at the exit," Ehri said.

"Wonderful," Donovan replied. "How are we supposed to get past them?"

"I know another way out."

"You seem to know everything."

Ehri smiled at the statement. "I am educated; that is all. I hunger for knowledge of all kinds. It is my reason for being. This way."

She led them off in another direction, bringing them through a second series of twists and turns until they finally reached a narrow passage that ran along the top corner of a massive hallway. Moonlight streamed in from a huge open portal at the end, and Donovan could see the green of the landscape growing around it.

"The launch tunnel," she said. "They won't expect you to go out this way."

"How do we get down there?" Diaz asked.

"There is a transport at the end, near the opening."

Ehri led them to it. Donovan stepped into the green light without hesitation this time, enjoying the feeling of the quick, controlled fall to the lower level. He waved open the hatch ahead of her, eager to get away.

They stepped out onto the floor of the ship, only a few meters away from the outside world and their freedom. Donovan could just barely make out the outline of Mexico City in the distance, a wisp of smoke still rising above it from the earlier battle there. The pipe had carried them a good ten kilometers.

He took a few steps forward.

One of the Dread stepped out in front of them from the side of the opening. Donovan recognized it immediately as the pur'dahm that had crossed their path earlier.

He had been unarmed that time. He wasn't unarmed anymore. A large rifle rested in his hands, and a large, primitive knife hung from a belt at his hips. The soldier was also wearing a mask with tubes coming out the sides, leading to something behind his back.

He barked something at Donovan, pointing the rifle at him. Donovan stood motionless, his weapon aimed back at the bek'hai warrior.

"Klurik," Ehri said, moving between them. "Step aside."

"You don't command me, lor'hai," the bek'hai said in choppy, guttural English. "Are you helping this lor'el?" He sounded amused. "I thought it was you. I knew you would come here."

Donovan glanced over at Ehri. It was obvious these two had some kind of history, and it didn't seem like a positive one.

"They were trapped. It is just to allow them to return to their kind."

"The Domo'dahm has ordered all lor'el dead."

"Then let them die with their own when you discover their hiding place. If you discover it."

The choking noise had to be a laugh.

"I will find it myself," Klurik said. His head shifted. Donovan couldn't see the bek'hai's eyes, but he knew the alien was looking at him. "Drop the weapon, and you may go."

Donovan tightened his grip on the rifle. Where was Diaz, anyway?

"I'm going with him," Ehri said.

Another laugh. "You are lor'hai. You do not make decisions on your own. Did Tuhrik put you up to this?"

"He asked me to accompany the human. He wants me to study them. I agreed to help this one escape in exchange for the chance to observe."

"The Domo'dahm-"

"Is above such things," Ehri said. "It was Tuhrik's decision to make."

"Very well. I cannot promise your safety when we locate the lor'el."

"I don't need you to protect me."

"There was a time when you respected me."

"And there was a time when you respected me," Ehri said. "Before you decided the lor'hai were not worthy of respect."

Klurik lowered his rifle. "Drop the weapon, and you may both go."

Donovan looked over at Ehri again. She nodded, and he threw the rifle to the ground. Klurik's head shifted to follow it. A plasma bolt burned past Donovan's ear, catching the bek'hai in the chest and throwing him to the ground.

"Got him," Diaz said. Donovan turned around, finding her at the edge of upper passage, aiming down at them.

Donovan hadn't realized he was holding his breath. He let it out, bending over to retrieve the rifle.

There was movement in front of him.

Donovan grabbed the weapon, dropping to his knees and turning toward the motion. Klurik was on his feet, the knife in hand. A slight burn mark was all that remained of Diaz's attack. The armor had absorbed the blast.

The bek'hai lunged at him, a rough growl pouring from behind the mask. Donovan fired the rifle, watching the plasma bolt hit the armor. It pushed at the alien, but he was ready for it this time, and he took the shot without slowing.

"Major, the switch on the left side," Ehri said.

Donovan knew the alien weapon well enough to know what she was referring to. He found the switch and flipped it down. The rifle began to vibrate, suddenly feeling lighter in his hands. Klurik was almost on him, the bek'hai completely airborne as it sought to run him through.

He pulled the trigger. This time, the plasma bolt struck the chest-plate, burning into the alien and through and striking the oxygen tank on its back.

It exploded.

The force of the blast threw Donovan and Ehri backward, covering them in the enemy's blood and gore.

Donovan cursed as his shoulder hit the floor and was wrenched back out of position. It hurt so much; he wanted to stay there and wait for it to stop throbbing. He knew he couldn't. He dragged himself up, getting to his feet at the same time Diaz reached him.

"Donovan," she said, running over and throwing her arms around him.

He threw his good arm around her waist to hug her while he turned to find Ehri. She was standing with her face dripping the bek'hai's blood; her expression horrified.

"We need to go," Donovan said. "Ehri?"

The clone looked back down the launch tunnel as if she were trying to decide what to do. She had come to observe how humans lived, not how her own kind died.

"Ehri?" Diaz said.

The alien scientist looked back at them.

"I'm ready," she said.

[34]

GABRIEL ROLLED OVER, TRYING TO IGNORE WALLACE'S attention as the dog attempted to get him out of bed. His bathroom was two levels up, and he had to go.

"Leave me alone," Gabriel said, pushing at the dog's side with his hand.

Wallace didn't quit.

"Okay. Okay."

Gabriel pushed himself up, turning to sit on the edge of his bed. He blinked the sleep out of his eyes, running his hand over his face. He hadn't shaved since the Council meeting, and a rough growth of hair was sprouting.

He stood up, ambling unevenly toward the door. Wallace rushed ahead of him, waiting and wagging his tail.

"Don't do that to me," Gabriel said. "There's nothing to be happy about."

Wallace ignored him. Gabriel opened the door, and the dog dashed out into the hallway. That was the problem with dogs. They were always happy. It didn't matter what went wrong. It didn't matter if you felt like your whole world was falling apart around you.

He ran his hand through his short hair, his door closing behind him. The corridor was empty save for the two of them, and he was thankful for that. It had been challenging to avoid everyone else on Delta Station for the last three days. He could imagine what they would say. He could imagine what they were already saying about him, about his father, and about the end of the war.

He was still wearing the same uniform from the Council meeting, wrinkled and messy and certainly smelling awful. He knew anyone who saw him like this would find his reaction pathetic.

Especially his father. He winced as his mind returned to the thought that he had run away instead of dealing with the outcome like a man and being the one to go to Theodore and tell him that his fight was done. He knew what he was doing was wrong. He could hear his father's voice in his head, telling him he was a coward, and that no St. Martin ever shirked their responsibilities because they didn't get what they wanted. He could hear him calling him a baby, a spineless gator, and worse. His father had a colorful vocabulary, and he was never afraid to use it.

So why was he doing it? Why was he wallowing in self-pity, when he should have been attending the meetings Colonel Graham had scheduled to prepare Delta Station for breakdown and abandonment?

Because it was his fault this was happening. It was a thought he couldn't shake. The Dread starfighter had chased him hard, and his ship had taken enough damage that it needed to be grounded and repaired. He had considered himself lucky at the time, but now he realized it was just another cruel joke, courtesy of the God he didn't believe in. How many times in the last few days had he been tempted to take the crucifix his mother had left him and crush it beneath his boot? How many times had he stood in front of his window and stared down at the Magellan as if he could will things to be different?

His mother had believed, so much so that she had stayed behind, sacrificing herself to get others on board in her place. So much that she had chosen the love of an unseen, un-present thing over the love of her husband.

This was how He was repaying her? Making her death for nothing?

He made his way down the corridor, redirecting Wallace to take the stairs up the two levels to the park. There wouldn't be any traffic on the stairs.

He moved like a robot, his emotions careening from angry passion to total despair, and generally settling on a simple numbness that drove his feet forward. Wallace ranged ahead of him until he went too slowly, and then the dog would return and nudge at his legs.

Daphne and Soon were in the park when the hatch slid open and Wallace ran in. Gabriel had a strong desire to turn around, to get out before they saw him. It was early. They should have still been in bed. Most of the station was. They noticed the dog and then turned to him. He could see the pity register on their faces as they took in the sight.

He hated it.

He hated himself more.

He knew he needed to get out of the malaise. He knew he was supposed to be stronger than this. He was General St. Martin's son. The Old Gator's son. Weakness wasn't supposed to be in the vocabulary. He didn't want to feel this way, but he didn't know how to stop it.

"Hey, Gabriel," Daphne said, approaching him with none of the caution her husband was displaying. "How are you?"

Gabriel took a few seconds to answer. "I've been better."

She stepped forward, putting her arms around him. The move took him by surprise, and before he knew it, he had tears in his eyes.

Soon joined them more slowly, standing beside his wife and putting a hand on Gabriel's shoulder. When Wallace trotted back over, he used his free hand to pet him.

"You've always been passionate," Daphne said, looking up at him. "You get that part from your father. You've always run on your emotions. I think you must get that from your mother because from what I've heard your father can run cold as ice in any situation. It makes you strong, Gabe."

"No, it doesn't," Gabriel said, trying to get control over himself. His father would be so disappointed in him. The thought made it worse. "I'm a damn mess, and I can't stop myself."

"It isn't your fault," Soon said.

"Yes, it is. It was my mission, and I survived it."

"Come on, Gabriel. You can't do that to yourself. The 'what if's, the 'if only's. It doesn't work. For anyone. Ever. If it weren't your mission, it would have been someone else's. It might have been mine. Would you prefer if I were dead?"

Gabriel shook his head. "No. I don't mean it that way."

"I know you don't, but you aren't looking at the whole picture. You're seeing it from one perspective. A selfish one that wants to punish you for being alive."

Selfish? How was he selfish to want to have died? To have given his life to keep fighting?

"You're hearing your father's voice in your head, aren't you?" Daphne asked, finally pulling away. "Telling you that you're a failure? Telling you that you aren't enough like him?"

"Sometimes," Gabriel admitted. "And sometimes I hear him calling me every Cajun curse he knows because of the way I've been handling the fallout. I'm a failure on both sides of the ball."

"You aren't a failure for caring," Daphne said. "You've poured all of your energy into this war for the last fifteen years. You've gone on more runs than any other pilot over that time by more than double. You've put your life on the line over sixty times."

"You've also had your share of loss," Soon said. "Nobody expects you to take this like it's nothing or Colonel Graham would be ready to court-martial you for failure to show for duty. You're beating yourself up when nobody else is."

"My father is," Gabriel said.

"You know that for a fact?" Daphne said.

"I know him. I know who he is."

"From what you've told me, he isn't conscious enough of the time to be beating anything up."

"He's been waiting for me to come to him and tell him we've

solved the secret of the Dread's armor. Every time I've been to visit him, I could see it in his eyes. Even when he barely knew where he was, or who he was, I could see it. I won't ever get to tell him that. And not only that. I should have been the one to tell him about the message from Earth, and I chickened out of that one, too."

"Gabriel-" Daphne started to say.

"And then there's my mother," Gabriel said, continuing over her. "Failing her memory is the worst of all. She was counting on us to win this war for her. It was her damn dying wish."

He could feel the anger rising again, the tears preceding it. He clenched his jaw and his fists, once more tempted to curse God for whatever part He had in this.

"It was always a long shot, Gabe," Daphne said. "You know that."

"It doesn't matter. I've always believed we would. I still believe we can."

"You heard the message from Earth."

"I don't care. I know our situation is bleak, but I don't know how to give up hope in it. I don't know how to let go of it."

"Maybe that's the real problem," Daphne said.

Gabriel froze, staring at them both. Was that the real problem? His entire life had revolved around the war with the Dread. He had literally been pulled out of cold storage and inserted into a surrogate womb to be born to fight them. Most children of the NEA were assigned to their future roles shortly after birth. They had assigned him before he had existed as anything more than a sperm and egg.

And now it was over, and he didn't know how to live without it.

"Gabe, are you okay?" Soon asked.

Gabriel nodded. "Not yet. I feel a little better. I should have talked to you sooner. Thank you."

Daphne smiled. "Anytime, Captain."

"Come on, Wallace," he said.

[35]

Gabriel went back to his quarters, finding a small measure of energy returning as he walked. He was still feeling depressed, and he still wanted to fall back on his bed and close his eyes.

He didn't want to do it as much as he had before he had taken Wallace up to the park.

It wasn't much, but it was something.

He fought to cling to that, to use it to push the feelings of hopelessness and loss from his head and his heart. He had handled Jessica's death better than this. He had mourned, of course, but he had also volunteered to pilot the next mission. There was no better cure for the loss than getting back out there and doing what they had dedicated their lives to do.

Now that there was no more getting back out there, he realized he had to find something else to do. Some other way to contribute. He had to put his mother's memory aside. He had to put his father's promise aside. He had to drop all that he had ever been and turn into something else.

How?

He slipped into his quarters, feeling the depression returning in a hurry. There was nothing else for him. He was a starfighter pilot. He was a soldier born into a war, and now that the war was over there was no place left for him. He didn't have any other skills. What good would a starfighter pilot be on Eden?

He went over to his small storage cabinet and opened it, finding a nutrient bar inside. He tore open the package and broke it up in his hand before tossing it on the floor. Wallace hurried over to it, gobbling it down before Gabriel could make his way back to his bed.

Wallace jumped on the mattress, blocking his path. Gabriel stared at the dog's face. The big eyes, the lolling tongue, the content smile. His spirit was fighting to bring him back. So was his pet.

"Okay," Gabriel said, fighting against himself. "I'll clean myself up."

He wandered into the bathroom, grabbing his razor and sliding it along his face. It took a lot of effort, and every motion left him feeling exhausted. He was tempted to quit a few times, but each time he began to turn around and let his face stay half-shaven Wallace was standing there, still looking at him.

He finished shaving, peering at himself in the mirror. He looked awful. Pathetic. He closed his eyes, pushing that thought away. If he couldn't accept himself for his loss, he was never going to get back on his feet.

He slowly removed his clothes, his muscles burning from the work though he was hardly out of shape. He stepped into the shower, finding just enough time to get his hair washed before the water ran out. He hoped the flow had gotten enough of the old sweat and dead skin cells from the rest of him that he didn't smell too badly. He dried himself off, wrapping the towel around his waist and moving back out into his bedroom.

He eyed the bed. Wallace was sitting on it, a ball between his front legs.

"I'm not playing with you," he said.

Wallace looked at him with hopeful eyes.

Gabriel noticed that his comm was flashing. It had probably been flashing for days, but he had been too lost to care. He circled around the bed, ignoring Wallace as the dog picked up the ball in his mouth and turned with him, dropping it on the other side.

He tapped the control pad and scanned the list of messages. Colonel Graham. General Cave. Major Choi. Miranda. Daphne. Captain Sturges. Reza Mokri.

He paused at the name, mixed in with the others. Reza? The same Reza who had been at the Council meeting?

He didn't know anyone else with that name.

He tapped the message. The list was replaced with Reza's face, a little too close to the camera.

"Captain St. Martin," Reza said. "Um. I'm sorry to bother you, sir. I. Um. I know you don't really know me, but I saw you at the Council meeting a few hours ago. Um. I saw your face after Colonel Graham played that recording, and I, um, I mean, everyone knows about your father."

Reza was nervous. His olive complexion was more pale, and his eyes kept dropping down from the camera. He glanced back over his shoulder every few seconds.

"I need your help," he said. "What I said at the meeting about the calculations. I. Um. I'm not wrong, Captain. I'm certain I'm not. There's something going on here. Something that smells." He glanced over his shoulder again. "Eden is real. It is. I believe that. We can't reach it. I know that for sure. I've run the numbers. I've run simulations. It won't work with everyone boarding the Magellan. We'll run out of food and water." He looked over his shoulder. "I. Um. I think the others may be planning something. I think they intend to leave some people behind. Maybe the military? I don't have any proof. I wish I did. I can prove the math doesn't work. Come to Gamma to see me, Captain. I'll show you. We need to convince General Cave. He's the only one who can stop it."

Gabriel could see the door open behind Reza. Guy and Sarah entered the room. He must have been sending the message from the lab. Did he not trust his personal comm?

Reza knew they had come in. He leaned in a little closer.

"Come to Gamma, Captain. Help me. Please."

The message ended, switching the screen back to the list.

Gabriel sat in front of it, shaken, but not in a bad way. He could feel his doldrums lifting like an evaporating cloud.

He had a new mission.

[36]

Gabriel smiled when Miranda's door slid open. "Hey, 'Randa."

Miranda looked surprised to see him. He had expected that. "Gabriel? Is everything okay?" She looked down at Wallace, standing beside him. "Hey Wallace. Who's my good boy." She kneeled down to pet him.

"Can I come in?" Gabriel asked.

"Of course." Miranda stood and led him into her quarters.

As a Senior Spaceman, she had her own room but it was a quarter of the size of Gabriel's. Soft music was playing in the background, and her comm was active, playing an old movie. He couldn't tell which one it was from a glance.

"What's up?" she asked as her door slid closed. "I heard from Daphne you were in pretty lousy shape this morning. You look okay to me."

"That depends on how you look at it. I've been pretty depressed since the Council meeting. This whole thing with Eden and the war. I'm sure you've heard."

"Everyone knows. I was at Colonel Graham's meeting earlier. They're planning to break down the fighters for their parts."

Gabriel felt a chill. "Already?"

"It's going to take a few weeks, but yes. Graham is under strict orders to get Delta Station out of operation within three months. They need the materials to refit the Magellan."

"Then we don't have a lot of time."

"Time for what?"

He hadn't realized he said it out loud. "Nevermind. I wanted to ask you for a couple of favors."

"Yes, I'll watch Wallace," she replied. "Where are you going?" She paused. "You aren't going to do something stupid, are you?"

Gabriel laughed. It felt good to laugh about something. "If I tell you, will you promise to keep it to yourself?"

"Gabriel, I know you're upset, but-"

"It isn't like that. Do you promise?"

"Fine. What?"

"Can I borrow your shower?"

"What?"

"I ran out of water, and I haven't bathed in three days."

"That's what you wanted me to promise?"

"No, but I'd like to finish cleaning myself up, and then I'll tell you."

She shook her head. "You're impossible. You're lucky I haven't used it yet. Go ahead."

Gabriel leaned down and kissed her on the cheek before heading into the bathroom. The small space didn't have a door, but he didn't mind. Miranda was like a sister to him. He quickly stripped, finished showering, and redressed himself.

"Now, spill it," Miranda said, pausing her movie as he came out of the bathroom.

"While I was out of commission, I got a message from a scientist named Reza Mokri. Do you know him?"

"It doesn't sound familiar."

"He's on Guy Larone's team. He was at the Council meeting the other day. He interrupted the meeting to try to tell the Council about a problem with Astronomy's calculations for the trip to Eden."

"What kind of problem?"

"According to his message, the trip is going to take a bit longer than advertised, and the only way to make it with enough food and water is to cut some of the population out of the exodus."

Miranda's face paled. "What?"

"Exactly. Reza suggested that there may be a plan in place to make sure it's the military personnel who get left behind."

Miranda was silent for a moment as she thought about it. "That doesn't make any sense. We have to be off Delta in three months. That isn't nearly enough time to get the Magellan ready."

"Are you sure? The ship is configured to support five-thousand right now. How long would it take to renovate some of the space into bunks, a hydro-garden, and a few extra recycling units for air and water? A month, at most?"

"Not for twenty-thousand."

"What about for ten-thousand?"

Miranda considered it, and then shook her head. "You can't be suggesting that there are people in the NEA who would leave others behind. They would essentially be murdering them."

"I don't want to believe it, and until I speak to Reza myself, I don't completely. He thinks it's true, and I don't get the feeling he's out of his mind."

"He could be looking for attention, or to get back at Guy for something. I've heard he can be a hard man to work for."

"It's possible, which is why I need to go to Gamma and talk to him. If there is something going on, I need to find out what it is and try to stop it."

"I don't know, Gabriel. You're a pilot, not a policeman. You should go tell Captain Tehrani about the message Reza left, and let him handle it."

"No. I can't. Reza came to me directly. He kept looking around like he was certain he was being watched. I don't know that I can trust Tehrani."

"She's a good person."

"She's also friends with Angela Rouse, who looked a little too happy about the message from Earth."

"What about your duties here?"

"I already put in a request for another week off. Colonel Graham granted it within five minutes. He knows there's nothing for me to do here."

"I'm not going to try to change your mind. God knows that I can't. You've got that St. Martin stubbornness. You're sticking your nose somewhere that you shouldn't. Be careful not to get yourself court-martialed or arrested."

"I'm only going to go talk to him. If anything does happen, you'll take care of Wallace? You're his favorite."

Wallace was laying on the bed, on her pillow.

"Something better not happen."

"If it does?"

"You know I will."

"Thanks, 'Randa. I left you access to my room. Feel free to hang out there if you want some more space."

Gabriel turned to leave. Miranda put her hand on his shoulder, and when he turned around she hugged him.

"Seriously, Gabe. Be careful. I already lost one best friend."

"They're scientists. They can't possibly be scarier than trying to outrun the Dread."

[37]

It had been seven years since Gabriel had been to Gamma settlement. He and Jessica had left their sperm and egg deposit with the registry on that trip, to secure their place as future parents once they were retired. Located on a small moon orbiting Taphao Thong, it was the most remote of the settlements, designed that way to both keep it obscured should the Dread ever show up in the system, and to protect the other settlements from the experimentation that occurred there. While the scientists took extra caution not to destroy anything, working with new technology meant there were never any guarantees.

Colonel Graham had authorized him to take a starfighter down to the settlement, since they would need to be delivered there for breakdown anyway. Sitting in the cockpit thinking that this might be the last time he was ever behind the sticks was a melancholy experience that might have led Gabriel back into his depression, if it weren't for the fact that his mind was otherwise occupied.

Miranda couldn't believe anyone in the NEA would be willing to let some of its people die to get the rest of them to Eden. While Gabriel didn't want to believe it, he was able to think that it was possible. He had seen Councilwoman Rouse's face when Guy had made his report, and how quickly she had sided with the Chief Astronomer. Was it because they were conspiring together, or was it because he was looking for something to fill the void left by the decision to end the war? Or maybe he was just looking for someone else to blame?

Gabriel adjusted his thrust as he neared the moon, bringing the fighter in more slowly than normal. The equipment in the settlement was sensitive to pretty much everything, which meant all kinds of extra rules around how things operated around it.

He eased the fighter through the open hangar, following a line of lights to the bay where they wanted him to land. He deftly maneuvered the vectoring stick, spinning the fighter in a neat one-eighty as he lowered it to the floor. He felt a wave of sadness as the small skids touched down, running his hand along the perimeter of the cockpit while he waited for pressurization. He lingered for a minute after the safety light had flashed to green before opening the shell and climbing out of his seat. He pulled off his helmet and set it down reverently, grabbing at his crucifix before hopping down and sending a thought to his mother.

The airlock slid open as Gabriel reached it. Lieutenant Curtis was on the other side, standing at attention as he approached.

"Captain St. Martin, sir," Curtis said, saluting.

"At ease, Lieutenant," Gabriel said. "I'm dropping SF-6 off for tear down. Has my return trip been arranged?"

Curtis shifted into parade rest. "Yes, sir. Spaceman Durvy will be ferrying you back to Delta in four hours."

Gabriel had asked Graham to arrange for him to have some time on the moon so he could tour the facilities. He hadn't been specific about the length of the trip to avoid possible suspicion, and he was happy to know he would have more than enough time to meet with Reza. He had sent only a single, obscure message to the scientist hours earlier in case the man's belief that he was being eavesdropped on was valid. Reza hadn't gotten back to him before he had left, so he figured he would find him now.

"Thank you, Lieutenant. Can you point me in the direction of Astronomy?"

"Astronomy, sir?" Curtis said, one of his eyebrows raising in curiosity. "Going to pick a fight?"

"Not quite," Gabriel said, smiling. "Would you want to assist if I were?"

"I'm friends with a lot of the team here, sir. Still, it would be tempting."

"I'll let you know if I change my mind."

"Yes, sir. Take the pod to the north wing, when you get off, go into the main concourse and turn left. Walk about half a kilometer."

"What about residential?"

"All of the scientists are segregated based on discipline. They don't like to be too far from their work. When you get to Astronomy, there will be a door to the lab in front of you. The passage to residential will be on your left."

"How do they manage it when an Astronomer marries a Chemist?"

"Excuse me, sir?"

"Never mind. I've got it. Thanks, Lieutenant."

"Of course, sir."

Gabriel took his leave of the hangar, casting one last longing glance back at the starfighter before he did. He followed the directions to the pod, climbing into the first that arrived and traveling the short distance to the central concourse. Like Alpha, this was where administration for the settlement was handled. Unlike Alpha, the area was nearly deserted in the middle of the day. He had always heard that scientists tended to be less social than other people, and his few trips to Gamma had proven it.

He crossed the concourse, drawing looks from the few people who were present. The soldiers in the space came to attention and saluted him as he passed while the others simply stared. He was sure most of them knew who he was, even if he had never met them. He was a rare enough sight in Alpha Settlement. He was like dark matter here.

A second pod ride brought him to the north wing of the settlement. The concourse was almost as quiet here, though it seemed they had chosen to use the hub as a food court. Three dozen scientists sat in random locations around simple tables, while a single cooking station prepared what smelled like fresh vegetables and synthetic meats. Gabriel had barely eaten in the last few days, and now that he was regaining some of himself the scent was more than tempting.

Like before, the scientists watched him pass. A few of them even waved or nodded their heads to acknowledge him. Others looked away when he made eye contact, embarrassed to be caught staring. He waved back to those who were friendly, and ignored the ones who weren't. He also scanned each face, looking for Reza.

He turned left and headed down the next corridor, stopping when he reached the full-sized hatch labeled 'Astronomy.' As he had guided the fighter in, he had seen the orbital telescope they used to scan the distant universe. Its construction had cost three times the resources as all of Delta Station, but both the science community and the Council had believed it was worth it.

He had been a child at the time, but his father should have seen the writing on the wall back then that the people were losing faith in their ability to overcome the Dread occupation.

He stepped up to the hatch. It slid open at his proximity, revealing another corridor that branched off into the science complex. He had no idea where he was going, so he just started walking.

He hadn't gone far when he nearly bumped into Guy Larone as he was exiting one of the rooms. The Chief Astronomer drew back in surprise at the sight of him, his posture and his expression instantly defensive.

Or was it guilty?

"Captain St. Martin?" Guy said. "I didn't expect to run into you here."

Gabriel struggled with his temper, fighting to keep it at bay. He really was getting back to normal.

"Reza invited me to have lunch with him," Gabriel lied. "Have you seen him?"

Guy's eyes twitched. "Lunch? I didn't realize you and Reza were friends."

"If you had, it would have given you more ammunition, right?" Gabriel replied, immediately angry at himself for not being more reserved. He smiled. "I'm kidding. We aren't friends, or weren't, I should say. We've been commiserating over the fate of the people of Earth together. There is one scientist in the NEA with a conscience."

He could have kicked himself for going over the line again. Guy stared at him, obviously angry. The scientist shook it off.

"Well, in any case, you won't find Reza here. He's been shipped off to Alpha."

"To Alpha?" Gabriel asked.

"After his performance in front of the Council, Mr. Mokri decided that it would be a good idea to try to hack into off-limits portions of our datacenter to prove his inane theories. Needless to say, built-in safeguards alerted the IT Department to his shenanigans, and he was summarily both fired and arrested. I'm sure he would have told you, had his comm access not been revoked."

It was Gabriel's turn to stew. Maybe if he had checked his messages earlier, the scientist wouldn't have done something so stupid. He had come to Gamma under a false pretense, and now he would need a reason to transfer between settlements.

"You believe him, don't you, Captain?" Guy said while Gabriel was trying to think of a good excuse to use on Colonel Graham for bringing the SF-6 to Alpha.

"I didn't say that."

Guy laughed. "You don't need to say it. I'm not stupid, Captain. I know you despise my team for our discovery, and for ruining your game of make-believe war. It wasn't us that drove the last rivet into the starship. You can thank General Rodriguez on Earth for his surrender. The idea that we would make up numbers that are the basis of transporting every life in the Calawan system to Eden is not only preposterous but personally hurtful. Just because we believe in two different ways forward doesn't mean that we're monsters."

"I never said you were," Gabriel said. "Like I said, we were supposed to have lunch. We set it up before I left Alpha the other day. I had no idea what he was planning. Anyway, to be honest, I did want a little more clarity regarding his statements. Considering that there's a question about the numbers at all, and considering my position and the position of my father, I don't believe that is out of line."

"No, it isn't," Guy agreed. "I would be happy to show you the calculations if you're interested. Just give me some time to prepare, and we can meet to discuss them."

"Why do you need time to prepare? They're only numbers."

Guy laughed. "Only numbers? If that were true, you could do my job. Do I tell you flying a starfighter is only a matter of manipulating a pair of sticks?"

"Maybe another time, then," Gabriel said. "I only reserved enough time to eat and run back to Delta."

"Very well, Captain. Let me know when your schedule allows a longer visit."

"I will," Gabriel said. "If you'll excuse me."

He turned and headed back toward the exit. He could feel Guy's eyes on him, watching him leave. The confrontation left him with a bad feeling that Guy was full of shit.

[38]

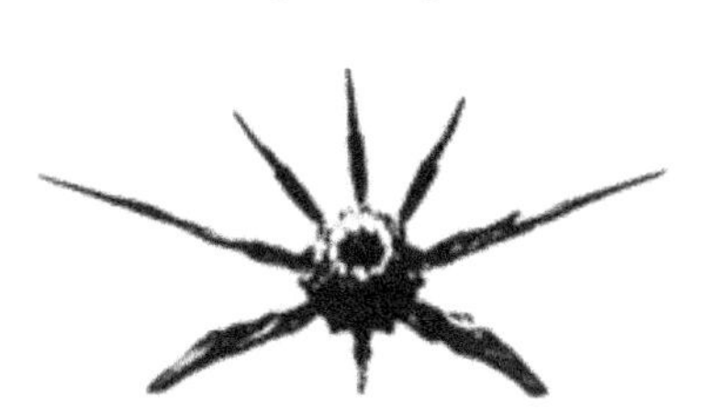

The prison on Alpha Settlement was located in the central hub, through a secured hatch that led down into a subterranean area above where the large dome's anchors had been sunk into the earth. It wasn't a large area. The vast majority of offenses in the NEA were minor things like fistfights or verbal altercations or the occasional theft or vandalism by a minor. These crimes often led to a maximum of a day or two in prison for the citizen in question and meant they only needed a dozen cells for the entire population.

When Gabriel arrived, he learned that only four of them were occupied. He didn't know what the other three offenses were for, but the guard in charge of documenting visitors to the prison was happy to talk to him about Reza. Mr. Mokri was the first hacker to be arraigned in at least twelve years, and between his two-week sentence and Guy's request that he be re-assigned, it turned out he was somewhat of a fifteen-minute celebrity in the settlement.

That fact worked to Gabriel's favor since he needed something to use to convince the Spaceman to let him in to see Reza. He had no official reason to stop by, but he also didn't think that whatever the scientist had to say could wait. The short hop from Gamma to Alpha had given Gabriel time to consider, and the idea that Reza had been framed had wormed its way into his head. It was Guy's attitude that had done it. Gabriel's father was arrogant, but the Lead Astronomer put that arrogance to shame. There was something there. Something Guy wasn't saying.

He was sure of it.

Fortunately, Spaceman Lee was a fan of Gabriel's exploits and an even bigger fan of the Old Gator. He was more than happy to let Gabriel in to meet Reza and to keep quiet about it. After all, what harm could Gabriel do in talking to him?

The cells weren't much different than the standard residential quarters, save for their slightly smaller size and open, barred entry. Each was identical, equipped with a simple bed and mattress, a small room with a toilet, and a comm unit for watching movies or reading.

Reza was laying on his stomach on the bed cradling his handheld, looking as distracted by it as he had at the loop station. He didn't notice when Gabriel approached with Spaceman Lee, continuing to tap on the device with his thumbs.

"You've got a visitor, Reza," Lee said.

"I thought I asked you not to let anyone in to see me," Reza said without looking up. "Are they media?"

"Reza, it's Gabriel St. Martin," Gabriel said.

Reza's head snapped in Gabriel's direction. He looked flabbergasted that the pilot had come to see him. "Captain St. Martin. You were the last person I expected here after I never heard back from you."

"Spaceman Lee, can you give us a few minutes alone?" Gabriel asked.

"Of course, sir," Lee said. "Do you want to go in?"

"Yes, please."

Lee put his thumb against the door. It unlocked, and he held it open for Gabriel, who went inside. Reza shifted to a sitting position so Gabriel could join him.

"I'll be back in twenty minutes," Lee said before leaving.

"Sorry it took me so long to come," Gabriel said. "I took the news about the resistance pretty hard."

"You're here now," Reza said.

"Why are you here?"

Reza shook his head. "Ugh. So stupid. When I didn't hear back from you right away, I thought maybe I could entice you to listen to me by getting at least a little bit of proof about my claims. I had seen Guy and Sarah's original workup on Eden on our servers, the one with the skewed numbers. I wanted to transfer a copy to you. But Guy knew I wasn't going to let things be, so he set a trap for me, and I wound up here. Like I said, it was stupid, but I needed to get your attention. You're the only one who can help me."

"Why am I the only one? If you had irrefutable proof that the math is wrong, then-"

"I tried to tell the Council," Reza said, interrupting. "You saw where that got me. The Larones have all the experience, and I'm just an upstart who switched out of mechanical engineering because I was bored."

"You switched out of ME? Because you were bored?" To Gabriel, there was nothing boring about trying to improve machines. Especially their weapons systems.

"Yes. I thought Astronomy would be fun. I've been trying to put together this theory on slipspace and phasing that I think could change the way we look at the streams, and maybe increase our time and distance estimates to ninety-nine point nine percent accuracy. That's what I'm working on now, and that's why I'm sure the numbers are wrong. The bulk of my astronomical effort has been with slipspace. So, Guy is trying to discredit me."

"Getting arrested doesn't help with that. I came over here with the idea that you might have been set up."

"I know, I know. It was so dumb. No, I didn't get set up. I did it to myself, and I probably lost the only tiny shred of proof I have."

"Only that the math is wrong. What about the other thing you said? What about the idea of leaving people behind?"

"Exactly. I told you; it doesn't work any other way, but I can't even get anyone to consider the possibility if I can't prove the smallest part of it. Well, except for you. You believe me, don't you?"

Gabriel stared at Reza for a few moments. "I'm not sure what I believe."

Reza leaned back, smacking his head against the wall. "Ugh. If I can't convince you, I can't convince anyone."

"You have to admit, the idea that there are members of the NEA conspiring to leave a good portion of the population behind is hard to swallow, when the worse offense we have around here is a food fight. You're talking about leaving people to die."

"They're willing to leave the people on Earth to die. What's the difference?"

Gabriel didn't have an answer for that.

"Who do you think is involved?" he asked.

"The Larones, of course," Reza replied. "Councilwoman Rouse. Councilman Giorno. Maybe a few others on the Council. Definitely some of the lead scientists beyond Guy. The head nerds are like an exclusive club, and they stick together."

"What about in the Space Force?"

"I'm not sure. I don't think so."

"It would be a major betrayal to go against one of your own," Gabriel said.

"Yes. The question is, how do we prove what they're planning?"

"Why did you say we?"

"The power of suggestion? I don't know how without the original, unaltered slipstream calculations, and I can't get them without you."

"You said they're locked away on a server on Gamma."

"They are."

"So how am I supposed to get them, assuming that I'm willing to help you?"

"You're a Space Force officer. You're legally allowed to request access to any file you want to see."

"I am?" Gabriel asked. He had never heard of that before.

"Yes. Since Space Force is also responsible for policing the settlements, you have rights to view any non-private document within the

NEA. Obviously, most pilots don't know about this, or if they do they don't care. It would be ripe for abuse if it weren't for the fact that, as you said, the worst offenses we have around here are usually food fights."

He shook his head, staring down at the floor.

"Unfortunately, not this time," he said.

[39]

"We aren't far now," Donovan said, pushing through the heavy brush.

It had taken the three of them nearly ten hours to make their way from the Dread starship to Chicoloapan, a suburb of Mexico City that had been leveled in the initial invasion. Like the capital, it was a ruined mess of destroyed buildings and dead vegetation, littered with debris and corpses picked clean by local wildlife.

"How can you keep your base so close, and remain undiscovered?" Ehri asked.

She had been incredibly inquisitive for the entirety of the journey, constantly asking questions of both Donovan and Diaz. Her energy level remained the same despite the trek while Donovan was just about ready to collapse.

"You'll see when we get there," Donovan said. Most of the answers he had given had been along the same lines. The bek'hai scientist was like a curious, impatient child.

They ambled along an empty street, with Diaz in constant motion, on full alert and scanning the sky for signs of enemy scouts, her captured plasma rifle held in a ready position. They had avoided a number of the machines getting away, with most of them tracking closer to the Dread colony. Ehri said it was because the pur'dahm in charge of the search wouldn't believe that they had managed to slip away. Apparently, arrogance wasn't a uniquely human trait.

There hadn't been any other sign of scouts in the last few hours, though there had been one flyover by a larger Dread ship, a starfighter. They had stopped and hid when they heard the whine of its engines approaching, watching it pass by pressed against the side of a rubble pile.

"How's your shoulder?" Diaz asked, checking in on him.

She had been much more attentive to him than she had ever been in the past, asking him how he was feeling every so often, her face strained with concern. It was a side of her he had never seen before, and while part of him liked it, another part wanted his cool as ice Lieutenant back. The whole episode had left him feeling all kinds of things he hadn't felt before, and he attributed it to loss of blood and lack of food and rest.

He expected that once both of them had slept the episode off they would go back to their professional respect and personal indifference.

"It hurts," he replied. "I need Doc Iwu to clean it out and make sure there isn't any shrapnel stuck in there. I bet there is."

"How do you manage such pain?" Ehri asked.

"The bek'hai don't feel pain?" Diaz said.

"Of course they can feel pain. We have medicines to remove it. Why suffer from something so unnecessary?"

"Pain teaches you to respect the fact that you're alive," Donovan said.

"In what way?"

"Because you never know how long you have. How many days or weeks or years before you get sick, or shot, or something."

"The bek'hai do not consider such things. We are each allotted the equivalent of one hundred of your years."

"Allotted?" Diaz said. "You mean you kill yourselves on purpose?"

"The bek'hai body cannot survive much longer than that because of the weakened genetic chain. Typically by that time we are ready to die. Perhaps once the integration has been perfected this procedure will change."

"I can't imagine surrendering my life," Diaz said.

"I cannot imagine wanting to survive in a body that no longer functions." Ehri said.

Donovan was about to chime in when he noticed a flash of light from a nearby rooftop. He glanced over at Diaz, whose eyes shifted, acknowledging that she had seen it, too.

"Ehri, whatever happens next, stay calm, okay?" he said. "I won't let them kill you."

"What?" Ehri said.

A dozen armed men and women poured out of the debris around them. They were ragged people in the same green cloth Donovan had been wearing earlier, except they had tattered boots covering their feet.

"Don't move," one of them said.

"Captain Reyes," Donovan said. He could imagine what the resistance soldiers were thinking, seeing him dressed in the enemy's cloth. "Major Donovan Peters. Identification code alpha-echo-foxtrot-four-seven-nine."

"Lieutenant Renata Diaz," Diaz said. "Identification code foxtrot-hotel-zulu-six-four-eight."

Captain Reyes froze along with the rest of the soldiers. He stared at Donovan, his eyes squinting despite the darkness.

"Donnie? Is that you?"

"I gave you my codes, Captain."

"The Dread take people. They make copies. How do I know you aren't one of those?"

"A copy wouldn't have the code. That's the whole point of using them. Besides, we've only been gone one day."

Reyes didn't lower his rifle. He pointed it at Ehri instead. "Who is this?" he asked.

"Captain, stand down," Donovan said.

Reyes stepped forward, his hands shaking slightly as he got closer to Ehri. "Who is this, Donnie?"

"We need to meet with General Rodriguez," Diaz said. "It's important."

"Is that a Dread plasma rifle?" one of the other soldiers, Corporal Wade, asked.

"Yes," Donovan replied. "But it's better than that, Miguel. It isn't secured."

A surprised murmur raced across the squad.

"Quiet," Captain Reyes said, still pointing the gun at Ehri.

She continued to follow Donovan's instructions, remaining completely calm, her hands at her sides, palms facing out. She reminded Donovan of a statue of the Madonna he had seen once.

"Who. Is. This?" Reyes asked again, his voice balancing fear and anger.

Donovan stepped toward him. Reyes backed up, pointing the gun at him again. "Don't. Just stay there, Donnie."

"That's Major to you, Captain," Donovan said. "Lower your weapon. That's an order."

"I don't think so. You walk in here dressed in whatever that leotard thing is, carrying an alien weapon with a freaking alien clone in tow, and you think I'm going to listen to you?"

"Julian," Diaz said.

"No. Shut up," Reyes said. "We haven't stayed hidden all these years by being stupid."

"You're being stupid right now. We're carrying active Dread plasma rifles. We could have already blasted you all to mush if that was what we wanted."

"Then you wouldn't know where the base is."

"I already know where the base is, jackass. I'll take you there if you stop pointing your gun at our prisoner."

"Prisoner?"

Ehri looked over at Diaz, unhappy with the title.

"Yes, prisoner," Donovan said. "We captured a Dread scientist. We need to bring her to General Rodriguez."

Reyes looked at Ehri again, his face twisting, losing its fear and turning to pure anger. "Dirty alien piece of-" He swung the gun toward her again.

Donovan stepped toward him, grabbing the rifle and yanking it up as Reyes pulled the trigger. The shot echoed across the landscape. Donovan wrenched the weapon from Reyes' hands, and then hit him in the face with the stock.

"You idiot," Diaz hissed. "They'll hear that for sure."

"You broke my nose," Reyes said, laying on the ground.

Donovan didn't care. His shoulder was throbbing, the wound pulled open by the motion. Reyes had always been too impetuous to be a good soldier, but beggars couldn't be picky. He was young and healthy and wanted to fight. Those were the only requirements, and even the young and healthy part could be overlooked.

"We need to get out of here," Donovan said. "Form up and let's go. That's an order, soldiers. You too, Reyes. Doc Iwu can fix your dumbass nose."

Reyes scowled, rolling over and getting to his feet. The group ran along the street, turning left after half a kilometer. Diaz took the rear, keeping a constant eye on the skies for signs of scouts.

They continued another eight hundred meters, to the edge of a collapsed building. A small space was visible at the bottom, barely large enough for a person to crawl out of.

"Let's go, people," Donovan said, stopping at the opening and waving the soldiers in. One by one they dropped onto their stomachs, rifles on their backs, crawling hand over hand into the small hole.

"No wonder they cannot find it," Ehri said.

"It gets better," Donovan replied. "You understand how much trust I'm putting in you right now?"

"Yes, Major. My touch is my bond."

"Right."

The rest of the soldiers went in ahead of them. Reyes glared at Ehri as he dropped to his knees. "She doesn't look like a prisoner to me," he said. "She isn't even bound."

"You have your own troubles to worry about, Captain," Donovan said. "Don't think I'm not going to report you for discharging your weapon in the open near the base like this."

Reyes was fuming, but he dropped to his stomach and disappeared a moment later.

"Anything?" Donovan asked when Diaz reached the hole.

She nodded. "Not drones. Something huge to the north, near the tree line. It's still a few kilometers away, but it definitely picked up the noise and is coming this way."

"A mechanized tactical armor," Ehri said. "You don't want to be out here when it arrives. I hope your base is well shielded from sensors."

Donovan smiled. "Don't worry. It is."

[40]

THE COLLAPSED SPACE THEY HAD TO CRAWL UNDER CONTINUED for ten meters at a slightly downward angle. For Donovan, it seemed more like a thousand meters, as every motion of his arm going forward to pull himself along like a snake sent waves of pain up his back, and they didn't have time for him to take it slow and easy.

There was a drop at the end of the tunnel that usually meant reaching out hands-first and rolling to the ground. Fortunately, Diaz waited with Corporal Wade and they helped him down. Ehri stood off to the side, turning in a circle to examine the space.

"What is this?" she asked.

There wasn't much to see just yet. The floor and ceiling were both thick lead with a small crease in the center, and there was a second lead-shielded door to their right. It was open for now.

"You'll see," Diaz said.

They made their way to the door, ducking through and into a narrow, winding stairwell that dropped over one hundred meters. Corporal Wade stopped and pulled the door closed behind them, spinning the central mechanism to lock it. Then they started to descend.

The ground shook above them as the Dread's mechanized armor neared the position.

"Are we out of range?" Ehri asked.

"We should be," Donovan said. "The space we crawled through is a reinforced and lined air vent, and the part of the ceiling that isn't collapsed is the same. The sensors shouldn't be able to penetrate it. That's how we've been able to stay so close without being found."

The vibrations above them stopped.

"We've heard them pass over before," Diaz said. "It won't find us."

They continued the descent, winding a spiral on the stairs. There was another reinforced door at the bottom that was also still open.

"Oh," Ehri said. Donovan looked at her. She was smiling. "I finally figured out what this is. A missile silo, right? For nuclear warheads."

"Yup," Donovan replied. "Sans missile. It was launched at one of the Dread ships during the invasion. I'm sure you know how that turned out."

"Clever. Very clever. It was designed to stay hidden from sensors. The perfect hiding place."

"It is for as long as your kind don't know it's here."

"How did you know it was here?"

"We found a schematic while we were looting a military base a hundred klicks from here, after we had to abandon our last hideout. We weren't sure we could make it without being spotted, but once we did, we've been safe here for quite a while."

They reached the bottom of the steps and approached the door. A figure swung around in front of them, blocking the path. He had a gun in his hand, and like Captain Reyes, he raised it and pointed it at Ehri's head.

"Prisoner, Major?" General Christian Rodriguez said. "Then why are you telling her your whole life story?"

Donovan stepped between Rodriguez and Ehri without thinking. "General Rodriguez, sir. Please. I can explain."

The General smiled. "I'm sure you can, Donnie. We're going to have to lock it in the fridge until you do."

"The fridge?" Ehri said.

"Don't worry. It's an old industrial refrigerator. It was used to store the rations for the crew that worked down here, in case of emergency. The cooling pumps blew out years ago. It's cold, but not that cold."

"Unless you have superhuman strength, you aren't getting out of it," Rodriguez said.

"There's no need to point the weapon at me, General," Ehri said. "I will go willingly."

"Diaz, Wade, bring her down. Donovan, you come with me."

"Yes, sir," Diaz and Wade said. They walked on either side of Ehri, through a small control center and down a long corridor leading to the living area.

"Yes, sir," Donovan said. "I need to see Doctor Iwu at your convenience, sir."

"Are you hurt?"

Donovan nodded, turning to show the General his back. Even though the material couldn't be cut, a large stain of blood covered the area around the injury.

"Ouch. Five minutes, and then you can see Iwu."

"Yes, sir."

Donovan followed Rodriguez through the base along the same path Diaz and Ehri had taken a few seconds earlier. The three of them were already well ahead, walking at a much brisker pace. Ehri glanced back at him once. There was no hint of fear on her face. Only the same look of intense interest and curiosity.

"Did Cameron and Sanchez make it back?" Donovan asked as they walked.

"Si. They told me you were separated when the mech showed up. That you and Diaz drew it away so they could escape."

"Yes, sir."

"It was a brave thing to do."

"I would expect anyone else to have done the same for me in that situation, sir. It was the right thing to do."

"You're braver than most, Donovan. That's probably why you're still alive."

"I wouldn't be if it weren't for Renata. I sent her away as a decoy. She came back for us."

"Disobeying orders?"

"It worked out for the best, sir."

"Yes, I suppose it did."

The connecting tunnel ended at another heavy door, which was hanging open. A guard stood to one side of it, ready to close it in an emergency. On the other side sat an open supply room, a special room the resistance called the Collection. The accumulated non-essential possessions of the resistance were piled inside, loosely separated as though bringing them together in such a way could knit back a history of humankind. It had seemed almost quaint at the time, but the twenty-third-century resurgence of physical nostalgia - photographs, books, handmade arts and crafts and the like - had been a Godsend to the wanderers of the present. It was a solid, tangible connection to the past, to all they had once had, and a memory of what they had lost.

They crossed a series of corridors and doorways from there until they reached General Rodriguez's office. Donovan did his best to ignore the stares he was receiving on the way through the base. He knew how out of place he must look. How alien. He was self-conscious of it, and at the same time proud. They had brought a treasure back with them.

The office was located in the corner of the first floor; a simple, barren, and rarely used space with an older desk sat in the center flanked by a pair of chairs.

"Close the door," Rodriguez said, moving to the other side of the desk. He remained standing.

"Yes, sir. Am I in trouble sir?"

He spoke as soon as it had shut. "In trouble? Are you joking with me, Donnie? Let me see it."

"What?"

"The weapon, Major."

Donovan had forgotten he was still holding the alien plasma rifle.

He held it out across the desk. Rodriguez took it, holding the grip and pointing it at the wall while staring at the active display.

"Wow," he said, shaking his head. He looked at Donovan. "Fifty years, Donnie. Fifty freaking years, amigo. How many of these things have we picked up, and they've been completely worthless? How many have we taken apart but couldn't get them to turn on?"

"It's better than that, sir," Donovan said. "We always wondered why they have that toggle on the side. Activating it changes the bolts somehow. They're able to pierce the Dread armor."

Rodriguez's eyes snapped from the gun to him. "You know this for certain?"

"We killed an armored Dread warrior with it."

"Seriously? You killed one of them? Do you have any idea what this means?"

"I have some idea."

"You don't know the half of it." He paused, wiping at the corner of his eyes. "I brought you in here because I didn't want the others to see me cry. I'm supposed to be the tough old General. Where did you get this? And those clothes you're wearing? That isn't cotton. Oh, and that woman you brought with you, the clone?"

"Just to be clear, General, you aren't mad that I brought her?"

"Should I be?" he asked.

"No, sir. She's earned my trust."

"That's good enough for me. You're a hero, Donovan. You and Diaz both. You may have just changed the entire face of this war." He paused again, lowering his voice. "I hope it isn't too late."

"Too late for what, sir?"

"We'll talk about it later. You need to see Iwu. We have a lot of work to do, and this changes everything." He shook the rifle. "Give me the short version."

Donovan spent the next few minutes briefing General Rodriguez on everything that had happened from the moment they had erected the needle. The General remained silent throughout, stroking the top of the weapon like the priceless artifact it was. His eyebrows went up as Donovan recounted in more detail how Diaz had killed the armored Dread, and a smile crept across his face.

"So we came back here. Everything was fine until Captain Reyes turned into an asshole with Ehri, like he's the only one whose family was killed by the Dread."

"I'll deal with Reyes. He won't be leaving the base again anytime soon. I know the Dread are sweeping the area right now because of his stupidity."

"Do you think they'll find us?"

"No. I sent Suarez up to collapse the vent just in case they decide to get too curious. It'll take a few hours to open it up again, but it's worth it."

"Yes, sir."

"Now, have Iwu clean you up and pass those threads over to Carlson so he can peek at it under his microscope. Here." He picked up the rifle. "Get this over to him, too. Tell him not to do anything to make it stop working, but we need to know everything we can about it, especially how it can get through the enemy's armor. Bek'hai, you said?"

"Yes, sir." Donovan took the rifle from Rodriguez. "What about Ehri, sir?"

"You trust her, and she looks like she trusts you. She'll stay under guard until you can escort her. I want to know everything she knows. I've been waiting a lifetime for an opportunity like this."

"Yes, sir."

"Dismissed, Major."

Donovan opened the door and left the room. He didn't see the wave of frightened concern that passed over General Rodriguez's face behind him.

[41]

DONOVAN FOUND CHIEF SCIENCE OFFICER CARLSON IN HIS usual location.

Face down on his cot in the barracks.

He had decided to drop the rifle and the alien clothing off first, grabbing a new pair of greens from Corporal Gosh in supply and carrying them with him to the bottom floor of the bunker. He didn't disturb Carlson right away, instead taking his time in getting the black cloth off his body. The pants were easy. The top wasn't. He grimaced in pain as he tugged at it.

"Whoever you are, and whatever you're doing, can you please stop?" Carlson said, his voice muffled from being buried in the pillow. "We have a separate room for that."

"Either shut up or help me get this off," Donovan said.

Carlson rolled over. He was an older man, a little pudgy, with thick gray hair and a large nose. He was disheveled in a button down collared shirt and slacks beneath an old and stained white lab coat. "Donnie. You made it back." He shifted back and forth a few times to get enough momentum to pull himself from the cot.

"Diaz and I both made it," he replied.

Carlson made a motion to give him a hug, but Donovan put up his hand.

"You wanted me to stop groaning, remember?" He turned so Carlson could see his back.

"Why aren't you with Iwu right now?"

"The General wanted me to bring you this." He pulled at the clothes. "And that." He pointed to the alien rifle, resting on an adjacent empty mattress.

"Is that-"

"Yes."

He forgot about Donovan, reaching for it. "How? What?"

"I'll tell you all about it later. The General said to examine it, but whatever you do, don't break it."

Carlson picked it up like it was an egg. "I don't believe it." He turned toward Donovan. "You're the damn messiah."

"I wouldn't go that far. Are you going to help me finish getting out of this, or what?"

"Right. Sorry, Donnie." He smiled as he put the weapon back down. "I got a little excited. Geez, I still can't believe it. I've been here since we found the place, and I never thought I would live to see the day."

"Is that why you spend so much time sleeping?" Donovan asked.

"I'm not sleeping. I'm thinking."

"Yeah, right."

Carlson grabbed at the alien cloth, helping Donovan wiggle out of it. The motion opened the wound again, and blood trickled warmly down his back.

"Don't waste your time with me," Carlson said. "Go see Iwu. I'm going to bring this down to the lab and get my people working on it. I'm glad I've been sleeping so much lately. I don't think I'll be resting again for a while. I'm so stoked."

"I thought you were thinking?"

Carlson laughed. "Shut up."

Donovan didn't put his shirt on, leaving his top half bare while he made his way back up one level to the infirmary.

"Where's Doc Iwu?" he asked George. The blonde-haired teen was one of the Doctor's four assistants-in-training.

"Hey Donnie," George said. "You've got a little blood on your side there."

"Thanks. That's why I came to see Iwu."

"She's in the back with Diaz. Let me take a look. Maybe I can help you? Take a seat over there."

He pointed at a small stool in the corner, near the racks of carefully labeled and organized medications that had been grabbed from anywhere they could find them.

Donovan sat down, turning his back to the boy.

"How does it look?"

"Hold on, I need to clean it out." He opened a few nearby drawers, removing some cloth and disinfectant. "This is going to sting."

"I'm used to it."

George worked at cleaning the wound. Donovan winced but didn't make a sound. The stinging was nothing compared to crawling through the tunnel.

"It's deep, but superficial. I imagine it's a bit sore?"

"You could say that."

"I'll stitch it up and get you a sling. Rest the arm for a week and you should be fine."

"George, don't take this personally because you're a good kid, and you're working hard at this, but I'd really like Iwu to take a look at it."

"I understand," George said. "Nailah's been teaching us that confidence is one of the most important traits of a good Doctor. You have to be sure that what you're doing is right. Which I am."

The slight turn on the statement wasn't lost on Donovan. "A little bit of arrogance doesn't hurt either, does it?"

"Nope. Nailah should be out any second. Diaz is in better shape than you."

"Doctors also need to not ogle their patients," Donovan said.

The door to the private examining room started to open. George lowered his voice. "I'm working on it, but between you and me, Diaz is gorgeous."

Donovan got to his feet. "Just wait until you reach puberty."

Diaz came out of the room first, smiling when she saw Donovan. She also had a fresh pair of greens on, though her alien outfit was still in her arms. "I'm glad Rodriguez didn't keep you too long," she said. "What did he say?"

"I'll tell you later," Donovan replied. "Is Ehri okay?"

"Why are you so worried about her? She's fine. It's probably boring for her in the fridge, though. There's nothing to look at, and nobody to interrogate."

Was that a hint of jealousy he was sensing?

Doctor Nailah Iwu was behind Diaz, and she also gave Donovan a wide, bright smile. She was an elegant woman, tall and thin, highly educated and well-spoken. "Major Donovan Peters," she said. "It looks like George has already started my work for me?"

"I'll catch up with you later, amigo," Diaz said, surprising him by leaning up and kissing his cheek. She left the room before he could respond.

"He has a laceration across his right scapula, ma'am," George said. "It's deep, but none of the muscles were cut. I recommended stitches, but Donnie wanted you to look at it first."

"George knows what he's doing, Major," Iwu said.

"I'm sure he does. It's just important to me that I'm ready for duty as soon as possible, and you can't argue that you're a master with stitches."

She laughed. "I've had too much experience. Come on back, I'll take a look. George, you too."

They followed her back into the examination room. It was necessarily low-tech, as it was difficult to keep the more advanced medical machinery operating with the limited resources they possessed.

"Sit facing away from me," Iwu said, patting the padded table.

Donovan did as he was asked. He felt Iwu's cold hands on his skin a moment later.

"George's prognosis is completely accurate."

"I told you so," George said.

"George," Iwu chided.

"Sorry, ma'am."

"Let me stitch this up. Keep the level of your arm below your head for the next week and you should be fine."

"No sling?" Donovan asked, looking over at George.

"I don't think that will be necessary."

George shook his head and looked away.

"Do you want something to bite down on?" Iwu asked. Stitches weren't a good enough reason for them to waste painkillers or numbing agents on.

"No, thank you."

"Suit yourself."

He could hear her moving behind him in quick, precise motions as she prepped the stitches.

"Here we go," she said.

He felt the first stab and closed his eyes, recalling his conversation with Rodriguez as she closed up the wound. The General had called him a hero. That was something to be proud of, and the part of the meeting he wanted most to hold onto.

He couldn't. Instead, his mind kept going back to a single statement the General had made and wondering what he had meant.

"I hope it isn't too late."

[42]

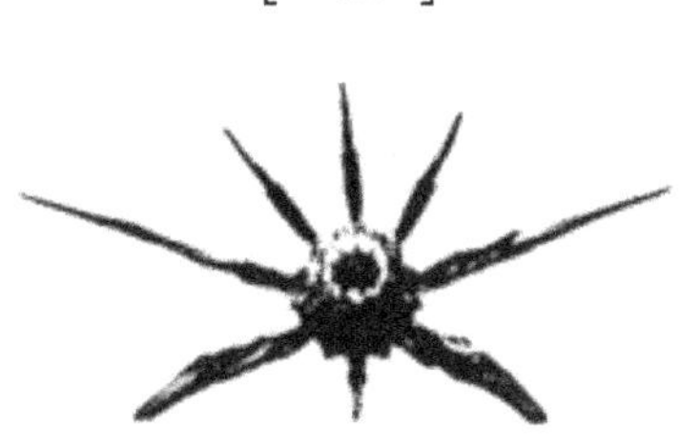

GABRIEL WAS BACK ON GAMMA LESS THAN TWO HOURS LATER, after making up an excuse for Colonel Graham about how he wanted one last ride in the fighter before turning it in. Graham was gracious in accepting the reason, even though it was within his rights to dress Gabriel down for his actions. Gabriel wasn't going to risk angering the Colonel, and so he arranged for the transport to return him to Alpha when he was finished on Gamma, ostensibly to visit his father.

Lieutenant Curtis laughed to see him back so soon, and he was even more amused when Gabriel took a few minutes to relate his conversation with Colonel Graham. Once he had Curtis loosened up, he made his next move.

"So, Lieutenant," Gabriel said. "I have it on authority that officers in the Space Force have the right to access any files stored on shared resources?"

Curtis seemed surprised by the question. "I haven't heard of that."

"Look it up if you aren't sure. Article seventy-one, paragraph three." Reza had shown him the law on his handheld. It was a real thing in the NEA law books.

"I believe you, sir," Curtis said. "I'm not sure why you're bringing it up, though."

"I need to make a copy of a file that I know is here on Gamma."

"I thought you came for a tour?"

"I did, but I also came to get the file."

Curtis seemed unsure. "I'll have to talk to Doctor Shore."

"Shore is a civilian," Gabriel said. "He has no jurisdiction over something like this."

Gabriel watched Curtis' expression. Reza didn't think any of the members of the military were in on the conspiracy. That didn't mean he was right. Curtis was stationed with the science team full-time. If any of the Space Force were going to side with them, it would be him.

"Look, it's not a big deal," Gabriel said. He made a face that he hoped looked somewhat pathetic. "I made a bet with the receptionist on Alpha. Danai. Do you know her?"

"No, sir."

"Well, she agreed to go out with me if I could prove the Eden mission was real, and that we really are going to get out of this system. I talked to Guy before I left, and he told me they had the report on their servers."

"Why didn't you ask Guy for the report?"

"Guy hates me," Gabriel said. "I only asked him to confirm it existed. You've probably heard I've been a little out of sorts the last few days."

"There have been some rumors, yeah. They said you and your father were both devastated over the resistance giving up the war."

"Exactly. I'm just looking for a little distraction; you know what I mean?"

Curtis smiled. "I hear you, Captain." He bit his lip. "It's on the books, right?"

"Yes."

"You promise?"

"Yes."

Curtis nodded. "Okay. I happen to be friends with the head of IT here. Come on, we'll go stop by her office. She can get you what you need."

"I assume you're referring to the file?" Gabriel asked.

The Lieutenant laughed openly. "Yeah. I would prefer if you keep it to business with Felicia. I've been trying to get her to go out with me for the last three months."

"Why won't she?"

"You know those types. They can be hard to get to warm up."

Gabriel didn't know. He smiled and nodded anyway. "Okay. I won't flirt with her. All I want is the file."

"Follow me, sir," Curtis said.

Curtis assigned one of his subordinates to keep an eye on things and then they made their way from the hangar to the loop station, taking a pod to the central hub. Once there, they took the elevator up to the second level. The door to the IT department was secured with a fingerprint scanner. Curtis put his finger to it, and it slid open.

The office was open and basic, rows of desks lined up neatly in the front, with racks of computer equipment behind glass in the back. The servers had originally been on the Magellan, and by the looks of it, there was early activity to disconnect it all and return it to the starship.

"There she is," Curtis said, pointing to a thin woman on the other side of the glass. She was with another tech, pointing at a neatly organized row of cables that dropped from the ceiling.

Curtis went over to the glass and knocked on it. Felicia looked at him, made a less than enthusiastic face, excused herself, and exited the room ahead of a blast of cool air.

"Can I help you, Lieutenant?" she asked.

"Hi, Felicia. How are you today?" Curtis said.

"I'm fine. I'm in the middle of something. Some of us have actual work to do."

Three months, and this was as far as he had gotten? Gabriel had a feeling she wasn't cold. The Lieutenant was just annoying.

"Excuse me, Felicia," he said, approaching them.

"Yes." Her eyes fell to the name badge to his shirt. "Oh, Captain St. Martin." She smiled. There was nothing cold about it. "How is your father?"

Gabriel glanced at Curtis, who responded with a shrug.

"He's doing well, thank you for asking. I'm sorry if we're bothering you, and I don't want to take too much of your time. I was hoping you might be able to help me with something."

"Really? I can't imagine how an IT girl would be able to help you with anything."

She was still smiling, her expression soft. He had told Curtis he wouldn't flirt with her as a joke, but it seemed she wanted to flirt with him.

"That's where you're wrong," Gabriel said. "I need to retrieve a file for Colonel Graham's review, but I have no idea how to locate it."

"Oh? I can probably help you there. Which file?"

"Astronomy's report on the Eden migration," Gabriel said. "Guy Larone wrote it."

"Why don't you get it from Guy?"

"You probably know he isn't a big fan of the military."

She laughed. "No, he isn't, is he? If it's his private report, you'll need his permission for me to pull it."

"Actually, he doesn't," Curtis said, trying to get back into the conversation. "Article... Which one was it again, Captain?"

"Article seventy-one," Gabriel replied. "NEA law says I don't need permission, which is good because he would never give it to me."

Felician bit her lip. "I've never heard of that law."

"How often does anyone need it? You must have a copy of the Articles you can pull up if you want to check."

"You don't mind if I take a look?"

"Why would I? I don't want you to get in trouble."

Felicia led them to her desk. It was sparse, save for a photo of a man Gabriel recognized, standing with a younger version of her.

"General Cave is your father?" he asked, suddenly feeling stupid for not putting two and two together. He knew the General had a daughter named Felicia.

"Yes. He used to talk about you and your dad a lot, you know. He has a lot of respect for both of you. There was a time he wanted the two of us to meet, to see if we hit it off. Then he decided he didn't want me to be involved with a pilot." She was speaking as she was navigating through the Articles on a large touchscreen.

"I can understand that," Gabriel said, his mind reaching back and inserting Felicia into a potential alternate timeline. She seemed like a nice enough person, and she wasn't hard to look at. "We don't tend to live very long."

"You have. Ah, here it is." She scanned the lines, reciting some of the words out loud. "It looks legit. I've got you covered, Captain."

She dove into a different part of the system, flipping through all kinds of data until she found what she was looking for. "Do you want me to push it to your account?"

"Actually, can you give me a copy?"

She reached down and opened a drawer, pulling out a small square. She tapped it against the touchscreen and then handed it to him. "Would it be possible for you to bring this back?" she asked. "We don't have an unlimited supply of these."

Gabriel had a feeling from the way she was looking at him that she wanted him to come back more than she wanted the storage square back. "Sure. I'll do my best."

"Great. Maybe we can get something to eat while you're here?"

He looked at Curtis again. The Lieutenant was shaking his head. "I'd like that," he said. "It may be a while though with everything going on."

"You'll have more free time once we're all on the Magellan," she said. "If I don't see you before that, I hope I'll see you then."

"I'll definitely return this to you by then," Gabriel said. "Thank you for your help."

"Anytime, Captain."

"Gabriel."

"Anytime, Gabriel."

Gabriel reached out and took her hand, giving it a light shake. He put the storage device in his pocket and headed for the door with Curtis trailing behind him.

"What was that, sir?" Curtis said once they were back on the elevator.

"I needed the file," Gabriel said. "Besides, I told you I wouldn't come on to her and I didn't."

"You could have been a little less open to her advances."

"Why? I'm not interested in her romantically. That doesn't mean she wouldn't make a good friend. By the way, I appreciate your help with this."

Lieutenant Curtis didn't look happy, but he seemed satisfied with the answer. "You're welcome, sir."

[43]

"I've got it," Gabriel said, holding the square up so Reza could see it.

The scientist lifted his attention from his handheld, his eyes falling on the square. "I knew I could count on you, Captain." He got to his feet, approaching the bars. Gabriel passed the storage device through.

Reza tapped it against his handheld and then navigated through to it. He scanned it quickly, nodding as he went while Gabriel waited.

"Well?" Gabriel asked a minute later.

Reza tilted his handheld so Gabriel could see the screen. It was filled with mathematical equations he didn't understand. "This is it. The original version. All of this is advanced math that you probably don't care about." He scrolled the data to the bottom. "Here's the important part. Look at that number."

Gabriel tracked Reza's finger to the line that said .001. "What is it?"

"The odds of reaching Eden. One thousandth of a percent."

"Those aren't good odds."

"No."

"I don't see how this proves anything."

"I have a copy of Guy's second report. The doctored one." He manipulated his handheld until he got to the same spot. "Take a look."

99.95.

"I can show you where he changed the calculation if you want. It's buried in the algorithms. Essentially, he reduced the variable until he got the number he wanted."

"Which variable?"

"Souls on board," Reza said.

The idea of it was chilling.

"And you swear that if you show this to the Council, they'll believe you?" Gabriel asked.

"If they don't, you'll know something is really rotten. I can share these two reports with any scientist on Gamma, and unless they're part of the conspiracy they'll jump all over this error."

"That's a problem, isn't it? It's going to be the good guys versus the bad guys. We need more proof than that."

"No, not proof, Captain. Support. If we can get enough people to believe this, we can at least get a stay of execution."

Gabriel considered it. If what Reza was saying was true, whoever didn't agree with his assertions would be outed as a possible traitor, which was good. It might not be enough to change the outcome, which was bad.

"We should bring this to General Cave," he said. "He was open to the Eden trip but he's not going to betray his soldiers to get there, and he has a lot of pull with some of the Council."

Reza nodded. "That sounds like a good start. Can you get me out of here so I can show him?"

"I don't know. I'll be right back."

Gabriel went to the front to find Spaceman Lee. The Spaceman stood and saluted as he entered.

"I'd like you to allow me to take Reza Mokri out of the prison," Gabriel said.

"Sir? What for?"

"He needs to speak with General Cave. He has some information that I believe the General would find valuable."

"I'm not allowed to do that, sir."

"I know you aren't supposed to. Does it explicitly say anywhere that you can't?"

"Not everything has to be spelled out for me to know that it isn't proper, sir."

"And in most cases I would agree with you, Spaceman. This is a bit of an unusual circumstance. You know you can trust me, and it isn't like there's anywhere for me to steal him to. I wouldn't ask if it weren't important."

"Even if I wanted to, I would need to get clearance from my Commanding Officer."

"Who is that?" Gabriel asked.

"Major Choi."

Gabriel smiled. "Can you reach her for me?"

Lee reached to the screen on his desk and tapped into the directory. Major Choi answered the request a moment later.

"Major," Lee said. "I'm sorry to bother you -"

Gabriel moved in front of the guard. "Major."

"Gabriel? What are you doing at the prison?"

"Where are you right now, Major?"

"Above your head in the concourse, getting something to eat. What's going on?"

"Would you mind meeting me down here? It's important."

He could tell she was thinking, trying to determine for herself why he was asking for her.

"This is about Mokri, isn't it? Gabriel, I know you're upset about the Council's decision, but-"

"Please, Vivian," Gabriel said. "For me."

Choi sighed. "Okay. Only because it's you. Give me five minutes."

"Thank you, Major," Gabriel said.

The screen returned to the directory. Gabriel left Lee and returned to Reza.

"Well?" Reza asked.

"I'm still working on it. Major Choi is coming down. I need you to show her what you showed me."

He looked unhappy about the news. "I thought you said General Cave would see me?"

"I have to get you out of this cell first. Major Choi is a friend of mine, and she's on our side. Convince her and she'll get you in front of Cave."

He seemed to relax. "Okay. Okay. I'm running a diff on the two reports that will show exactly what changed between versions. That should help me explain everything more easily."

"Whatever helps."

Reza continued staring down at his handheld while Gabriel waited, leaning against the wall. Major Choi arrived early, entering the cell block with Lee behind her.

"Major," Gabriel said, coming to attention and saluting.

"Relax, Gabriel. I'm here as your friend. Mr. Mokri."

"Major," Reza said, looking nervous.

"Spaceman Lee, you're dismissed," Choi said. The Spaceman saluted and left them. "Gabriel, what is this all about."

Gabriel explained the situation as best he could, with Reza filling in the details. Major Choi seemed unconvinced until he described how he had gotten the original file from the servers on Gamma, and Reza showed her the discrepancies.

"I don't want to believe this could be true," she said, staring at Reza's handheld. His diff program had highlighted the changed number in red. "Never mind what this means for the Eden mission. What does it mean for humanity if we're willing to sacrifice so many?"

"It means people are getting desperate," Gabriel said. "I understand why they would want to get out of Calawan and go somewhere green. I've seen Earth. So have you. Neither one of us is stupid. The allure is there."

"And the temptation may be too strong for some."

"Strong enough they'll let thousands of people die," Reza said. "It isn't right."

"No," Choi agreed. "It isn't. Both of you are coming with me. We're going to find General Cave, and we're going to put a stop to this right now while we figure out what the complete truth is."

"I knew I could count on you," Gabriel said.

Choi smiled, putting her hand on his cheek. "Always, Gabriel."

[44]

GABRIEL WAS THANKFUL HE HAD ENLISTED MAJOR CHOI'S HELP. All of the activity around planning for the trip to Exodus left General Cave's schedule full, and would have made it nearly impossible to get a minute to speak with him without her influence.

As it was, she had to put in a communication with Colonel Graham to explain that Gabriel was helping her with an important task, and to request he be permitted to spend the night on Alpha. Graham was not only understanding but discreet as well. He didn't ask her why she needed him.

It was evening by the time they arrived at Space Force headquarters on the top floor of the central dome. They were standing in the lobby and waiting for Cave to finish a prior meeting. He had ten minutes between appointments. Ten minutes the General had been planning to spend eating his dinner, which would now have to be skipped until the early morning.

"It better be good," Cave had said to Choi. "If it weren't coming from a St. Martin, I wouldn't bother at all."

Gabriel knew it was good. He wasn't sure if it would be good enough. Reza had been heads down, staring at his handheld since Choi had released him from the jail. The astronomer was doing everything he could to arrange the data in a way that would be digestible to non-scientists.

"You should see your father after this," Choi said.

He didn't like that the Major had to keep telling him how to be a minimally responsible son. At the same time, he was more nervous than ever about seeing his father. It was Choi who had told Theodore about the resistance's message, and the plan to abandon Calawan. She said he had responded very similarly to Gabriel, turning over in his bed in silence and refusing to speak to anyone since. His condition was also getting worse, and the doctor had doubled his dose of medication to keep him nearly unconscious.

"I know. I'm going to. I should have been the one to tell him. I still feel like dirt about that."

"Good," Choi replied. "Let it bother you until we talk to Cave, and then let it go. We have bigger things to worry about now, and you can't change the past."

"Right."

"Major Choi," Spaceman Owens said. "The General will see you now."

"Thank you," Choi said.

They followed Owens through the corridors, past the visitor offices to the rear of the HQ. Owens approached the door first, knocking lightly. It slid open a moment later.

"General Cave, sir," Owens said, saluting and standing at attention. "Major Choi, Captain St. Martin, and Mr. Reza Mokri here to speak with you, sir."

"Send them in, please," Gabriel heard Cave say.

"Yes, sir." Owens shifted his hands to motion them into the room.

"Major Choi reporting, sir," Choi said, saluting and stepping to the side.

"Captain St. Martin reporting, sir," Gabriel said, doing the same.

"General," Reza said. His voice was barely more than a whisper as his nerves started to get the better of him.

"Relax, all of you," Cave said. "Take a seat."

The General's office was the largest in the NEA, as well as one of the fanciest. It not only contained the standard desk and chairs, but also a large conference table with a holographic projector in the center. An oil painting was also mounted on each wall of the room. The three of them each chose a seat on one side of the table.

"We can start in one minute. I'm waiting on, ah, there you are."

Gabriel was confused. He hadn't expected anyone else to be at the meeting. He turned his head toward the door as Guy and Sarah Larone walked in. Angela Rouse trailed behind them.

"I feel like we just walked into an ambush," Choi whispered.

"How the hell did they know about this?" Gabriel replied. He had a feeling he knew. He could picture Lieutenant Curtis running to Guy after Gabriel had left, eager to tell him what had happened to get some kind of childish revenge because Felicia liked Gabriel and didn't like him. Was it any wonder why?

"This isn't good," Reza said. "Not good at all."

Guy met Gabriel's eye as he was greeted by General Cave, letting a small smirk crease the corner of his mouth. Sarah was less subtle, glaring angrily at them while Councilwoman Rouse wore her same general look of amusement.

"Please, sit," Cave said, directing everyone to the table. He moved to the head. "I only have ten minutes, so we'll make this quick. Before anyone says anything, Gabriel, I understand that you went behind Guy's back to get a copy of a specific file from the servers on Gamma and that you got that file from my daughter."

"It was perfectly legal, sir," Gabriel said.

"Yes, it was. That doesn't make it acceptable behavior for an officer."

Gabriel wasn't surprised at the General's reaction. "You are correct, sir. Given any other option, I would have chosen a different course."

"You're undermining everything we're working for, Captain," Guy said.

"Be quiet," Cave said, forcefully enough to cause Guy to sit up a little straighter. "I wasn't done. I've spoken with Councilwoman Rouse about this situation. I understand what the contention is, and what you are trying to prove. Gabriel, Vivian, Reza, the truth is that you are only looking at half the story. As hard as it may be for you to accept, the resistance on Earth has chosen to disband and disappear. Without them, there's no reason for us to continue our military efforts. We don't have the resources to make a true attempt to take back Earth on our own. Is that part understood?"

"Yes, sir," Choi said immediately.

Gabriel was more hesitant, but he reluctantly agreed. "Yes, sir."

"That being the case, the only issue I see here is whether or not Eden is truly a viable planet to send the people of the New Earth Alliance to. My answer is that we have been scanning the stars for the last fifty years, and this is the first real possibility we've had. We can't stay here forever. You all know that."

"You're saying that even if half of us die, it's better than being here?" Reza asked.

"Half of us will not die," Sarah said. "That's a story you keep making up to scare people."

"I do not. General, let me-"

"I said, be quiet," Cave said, his voice low and harsh. It was more frightening at a whisper than it was at a shout. "I'm saying that what you're calling a conspiracy is a possible reality we may just have to deal with. If we can't go to Earth, and we can't stay here, then we have to go somewhere else. If Eden is the only somewhere else even some of us have a chance of reaching, then that is how it has to be. In other words, it doesn't matter which of you are right or wrong. The facts are the facts. There is only one way any of the human race survives, and that way points to Eden."

Reza sighed and slumped back in his seat. Gabriel stared at the General, a painful mixture of emotions stirring in his gut.

"You used to be a man I respected," he said, unable to stay quiet. "A man who would never give up. You promised my father you would be there with him. You swore you would help him avenge my mother's loss, as well as the loss of billions of others. You have given up, though, haven't you? You're too old, you've been away for too long, you miss the air and the grass and the rain.

Whatever your reason, you've aged into nothing but a damn coward."

"Gabriel," Choi said beside him.

Cave didn't react to the outburst. He was calm when he spoke. "You need to open your eyes, Captain. We've lost Earth, and the only way we don't lose everything else is to go to Eden. In your head you know it's true. Your heart is loyal, and I admire that in you. Don't let it lead you to foolishness."

Gabriel felt his pulse racing. He was going to be court-martialed if he wasn't careful.

He didn't care.

"It already has, or I wouldn't be sitting here. I was stupid to think you would come through for my father. You admire my loyalty? You've forgotten what that is. I'm sorry, Reza. I tried. This whole colony is being run by a bunch of-" Gabriel stopped himself, shaking his head. "It doesn't matter." He looked over at Angela. "Congratulations. You've managed to convince one of the people I used to respect the most to agree to genocide. I hope you're proud of yourself."

Angela gasped and opened her mouth to reply. Gabriel stood and headed for the door.

"I haven't dismissed you, Captain," General Cave said.

"Go to Hell," Gabriel replied. His training had taught him to respect those above him in rank, but he couldn't pretend he had any respect left for the General.

He was a warrior without a war.

What did it matter anyway?

[45]

GABRIEL'S MIND WAS A CHAOTIC MESS OF ANGER AND disappointment, sadness and rage. He stormed from the Space Force offices, shoving Spaceman Owens aside as he tried to respond to the General's request to stop him. It was too bad very few of the military personnel on Alpha were actually armed.

He made it to the elevator and headed for the ground floor. Cave would be livid with him, he knew. The General would have him arrested and brought to the prison he had just gotten Reza out of. Then he would be left to rot for a while until Cave came to see him, spoke to him calmly, rationally, and logically, and then let him go. The old man didn't have the fire left in his gut to give him a real dress down. He didn't have the energy to chew him out like a soldier.

Gabriel wasn't ready to be brought in. Not yet. He could feel how his emotions were swirling within him. He knew he had only two options left. Fall back into his terrible depression, or stand up and fight like the soldier he was. Like the man his father would be proud of. Even if the only victory he could muster would be to evade the MPs long enough to go and see Theodore.

General Cave was siding with the scientists. The idea of it was so alien to him; he could barely believe it was true. Cave owed

Theodore his life. He owed him his daughter. It didn't matter that the resistance on Earth had failed. As Cave himself had said, that wasn't the point anymore. The point was that he was alive because Juliet St. Martin hadn't abandoned him. He was here to make the decision because he was saved by an act of charity that he refused to pay forward. Would he rather let half the colony die than stay here for a while longer? Would he rather turn his back on her sacrifice than make one of his own?

What if the entirety of the NEA voted on the decision with all of the facts in front of them? How many would want to risk being one of the ones left behind? How many would want to determine the fate of their friend or neighbor?

The problem was that neither General Cave or Councilwoman Rouse would let them know the full extent of the truth. He wondered if the rest of the Council even knew what decisions were being made without them.

The thoughts fueled him as he reached the loop station. He was happy to discover there were no guards nearby. Would Cave go through the trouble of calling them in for emergency duty just to grab him? The General may not have liked being told to go to Hell, but he didn't think so.

A pod arrived a minute later. Gabriel climbed in, taking the short ride to Residential. His mind was still a maelstrom of emotion as he hurried through a quiet concourse and up to his father's apartment. He had half-expected to find an MP waiting for him there, but the area was still clear. If Cave wanted him that badly, he would send someone here to look for him, which meant he didn't have a lot of time.

Sabine was asleep on the sofa. She woke with a start when his entry caused the lights to go on.

"Huh? Gabriel? Is that you?"

"Sabine? It's okay. I'm sorry. I need to talk to my father. It's important. What are you doing here?"

Sabine sat up. "Your father's sleeping. The doctor raised the doses on all of his medication. I was ordered to stay and keep an eye on him. He isn't doing well."

"Is he dying?" Gabriel asked.

The fight began draining from him in a hurry. A part of him had always believed that his father was only alive to continue the war, and that learning it was over would kill him. At the same time, the idea of it seemed like uneducated superstition. If only people had such complete control over their mortality.

Either way, he wasn't ready to lose his father. Not yet. He had run away before. Now that he knew the truth of things, he wasn't going to do it again. Not when it meant thousands of people might die.

"He's old, Gabriel. His injuries have taken a toll on him, and his will to live is fading."

"How much longer does he have?"

Sabine shook her head. "I don't know. If it was imminent they would have contacted you. A week or two?"

A chill coursed through him. He had so little time left to spend with Theodore, and he had been wasting it feeling sorry for himself.

"I'm going to talk to him anyway," he said, heading toward the bedroom. "If the Military Police or General Cave show up, can you stall them for me?"

"What? Gabriel, are you in trouble?"

"Nothing I can't handle, but I need to see my father first."

He ducked into the bedroom before Sabine could answer.

Theodore St. Martin was lying in bed, eyes closed, hands out at his sides. An IV hung beside him, the end of it jabbed into his wrist, while a monitor was connected to his finger, taking his vitals and projecting them on the wall behind the bed. A blue line ran in a slow, rhythmic pattern across it, showing a currently steady pulse.

None of the equipment had been there four days earlier, and the sight of it helped return some of his anger. At that moment, he saw his father's condition as a symbol for everything he had ever believed in. Sick. Dying. On life support.

It was no way for anything or anyone to end. Especially someone like Theodore St. Martin.

"Dad," Gabriel said, sitting in the chair next to him. "Dad, wake up."

Theodore's eyes opened. He turned his head to the side, staring at Gabriel with a clarity the younger St. Martin hadn't seen in months.

"Gabriel. About damn time you got here. Thought I'd go near insane waiting for you to show and send your old man off to the bayou in the sky with the respect I deserve."

Gabriel stared at Theodore, trying to figure out what was happening. His father was supposed to be near death. Instead, he seemed full of life. He had heard that people who were sick often regained all of their faculties right before they passed on as if God gave them one last round to say their goodbyes. He felt his eyes begin to tear, realizing that his father had been waiting for him so that he could finish his journey.

"What are you choking up for, son?" Theodore asked.

"I'm sorry," Gabriel said.

"What for? Come on now, Gabe. Don't sit there blubbering like a little school girl. Spit it out."

"I should have been here more often. I should have come sooner. I should have been the one who told you about Eden."

"Yeah. Damn right you should have. You can make it up to me now by helping me get the hell out of here."

"What?" Gabriel said, his emotions swinging again. He was completely confused. "Dad, what do you mean get out of here?"

Theodore reached over with one hand and grabbed the IV, pulling it slowly from his wrist. He held it up to Gabriel. "You know what this is, son?"

"Yes. It's the medicine that's keeping you alive. Dad, I don't want you to die. Not yet."

Theodore's dry lips curled into a smile. Gabriel hadn't seen that expression since before the accident. "Who said a damn thing about dying? There ain't no meds in that there bag. It ain't nothing but saline."

"What?"

"You having trouble with your ears? You keep saying what? What? What? I need your help, son. There's trouble brewing, and we don't have a lot of people we can trust."

Gabriel started to say "what" again. He stopped himself, shaking his head. "I don't believe this is happening."

"Get your head out of your ass, Gabriel. This ain't no dream. Geez, it's a damn nightmare more like. They're spitting on her grave, son. Your mother. My bride. General Cave thinks I'm going just to sit here like a damn fool invalid while he destroys her memory? Son of a bitch tried to poison me, son." He waved the IV needle at him. "Medication? This ain't medication to help. You get me? It's control."

Gabriel couldn't believe what his father was suggesting. "You're saying Cave has been drugging you? Why?"

"To keep me quiet. I've still got a lot of pull in this colony. He doesn't want anyone interfering with his plan to get to greener pastures."

"I'm totally confused. Four days ago you were pathetic and broken."

"You ever call me that again, I'll whoop you so bad you can't sit for a week." He smiled. "I was, son. I was. Just like you, I ain't immune to it. You want to apologize to me for wallowing? No. I've been stuck in the mud for years. Ever since I lost my wheels. It took your mother's intervention for me to open my eyes."

"What do you mean, mom's intervention?"

"When you didn't stop by after the Council meeting the other day, Cave did. He told me about the message. Hell, he showed me the damn thing. I was barely lucid then, but maybe more than he was expecting. I could see the satisfaction in those eyes when he played the message you picked up from Earth."

Theodore removed the finger monitor and pushed himself to a sitting position. He wasn't wearing civilian clothes beneath the covers. He was wearing SBU fatigues.

"Grab my chair," he said.

Gabriel did, rolling it over and positioning it for Theodore. His father swung himself over and into it, looking ten years younger as he did.

"He didn't recognize General Rodriguez," Theodore continued. "I did. He was only seventeen the last time I saw him. Not Space Force. Army. Nothing but a Private back then. He was in the platoon in charge of guarding the Magellan. Stick your hand under the pillow."

Gabriel leaned forward and reached beneath Theodore's pillow. His hand landed on metal, still warm from his father's head. He pulled the gun out, turning it. It was his father's original service piece. A standard projectile pistol. Bullets, not plasma.

"Dad? Why am I holding your gun?"

"I recognized General Rodriguez," Theodore repeated. "That dog is still alive. Which means your mother might be, too."

[46]

DONOVAN HAD ONE MORE STOP TO MAKE BEFORE HE WENT BACK to General Rodriguez, leaving the infirmary and heading across to the nursery.

"Hey, Mom," he said, opening the door and stepping in. He instantly found himself surrounded by toddlers, six in all between one and three years of age. Wanda Peters was sitting in the middle of them with one of the children on her lap, asleep. She looked weary and worried.

At least, she did until she saw him.

"Donovan," she said, a huge smile growing across her face. "You're back."

"Rodriguez didn't tell you?"

"No. When did you get here?"

"About an hour ago."

Wanda lowered the child to the floor. He didn't even seem to notice he was being moved. She got to her feet and wrapped Donovan in a hug.

"I was worried about you."

"You always worry about me. I always come back."

"Thank God. That doesn't mean you always will."

"Then I'll die happy, knowing I was trying to make a difference. Tell me you slept?"

"A little. I'm almost starting to believe you're as invincible as you do."

"You'll probably find out soon enough, but Diaz and I did it, Mom. We got into a Dread city and captured two of their weapons. We killed a Dread."

His mother nodded. "Never be proud of killing anything, Donnie. That's the road to Hell."

Donovan wasn't surprised at her statement. For all the Dread had cost them, she remained adamant that life was precious. All life. Maybe that was why she surrounded herself with it.

"Okay, Mom. I'm not as much proud of that as I am that we got the guns. If Carlson can figure out how they work, it can change the entire face of the war. We might be able to fight back."

"Good. Maybe if they see we aren't so helpless they'll decide to leave."

The door opened behind them. Donovan turned to see Matteo's head poking through it.

"Major Peters," his friend said, entering the room. Matteo Diaz was an olive-skinned, athletic god. At least, that's what most of the women on the base whispered to one another. His dimpled smile cemented the reputation. "I figured if you were done with Iwu I would find you over here."

"Matteo," Donovan said, clasping hands with him. "Your sister told you where I was?"

"Actually, it was General Rodriguez. He wanted you to go see him as soon as you were done with Doc Iwu."

Donovan was eager to find out what Rodriguez was thinking. The General's words still resonated, chilling him to the core.

"Doc Iwu?" Wanda said. "Did you get hurt?"

"No. Standard operating procedure, you know that. I've got to go."

"He leans too hard on you, Donnie," Wanda said. "You just got back, and he won't even give you time to sleep?"

"I can sleep later. Thanks for caring, Mom." He kissed his mother on the cheek.

"I'm glad you're back. I love you."

"I love you too, Mom. I'll stop by again later."

"Get some rest first. That's more important than checking in on your mother and a bunch of rugrats."

"Yes, ma'am," Donovan said, saluting.

"Get out of here," Wanda replied, slapping him on the arm.

He held back from wincing at the twinge of pain. He didn't want her to know he had been injured. She worried enough already.

He left the nursery with Matteo, heading toward the stairs.

"Renata told me you got hit."

"Yeah. Some debris buried itself in my back. We were this close to getting blown to ash." He put his thumb and forefinger together. "Iwu cleaned it out and stitched it up. It wasn't bad enough to waste meds on."

"How does it feel now?"

"As long as nothing hits it and I don't have to raise my hand, I'm fine."

"So, you know it's my birthday this weekend, right?"

Donovan laughed. "Are you serious? I almost died."

"Yeah, but you didn't. Which means you got me something, right?"

"I've got something for you. You aren't going to like it."

"Oh please, amigo. You say that every year, and every year you get me something great. Like that date with Ronnie. Man, I wanted to kiss her forever."

"I didn't have to do much to get her to go out with you. Have you looked in a mirror lately? Besides, that ended in disaster."

"Beautiful disaster."

They ascended the steps to the first floor and headed toward Rodriguez's office.

"Are you in on this?" Donovan asked.

"No. Officers only. I'm just a lowly handyman."

"This base wouldn't run at all without you and your father."

"Thanks for saying so. Which reminds me, I've got a leaky pipe I need to patch. I'll talk to you later, bro."

"Later, Teo."

They split up at the next corridor, with Donovan continuing on to Rodriguez's office.

"General Rodriguez," Donovan said, walking in. "Major Peters, reporting as requested." He saluted sharply.

"At ease, Donovan," Rodriguez said. He was standing behind his desk, a concerned look on his face.

Donovan quickly scanned the room, noting the presence of Colonel Montero, Major Sharma, and Diaz.

"Lieutenant Diaz, can you get the door?" Rodriguez asked.

"Yes, sir," Diaz replied.

"Donovan, I've already briefed Colonel Montero and Major Sharma on what you told me earlier. The reason I called you back so soon is because I have some time-sensitive information that I believe it's important to share."

Donovan glanced at Diaz, who shrugged.

"As you know, we've been in contact with other resistance bases around the globe for some time, including the installation in New York where General Parker is based. Three weeks ago a missive went out from General Parker, outlining the movements of the Dread as they had been reported in. Mexico isn't the only region that is falling under expanded enemy scrutiny, and it was reported that a number of bases around the globe were discovered and destroyed."

Rodriguez paused to let that information sink in.

"The result of this series of defeats led General Parker and his advisors to re-examine the resistance's strategy in dealing with the Dread occupation. The outcome of this is that he passed a message to every known resistance base across the globe that we were to disband at once into smaller groups and make every effort to avoid the Dread."

"What?" Diaz said, beating the rest of them to it. Donovan felt his pulse quicken, and the chill returned. Looking at the other officers, they were feeling the same thing.

"He ordered us to stop fighting and focus on survival," Rodriguez said. "He also made a special request to have me record a message informing the space forces of his decision."

Donovan shook his head. He couldn't believe it. "No. You've got to be kidding me," he said, not meaning to voice his feelings out loud.

"I'm sorry, Donovan. You're a little too good at your job. Your team delivered the message yesterday."

[47]

"You're saying we told our only allies in this fight not to come back? On the same mission we recovered a weapon that can kill the alien bastards?" Diaz asked, a tremble in her voice.

"General, why didn't you tell us about General Parker's orders?" Colonel Montero asked.

"I was waiting to ensure the message was delivered. Then I was waiting to see if Major Peters and Lieutenant Diaz made it back. How could I know what they would bring back with them?"

"You couldn't, General," Major Sharma said. "None of us could."

"What's done is done," Donovan said. "We have to decide what to do about it. You said before that you hoped it wasn't too late. I think I know what you meant now."

"Thank you, Major," Rodriguez said. "I appreciate your attitude. That's why this couldn't wait."

"What do you mean?" Montero asked.

"You want to make another t-vault, don't you sir?" Donovan asked.

"Yes."

"Sir, you just told us you sent a message to the colony not to come back," Sharma said.

"I did. And it is highly likely that they will follow that directive. It's also entirely possible that they won't."

"They've been returning like clockwork for over twenty years," Donovan said. "We know they've lost ships doing it, and yet they keep coming."

"There is a chance they'll make one more trip to confirm the message. There's a chance they'll keep coming even if no one ever replies. We stopped transmitting for months and they still came."

"We didn't tell them not to," Sharma said.

"It's foolish to assume they'll come back," Montero said. He smiled. "It's also foolish to assume they won't."

"My thought exactly," Rodriguez said. "We have to stay on schedule and make another run, to tell them what we've discovered. We have a couple of weeks. Maybe we can even uncover the secret to overcoming their shields by then."

"That's a big maybe," Diaz said.

"It is, but at the very least we can tell them we have an active weapon, we know it can hurt them, and we're working on it. We can tell them to disregard the previous message."

"What about General Parker in New York?" Donovan asked.

"We need to get a message to him, too. We have to hope just as much that it isn't too late to keep the resistance from falling apart here on Earth as we do out among the stars."

"It should be easy enough to get a message to them," Major Sharma said.

"It still takes time," Rodriguez replied.

Messages flowed from one base to another over an Internet of sorts; a collection of computers connected via a spiderweb route of cables that the Dread had so far ignored. It was all peer-to-peer, incredibly slow, and often subject to blackout. From the way Matteo had explained it, it was a miracle that the system worked at all. Fixing pipes wasn't the only thing he was handy with.

"When is the next expected match in the pattern?" Donovan asked.

The space forces always returned when the slipstream matched a specific set of wave patterns, ostensibly to keep the Dread from guessing when they would arrive. It was more than likely the Dread knew but didn't care.

"Three weeks," Rodriguez said.

"That's plenty of time for my arm to heal," Donovan said.

"We have a bigger problem than that, General," Diaz said. "Most of our team was killed during the last mission, and we lost the transmission equipment."

"Understood," Rodriguez said. "I'm going to put the word out to the base looking for volunteers for this run. As far as our chain-of-command is concerned, we aren't even supposed to be continuing operations right now. I'm not going to order you two back out there, either. There's no guarantee the space forces will return. In fact, it's more likely you'll be killed out there for nothing."

"I wouldn't call it nothing, sir," Donovan said. "I would call it hope."

Rodriguez smiled. "You keep going like you are, Major, and you'll have my job soon."

"If I survive."

"I'm not making you go, Donovan."

"I know, sir. Consider me volunteered."

"Me, too," Diaz said without hesitation.

"Sir, if I might," Colonel Montero said. "I'd like to volunteer as well."

"Are you sure, Jose?"

"Yes, sir. The bigger the team, the better the chance we can pull this off. Besides, I'm getting soft sitting on the sidelines and watching cadets beat each other up."

"Very well. Harpreet, do you want to throw in as well?"

"I would sir, but we all know I would be more hindrance than help with this bum knee of mine." Major Sharma turned to Donovan. "If there's anything else you need, I'll do whatever I can."

"Thank you, Major," Donovan said.

"We've got three weeks, people," Rodriguez said. "Donovan, if you can stay behind for a moment? The rest of you are dismissed."

"Yes, sir," they said, filing out of the room and leaving Donovan alone with Rodriguez again.

"About the prisoner," Rodriguez said.

"Her name is Ehri," Donovan replied.

"I wasn't sure if I should say anything. I'm not even sure if it's important or not."

"What is it, sir?"

"The clone. Ehri. I've seen her before."

Donovan could tell the General was uncomfortable with the subject though he had no idea why. "I'm sorry, sir. I don't know what you're talking about."

"I was there. Did you know that? In New Mexico during the invasion. I was only a Private then, a freshly minted soldier put on guard detail. It was a boring job for the first three months. Every day, I would head in and stand in front of a pair of locked doors leading to the biggest underground hangar you could ever imagine." He smiled.

"I've heard this before, sir. You were stationed in New Mexico, guarding the Magellan."

"I knew the Captain who was in command of her. Not well, but I knew him. Theodore St. Martin. They called him the Gator because he was from an old Louisiana family, and because he was an incredible pilot. They said that once he got something in his teeth, he never let it go. He also liked to curse in cajun."

Rodriguez's eyes were distant as he recounted the memory.

"I knew his wife, Juliet, too. She was the sweetest, most kind-hearted person I've ever met in my life. Compassionate, sensitive, devout. They don't make a lot of people like her.

"Anyway, the invasion had been going on for three days when the order came to round people up to evacuate on the Magellan. She wasn't fully ready for travel, but they didn't have a choice. The top brass chose who would go. Military mostly, with training in every discipline they thought would be useful to a new world, plus their families. I wasn't invited.

"The Dread found out about the Magellan the second they fired up the reactors. They couldn't see her because she was underground, so they didn't get the position precise. That's the only reason she made it off the ground in the first place. Like I said, I wasn't invited, so I was doing my best to help the others on board. The problem was that they weren't ready, and the Dread attack turned the whole thing into chaos. They had to leave in a hurry, and they were going to wind up with only half a boat full of people.

"Then Captain St. Martin's wife, Juliet, appears out of nowhere, running through the base and screaming at the admins and the janitors and everyone she could find to get the hell on board. She yelled the same to me. I had a choice then, Donovan. A choice to leave or to stay. To die right then and there, or maybe live a full life out in the stars. You know which choice I made. I stayed with Juliet, helping her get people onto the ship. I stood next to her on the surface and watched the Magellan get off the ground. I watched how Theodore piloted that behemoth like it was a schooner on a lake of glass. I've never seen anything like it. The plasma flumes were so heavy into the pit, and somehow he got the Magellan around them. It was like he knew where they were going to be before they got there."

His eyes refocused, and he stared at Donovan.

"We escaped from the base in New Mexico, heading south. We got caught in one of the Dread's round ups. I escaped. Juliet was taken."

"Ehri is a clone of Juliet St. Martin?" Donovan said.

Rodriguez nodded. "I don't know how much of her originates with her creation by the Dread, and how much comes from her genetic relationship with Juliet St. Martin. If she's anything like her template, she may be way more important to this war than those rifles could ever be."

[48]

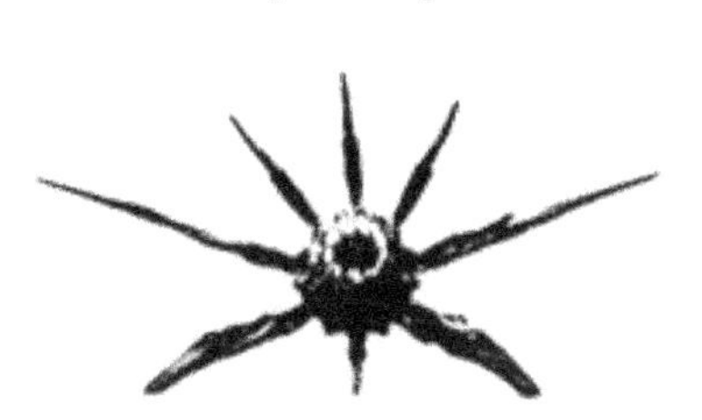

Gabriel put the gun down on the bed. "You can't be serious. You're seventy-eight years old. She would be eighty. Living on Earth. No medical care. Being hunted by the Dread."

"You didn't know your mother. Pick up the gun."

"Why?"

"Because I need my hands to roll the damn chair. Pick it up, Captain."

"Don't start using my rank on me. You aren't enlisted anymore, remember?"

"I'll tell you where you can put that piece in a second. That wasn't by choice."

"You crashed a fighter into a transport and killed four people because you were so afraid you had lost your touch. You had to get out there and prove you could still do it, and guess what? You couldn't."

This was an old fight. One that had been continuing whenever Theodore was alert enough to have it.

"It was a damn mechanical failure," Theodore said.

"The engineers said-"

"Engineers? They said what they had to say to cover their own asses. Don't you get it, son? This is the way things work. Just like General Cave and that bitch, Rouse."

"The investigation didn't turn up anything."

"Because the investigator had to rely on the engineers. Pick up the damn weapon."

"Why? To do what, Dad? Go and kill General Cave?"

"That traitor should get off so easy. He knew I would fight his decision, so he had the doc jack me up so full of shit that I could barely think. All I could do was sit here and die. He didn't know I recognized Rodriguez. He didn't know what that meant to me. He thought I was inconsolable. He left, and ten minutes later Sabine comes in and says I've been ordered a higher dose of meds. It took every ounce of strength for me to tell her no.

"Vivian, bless the woman, came by an hour later. I was in and out the whole time, but after seeing Rodriguez, I wasn't going to let anything in the world stop me. I told her what I saw. She told me everything that Cave didn't. I ain't a highly educated man like them scientists, but I ain't stupid either. I told her I needed to get clean, and I couldn't do that with Cave trying to keep me quiet. So when they came with the IV, she followed up and swapped it out for a placebo."

"Sabine told me you were in a bad way."

"Withdrawal from the meds. Damn near killed me, for sure, and my stumps hurt like a son of a bitch. I've got a couple of bottles of pills to help keep me going insane from it, but I have to say, drugged ignorance was bliss. Will you pick up the damn gun now?"

"No," Gabriel said, eyeing the weapon. "I still don't know what you want me to do with it."

"Why'd you come here, son?"

"What?"

"Why did you come to see me now, at this particular late hour?"

"I wanted to see you. To apologize-"

"Don't try to bullshit me, boy. I've been able to tell when you're lying since you were in diapers. What's the real reason?"

"I had a meeting with General Cave. Rouse and the Larones were there, along with Vivian and the scientist who said they lied about the math, Reza Mokri. Cave basically said that it doesn't matter if half the colony dies to get to Eden, we're going to Eden."

"Instead of heading back to Earth," Theodore said. "Fifty-percent casualties for a half-promise. Or we could be going home."

"We can't fight the Dread."

"You can't fight slipstream equations either, son. That isn't stopping them from trying. Besides, those are the words of a quitter, and I didn't raise a damn quitter. I know what happened next because as much as you hate it, you're still too much like your old man. You told Cave off and stormed out, didn't you?"

"Yes."

Theodore laughed. Gabriel couldn't remember the last time he had heard his father laugh. "And then you came here. Why?"

"I wanted to talk to you, to ap-"

"Don't bullshit me, boy."

"I wanted your advice. I wanted to know what you would do with everything I've learned."

"Now we're getting somewhere. Pick up the gun, Gabriel. You want to know what I would do? That's step one. I knew you would be by once you couldn't take it anymore. Once you saw Cave for the worm he's become. I was hoping it wouldn't come to this, but we've just about run out of reasonable options."

"Come to what?" Gabriel said, reaching for the gun again.

"I made two promises to your mother. I promised to keep fighting, and I promised to take care of the people who made it out because she didn't. I ain't letting them break those promises. I ain't letting them kill thousands on a wing and a prayer, and I ain't giving up on Earth without a fight."

Gabriel wrapped his hand around the grip and lifted the weapon. His father was putting into words everything he had been feeling. The difference was that his father had the experience to have already guessed it would be up to them to do something about it.

"So what are we going to do?" he asked, putting his other hand over the crucifix around his neck.

"I knew you wouldn't let me down, son. You're everything good about your mother, and everything bad about me." He laughed again. "The Magellan was given over to my care before we ever left Earth. As far as I'm concerned, that means the old girl is mine.

"You and me, we're going to take her."

[49]

"You want to steal the Magellan?" Gabriel said, his grip on the gun loosening slightly. "We'll be executed for treason."

"Like I said, it ain't stealing. Maggie is mine, placed into my care by General Tomlinson fifty years ago. I'm still on the docket as the registered CO. Idiots never bothered to take my name off because the old girl isn't going anywhere. At least, they don't expect it to be going anywhere."

"That doesn't mean you can lift off without permission. Like it or not, you aren't commissioned."

"Which explains why I was waiting on you. According to Choi, it's a legal gray area."

Gabriel was surprised. "Choi knows about this?"

"Hell, yeah, boy. I told you; she was swapping the spit for me."

"I know. She knows you plan to take the Magellan?"

"She knows. She wasn't too keen on the plan, but I think she'll have a new opinion after your little meeting with Cave. Come on."

Theodore rolled his chair toward the living area. Gabriel grabbed the back of it, holding him.

"Wait a second, Dad. If we do this, we're going to leave everyone here stranded. There aren't enough materials in this system to print another Magellan."

"Then I guess we ought to bring her back in one piece, eh? If we succeed, everyone lives. If we fail, at least everyone gets stuck together. Why the hell do we want to perpetuate a race of backstabbing, immoral, idiot babies? All or nothing. That's the only way to play it."

Gabriel couldn't stop himself from smiling at that statement. It was a classic comment from his father, and he had missed it.

"Now, either let go of my damn chair and be part of the solution, or give me the gun so I can shoot you myself. I'm not going to have my only son be part of the problem."

Gabriel let go of the chair. At the same time, the tone for the front door of the apartment sounded.

Gabriel slipped around the front of Theodore, rushing to grab Sabine's arm before she could respond to the tone. "Wait a second."

Sabine turned around, surprised and angry. Her eyes began to tear when she saw Theodore roll out into the room.

"General St. Martin," she said, hurrying to him and bending over to give him a hug. "You're awake."

"No thanks to the garbage they were poisoning me with," Theodore said, tapping Sabine's back in a more cordial embrace. "You're fired, by the way. I won't be needing a nurse anymore."

"What are you two planning?" Sabine asked, noticing the gun.

The tone sounded again. Gabriel trained the gun on the door. Theodore commanded it to open.

Major Choi stood in front of it, clutching Reza by the arm.

"Gabriel." Her eyes fell on the gun. "I see you talked to your father." She looked past him. "We don't have a lot of time, sir. I talked Cave into letting me deal with Gabriel, but when we don't come back he's going to get suspicious."

"I'm ready to go," Theodore said.

"Where are we going?" Reza asked.

"You wanted to save people?" Choi asked.

"Yes, ma'am."

"Now's your chance."

Gabriel led his father out of the apartment, tucking the gun in the back of his pants and covering it with his jacket. He couldn't believe everything that was happening. First, his father was awake and in relatively good health, and now he was on the verge of stealing the New Earth Alliance's only starship. It was crazy and exhilarating at the same time.

"We can't fly the Magellan with four people," Gabriel said as they hurried across the upper level to the elevator.

"I've got a plan for that," Theodore said.

"Fly the Magellan?" Reza said. "Wait a second. Are you serious?"

"Vivian tells me you're an engineer, and that you have a specialty in slipspace. Is that right?"

"Yes."

"Do I look like some damn teenage girl or your friend from astronomy class or something?" Theodore snapped. "Yes, what?"

"Yes, sir," Reza said, his face turning red.

"Good. You're exactly the kind of person we need."

They reached the elevator and rode it down to the main concourse. Once there, they began moving across it together, drawing stares from the few residents who were still awake. They probably thought they saw a ghost to see General St. Martin crossing the space in his wheelchair.

They were halfway to the loop station when a pair of MPs entered the concourse. They were each holding a plasma rifle, and they took up a guard position on either side of the station entry.

"Damn," Choi said. "I guess he doesn't trust me, either."

"Or Sabine told him what was going down," Gabriel said. "You shouldn't have been so obvious in front of her."

"Me?" Theodore said. "You're the one holding the gun."

"Have you looked in a mirror, Pop? The fatigues don't exactly say 'out for a stroll.'"

"How do you want to handle this, General?" Choi asked.

"My eyes are still a little fuzzy from being half-dead. Do you know the soldiers?"

"Hafizi and Diallo," Choi said.

"I don't know Hafizi. I know Diallo. Gabe and I will handle this."

They approached the loop station entry. As they neared, the two soldiers blocked the way. "Captain St. Martin. We're under orders from General Cave to bring you back to Space Force HQ."

Theodore cut Gabriel off before he could speak. "Lucy. It's been a while."

Diallo shifted her attention to him. "General St. Martin? I thought you were sick."

"I'm feeling much better. I'm afraid Gabriel can't come back to HQ with you. I'm a frail old gator, and I need his help."

Diallo laughed. "You don't look that frail to me, sir."

"You're right. I lied. The truth, Sergeant, is that General Cave is a yellow-bellied couillon, and if he wants Gabriel he'll have to come and get him personally. Now, me and mine are heading over to the Magellan so we can win the war General Cave is afraid to fight. That leaves you with two options, Sergeant. One, shoot us. Two, help us. What's it going to be? And don't take forever to decide. We're on a tight schedule."

Diallo glanced over at Hafizi, who looked uncomfortable with the whole situation.

"I said no lollygagging, Sergeant," Theodore said.

Diallo shifted her rifle, leveling it at Hafizi. "I'm with you, sir. Ali? Come along or hand your rifle over to Captain St. Martin."

Spaceman Hafizi hesitated for a few seconds before shouldering his weapon. "I'm in," he said. "I never served under you, sir, but your reputation precedes you."

"Good man," Theodore said.

"This is outright treason," Reza said nervously.

Theodore spun his chair on one wheel to face the scientist. "Treason, boy? Treason is breaking promises to thousands of people stranded on Earth. Treason is poisoning your best friend to keep him quiet. Treason is making up numbers to support personal goals, and treason sure as shit is giving up ten thousand souls for the sake of a new home world. This ain't treason, son. This is justice."

Reza's face was red again, but he nodded in agreement. "Yes, sir."

The growing group entered the loop station. An empty pod entered less than a minute later, and they filed in, with Hafizi helping Gabriel get his father into the transport.

"You sent a message to Sturges?" Theodore asked.

"Yes, sir," Choi replied. "He's passing the word on to the crew on Delta that he trusts."

"Delta?" Gabriel asked. "What word?"

"Boy, you sound like a parrot," Theodore said. "As you were so kind to point out, you can't fly a damn starship with four, nay, six crew members. And we sure as hell can't run reconnaissance on Earth without any starfighters. We need people that will follow you and me, and that means Delta."

"Me?" Gabriel said. "I'm just a Captain. I'm not anything special."

"That's your mother talking again," Theodore said. "To which I say, bullshit. You're the most decorated pilot in the NEA. You've survived over sixty-eight sorties. You're the only one ever to do that. You could be sitting pretty on Alpha making babies with any lady in the universe, and instead you're still going back out there. Where I'm from, that's called having balls, and people respect men with balls."

Gabriel smiled. His father had that special way with people that few others possessed. He knew exactly what to say to build a person up or tear a person down.

The pod came to a stop, and they climbed out. There was no direct route from the settlement to the Magellan. They would have to take a transport to the starship.

They hurried from the loop station to the hangar. Bay Six was occupied, and Choi steered them toward it.

"How long do you think it will take for you to be missed?" Gabriel asked Diallo.

"We're supposed to report in when we have you." She pulled a handheld from her pocket and checked the time on it. "I suppose we should have you by now." She held down a button on the device. "This is Diallo. We have Captain St. Martin in custody, and are en route to HQ."

"Affirmative, Diallo," Owens replied.

She pocketed the handheld. They reached the airlock for Bay Six, and Choi put her thumb on the scanner to open it. A transport was waiting inside, with Captain Sturges and his wife Siddhu standing on the ramp leading into the BIS.

"General St. Martin," Sturges said, snapping into an attentive salute.

"Captain Sturges," Theodore replied. "Siddhu. It's good to see you both."

"You too, Theodore," Siddhu said, leaning down to kiss his cheek.

"We don't have any time to waste," Sturges said, waving for them to board the transport. Theodore wheeled himself up, looking to Gabriel as if he were getting stronger with each passing minute. "I've got clearance for a supply run to Delta." He pointed to the pallets of food and materials to bring to the station. "I think that stuff will come in handy on the Magellan, don't you?"

"Damn handy," Theodore said.

Sturges hit the control to close the ramp and headed toward the cockpit. Gabriel followed him, taking the co-pilot seat.

"You could have told me about this sooner," Gabriel said.

"And ruin the surprise?" Sturges replied. "Your father said you needed to understand before we could count on you to bring your best game. We have no margin for error here, Gabe."

"I know. Whatever happens, thank you for being part of it."

"I'm loyal to your father and you to the day I die, Gabriel. Thank you for giving this old pilot one more mission that will mean something."

"Are you sure it will?"

"Absolutely. Now, let's steal a starship."

[50]

"BIS Two, this is Control. You're off course. Is everything okay, sir?"

Sturges looked over at Gabriel. "I guess they noticed that I'm not headed toward Delta Station." He leaned over and tapped the comm. "Control, this is BIS Two. I appear to be having a vectoring thruster malfunction. One of the venting ports may be jammed. I'm investigating."

"Roger, BIS Two. Do you need recovery, Captain?"

"Not yet. I'll let you know if I'm about to float off into space."

"Yes, sir."

"How much time will that buy us?" Gabriel asked.

"Enough."

Gabriel looked through the viewport. The Magellan was already below them, but Sturges was letting the transport drift past it to keep up the ruse.

"The bigger problem is that there's already a transport docked to it," Sturges said, pointing to the rear of the ship, near the port-side slipstream nacelle. It was tiny compared to the starship.

"Who is that?" Gabriel said.

"No idea. I've been keeping an eye on the work orders. There isn't anything scheduled to start until next week."

Gabriel pulled the gun from his waist. "I hope I don't need to use this thing."

"Me, too."

"How long until we dock?"

"Five minutes."

"I'll tell my father about the other transport and get everyone ready."

"Roger."

Gabriel moved to the back of the transport. His father was already holding court, positioned in the center of the group and telling the assembly about Gabriel's mother.

"Dad,' Gabriel said, cutting him short. "Sorry to interrupt, but we're almost at the Magellan. There's a small problem. Another ship is already docked there."

"What?" Siddhu said. "There were no work orders on her this week."

"That's what your husband said," Gabriel replied. "I guess plans changed."

"Or someone else is trying to take her before we do," Theodore said. "I'm glad we picked you up on the way over, Sergeant."

"I don't want to kill any of our own," Diallo said.

"Me neither," Theodore agreed. "Although I have found that an active plasma rifle pointed at your face can be a very effective negotiating tactic." He spun his chair toward Gabriel. "I want you to take point with Diallo and Hafizi."

"I'm a pilot, not a foot soldier."

"I think I've been asleep a little too long, son. You used to recognize when I was asking, and when I was giving you an order. Or has this old gator lost your respect?"

"No, sir," Gabriel said, snapping to attention. "My apologies, sir."

"Good man. Sweep the corridors up to the bridge and clear a path. If whoever is on the ship ain't there and they get stuck riding along, too damn bad. Major, if you would do me the honor of escorting myself and Mr. Mokri here to the bridge, I would be much obliged."

"Of course, General," Choi said.

"Siddhu, wait for your husband and stay with the transport, just in case."

"Yes, sir," Siddhu said.

Gabriel joined Hafizi and Diallo near the docking collar on the side of the BIS, a rounded rectangular hatch with an airlock between them and the vacuum outside. He could see the side of the Magellan growing larger ahead of them, the massive scale of the starship stealing his breath. He had only been on the ship a few times before, and not since before he had gone to officer training. He had forgotten how majestic the Magellan was.

"Wow," Hafizi said beside him.

"First time?" Gabriel asked.

"Yes, sir. I've only seen her from a distance."

"Imagine what she would look like with guns," Diallo said.

"I don't want to imagine it," Gabriel replied. "I want to make it happen."

"Yes, sir."

They stood and watched as the ship drew close enough that the matching docking collar came into view. Captain Sturges guided the transport expertly, getting it aligned right next to the collar before the vectoring thrusters pushed the two together. Gabriel pressed the control pad next to the airlock and felt the slight vibration as the clamping mechanism shifted into place, taking hold of the BIS and pulling it the last few inches to the collar. Once the two ships were joined the outer hatches of each opened, revealing similar airlocks on both sides. Gabriel waited while the two corridors pressurized, and then those doors also slid open.

"Stay close, don't shoot anything unless it shoots at you," Gabriel said. "These are our people, and they probably don't know why we're here."

"Yes, sir," Hafizi and Diallo replied.

The three of them walked through the joined airlocks, passing from the transport into the Magellan. The inside of the starship was dark, with only emergency lighting providing a dim glow.

"They didn't even turn the lights on," Diallo said.

"They probably can't," Gabriel replied. "Only a registered officer has control over Maggie. I don't know which Major is assigned to the retrofit."

They moved out into the corridor. The Magellan would be a maze to anyone who was unfamiliar with her layout, due to hundreds of corridors that all looked nearly identical. While there were plenty of physical signs indicating the current floor and the direction of the passage, even that was of limited help when everything looked the same.

Fortunately, the route to the bridge was one of the easiest, and Gabriel still remembered it from his last time on board. He led the two MPs in that direction ahead of the rest of the group.

"I can't believe this ship was made on Earth," Hafizi said, reaching out and running his hand along the cold metal walls. "So much history."

"What's it like, Captain?" Diallo asked. "Earth, I mean."

"It's beautiful from a distance," Gabriel replied. "White clouds. Blue oceans. When you get closer, you can see how much it's hurting. The Dread haven't been kind to the planet. Their structures litter most of whatever landscapes they didn't burn from orbit. It's home though. Our true home. Not some far away place that half of us might never see. It isn't too late to fix it, if we can get it back from the enemy."

"Yes, sir," Hafizi said.

They reached one of the three dozen or so elevators sprinkled throughout the ship. This one would bring them up into the quarterdeck. The bridge was on QD3. Only the sensor equipment and a maintenance level that had been converted to a damage control buffer sat above the large, open layout of the ship's command center.

Gabriel put his hand to the control pad of the elevator, expecting it to light up with a list of destinations. Instead, a red 'X' flashed on the interface above a message that read, "Access denied. Security lockout."

"What does that mean?" Hafizi asked.

"The elevators were locked out the last time a crew was in here working on things."

"Can we still get to the bridge?"

"Yeah. We have to take the stairs. It's only twenty floors."

"It figures," Diallo said.

"We could wait here for the General," Gabriel said. "His fingerprint should override the lockout. Of course, I don't think he would be too pleased to find us hanging out here."

"I'll take the stairs," Diallo said.

"Sounds good to me," Hafizi agreed.

The emergency stairwell was in an adjacent corridor. They opened the manual hatch and ascended quickly, not wanting to arrive behind the rest of the group. They exited into a second corridor and turned left, taking a short walk to the bridge's entry.

As they neared, Gabriel could hear low voices speaking inside. He raised his hand, ordering the MPs to a stop.

"This is going to be our salvation," one of the voices said. A man, judging by the tone of voice.

"For some of us," a female voice said. "Not all."

"You can't back down now, Sarah. Not when we've made it this far."

Sarah? Gabriel took in a sharp breath. He recognized Guy Larone's voice. Was this a joke? Were they going to be everywhere he went?

"I'm not backing down. It's just. It's troubling. You heard Captain St. Martin. I'm sure he isn't the only one who feels that way. I bet most of the military does, and they're the ones with the weapons. If General Cave can't reign him in, he can make a lot of problems for this trip."

"General Cave will get him under control. Take a look out there, Sarah. What do you see?"

"Gas clouds, stars, the usual."

"But no home."

"No."

"That's why I wanted to bring you here. I wanted you to see. I wanted you to be able to picture it more clearly. In six months, we could be staring out this same viewport at a pristine oasis of life. A perfect blue and green marble. A new home for humankind."

"I hope so. I want to see it. But the sacrifice-"

"There are no easy decisions left, love," Guy said. "The Dread took them all away. My father used to tell me about the invasion. About the pillars of fire, and how every military in the world was powerless against them. He was so grateful to have escaped, and yet so pained by what we had all lost. In two or three generations, no one will remember the ones who were left here or on Earth. No one will remember ever living in Calawan at all. Even Earth can be erased from people's memories. Destroy the videos and images, and in time it becomes nothing more than a myth. A bad dream. That is the beauty of time. A beauty matched only by your own."

Gabriel glanced over at Diallo and Hafizi. Diallo made a face like she was about the vomit, while Hafizi rolled his eyes. Was Guy trying to solidify his wife's resolve, or was this foreplay? And where was the pilot who must have brought them here?

"I love you, Guy," Sarah said.

"I love you, too."

Gabriel stepped quietly forward, pausing as he reached the open archway onto the bridge and looking up at the engraved plaque hanging above it. "IN GOD WE TRUST. U.S.S.S. Magellan. 2264." He could hear the couple kissing just out of his view.

He was going to enjoy this part.

He held up Diallo and Hafizi, stepping around the corner on his own, raising the gun and pointing it at Guy and Sarah's interlocked faces. They didn't notice him until he let out a soft cough.

"Hello, Guy. Sarah."

The scientists broke their embrace, their faces turning pale with sudden fear.

"Captain St. Martin? What are you doing here?"

"Apparently, we're stopping you from erasing as much of human history as you can. You had good reason to be worried about me before. You have even more reason to be worried now. We're taking the Magellan before you can fulfill your dream of leaving innocent people to die so that you can reach your Utopia."

"On what authority?" Guy asked. "You don't have access to this ship's control systems."

"He doesn't," Theodore said, rolling around the corner, flanked by Choi, Reza, Diallo, and Hafizi. "But I do. Good evening, Maggie."

[51]

THE BRIDGE JUMPED TO ATTENTION IN FRONT OF THEM. FIRST, the lights that ringed the large space faded on to a comfortable brightness. Then the screens in front of each of the stations flashed to life like a row of dominoes, starting with the smallest screen on the right side of the raised Command chair and dropping down into the pit in front of it, running right to left across half a dozen pods organized around a large starmap station that dominated the forward position ahead of Command.

"Good evening, Colonel St. Martin," the ship's computer replied in a neutral female voice.

"It's General now, Maggie," Theodore said. "I know it's been a long time."

"Twenty two years, six months, eighteen days, twelve hours, forty-seven minutes, sir," Maggie replied. "Congratulations on your promotion."

Theodore chuckled. "You're a little late, but thank you. Gabriel, you'll take the helm. Reza, that pod over there is navigations. Go sit there and don't touch anything. Vivian, I expect you'll be my XO."

"Yes, sir," Gabriel said.

"I'm honored, sir," Vivian said. "What about Colonel Graham?"

"If the Colonel joins up, he'll be in charge of operations, same as he is on Delta."

"You can't do this," Guy said, remaining stationary with the gun aimed at him. "I'll have you arrested."

"Are you some kind of dumbass, boy?" Theodore said. "You're alone on a starship that I control, with no way out except past the gun pointed at your head. How exactly are you going to have me arrested? By the way, Gabriel, you can lower the weapon and get us underway."

"Yes, sir," Gabriel replied, lowering the gun. "Sir, you need to clear the security locks."

"I do, don't I? Maggie, can you clear all security protocols?"

"Protocols cleared, sir," Maggie replied.

"Thank you."

Gabriel stuck the gun back in the waist of his pants, grinning at the Larones as he descended the raised platform into the pit and took a seat in the front pod. The seat was very similar to that of a starfighter, as were the flight controls. The Command chair had a similar setup, as it was typically the ship's Commander who did the most intense piloting. The helmsman generally served as a backup when the Commander was attending to other duties, and to keep the ship on course during more mundane travel.

He dropped his right hand to the control pad there, navigating through it without looking until he brought the systems status up. The software on the Magellan was identical to the operating system on the starfighters, except a little more complex.

"Vivian," he heard his father say. "You've read the technical manual, correct?"

"Yes, sir. It was at least fifteen years ago."

"I'm sure it'll come back to you. I'm an old gator, and I still remember how it all works. Can you take the engineering pod for now? We need to heat the reactor up, and she can be a little temperamental. I need you to monitor the subsystems to make sure we don't go killing ourselves."

"Of course, General."

Gabriel looked back and up to where the Larones were standing near the edge of the pit.

"As for you two," he heard his father say. "We don't have a brig, or I'd lock you up there. We also aren't about to go shooting people because that would make us killers like you. I can't let you leave, since you've already threatened to have me arrested, and I didn't like that. Let me see, what's left?" There was a pause while Theodore considered. "I'll tell you what. You promise to follow my orders, and I won't ask Sergeant Diallo here to rough you up a bit."

"You just said you wouldn't hurt us," Guy said, sounding frightened and angry.

"I did not, boy. I said I wouldn't kill you. Hurting is another matter entirely, and if you keep testing my patience I will proceed with putting it on. Are we clear?"

"You won't get away with this," Guy said, remaining defiant.

"Guy," Sarah said before Theodore could respond. "I'm sorry, General. We'll follow your orders."

"Your wife is a smart woman. Pretty, too. It's a shame you two are so cold. You could be such a boon to the colony. I'm taking her word as yours. I hope it's good."

"It is, General," Sarah said. Guy remained silent.

"Go on down and join Reza at the nav station. If he tells you to jump, you damned well better jump. Understood?"

"Yes, sir," Sarah said. She and Guy appeared on the steps a moment later. She was pulling him by the arm, with Hafizi staying close behind.

"Maggie," Theodore said, his voice shifting as he moved to the Command Station. "Initiate startup series."

"Yes, sir," the computer replied. Immediately, the ship began to hum and shake.

"I don't remember that from last time," Theodore said. "Vivian, do we have an issue?"

"We blew a power converter on the secondary reactor," Major Choi said. "Diverting power through the alternates. I hope."

The ship stopped shaking, the hum vanishing as well. From the bridge, there was little indication that the starship was waking up.

"Main positron reactor stable," Choi said. "Secondary and tertiary stable. Quantum phase generator online."

"Navigation looks like it's online," Reza said.

The screen in front of Gabriel changed, revealing a three-sixty view of the Magellan, positioned in the center as a skeletal frame of the starship.

"Helm is online," Gabriel said.

"All systems are nominal," Choi said.

"After all of these years," Theodore said. "You still purr like a kitten, Maggie."

A tone sounded from the empty pod next to navigation.

"I can only think of one person that might be calling me already," Theodore said, receiving the same communication alert at the Command station.

Gabriel tapped his control pad a few times. The controls unlocked as the starship finished its initiation sequence. "We're ready to go, General."

"Do me a favor, Captain, get us on course for Delta Station while I take care of this couillon," Theodore said. There was an audible click as he sent the communication to the entire bridge.

"Teddy, what the hell do you think you're doing?" General Cave said, his voice sharp with anger.

"Why, hello there Alan," Theodore said. "I was hoping maybe you would give me a shout. In case you failed to notice, I'm taking my ship, and I'm moving it away from assholes like you."

Gabriel adjusted the suppressor energy levels, trimming the gravitational pull and using a small amount of hull thrust to begin lifting the Magellan from the surface of the planet. As he did, a cloud of dust began to rise around the fringes, rising into the atmosphere and swirling around the ship like a cape.

"You have no authority to do any such thing, Theodore," Cave said. "You were honorably discharged. Don't make me change that to dishonorably."

Theodore laughed. "Honor? You want to lecture me on honor? Take a look in the mirror, Alan, and hope it doesn't crack at the sight of your lying mug. You're slipperier than a gator in a swamp, and I ain't about to let you poison the few good and brave men and women of the Alliance who still believe in it."

"We've been friends for a long time, Theodore. Don't make me-"

"Make you what?" Theodore said. "You ain't got a damn thing that can hurt the Magellan, and so you ain't got a damn thing that can hurt me. Hearing you were going to abandon Juliet's memory and the people we left behind, that was the worst you could do. You know what happens when you disturb a viper's nest, Alan? It bites."

The communication cut off abruptly. Gabriel turned his head to look back at his father. Theodore was looking at him, and they shared a moment of satisfaction.

"Let's hurry things up a bit, son. I don't want to give Cave time to do something stupid."

"Yes, sir," Gabriel said, increasing the thrust.

The Magellan was already ten kilometers from the surface of the planet. Gabriel increased the power to the main thrusters, arranged in an 'X' pattern along the back of the starship. At the same time, he decreased the power to the outer suppressors. They were high enough that the weak gravity would no longer tether them to the ground.

"Reza," Theodore said. "Can you start plotting a slipstream path? Not too close to Earth, we don't want to get blown up before we can plan our next move."

"I've already started, sir," Reza said, flipping through the interface with the ease of someone who spent most of their life staring at a screen. "When we have some time, I can also make corrections to the operational algorithms to improve path efficiency."

Theodore raised his eyebrow. Gabriel smiled at the sight of it.

"Good man," Theodore said. "Captain Sturges, do you read me?"

The comm station clicked again. "Roger, General."

"Is everything on schedule?"

"Yes, sir. Captain Kim reports we have over sixty percent of Delta Station on our side."

"Sixty? That's low. Damn low."

"You've been out of action for quite a while, Dad," Gabriel said. "There's a lot of young blood on Delta that doesn't even believe you're real."

"Bah. It's enough to handle Maggie. It'll have to do."

Gabriel smiled, turning back to the helm. Delta was approaching in a hurry.

A green triangle appeared on the HUD in front of him, a fighter launching from Gamma. The same one he had delivered earlier.

The triangle flashed, turning from green to red as the Magellan's new combat systems picked up an active weapon signature locked onto the starship.

"Uh, Dad," Gabriel said. "We have a small problem."

[52]

"You've got to be kidding me," Theodore said, getting his own view of the incoming fighter. "Who the hell did Cave find to send out here?"

Gabriel had a feeling he knew. There was one soldier on Gamma who might want to get in the General's good graces, and would certainly enjoy a chance to be a thorn in his side.

"Lewis," he said. "He's an asshole Lieutenant in charge of security on Gamma. He doesn't like me because Cave's daughter came onto me. I didn't know he was trained to fly a fighter."

"Felicia?" Theodore said. "Heh. Alan kept trying to keep her away from you. I'm happy to hear all of his efforts were for nothing."

"I'm not interested, Dad."

"Why not? She's a good looking girl. She's got good hips."

"Hips?" Gabriel said. "Who says that?"

"Do you think you could try paying attention to that fighter out there?" Guy said. "It's shooting at us."

"What does Maggie look like to you?" Theodore snapped. "This is a starship, not a damn speedboat. There's a reason combat starships carry fighters."

Gabriel looked up, watching the fighter zip past the bridge, firing its ion cannon at the surface of the Magellan. The heavy armor absorbed the attack without flinching, but that was the idea. Cave wanted to show Theodore he was serious, not inflict costly damage to the ship.

He watched the triangle circle around the skeleton of the Magellan, returning for a second run. The comm station toned.

"I knew you'd be calling me back," Theodore said.

"I don't want to make this hard," General Cave said. "Gabriel, put the Magellan back where you got her, and I promise we won't imprison you or your father."

Gabriel looked back at Theodore, shaking his head. The starfighter came back around, strafing the heavy armor with its ion cannon again.

"General, do you remember when I told you to go to Hell? Why are you still here?"

Cave didn't respond to the statement. "Theodore, if you want to be a hero, this isn't the way to do it. I can have Lewis target your thrusters and cause damage to the Magellan that can't be repaired. And then what, Teddy? The people of the NEA will hate you for breaking the most important asset we have, and neither one of us will get what we want."

"You wouldn't," Theodore said.

"Oh, no? Do you want to try me?"

Theodore was silent while he considered. Gabriel watched as four green triangles appeared on the HUD, all of the starfighters on Delta Station launching at high velocity and making a hard turn to head their way.

"You know what, Alan? I think I do," Theodore said, having seen the fighters as well. "You're a snake in the grass, and I just found myself a few mongooses."

He was the one to close the connection this time, cutting Cave off before he could respond.

The fighters were closing on the Magellan. Lewis must have noticed them, because he altered his vector, gaining some distance between them.

"General St. Martin," a new voice said over the comm. "This is Captain Soon Kim, Alpha Squadron Leader. It looks like you could use an escort."

"Damn right we can, Captain. It's good to have you with us. My boy tells me you're a stellar pilot."

"He does? He's never told me that."

"I didn't want it to go to your head," Gabriel said.

"Too late," Soon said, laughing. His fighter buzzed past the bridge before spinning around and taking position above and to the front.

Delta Station was getting close, and Gabriel began slowing the ship for docking. Lewis' red triangle was growing ever more distant on the display.

"I'm going to ease her in," Gabriel said, switching his attention between the view from the bridge and the representation of the Magellan's position on the screen.

"No need, son," Theodore said. "Maggie can take it from here. Maggie, initiate docking procedure Delta."

"Yes, sir," the computer replied.

"Come on, Gabe. We've got some new guests to meet and greet."

Gabriel rose from his seat, joining his father. Theodore had already managed to swing himself from the Command Station to his wheelchair.

"Impressive," Gabriel said.

"Hurts like a son of a bitch," Theodore said, pulling one of the pill bottles from his pocket. He popped the top and dumped two of the red capsules into his mouth, swallowing them dry. "Hafizi, you're with us. Vivian, you have the bridge. Maggie, add security protocol beta for Choi, Vivian. Rank of Colonel."

"Yes, sir," Maggie replied.

"Colonel?" Major Choi said. She abandoned the engineering station, ascending the steps and taking over the Command chair.

"We can't have Graham getting too pissy about his assignment."

"You aren't authorized to raise my rank."

"Hah. I'm not authorized to do a damn thing, according to all of you people. And yet, when I look around, it seems that I'm still the one in charge."

Choi smiled. "Yes, sir."

"Keep her warm for me," Theodore said, rolling off the bridge ahead of Gabriel and Hafizi. They had to move quickly to keep up.

"Your father is something else," Hafizi said.

"You have no idea," Gabriel replied.

It had been so long since he had seen his father. He had gone to visit his physical husk a few times, sure, but the mind had been missing for years. To watch him up and at it gave him a pleasure he hadn't even known he was lacking.

Whatever happened from here on out, there was nothing that could take that away.

[53]

THE AIRLOCKS BETWEEN DELTA STATION AND THE MAGELLAN slid open. Gabriel stood beside his father, eager to see who had decided to join them.

He smiled when Wallace was the first one through, running ahead and jumping up at him excitedly.

"Hey, buddy," Gabriel said, patting the dog's side.

Wallace shifted his attention to Theodore, sticking his nose in the General's face and trying to lick him.

"Okay, okay," Theodore said, trying to gently shove Wallace's face away. "I know, it's been a long time. Yeah, yeah. You can be my XD. Okay."

"General St. Martin," Colonel Graham said, having crossed the space between them while they were being assaulted. He came to attention and saluted sharply.

Gabriel looked up. The crew of Delta Station was waiting behind their Commanding Officer, at strict attention with spacebags on the ground beside them.

"Colonel Graham," Theodore said, returning the salute. "At ease, James."

The Colonel shifted to a parade rest. "I can't believe you did this, sir," Graham said.

"I've been acting a fool for a long time, I admit. I wised up. So did you."

"Yes, sir." Graham's eyes shifted to Gabriel. "I was looking for a sign. I wasn't expecting it to park right outside my station." He looked back at Theodore. "I'd like to present most of the crew of Delta. They're all loyal to you and the mission, sir."

"Are they good men and women?" Theodore asked.

"The best," Graham replied.

"Let me see."

"Yes, sir." Graham turned around. "Company. Present."

The members of the crew marched forward in a perfect line, doing a good job remembering their days as cadets. They stopped when they reached the edge of Delta's airlock, a line of people that vanished back into the station. Gabriel could see Miranda a few rows back, and if Soon was out there running escort he was sure Daphne was in the mix somewhere as well.

Over one hundred hands snapped up in a sharp salute. Theodore and Gabriel both returned it.

"My fellow members of the New Earth Alliance Space Force," Theodore said, raising his voice loud enough that even the crew in the back were sure to hear. "I wish I could say this is going to be easy, but it ain't. Most likely, we're all going to die. As I like to say, it's better to die for something than to die doing nothing. If you don't agree, now is your chance to walk away."

They waited in silence. None of the assembled soldiers moved.

Theodore smiled. "In that case, welcome aboard." He lowered his voice, looking at Graham. "Colonel, I want you to be my Operations Officer."

"Not XO?" Graham asked. He was clearly disappointed.

"Please don't hurt an old gator's feelings, Jimmy. You know I respect the hell out of you. Right now, I need everyone to do what they do best and for you that's getting these people and this ship organized. What do you say?"

Graham nodded. He was a loyal soldier. "Of course, sir. Who do you need on the bridge?"

"A couple of engineers, someone to handle the comm, and a pair of systems techs. That should be enough to start."

"Consider it done. I'll send them up once I find them in the line."

"Uh, sirs?"

The new voice came from behind them. Gabriel spun, surprised that he hadn't heard anyone coming. Graham glanced up, and they all stared at the newcomer. She was young, maybe nineteen or twenty, with short brown hair and a pretty face. She couldn't have been more than three months out of training.

"My apologies. I'm Second Lieutenant Sandra Bale, sir."

"You're the pilot who brought the Larones over?" Gabriel guessed.

"Yes, sir," she replied. "I was waiting in the transport for them to come back. When the Magellan took off, I left my ship and found Captain Sturges. We talked about what you were doing, and he told me to find you." Wallace stepped over to her, sniffing her hand. She looked down at him and smiled, running her hand along his fur. "I've never seen a dog before. He's so soft."

"Lieutenant Bale, don't take this the wrong way," Gabriel said. "But where did you come from? If you're a recent graduate, you should have been assigned to Delta Station."

"And I don't know you," Graham said.

Bale's face turned red. "This is awkward," she said. "I haven't actually graduated yet."

"What?" Theodore said.

"General Cave needed someone to bring the Larones over to the Magellan, sir. He asked me to do it."

"How do you know him?" Gabriel asked.

She looked even more embarrassed. "We met last year, sir. At one of the restaurants on Alpha."

"Hoo-boy," Theodore said. "You're doing the dirty with him?"

"Dad," Gabriel said.

"It ain't none of my business, I know, but last I knew Alan was a married man. You're telling me you're his mistress?"

"I prefer not to think of it that way, sir," she replied. "Yes, we were in a relationship."

"And now you want to get off my boat. Is that it?" He pointed to the airlock, where Delta's soldiers were still standing at attention. "There's the exit. I'm keeping the transport."

"Actually, sir, I want to stay."

Theodore's eyes narrowed. Gabriel could tell his father didn't trust her. "Really? Why?"

"I didn't know what he was doing. What they were planning. I don't agree with it."

Theodore rubbed his chin. "Bale. Bale. Where do I know that name from? It sounds so familiar, but I just can't get it solid in my noggin."

"My father was David Bale, sir. He was a scientist. His father was Roland Bale. He was an administrator who happened to work on the base where the Magellan was docked. Your wife saved him. I mean, I know everyone is here because of you, but it's more than that."

"Is it?" Theodore said. "I don't remember every civilian that made it onto the Magellan. I suppose it doesn't matter. Even if Alan wants you to spy on me, there ain't much you can do from out here."

"I'm not a spy, General," Bale said. "I care about the people of the NEA. All of them."

"Then welcome aboard, Lieutenant. Colonel Graham here will get you settled with everyone else."

"Thank you, sir," she said.

"Go and join the others," Graham said.

"Yes, sir."

Bale went over to stand at attention at the front of the line.

"Do you really think she's a spy?" Gabriel asked.

"Her? I doubt it, but you never really know a person, do you? I thought I knew Alan Cave and I hate being wrong."

"Amen to that, sir," Graham said.

"Get your people loaded and ready, Colonel," Theodore said. "I want to be underway within the next half-hour."

"Yes, sir."

"Let's go, Gabriel. And bring Wallace with you. He is the XD, after all."

"Executive Dog?" Gabriel asked.

"Damn right."

"Yes, sir."

Gabriel walked beside Theodore as they made their way back to the elevator while Wallace ranged ahead and sniffed at different spots along the wall.

"Was there anyone you didn't see in the crowd that you were hoping to?" Theodore asked.

"It was hard to see to the back. We have enough pilots for the Magellan and the starfighters, and then some. Assuming you let Second Lieutenant Bales fly, that is."

"Why wouldn't I let her fly? She may be a cute little dollie type, and she may have messed around with Alan, but I don't think she's dumb enough to try anything that stupid."

"Let's hope not. So, we have a ship. We have a crew. We're going to Earth. Then what?"

"What do you think? We need to make contact with the resistance."

"We don't contact them. They contact us."

"Well that's the problem right there, ain't it?"

"A problem we haven't been able to solve in twenty-seven years."

"Not true, son. We know how to solve the problem. We just ain't ever had a good enough reason to order someone to do it."

Gabriel stopped in the corridor. He knew exactly what his father was suggesting. And who he was suggesting.

Theodore turned his head to lock eyes. "You know I wouldn't ask you to do it if I didn't think you could."

"I barely made it out last time at full tilt," Gabriel said. "What makes you think I can enter the atmosphere and survive at air speeds long enough to broadcast."

"Because you're my boy, and you're the best."

"That isn't a great reason. You're biased."

"I ain't biased that you're the best. You've proven that you are."

"I've never flown outside of a vacuum."

"Same thing. Mostly."

"You know it isn't. You can't flip a fighter over in place when you've got friction and gravity."

"Nope. Neither can they."

"So what if I pull it off? What if I can contact them? Then what?"

"We'll tell them what you told Graham and Choi. That the enemy's weapons can damage the armor, and that they need to get their hands on some."

"You don't think they already know that?"

"Nope. They never reported that they did, only that the weapons have some kind of security on them that they can't crack. Hell, if we can get one of those maybe we can crack it ourselves. We've got Mr. Mokri on board, and from what I've heard, he's a regular Einstein."

"Someone would have to land on the planet's surface to pick it up."

"Yup."

Theodore was still looking at him.

"Right," Gabriel said. "Survive the frying pan, jump into the fire. I get it."

"This is about the entire human race."

"I know. It's bigger than both of us. That doesn't make it any less frightening."

"Fear is a gift, Gabe. Fear gives you the edge you need to stay alive."

"Then I must have the sharpest edge around."

"You damn well better. I lost your mother. I don't want to lose you, too."

[54]

"We're away, General," Gabriel said, increasing thrust to put some distance between the Magellan and Delta Station.

He watched out the viewport as it vanished off the port side and they made their way toward empty space. His conversation with his father had left him equal parts frightened and excited. He had been born to be a warrior. He had been born to fight back against the Dread. When he had been at his lowest, all he had asked for was the chance to do something. Now that he had that chance, he didn't want to waste it.

"Mr. Mokri," Theodore said from his position at the Command Station.

"Yes, sir," Reza said.

"How are those calculations coming along?"

"They were done ten minutes ago, sir. I'm sending the sequence over to the helm now."

"I've got them," Gabriel said. "Setting slipstream sequence."

"Maggie can handle this for you, if you want, Captain," Theodore said.

"No thank you, sir. I prefer to handle it myself."

"As you will."

Gabriel tapped out the commands that would finalize the coordinates. Then he adjusted the throttle, opening up the thrusters. From inside the ship, there was little indication of the change in power or speed. Instead, Gabriel relied on the display to alert him to their current velocity. They had a nice long runway to get the Magellan into the slipstream.

"Sir, I'm getting a ping from Alpha," Spaceman Locke said from her position at the comm station. Gabriel had been pleased when she had entered the bridge with the rest of Graham's picks for duty. "It's General Cave."

Theodore laughed openly. "Put him on the general broadcast."

"Yes, sir."

"Alan. Here to wish us luck?"

"Believe it or not, Teddy, I am," Cave replied. "Whatever you think of me, I'm not your enemy. The Dread are. I want you to succeed, and I want you to bring the Magellan back in one piece. It's the only way any of us survives."

"That's awful gracious of you, Alan. I have every intention of bringing her back. Thank you for your support."

"I'm sorry it had to come to this."

"I'll take it any way it comes," Theodore said. "In your own convoluted way, you saved me from myself. I'll remember that." He used his controls to close the channel.

Gabriel watched the counter continue to climb, the Magellan nearing slip velocity. He tapped his control pad, preparing to activate the quantum phase generator. A silent reverence settled over the bridge as the rest of the assembled crew seemed to realize all at once what it was they were actually about to do.

He looked around the room. Miranda caught his eyes with hers, responding with a smile. Reza nodded to him. Guy and Sarah glowered, but Sarah nodded as well, showing him a hint of respect. The three engineers Graham had chosen huddled over their monitors, keeping a close eye on the systems as they prepared to slip.

Up on the dais, Theodore was leaning forward in his seat, watching space outside with an expression of eager determination.

He had waited fifty years to return to Earth. Fifty years to attempt to avenge what the Dread had done.

That wait was nearly over.

Gabriel returned his attention to the display, holding his finger over the control pad. As the indicator hit slip speed, he dropped his finger and set the QPG to work. A sudden deep rumbling rippled through the Magellan before fading away.

"All systems nominal," the Chief Engineer, Technical Sergeant Abdullah said. "Everything looks good."

"Entering slipspace," Gabriel said. He couldn't see the nacelles, but he didn't need to. They bore the same distinctive construction as the wings of each starfighter, and would carry the remainder of the Magellan out of phase and into the slipstream with them. He knew it was happening when the stars began to fade away, and the ship started to shake slightly as it surfed along the edge of the wave.

"What's the ETA, Mr. Mokri?" Theodore asked.

"Seven hours, sir," Reza replied.

"Not bad," Theodore said. "Not bad at all."

Gabriel clutched at his crucifix, closing his eyes. He had never been sure about God, but he figured it couldn't hurt. The ship stopped shaking, and everything went silent and still. He opened his eyes and stared out at the empty black expanse ahead of them.

"Slipstream joined," he said.

They were on their way.

[55]

"I'M HERE TO RETRIEVE OUR GUEST," DONOVAN SAID, approaching the woman standing guard in front of the fridge.

Sergeant Wilcox saluted. "Yes, sir," she said, shouldering her rifle and moving to the handle of the large, stainless steel box.

"Thanks, Amanda," Donovan said. He had known Sergeant Wilcox for almost his entire life. Their parents had met up during the escape from Los Angeles and traveled to Mexico together. They had dated for a little while in the past, and she was still the only girl he had ever been with.

"I can't believe you caught an alien," she said, putting her hand on the cool metal. "What are you going to do with it?"

"Number one, I didn't catch her. She came voluntarily. Number two, she's a she, like you are. Not an it."

"She wasn't born. She came out of a tube or whatever as an adult. As far as I'm concerned, that makes it an it."

Donovan was tempted to chide her for being out of line with a superior officer. How dumb would that look? He was the one who had made the conversation casual. "She has breasts and a vagina, and her DNA is one-hundred percent human."

"Are you sure? Have you seen her naked already?"

Donovan shook his head. He wasn't even sure about the DNA part. The military clones were genetically altered. It was more than likely Ehri was, too. As for seeing her naked, he liked to think of himself as a gentleman. That didn't mean he didn't think she was attractive.

She was also the enemy. Whether he trusted her or not, that didn't change. She was confident the bek'hai were going to stomp them to dust, which was why she had helped them in the first place.

"Just open the door, Sergeant," he said, smiling. They had only dated for a little while because she had been too argumentative. It was as if having sex had given her leave to question or counter everything he said from then on, for no other reason than she seemed to enjoy it.

"Yes, sir," Wilcox replied, a hint of amused smugness in her voice. She wanted to get to him, and she had. She pulled the door open.

Ehri was sitting in the back of the fridge on a few sacks of grain they had managed to harvest from a field further up the mountain, and surrounded by a multitude of long-preserved edibles that had been foraged from anywhere their scouts could find them. She had a pleasant, slightly bored look on her face, which brightened instantly when she saw him.

Donovan stared at her for a moment before speaking. He still wasn't quite sure what to make of the story General Rodriguez had told him. Apparently, Ehri was a clone of a woman the General had known. A woman who had not only saved the lives of thousands, but who had also worked incredibly hard to help organize the early resistance. Obviously the Dread had also found value in her genes if they were using her as a template for their scientists.

"Are you okay?" Donovan asked.

"Yes, I'm fine," Ehri said, getting to her feet.

She looked different. Less alien. Donovan realized it was because they had taken her dress and replaced it with whatever surplus they had found to fit her. A simple pink t-shirt that Donovan knew belonged to Diaz, and an old pair of jeans. They had also been kind enough to give her sneakers. He doubted her feet were as used to being bare as his own.

"They are interesting," she said, tugging at the sleeve of the shirt. "Not as soft or as warm as I am accustomed, but I do feel a sense of-" She paused, trying to decide on the word. "Freedom, maybe? I have always appeared the same as the others, and now I don't."

"You look like you were born here," Donovan said.

"I am happy to try to fit in. Subjects do not act the same when they know they are under observation. It takes time for them to forget you are there."

"I thought you haven't studied humans directly before?"

"I haven't. We also do research on the drumhr to measure the integration and ascertain fit."

"What does that mean?"

"Splicing bek'hai genetic code with human genetic code tends to introduce new traits. Those traits are human in some cases, and entirely new in others. We have to monitor these traits to ensure we don't create something we do not want."

"Such as?"

"Earlier alterations produced drumhr who were extremely violent."

"You killed billions of humans. Isn't that violent?"

"No. That is war. By violent, I mean they would attack others with no provocation. They would eviscerate them, decapitate them. There was one case of what you would call rape."

"Are you sure that wasn't too much of the human traits?" Donovan asked. The end of human civilization hadn't only produced rebels. It could be a very dangerous world out there.

"I did not say it wasn't. Either way, it was an unacceptable alteration. This was all before I was made. I know these things from research notes."

"I see. Well, General Rodriguez put me in charge of keeping an eye on you. He's also given me permission to allow you access to most of the base as long as I'm with you."

"What about when you aren't with me?"

"You'll either be in here, or in the nursery."

"The nursery?" She made a face that was both nervous and touched. "You would trust me with your children?"

"They aren't mine. And yes, I do trust you, though not everyone here will or does. I expect you'll get a lot of looks, and you'll probably hear whispers."

"I have studied humans. I expect as much."

"Right. As for the nursery, I'll leave you there when I can't be with you because my mother runs it. She'll keep the others off your back."

Ehri smiled. "Your mother? I should very much like to learn of this kind of familial interaction. The bek'hai no longer have a concept of parenthood, or of children."

Donovan had already guessed that. So had General Rodriguez. They had decided to leave Ehri with Wanda at times for that very reason. The human she was created from, Juliet, had been extremely compassionate and loved children though she had none of her own. And of course, they wanted to win Ehri over to their side. It could lead to her revealing more valuable information than she otherwise would. They hoped that connecting her to the inherent qualities of Juliet St. Martin would be the path of least resistance.

"Good," Donovan said. "I was hoping to give you something you would find of value to your study. In payment for what you gave us."

"You would have figured out the plasma weapon eventually. The bek'hai will never understand the value of natural offspring. It has been lost to them for too many centuries. This learning will be of great benefit."

"I get the feeling you want me to go away and leave you with my mom right now."

Ehri laughed. "I am excited about the prospect, yes. I also enjoy your company, Major."

Donovan felt a twinge in his chest. He pushed it aside. "Right now, I'm to bring you to Doctor Montoya. He's the administrator for our base, and as a former psychologist, he's also a bit of a sociologist himself. He wants to ask you some questions about the bek'hai."

"Yes. Of course. As I said, I will share whatever information I can. I do have two questions."

"What is it?"

"One, are we going to eat soon? I have not had a meal since we met."

Donovan smiled. "Yes. Right after we speak with Doctor Montoya. I haven't eaten in almost two days myself. I'm so used to it; I hadn't even noticed."

"Do you have a shortage of food?"

"No. We have this storage, plus a larger one downstairs where we keep the game we catch. It's cooler down there. We're lucky the ovens still work here. It's because I spend a lot of time out of the base. On missions to transmit our signals mostly, but I've also gone with the scouts on occasion to search for things we can use. What was your other question?"

"Do you have a place to void?"

"Void?"

"A toilet?"

"Oh." Donovan could feel his face turning red. How had he forgotten she would need to relieve herself? Her body was still human. "Of course. I'm sorry."

"I know you are unaccustomed to me, as I am unaccustomed to you. We will each learn from the other, and regardless of when or how the bek'hai destroy your people, we will perhaps change the course of the universe through this understanding."

"I'd rather do it without being destroyed," Donovan said.

"I know, and I am sorry for that. The will of the Domo'dahm cannot be altered by any of us."

Donovan's mind wandered back to the sight of the plasma bolt cutting through the Dread warrior's breastplate. Maybe Ehri's statement wasn't as true as she thought it was?

He was going to do anything he could to make it false.

[56]

Walking Ehri through the halls was as surreal an experience as Donovan had ever experienced. He had expected that she would receive angry stares, comments whispered just loud enough for her to hear, and maybe even an attempt at violence from someone as stupid as Captain Reyes.

He was wrong.

Of course, the people watched her. They stared as he escorted her out of the fridge and through the hallways, first to the bathroom and then to Montoya's office. They kept their eyes glued to her in a curiosity mixed with wonder and some small bit of resentment. The outright hatred wasn't manifest, though. Was it because they had heard about the weapons they had brought back? Had word already spread that she was responsible for helping them escape? Or had General Rodriguez sent his own whispers throughout the base, asking the people to be calm and kind and welcoming because this clone could hold more keys to defeating the Dread than they even understood right now?

Whatever the reason, Donovan was thankful for it. He could tell Ehri was as well. She smiled at the people who looked on her with wonder. Her expression was priceless as she took it all in. And when she saw a young girl run across a hallway in front of her, she nearly had tears in her eyes for the experience.

"What do you think?" Donovan asked as they reached Montoya's office.

"This is everything I ever dreamed of. The videos and photos do not compare. I will be a hero to my peers for the information I am gathering."

"What about the child?"

"Amazing. Beautiful."

Donovan opened the door to Montoya's office. The doctor was sitting behind the desk, leaning back in his chair with an ancient book cradled in his hands. He set it down carefully before standing at attention.

"Major," Montoya said. He was middle-aged, with a bald head and a pair of old, round glasses resting on a small nose. He was dressed in a worn pair of slacks and collared shirt. "And Ehri, is it?" He circled the desk as they entered, reaching out to shake Ehri's hand and smiling broadly. "I can't tell you what a pleasure it is to meet you. I've studied everything I can about the Dread, but there's so little that we know. Every word you speak will be new information for us."

"Surely not every word, Doctor," Ehri said.

"You speak English so well."

"I speak seven human languages."

"Incredible. Please, both of you, have a seat."

There were two chairs against the wall. Montoya grabbed them and dragged them over.

"You have an hour, Doc," Donovan said. "Ehri hasn't eaten, and neither have I."

"Oh. I can't possibly get through all of my questions in an hour."

"She'll come back."

"Okay. Let me do my best then." He returned to the desk, reaching down and taking a legal pad from a drawer, along with a pencil.

It was low-tech, the best they could manage. There were only three functional computers, and they were needed to maintain the link to the other resistance bases. Anything he wrote now would be transcribed and distributed later.

"Please state your name, age, and place of birth for the records."

"My name is Ehri dur Tuhrik. My physical body is equivalent to that of a twenty-four-year-old human. I was released from the generation chamber seven years ago. My place of birth is the bek'hai mothership."

Doctor Montoya was writing everything down as quickly as he could.

"You say you were released from the generation chamber. Can you describe what a generation chamber is, and how it functions?"

"Of course. The generation chamber is how the bek'hai reproduce. It is what you would call a cloning device. It is essentially a vat of nutrients in which base genetic material is submerged and excited in order to make it grow. A generation chamber produces a fully formed and adult bek'hai in approximately eight weeks."

"Eight weeks?" Donovan said. "You went from a single cell to a seventeen-year-old human in two months? And you've been alive for seven years since then? How do you have such an extensive education?"

"If you don't mind, Major," Montoya said. "I'll ask the questions. Ehri, go ahead. I'm also interested to know."

"First, during the generation process, targeted electrical currents are used to implant a standard set of directives and information into the developing brain. We leave the generation chamber already able to speak the bek'hai language, dress ourselves, and perform other functions an adult bek'hai is expected to perform. Second, each lor'hai, or clone, regardless of type, has a purpose. A specific job that they are intended to do. As a scientist, I dedicated all of my time to study beneath Dahm Tuhrik, eventually becoming his Si'dahm. His second."

"So you're saying you have no children at all?" Montoya asked.

"No. The bek'hai culture had children once, many hundreds of years ago. That has not been our way for quite some time."

"Then do you have relations?"

"Relations?" Ehri asked, confused.

"Sexual relations. Intercourse."

"No. It is a process that my team would like to re-introduce. As it is, the bek'hai can generally be divided into three classes. If you are not a warrior or a scientist, you are a servant of warriors or scientists."

"You said you want to re-introduce sexual intercourse? Why?"

"Our survival depends on it. Only certain kinds of genomes are acceptable for us in the generation chamber, despite many years of efforts to perfect the technology. Over time, this greatly retards genetic diversity. With our integration of humankind, we have a much larger pool of potential genetic code, but without natural reproduction, this pool will shrink and dry up once more."

"What kind of challenges have you faced?"

"Neither warriors nor scientists see the value in what you call relations. To them, it is primitive and animalistic. We have had some success with the servants, but their value is limited and we don't desire to over-diversify them."

"So you're saying that because servants are inferior, you don't want too many of them?"

"Yes."

"Like humankind?"

"There are parallels that may be interpolated, yes."

"You sound like a lawyer I used to know."

"Lawyer?"

"Never mind. You aren't an alien, in a sense, correct?" Montoya said. "You're a clone of a human woman."

"That is correct."

"What about the aliens? The real Dread? What do they look like?"

"I do not know."

The answer surprised both Doctor Montoya and Donovan.

"You don't know?" Donovan said, forgetting himself.

Ehri smiled at his speaking out of turn. She looked at him. "I have never seen a pure bek'hai. There are very few remaining. Even the Domo'dahm is a drumhr."

"Drumhr?" Montoya said.

"Half-human, half bek'hai," Donovan said. "I've seen them. You said you live around one hundred Earth years. Your kind has only been here for fifty. Why aren't there more of the original?"

"Major," Montoya said, trying to take charge of the interview again.

"Do you want to know?" Donovan asked.

"Yes."

"Then stop correcting me and get your pencil ready."

Montoya made a rejected face and readied his pencil. Ehri almost laughed at the reaction, her mouth parting in a small smile.

"The bek'hai were very sick. Only a small percentage have survived to the date of their surrender. The years since we arrived on this planet have produced healthier bek'hai in the form of the drumhr, but even they have their limitations. We are improving with each generation."

"I think I understand," Montoya said. "I want to come back to speak more on Dread, er, bek'hai culture, but for now let's talk about something else. Can you tell me more about your technology. Things like communications, transportation, computation."

"Shields," Ehri said. "Or the plasma weapons? I know you very much want to know how the bek'hai are able to both protect themselves and harm themselves the way they do. Even if I could answer that question for you, I wouldn't. That is something you will have to work out for yourselves, if you can."

Montoya stared at her, a sour expression crossing his face. "I have one more question, and then we can break for the day so you can get more settled. What do the bek'hai think about your treachery? How does such an action make them feel, in context with your culture?"

Donovan could tell by Montoya's face that he had been hoping the question would shake her, maybe as a test of her loyalty to both the Dread and the promise she had made to him.

She reacted with the same calm confidence as she had handled everything else.

"Some would label me a traitor, and wish me dead. Others will call me a hero for what I have sacrificed to be here, and for the knowledge I will gain if I survive."

"What do you mean, if you survive?" Montoya asked.

"This base is well protected, and well hidden. I believe you will survive here for some time. You will not survive here forever."

"Is that a threat?"

"No, Doctor Montoya. That is the simple truth of your situation. It requires no intervention from me, and I plan to provide none. As I have told Donovan, the Domo'dahm wishes all resisting humans dead within the year. The pur'dahm will do all in their power to make it so."

Montoya's face was pale, his hand shaking with a combination of fear and anger as he finished writing his notes. "Major, will you bring Ehri back tomorrow at the same time? I'll prepare follow-up questions based on what I've learned today."

"Sure," Donovan said. "Do you want to head to the cafeteria with us, Doctor?"

Montoya looked at Donovan as if he were insane. "No, thank you. I don't have much of an appetite right now."

[57]

"THAT WENT WELL," DONOVAN SAID, LEADING EHRI DOWNSTAIRS to the cafeteria. "Did you have to mention the part about your kind killing all of us again?"

"My apologies, Major. It is only-" she trailed off.

"Only what?" he asked.

She pursed her lips. She seemed conflicted to him. "I have seen little of this base or its people so far, I admit. Even so, I get this sense of an attitude that is permeating through both. It seems that while your kind believes things are bad, it is simply the new normal. That you have grown accustomed to it, and have become complacent and satisfied as a result."

Donovan glanced over at her. "You picked all that up just from talking to Montoya?"

"It isn't only Montoya. I saw it in you when we met as well. Even trapped in the bek'hai mothership, you seemed almost arrogant, despite your situation."

"Arrogance is a very human trait," Donovan said. "As is selfishness and jackassery."

"Jackassery?"

"Acting stupid. Like Reyes did. It's true that some of the people here have gotten too comfortable with how things are. Most of those people are refugees and civilians. They have important roles here on the base, but they never go out there. They don't see how the world has been burned. The arrogance you sense is a defense. A way of controlling fear. When you've been living afraid for so long, it just becomes a way of life. Montoya was not as much afraid of you as he was of what you represent."

"What I represent?"

"Yeah. Superiority. The future. I think everyone here knows the score. Humankind is dying, and unless we get lucky or do something smart we won't be here a year from now. We've been fighting an uphill battle for fifty years. A war where we were the only casualties until today."

"I understand. How do you manage it so well, Major?"

"Fear?"

"Yes."

"I invite it. It shows me how much I care. The alternative is to drown in it, and I can't stand the thought of that. You don't seem to be afraid of being here. You didn't hesitate to come back with us, and you seem more excited than frightened."

"I'm not afraid. Not of this. Perhaps because the bek'hai do not value life the way humans do. We are made to adults in a number of weeks while you take years to mature. It is even worse for clones. Even clone scientists are servants of a kind."

"That's what I don't understand," Donovan said. "Don't take this the wrong way, but what are the bek'hai's overall purpose? Do you love one another? Do you experience things outside of your assigned roles? Do you even have free time to do anything you want to do? It seems that as a whole, you're missing a lot of what makes life worth it. Maybe that's the real reason you don't value it very highly."

"I loved my Dahm. I love learning."

"What about music? Dancing? Jokes? Laughter? Celebrations?"

"Perhaps there is some of that among the pur'dahm," Ehri said. "I was made for a different purpose."

"And you don't desire anything else?"

"No."

She said it softly. Donovan wasn't convinced. "So being here to learn is the only reason to enjoy being here? What about the experience of what you learn? What about the meal you are about to eat? Or the emotions and the personalities of the people you will talk to?"

"I came to observe you, and I will return my observations to whoever is named the new Dahm."

"You were the Si'dahm. Shouldn't you become Dahm?"

"I cannot. I am not drumhr."

"And that's okay?"

"Yes. That is our way."

Donovan looked over at her again. They were almost to the cafeteria, and her face was flushed, her eyes cast down to the floor. He would ask her again once she had experienced a little more of a life of freedom.

Maybe she would be honest with him then.

[58]

"Colonel Choi, Captain St. Martin, Mr. Mokri, Mr. Larone, Mrs. Larone, come on up and join me, will you?" Theodore said in a booming voice.

Ten quiet, tense minutes had passed since the Magellan had entered slipspace, riding a wave of distortion across the vastness of the universe toward Earth. Most of the crew knew one another, or at least knew of one another, but it didn't diminish the level of eager discomfort they were feeling. They had disobeyed their superior officer. They were traitors and deserters, all of them.

At the same time, they respected Theodore and his point of view, one that fell much closer in line to their upbringing and training. To a man, with the exception of the Larones, they didn't want to run off to another planet. They wanted to stay and fight, even if the odds were impossibly stacked against them.

Gabriel rose from his pod, smiling at Miranda as he headed toward the back of the bridge with the scientists. Now that they were in the slipstream, he didn't need to do anything. Nobody did. Once the wave was joined, they would only need to worry about disengaging at the right place and time.

"Yes, sir?" Colonel Choi said, saluting Theodore when she reached him.

"Let's take a walk, shall we?" Theodore said. "There's a conference room across the corridor. I already called for Colonel Graham. I want to talk to the five of you."

"What do you want from us?" Guy said, looking at his wife. "Do you think we're going to help you?"

Theodore laughed. "I know you're going to help me, son. Because if you don't, this ship is going to get blown to flotsam, and you're going to be on it when it does."

"You're a damned psycho," Guy said, getting angry. "Keeping us here against our will, forcing us to take this trip with you. You don't get it, do you old man? Nobody in the NEA wants to fight this war anymore. They want a real home. A place where food grows in the ground, not on a wall."

Theodore leaned on his arms as if he was going to try to stand. He paused when he realized he couldn't, keeping himself in the position.

"Nobody?" he shouted, causing Guy to flinch and step back. "Who in the damned hells are you calling nobody? There ain't a soul in this universe who calls my son a nobody, you son of a bitch. There ain't a person on Earth or on Calawan that questions the value of the men and women who gave up everything to be on this ship, to fight for what they believe in, and to have the guts that you so sorely lack. Now, you will get in line, you will help us do what needs to be done, and you will do it with quiet respect, or I will throw you off of my starship. Do you hear me, boy?"

Guy clenched his jaw, somewhere in between anger and fear. Sarah stepped in front of him. "I'm sorry, sir," she said. "Guy doesn't handle change well."

"Well ain't that sweet," Theodore said. "Welcome to the present, Mr. Larone. Change is inevitable. I'm an old man, and I ain't afraid of a little change. I invite it. Now, let's take that walk."

Gabriel helped his father into his chair this time. Theodore's arms were shaking and tired from holding himself erect to yell at Guy.

They followed as he wheeled himself off the bridge and a few meters down the hall. The opposite door was open. Colonel Graham was already present, and he saluted sharply as Theodore entered.

"At ease, Jimmy," Theodore said. "Everybody grab a seat."

The chairs on the Magellan were plush cloth, much finer than anything they had in the settlements. Gabriel was surprised at their comfort as he took his seat next to his father. Not surprisingly, Guy took a position at the opposite end, keeping himself separate from the others while Sarah sat halfway between.

"You always been a peacemaker, Mrs. Larone?" Theodore asked.

"I don't see the point in conflict. Not now. If the only way we survive is to help as best we can, then that is what both of us will do." She glared at Guy. "Or you can find a new wife."

Guy looked like he wanted to say something. He remained quiet.

"The reason I asked you here is so that we can plan our first mission," Theodore said.

"Which is?" Colonel Graham asked.

"I'm going into the atmosphere," Gabriel said.

"What?" Colonel Choi said. "General-"

"I'm doing it," Gabriel said. "Thank you for your concern, Colonel. I can take care of myself."

She didn't look happy, but she nodded.

"Gabriel is going to take one of the fighters in and fly it low to try to get in contact with the resistance," Theodore said.

"The resistance is disbanding," Guy said. "You heard the message."

"I heard it," Theodore said. "But I know how people like me think. Just because one man wants to stop doesn't mean they all do. Besides that, we have information for them that they might find valuable. Hell, it might change the whole face of this war."

"How are you going to transmit to them?" Reza asked. "You have no idea what band they'll be listening on, if they're listening at all."

"That's why I need scientists, Mr. Mokri. Scientists like you and the Larones. You have a background in engineering, and they have both broad-based theoretical training and a specialty in waveform patterns. I ain't the smartest berry on the tree, but I think that ain't too different from slipstream patterns, is it?"

"No, sir," Sarah said. "I have some experience with communications systems. I spent a year over there during my training."

"That was fifteen years ago," Guy said.

"I remember most of it. Seriously, Guy. Either help or shut up."

"Fine. I've done some work on the fighters in the past. The phase generators, mostly, but I have a general understanding of the equipment on board."

"Good man," Theodore said, warming immediately with Guy's compliance. "I knew we could count on you. Now, what do we need to do to get the message to the resistance?"

"Besides a low altitude sweep?" Reza said.

"Yes."

"Well, what can you tell me about Earth communications before the invasion, sir?"

"There was nothing but dirt and smut on the Internet. I can tell you that much."

"The Internet, right. A hardened communication system, designed to withstand disruption by any number of natural disasters, or in this case an alien invasion. That's our best bet for an attack vector."

"I like how you speak, Mr. Mokri."

"Thank you, sir," Reza said, blushing. "So, without satellites or wireless links, they'll have to be using wired connections. It's unlikely the Dread attack damaged underwater or underground cabling, so we should be in luck there."

"You can't transmit a wireless signal into a wire," Sarah said. "It needs to be received wirelessly."

"There has to be a receiver still active somewhere. It's a network, so all we need to do is hit one access point. I assume the data transfer protocols are the same as what is on the Magellan, sir?"

"There ain't been anyone to update them."

"Okay, so if we can get the gain high enough we can pump the signal out, and hopefully it will hit a functional device that can transfer it to whatever resistance computers may be up and running. If we assume that technology has been dormant on Earth, we can base our design on the equipment here on the Magellan."

"We'll need a lot of power to put out that kind of signal," Guy said. "Add to the friction of the atmosphere, and we will need to boost the starfighter's energy stores significantly."

"I have techs that can help with that," Colonel Graham said.

"I knew you would," Theodore said. "Now, you see what we can accomplish when our backs are against the wall?"

Colonel Choi was shaking her head. "So, Gabriel flies his starfighter into the atmosphere and makes a sweep of the surface, transmitting a signal to the resistance. I'm going to assume he makes it because he always has. I'll assume the resistance gets the message, too. Then what?"

"We'll wait near Mars, using the planet to stay hidden. Gabriel comes back, and then we wait. Mr. Mokri, how long until the next regular reconnaissance slip?"

"Sixteen days, sir."

"We'll wait sixteen days. Then Gabriel will go back to pick up whatever message they left for us. We'll decide what to do after that once we can reestablish communications."

"What if the Dread come looking for us?" Sarah asked.

"Then we'll play 'spot the gator' until we either launch the mission or die," Theodore said.

"You've got it all figured out, don't you?" Colonel Graham said.

"You're damned right I do," Theodore replied. "Everybody does their part, and maybe we can start turning the tide of this war. Now, let's get to it. Dismissed."

[59]

On a ship as large as the Magellan, slipspace was a chance to finally get a little downtime. It hadn't occurred to Gabriel that he had been running for nearly twenty-four hours without sleep until Colonel Graham had been summoned to the bridge along with a small replacement crew, and they had all been sent to their quarters to get some sleep.

"I didn't even know I had quarters," Gabriel said.

"We did yours and your father's first," Daphne replied.

They were walking down to his room. Theodore had requested Gabriel be put a little closer to the launch tubes, so that he could be ready if he was needed. Ready for what? He had no idea.

It didn't matter. He felt alive on the Magellan, as if all of his years of training and all of the missions he survived had all been leading up to this moment. Unlike some of the other crew, he didn't share the mixed emotions over disobeying Cave's orders.

"How do you like her?" Gabriel asked.

"The Magellan? The corridors are a little claustrophobic, and the bunks are tiny. Otherwise, I have no complaints."

"I'm glad you decided to come."

She laughed. "It wasn't much of a choice. I'm not going to leave

Soon to fend for himself, and he wasn't about to let you go off and steal all the glory."

"He said that?"

"Word for word."

"I think there will be plenty of glory to go around."

"Me too. Even for logistics officers like me."

They reached the door to Gabriel's quarters. Daphne pulled the handle, giving it a shove with her shoulder to convince it that it wanted to open.

"The hinges need a little attention," she said. "Well, what do you think?"

Gabriel stared in at the room. He had been expecting something simple, like on Delta Station. Instead, the quarters were expansive, with carpeting and couches, and a raised bed, a real bed, on a platform near the back. To the left of it was a large viewport, and to the right an archway leading into a large bathroom.

"You're lucky, you get your own shower. No three minute rule here," Daphne said. "Every drop of liquid on this boat gets processed and recycled, and the tanks are large enough for a crew of thousands, not hundreds. This is the Orbital Group Commander's quarters."

"The COG's quarters? My father didn't say anything about that to me."

"I guess he figured it was obvious."

"I don't know. Soon is just as qualified for the job."

"Your humility would be annoying if you weren't so sincere. Nobody is as qualified as you. Do you like it?"

"It's amazing. I didn't know the Magellan was so opulent."

"Most of it isn't, but it's still a step up from Delta, at least for as long as we have such a small crew. If you think this is fancy, you should see the General's quarters."

"I'm sure I will at some point. Hey, where's Wallace?"

"Soon is keeping an eye on him. I'll send him over."

"Thanks, Daphne."

"You're welcome. Try to get some rest, will you. You can't be a hero with your eyes closed."

Gabriel gave Daphne a quick hug. "You, too. You can't organize a starship with your eyes closed either. You'll keep running into walls."

Daphne turned to leave at the same time Wallace appeared in the doorway. He hurried over to Gabriel, putting his head down to be pet.

"I found this mangy thing hanging out next door," Soon said.

"Are you talking about yourself, dear?" Daphne asked.

"Of course."

"Thanks for running interference out there," Gabriel said. "It's good to have you with us."

"Us pilots have to stick together. I've always got your wing, Captain."

"And I have yours, Captain."

"Come on, Soon. Let's leave the man and his dog to relax for a while."

"Whatever you say, boss." Soon replied. "See you later, Gabe." He put his arm around her waist, and they headed off together.

Gabriel pushed the door closed, and then scanned the room again. In eight hours he would be suiting up to make a run on Earth. A run unlike any other he had made before. He had confidence in his abilities, but he had never flown outside of a vacuum before. None of them had except for his father. He had used the simulator, of course, but that wasn't the same thing.

Nothing was chasing you in the simulator.

He looked over at the bed, and then to the bathroom. He began stripping off his clothes.

If he was going to die soon, he would die clean and relaxed and having enjoyed the longest shower of his life.

[60]

"CAN YOU HEAR ME OKAY?" MIRANDA ASKED.

Gabriel adjusted his helmet, tapping on the side. "Try again."

"Testing. One. Two."

"It has to be on your side."

"I'll get one of the engineers to look at it while you're gone. It should be fixed by the time you get back."

"It better be."

Gabriel leaned back in the seat of the starfighter, holding his mother's crucifix. He closed his eyes, concentrating on his breathing. This mission wasn't like all of the others. Not just because of the atmosphere. There would be no slipstream ride to Earth. The Magellan would fire him at max power from its launch tubes, bringing him up to speed in a matter of seconds. After that, he would do a light, continual burn that would get him to Earth within ten hours.

He was nervous, and that was okay. It was normal. The fear was normal. If he didn't feel it, he knew he would get sloppy and die. He felt ready. He had showered, slept for a few hours, and woken to a hot bowl of oatmeal waiting at the end of his bed. It was the best food he had tasted for some time, so much better than the nutrient bars.

Gabriel tapped his control pad, and then eyed his power levels. Guy and Colonel Graham's crew had been hard at work during the entire slip, using a spare cell that had been loaded into storage and somehow finding a way to shoehorn it into place beside the primary. It had meant removing the ion cannon's targeting computer, but what good would that do him anyway?

Reza and Sarah had also done their part, running tests against the Magellan's onboard network to determine when they had solved the transmission problem. From there, Reza had gotten the circuit boards in the fighter pulled so he could do some additional soldering on them to expand the capabilities of the equipment. They had done a simple test only minutes earlier, ensuring that the whole package functioned as expected.

As far as Gabriel was concerned, if anyone was going to be called a hero for this, it should be the scientists who had even made his run possible. He hated to admit it, but that included Guy as well. For all of his complaints, the man had come through when it mattered the most.

"We're going to be getting a clear shot in one minute," Miranda said. "Try not to hit anything on your way in."

The Magellan was sitting about three quarters of the distance between Earth and Mars, as close as Theodore dared to take it without risking discovery.

Gabriel laughed. "I'll do my best."

"Gabriel, this is your father," Theodore said, his voice cutting into the comm. "I don't need to tell you what to do, or how to do it. I know we've had our differences over the years, but then, who hasn't? You're a St. Martin, and that makes you a stubborn gator by default. But you're a damn fine pilot and a damn fine son. I want you to know your old man is proud of you, and I know your mom would be proud of you too."

Gabriel felt a chill wash over him. Who didn't want to make their parents proud?

"Thanks, Dad."

"Captain, prepare to launch on my mark," Miranda said, switching the tone of the conversation to a purely professional one.

"Roger. Wish me luck."

"Good luck, Captain," Theodore said. "May God be with you."

Gabriel squeezed the crucifix one last time before letting it drop and taking hold of the control sticks. He took one more long breath and held it for a few seconds before releasing.

"Launching in three. Two. One."

Gabriel was pushed back in his seat as the magnetic launcher pulled him forward through the tube. The lights were a growing blur while he streaked through the tunnel, his pulse quickening in an instant.

Then he was out, rocketing forward through space. Mars was at his back, small and red. Earth was a distant speck ahead of him. It wouldn't be for long.

He turned his head, looking back over his shoulder at the Magellan. It was shrinking fast, growing more distant with each passing second. He could picture his father up on the bridge, watching the starfighter vanish within moments. He wondered what he was thinking, smiling as he did. He imagined his father was telling him to hurry the hell up.

He put his eyes forward again, keeping his attention on the HUD and ready to fire the vectoring thrusters should any solid masses pop up in front of his course.

Ten hours quickly became nine, and then eight, and then seven. The Earth began to come into view as he reached the one hour mark, continuing to grow larger ahead of him, slowly morphing from a bright point of white light to a more bluish tinged point, to a small blue sphere.

His thoughts redirected to Jessica. He knew how much she would have wanted to be a part of this. She had always been so passionate about her beliefs, and the war was something she had believed in. It was that passion that had led them to fall in love. It was the same passion that had sent her to her death. He used it now to steel himself against the coming storm. To find strength and focus.

He was a warrior, a soldier on a mission.

He wouldn't be denied.

[61]

"GENERAL RODRIGUEZ," DONOVAN SAID, STANDING AT attention and saluting.

"At ease, Major," Rodriguez said.

Donovan adjusted his stance before making eye contact with the rest of the assembly. He had come running when one of Carlson's assistants had found him and asked him to head down to the lab right away, but it seemed even his best time was slower than the General, Diaz, Montero, and Sharma.

Maybe if he hadn't dropped Ehri with his mother first.

It had been three days since Donovan had brought the alien clone back to the resistance base. They had been the three busiest and most fulfilling days of his life. When he wasn't escorting Ehri around, teaching her about human life, or in many cases just allowing her to observe his routine, he was working to organize and prepare for his next mission to make one last ditch effort to contact the space forces. It was more work than usual, mainly due to his need to find at least six more volunteers for the mission, though he preferred to take as many as he could find. The resistance base had a limited pool of potentials to begin with, and many of the fighters weren't in good enough physical condition to make a good runner.

As for Ehri, she was absorbing what it was like for them with alarming aptitude, quickly adjusting her speech patterns to better match theirs, as well as learning everything she could. She spent time with Doctor Montoya, answering his questions. She spent time in the kitchens learning to cook. She spent time with the seamstresses learning to sew. She even spent time with Matteo, watching him repair this and that around the base, and quickly making everyone on the base forget she wasn't human or truly one of them.

Of course, it was the nursery where she was the happiest. Every moment with a child was a learning experience for her, and she delighted in their generally unpredictable nature, finding a great challenge in trying to understand how they thought and functioned, and somehow maintaining her patience when she couldn't. She also enjoyed his mother's stories about him, and about how he had been as a child. Rambunctious and independent. He hadn't changed since then.

"Carlson, we have everyone here," General Rodriguez said, giving the CSO the floor.

"Thank you, General," Carlson said. He had a smile on his face, though his hair was dirty and messy and he looked as if he hadn't slept since Donovan had returned.

Donovan realized he probably hadn't. Carlson had joked about it, but it was no joke at all.

"I've been working on the alien tech that Major Peters and Lieutenant Diaz returned after their last mission. I wanted to give you all a quick update on what I've discovered."

"Do you know how to defeat their armor?" Rodriguez asked bluntly.

Carlson shook his head. "Well. No. Not yet. But we're working on it. The rifle is incredibly complex, and of course, we need to make sure that our work on it doesn't damage it in any way. It's made reverse engineering it a bit of a challenge. We have made progress on the power supply; however, and I think we may be able to design something similar based on it. I know the reactor keeps this place going, but it isn't exactly portable. That's not why I asked you to come down."

"It isn't?" Montero said.

"No. I wanted to talk to you about the cloth."

He had a pair of the pants hanging against a heavily shielded wall beside them, and it was clear he had tried to puncture them with gunfire.

"This material is unlike anything I've seen before. Completely bulletproof, it actually hardens in direct opposition to the amount of force placed against it. Meaning, the harder you hit it, the harder it gets. We've been examining it, and it appears as though it is constructed of nanometer-sized particles that act kind of like springs, loose in general, but coiling up as pressure is applied."

"That's interesting, Carlson, but not that useful," Rodriguez said.

"You're so impatient, Christian," Carlson said. "Okay. This is the super cool part that's got me all excited. So, we left one of the shirts sitting under the microscope while we switched gears to look at the rifles. When we came back, the spring's molecules had reorganized."

He opened his mouth, mimicking his total amazement and expecting the gathered officers to respond in kind.

"I don't know what that means," Diaz said.

"Ah. Uh." Carlson shook his head. "I should have known better. It means the cloth is alive."

"What do you mean, alive?" Donovan said.

"I mean, the thing that makes it so impervious is a nano-organism. There are billions of them living on the base fibers of the cloth, which is made of some kind of silk. They seem to be feeding on the cloth, so I imagine that over time it wears down to point of uselessness. This is nothing that you can find here on Earth."

"Okay," Rodriguez said. "I understand why you're excited, I think, but was this really something worth calling us all down here for?"

"Yes, sir," Carlson said. "Don't you see? This cloth is an example of using a biological ingredient in making super strong cloth. What if this is a primitive version of the Dread armor? If we can find a way to kill these creatures, maybe we can do the same to destroy their shells?"

"We have a way to destroy the shells, Carlson," Major Sharma said. "The rifles Donovan brought you can do it. What you need to do is figure out how."

"I said, I'm working on that."

"You were wasting time on a shirt when you could have been learning about the weapons technology. You do understand we're at war, and on the verge of losing it?"

Carlson's face turned beet red. "I understand completely. If you would open your mind the teeniest bit, you would be able to conceptualize the parallels between the cloth and the carapace. The goal here is to defeat the enemy shields, and understanding how they work is the best key to doing so."

"Assuming they are even remotely the same."

"Yes. I do believe the armor is biological in nature, at least in part."

"But you don't know for sure."

"No. What I do know is that I don't have the equipment here to do a more thorough analysis on this. I've seen these rifles before. I've broken them down and scanned them under a microscope. The problem is that even with it turned on, there's nothing new for me to discover here. At least, nothing new that I'm capable of discovering. Considering the nano-tech in the cloth, it is reasonable to assume there is other nano-tech within the weapon."

"The rifle has a switch on it," Donovan said. "A clear indication that it has two different modes. You can't figure out which is which?"

"I can't figure out which does what. Something is happening when I flip the toggle. I can hear it; I can sense it. I can't see it. Not with the equipment we have here. I could try taking the weapon apart and hope that I can put it back together, but that is precisely what you ordered me not to do."

"Damn," General Rodriguez said. "So close, and still so far."

"I can try taking it apart,"' Carlson said.

"No. Not yet. Let me think about it."

"We don't have a lot of time, sir," Montero said.

"I know. We only have two. We can't risk losing either one without being certain we can get what we need from it. Carlson, how confident do you feel that you can take the weapon apart and put it back together in working order?"

"We have some older disabled weapons in storage, maybe if I practice on those a few more times, I can be more sure."

"Okay. Do it. But don't start breaking down either of the active weapons until you come and see me."

"Yes, General."

"And keep your people on the cloth. See if you can find something that will kill the organisms. It was good thinking, bad timing."

"Yes, General."

"Donovan, walk back to my office with me. The rest of you are dismissed."

"Yes, sir," Diaz, Montero, and Sharma said.

Rodriguez exited behind them, with Donovan at his side. "How are the preparations for the run going?"

"As well as can be expected, sir. I only have six in my squad. That's a bare minimum for any run, and considering how heavily the Dread have been coming after us any time we expose ourselves, it doesn't leave me feeling that positive."

"Understood," the General said, rubbing at his mustache. "I can't order people to do this. Not in good conscience."

"I'm not asking you to, sir. If we have to use six, we'll use six. Even if we don't make it back, we'll get the message sent."

"I know you will. I've been reading Doctor Montoya's reports on Ehri. The bek'hai culture is interesting, wouldn't you say?"

"It's different, that's for sure. I can't imagine a world without children, without intimacy, where intelligent beings are so easy to make that most of them are expendable."

"Agreed. Have you been able to get her to tell you anything she hasn't told Montoya?"

"Not yet. I'm still trying to win her over. She loves spending time in the nursery, so I think that's helping. She needs to give us the information willingly, without feeling like I'm attempting to trick her.

Anyway, I don't know if she knows any more than what she's said. Her role with the bek'hai was to study us."

"She may not, but like I told you earlier, if genetics play any role in who a person is then getting her on our side can be one of the most important things we do."

"I'm still not sure how," Donovan said.

"Neither am I. Maybe it's because I held Juliet St. Martin in such high esteem. I don't know. It's a gut call."

"One that I don't disagree with, sir."

"Are you still planning to take your team off-base tomorrow?"

"Yes, sir. We all need to stay sharp somewhere that isn't as safe as down here."

"What about your shoulder?"

Donovan lifted it over his head, ignoring the twinge of pain as he did. He couldn't afford to let Rodriguez know it wasn't healed yet. "Almost as good as new, sir."

The General smiled. "Good. Dismissed, Major."

"Yes, sir."

[62]

"CAPTAIN GABRIEL ST. MARTIN MISSION RECORDING SIXTY-nine," Gabriel said, starting the in-flight recorder. "Time to Earth, nine hours and thirty-four minutes. Engines online. Weapons systems deactivated. All other systems nominal."

He had been firing reverse thrusters for the last ten minutes, slowing the starfighter down to a more acceptable speed. He was close enough now that he could see the orbital defense ring up ahead as a solid line of black that seemed to split the planet in half.

He tapped the control pad until he found the new menu item that had been tacked on. It was nothing but a simple toggle to activate and deliver the transmission his father had recorded earlier. It was also the most important button on the pad.

His pulse had calmed during the journey from the Magellan, and it remained calm as he grew ever closer to the Earth. He was in his element now. He had done this so many times before. True, entering atmosphere would be a new experience, but it didn't change who he was or what he knew, or how much he had experienced. His fears and doubts vanished as he traveled further and further from the starship and his father. Sometimes he wanted so much to make Theodore proud that his reputation became more hindrance than help.

"I'm beginning my run," he said, using the second stick to fire the planar vectoring thrusters and put the ship into a wobbly spin. He needed more than ever to conserve his energy, and making an effort to confuse the defense system before he reached it was one way to do it.

The spheres began to activate as he approached, short bursts of thrust turning them as they extended their weaponry. Gabriel kept his eyes focused on them, ignoring the way the universe was spinning around him.

They started to fire, their blasts of plasma streaking out toward the fighter. Gabriel kept his rotation, turning the stick in tight, precise motions to bring himself out of harm's way. He found an opening in the pattern and swung toward it, bright flashes of energy all around him.

The ring seemed tighter to him than the last time, and it began to close as he maneuvered towards the space. He couldn't spare the energy to go back and make another approach, and if he tried to run horizontal he would be blown to pieces. There was no other choice than to try to go through.

He gritted his teeth, the satellites so close to his ship that he could see the way the plasma formed at the tip of the cannon before firing, so close that each shot nearly blinded him. Somehow he got the starfighter through it, angling the wings and changing his direction just enough to keep himself alive. There was no thought behind it. No planning. It was all instinct and muscle memory.

It was what separated the good pilots from the rest.

Then he was in, past the orbital defense and racing toward the atmosphere. He tapped his control pad, adding a new layer to his HUD to help guide him to the correct angle to spear his way through. A line appeared on either side, moving toward the center as he adjusted. He checked his power supply. Getting in wouldn't use nearly as much as going back out.

The front of the fighter lit up as he sank deeper toward the surface, the heat pouring from the surface. Within seconds he was through, dipping toward the ground. The fighter shook and jostled as it cut through the air. It was similar to joining the slipstream, but felt less controlled, and Gabriel fought to maintain his focus and his nerve. He released the vector control stick, it wouldn't do him much good here, and put both hands on the main.

The alien structure looked so different closer in, and he felt his breath catch at the sight of it. It may have looked large from space. From within the atmosphere it was massive, stretching for miles and seeming to overtake the entire planet. The spires cut high into the air below him, and he could see motion along the black, armored surface.

He jumped in his seat when the first plasma bolt passed next to the fighter. He cut the stick hard, feeling the fighter shake more, the airframe working to meet his command. Inertial dampeners kept him from being knocked unconscious by the move, and he cursed himself for being stupid. He flicked the stick in more controlled motions, sweeping side to side as he continued the descent. He could see the world beyond the Dread approaching, brown and green in the distance.

"I'm inside the atmosphere, heading toward North America."

They knew the transmissions generated from somewhere around Mexico, though not exactly where. He tapped the controls to return to the toggle. He was almost in position.

A warning tone sounded in the cockpit as a pair of Dread fighters rose from behind him. He dropped the fighter, sending it straight down toward the enemy city, going into a slight spin as the plasma cut the sky around him. He needed cover, and it was the only cover he was going to get.

A massive machine appeared ahead and to his right, a squat torso on huge legs, with some kind of weapons hanging on either side. It rotated to face him, raising the guns and firing. Red blobs rocketed up at him, and he rolled and dove a little more, getting under them before coming up straight and breaking the descent. He angled to the left, barely skirting around a tall spire before moving back to the right. The Bats were still behind him, struggling to maneuver as well as he could. He recognized he had the advantage as he located a narrow channel in the structure and dove down toward it. A second mechanized ground unit appeared near the top of the channel, unable to angle its weapons in time to fire on him.

Gabriel raced through the channel, his heart beating calmly, nothing but ice in his veins. Fear was foreplay. Now there was only determination.

The channel ended at another spire, and Gabriel pulled back hard on his stick while increasing thrust, launching vertically out of the channel and climbing the side of the structure. The fighters had held back to wait for him, and they didn't dare fire without the risk of hitting their own structure. Now that Gabriel knew the weapons would damage it, he felt safe to use it as a shield.

He rolled his starfighter again, finding his direction and adding more thrust. He wouldn't get as wide of a spread coming in low, but he didn't have a choice. He cleared the edge of the Dread city, shooting over a former human city that had been reduced to brown earth and a mixture of partially standing buildings, rusted steel, and rubble. He hit the toggle on the control pad, transmitting the message downward. The enemy fighters had lost some ground, but they were still behind him.

"Transmitting," he said. "I pray to God that someone hears it."

[63]

Donovan's eyes passed over the five men and women who had volunteered to join him on the t-vault. Diaz, Montero, Cameron, Sanchez, and Wade. They were standing at attention beneath the cover of a hollowed-out building, dressed in greens and barefoot. Two buckets of water and a third of orange clay sat on the ground beside them.

"First, I want to thank you all for volunteering for this mission. Your support of what we're trying to do is a testament to your courage and your faith."

"Thank you, sir," all five replied. They kept their voices low, not wanting to be discovered by a passing enemy drone.

The area around the base had been warmer since Reyes had fired his rifle. The mechanized armor on the scene had been replaced by clone patrols, and then with drones. Only the scouts had gone in or out for the last four days, and even then it was to quickly monitor the situation and get back inside.

Donovan was thankful for the opportunity to bring his team outside. Scanning the soldiers, he could tell that only Diaz wasn't nervous to be too far from home to escape should they be sighted.

Getting used to that fear was one of the most valuable experiences he could give them.

"Lieutenant Diaz, prepare the squad."

"Yes, sir," Diaz said, breaking rank and going over to the water.

She lifted the bucket with one hand, grabbing an attached spray nozzle in the other. She proceeded to douse each of the soldiers with it, soaking their shirts and pants. Once that was done, she retrieved the bucket of clay. "Cover yourself as much as possible. Clothes, too. The clay will dampen your heat signature. Help each other in the places you can't reach."

"Yes, ma'am," they said, approaching the bucket.

Donovan watched and waited while they coated themselves and one another. Diaz brought him the bucket once they were done.

"Would you like some help with that, sir?" she asked playfully.

"I've got it," he replied, smiling. "Thanks."

"Yes, sir."

Donovan grabbed the clay, quickly spreading it over his body. Then he headed for the open air.

The others followed him, quickly moving into a standard wedge formation. Only Wade lagged behind, his slowness immediately drawing Diaz's attention.

"Wade," she hissed. "This isn't a walk in the park. If you dawdle, you die."

"Yes, ma'am."

Donovan scanned the street. They were a good kilometer away from the base, closer to the edge of the city so that if they were caught the Dread might think they were hiding in the mountains. He watched the sky for signs of scouts. He didn't see any.

"Okay, people," he said. "We're going to cross to that rubble over there, as fast as we can. Stay in formation, eyes up and alert. Diaz, you're on point as the spotter. If she sees anything, her hand will go up like this. You see the hand, you find cover, and you stay there until she opens her fist to signal the all clear. Understood?"

"Yes, sir," they replied.

"What if they see us?" Wade asked.

"Rendezvous point is two klicks north. We split up, try to lose them, and meet back there when it's clear. We wait two hours for survivors. If you aren't there in that time, you're probably dead."

"But not always, sir," Montero said. "You weren't."

"We were lucky once. I doubt that will happen again."

"Yes, sir."

"Diaz, on your mark."

Diaz moved up ahead of him, and he replaced her position in the wedge. As the fastest runner, she could afford to watch the sky while she sprinted.

"Okay, let's-"

They all froze, as a heavy clap echoed across the sky, followed quickly by a second.

"What the hell was that?" Diaz said.

"I don't know," Donovan replied. "Can you see anything."

Diaz lifted her head, looking up, turning in a circle as she did. "I don't. Wait. Major, you have to see this."

Donovan joined Diaz, following her finger as she pointed.

"What is that?" she asked.

A dark speck was falling from the sky in a hurry, trailing vapor. It looked like it was out over the Dread city.

"Maybe one of their satellites malfunctioned and lost orbit," he said.

"And is coincidentally falling right on top of their heads?"

"You never know." He watched the speck continue to tumble, and then straighten out and move horizontally. "Okay, not a satellite."

"It's a ship. It has to be."

"A Dread fighter? Why would it be out there? They don't launch them unless they pick up one of ours."

The speck was getting slightly larger, moving in their general direction. Two more joined it a moment later, rocketing upward from the Dread city.

"I don't think that's a Dread ship," Diaz said.

"The run isn't for another twelve days," Donovan replied, his pulse quickening nervously. "If it's the space force, they're way too early."

"Why would they be coming in this low?"

Thin bolts of plasma began to pierce the sky around the black spot, which turned and jiggled to avoid them.

"Definitely not theirs," Donovan said. He noticed the others had moved into position to watch as well.

"If he's one of ours, he's damn good at avoiding them," Montero said.

The three dots continued to descend until they vanished behind their line of sight.

"I wonder what he's doing here?" Diaz said. "There has to be a reason for it."

"I don't know," Donovan said. "We need to get back to base and inform General Rodriguez. Come on."

Donovan sprinted away from the building, heading back the way they had come. He had only reached the end of the first street when he felt the first vibration. He recognized it immediately and threw up his fist before pressing himself against the closest standing wall.

The vibrations intensified in a hurry, coming one after another in rapid succession. Donovan slid along the wall, reaching the end, and then peered around it. He could see down the long main thoroughfare, and while it was littered with debris, the mech was easily large enough for him to spot.

His pulse moved to triple-time, and he made sure to keep his arm up, fist closed. They were still encased in clay. They were still damp. They would be safe as long as they were quiet and remained hidden.

He watched it approach with a measure of awe. He had never had a chance to observe one before. He was impressed with the size and how easily it seemed to move with its near-humanoid shape. It pushed some of the rubble and old cars out of the way as it moved ever closer to him.

Had it seen him? He didn't think so. It would have blown him to ash already if it had. What was it doing?

It stopped halfway to him, the upper half turning, the arms lifting toward the sky and began firing projectiles. Donovan heard the soft whine a moment later, his mouth falling open in wonder as the starfighter rocketed past, barely a hundred meters overhead and angled on its side. He saw the pilot for the briefest of instants before he was past, somehow avoiding the enemy fire and continuing beyond the city.

The mech turned to follow the fighter, and so did Donovan, losing it behind the building before finding it again, headed along the slope and up the mountain. Two heartbeats later a pair of Dread fighters screamed overhead in pursuit.

"Come on, buddy," he said, shaking from the excitement. "You can do it."

The fighter shrank into the distance. The mech started to move, heading back the way it had come and giving up its part in the battle. The two Dread fighters took over for it, resuming their plasma attack.

Once more, the pilot managed to avoid the fire. Then it dipped suddenly, heading for the trees, so low he was amazed it hadn't crashed into them already. The Dread angled down, so intent on hitting him they weren't paying attention to the altitude.

The fighter shifted vectors and streaked up, barely whipping around the side of the mountain and disappearing beyond. The enemy ships weren't as fortunate, and he could hear the echo as they crashed into the woods.

"Yes," he whispered, holding himself back from screaming and remembering to keep his fist up.

He stayed that way for thirty seconds, waiting for things to calm down. There was no smoke coming from the area where the Dread had crashed, just a swath of downed trees. The armor would have protected them from damage, but could they get airborne again from that position? He didn't know.

He looked around, finding Diaz to his left next to a car, with Wade right beside her. He opened his hand. Montero, Cameron, and Sanchez appeared from their cover, and they ran to form up on him again.

"Dios Mio, did you see that, amigo?" Diaz asked excitedly.

"Shh," Donovan replied. "Take us back to base. Silent until then."

She nodded, moving to point and bringing them home.

[64]

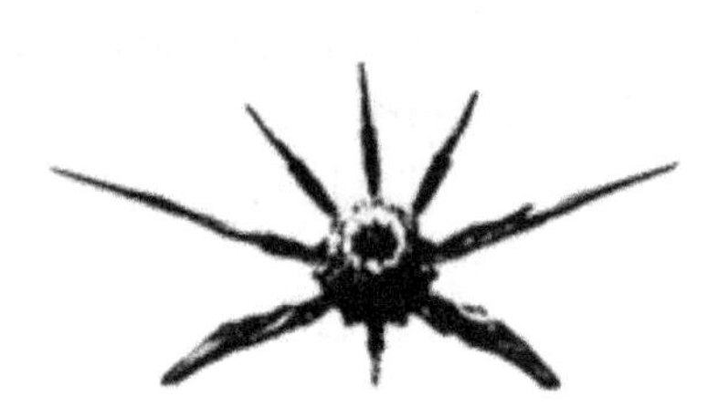

"Major. You're back," Sergeant Wilcox said. "We could feel the rumbling over the base and thought you might have been spotted. General Rodriguez was worried about you."

"We're fine," Donovan said. They were standing at the entrance to the corridor between the silo and the control center. Wilcox had been posted there to guard the door and open it upon their arrival. "Where is the General?"

"He was meeting with Carlson again. What happened out there?"

"I'm sure you'll hear about it. I need to speak to Rodriguez."

Wilcox nodded and moved aside, allowing them to file in. Donovan and the rest of the t-vault team ran through the connecting corridor while the Sergeant closed the door behind them.

They reached the base, and Donovan headed for the stairs down to the lab. He was standing in the doorway leading to them when he heard a shout behind him.

"Donovan, wait," Matteo said. The entire squad turned as one, watching Matteo pull to a stop in front of them, his breathing heavy.

"What's going on"? Diaz asked.

"Do you know where General Rodriguez is?"

"Science lab," Donovan said. "I was headed down there now."

"Tell him to come up to the comm room right away."

"Why?"

"Just tell him, amigo. It's important."

"I will. The rest of you wait here," Donovan said. "Don't say anything to anyone about this until the General says it's okay."

"Yes, sir."

Donovan continued down the steps, hurrying to the lab. He found General Rodriguez on his way out.

"Major," Rodriguez said, his eyes checking Donovan for injury. "There was some action outside. I was afraid your team was in trouble. Is everything okay?"

"We're fine, sir," Donovan said. "I'm not sure if everything is okay. There's something happening out there. Matteo said to ask you to come to the comm room immediately. He said it was important."

"Let's go, then. Tell me what happened to you."

They started walking together, taking a brisk pace back.

"A ship dropped from orbit. At first, we thought it was a Dread ship, but then it leveled out, and the Dread came up and started shooting at it. There must have been a mech nearby because it moved closer to our position and also started shooting. General, it was unreal. The ship was one of ours, and it flew right over our heads, so close I could see the pilot inside."

"Did he engage the enemy?" Rodriguez asked.

"No, sir. It didn't look like he had any weapons."

"Then why would he come in so low? What would he be doing here, anyway? They're early."

"Very early."

They reached the steps, climbing them two at a time. Donovan's team was still waiting at the stairwell for him, and they came to attention and saluted when the General appeared.

"At ease,' Rodriguez said. "I'm glad you're all safe. Donovan told me you had a bit of excitement."

"Yes, sir," Diaz said.

"Follow me. Whatever is happening, you're all an important part of it now."

The soldiers trailed behind Donovan and Rodriguez. They entered the communications room, where three small computers rested on an old metal desk, and wires snaked across the floor to the wall. Matteo was behind the desk, leaning over an old touchpad and staring into the monitor. He looked up.

"General," he said, saluting even though he wasn't part of the military.

"Matteo. What do you have?"

"I still can't quite believe it, sir. I mean, after all of this time, and-"

"What do you have?" Rodriguez repeated.

"Sorry, sir. Our monitoring software picked up an incoming message about ten seconds after the first round of vibrations stopped. It kind of caught me off guard with how fast it transferred because that meant it had to be a local send. But what really blew my mind were the headers."

"Headers?" Diaz asked.

"Information on where and how to send," Matteo said. "General, the message was directed to you, using an old identification tag you provided when we setup the system. According to the headers, it came from a General Theodore St. Martin?"

Donovan felt a chill run through his body. He glanced over at Rodriguez, who had frozen in disbelief.

"Did you say Theodore St. Martin?" he said, his voice barely more than a whisper.

"Yes, sir," Matteo said.

"What did it say?"

"It was sent to you. I haven't looked at it. I came to you right away."

General Rodriguez smiled. There was a tear in the corner of his eye. "That son of a gun. I knew if he were still out there he wouldn't let me down. Let me see it."

Matteo turned the monitor so they could all see. He tapped the pad, and an older man appeared. Donovan assumed it was General St. Martin. The look of recognition on General Rodriguez's face confirmed it.

"Christian," Theodore said. "You may not remember me, son, but I remember you. I can't say I'm surprised to know that you're still alive down there. You always had this look about you that told me you were a survivor. We got a message from you not too long ago, saying that the resistance was giving up the fight and going into hiding." Theodore leaned forward on his arms, getting closer to the recorder. "Christian, don't you dare do something as foolish as that. This fight ain't over yet. Hell, son, it's just getting interesting."

"He has no idea," Diaz said.

"Shhh," Rodriguez replied.

"If you're watching this recording, it means my son, Gabriel, managed to break through the Dread's defenses and transmit it down to you. Hopefully, it means he also managed to get himself back out. The point is, I risked my own boy to get in touch with you, and I did it for a damn good reason. Gabriel witnessed a Dread fighter firing on the defense satellites in orbit around the planet. He says the Dread's plasma cannon was able to destroy them, meaning their weapons can defeat their armor."

"We already knew that," Diaz said.

"Shhh," Rodriguez repeated.

"What I want you to do is try to capture one of their weapons. I've got a scientist up here who's a real genius, and I think if we can get our hands on one, he can figure out what makes it tick and find a way to use it against the enemy. Now, I know it may not be easy to get one of these weapons, but son, this is it. The last hurrah, if you will. The New Earth Alliance was considering abandoning Earth before we received your message, and I had to take the Magellan despite their protests to keep them from turning tail and leaving you stranded. If you have to give up every last man and woman you've got to make this happen, you need to do it. It's more than just their lives at stake. It's the lives of everyone left on Earth, and at least half the population of the NEA as well. Me and mine are waiting out near Mars for the next standard recon cycle. My son, Gabriel, will be back then. Send a transmission, tell us if you've got it or what the next move is. We'll be waiting."

Theodore leaned back. It seemed as if the recording would end, but then he leaned forward again.

"Oh, and Christian, if you know the whereabouts of my Juliet, I would be much obliged for that information as well. I know it seems a long shot, but there's a part of me that can't let go and is very much praying that she's still alive."

The screen went dark.

[65]

"Sir?" Donovan said.

Thirty seconds had passed since the recording ended. General Rodriguez hadn't moved a muscle. His eyes were glued to the dark screen; his hands clenched into fists.

The rest of the squad waited silently.

The seconds continued to tick by.

"Matteo," General Rodriguez said at last. "Get a message out to General Parker in New York. Tell him that Mexico base will not stand down, and my recommendation is for him to rescind his order, at least temporarily."

"Yes, sir," Matteo said, immediately shifting the screen back around and sitting at the desk to prepare the message.

"Donovan," Rodriguez said, turning to him. "I don't want to put undue pressure on you, but I can't even begin to express how important your next mission is going to be. I-"

"General Rodriguez, General Rodriguez, sir!"

Sergeant Wilcox barreled into the room, barely stopping before knocking Corporal Wade over.

"General Rodriguez."

"What is it, Wilcox?" he asked.

"Sir." She swallowed, trying to catch her breath. "If you remember, sir, Sergeant Yung and his team left yesterday on a supply run. They just returned a minute ago. They were out of breath from running to get the message back to you, so I ran here for them. Yung said the Dread were headed this way in force."

Rodriguez's eyes bore into her so fiercely she looked away.

"Damn it," he said. "They got us the message, but they attracted too much attention doing it."

"The fighter flew right over the base, sir," Donovan said.

"Between that and Captain Reyes firing his weapon the other day, they have to suspect we're here somewhere," Diaz said.

"Did he say how many?" Rodriguez asked.

"No, sir. He said it was more than he had ever seen in one group before. Both regular clones and others in armor."

"Should we evacuate, sir?" Montero said.

Rodriguez didn't answer. They all knew it was a difficult decision to make. How could everything be falling apart at the same time it was beginning to come together?

"Sir?" Donovan said.

"Yes, Major?"

"General St. Martin said they have a scientist with them who he thinks can figure out how the alien weapons work. He wanted us to get a gun, but we already have one. What we need to do is to get it to them."

"In twelve days," Rodriguez said. "Maybe we can stay hidden down here for that long, but then Gabriel is going to come back, and there will be nothing for him to pick up. They'll assume we've either given up or died, or maybe that their transmission never made it through, and they'll leave again. That's assuming we can stay hidden. If the Dread are sending a large force, I don't think they'll give up until they've found something."

"Or we can evacuate and make a run for it," Montero said.

"Where are we going to go?" Donovan asked. "We've already been on the run. How many will people die if we do? Besides, we know from Ehri that the Dread leader wants us all dead. Who's to say we'll make it out this time?"

"So you want to hide down here and wait for them to storm in and kill us all?"

"Of course not. I think we need to focus on our priorities. I hate to say this, but this base and everyone in it is secondary to getting the weapon out of the area and up to General St. Martin. If all of us have to die to do it, then that's our fate. We're part of the resistance. We have a duty to the mission. We have to fight to the last man, to the last breath to get the Dread off our planet."

"Tell that to my daughter," Montero said. "She's only four years old."

"I'm sorry, Colonel," Donovan said. "I know it sounds cold, but this is the world we're living in. If we don't get that gun off the planet, we're all as good as dead. Not just you and me. Every last human on Earth."

Montero turned to Rodriguez. "I'm not going to sit here and wait for her to die, sir."

"No one wants their child to die," Rodriguez said.

"General," Donovan started. Rodriguez put up his hand to silence him.

"Give me a minute, Major. I didn't survive this long by rushing into things."

"We don't have a lot of time, sir," Diaz said.

"I'm aware, Lieutenant. Matteo."

"Yes, sir."

"You said the transmission was received locally. Do you know where?"

"Give me a minute, sir." Matteo's eyes locked onto the monitor, his hands gliding across the control pad.

"What are you thinking, General?" Montero asked.

"I have an idea. It may get us all killed, but it may also be the best chance we have."

"I ran a packet trace, sir," Matteo said. "The transmission was picked up by an antenna thirty kilometers east of here."

"East?" Montero said. "That would be near the top of Mount Tlaloc. There's nothing out there, never mind anything with a power supply. That can't be right."

"The antenna id was MTTC-DSN-110. I've got the IP address." Matteo did something with the control pad. "I just pinged it. Whatever it is, it's active."

"Another group?" Donovan asked.

"If it is, they may not be friendly," Diaz said.

"I'm telling you, there's nothing out there," Montero said. "I'm from this area. I would know."

"Matteo, how sure are you about the location?" General Rodriguez asked.

"It isn't a perfect system. Seventy percent?"

"It will have to be good enough. Major Peters, I need you and your team to head out to the transmission site. Matteo, I want you to go with them."

"Me?" Matteo said. "Why?"

"Whatever that place is, it has power and an antenna. We can't wait twelve days for the recon flight to return. We know General St. Martin is waiting near Mars. We need to get a signal out that way, to tell them we have the weapon and that we're waiting for them."

"Waiting where, sir?" Donovan asked.

"On the mountain. You'll bring the guns with you."

"Guns? Both of them?"

"Yes. We can't afford to lose them. Not now. I'd send Carlson with you, too, but he's too damn slow. I do want you to bring Ehri."

"I don't understand?"

"It's like you said, Major. Our top priority is to get the weapon to General St. Martin so his genius can try to do something with it. Unfortunately, right now I think that's also the safest place for anyone to be. Our second priority is to protect the people here who can't protect themselves. I have an idea on that, too. Montero, go ask Major Sharma to help you get our people together in the cafeteria so that I can go over the details."

"Yes, sir," Montero said, leaving the room.

"Sir," Matteo said. "I don't know if this will work. I've read everything we have here about communication systems. It takes a pretty big antenna to reach out into space with any kind of authority. What if we get there and it's somebody's homebrew needle or something?"

"Then you stay alive for twelve days and wait for Gabriel St. Martin to return. You can use the needle to transmit to them. Either way, we'll get a message off."

"Are you sure you want us to bring Ehri, sir?" Donovan asked. He didn't mind keeping her out of harms way, but he wasn't sure what value she would add to the mission.

"Yes. She knows how her people operate, and she seems to have a soft spot for you. She may be able to help you evade the Dread long enough to deliver the message."

Donovan was surprised by the comment. "A soft spot?" he asked.

"That's what your mother told me."

"You've been talking to my mother?"

"I get reports from everyone who is in charge of anything around here, Major. That includes the nursery."

Donovan felt a mixture of excitement and guilt. It had never occurred to him that Ehri might become fond of him. The children, maybe. Not him.

"She's also highly educated and intelligent. She may be able to help with the transmission."

"Yes, sir," Donovan said.

"Take Diaz down to the lab to get the weapons from Carlson. Take the Dread cloth, too. All of it. Use it to stay alive. Come to the cafeteria after."

"Yes, sir. One more question, sir."

"Yes, Major?"

"Thirty kilometers to the top of the mountain? It's going to take us at least a day to get there. If the Dread see us, there's no way we can outrun them."

Rodriguez smiled. "I'm a survivor, remember? I've got a plan for that, too."

[66]

DONOVAN AND DIAZ LEFT THE SCIENCE LAB, EACH WEARING THE alien clothing beneath their green uniforms and carrying a Dread plasma rifle. Donovan also had Ehri's black dress in a bundle beneath his arm.

They were on their way to the cafeteria, following a short distance behind Carlson and his team as they answered the General's call for all hands. They were close enough to the open space that they could hear the general hum of the assembled as each of the gathered members of their community worked to guess why they had been summoned or calm their suddenly fraying nerves.

"This is it, isn't it?" Diaz said, her voice low. "What did General St. Martin call it? The last hurrah."

"This may be our most important mission, but this isn't it," Donovan said. "If we make this happen, we'll be on the road to fighting back for the first time in half a century."

"Can we make this happen?"

Donovan nodded. A strange calm had come over him since they had left the communications room. After barely surviving so many t-vaults, the idea of having something tangible come from it meant that all of the friends and comrades he had lost over the years had died for something. He would do his best to make sure of that.

"Yes. No one would ever have guessed we would wind up in a Dread starship and make it out alive. Last week, it seemed impossible that we would be able to get our hands on one of these." He shook the rifle. "We can do this, Renata. You and me and our team."

She smiled. "You seem convinced."

"I am."

She stopped walking and turned to face him. "Can I ask you something? Something personal?"

He paused. "Of course. We've known each other for a long time."

"Do you ever think of me? As anything other than a friend or Matteo's sister, I mean?"

Donovan stared at her. He knew there was something passing between them. Two weeks ago he had only ever thought of her as his best friend's sister, and now he saw her as a friend and equal. He appreciated the way they interacted, and the trust he had in her ability to help keep him and the team alive. Maybe there was something more to it? He really didn't know. He had bigger concerns right now.

"Renata," he said. "This isn't the best time."

"There is no best time, D. You know that. Is it a hard question to answer?"

"I can only tell you what I know, which is that I'm glad we're here together, and that we're fighting this war together. I trust you and have faith in you, and I genuinely enjoy your company. I don't know exactly where that fits in the hierarchy of male and female relationships."

He could tell that wasn't exactly what she wanted to hear. A flash of disappointment crossed her face.

"Is it because of Ehri?"

When she said it, she didn't sound like the confident woman she had grown into. She seemed more like a little girl about to have her heart crushed.

"No. It isn't that. My job is to complete the mission and keep as many of you alive as I can. That's all that matters to me right now."

The confidence returned in an instant. "I know. I'm being ridiculous, and I'm sorry. It's just that I've had this crush on you since I was twelve years old, and you never noticed me. You did a little bit when we were trapped on the Dread ship. Maybe it was just because you had lost so much blood. Maybe it was something else. Whatever. I didn't want to die without having said anything. I didn't want to die without letting you know how I feel."

"You aren't going to die. Is that understood, Lieutenant?"

"Yes, sir," Diaz said. Then she surprised him, stepping forward and leaning up on her toes to put her lips on his.

He didn't respond to the kiss, caught off guard and unwilling to complicate things. It passed quickly. She pulled away, looking up at him. "I'm sorry, Donnie. I always dreamed of kissing you, and I didn't want to die without doing that once either."

She turned on her heel and continued toward the cafeteria. Donovan watched her for a moment before trailing behind.

The cafeteria was already full when they entered, with all three hundred plus members of the community crowded around the tables and benches, and standing along the walls. They drew some stares when they walked in armed, and some of the people quieted. Donovan scanned them, finding Ehri and his mother standing with the parents of the children in the nursery. Ehri smiled and waved when she saw him.

He made his way over to her, Diaz hanging close at his side.

"What's going on?" his mother asked. "Why did General Rodriguez bring us all together?" She glanced at the gun. "I can guess it isn't anything good."

"Things are going to get rough, Mom," Donovan said.

"We've done rough before. We'll do it again."

"Yeah, we will." He turned his shoulder with the bundle under it to Ehri. "Your bek'hai clothing. Rodriguez wants you to wear it for whatever protection it can offer."

"Why?"

He looked at his mother again. "Some of us are leaving. We have a chance to deliver one of these guns to the space forces. To someone who may be able to decipher the technology."

"Ehri's coming with you?"

"Yes. General Rodriguez wants you with us."

"He believes I can be of use?"

"Maybe. Would you help us if you could?"

Ehri looked at Wanda, and then back at the children. Donovan could see the conflict on her face. She had come to observe, not to help. Except she had started this in the first place by leading them to the weapons. Confident in her kind's success or not, she had to know she was at least partially responsible for what was happening.

"Attention!"

Colonel Montero's voice echoed across the room, bringing the assembled soldiers to attention and silencing the non-combatants. He also spared Ehri from having to answer the question.

General Rodriguez entered the cafeteria a moment later. Donovan couldn't help but notice how old he suddenly looked.

"I'm sorry to bring you all here under these circumstances," Rodriguez said, not wasting any time. "We have a report from Sergeant Yung that the Dread forces are heading this way in a number that suggests they intend to do whatever they must to find this base."

He waited a moment while the crowd reacted.

"I have a plan. Two plans, actually. First, Major Peters and the t-vault squad are going to be heading out following this meeting. Their mission is to deliver one of the captured alien weapons to a member of the space forces that we have been communicating with for all of these years. Both their General and I are of a belief that together we can find a way to defeat the alien armor and start fighting back against the Dread for real."

"Why don't we just offer them their clone back in exchange for our safety?" someone said from the back of the room.

Donovan glanced at Ehri. She didn't seem phased by the comment. In fact, she looked intrigued.

"Yeah. If we had never brought her here in the first place, this wouldn't be happening," someone else said.

"Yeah," one of the women right behind them said. "Why did you have to come here, anyway? Go home you alien bitch. You don't belong with us."

Ehri's face froze at that comment.

"Be quiet," Rodriguez shouted, quieting the crowd. "Are you all loco? This has nothing to do with her, and if you think the Dread give a crap about one wayward clone when they have hundreds more just like her, you're really out of your mind. In case you've forgotten, this is a rebel installation. A military base, dedicated to continuing the war with the Dread. Have you all gotten so comfortable here, you've gone soft? Do you think you have a right to question any of the decisions I make? You know how to get out if you do."

The people were silent.

"Now, here's the second part of my plan, and I need your help to make it work. We're going to leave a small number of soldiers here along with the mothers of the children, or fathers if the mother isn't with us. Everyone else is going to pack up everything they have and we're going to make a run for it. With any luck, the evacuation will lead them away from the base and keep its location secret. Except we won't be evacuating. We can double back once we've split up and lost them."

The crowd was silent this time, but a thick tension was heavy in the air. The plan wasn't that much of a plan at all, and everyone in the cafeteria knew that it meant many of them were going to die. At the same time, they also knew there was nowhere else for them to run to. There was nowhere to go that was as safe as it was down here. In a sense, the idea was brilliant in its simplicity. Some of them would escape and make it back.

Some was better than none.

"Major Sharma and Sergeant Wilcox are going to organize you into groups. Everyone needs to head in a separate direction for this to be believable. I'll be bringing the bulk of the soldiers with me, and we'll do everything we can to draw them away. Understood?"

The room remained silent. Even the soldiers were too shocked to reply. Everything had happened so suddenly; it was hard to digest.

"I said, understood," Rodriguez repeated in a drill sergeant tone.

"Yes, sir," came the reply, loud and strong.

"I'm proud of all of you. Major Peters, gather your team and meet me on the first level immediately."

"Yes, sir," Donovan said.

Rodriguez strode confidently from the room, while Sharma and Wilcox began moving through the gathered crowd.

"Mom," Donovan said, turning to his mother. "I-"

"Shh," Wanda said. "You be careful. Stay alive, and finish this mission. This is bigger than the people here. It's bigger than me. I love you, and I'm proud of you."

Donovan hugged her. "Thanks. I love you, too."

"I know."

He let go and looked at Ehri. She was standing stiff and distant. He knew the Dread didn't value one another as a whole the way humans did. He wondered if they could ever be as downright mean to one another.

"Goodbye, Ehri," Wanda said, approaching her. She wrapped her arms around the clone, hugging her. "I know you want to learn," Donovan heard her say. "Sometimes fear makes humans say and do terrible things, but that's all it is. The fear coming out in words. They don't really mean it. None of this is your fault."

Ehri's face softened, and she raised her arms and hugged Wanda back.

"Now, don't keep the General waiting," Wanda said.

[67]

"Diaz, go round up the others," Donovan said. "I need a minute with Ehri."

Diaz almost covered up her displeasure before he noticed. "Yes, sir."

"We can talk in here," Donovan said, leading Ehri to one of the offices.

"Your General won't be happy when you're late."

"I know. Are you okay?"

"Yes. Why do you ask?"

"The things the people were saying. I know they must have hurt."

"No. Not at first. Only when Carol turned on me. I thought that we were friends. I watched her son every day."

"My mother was right. It was only fear."

"I know that now."

"I need to know if you're with us, against us, or neutral."

"Major, I don't know."

"You have to know, Ehri. I have to know. Rodriguez wants you with us because he thinks you can help us. You helped Diaz and me back at the bek'hai mothership because you knew this day would come, though I don't think you imagined it would come this soon. You knew the Dread would find us and crush us sooner or later, and then you could go back to your life as a slave."

Donovan bit his lip. He hadn't meant to say slave. After all he had heard of her life as a member of the lor'hai, it had spilled out.

"I'm not a slave," Ehri said. "No one owns me."

"Do you have freedom?"

"I'm here, aren't I?"

"Yes. Here you're free. What about back there? What will happen to you then?"

"I will be Si'dahm to the new Dahm in charge of my team. I will continue to study human culture, and I will write my own discourse on what I have learned of humans in these last few days."

"And then what?"

"What do you mean? That's all."

"Do you think you'll enjoy watching fifty year old videos of humanity, after you've experienced the real thing? Will your work even matter when the Domo'dahm gets his wish and all of us are gone? Will they even need you anymore?"

"Of course. There are always things to study and to learn."

"Really? And the pur'dahm will have a use for an aging clone whose field of science is obsolete? I've been to all of your interviews with Doctor Montoya. You're lying to yourself if you think that will happen."

"I'm not a traitor, Donovan."

Donovan couldn't help but laugh at that. "You gave us the guns. The key to this entire war. You handed them over without a second thought."

"You know why."

"You helped Diaz kill Klurik."

"I did not."

"Come on, Ehri. You distracted him while she aimed her shot. You could have told him she was there."

"It had to be done in order for me to continue my work. That is an acceptable reason in bek'hai culture, and I will face no punishment for it."

"It was more than that, wasn't it? You didn't like Klurik. That much was obvious."

"You're saying I wanted to kill him?"

"Maybe. You didn't like the way he treated you. It made you feel like you were nothing. That's what you want to go back to?"

"There is more to it than that. I miss my sisters."

"You're lying."

"I am not. How do you know when I'm lying, anyway?"

"Your nose wrinkles. It's kind of cute, to be honest with you."

Ehri paused, staring at him. "Donovan, I'm scared."

He hadn't expected his simple, silly compliment to be the thing that drove down her defenses. "Why?"

"I." She shook her head. "I don't know who I am, anymore. I don't know what I am. I followed what Tuhrik taught me. I did what I believed he would have wanted. Only it didn't give me answers, only more questions to go with experiences I never believed I would have. Children." She smiled sadly. "The bek'hai are not evil, Donovan. They seek to survive, like all living things do. Like your people are trying to do now."

"I know they aren't. But they messed up their world. They don't have the right to ours. Don't you understand that?"

"Yes. I do. That is why I'm scared. I understand that they're wrong. I understand that they use me, as they use all lor'hai. We aren't slaves, but we aren't free, either. I feel guilty for hating them for that, the way I hated Klurik for how he treated me. Like a thing instead of an intelligent being. I am alone here, Donovan. The only one of my kind. My DNA may be fully human, but as much as you might accept me, I'll always be set apart. I'll always be different."

"You aren't alone," Donovan said. "I'm here."

"For now. Until they kill you."

"Then help me stay alive. If you know the bek'hai are wrong, maybe together we can do something about it. Maybe we can fix things for everyone, including the lor'hai."

"I'm only a scientist."

Donovan remembered what Rodriguez had said about Juliet St.

Martin. "No. You're more than that. You proved that when you helped us escape. You're proving that right now."

"I. I don't know. I-"

Donovan didn't think about what he was doing until he was doing it. He wrapped his free arm around her, pulling her to him, leaning his head down and finding her lips. He kissed her, trying to pour every ounce of his desire for her to stay and help them into it.

She didn't resist him. She melted in his arms, her lips responding awkwardly. She had never kissed anyone before.

"Please," Donovan said. "Help us. Whatever happens, we can do it together, as free people."

She pulled her head back to look into his eyes.

"Please," he said again.

She nodded. Her entire body was trembling.

Donovan wondered if he had just done the right thing. He had no idea how this mess was going to turn out. He could barely believe how quickly they had ended up in it to begin with. He wanted Ehri on their side. So did General Rodriguez. But had he kissed her to win her over, or simply because he wanted to?

He wasn't even sure of that one himself. One mess at a time. It wouldn't matter if he were dead twenty-four hours from now.

"Come on," he said. "We have a delivery to make."

[68]

GABRIEL FELT A MASSIVE SENSE OF RELIEF AS FIRST THE PLANET Mars came into clearer view, and then the starship Magellan appeared ahead of it. It was a black speck at first, a mote of dust against the red planet.

He had never been more grateful to make it back.

It hadn't been easy. The Dread ground defenses had been tight, and only some fancy flying that he couldn't even believe he'd managed had gotten him out of harm's way and back into space. He had seen the two Bats slam into the trees and vanish from his HUD. It had been his last ditch effort to lose them by taking advantage of his fighter's more Earth-friendly design and agility. Fortunately, it had worked.

He didn't know if the resistance forces had received the message. He wouldn't know until he was back on board the Magellan and Guy could check the logs of the equipment. He was almost sure he had caught a flash of movement from the ground and seen someone there in a green uniform, but everything had happened so fast it was just as likely a figment of his imagination.

He hoped not.

He tapped his control pad, activating his comm. "Magellan, this is Captain Gabriel St. Martin. Do you copy?"

"Captain St. Martin," his father's voice replied a few seconds later. "This is Magellan. We hear you, son. Welcome home." He paused again as if trying to decide whether or not to break protocol. "I knew you could do it, Gabe," he continued, throwing protocol aside. "I'm just about pissing myself that you made it back to us."

Gabriel smiled. "Thank you, General," he replied. "I don't know if the mission was a success or not. The enemy position is pretty strong down there."

"Understood. Bring her in and we'll see what we've got."

"Roger. Captain St. Martin, out."

Gabriel navigated the fighter to the waiting hangar, bringing it into the first bay and waiting while the system re-pressurized it. As soon as the light turned green, he popped out of the cockpit, climbed down, and headed to the airlock. A crowd was waiting to greet him as he opened it and stepped through.

"Welcome back, Gabriel," Miranda said, hugging him.

"Nice work, Captain," Soon said, also giving him a hug.

"Gabe," Colonel Choi said, squeezing his shoulder.

Gabriel suddenly found himself face to face with Guy. The scientist looked different, and Gabriel was taken off guard because he was smiling.

"Welcome home, Captain," Guy said, extending his hand.

They locked eyes for a moment. It was obvious to Gabriel that Guy still didn't like him, but he had made the decision to be a team player.

"Thank you," Gabriel said, taking the hand.

"We're glad you made it," Sarah said, hugging him.

"Your father said to go clean yourself up and then to stop by his quarters for a debriefing," Choi said.

"Yes, ma'am," Gabriel replied.

"We should have the logs analyzed by then," Guy said. "Colonel, I'll send the report up to the General as soon as I have it."

"Thank you, Guy."

The crowd dispersed, each member of the crew returning to their duties. Gabriel made his way back up to his quarters with Colonel Choi at his side.

"How is it down there?" she asked.

"Not good," Gabriel replied. "It looks worse from close up."

"This whole thing is such a long shot."

"It's worth it."

"Don't get me wrong, Gabriel. I agree completely. The fact that you're here proves that we can still fight back. We don't have to be victims."

"No, we don't. How is the General holding up?" He couldn't ignore the fact that his father had been bedridden up until two days ago.

"I convinced him to sleep a few hours. He seems twenty years younger to me since we boarded this ship. He's acting it, too."

"He's in his element out here. A man on a mission."

"A man of war."

"Because he has to be. We all have to be. You saw what the alternative is. The kind of people we become."

"It helps that you're with him."

"You, too. You've always been there for both of us."

"How could I not, Gabriel? I can still remember how hard you used to kick me." She put her hand on her stomach. "I've never been more proud than to help give Theodore and Juliet their son, after what they did for me."

They reached Gabriel's quarters. Gabriel was going to salute Colonel Choi. He decided to embrace her instead. "Thank you," he said.

"You're welcome."

[69]

"Captain St. Martin reporting, sir," Gabriel said as the door to his father's quarters opened. He was greeted there by Sergeant Diallo.

"The General will be with you in a moment," she said. "Welcome back, Gabe."

"Thank you."

His father's quarters were twice the size of his own, leaving room for both a sitting area and a conference table, in addition to the bed. Gabriel started moving toward the sofa until he heard Theodore coughing from the bathroom and the soft splash of water. Was his father vomiting?

"Is he okay?" Gabriel said, taking a step in that direction.

Diallo moved in front of him. "He's fine. He said it was the pain medication. It makes him nauseous sometimes."

Gabriel wanted to go and check on him but resisted. If Theodore had asked Diallo to keep him away, he would respect that. He went to the sofa and sat.

His father emerged from the bathroom a minute later. Gabriel stood as he rolled over, noting how pale his face was. Colonel Choi had mentioned how much better he looked not twenty minutes earlier. Did she know the pills were making him sick?

"Gabriel. Damn glad to see you again, son. Damn glad."

Gabriel saluted him. His father returned the salute.

"Now, don't ever do that in here again," Theodore said. "In here, we're father and son, you hear me?"

"Yes, sir," Gabriel said. His father glared at him. "Okay, Dad," he said in correction.

"Good man. Go ahead and sit, son. I got word from Guy and Reza. They'll be bringing the report up any minute now."

"Dad, are you feeling okay?" Gabriel asked. He cared more about that than the report.

"I'm fine. Just a little nauseous from the meds is all. They were giving me anti-emetics back on Alpha. I don't have any here." He shrugged. "Tell me, what's it like on Earth? It's been so long since I've seen it, and back then most of it was on fire."

"It isn't on fire anymore, at least. There are still things growing there. I saw trees up close for the first time in my life." Gabriel couldn't help but smile at that. Even while trying to escape the Dread, a portion of his brain had been able to marvel. "I might have seen a person, too, but I'm not sure."

"They're down there. With any luck, they saw you. Even if the transmission didn't make it, having you pass so close to the surface has to send a message of its own."

"If they were there, I'm sure I was hard to ignore."

A tone sounded from the door. Diallo was standing next to it, and she stood in front of the hatch and opened it.

"Uh, is General St. Martin here?" Reza said.

"Lucy, I know you want to help me, and I appreciate it from the bottom of my ancient ticker, but I don't need a keeper," Theodore said.

"I'm sorry sir," Diallo replied, stepping aside. "It's the training."

Reza, Guy, and Sarah entered the room with Colonels Choi and Graham.

"Sir," the soldier said, saluting.

"Relax," Theodore said. "We're all friends and family in here."

"We have the results of the logging, Theodore," Guy said.

"Well, don't keep us all squirming. Spill it."

"The transmission was a success," Reza said, his voice giddy. "It was sent, anyway. Obviously, we have no way to know if General Rodriguez, or anyone for that matter, heard it."

"It worked," Theodore said. "Y'all are geniuses. All of y'all. If I had any cigars, I'd give you one."

"Cigar?" Reza asked.

"They're made from a plant that grew on Earth. Tobacco. You cultivate it, dry it out, roll it up, and smoke it."

"Oh. Why?"

"What do you mean, why?" Theodore asked.

"I'm sorry, sir. I mean, what is the purpose of it?"

Theodore stared at him for a moment before laughing. "Heh. You know, I never really thought about it. I ain't sure I know anymore. The point is, the mission was a success. A real team effort, too. Y'all make me proud. Now, we need to start planning ahead."

"We'll assume that they received the message," Choi said. "That means that you'll be making another run in twelve days, Gabriel."

"Standard operation this time," Theodore asked. "Easy-peasy for you." He looked over at the scientists. "You three have some tougher work ahead of you."

"What do you need?" Reza asked.

"We have to assume the ground forces will do their damnedest to get us one of the enemy weapons. Once they do, we'll need to get on the ground to retrieve it."

"I barely made it skimming the surface," Gabriel said. "Dad, there's no way we're landing without getting killed."

"Now Gabriel, don't make me embarrass you in front of the others. No soldier of mine is going to use words like 'no way' without getting under this old gator's skin. Nobody's saying it'll be easy, but we have to believe it can be done."

Gabriel felt his face flush, even though Theodore had gone easy on him that time. "You're right. I'm sorry."

"Reza," Theodore said. "You've been doing a lot of work on slipstream algorithms. What is your opinion on the possibility of exiting a slipstream inside of Earth's atmosphere? And remember what I just said to Gabriel."

Reza looked uncomfortable under Theodore's gaze. "Uh. Hmm. It's a good question, sir. I gather you want Gabriel to be able to leave the slipstream already past the Dread defenses?"

"That's right. I want to take them by surprise. That way we get in and out before they can organize a defense."

"Well. You know. I mean." He paused.

Gabriel could tell he wanted to inform the General that it couldn't be done. That it was impossible. After all, it wasn't a new idea.

"I've done a lot of reading on this subject. There are three main problems with the concept. The largest is that while slipstream velocities are somewhat predictable, they aren't consistent. Right now we can estimate time to arrival with a certain margin of error, but to phase out in atmosphere doesn't have any margin. The disembarkation would have to be millisecond precise, as would the velocity calculations. One tick in the wrong direction, and you could come out in the center of the Earth, or shoot past it by a million kilometers."

"But the shorter the distance, the less error there is," Guy said.

"Right," Reza agreed. "Which is a second problem. There is a minimum distance to phase. Otherwise, you would never be able to turn the system on and off fast enough to arrive at your destination instead of shooting past it. Not to mention, you need to get up to slipstream join velocity in the first place."

"Even at a minimum distance there is still some error," Sarah said. "One thousandth of a millisecond could be the difference between life and death."

"Another problem is exit velocity," Guy said. "You'll be coming out of the slipstream at over twenty thousand KPH. A fighter will be torn to pieces by the sudden air resistance and pressure. Even if it could survive the exit, it would be a challenge to slow enough to keep from crashing into the surface."

"Reza, you told me back on Alpha that you were working on improved slipstream algorithms to better calculate velocities," Gabriel said. "Can you eliminate the margin of error?"

Reza started to shake his head before thinking better of it. "There is still some error. It's much, much less, but it isn't zero."

The assembly fell silent. Gabriel turned his attention to his father, who was sitting stiff and stoic, a thoughtful expression on his face.

"Well," he said at last. "It looks like y'all have your work cut out for you. I want to know what the margin of error is. I want calculations on the effects of air pressure and resistance at speed, and I want proposals on how to mitigate both as much as possible. We don't have the luxury of 'can't' right now. Is that understood?"

"Yes, sir," Reza said. Guy and Sarah nodded.

"You have twelve days. I know you won't let me down. Dismissed."

Gabriel stood with the others. He started to salute Theodore before remembering what he had said. "I'll see you on the bridge, Dad," he said instead.

Theodore nodded. "Take a day off, son. You've earned it."

Gabriel wasn't going to lay around and relax when he knew Reza and the Larones would be working nonstop. "I'll see you on the bridge," he repeated.

His father smiled. "Have it your way."

[70]

General Rodriguez, Diaz, and the rest of Donovan's t-vault team were already assembled by the time Donovan and Ehri joined them, with Ehri now wearing her original Dread clothing.

"Time is not on our side, Major," Rodriguez said.

"Yes, sir. I'm sorry, sir."

"It was my fault, General," Ehri said. "I-"

"It doesn't matter," the General replied. "All of you, follow me."

The group trailed behind Rodriguez as he moved away from the silo. Donovan hung back to walk next to Matteo, who looked lost and alone amidst the armed soldiers.

"Are you okay, amigo?" he asked.

"Sure. Why wouldn't I be?" Matteo said. "No sweat."

"I've got your back. Don't worry."

"I don't know if I can update the system to transmit. Hell, I don't even know what the system is."

"You'll figure it out. You've read every technical manual we have."

"That isn't saying much."

"I have faith in you," Donovan said, clapping Matteo on the shoulder.

"General, where are we going?" Diaz asked. "The exit is that way."

Rodriguez turned his head back. "There is an exit that way, yes. It's a little too open."

"Too open for what, sir?" Wade asked.

"You'll see, Corporal." He smiled. "I've been saving this surprise for a special occasion. I hoped I would never need to share it with anyone."

They reached the General's office. He circled his desk and stood next to the wall.

"I always figured there had to be another way out," he said. "Even though it wasn't in the schematics we found. I mean, you never know if you might need to evacuate, and exiting near a nuclear warhead seemed a bit stupid. I found this by accident a couple of weeks after we arrived here."

He ran his hand along the wall, feeling for something. When he found it, he pushed.

The solid cement wall suddenly gained a seam, and then it clicked and swung inward.

"Oh, man," Sanchez said. "A secret passage? Too cool."

"If there's another way out, why haven't the Dread found it?" Wade asked.

"And why didn't you tell the others about it?" Donovan asked. "They can use it if the Dread find their way in."

"Your mother knows about it, Major. She'll lead the others here and try to keep them hidden if things get bad. If the Dread are already coming into the base, it's likely they'll be killed if they attempt to leave whichever way they go. That's why we're trying to draw them away."

He brought them into the passage. It was dimly lit by emergency strips along the cement walkway, guiding them a hundred meters forward until dipping down.

"Where does it come out?" Donovan asked.

"You'll see."

Rodriguez started jogging, and the others picked up the pace with him. They followed the corridor nearly half a kilometer. Finally, they reached a heavy lead hatch that was hanging open. An earthy, damp smell permeated the tunnel, making Donovan nauseous.

Rodriguez slipped through the hatch, which led to a ladder.

"The ladder goes down into the sewers," Rodriguez said. "What you're smelling is fifty-year-old shit, garbage, and corpses. I think the stench is too much for the Dread, and that's why they never came this way."

"The bek'hai consider delving beneath the ground to be a sign of weakness," Ehri said. "They think it is degrading, even for a lor'hai. That is why they never search the sewers." She paused. "With the Domo'dahm's new orders, I don't know how much longer that will hold true."

"You learn something new every day," Rodriguez said. "But I guess when your enemy can't hurt you, you don't need to go soil yourself to hunt them down. In this case, it works out in our favor."

Rodriguez descended. The others followed. When he reached the bottom he pulled a wrist light from his pocket and slapped it on.

"The Dread have the right idea," Diaz said, holding her nose with her free hand.

Donovan looked around, feeling even more sick at the sight of the bloated, rotted, bodies that mingled with the rest of the debris in an inch deep layer of brown muck.

"We should have gone out the other way," he said.

"Come on."

Rodriguez led them another kilometer through the sewer to another ladder.

"I'll go up first and make sure it's clear. Wait here."

He climbed the ladder, reaching the top and then using his back to lift the heavy cover enough to see out. Once he was convinced it was safe, he slowly moved the cover off to the side and finished his ascent.

They joined him a minute later, standing in the back of a dark, enclosed space.

General Rodriguez made his way to the wall and pressed a switch. A single light faded on above them, revealing his secret.

"Is that a car?" Matteo asked.

They were in an old garage somewhere within the city. A bench of tools sat along the north wall. A hatch leading out was to the south. The west wall was intact, while the east had collapsed, destroying the rest of the building but managing to keep the single bay hidden.

Rodriguez smiled. "An old car. I think it was parked in here when the Dread came. Maybe they were working on restoring it? You can imagine my surprise when I happened across it."

"It has wheels," Diaz said.

"And an electric motor," Rodriguez said. "Fortunately, it was still holding a charge."

"What year do you think it's from?" Sanchez asked. "Twenty-two hundred?"

"Earlier than that. This thing was probably already a hundred years old when the Dread showed up. I've been coming here every week since I discovered the secret passage, trying to fix her up. It took me three years, but I got her running again."

The group circled the car. It had large, rugged tires and a boxy shape, and was covered in a layer of thick armor-plating.

"I can't believe you were coming here to work on this, sir," Donovan said. "Nobody else knows?"

"Major Sharma knows," Rodriguez said. "He made excuses for me now and then so I could come here. I had a feeling we would need it one day."

"How does it work?" Montero asked.

"I know how it works," Ehri said. "I have studied human transportation extensively."

"Ehri is driving," Donovan said.

"Major, I said I know how it works. I have never driven before."

"None of us have, except for the General."

"It's been a long time," Rodriguez said. "I always hoped I would be able to take her for a spin." He smiled sadly. "It's electric, so it won't give off too much heat for the first five minutes or so. After that, if there are any scouts around, they will spot you. Try to get as far as you can up the mountain before you have to abandon it." He reached into his pocket, withdrawing a small, gray block and a remote. "Explosives. After you ditch the car, blow it up. The heat will help hide you, and if you're really lucky they'll think you crashed and burned, or that they killed you themselves."

Donovan was reluctant to take the explosives. The General had spent so much time to restore the car, only to have to destroy it. It didn't seem fair.

"It's okay, Donnie," Rodriguez said. "It's a tool. A means to an end. Nothing more."

"Yes, sir."

"Now, get in. I'll get the door for you. Don't look back, don't slow down. Three blocks straight out, turn left, head up two klicks. You'll see the old highway there. Head over to it and follow it until you reach the tree line. Head into the trees and go as far as you can as fast as you can. Their mechanized armor will have trouble through the brush. The canopy should help absorb some of the plasma if they send fighters after you."

General Rodriguez took a step toward the hatch. There was no power to open it, so it would have to be pushed up manually.

"General, wait," Donovan said, approaching him.

"What is it, Major?"

"I hope I'll get to see you again, sir. If I don't, it's been an honor."

"The honor is mine, son. That goes for all of you. The bravest of the brave. You know what you have to do."

"Yes, sir," they replied, sharp and low, saluting at the same time.

Donovan retreated to the car, opening the passenger side door. Ehri climbed in behind the wheel to his left. She stared at the controls for a moment while the others piled into the back.

"You're sure you know how to work this thing?" Donovan asked.

She reached up and pressed the ignition. It didn't make any sound, but the dashboard lit up. She put her foot on the small, thin pedal on the right at the floorboard and depressed it slightly. The car inched forward. She moved her foot to the larger pedal and it stopped.

"Yes," she said.

General Rodriguez gave them the thumbs up, and then bent down and grabbed the small handle at the bottom of the hatch. He pulled hard, lifting it up and over his head, getting it just high enough for the car to fit below. He stood there, holding it while Ehri accelerated out into the fading light.

The General had said not to look back, but Donovan did anyway. He saw Rodriguez vanish behind the door.

"We're on our way," Matteo said, his voice shaking.

"Don't worry, bro," Diaz said. "We'll be there in no time."

A figure moved out into the street ahead of them.

A Dread clone, its plasma rifle already raised and ready to fire.

[71]

THE CAR BUCKED FORWARD AS EHRI SLAMMED ON THE BRAKES.

"What are you doing?" Donovan started to say, a sudden feeling of betrayal worming its way into his head.

The Dread soldier's shot was short, judged on where they would have been if she hadn't slowed. She immediately accelerated again, swerving to the left as the soldier adjusted his aim. The next shot grazed the side of the vehicle, leaving a scorch mark on the armor.

Corporal Wade aimed his rifle out the window, returning fire. The clone ducked back and away as they sped past.

"We made it, what, twenty meters?" Matteo asked.

"Relax, bro," Diaz said. "Ehri clearly knows how to handle this thing."

They crossed the three blocks in less than a minute, with Ehri making a hard left turn that threatened to tip the car. More Dread clones were appearing in the streets, answering the call of the first and trying to keep up with them.

"How the hell is the General going to get through this mess?" Montero said. "They're already crawling all over the city."

"We're still a klick out from home base," Donovan said. "It could be less crowded back that way."

The car was whipping past the ruined streets, with Ehri deftly steering it around the rubble. The large tires allowed them to clear large pieces of debris, bouncing the team around inside.

"Drive faster, drive faster," Sanchez said.

Donovan turned his head back to see her staring out the rear. He cursed under his breath as the mechanized armor turned the corner and took aim.

"Ehri, we've got a mech on our tail," he said.

Fire spewed from its arms, and the ground behind them began to explode, creating a cloud of fragmented pavement behind them while the machine adjusted its aim.

Ehri reached a street corner and turned left, escaping the strafing fire as it tore up their expected position.

"We're going the wrong way," Matteo said.

"Would you rather be dead?" Diaz asked.

Ehri turned right at the end of the block and immediately brought the car to a stop.

The road was blocked by a twenty-foot high pile of rubble.

"Back up," Donovan said, keeping his eyes to the rear.

"I don't know how," Ehri replied, looking at the dashboard.

"We can't just sit here," Wade said.

"You'll figure it out," Donovan said, opening the door and climbing out.

"What are you doing, Major?" Montero asked.

Donovan returned to the corner and peered around it. A squad of Dread soldiers had already covered the position, and the mech was still incoming. He aimed the plasma rifle and fired, the first few shots going wide before he adjusted for the lack of recoil. He let the base of the building absorb the return volley, and then fired back again, hitting each of the clones in turn.

They weren't even trying to hide. Not with the mech at their backs.

The car began to go backward, stopping next to him. He jumped in and they continued onward. They were turning right when he saw the mech reach the corner. It was too slow.

The vehicle jumped forward, accelerating quickly through the mess. Ehri steered like a pro, getting them toward the city center where a park had once rested. Now it was a wide-open space, one that they would have to cross to get to the highway beyond.

"Go as fast as you can," Donovan said, scanning the area. A line of soldiers was entering from the west. He could feel the ominous presence of the mech approaching from the south.

Ehri went even faster, letting the car hit the edge of a burned out vehicle and throw it violently to the side. Then they were up and over what had once been a grassy area, now turned to brown wasteland. The Dread mech appeared to their right. The first shots hit dangerously close, sending up a spray of dirt through the open sides before the remainder struck the tail end, the force of the projectiles it was firing hitting the armor rocking the car.

Then they were across, breaking the mech's line of fire and racing toward the highway. The lane ahead of them was clear.

"I can't believe we made it," Matteo said.

Donovan caught motion to his right. A dark blur launched toward them, hitting the side of the car and sending it sideways. Ehri's hands gripped the controls, fighting to keep it stable as it began spinning from the force. Donovan got a glimpse of a pur'dahm soldier rising to its feet and bringing its rifle to bear.

The car hit the side of a wall and came to a stop. A bright flash nearly blinded them as a plasma bolt struck the armor, sinking in but not through. A second passed through the opening and into the wall on the other side, so close that Donovan could feel the heat of it.

A return volley caught the Dread in the shoulder, burning through the armor and damaging its arm, which fell limp to the side and dropped the gun. The pur'dahm vanished a moment later, springing away as Ehri got them moving again.

"Wow," Montero said. "Nice shot, Lieutenant."

The car began picking up speed again, breaking free from the edge of the city and bounding up and across a swath of long-dead grass and trees. Donovan could see the highway up ahead, a long strip of decaying pavement that continued on toward the tree line leading up the mountain. Donovan watched their rear as they crossed the area.

"It stopped following," he said. The echo of rifle fire created a sudden burst of sound.

"The General," Diaz said.

"Godspeed to him," Montero replied. "And to all of them."

"Do you think we're safe now?" Matteo asked. "Maybe they think we're just part of the evacuation and not worth the effort."

"I doubt that," Donovan said. The pur'dahm must have seen that Ehri was driving the car.

Two black dots appeared in the distant sky behind them.

He knew the Dread fighters were headed their way.

[72]

"WE'LL MAKE THE TREES," EHRI SAID, KEEPING THE CAR MOVING faster and faster.

"I don't think so," Donovan replied.

The fighters were closing so quickly there was no way to outrun them.

"Diaz, we have to keep them off-guard."

He cradled the plasma rifle, leaning out through the side of the vehicle, facing the rear. The odds of hitting the fighters were ridiculously low, but if he could at least make them wary, it might be enough.

Diaz joined him on the opposite side, holding tight with her legs and aiming the weapon. They both began to fire into the distance, the plasma bolts piercing the sky, covering a thousand meters before fading.

Ehri swung the car left, nearly peeling Donovan from his perch. The fighters fired back at the same time, swooping down to send plasma bolts at them. They burned the ground next to the car, over and over as Ehri zigged and zagged before momentum carried them past and forced them to turn around and reset.

Donovan looked in at the Dread scientist, her eyes fixed on the road and her tongue sticking slightly out of her mouth in concentration. She had steered them away from the Dread's attack as if she knew when and where it was coming. Was that even possible?

The fighters were coming back. The trees were growing closer. The off-road path had to be close.

"Diaz," Donovan shouted, resuming his cover fire. Diaz did the same, their aim improving enough to force the fighters to wobble slightly. The next volley missed wide; the pilots' aim disrupted.

"Over there," Montero shouted. "The break in the trees."

Ehri turned her head, and then the wheel. They bounced off the pavement and onto the grass, the car jostling over the terrain toward the slope. The fighters were coming back for a third approach.

Then they were below the canopy, smashing through the lighter brush. Ehri had to slow to maneuver around the trees, and Donovan and Diaz ducked back inside before they were decapitated by wayward branches. They had covered a lot of distance in a short time.

Maybe they would make it after all.

They continued up the slope. Donovan tried to watch the sky, but the growth above them made it difficult to see. He was sure the fighters were up there, and he knew they would fire on them sooner or later.

The attack came. Plasma bolts rained through the branches, burning holes in trees and igniting the brush around them. They were tracking the heat signature; their aim pushed off by the interference. Each volley began to come closer and closer.

"I can't shake them in here," Ehri said. "The trees force me into an almost straight line."

A plasma bolt hit the front of the car, digging deep into the armor, which managed to withstand the attack.

"It's time to ditch," Donovan said. "Everybody else out."

"We're still moving," Matteo said.

"If we stop, we die for sure."

Diaz kicked open her door and grabbed Matteo's arm. "Come on," she said, throwing herself out and dragging him along.

The other soldiers opened their doors and jumped out, rolling along the ground. More plasma bolts came down, two of them hitting the rear of the car where the passengers had been moments earlier.

"Ehri, we need to jump," Donovan said. He shoved the explosive against the dashboard and took hold of the detonator.

Ehri pushed open her door and vanished, leaving him alone in the car. He waited for the next plasma bolt to hit before throwing himself from the car and hitting the trigger on the remote at the same time.

The car exploded calmly, the armor keeping it from sending shrapnel everywhere. It was enough to set the interior on fire, and blow through to the engine compartment. Thick smoke rose from the front, and two more plasma bolts immediately dug into it, damaging it further.

Donovan waited thirty seconds before getting to his feet and scanning behind him. The others were still on the ground, likely watching him. He looked up through the brush and didn't see the Dread fighters.

Hopefully, the enemy thought they were all dead.

He waved back and signaled ahead. The rest of the squad began to rise, heading in the direction he had motioned while merging into one unit. They started picking their way through the woods in tense silence, listening for any sign of pursuit.

There was none.

[73]

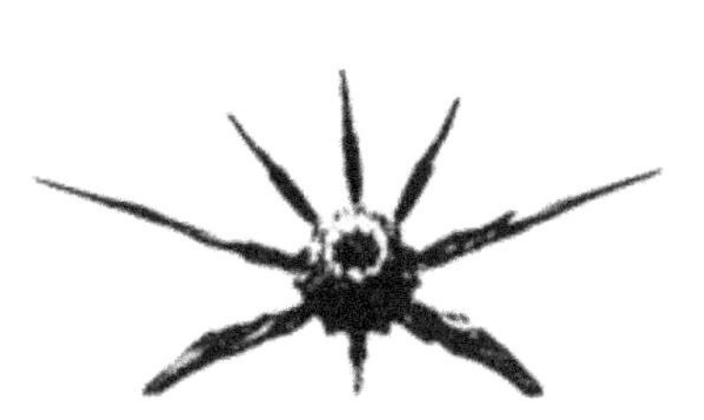

THE ECHO OF GUNFIRE HAD FADED TO NOTHING BY THE TIME Donovan and his squad neared the position where Matteo claimed General St. Martin's transmission had originated. They had climbed ten kilometers up the mountain in less than two hours, a pace that left them all tired and breathless.

"Do you think anyone is still alive down there?" Corporal Wade asked.

"They have to be," Sanchez replied. "No way General Rodriguez goes down like that."

No one else spoke. The words only made them more tense.

They traveled another half-kilometer before they reached their target.

A large building, half-buried beneath trees and moss and vines, the side of it appearing as if out of nowhere directly in front of them.

"I think this is it," Matteo said.

"What is it?" Diaz asked.

"I don't know."

Donovan approached the wall, pushing some of the leaves in front of it aside. He followed the parts he could see upward. It appeared there was a dome on top, though time had merged it with the vegetation.

"I think this is the side," he said. "We need to find the front."

They continued, staying close to the side and moving clockwise around it. It took another few minutes before they discovered the entrance in the form of a dark shadow beneath a line of vines and spider webs.

"Anyone have a light?" Donovan asked.

"I do," Matteo said producing a wrist light. He slapped it on and stayed close behind as Donovan pushed the vines and webs aside.

There was a soft light coming from somewhere inside, allowing them to see the long corridor the entrance became. The illumination was sourced through a window in a simple red door.

"There," Donovan said. He led them to it, running his fingers over the lettering etched into the glass when they reached it.

"Control," Ehri said, reading it.

Donovan looked through the glass. The light was brighter now, and was joined by others. Control was a small room with a monitor and touchpad, along with some other equipment he was sure Matteo would recognize.

He tried the door, finding it unlocked. He pushed it open.

"It's all yours, amigo," he said to Matteo.

"Thanks," Matteo replied. He entered and sat on the stool in front of the monitor, running his hand along the control pad. "This thing is old."

"What is it?" Donovan asked.

"It looks like a mainframe for something. I bet it was on low-power standby for all of these years, waiting for instructions that no one was around to give."

"Until now."

"Yeah." He explored the different screens while the others waited in anxious silence. "If I'm not mistaken, it looks like this building is connected to an antenna outside."

"I didn't see an antenna," Donovan said.

"I think it was on the opposite side."

"Does it transmit, or only receive?"

"I don't know yet. I'm picking through the pieces here." He moved through a few more screens. "Give me time."

"We don't have a lot of time."

"I know."

"Major," Ehri said. Donovan turned and found her standing outside of the control room. "You should come and see this."

Donovan left the others, following Ehri through a second hallway. Each door had a small window in it, and looking through he saw a series of rooms, dimly lit by backup lighting: a small room with a pair of bunk beds, a kitchen, a gym, and finally three adjacent offices.

There was a single book resting on the desk of the first. He pushed open the door and approached it. A layer of dust coated the cover, and he picked it up and wiped it off. Ehri stood behind him, looking over his shoulder.

The book was a plain navy blue with white writing. "Mount Tlaloc Deep Space Network Station 110," Donovan said, showing it to Ehri.

"Deep Space Network?" she said, reaching out and taking the book. She flipped through a few pages. "This is an operations manual for the base."

"Whatever the Deep Space Network is, it sounds promising."

"I know what it is, Major. The DSN antennas were originally installed to communicate with satellites and probes your people launched in the twenty-first century. As your technology improved and interstellar travel became possible, they were updated and increased in number to communicate with and track outbound ships. The bek'hai destroyed all of them during the initial invasion. Or at least, they believe they did."

"This one looks like it was out of use before the invasion," Donovan said. "The entire forest has grown around it."

"Which is likely why the bek'hai didn't know it was here."

"If what you're saying is right, then this base should be able to get a message out to Mars."

"Yes, Major."

Donovan couldn't believe it. Just when everything had started to look hopeless. Just when the head of the resistance had decided it was better to run and hide than to continue the fight. The one thing they needed most had been sitting right in their backyard, waiting for them.

"We need to tell Matteo."

They rushed back to the control room. Matteo was tapping on the control pad.

"I think I have this mostly figured out," he said.

Ehri placed the book on the desk next to him. "This might help."

"Deep Space Network?" Matteo said. "Does that mean what I think it means, amigo?"

"Let's hope so," Donovan said. He turned to Diaz. "We need to secure the area. Take Wade, Cameron and Sanchez and form a perimeter. Do not engage. If you see any Dread coming, send a warning."

"Yes, sir," Diaz said. "You heard the Major."

The other soldiers followed Diaz from the room.

"What should I do?" Colonel Montero asked. It was still strange to Donovan to give orders to someone who outranked him.

"Cover the door, sir. Help pass any messages in from outside."

"Of course, Major."

"This screen has a list of numbers on it," Matteo said. "I wasn't sure what they were, but knowing what this place is helps. I think they're coordinates."

"May I see?" Ehri asked.

Matteo rolled the stool to the side so Ehri could lean over and see the screen. "Yes, you're right. They're updating in realtime."

"Is one of them Mars?" Donovan asked.

Matteo scrolled the list. He went halfway before pausing.

"Si, amigo. One of them is Mars."

[74]

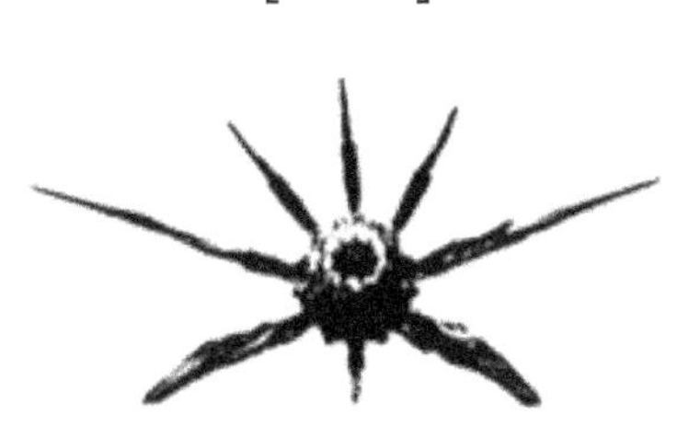

Gabriel was already on the bridge when Theodore arrived. Only fifteen minutes had passed since their meeting with the scientists, and he was pleased when he noticed that the color and health had returned to the General's face.

There wasn't that much for him to do on the bridge while the Magellan was in a static position near Mars. In fact, there wasn't much for anyone on the bridge to do except sit and wait. Even so, he felt an obligation to be there. He didn't want anyone to think he was getting off easy because he was the General's son. Maybe it forced him to push himself harder than he would otherwise, but he was okay with that. If his efforts motivated the people around him, all the better.

"General on the bridge," Colonel Choi said as the elder St. Martin rolled in. The rest of the crew stood and saluted him.

"At ease," Theodore said.

He got himself to the Command Station and transferred himself from the chair. Then he leaned back in it, taking a breath, before fixing his gaze out of the front viewport. They had shifted their position, moving closer to Mars and leaving the red planet visible on the port side, large and beautiful. There was nothing but empty space dead ahead.

"Systems report," the General said.

"All systems operating smoothly, sir," Sergeant Abdullah said. "She's as content as a kid in a candy store."

"Heh. Where did you hear that simile, Sergeant?" Theodore asked. "You ain't old enough to have ever seen a candy store."

"My father used to like to say it, sir," Abdullah replied, turning back to face him. "He told me it reminded him of Earth. He was only seven when the Dread came. Was my usage incorrect?"

"No, Sergeant. It was spot on. I was just curious. Carry on."

"Yes, sir."

The bridge fell into a comfortable silence. Gabriel sat back in his pod, mimicking his father by staring out the viewport. Was this the calm before the storm?

"Sir," Miranda said, spinning around from the comm station. "I'm picking up an unidentified signal on the X-band."

"X-band?" Theodore said, sitting forward on his arms. "That's a military frequency. Are you receiving?"

"Let me check, sir," Miranda said, operating her station. "I'm sharing with your station." Her voice was quivering. She glanced over at Gabriel, her surprise obvious. "It's coming from Earth, sir."

"I see that, Spaceman Locke," Theodore said. "Well I'll be. That sly son of a bitch, he's way ahead of me." He paused as the message continued to receive. "Damn it. Those alien couillons. It ain't going to end like this."

Gabriel looked back at his father, his pulse quickening. A message from Earth? How could that be? And what was his father muttering about?

The message must have finished. Theodore's expression gained an even higher level of intensity and focus.

"Colonel Choi," Theodore said. "Get me Reza and the Larones and bring them to the conference room."

"Yes, sir."

Colonel Choi left the bridge to find them.

"Captain St. Martin."

Gabriel stood and faced his father. "Yes, sir?"

"Contact Captain Kim and tell him to get the other pilots organized."

"Sir?"

"Don't question, son, just do."

"Yes, sir."

Gabriel returned to his station, using his control pad to contact Soon.

"Gabriel?" he said, answering the call. He sounded as if he had been sleeping. "What's up?"

"I'm not sure yet. I have orders from the General to prep the flight crew."

"Are you serious?"

"Very."

"Yes, sir."

"Captain Kim is prepping the flight crew, sir," Gabriel reported.

"Follow me, Captain," Theodore said. "Sergeant Abdullah, you have the bridge."

"Yes, sir," Abdullah said.

Theodore was in his chair by the time Gabriel reached him. He had to jog to keep up with his father as he sped down the hall.

"What's happening?" Gabriel asked.

"The resistance got our message. They already have a couple of alien rifles, if you believe that. Not only that, they've used them to kill a couple of the aliens."

"That's great news," Gabriel said. It was about time they had managed to do a little bit of damage against their enemy. "How did they manage to send a signal out here?"

"That's the bad news. The Dread are swarming their position, which may or may not already be overrun or lost. A small team led by Major Donovan Peters traced the source of our message back to an old Deep Space Network station of all things. Hah. They used it to transmit out here. They want to organize a pickup."

"It's ten hours back to Earth," Gabriel said, his earlier misgivings about landing on the surface lost in the moment. "Can they last that long?"

"No. Not now. They had to burn the station's backup power supply to adjust the antenna position and get the message out. Not to mention, the motion is bound to attract the Dread."

"Which means they may be dead already."

"We ain't going there, son," Theodore said.

They reached the conference room. Colonel Choi and the scientists joined them less than a minute later.

"I don't understand," Guy said. "We just spoke to you."

"You remember all that stuff I asked you for twenty minutes ago?" Theodore said. "I need it now."

"What?" Guy said. "General, we can't possibly produce any kind of accurate information in less than twenty minutes. We need time to-"

Sarah put her hand up, cutting her husband off. "I thought we had twelve days?"

"Things change fast in war," Theodore said. "We've got one shot to get our hands on an alien weapon, but the only way we make it is if you get us to Earth in the next thirty minutes."

"Thirty minutes?" Reza said. "General, it can't-" Theodore flashed him an angry look. "Okay. I mean, my algorithm hasn't been tested, but we're far enough out we should be able to get it to work. I assume you want to bring the Magellan close to Earth, but far enough out that the orbital defenses won't start shooting at you?"

"No, Mr. Mokri. I want you to bring the Magellan in past the orbital defense ring."

"What?" Reza and Gabriel both said at the same time.

"General, that's suicide," Guy said. "You'll kill every one of us."

"Maybe I will. Mr. Mokri, what's your margin of error?"

"I'd have to check, sir."

"Guess."

"Plus or minus one hundredth of a second?"

"A slipstream ride from here to Earth will take less than two seconds," Guy said. "That's more than enough to throw the position completely."

"I can get it to one ten-thousandth if I can run the calculations," Reza said.

"You can not," Guy replied.

"Yes, I can. General, I'm sure I can. I have an idea."

"That's the spirit," Theodore said. "Go do what you need to do."

"Yes, sir." Reza turned and ran down the hallway toward his quarters.

"General, this isn't going work," Guy said.

Theodore glared at Guy, opening his mouth, ready to explode.

"Guy, we're doing this one way or another," Gabriel said, interrupting. "Two seconds is too fast for a human to start and stop the QPG. We'll need to automate the shutdown."

"Me? I'm not a software engineer."

"Then go back to your room and get out of my face," Theodore said. "I thought you were coming around to our way of thinking, but I guess you're just a yellow-bellied couillon after all."

"I can do it," Sarah said. "But I need full access to the ship's computer."

"You can use the Command Station. Access code is 7-2-4-8-9-1-5-6. Can you remember that?"

"7-2-4-8-9-1-4-6," Sarah repeated. "I've got it."

"You're a smart cookie. Be careful with Maggie, Mrs. Larone. She's a delicate flower."

"Yes, General." She eyed Guy angrily before rushing from the room.

"Captain, head on down to the hangar and prep your squad. If we survive the slip, you'll be launching directly into the thermosphere."

"And then what, General?" Gabriel asked.

"One of your team needs to touch down on top of Mount Tlaloc in what used to be Mexico. You probably flew over it on your pass. Collect the alien rifle from the ground team and get the hell out of there. The rest of the squad runs interference."

"Interference? We don't have any firepower."

"I don't care how you do it, Captain. Ram them with your fighters if you have to. We need to get that weapon back to the Magellan."

"And then we need to get the Magellan away from Earth."

Theodore smiled. "You let me handle that, son. I beat those bastards once, and I'm damn well going to do it again."

[75]

"Did it work?" Donovan asked.

"I think so," Matteo said, turning away from the now dead computer.

It had taken nearly twelve hours for Matteo and Ehri to get the transmission sent. The complexity and age of the system had been a challenging barrier to overcome, even with the help of the operations manual. On top of that, their first attempt to reposition the antenna to Mars' azimuth had been met with total failure, as a frayed wire connecting the station to the parabolic transmitter caused the commands to die silently.

The two of them had eventually figured it out, and the message had been sent.

He could only pray that it would be received and acted on.

"Let's round up the rest of the squad," he said. "We need to be out of here and up the mountain to the rendezvous point."

"Do you think the Dread noticed?" Matteo asked. "The antenna wasn't exactly quiet."

They were lucky it had moved at all with nearly one hundred years of vegetation attached to it.

Donovan glanced at Ehri, who shrugged. "I don't know. Anything is possible, which is all the more reason not to linger."

They abandoned the control room, heading for the exit. Colonel Montero was standing against the wall there, staring out into the night.

"Major," he said when he saw Donovan. "Success?"

"Yes."

"Excellent."

Donovan put his fingers to his mouth and blew softly. A reply came a moment later. Then another. Then another.

"Only three," Montero said.

Donovan made the signal again. Again, three whistles in reply.

"Why aren't there four?" Matteo asked.

A plasma bolt lit the night, a red flash that struck Colonel Montero in the chest, sending him flopping backward and to the ground.

"Mierda," Matteo said, ducking back into the building.

Donovan shoved Ehri against the wall, scanning for the source of the shot. No others followed.

"They're on to us," Donovan said. "Damn it." He put his fingers to his mouth and blew a new signal, warning the others. He saw a flash in the trees to the north. Who had gone that way? The echo of rifle fire confirmed the position was under attack.

"We can't stay here, Major," Ehri said.

"I know. We have to get up the mountain."

"What about the others?" Matteo asked.

"They'll follow if they can."

He stuck his head out from the entrance, trying to scan the trees in the darkness. "Their soldiers can see in the dark. Can you?"

"Better than you, but not like them," Ehri replied.

"Do you see anything?"

"No."

"Come on."

He stared out of the building, keeping the Dread plasma rifle raised and ready. He only made it a single step when he heard a branch snap to his left. He backpedaled just in time to regain the cover as a plasma bolt seared into the wall.

"We're pinned down," he said. The soldier had vanished into the woods again, taking advantage of its superiority in the dark.

"We can't stay here," Ehri repeated. "They'll send a fighter to blast this building to dust if the lor'hai can't root you out."

"I don't suppose we can reason with them?"

"No. They haven't been exposed to freedom the way I have. They won't understand it. Not yet."

"So, what do you suggest?"

"We have to make a run for it."

Donovan looked back at Matteo. He was pressed against the wall, his face pale.

"Matteo, are you with me, amigo?"

Matteo didn't answer.

"Matteo? Come on, bro. You need to snap out of it."

More gunfire sounded from the east, and the sky flashed again. The shooting stopped. They were being picked off one at a time.

"Matteo?" Donovan said, grabbing his arm. "I don't want to have to leave you here."

Matteo's eyes shifted. "Donovan?"

"Come on, amigo. It's time to run."

"I don't want to die."

"Stick with me, you won't die. I promise. Okay?"

"Okay."

Donovan inched to the edge of the doorway again, looking out into the darkness once more. He jutted his neck out once more, peering through the opening.

A bright flash ahead of him caused him to duck back, but nothing hit the wall.

He looked out again. Diaz ran to the doorway.

"You're clear, Major," she said.

"The others?"

She shook her head. "I don't think so. I saw Wade get hit. I nailed the bastard who killed him."

He would have time to mourn his people if he survived.

"Fast feet, eyes open," he said.

"Yes, sir."

They sprinted from the doorway, into the trees and away. Branches slapped Donovan's body as he barreled in front of the remainder of his squad, absorbing the blows with the alien cloth. The drop point was five kilometers up the mountain. General Rodriguez had chosen the spot because they could reach it on foot and because there was a small plateau where a starfighter could likely land. It was fairly close. Right now, it seemed impossibly far.

Not that it mattered. It would be nearly ten hours before General St. Martin would be able to reach them from Mars. They had to stay in the area, which meant there was no way to lose the Dread soldiers.

They had to fight, but how? The enemy could see them, but they couldn't see the enemy.

He tried to ignore the cold truth of their situation, but it began creeping through him, a chill that started at his chest and started working its way outward.

They were going to die.

Worse, they were going to fail.

[76]

"This is Leader One. Fighter Squadron Alpha, sound off," Gabriel said.

"Alpha Two, standing by," Captain Kim said.

"Alpha Three, standing by," Lieutenant Ribisi said.

"Alpha Four, standing by," Second Lieutenant Bale said.

"Alpha Five, standing by," Second Lieutenant Polski said.

Gabriel tapped his control pad. "Fighter Squadron Alpha is standing by, General."

"Roger," Theodore replied. "Hold position and prepare for launch."

"Roger."

Gabriel looked out at the bare metal walls of the launch tube he and his fighter had been placed in. The rest of the squad was arranged in the other four tubes on either side of his, part of the half dozen that lay on each side of the Magellan. He wished he could see into space from where he was. He wasn't claustrophobic, but riding blind when he was used to being in control was making him a little tense.

It had taken Reza almost an hour to return to Theodore with his calculations and an updated slip algorithm that he swore was almost error free, with the important word being almost. Reza had started to try to tell the General that perfection was impossible, but had stopped himself before he got in trouble. Instead, he had turned the algorithm over to Sarah Larone, who used the Command Station to make the changes to Maggie's software. Between that untested math and the better half of the Larones' untested hack into the QPG controls, Gabriel figured there was a one percent chance or so that they would even survive the entry and exit from the slipstream.

And that was being generous.

Even so, he was able to hold on to a certain calm. Either it was all going to end, or perhaps something new would begin. A chance to fight back against the aliens who had taken their world. A chance for humankind to rise up and prosper once more.

To him, it was a chance worth dying for.

"Stand by, Alpha Leader," Miranda said through his comm.

"Beginning acceleration to slip velocity," Theodore said. He had left the comm open so that the squadron could hear.

A soft hum rose in the launch tube as the main thrusters on the rear of the Magellan began to fire.

Gabriel reached down and clutched his mother's crucifix, bringing it to his lips and kissing it. He closed his eyes, thinking of the picture of her that he had grown up with. "We're keeping our promise, Mom," he whispered. Then he smiled. "I bet you always knew we would."

"Ten-thousand," Theodore said. "Maggie, prepare the QPG."

"Yes, General," the computer said.

"Fifteen-thousand," Theodore said. "Get ready."

Gabriel lowered the crucifix, moving his hands to the fighter's control sticks. The slip was going to be short. Shorter than should even be possible. Shorter than might be possible. They were fortunate there was even a current to carry them.

"Eighteen-thousand," Theodore said. "Maggie, darlin', you know what to do."

The ship shuddered slightly as the QPG was engaged, beginning the process of phasing the starship into slipspace. Gabriel breathed in, finding that breath caught in his throat.

"One one-thousand, two one-thousand," he counted in his head.

"Launch Alpha Squadron," Theodore barked crisply.

"Launching," Miranda replied.

Gabriel was shoved back in his seat as the fighter was rocketed forward through the tube. They were still alive, which meant the slip had been successful. He wouldn't know if they had come out as intended until he reached open space.

He remembered to breathe out.

The fighter burst from the side of the starship in unison with the rest of the squadron. Earth was directly ahead of them. The Magellan was already yawing to allow them an easy departure into the atmosphere.

"I can't believe he did it," Soon said over the comm.

"Stay focused," Gabriel replied. "Bring weapons online."

"They won't do anything," Ribisi said.

"Bring them online," Gabriel barked.

"Yes, sir."

They hit the atmosphere, blinding heat pushing off the front of the fighters as they descended. The Magellan lumbered behind them, crossing the planet just out of reach of the gravitational pull, safely behind the net of deadly satellites.

"Follow my lead," Gabriel said. "If anything happens to me, you have to get down and retrieve the weapon."

"Yes, sir," the pilots said.

They continued to descend, coming in hard and fast. The sun was on the other side of the planet, leaving it draped in darkness as they burst into the sky. The Dread had no time to prepare for them. There was no advance warning from the outer defenses. The squadron raced across the landscape, headed for the mountain.

Ten seconds passed. Twenty. The mountain came into view ahead of them, lit only by the multitude of stars and outlined on Gabriel's HUD.

"Cut throttle. Form up, pattern bravo. Eyes open."

He slowed his fighter. The mountain was approaching in a hurry. Even in the dim light of the stars he could see the line of downed trees where the two Dread fighters had crashed. It looked like they had managed to get airborne again.

"Alpha Leader, are you seeing what I'm seeing?" Bale asked.

He wasn't. "What do you have, Alpha Four?"

"The mountain, sir. The western side. It doesn't look like it's very far from the drop point."

Gabriel turned his attention to the area. He didn't see anything at first. Only the shape of the canopy in silhouette against the dark.

A sudden flash below the trees sent light rippling out and around. Three more followed.

"That looks like plasma," Kim said.

"It has to be the resistance," Gabriel replied.

"Alpha Leader, we've got company," Polksi said. "Two bogeys, headed our way from the direction of the Dread city."

"Probably the same two I sent into the trees once already. Alpha Four, Alpha Five, peel off and see if you can keep them distracted. Remember, they can't maneuver as well as you can."

"Yes, sir," Bale and Polski said, breaking from the formation and turning to engage.

"What about us?" Ribisi asked.

"Low and slow, Alpha Three. It doesn't matter if we make it to the drop zone if the rebels don't."

[77]

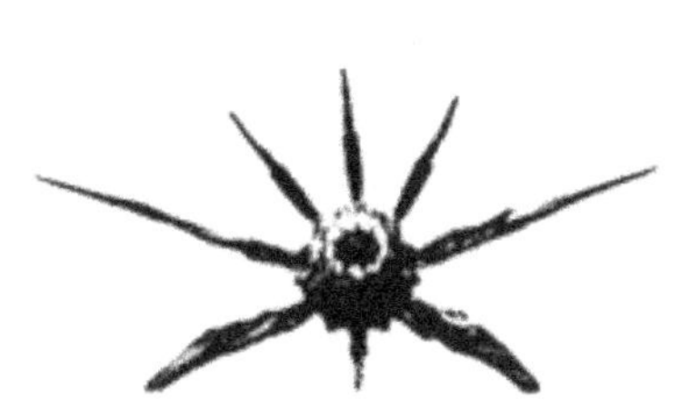

DONOVAN GRABBED MATTEO'S SHOULDER, PULLING HIM TO THE side and behind a tree as a bolt of plasma pierced the spot where he had been standing.

"You can't come out from cover like that, amigo. You're going to get yourself killed."

Matteo looked up at him, his eyes glazed over with fear.

They had been making a slow but steady retreat from the Deep Space Network Station to the pickup site, backing toward it while trading fire with the Dread clone soldiers. The battle had started fairly intense, but at this point it was becoming tedious. Donovan had been hoping Matteo would get used to it after he didn't get hit with the first three hundred or so rounds. He couldn't believe his friend was so skittish.

"We can't keep this up," Diaz said, leaning against the trunk of the tree next to Ehri. "We're going to kill our guns before we can hand one over."

"I think we're almost there," Donovan said. "It can't be more than another half-kilometer."

Diaz leaned out, searching the night for the soldiers. "I think we have a break. Let's move."

Donovan grabbed Matteo's shirt and pulled him up. They raced as one unit toward the next line of trees a dozen meters ahead. Plasma bolts flew by, one of them passing so close to Donovan's foot that he felt the tingle as it burned.

They slipped behind the tree, with Diaz firing back as they did. Two shots to conserve power.

"We only need to do that about fifty more times," she said.

"We've already done it at least a hundred," Donovan replied.

"I want to go home," Matteo said.

"You need to man up, bro," Diaz said. "I can't believe my big brother is such a baby."

"Screw you, Ren."

"Shhh," Ehri said, silencing them. "Do you hear that?"

Donovan listened. He could hear the soldiers in the woods. That was nothing new. "I don't hear anything different."

"We need to move faster," Ehri said. "They're losing patience."

"How do you know?"

"Listen."

Donovan did. "I can't hear it, whatever it is."

"The trees are too thick for mechanized armor. They aren't too thick for pur'dahm hunters."

"hunters?" Matteo asked.

"Elite warriors. They organize in teams, and fight to the death for sport."

"So much for civilized," Diaz said.

Ehri didn't reply to that. "We need to move faster," she repeated.

"Okay," Donovan said. "Let's go."

"We aren't clear," Diaz said.

"It doesn't matter. If we don't make it-"

"Then what, D? What if we don't make it? General St. Martin isn't coming for at least another nine hours. Nine. We're going to be out of bolts way before then, and if we aren't it will only be because we're dead. I know you're being the strong commander, but you have to know that's true."

"We aren't dead until we're dead," Donovan said. "Now move it, Lieutenant. That's an order."

Diaz clenched her jaw, nodded, and got to her feet. "Fine."

They started to run. A hail of bolts pounded the area around them, forcing them back into safety.

"They're laying down suppressing fire to keep us pinned," Diaz said.

"We have to try again. We don't have a choice."

"I knew you were going to say that."

They prepared themselves a second time. They were just about to break cover when a series of rumbling pops echoed across the mountainside. He looked over at Diaz, who was looking back at him.

"It couldn't be," he said.

"Those were sonic booms," Ehri said. "At least six of them."

"Is he here already?" Diaz asked.

"We have to get to the drop point. Now."

The assumed arrival of the space forces gave them new energy. Donovan pulled Matteo up again, holding on as they made a run for it. He ignored the enemy fire at his back, focusing only on making it through the brush without tripping on a branch or a root. He had no idea how General St. Martin could have gotten here so fast, but they had to make it to the plateau. It was the only thing that mattered.

They kept going, slipping through the foliage and somehow managing to make it through without being hit. They covered fifty meters, then one hundred. Donovan's legs were burning, but he didn't dare stop. The fact that he was still alive was a miracle in itself.

They pushed through the trees and into a small clearing. It took Donovan a few seconds to realize he was standing on the plateau.

The pur'dahm hunters were already waiting there for them.

"That's why they kept missing us," Diaz said, pulling up short, her breathing hard. "They were herding us here."

Tense seconds passed as the two sides stood and stared at one another. Donovan glanced over his shoulder at the movement in the trees. A dozen clones spilled out behind them.

"I'll go talk to them," Ehri said.

"Why?" Donovan asked.

It was too late. She was already ranging ahead.

"Who speaks for you?" Ehri shouted to the pur'dahm.

They looked different than the other bek'hai soldiers he had seen. Their black armor covered every inch of them, encasing them in an impenetrable carapace. Donovan shifted the plasma rifle in his arms. It wasn't impenetrable right now.

"Buhr gruhmn. Orik dur Lorik."

"Speak English, Orik dur Lorik," Ehri said.

"I do not take commands from the lor'hai," Orik said. He reached up and tapped the side of his armor. It slid away, revealing his face. Tubes ran from his nose to the oxygen tank Donovan knew would be on his back.

"And yet you did as I asked," Ehri replied.

Orik's face twisted in anger. "I chose for myself. This is not your affair, Ehri dur Tuhrik. You have had your time to study the humans, as your Dahm wished, even though it cost his life."

"Four days? What was I to learn of them in four days?"

"You shouldn't have armed them with our weapons if you wanted more time. You shouldn't have let them kill Klurik."

"He wasn't one of yours."

"It matters not."

"The Domo'dahm promised me time."

"And you promised not to interfere."

Donovan stared at Ehri. She was speaking as if she had been planning on joining them. How could that be if their entry into the Dread ship had been an accident?

Unless it hadn't been an accident.

Had she manipulated the entire thing? It seemed impossible, but if they had been spotted scouting out the transmission site, it could be that she had arranged for the clone soldiers to attack in a way that would steer them toward the elevator shaft. It could be that she had seen them enter the ship, and had arranged for Tuhrik to leave his quarters at the same time they arrived.

"I needed a proper catalyst," Ehri said.

"The Domo'dahm did not approve it."

"He gave me approval when he allowed the study. Do what you must to learn what you must. Those were his exact words."

"The Domo'dahm have always been illogical to that face," Orik said. "I don't know what he ever saw in that human, to give her such favor. Her genetics weren't even compatible."

"I need more time," Ehri said.

"It is over, Ehri. The human base is destroyed. The ones who were trying to escape are all dead."

Ehri looked back at them, her eyes apologetic. Donovan shook his head, silently pleading with her not to turn them over to the Dread.

Diaz reacted differently, whipping the plasma rifle up. "You alien bitch," she said. "We trusted you."

The pur'dahm raised their weapons on the other side of the plateau, five rifles all pointed at Diaz.

The entire clearing erupted.

[78]

Gabriel squeezed the trigger, loosing pulse after pulse of ions at the line of Dread soldiers standing near the far side of the plateau, while a similar assault tore at the clone soldiers standing behind the rebel fighters. Captain Kim and Lieutenant Ribisi's attacks were more effective than his, the ions shredding both the stone around the clones and the clones themselves, sending them sprawling in sprays of blood and gore.

The armored Dread weren't completely immune, the ions still powerful enough to push at them, knocking them off-balance and causing them to fall.

Then he was past, shooting by the drop point and making a tight vector to come back around again. He didn't know if their intervention would be enough to give the resistance the upper hand. If he was quick enough, he could knock the Dread soldiers back a second time.

"Alpha Leader, this is Alpha Four. We just lost Alpha Five."

Gabriel felt the wrench in his heart at the sudden news.

"I could really use some help back here."

"Alpha Two, pick up the slack for Alpha Four," Gabriel said.

"Yes, sir," Soon replied, breaking away.

"The enemy assholes are up again, sir," Ribisi said.

"Then we knock them down."

He dropped back toward the clearing, getting visual on the alien fighters. They had reassembled, spreading apart to minimize the chance of being hit. Half of them were turning their weapons to the sky while the other half were aiming for the resistance soldiers. The one who had moved ahead of the rest was on her stomach between the two sides. He didn't know if she were dead. Had they hit her by mistake?

He fired the ion cannon again, the pulses cutting into the line of Dread soldiers a second time. Once more, they fell away under the weight of the assault, losing their aim. He saw a plasma bolt launch from the resistance side and hit one of the Dread in the chest.

"Alpha Leader, this is Alpha Two. We can't shake them."

Gabriel watched his HUD. All of the airborne targets were visible in it as red or green triangles. The greens were moving every which way, and the reds were managing to keep up despite their lesser maneuverability.

"Alpha Three, see if you can sneak up on them. The cannons may at least disrupt their aim."

"Yes, sir."

The final fighter moved away, leaving him alone to finish trying to clean off the mountain. He was running out of time.

He adjusted his flight pattern, setting up to make a third and hopefully final run.

[79]

Donovan pushed himself to his feet, quickly scanning the line of hunters ahead of him. They were recovering from the starfighter's second approach, preparing to attack once more.

He ran toward Ehri. She was lying face down and motionless in the center of the clearing. Was she dead? Why was he running toward her, anyway? She had betrayed them. She had lied to them. She had used them like some kind of laboratory experiment.

Was he going to help her or make sure she really was gone?

Motion from the other side alerted him to the Dread soldier who had gotten back up and was now running toward Ehri as well. The one she had called Orik. Donovan fired his plasma rifle, the poorly aimed shots going wide. Orik did the same, his targeting equally poor.

It was a race to reach her. He didn't know what the Dread was planning to do with her. What he did know was that he wanted to be the one to decide her fate. He pushed himself to run faster.

Orik's shots were getting closer. His return fire was still no good, and he was just too damn slow. He wasn't going to make it.

The pur'dahm reached Ehri as Donovan came to a stop, intending to retreat. He had forgotten about the rest of the Dread soldiers in his desperate run, and now he looked further ahead. Only three were still moving, keeping a low profile and shooting back at Diaz, who was covering him. He started adjusting his aim again, a sudden sense of hopelessness overwhelming him. He had been reckless. Careless. Orik stood over Ehri, the bek'hai's rifle already trained on him.

A hand reached up from the ground. Ehri rolled over, grabbing the pur'dahm's wrist and pulling it down, bringing it into her other hand and continuing to yank on it as she shifted. The hunter was brought off balance, and she used his momentum to get to her feet, spinning like a top and kicking him hard in the side of his bare head. The blow knocked him back a step and pulled the oxygen tube from his nostril, and she used the chance to grab his rifle, turning it in her grip and firing at point blank range before he could react.

She shifted to face Donovan, pointing the rifle in his direction. How was she even able to use it?

A starfighter streaked past. It didn't attack.

"Ehri?" Donovan said. He dropped his gun, holding his arms out in submission.

The battle seemed to pause, as both sides stopped their assault while they waited for Ehri to resolve it.

"I'm sorry, Major," she said.

"Me, too," he replied. He didn't know why. It seemed appropriate.

An explosion echoed from the sky behind him. One of the starfighters, no doubt.

"I didn't mean for this to happen," Ehri said. "I only wanted to learn about humankind. To understand in a way that none of the others do."

"I know," Donovan said. "You started this. It's only right that you finish it."

He spread his arms wide. He wouldn't close his eyes. He wouldn't make it that easy for her.

"Thank you, Major," Ehri said.

"For what?"

"For showing me the truth."

He didn't know what that meant.

Not until she turned, spinning on her heel like a dancer, dropping into a crouch and firing one, two, three plasma bolts. Each one of them struck one of the pur'dahm hunters directly in the center of the head. They dropped in a neat line.

"I know I tricked you into coming for me," she said, looking back at him. "I wanted to learn about humanity, and in doing so, I realized it was the element of your kind that the bek'hai most sorely lack, and most desperately need. I said I would help you, Donovan. My touch is my bond."

Donovan smiled, remembering the tingling feel of her fingers against his.

"I shouldn't have doubted you," he said.

"Yes, you should have."

A soft whine rose to their left. They both turned in the direction of it, watching as the starfighter approached them.

[80]

Gabriel gritted his teeth as the sky lit up in the distance and Lieutenant Ribisi's starfighter vanished in a storm of flame and fragments. His pilots were dying, and dying fast. They had to finish this, now.

He was coming in fast toward the plateau, ready for one more assault. There were still a few of the Dread fighters trading shots with the resistance on the ground, and while he couldn't hurt them, he could stop their fire, maybe long enough that the soldiers could finally take them out.

He rocketed toward them, suddenly noticing that one of the Dread warriors and one of the resistance soldiers were both up and running, converging on the body in the center of the action. Who was she, that they both thought she was so important?

He angled the fighter, prepared to strafe the area again.

"Alpha Leader, if you're going to land, you need to do it now," Soon said, his voice desperate. "We've got more fighters incoming."

More? They couldn't handle two. Gabriel quit the attack, launching past the field and beginning a tight turn to get him to the plateau. He was going in, whether the fighting was over or not.

The fighter complained at the force of his reverse, the frame shuddering against the motion, the dampeners working to keep him from passing out. He felt it all the same, ignoring it as best he could. He pointed the fighter back to the plateau and leveled out, checking the HUD. Three more Dread fighters had appeared; they were at most thirty seconds out.

He began his descent, dropping hard and fast. He hadn't seen the action, but somehow the resistance force had won. The Dread were all motionless, and the male soldier was standing with the woman near the center of the area. He adjusted slightly to bring the fighter down right in front of them.

Their heads turned to look at him as he approached. He nearly crashed when he saw the woman's face.

Gabriel's heart began to pound, his mind trying to make sense of what his eyes were telling him. He finished his descent, tapping his control pad to open the cockpit before he had even touched down. The fighter bounced slightly before settling, and he unbuckled himself and jumped from the cockpit.

The two people rushed over to meet him. Two more were running their direction from the other side.

"Mom?" Gabriel said softly as they all coalesced. His hand had absently fallen to the crucifix, clutching it tightly.

The woman's expression changed, softening slightly. She was the spitting image of his mother. There was no doubt about that. He felt a tear on the corner of his eye. Damn it, that wasn't Juliet St. Martin. He knew the Dread used people to make clones. He could barely stand the thought of what that meant for his mother's fate. How would he ever tell his father about this?

"Captain Gabriel St. Martin?" the man asked.

Gabriel nodded.

"My name is Major Donovan Peters." He held out the alien rifle. "I brought you this."

Gabriel was numb as he reached out and took it, his eyes having trouble escaping the clone. He had never met his mother. He had never had the chance to see her in flesh and bone. Maybe she was a copy, but at least he could take this memory and juxtapose it with the others.

"Thank you," Gabriel said, forcing himself to keep it together. "We'll get this back to our ship and handed off to our scientist. How can we contact you, once we reverse the engineering?"

"The resistance headquarters are in New York. If you can, fly over there and send a message, just like you did before. Someone there should hear it."

Gabriel was about to say something to the clone. What was she doing, helping the rebels, anyway? How had they managed to get one of them on their side? There was no time to speak or wonder. The Dread fighters were closing in.

"I have to go," he said. "It was an honor to meet you, Major." He passed his eyes over the others. "It was an honor to meet all of you. You need to clear the area; there are more Dread fighters on their way."

"Yes, sir," Major Peters said. Gabriel didn't understand why. He was the ranking officer.

"Good luck, Captain," the clone said. "Be safe."

Gabriel felt his heart about to burst anew to hear her voice. He clenched his teeth and nodded, and then grabbed the wing of the fighter and pulled himself up. He sat down, placing the rifle between his legs, getting the starfighter back into the sky before the cockpit had sealed.

"Alpha Two, report," Gabriel said, firing his thrusters and launching away from the site.

There was no reply.

"Alpha Four, report. Bale, are you there?"

Again, no reply.

It didn't mean they were dead. He hadn't heard any explosions.

They had the alien weapon.

Now they had to escape.

[81]

Captain Kim and Lieutenant Bale weren't dead after all. He spotted them as they streaked upward, climbing vertically from a nearby river valley. The topography had interfered with both the HUD and the comm system.

A single Bat was rising behind them, taking a less steep vector as it tried to line up a shot.

The other Dread fighters were almost on them, their thrusters visible in the distance against the night sky.

"Alpha Squadron, this is Alpha Leader. We have the package. It's time to evac."

"Roger, Alpha Leader," they replied.

"Did you see? We managed to dunk one," Soon said.

"Good work," Gabriel replied. "Let's break away from our new friends and get ourselves home."

"Yes, sir."

Gabriel changed direction, ascending in a vector that would put him into formation with the others as they climbed away from the planet. He checked his power supply, noting that he had burned more than half of his reserves. It was enough to get him back to the

Magellan as long as he didn't waste any more energy on the ion cannon.

The Bats started shooting, sending streams of plasma bolts toward them. Gabriel shifted the control stick, winding his way through the sudden rain. Bolts flashed in front of the cockpit, his onboard computer sounding off in both warning and complaint. He glanced to the left, to Captain Kim, who was managing to wiggle enough to keep the enemy off the mark. He couldn't see Bale, but her green arrow was still on his HUD. He hoped it would stay there.

They continued to climb, pushing higher and higher. The Dread couldn't ascend as quickly and began to fall behind. The growing distance caused them to intensify their fire, filling the air with so much plasma that Gabriel had no idea how they were avoiding it. Was it divine intervention, or just unbelievable luck?

Whatever it was, it ran out a heartbeat later.

His computer beeped in rapid pulses as he became blinded by the light of a plasma bolt and the starfighter started to wobble. He cursed, checking the HUD for a damage report.

Everything was still operational. The shot had grazed him.

"Alpha Leader," Soon said. "Gabriel. I'm hit. One of the cells is offline. I don't have the power to make it into orbit."

Gabriel looked over at the other starfighter again. It was trailing smoke, and there was a gaping hole in the fuselage.

"Yes you do, Alpha Two," Gabriel said. "Get in behind me and I'll cut the air for you."

Soon's fighter spun sharply, avoiding more enemy fire as he worked his way over. Lieutenant Bale tightened her position up as well, aligning next to Gabriel's wing. They were way up above the Earth now, and he could make out the shape of the Magellan silhouetted against the stars.

They were almost there.

"Alpha Two, what are your power readings?" Gabriel asked.

"Not good, Alpha Leader," Soon replied. "I'm reaching critical."

Gabriel checked his own levels again to compare. He had nearly drained the primary cell, but the secondary was still at half. "You can make it, Soon. Hang in there."

A plasma bolt flashed by, crossing within a meter of the cockpit. The Bats had fallen back. Not far enough.

"Alpha Leader, I'm turning around," Soon said.

"You'll make it," Gabriel repeated.

"No. I won't, and when I run out of power I'm going to fall back to Earth. I'd rather land than crash, and maybe I can draw your tail away. At the very least I can disrupt them and help you escape. Anyway, I'll hook up with the resistance if I can. At least I'll get to spend some time planetside. It looks incredible, even if the Dread are ruining the view."

Gabriel was going to try to argue. He decided against it. Soon had made up his mind, and was already decelerating and rolling the fighter over.

"Damn it, Soon," Gabriel said. "Be safe down there. We'll be back for you. I promise."

"I know you will, Captain. I'll be waiting for you. Tell Daphne I'll be waiting, too, and that I love her."

Gabriel tightened his jaw. "I will."

He watched the fighter in the HUD, accelerating back down toward the Bats. It didn't matter if they collided with him or angled out of the way, as soon as they broke off the chase he and Bale would escape.

The Dread ships parted to allow Soon through, realizing that it was more efficient than being knocked off course in a collision. Even so, they lost nearly a kilometer of ground in the few seconds the evasive maneuvers took.

Gabriel looked forward again. The Magellan was looming large ahead of them as they plowed into the thermosphere, climbing higher and faster. The enemy fire had finally started to ease, and they would be home safe with the Dread weapon in less than a minute.

Without Captain Kim.

Without Lieutenant Ribisi.

Without Second Lieutenant Polski.

Gabriel was used to losing his friends and comrades. So many had died skirting the atmosphere to communicate with the resistance. Seeing it happen felt so much worse. It made it more personal. More painful. He could only imagine what the people on the ground were experiencing.

He glanced down at the Dread plasma rifle.

Not for much longer.

The two remaining fighters cleared the remainder of the atmosphere. General St. Martin's voice carried crisply through their comm systems as soon as they did, breaking protocol by not waiting to be hailed.

"Welcome back, son. What's the verdict?"

"We have the alien weapon, sir," Gabriel said. For all his upset over the deaths of his wing mates, he couldn't help but feel proud of what they had accomplished. All of them.

"I knew you would," Theodore said. "What about Kim, Ribisi, and Polski?"

"Ribisi and Polski are dead, sir. Captain Kim's fighter was damaged, and he was forced to land."

"I'll say a prayer for their souls. Soon is still alive?"

"I hope so."

"He's a good man. He'll survive. Hangar B is open. Bays One and Two."

"Yes, sir."

Gabriel leaned his head back in his seat, closing his eyes for a moment and sending a quick prayer into the universe, that Ribisi, Polski, and all the others would have a peaceful and happy eternity. Then he vectored his fighter to the waiting hangar, guiding it smoothly into the open bay.

He had done his part.

The rest of it was up to his father.

[82]

DONOVAN STOOD AT THE EDGE OF THE PLATEAU AND WATCHED the sky as Captain Gabriel St. Martin's fighter rose into it and raced away. His eyes did their best to follow the small glow of the ship's thrusters through the night, finding it difficult with the twinkle of the stars behind it.

Ehri stood next to him in silence, while Diaz and Matteo sat on the ground where the starfighter had been a moment earlier. Matteo had his head in his hands. He was ill from all of the violence. Diaz was trying to comfort him.

"Why did you do it?" Donovan asked without looking.

"I told you why when we met," Ehri said. "All of those words were true."

"What wasn't true?"

"The decision wasn't spontaneous. I spent weeks devising a plan to lead one of you to our ship. The water was the most challenging part. The bek'hai cannot control the weather."

"You set me up to kill your Dahm."

"Yes."

"Why?"

"He was old by drumhr standards. He was one of the first

successful splices. The Domo'dahm, the previous one, gave him fifty years, and he had seen forty-eight."

"He was going to die soon anyway, so he sacrificed himself for your plan?"

"Yes."

"You spoke about the Domo'dahm as if you know him personally. How?"

"I am a clone of his heil'bek." She paused. "It is a difficult word to turn into English. It is similar to a significant other, but that meaning is imprecise because the bek'hai do not take mates. Perhaps best friend is more appropriate? I am unsure. As I told you, we all have our own personalities. He always said that mine was most similar to hers. It allowed me to persuade him to approve my study."

Donovan knew she had to be talking about Juliet St. Martin. The question was, did she know? "Did you know the human woman you're a clone of?"

"No. I never met her."

He wondered if he should tell her. Was there any value in it?

"I've always found your kind fascinating," she said. "I wanted to walk among you from the day I emerged. I wanted to understand how any intelligent life could continue with such tenacity and persistence in the face of elimination. I told Orik that four days were not enough, but in truth it took only hours for me to discover those answers. Once I had, I found that I did not want to leave. As I told you, for all of the freedom the Domo'dahm allowed me because I reminded him of his heil'bek; before I came with you I had never been free."

Donovan was silent as he scanned the sky. He could see the flashes of light high above them, the Dread giving chase to Captain St. Martin and his team. He wished there was some way, any way that he could help.

He finally turned to face Ehri, looking her in the eye.

"Is there anything else you weren't completely honest about?" he asked. "Maybe like how you're able to use that weapon."

Ehri was still holding Orik's plasma rifle. She shifted it in her hand. "The hunter's rifles are not biologically secured. It is a point of pride for them to risk being killed by their own weapon."

Donovan glanced over at the dead hunters further back on the plateau. Each of them had been carrying one of the guns. "Even if it means us humans have a better chance of fighting back?"

"Especially because of that. They believe that if you can defeat them in battle, then you deserve what you have earned."

"Did you hear that, Diaz?" Donovan asked, looking back at her.

She glanced up at him, but didn't speak. He could tell by her face she was both worried about Matteo, and still angry at Ehri, even though she had saved their lives in the end.

"There is one other thing," Ehri said.

"What is it?" he asked.

"I know how to fight."

"I noticed."

She smiled. "I studied under Klurik for many years. That is how we knew one another. At one time I thought he might ask me to be his heil'bek. Instead, he turned his back on me because I am lor'hai. I told Diaz to wait in the back and take him by surprise. You would not have defeated him any other way."

Donovan was about to respond when a soft rumble rippled across the landscape. The ground started to shake a moment later. He returned his attention up and out. The flashes of light were gone. He scanned the forest, looking for incoming mechs.

He didn't see any.

Ehri didn't react. Instead, she pointed out toward the Dread city. "The Domo'dahm is worried about what we have done, Major."

Donovan followed her finger. He could see the lights rising in the distance. A portion of the alien structure had broken away and was slowly ascending.

"They can't fight that thing," Donovan said.

"No. If it catches up to them, they'll die."

They stood and watched it. Even Matteo lifted his head to see. It continued to rise, gaining speed as it gained altitude, a series of thrusters in the back leaving long trails of heat that brightened the entire sky.

"Donovan, look," Matteo said. He pointed to another point in the sky, to a small dark spot illuminated by the Dread starship's thrusters.

"It's one of the human ships," Ehri said.

Donovan watched the dot cut across the sky. It was growing larger, flattening out a bit and heading in their general direction. Smoke poured from its side.

"It looks like it's damaged," Matteo said.

"But not out of control," Donovan said, trying to guess where it would come down. "I think it's going to land."

"They won't survive ten minutes out here," Diaz said.

"Not on their own," Donovan replied. "We're done here, anyway. Let's grab the hunters' weapons and go help him out."

There was no questioning. No hesitation. They sprang into action, grabbing the unsecured Dread plasma rifles and vanishing into the woods.

This battle was over. Despite everything, they had won.

Now the real fight would begin.

[83]

"Sir, sensors are detecting an enemy ship incoming from the surface," Spaceman Locke said.

General Theodore St. Martin moved his hand across the Command Station's control pad, switching his main view to see below the Magellan's belly. The shape of the rising alien starship was obvious when contrasted against the blue marble below it.

"I knew it wouldn't be that easy," he mumbled. Gabriel had made it back safe with one of the Dread's weapons. It was only fair that he would have to find a creative way to get them all away from the planet in one piece.

"Maggie, sound the red alert," Theodore said.

"Yes, General," the computer replied.

The shrill tone of the alarm echoed in the hallway beyond the bridge. Theodore adjusted his position in his seat, using his elbows to sit up a little bit straighter so he could see his crew. He wanted a reminder of the consequences of failure.

He was responsible for every soul on this ship, and he had no intention of letting them die.

He took hold of the Magellan's controls, shifting again in an effort to get comfortable. He had taken a pill not too long ago, but he wanted another one or two to take more of the edge off the pain that was flaring out from the stumps of his legs. There was no way he was going to. They cut back on the agony, but they also made him sick and tired and unable to think.

Right now, what he needed most was to think.

"General, Lieutenant O'Dea reports that Captain St. Martin and Second Lieutenant Bale are safely aboard and Hangar B is sealed," Miranda said.

"Thank you," Theodore replied, immediately pushing the throttle forward. A soft groaning noise could be heard from somewhere in the ship, and the Magellan started to move out of its synchronous orbit. "Time to intercept?" he asked.

"Forty three seconds and closing, sir," Colonel Choi said. "General, how are you planning on getting us through the orbital defense satellites?"

"I'm working on that," Theodore replied.

He had been in this situation before. He could still remember it like it was yesterday, even though it had happened over fifty years earlier. The Dread had been coming down to the surface then, while he had been trying to escape it with nearly ten thousand souls on board. He had zigged and zagged and vectored the massive starship using every trick he knew and a few he had improvised, somehow charting a course through the rain of heavy plasma that was decimating cities around the globe. His ship had been the only one to escape, and yet he had never questioned the how or why of it. As far as he was concerned, it was the Will of God plain and simple, in restitution for stealing his bride from him and in a great desire not to see his creations completely wiped out.

He had always known that God would call him back here. He had always known a showdown would come. That knowledge was the only thing that kept him alive in the years that had followed the escape. It was the only reason he hadn't taken a knife or a belt to his throat after the accident that had taken his legs.

That, and Gabriel.

He had taught his boy to be strong, and he wasn't going to ruin that by taking the coward's way out. His life would end the way it was intended.

Going down fighting.

"But not today," he said to himself.

The ship was too large to steer through the viewport, so he focused his attention on the HUD instead, watching the position of the Dread starship as it grew ever closer, and taking note of the orbital defense ring above. The slip calculations Reza had done had been impressive in their perfection, getting them to the safe side of the satellites. He had told the crew he had an idea on how to get back out, but the truth of it was that he didn't. In part it was because there was a piece of him that hadn't believed they would succeed. In part it was because he had assumed he would think of something before the situation went critical. He had always been better under pressure. He was a sly old gator, and he had a knack for getting himself out of tight spots.

Except the situation had gone critical, and he was still struggling for an idea. He couldn't try to fight back against the Dread starship. Not without any weapons. He also couldn't outrun it. He clenched his teeth.

He had to think of something or they were all going to die.

The Dread's first shot across the Magellan's bow solidified that fact. It was made as a singular gesture of warning, a prelude to the real attack, set to begin at any moment. An attack that would tear the ship to pieces. It would happen more slowly with the extra armor that had been added to the old girl, but slow or fast, dead was dead, and he couldn't let it happen.

The starship shuddered, and something at one of the pods began beeping in a shrill tone.

"We're under fire, sir," Colonel Choi said from her station.

"She can take it," Theodore replied. "Can't you Maggie?" Even so, he adjusted his flight path, rotating the Magellan to give their attacker a smaller target.

The ship shuddered again from another hit.

"We have damage to a power conduit," Sergeant Abdullah said. "Deck 17. Seal door is closed."

Theodore shook his head. They were taking damage already? It shouldn't have been that easy.

Gabriel ran onto the bridge, pausing at the Command Station.

"Captain St. Martin reporting for duty, sir," his son said, standing at attention, holding to protocol in front of the others, even in the middle of an attack.

"Head on down to your pod, son," Theodore said, using his hand to wave him closer. Gabriel stopped next to him. "By the by, if you've got any ideas on getting past the orbital defense, I'm all ears."

Gabriel leaned over to see the HUD. He turned his head, putting his face level with Theodore's.

"I thought we were going to go out the way we came in?"

"What do you mean?" Theodore said. He shouldn't have taken that other pill. It hadn't helped the pain much and it was hurting his ability to think more than he realized.

"Reza," Gabriel shouted up to the scientist, who was sitting at one of the pods with a terrified look on his face.

Reza turned his head at the sound of his name. "Yes, Captain?"

"We need a slipstream. What do you have?"

The ship shuddered again. Another tone sounded from the engineering station, and Sergeant Abdullah shook his head as he tapped furiously on his control pad.

"I don't keep them in my pocket, Gabriel."

"Not the time for jokes," Gabriel replied. "Is there a stream running through the Earth or not?"

"Through the Earth?" Theodore said.

Gabriel looked at him. Theodore recognized that face. He understood the spark of anger in his son's eyes. He had been that way once, a long time ago when he hadn't been a crusty old coonass. When he had been able to think straight. He was losing it, he knew. His reflexes. Maybe his mind. Nothing was right anymore. Nothing was the way it used to be. He knew it by the fact that the answer was so obvious, and yet he had been unable to see it.

He wanted to both laugh at Gabriel's genius and cry at the loss of his own. Instead, he pushed Gabriel gently aside.

"Good man," he said. "I'm smelling what you're cooking."

The ship shuddered.

Theodore worked the controls to the starship, changing their course.

"You had better find me a stream, and you had better do it now, Mr. Mokri," he said.

Reza looked out the forward viewport, and then back at Theodore. "General?" he said softly.

The Earth had rolled into view ahead of them. Theodore continued to angle the starship toward it, pushing the throttle the rest of the way open.

"I said find me a stream, son," Theodore repeated. "Or we're going to make an awful mess on the surface of the planet."

Reza's face paled, and he turned to his station's controls.

"Maggie, prepare the QPG," Theodore said.

"No sequence has been input, General," Maggie replied.

"Nope, and it ain't going to be. Command override three nine seven."

"Command override accepted. Deploying QPG nacelles."

"You can't do this, General," Reza shouted, even as he continued his work. "You can't enter a slipstream inside a planet's atmosphere."

"Why the hell not?"

"You need to get up to join velocity for one," Reza said. "For another, the planet's gravity will make a mess of the stream path and pattern. We have no way to know where we're going to wind up."

"Space is a big place, Mr. Mokri," Theodore said. "As long as it ain't smashed into the ground, I'll take it."

"You don't understand, sir. The gravitational fields accelerate the stream. We could wind up too far from anything to ever get back."

The edges of the Earth vanished to the sides of the viewport. The long bow of the Magellan was pointed straight toward the planet while the Dread ship was on her port side, slowly rolling over to get its weapons aimed and fired once more.

"Stop complaining and start producing," Theodore said.

"Sir-" Reza said again.

"Get me a stream, damn it," Theodore roared.

The Magellan passed into the atmosphere. Theodore checked their velocity. Fifteen thousand kilometers per hour. They were almost there, but the planet's surface was rising in an awful hurry. They had seconds to escape.

"Got it," Reza said, sounding pleased with himself.

"Put them in," Theodore said.

"Yes, sir." Reza tapped his control pad. "Sequence entered and accepted."

They were falling ever faster, passing from the darkness into the great blue below. Seventeen thousand, eighteen thousand. The world was rising to meet them, opening her arms and preparing to take them in.

The ship began shaking violently, the air shoving against the irregular shape of the craft. It was intended that the suppressors would be used in gravity, not the main thrusters. Theodore had no idea if she was sturdy enough to hold together. He thought she was. He prayed she was. He pushed a little harder on the throttle, trying to eke out just a little bit more.

Nineteen thousand. Collision warnings began to sound, and Gabriel had to grab onto the back of the seat to keep from falling over.

"Son, if we don't make it," Theodore said. "I want you to know-"

"We're going to make it," Gabriel replied.

They were out over the ocean, getting so close that Theodore could almost see the outline of the waves below, the Magellan a meteor about to strike.

In that moment, his mind settled on a single instant from the past. The one where he and Juliet stood on a beach in Hawaii, the water up to their ankles as they gave their vows. It wasn't the church wedding she had always wanted, but they had decided they couldn't wait that long.

He closed his eyes, remembering the feel of her hands on his, her lips on his. Whether they lived or died was out of his control now.

He counted his heartbeats.

Thump thump.

Thump thump.

Thump thump.

Thump thump.

The Magellan became translucent, phasing into slipspace, her bow slicing into the water without breaking the surface, sinking like a ghost ship until she vanished entirely.

Theodore opened his eyes.

He was still alive.

All of them were.

2. WEAPONS OF WAR

[1]

THERE WAS NOTHING IN SLIPSPACE. NO STARS. NO PLANETS. NO dust. No light. There was only pitch black, pure and perfect in its simple depiction of nothingness. A place positioned somewhere outside of reality, where time and space changed meaning, and sometimes it seemed as if anything were possible.

Gabriel had flinched as the Magellan had reached the surface of the Earth. He had felt his stomach clench, his body reacting to his sudden fear and tension. He had thought that he was going to die. That everyone on board the starship was going to die.

He thought his father had failed him. Had failed them all.

And General St. Martin would have had Gabriel not reached the bridge when he did. He didn't have to think it. He knew it, as sure as anything.

The ship had made it into the aether, riding the waves of phased distortion through the planet and out the other side. Maybe his first thought should have been to jostle his father, to remind him to command Maggie to get them out of this place and back into realspace, to keep them from riding the crest too far, too fast. Maybe he should have given the command himself, and hoped the starship's intelligence would obey, even though he already knew it wouldn't. Maggie only listened to one person, and that was the General.

Besides, it was so peaceful here. So quiet. So calm. After the chaos and fury that had seen him escaping from the planet with one of the Dread's weapons only to nearly crash back to the Earth, he was anxious for the break and eager for the suggestion of possibility.

He welcomed this place outside of time where he could believe his mother was still alive, and his father was still fit for duty.

He wished at least one of those statements were true.

He counted four heartbeats. Five. Six. He wrenched himself from his inner dialogue, his eyes casting out around the bridge, to the men and women manning their stations, the same look of fear and surprise on their faces that he was sure was written all over his.

It had been that close.

"General," he said at last, remembering what Reza had said.

The Earth's gravity would intensify the strength of the stream, and in turn, would send them further, faster. The Magellan had means to sustain them, but not forever. And besides, they had woken the sleeping giant, drawn one of the Dread's massive, city-sized starships to leave its moorings on the surface and give chase. Maybe they had escaped. Maybe they hadn't. Either way, they had gained an advantage against Earth's usurpers that they had never held before. They had captured a weapon that could defeat the enemy's shields. A weapon that could damage them. A weapon that could kill them.

Retaliation, no matter what form it took, was inevitable.

"General," Gabriel repeated, loudly this time.

His father jerked as if taken by surprise. He was as lost in his thoughts as Gabriel had almost been. His eyes darted to Gabriel, an embarrassed expression crossing his wrinkled face. It vanished in an instant as he gathered himself. The fact that Gabriel had seen the emotion at all told him he wasn't wrong in his assessment that his father was losing it. Was it his age? The pills? A momentary lapse? He had been concerned when he saw Theodore bent over and vomiting in his quarters. Their near death had proven that the General's judgment was impaired. Hadn't it?

Could he afford to risk that he was wrong?

Could the crew?

The Magellan shuddered suddenly, a warning tone sounding across the bridge. It was a sound Gabriel didn't recognize, but he could tell by feel what was happening.

The ship was coming out of slipspace of its own volition.

"Maggie?" Theodore said softly.

"Slipstream velocity lost," Maggie said. "Quantum phase generator powering down."

The stars expanded in front of them until everything looked normal once more.

Except nothing was normal. Nothing would be the same. They had scored their first victory against the aliens who had stolen their home world. He had seen a clone of his mother among the rebels on the ground. He had witnessed a Dread gun cutting through Dread armor like cloth. They were alive.

Thank God, they were alive.

The bridge was silent as the starship came to a full stop. Nobody moved. Nobody dared to breathe. Gabriel stood next to his father, waiting for orders. He would have to confront him, he knew. He would have to challenge him on his lapse, and on the potential for future lapses.

Not now. Not yet. He was a good soldier and a good son. Some things were better discussed in private.

"Damage report," General Theodore St. Martin shouted, breaking the silence as he finally leaned back in the command chair. Gabriel caught the grimace of pain as he did.

"Data is still filtering in," Abdullah said, watching his screen. "We had a hull breach on Deck 17. The emergency bulkheads have sealed it, but we lost a power conduit. We won't know how that will hurt us until we have a better picture of our overall status."

"Understood, Sergeant," Theodore said. "Casualties?"

"None reported, sir," Spaceman Miranda Locke said.

"Only 'cause the old girl is four-quarters empty," Theodore said softly to himself. Gabriel still heard it. "That was close. Too damn close." He looked at Gabriel. "You saved all our bacon, son."

"General-" Gabriel started to say. Theodore put up his hand.

"I'm tired, son. Suddenly so damned tired. Came at me like a snake in the bayou."

"General-" Gabriel tried to speak again.

"Colonel Choi, you have the bridge," Theodore said.

"General?" Choi replied. "What about-"

"Captain St. Martin, I'll expect you to provide the Colonel with a full debriefing," Theodore said, ignoring her protest. He leaned forward on his hands again, his arms shaking from the exertion. "The rest of you, thank you for a job well done. Especially you, Mr. Mokri. For a civvie, you sure have a big set of balls."

"Uh, thank you, sir," Reza said.

Gabriel could feel the tension on the bridge, and it only grew as the General swung himself into his wheelchair and rolled away without another word.

[2]

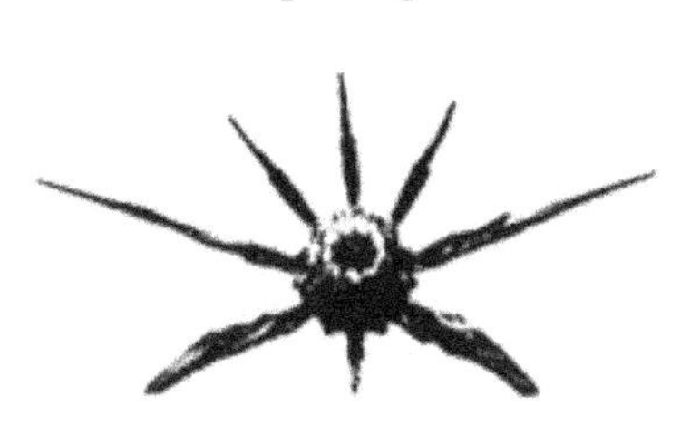

Gabriel looked at Choi. Her face was hard, her lips a taut, thin line.

"I should go talk to him," Gabriel said.

"No, Captain," she replied. "Give him some time. He's never been in this situation before either."

Gabriel looked back the way his father had gone. He knew Choi was right. Even so, it was hard for him to stand there.

"Colonel Choi, I've got an update from engineering, ma'am," Abdullah said.

"Go ahead, Sergeant," Choi said.

"According to Corporal Rogers, the blown conduit can be rerouted through one of the internal circuits, getting us back to full power. There's also some damage to secondary plumbing that is causing a loss to water reserves."

"What kind of loss?"

"Zero point three percent per hour at the current rate," Abdullah said.

"How long to patch it?"

"Three hours, ma'am."

"Not bad. Get on that first. Right now, water is more valuable than engine thrust."

"Yes, ma'am."

"Mr. Mokri," Choi said, calling out Reza. The scientist was sitting at his station, checking the star charts. "Do you have any idea what just happened, or where we are?"

"I think we hit a dead zone, Colonel," Reza said.

"Dead zone?"

"Yes, ma'am. There are areas in space the slipstreams don't cross. I'm still calibrating, but I think we're in one of them. It would have been easier to pinpoint if we had a target for the slip."

"Understood. Interrupt me whenever you have our position."

"Yes, ma'am."

Choi returned her attention to Gabriel. "So. Do you have it? The weapon?"

Gabriel nodded. "I left it with O'Dea. We'll have to bring Reza to take a look at it."

"It really works?"

"It does. I saw the ground forces take down armored Dread soldiers that my guns couldn't touch." Gabriel lowered his voice and leaned in closer to her. "There's something else. They had a girl there with them. I think she was one of the enemy's clones. They copied her, Vivian. They copied my mother."

Colonel Choi froze, her surprise obvious. "If they copied her-"

"It means they captured her. I know. As if things aren't going to be hard enough with Theodore. When he finds out about this-"

"You can't tell him, Gabriel."

"I have to. He's going to ask for news about her. You know he will. He almost cared more about Rodriguez updating him on her whereabouts than he did about recovering the weapon."

"It's going to break his heart."

"His heart is already broken. It's going to piss him off, make him irrational. He's already not thinking clearly."

"That's the medication."

"It doesn't matter what it is; he isn't thinking clearly. That's dangerous territory considering what we just did."

"I know," Choi said. "Like I said, you can confront him on that later."

"Colonel Choi," Reza said, standing at his station. "I have it."

"So where are we, Mr. Mokri?"

"There's some math involved here," Reza replied. "So the projection may be slightly off. I've had to recenter based on the position of Earth in relation to the rest of the known universe, and then estimate the wave speed based on the data collected by the QPG nacelles."

"The short version, Reza," Gabriel said.

"Uh. Right." He smiled. "About six hundred light years beyond Earth."

"Six hundred light years?" Sarah Larone said. "We were in the slipstream for what? Twelve seconds?"

"Thirteen seconds," Reza said. "We traveled approximately forty-three light years per second."

"Are you certain that's right? At that speed, we would be able to reach Calawan in less than two seconds."

"From Earth. Not from here."

Gabriel had been too busy to look out the viewport ahead of them. He did so now, staring out into the expanse of emptiness beyond. It was difficult to differentiate from any other part of space. There was a red dwarf star nearby, close enough to be a little more than another white dot against the black backdrop. Otherwise, there was nothing.

"It would still only take about twenty-two days," Choi said. "We have more than enough reserves for that."

"Yes, ma'am, that's true," Reza said. "There is one complication."

"What is that?"

"I'm scanning for streams, ma'am. As near as I can tell, there aren't any."

Gabriel forgot about the view. His head snapped toward Reza, as did every other head on the bridge.

"Excuse me?" Colonel Choi said, not quite sure she had heard correctly.

"I know," Reza said. "It seems impossible, but there's nothing."

"We came here on a stream," Gabriel said. "That means there has to be one in this area. Doesn't it?"

"That's not how slipspace works, Captain," Sarah said. "The paths aren't random, but they also aren't constant. Are you familiar with the tides on Earth?"

"Caused by the gravitational pull of the moon, sure," Gabriel said.

"Slipstreams are like the tide," Reza said. "During high tide, they'll extend further than during low tide."

"It's only been five minutes."

"For us, Captain," Sarah said. "Remember, slipspace sits outside of our conceptualization of time. We know a lot about how it works, enough that we can plot courses with some measure of accuracy, but only to a certain point."

"And we're beyond that point," Reza said. "It was nothing but insane luck that we were able to even find a slipstream to ride that was passing through the Earth. We should all be dead right now. That stream has crested, though. It will pass through here again, but without a point of reference, it may take weeks to figure out when that will be."

"What's the bottom line?" Choi asked.

"We took a calculated risk to escape the Dread the way we did," Reza said. "That part of it worked out for us, and we made it out alive."

"But?"

"But Captain, unless something changes, we're stranded out here."

[3]

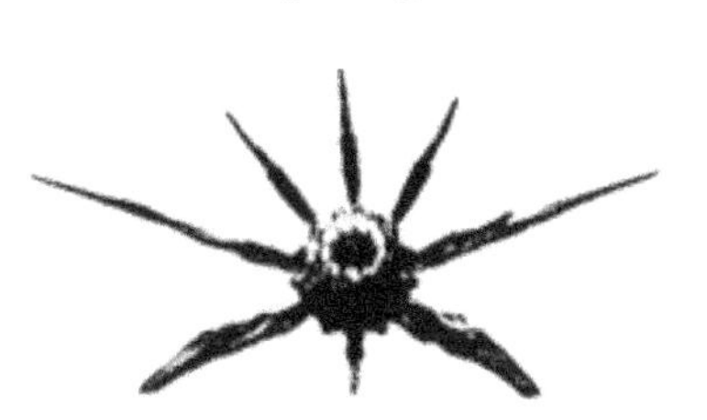

"It can't be much further," Major Donovan Peters said, pushing past another bit of low-hanging brush. His eyes drifted above him, to the wisps of smoke illuminated by the starry night sky. They had been tracking the fallen starfighter for the better part of two hours, making their way back down the mountain toward the area where they had seen it touch down in a controlled crash.

"Wait," Ehri said, grabbing his shoulder to slow him down. "Look."

She pointed through the trees, to where a large shape stood sentinel. At first, Donovan thought it might be one of the bek'hai mechs, before realizing it was too small. An armored Dread soldier.

Where there was one, there had to be more.

"I've got a clear line of fire," Lieutenant Renata Diaz said, hefting one of the Dread hunter's rifles to her shoulder. "One shot, one kill."

"At ease, Lieutenant," Donovan said. "We don't know how many more are out there."

Of course, the bek'hai had reached the site before them. They were on foot and tired, while their enemy had powered armor and genetically enhanced human clones to send out to survey the scene of the crash. Had they already found the pilot? Captured him? Killed him? They had moved as fast as they could to reach him ahead of the Dread.

They were too late.

Donovan motioned to Diaz. "See if you can find a good line of sight that way. Don't shoot until I do."

"Yes, sir," Diaz said.

"Ehri, you're with me. Matteo, stay low and out of sight. If you get in trouble, don't be afraid to use that thing."

Matteo glanced down at the Dread rifle. Donovan could see his friend's hands were shaking slightly, but the tech didn't complain.

"Okay," Matteo said. Then he took a few steps back to hide behind the brush they had just pushed past.

Diaz headed off to the left, vanishing into the woods a moment later. Donovan kept an eye on the Dread soldier, making sure it didn't notice the movement. It continued to sit motionless, watching whatever was taking place near the wreckage. Donovan was sure he could hear soft voices now, coming from that area.

He headed to the right of the Dread soldier, creeping slowly through the brush with Ehri right behind him. She was so close he could feel her breath on the back of his neck, calm and even. Did anything make the bek'hai scientist nervous? He doubted it.

It took a few minutes for him to get a better vantage point. He stopped when he caught a glimpse of the source of the wisps of smoke, the side of the starfighter where a scorched hole in the fuselage had burned through one of the thrusters and left it unable to climb out of the atmosphere.

"There," Ehri said, tapping his shoulder and whispering into his ear.

She pointed to the left of the fighter, to a small area in front of it. Two female clones were kneeling beside a man laying on his back. The pilot. They had pulled his flight suit down to his waist and were talking quietly to one another while they placed a bandage over his abdomen.

"What are they doing?" Donovan asked.

He continued scanning the area. A second armored Dread

soldier was standing perpendicular to the first, at the edge of the small field. A handful of clone soldiers stood in formation beside him. None of them seemed concerned that they might be attacked, or that they were in any danger. They had to know what had happened up on top of the mountain. They had to know their hunters had been defeated, their weapons falling into the rebel's hands.

Didn't they?

"He must have been wounded," Ehri replied. "The salve is similar to the restorative bath the drumhr use to keep their skin healthy. It will heal most of the damage within hours."

"Why are they healing him? Why not kill him?"

"Why do you think, Major? The Domo'dahm will want information about the ships. Especially where they came from. The bek'hai have been monitoring the activity for years, but were never concerned enough by it to seek out the source."

"Until tonight."

"If they escaped with the weapon, then yes. Until tonight. To use a human expression, the tides have shifted, Major. Yesterday, the bek'hai were invincible to the human rebellion. Now, they are not."

"Thanks to you, in part," Donovan said. "Those soldiers don't seem that concerned to me."

"They have grown complacent over the years. Some will take the threat more seriously than others, at least until you start winning more battles."

"Which I have every intention of doing," Donovan said, his thoughts drifting to his mother. Had the Dread discovered her and the children? Was anyone from their base still alive? "We can't let them take him."

"No."

"What about the female clones?" Donovan asked, putting his eyes back on them. They were nearly identical to Ehri, created from the same base DNA. "Are they a threat?"

"They can't be permitted to escape."

"Is there anything else you can tell me that might be helpful?"

"The armored soldiers. Aim for the helmets. Severing the connection to their oxygen supply will kill them. Be careful not to hit the tanks. At this distance, you'll wind up killing the pilot."

Donovan remembered the explosion that had followed when they had killed the bek'hai hunter, Orik. "Affirmative. I'll take the one on the right. Can you hit the one on the left?"

Ehri raised her rifle. She had confided that she had trained with Orik for a number of years. She knew how to fight, better than he probably ever would. "Of course."

"On my signal. I expect Diaz will open up as soon as she sees the plasma."

"Affirmative."

Donovan lifted the Dread plasma weapon, sighting along it to the armored soldier, getting a bead on the helmet. He focused on his breathing, making sure to keep himself centered and steady while he took aim. He couldn't afford to miss. Not this time.

He was about to take the shot when a flash to his left broke his concentration.

A scream pierced the night.

[4]

"Matteo," Donovan said, lowering the rifle and breaking back toward where they had left him.

His motion drew the attention of the Dread soldier, and a moment later a heavy plasma bolt hit a tree right in front of him, sending hot splinters into the alien cloth he was wearing. The second skin absorbed the attack, deflecting it without harm, and he continued to run.

A second bolt came a little closer, flashing past his chest, nearly cutting him down. He dropped to his stomach, sensing the light and heat of the third shot crossing over him.

The shooting stopped.

He got back up, running toward the trees. He could see the light of rifle fire to his right, back at the clearing. It had to be Diaz and Ehri covering him.

A face appeared to his left. A clone soldier, nearly on top of him. He didn't hesitate, swinging the Dread rifle like a club, smashing it across the soldier's jaw. The clone collapsed into a heap, replaced with a second a moment later. It tried to tackle him, but he fell to his knees, turning the rifle and shooting, catching the clone in the chest. He rolled away before the body fell on top of him.

"Matteo," he shouted. The enemy already knew he was here; it didn't matter if they heard him.

"Donovan," his friend replied.

"Where are you?"

"Help!"

Donovan followed the sound, rushing through the trees. He had managed to break away from the attack, to escape the Dread's attention.

He caught sight of Matteo a moment later. The tech's back was against a tree; the rifle cradled in his arms. His expression was fearful and tense. A dead clone was on the ground in front of him. Three more were approaching his position.

Where had this group come from?

Donovan dropped below a stump, resting his weapon on it and taking aim. He didn't have time to worry about accuracy. He started firing, sending bolts of plasma across the distance and into the enemy line.

One fell. Then another.

Something came at him from his left, cracking through tree branches and landing right beside him. A bek'hai warrior. It kicked the rifle away from him, giving him just enough time to stumble back and fall onto his ass.

"Shit," Donovan said, eyes frantically searching for a way out. The soldier said something to him in the alien language as it approached, rifle pointed at him. Why didn't it shoot?

"Surrender," the soldier said, switching to English.

Information. That was why it didn't just kill him. The rest of the Dread didn't know everything that had happened on top of the mountain, but they wanted to.

"Go to hell," Donovan said. It probably wasn't the smartest thing to do, but he wasn't going to tell them anything.

The soldier came at him, faster than Donovan could believe. It grabbed him by his throat, lifting him easily and shoving him against a tree. "Druk'shur. How did you defeat Orik?"

"He had help," Ehri said, appearing from the brush.

She fired, the bolt tearing through the Dread soldier's helmet and head and passing out the other side. Donovan felt the pressure on his throat release, and then he slid down the trunk as the soldier collapsed.

"Thanks," he said, looking back to where he had last seen Matteo. He wasn't behind the tree. "Where's Matteo?"

"I didn't see him," Ehri said.

"What about the pilot?"

"Diaz is with him."

"The enemy soldiers?"

"Dead."

"Your clones, too?"

"I told you, they couldn't be permitted to leave."

He watched her face for signs of remorse. There wasn't any. Death didn't have the same meaning to the bek'hai as it did to humans. Not when they reproduced like toys in a factory, instead of unique living, breathing, feeling creatures with hearts and souls. Ehri was starting to see the truth of that perspective, but she wasn't there yet.

He found his rifle on the ground, picking it up before heading over to the spot where Matteo had been standing. He was half-afraid to find his friend's corpse among the dead clones, half-relieved when he saw it wasn't. Where had he gone?

"Matteo," he said as loudly as he dared. "Matteo."

There was no reply.

"Did any of them escape?" he asked.

"I didn't see any fleeing, but their numbers are hard to judge in the cover and the darkness."

"Did they take him?"

"It is possible."

Donovan cursed, leaning against the tree. If the Dread had ordered Matteo to surrender, it was likely that he had. Matteo was smart, creative, resourceful. He wasn't a soldier.

"What am I going to tell Diaz?" he said. He felt responsible for losing him, and he knew she was going to blame him, too. Even if she didn't admit it. Even if she would never say it. He had been so close. He should have protected him.

"It isn't your fault," Ehri said. "He may still be out here."

A soft rumble in the sky caused Donovan to look up. A Dread fighter streaked overhead, momentarily blotting out the stars.

"We don't have time to look for him," Donovan said. "They're going to send more soldiers."

"Mechs," Ehri said. "I can hear them in the distance. We don't want to be near here when they arrive."

Donovan wasn't going to run away from his responsibility. He led Ehri back to the downed fighter, where Diaz was positioned over the pilot, keeping an eye out for more of the enemy.

"Diaz, we have to move," he said, approaching them. He glanced down at the pilot. He was small and thin, with a delicate frame and a kind face. "Can he be carried?" he asked, looking over at Ehri.

"Do we have a choice?" she replied.

"Where's Matteo?" Diaz said.

He kneeled down next to her. "I'm sorry," he said.

She kept her expression flat. "Dead?" There was no emotion in the question.

"I didn't find his body. They may have taken him. I was close. I should have-"

"Shut up, D. We're not going there. We're all doing our best." She blinked away a tear that found its way to the corner of her eye.

"I'm sorry," he said.

"I told you to shut up," she replied. "We need to get this guy out of here, or we lost him for nothing."

Donovan nodded and then lifted the pilot over his shoulder. The man was unconscious, but he groaned slightly as he was moved. The Dread fighter passed over a second time. It would be sensing their heat, communicating their position. They had done well so far, but they were nowhere close to being safe.

How the hell were they going to get out of this alive?

[5]

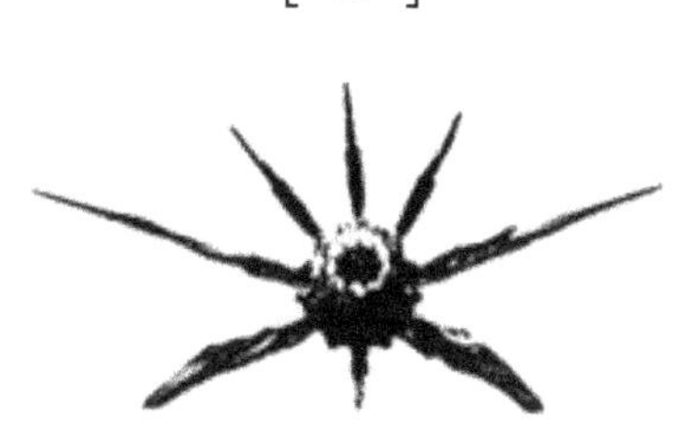

Tea'va Dur Orin'ek stood in the antechamber to the court of the Domo'dahm. His mottled face was wearing what he intended as a scowl but was distorted by the overall structure of his flesh and bone into something closer to a smile. It was an unfortunate side effect of the cloning process that had made him, and of the in-between state of the bek'hai and human genetic splicing. He was ugly as both a pur'dahm and a human, trapped in a phase of change that had left him alienated from the other dahm, while at the same time revered by the scientists that had created him.

Beauty was in the eye of the beholder, and to them, he was the future.

The Domo'dahm's antechamber was a dark place, lit only by a thin line of luminescent moss that had been compounded and packed into narrow channels along the surface of the lek'shah; the material that was used in nearly all of the bek'hai construction. Super strong, impervious to nearly everything, it was the only reason they had survived for as long as they did. From what Tea'va had learned, when their homeworld had started to die, it was the lek'shah that had saved them.

That was all history. Ancient history. For hundreds of cycles they suffered under the weight of their failures, each rotation of time leading them closer to the final destiny.

And then they had found this Earth. A planet rich in resources, including an intelligent life form that had not only overcome its failures, but that held the key to saving them as well. It had taken the prior Domo'dahm little time to decided that the planet would be theirs and that these so-called humans would be both savior and slave.

So it had been for fifty of the planet's cycles. They had first conquered the humans and then begun to use them, harvesting the strong to assist in their splicing experiments, using the middling as labor while they replenished their strength, and breaking down the weak for sustenance. Of course, some of them had evaded their grasp. They were intelligent life forms after all, able to think and reason and learn. It didn't matter if some escaped. It didn't matter if they tried to resettle their planet, to learn to live alongside their masters. And the bek'hai were the masters. They both knew it.

Most of them, anyway.

A hatch slid open. A female lor'hai in the traditional white robes of the sur'Domo'dahm, the servants of the Domo'dahm, stepped through it to meet him. Unlike many of the clones within the capital, she wasn't a copy of the un'hai. She was one of the Mothers, a larger-framed model that was being produced for their higher levels of fertility and genetic compatibility. The idea of the clone type was lost on Tea'va. Some of the dahm, like Tuhrik, had been adamant that the key to their survival was to re-learn to reproduce in the fashion of the humans, a method they had abandoned long ago. He could still remember Tuhrik's impassioned plea for Tea'va to open his mind to the idea. He was one of the few pur'dahm who had fully functional genitals, and who had the potential to impregnate a Mother.

The idea of it disgusted him, and as a pur'dahm he couldn't be forced. Turhik had gone so far as to attempt to lure him to first experiment with his si'dahm, Ehri, a clone of the un'hai. Rorn'el had always been infatuated with the human who had sourced Ehri's genetics, and some of the other pur'dahm had found the si'dahm particularly intriguing. He wasn't one of them. The bek'hai had abandoned sexual reproduction for a reason.

"Domo'dahm Rorn'el is prepared for you," the Mother said, smiling widely at him. Her face was soft and gentle. He saw nothing appealing in it.

Tea'va followed behind her, into the court. It was a large, open room, though the lek'shah here was molded thickly to protect their leader, hanging from the ceiling in wide spines and covering the floor in intricately carved plates. There were a few other pur'dahm already present, those that had positioned themselves into the top ranks of their pecking order. One of them would be the next Domo'dahm within thirty cycles.

Tea'va knew he should have been standing there with them, instead of approaching them under these circumstances. He had played the game differently than the others, his more successful splicing leaving him with no choice but to prove that he was, in fact, superior to them. The scientists wanted to believe that he was because it would validate all that they had done since they had found this planet. Subjugating another intelligent race had never been a desire.

It had been a necessity.

The assembled pur'dahm stood beneath the warm glow of bright lamps that mimicked the sunlight outside and cast shadows across the space, shadows that hid the Domo'dahm from clear view. It was a tradition that had continued after the death of Kan'ek, the Domo'-dahm who had brought them to Earth. The original bek'hai form was against their laws to be gazed upon. It had been decreed that the human design was their future and that looking upon their past would predispose them to reject it.

Tea'va understood why Kan'ek had made it so. He had never seen what a true bek'hai looked like, and he still rejected being more human. He knew he wasn't alone in that. Though Rorn'el had been taken with a human slave, he had little love for the rest of the lesser species. It was the reason he had decided he would no longer tolerate their presence on the planet. They had what they needed from them, and their consistent uprisings were a wasteful distraction. There was no logical reason to risk that they might ever find a way to overcome the lek'shah.

Tea'va lowered his head at the thought, staring at the floor plates as he approached the gathered pur'dahm. They had been etched with a written and pictorial history of the bek'hai, from the early days before they had invented an alphabet, to their first forays into space, to their arrival here on Earth. Parts of the design had been scorched over; the images that had once depicted the original bek'hai body.

"Domo'dahm," Tea'va said, reaching the front of the room. He fell to his knees, prostrating before his Master.

[6]

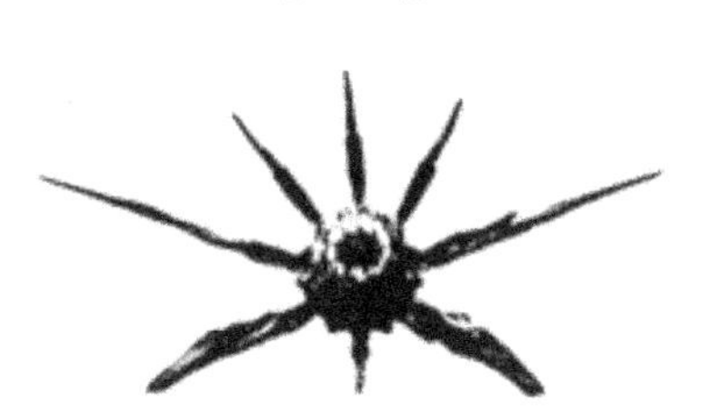

"PUR'DAHM TE'AVA," DOMO'DAHM RORN'EL SAID. HIS VOICE WAS light and scratchy. He spoke in English, though it was difficult for him to do so. "Rise."

Te'ava got back to his feet. He forced himself to make eye contact with each of the other pur'dahm. They glared at him with flat expressions. They knew what he had done. All of them knew what he had done. It wasn't all his fault. Tuhrik had a hand in this. A bigger hand than his? It was difficult to say. Difficult for him to judge. It was up to Rorn'el to determine that.

Of course, Tuhrik was dead, and his si'dahm was a traitor. Rorn'el should never have allowed Ehri to study the humans so closely. He had tried to do right by Kan'ek, to continue the work the prior Domo'-dahm had started and bring them closer to full integration. The failure was as much his as it was Tea'va's.

Not that he would ever suggest as much. To do so would mean challenging Rorn'el's wisdom, which in turn would mean matching the Domo'dahm in a game of intellect. A game Tea'va knew he couldn't win. A loss that would mean his immediate death.

"Domo'dahm Rorn'el," Tea'va started. He would be aggressive, speak first and state his case before any of the assembled pur'dahm could take the opportunity to twist his words and use them against him. They all wanted to take Rorn'el's place, and discrediting one another was part of the game. "I believe the latest human activity has proven that my initial concerns were accurate. Allowing the external-"

"Silence," Rorn'el said softly.

Tea'va stopped speaking.

"Why do you suppose, after fifty years of absence, the human ship returned?" Rorn'el said.

"Domo'dahm?"

"Something made them bold, wouldn't you say, Gr'el?"

"Yes, Domo'dahm," the pur'dahm replied. "Perhaps it was related to one of our gi'shah pilots giving chase through the mesh?"

"A desperate attempt to destroy another of the human's small starcraft," a second pur'dahm, Orish'ek, said. "To what end, when we have already destroyed so many, and still they continue to come?"

"You didn't question my motives at the time," Tea'va said. "You believed it wise to try to destroy the one you call Heil'shur. The one who has always evaded us. You believed he could be dangerous."

"I told you the pilot's success was a minor concern," Rorn'el said. "If he could teach the others to defeat our defenses so regularly. A minor concern, Tea'va, because they still couldn't harm us."

"Tell us you weren't trying to prove your worth as a hunter, Tea'va," Orish'ek said.

"Tell us that you weren't trying to prove that you are better than we are," Gr'el said. "Because you can breathe their air without assistance. Because you can mate with the Mothers."

"Why would I ever want to mate with the Mothers?" Tea'va spat. "You insult me."

"The scientists believe our future depends on it," Rorn'el said. "Whether you agree with the practice or not, the potential of your splicing cannot be ignored. You insult us with your pride."

"A Domo'dahm must be proud," Tea'va said. "To make the right decisions, a Domo'dahm must be strong in their beliefs. That is what the pur'dahm are taught. That is what all of us were taught."

"Being steadfast and being stubborn are two different things, Tea'-va," Rorn'el said. "That is why you are here as a disgrace, instead of standing among us."

"I almost had him," Tea'va said. He regretted the outburst immediately. He couldn't win the game if he couldn't keep his emotions in check.

"Pride, again," Rorn'el said. "What has your pride gotten us? One ship escaped from Kan'ek. One ship capable of riding the slipstream. One ship capable of returning to this planet."

"It is only one ship," Tea'va said. "It cannot defeat the lek'shah."

"That is what even they believed before you fired so recklessly into the mesh," Gr'el said. "You showed them that the lek'shah is not invincible, that there is a way through it. That we are vulnerable."

"The smallest light of hope soon grows into a star," Rorn'el said. "Letting the humans remain was a risk I no longer wished to take. That is why we have expanded our patrols. That is why we seek to root them out."

"And that is why you allowed Ehri her experiment?" Tea'va said. He tensed as he realized he was doing more harm than good.

"We could have kept her under control. Even with the weapons she stole, without the help of the external forces she would never have held them. Even now, I expect that we will have her back here before long."

"Back here? Don't you intend to kill her?"

"No. I want her back."

"Why?"

"She is different. I am curious."

"Domo'dahm, that is a mistake."

"You should not be the one to judge mistakes. Ehri exhibits many of the same traits as the un'hai. I wish to understand how that has come to pass."

"None of this would be a concern if the ship hadn't returned," Gr'el said.

"Or if the pilot hadn't escaped," Orish'ek added. "Again."

Tea'va bowed his head. It was his fault the starcraft had made it back to the larger starship with the weapon. He had hit one of them, but it had been the wrong one. The human had escaped him a second time. Then, the forces he had sent to retrieve the downed pilot had been overcome by the freshly armed human rebels and the lor'el that Rorn'el was so infatuated with. Everything had been spiraling out of control for him since he had given chase through the mesh.

It was a mistake he didn't know if he could recover from. He had to try. First, he had to stop letting his defensiveness get the best of him.

"Domo'dahm," he said, bowing his head deeper in further submission. "I accept that my actions have threatened the security of the bek'hai, and given the humans that light of hope of which you spoke. I take responsibility for the deaths of the other pur'dahm, and for my failure to destroy the Heil'shur on two occasions." He looked up, barely able to make out the Domo'dahm's form in the darkness. "I implore you, Domo'dahm. Allow me to take command of the Ishur, and I will find the humans. I will destroy them before they can learn how to defeat the lek'shah. I will hunt them to the ends of the Universe, and I will not fail you again."

"Take command of the Ishur?" Orish'ek said. "You wish to be rewarded for your failure?"

"I wish to redeem myself," Tea'va said. "Domo'dahm, you have held the belief that the success of my creation is a herald of our next age. Please, allow me to prove that your trust is not misplaced. I have erred in the past. I will not do so again."

A silence fell over the court. The other pur'dahm's eyes suggested they were furious that Tea'va had asked. Tea'va didn't care. His advanced genetic makeup was the only thing he had to bargain with; he wasn't going to waste it. And, if he could find the human rebellion and destroy it, he would be able to return to Earth as second in line to the Domo'dahm.

"You intrigue me almost as much as she does," Rorn'el said at last. "I will acquiesce to your request on two conditions."

"Domo'dahm," Orish'ek said. "You can't-"

"Do not presume to tell me what I can and cannot do, Orish'ek," Rorn'el snapped. "It took you ten years to reach this cell. I can expel you from it in seconds."

Orish'ek cast his eyes to the floor and lowered his head.

"What are your conditions, Domo'dahm?" Tea'va asked. He would do anything for the chance to recover from the failures Rorn'el believed he had made.

"First, Gr'el will accompany you as your si'dahm. He will report your experiences back to me. If I see a need to remove you from command, I will do so without hesitation."

Tea'va glanced at Gr'el. He hated the idea of having someone watching over him. He also knew he had no choice. The former hunter was an easier choice to live with than Orish'ek, who was more likely to let personal grudges guide his thinking.

"And the other?" Tea'va asked.

"When you return, you will mate with the Mothers. As many and as often as needed to further our learning."

Tea'va felt the distaste rising in his throat. He fought against it, though it was almost enough to break his resolve. Was he willing to submit himself to something that disgusted him for the opportunity?

"Very well," he said, unsure if the bitterness was held from his voice. "I agree to your terms, Domo'dahm."

"Good," Rorn'el said. "The Ishur is yours. She is waiting in orbit while we calculate the stream patterns. The human's strategy was unorthodox and effective, but it will not prevent us from catching up to them."

"Yes, Domo'dahm."

"Do not fail us again, Tea'va. It would be a shame for all of us to have wasted these years on the wrong genetic considerations."

"Yes, Domo'dahm."

Tea'va glanced at each of the pur'dahm and then turned and walked away without another word. When the Mother met him at the end of the chamber to escort him out, it was all he could do to keep himself from throwing her against the wall. He would take the

Ishur, find the humans, and destroy them. Then he would return not as a triumphant pur'dahm, but as a challenger to the bek'hai leader.

Nothing was going to get in his way again.

[7]

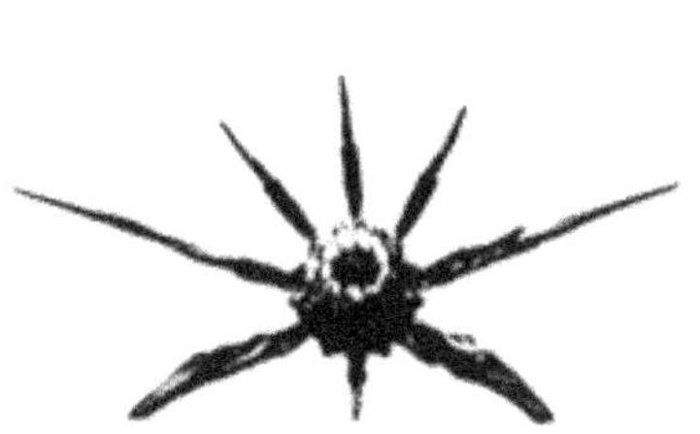

DONOVAN GRUNTED, SHIFTING THE UNCONSCIOUS PILOT ON HIS shoulder so that he could take aim at the Dread clones behind them. He fired a few times, appreciating the lack of kick on the enemy plasma rifle. If he were carrying a standard issue Resistance weapon, his entire arm would be bruised and sore.

Even so, he was exhausted, and the pilot he was carrying seemed to gain weight with every heartbeat. He was so heavy by now that Donovan was surprised he was still able to stand, still able to fight.

When the other option was to die, it made things a little easier.

"Where are we?" he asked. They had been running for so long, fighting for so long, he had lost all sense of bearings. They were somewhere in the jungle near what had once been Mexico City. That was the best he could do.

They had chosen the direction based on geography. There was a river somewhere to the south of their position that would offer their one, slim opportunity to make a good break from the Dread forces that were pursuing them. Forces that by all rights should have killed them a hundred times already, but had always eased up at the moment he believed they were about the be obliterated.

Ehri had told him that she believed the Domo'dahm wanted her alive, and he had no reason to doubt her. Their continued survival wasn't accidental, and it wasn't because of anything special they had done. The fighters that continued to pass overhead didn't risk strafing them and hitting her, and the mechs had remained further back while the clone soldiers harassed them with their more precise fire. It was fire that had damn near killed both him and Diaz a couple of times already; plasma bolts that had split hairs to find their way between the foliage and Ehri.

"The river should only be another few hundred meters ahead," Ehri said.

"You have global positioning built-in?" Diaz asked. Despite her efforts to push reality aside, losing Matteo had made her understandably upset, and she was taking her anger and frustration out on everything around her. Donovan had been forced to order her to turn over her Dread weapon out of fear she would expend the power source that made it work.

"I have studied this area extensively," Ehri replied. "If we make it to the river, we can become much more difficult to track from above."

"And then what?" Diaz said.

"We lose or kill the clones, and then we find somewhere to hole up for the night," Donovan said. "Hopefully, this guy will wake up at some point and be able to walk on his own. At that point, we go back to base and see if that hunter was lying about killing everyone."

"What if he wasn't?"

"We keep fighting, Diaz. That's all we can do."

They continued through the trees. Every step Donovan took hurt, his legs and shoulders burning. A part of him had been tempted to abandon the fallen pilot more than once, knowing he was slowing them down. He would never have done it, but he couldn't avoid the thought. He gritted his teeth and kept going, one step at a time, refusing to quit. They were almost at the river, and then they would have a chance.

Bolts continued to light the area around them, pulses of plasma striking the foliage on either side, each explosion of sparks and smoldering wood a reminder of what would happen if any of the shots landed. Donovan and Ehri continued to fire back from time to time, their attacks measured, their goal to disrupt the clone soldiers more than to hit and kill them. They pushed on until Donovan could hear the soft churning of water over rocks, the signal that they were in the final stretch.

One last step, and then Donovan found himself on a steep slope, the river spreading out below the bank. He almost collapsed right then and there from his exhaustion, and would have fallen over if Diaz hadn't grabbed his shoulder to keep him upright.

"We made it," she said with a smile, even as the Dread fighters passed overhead once more. "We'll be invisible to their sensors by the time they circle back."

"But not to line of sight," Donovan said, pointing to the trees where the clone soldiers were still approaching. He took a few shots at them before stumbling down the incline a few steps.

"We can lose them in the current," Diaz said. "Come on."

She continued down the slope ahead of him, putting her arms out to balance. He followed behind, each step threatening to knock him to the ground.

He was almost to the water when he realized Ehri wasn't with them.

He looked back. He hadn't seen her get hit. He hadn't heard her cry out. Where was she? Had she decided to rejoin the bek'hai after all? Or had she sacrificed herself to help them escape?

"Where's Ehri?" Diaz asked, her sudden concern surprising him.

"I don't know," he replied, still scanning the tree line.

The grade and distance had given them a short respite from the Dread soldier's harassment fire. He could hear the fighter's engines growing louder as they approached for another pass. He heard something else now, a crashing sound from the other side of the bank a hundred meters distant. It was the sound of tree branches breaking against something substantial.

Something like a mech.

"Hurry," Donovan shouted, giving up on trying to keep his balance. He scrambled down the slope, slipping onto his back, barely managing to maintain his hold on the pilot. Diaz moved ahead of him, reaching the water's edge and wading into it.

Was the water even deep enough for them to hide?

The trees on the other side began to part, the Dread mech making its way through the foliage. Donovan looked back over his shoulder. Ehri was still nowhere to be found. Where could she have gone?

She had abandoned them at the worst possible time. Without her, the mech would have free reign to open fire.

He got back to his feet, skipping the last few meters to the water's edge. Diaz was in up to her waist and had turned back to face him, holding out her arms to help him in. The mech was clearing the trees, its arms swiveling to target them.

"Get down," Donovan said, throwing himself into the current.

Then he was submerged, his ears hearing nothing but the rushing of the water as it began to carry him away. He lifted his head to take a breath, shifted his body to ensure the pilot's head was clear. The echo of the mech's weaponry discharging drowned out his hearing again, rounds splashing into the water behind them as the machine's driver worked to get completely clear. Donovan looked around frantically, searching for Diaz, finding her a dozen meters ahead of him, letting the current carry her away.

The Dread clone soldiers reached the edge of the bank, and suddenly Donovan found himself under fire from both sides. Plasma bolts joined with projectiles, striking the area around him and vanishing in gouts of steam and bursts of water. He knew he was hard to see and hard to pick up on sensors submerged the way he was. It didn't matter. The volume was more than enough that he would be struck sooner or later.

He tried to swim a little, to push himself further and faster, to escape the range of the attack. He felt a biting in his leg, a bolt sinking into the water and hitting him, striking the Dread cloth at a reduced strength, burning him but not destroying the flesh and bone. Another hit his shoulder, only inches from the pilot's face. He was too slow, their escape too late. They had taken Matteo, Ehri was missing, and he was going to die at any moment.

At least he would fight to the last breath.

He rolled over onto his back, positioning the pilot on top of him and bringing his Dread rifle from the water to rest it in front. He pulled the trigger, aiming wildly at the soldiers on the side of the river, fighting back until the last. He smiled when he saw one go down. He laughed when he saw another fall.

He froze when he realized he wasn't the one shooting them.

The mech was.

[8]

DONOVAN LOWERED HIS BODY, TRYING TO FIND THE BOTTOM OF the river with his feet. He kept his eyes on the scene ahead of him the entire time, watching in awe and confusion as the mech on the south side of the bank decimated the Dread clones on the north side, tearing them apart with heavy projectile rounds.

"Dios mío," he heard Diaz say behind him, as she caught sight of what was happening.

He started swimming toward the shore as the last of the soldiers vanished beneath the onslaught. A Dread fighter streaked overhead, sending streams of plasma into the mech. It burned into the machine's armor, making deep scores but not taking it down. The mech pivoted to track it, missiles suddenly launching from hidden compartments on its shoulders. They streaked behind the fighter like a swarm of angry insects, exploding prematurely as the fighter pilot released some kind of chaff to distract them. A second Dread fighter appeared overhead, also targeting the mech.

The mech moved almost gracefully, sliding down the decline toward the water, shifting to fire at the newcomer. Plasma beams and projectiles crossed over one another, leaving the mech down an arm and the fighter without the rounded wing on its left side. It vanished behind the trees, the thunder of its crash and a cloud of smoke appearing seconds later.

"What the hell is going on?" Diaz said, reaching him.

"I don't know. Help me get the pilot closer to the shore."

Donovan and Diaz pulled the pilot further to the side of the river, where grasses overhung the water and gave them somewhere to hide while the battle continued to unfold. The mech had made its way into the water, moving toward the center and submerged to its knees. The first Dread fighter was circling back, coming in for another strafing run.

"It's wide open out there," Diaz said.

Donovan didn't respond. She was right. The mech pilot had left the cover of the trees and made the machine a massive target.

He watched in fascination as the two Dread weapons faced off. The fighter continued its trajectory, heading right at the mech while the mech responded in kind, raising its remaining arm and unleashing a barrage of missiles to go with projectiles and plasma bolts. Firepower met firepower, each machine generating small explosions as the attack caused extensive damage to both. The fighter passed fifty meters over the mech before spinning out of control, veering hard to the left and smashing into the trees. The mech groaned, pushed back by the assault, before flopping backward and slamming into the water.

Donovan turned his head away as the resulting wave crashed over them. Once it had passed, everything fell into silence.

He stared at the carnage upstream, barely able to breathe. His heart thudded in his chest, while his mind worked to make sense of what had just happened. Why had the mech pilot decided to defend them instead of killing them? It didn't make any sense.

A minute passed. Then another. Everything remained quiet. No other fighters flew over. No other mechs arrived on the scene. It was the closest thing to a miracle Donovan had ever seen.

"We're still alive, amigo," Diaz said, her face telling him she was as shocked and pleased as he was. "Someone up there is looking out for us."

"I guess so." He put his hand to the pilot's neck, feeling the steady pulse below his fingers. "For all of us."

"Not all," Diaz said.

Donovan flinched. He shouldn't have said that. "Diaz, you know-"

"Forget it. I know what you meant. It isn't your fault. We need to head downstream. We may not be alone here for long."

"Ehri's gone."

"I know. I'm sorry."

"You are?"

"Why not? I know you like her. I'd be an asshole not to care if you lose someone important to you, even if I'm not as fond of them. Or if I'm jealous of them."

"Jealous?"

"You know how I feel, D. We don't need to rehash, especially now. We need to get the hell out of here, stay alive and do something with these weapons. We can't count on St. Martin to come back and save us, not when he's got a Dread starship on his ass."

"The Dread ship didn't leave," Donovan said. It was large enough that they had seen it hanging in a synchronous orbit above the Dread fortress before the trees had blocked their view.

"Not yet. It will, or it would have come back down."

"Yeah, you're right. Hopefully, General St. Martin and his son will make it back, but we need to be able to handle ourselves either way." Donovan shifted his grip on the pilot. "Let's head another kilometer or two down the river, and then we can set up a camp for the night. I can barely think straight."

"Yes, sir," Diaz said, climbing out of the water, and then reaching out.

Donovan shifted the pilot's weight, turning him over to Diaz so she could pull him out by his shoulders. He hoped they weren't doing lasting damage to the man with as rough as they had been forced to be with him.

He planted his arms on the side of the river and lifted, pulling himself up and out. He paused on his hands and knees, a sudden feeling of nausea nearly overwhelming him. He was exhausted beyond any limits.

He dry heaved then, coughing and sputtering. Diaz lowered the pilot gently to the ground, and then came to his side, rubbing his back as he continued to choke.

"It's okay, D," she said. "Relax. You'll be okay."

Donovan nodded. He would. He had to. He coughed again, and then turned his head to the side, back toward the fallen mech. The front of it looked different now. The enclosure near the shoulders was open, revealing part of the internals. It was composed of wires and some kind of organic compound coated in a layer of gel that pulsed with light.

Someone was in the water, swimming toward them.

"Diaz," Donovan said. He had two of the Dread rifles hanging from his body, and she took one and lifted it from him, aiming it at the approaching figure. "Don't shoot."

She grunted in response. He wasn't sure if she was going to listen or not.

The figure was ten meters away when it stopped swimming and stood in the waist deep water.

Donovan fell back onto his rear, the tension draining from him, the exhaustion making him dizzy.

"I don't know how you did it," he said, "but I'm glad you did."

Ehri's face was covered in a layer of grime, her hair had been singed, her left arm was cut and bleeding, and she had another wound across her abdomen. Despite all of that, she was alive, her expression serious as she approached them.

"I've bought us some time, Major," she said. "Let us not waste it."

[9]

GABRIEL STOOD IN FRONT OF THE HATCH LEADING DOWN INTO logistics, staring at the cold metal. It was the only thing remaining between him and Lieutenant Daphne O'Dea. The only remaining barrier before he would have to be the one to deliver the bad news.

"I'm sorry, Daphne," he whispered to himself. "Soon didn't make it back."

He wasn't sure how she would react when he said it for real. She was a soldier, and she had fallen in love with the pilot and married him knowing that he would likely die somewhere near Earth. She might be coldly accepting of his fate. She might fall apart. He needed to be ready for either reaction. The silver lining was that there was a chance, a small chance, that Soon wasn't dead. He was landing the starfighter, not crashing it.

He heard a noise behind him and glanced over his shoulder. A tech crossed the corridor behind him, pushing a heavy cart of tools. Two hours had passed since they had come out of slipspace, somehow still alive. Two hours since Reza had informed them that they were essentially trapped out in the middle of nowhere, right after they had kicked the hornet's nest and sent the Dread searching for them.

It was a truth that didn't sit well with him, or with anyone on the bridge who knew about it. Calawan was only fifty light years from Earth, close enough that if the Dread wanted to find it, they would be able to find it. Nobody had any doubts about that. Meanwhile, the only chance they had of defending the settlement was resting in a makeshift laboratory near the hangar, waiting for Reza and Guy Larone to be able to take a break from calculating possible stream positions to take a look at it instead.

Meanwhile, the Magellan was almost twenty generations away from the planet, and away from Earth, unless those calculations bore quick fruit. Plus, with the damage to the fluid systems, the starship only had three months of potable water. It sounded like a lot, but Gabriel knew it wasn't.

He put his hand to his chest, feeling his mother's cross beneath his shirt. He traced the lines of it, tentatively asking for strength. For all that had gone right in retrieving the weapon, so much had gone wrong immediately after.

He knew he would have to go and see his father soon. He wasn't going to make the mistake of abandoning him again. He just couldn't deal with all of the conflicting emotions that went along with it right now.

He tapped on the control panel beside the hatch. It slid open slowly, groaning as it did. The ship hadn't been in the best shape when they took it. The Dread's attack had only made it worse. There were dozens of doors within the ship that wouldn't open at all, and enough damage it would take their crews weeks to get to it.

Lieutenant O'Dea was standing in the middle of the large cargo area, holding a tablet in her hands and shouting to a dozen crew members as they dug through bins of replacement parts, bolts, and screws. The Magellan had been expected to break down during her journey to the stars, and so had come with a supply of pieces to keep her running. That supply had dwindled over time and seeing the way the crew dug into it signaled to Gabriel that it was running thin.

He had wondered if news of Soon's fate had leaked from the bridge ahead of him. He could tell by the way Daphne was working that it probably hadn't. He was proud of the crew for the level of professionalism they had shown. Most had spent their entire lives groomed to occupy Delta Station, to practice war but not to live it. They were holding up well.

"No, we need six of the inverse capacitors," she was saying as he approached her.

"We only have four, ma'am," one of the crew members said.

She shook her head. "We need six. See if you can find them in one of the other bins."

"Lieutenant O'Dea," Gabriel said.

She looked over at him. Her face immediately froze, paling and falling flat in a moment's time. He should have realized he wouldn't need to say anything. It should have been Soon coming to see her, not him.

"No," she whispered, blinking a few times.

"I think I found one," the crew member said. "Why didn't we get a decent inventory before we stole her?" He laughed for a second before looking back at Daphne and Gabriel.

"Sergeant Keene, is it?" Gabriel said.

"Yes, sir," Keene replied.

"Take over for Lieutenant O'Dea. I need to speak with her privately."

Keene nodded curtly, his whole demeanor shifting.

"Gabriel," Daphne said softly.

"Come on," Gabriel said, leading her from the large room.

He got her out into the side corridor where he came in from and tapped the door control. It groaned again and didn't close.

"Damn door," he cursed, his own control slipping at the mishap. Soon was his friend, too.

"What happened?" she asked, the tears beginning to run from her eyes.

"We were taking heavy fire from Dread Bats. Heavy fire. He was hit. He didn't have enough power left to make it out of orbit. He saved my life, Daphne. He distracted the Dread, gave us the time we needed to make it back out. He's a hero." Gabriel felt the wetness in the corners of his own eyes.

Daphne responded with a small smile. "I bet he made a joke while he was crashing."

"He didn't crash. He had enough control to land the fighter. There's a good chance he's still alive."

"If the Dread didn't capture him. Or kill him."

"Yes. He wanted me to tell you how much he loves you."

"Thanks, Gabriel. I already know that."

"I don't think we should give up on him. The rebels on Earth captured some of the Dread's weapons. They're able to fight back. The tides of war may be turning."

"What about us? What are we doing?"

"Trying to get back into the fight. Our slip away from Earth didn't go as well as it could have, but we'll recover. Reza's a genius, and for as much as I hate Guy Larone, he's got a good head on his shoulders when he wants to."

"We're going back to Earth, though, right?"

"Not right away, but yes, we'll be going back."

"You got the enemy weapon? Do you think we can use it?"

"They'll figure it out. They have to."

She took a deep breath, straightening up and wiping her eyes. "I was always worried he would die making a run. Knowing he has a chance, that's all I need. Don't ever talk to me like he's gone, Gabriel. Until someone proves otherwise, Soon is alive on Earth, helping the rebels take the fight back to the Dread."

"Okay," Gabriel said, wiping his eyes. "We'll save him. We'll save all of them."

"I know that, too. You and your father, you're cut from the same cloth. Neither one of you will be able to die before we're living peacefully on Earth again."

"I hope you're right about that," Gabriel said, his thoughts turning to Theodore again. "Are you going to be okay?"

"I won't lie and tell you that I'm one hundred percent. I'd rather have Soon here with me, and I'm going to miss the hell out of him. I'll survive, just like he will."

"I can bring Wallace over if that helps. So you don't have to be alone."

Daphne laughed at that, stepping into Gabriel and wrapping her arms around him. He returned the embrace, holding her in silence for a minute and letting her decide when to pull away.

"I don't need his hair all over my bed," she said. "But maybe I'll stop by and take him for a run."

"Anytime."

Daphne straightened her uniform, and then flattened her hair and wiped her eyes one last time. She looked back in at her team, pretending to be busy while they kept an eye on her.

"I'll tell them what happened," she said. "We're stronger together than we are alone."

Gabriel nodded. He knew it was true.

Now he just had to convince his father of that.

[10]

SERGEANT DIALLO WAS STANDING OUTSIDE THEODORE'S quarters when Gabriel arrived. She had a stern look on her face, one that suggested at her strict loyalty and stricter orders not to let anyone past.

"Colonel Choi was already here," she said as Gabriel approached. "She didn't get past me, and neither will you, Captain. General's orders."

"I'm not here as an officer," Gabriel said. "I'm here as a son."

Diallo shook her head. "I'm sorry, Gabriel. He doesn't want to see anyone."

"I know. That's why I came."

"He knew you would. So did I. He specifically told me not to let you in."

"And you're going to listen to him?"

She bit her lip. "Please don't make me choose. I promised your father I would follow him. If I renege on that, he'll never forgive me."

Gabriel thought about it. He appreciated the woman's loyalty to Theodore, even if it was getting in the way of his mission. "Okay. I won't ask you to choose. Can you just pass a message to him for me?"

"That I can do."

Gabriel paused. He wasn't sure it was a card he wanted to use, but what choice did he have? His father had holed himself up in his quarters, feeling sorry for himself instead of taking charge. It was an embarrassing response to his moment of failure. A response that Gabriel wasn't going to let him get away with.

"Tell him I have news about my mother. About Juliet. He doesn't get to know what it is unless he lets me in."

"Do you really have news?" she asked.

"Yes."

"Do you swear?"

"I very rarely lie, Sergeant, and only when it's important."

She raised her eyebrow.

Gabriel smiled. "I promise."

"Fine. I'll tell him. Step back a little. I don't want you trying to sucker me."

"Would I do that?"

"I think if it were important."

Gabriel took a few steps back, putting his hands behind him for good measure. Sergeant Diallo smiled and then opened the hatch to Theodore's quarters. Gabriel looked past her. His father wasn't sitting out in the open. It was more likely that he was in that bathroom sick, or in bed, tired.

She vanished inside, the hatch closing smoothly behind her. Of course, that one would be in good working order. Gabriel leaned back against the bulkhead to wait, keeping his arms folded behind his back.

He didn't have to stand there for long.

"He said he'll see you," Diallo said as the hatch opened. "Provided, as he says, 'you keep your coonass opinions of my fitness for duty to your damn self.'"

Gabriel smiled. At least there was still some sass in his old man. "You know I won't," he said.

"I know," she replied, stepping aside to let him in. "Be gentle with him, sir. He isn't feeling well."

"He's my father, Sergeant. First and foremost. I want to help him."

"Yes, sir."

Gabriel entered the living space, closing the hatch behind him. He could smell the vomit in the air, and he noticed the stain of it still on the floor.

"You come to tell me I'm a screw-up?" Theodore St. Martin asked, moving into the room. He was wearing his full dress uniform, crisp and tight. "You come to tell me I don't deserve to lead these fine men and women?"

"Dad," Gabriel said.

"We ain't stupid, son. Neither one of us. We both know what happened out there, and we both know the cause."

He pulled something from his pocket. The remainder of his pills. He tossed them to Gabriel, who caught them smoothly.

"I ain't hiding from my responsibility in here, Gabe. I'm getting my ass clean. Two hours ain't much so far, but I need to be stronger. I need to deal with the pain. Those people are counting on me. They're trusting me to take care of them, the way I did all those years ago. To get them away from harm." His voice cracked as he said it, his emotions threatening to break through the resolve of a General.

He paused, turning away so Gabriel couldn't see his face. It was just as well. Gabriel had never seen his father like this, and it was waging war on his composure, too.

"They still believe in you," Gabriel said. "They don't blame you for this. You did the best you could."

Theodore's head whipped back. "Best I could? No, I did not do the best I could. I gave in to the demon of pain. I let my weakness get the better of me, and I damn near got us all killed. If you hadn't been so quick up to the bridge, we'd all be one with the Atlantic Ocean right about now." He walked over to the sofa and sat down. "I blanked, son. Completely blanked. Couldn't think a lick. All I could see was your mom and me on the beach in Hawaii. What a time that was. No Dread, no war. No outpost in the middle of a sea of nowhere."

"Because of these," Gabriel said, shaking the bottle. "When you don't take them, you get sick."

"I'd rather be floating in my own vomit than losing my head when it's needed the most. Oh, don't get me wrong, son. I want them. I really want them. I'm damn near ready to tear your head off to get another hit. I ain't going to do it. I have a responsibility to these people. They're following me because I promised to give them everything I had to take back what's ours. You got us the gun. You gave us that chance. I need to hold up my end."

"I'm not arguing with that as a soldier," Gabriel said. "As a son, I don't want to see you in pain."

"I appreciate that. I do. There ain't no way around it. Not this time. I'm going to hurt. I'm going to hurt bad for the next few days. You want to help me? Don't tell anyone."

"Why not?"

"Ain't none of their business for one. It will be more effective when I reappear clean and sober for another."

"Okay. You know our situation?"

"Diallo passed the info along to me, yeah. Up shit's creek and we ain't got a paddle."

"Huh?"

"I guess you're too young for that one. Point is, we ended up in a bad way thanks to me. Now, the only reason I let you in here is because you know something about your mother. Vivian tried to use that line to get in here too, but I wanted to hear about it direct."

Gabriel clenched his jaw. He had been holding onto the slim hope his father would forget. As if that would ever happen.

"It isn't good news," he said.

"Fifty years," Theodore replied. "I wanted it to be. I was hoping she was with him. General Rodriguez. I wanted it so bad." He leaned forward, putting his head in his hands. At first, Gabriel thought he was going to cry, but then he rubbed his face and sat back up. "It was all wishful thinking, wasn't it? Selfish, wishful thinking. God's always had a plan for my Juliet. I wish it had included me for all of my days, but that ain't His way, is it?"

"I don't know," Gabriel said.

"I do. You don't get to choose when to believe and when not to believe. That ain't faith. I have to believe there's a reason she was taken from me. So, what did you learn?"

Gabriel sat down next to his father, turning toward him. "The resistance soldiers that gave me the weapon. There was a woman with them. She was human, but clearly not human."

"One of their clones?"

"Yes. I never met mom, but that picture of her that you always projected onto the wall of our apartment, that's etched into my brain. I don't even need to think about it to call it up. The woman, she was the spitting image. An exact duplicate."

"They cloned Juliet?"

"It seems that way."

"So they caught up to her, and they took her?"

"I think so."

Gabriel expected his father to fall apart again. To take the news hard, like he and Colonel Choi had both believed he would. Instead, he started to laugh. A hard, deep laugh.

"What's so funny?" Gabriel asked, as his father leaned forward, beginning to cough from the effort.

"They made copies of your mom," Theodore said. "Do you have any idea what that means?"

"It means she was captured. It means she's most likely dead."

"She was always most likely dead, son, as much as I hate to admit it. No, I'm laughing because it means that those couillons have no idea what kind of reckoning they've brought down on themselves. None at all. A spirit like Juliet's can't be quelled forever. They're going to learn that the hard way if they haven't learned it already.

"It's like I said, son. God has a plan, and it's a doozy."

[11]

TE'AVA SHIFTED SLIGHTLY IN THE CONFINES OF THE GI'SHAH, the suspension gel of the cockpit cold and damp against his more sensitive, more human-like flesh. For older drumhr, the koo'lek was a necessary ingredient, as it was filled with nutrients, hormones, and chemicals that would make the pilot a more efficient fighting machine. For them, it would remove waste and add back needed fluids, as well as act as a transmitter to the bek'hai's every thought, transferring electrical signals into activity that would pass to the organic control system of the gi'shah. For him, it did little more than cling to his body, attempting to fulfill its design and failing miserably. Instead, he had to wear a cap and suit composed of the gori'shah, microscopic symbiotic organisms that were often grown to maturity woven into their more recently developed clothing.

It was the gori'shah that would enable the transfer for him. This made flying the craft less efficient for him than was for the others, and was one of the reasons he had given chase to the Heil'shur. He had wanted to prove that his more genetically advanced form strengths were greater than its current weaknesses.

He had failed.

It didn't matter. The Domo'dahm had listened to his plea. Had allowed him another chance. While the other pur'dahm ridiculed him, the Domo'dahm believed in him and his future. If only Rorn'el didn't insist on his mating with the Mothers, the situation would have been perfect.

He saw the Ishur growing nearer through a tiny transparent slit at the head of the gi'shah, slightly distorted by the fluid he had to look through. A thought sent the fighter into a slight vector change, decreasing thrust and angling for the ship's hangar.

"My bek'hai splice was second to Kan'ek," Gr'el said through their communication system. His voice was muddled by the transfer from the koo'lek to the gori'shah, to Tea'va's ears. "He commanded the Ishur during the invasion."

"Was it your splice who allowed the human ship to escape?" Tea'va replied.

"Drek," Gr'el cursed, speaking in bek'hai. "The human ship evaded the entire fleet. It makes no less of any of the bek'hai involved. Must you always be so abrasive?"

"It was an innocent question," Tea'va said.

"The Ishur has a growing history of failure," Gr'el said. "Perhaps that is why the Domo'dahm allowed you to command it?"

Tea'va felt his upper lip curl at the remark. He didn't respond to it. Rorn'el would be receiving reports from Gr'el about his performance. He knew he should be working to be friendly with the pur'-dahm, not taunting him about his heritage.

"We will change the Ishur's fortunes together," Tea'va said. "When we destroy the humans, we will both gain rank in the eyes of the Domo'dahm."

"Yes, we will," Gr'el agreed.

Tea'va didn't speak again after the exchange. He watched the Ishur as it drowned out the entire viewport of the gi'shah. The hangar was little more than a thin line of white light along the huge lek'shah surface. It took nearly two hundred cycles to produce enough of the material to build a star fortress. He had heard it would take even longer now. Apparently, the Earth's atmosphere was not as favorable to the production process.

Gr'el was already a problem. He would become a bigger problem as time passed. Both were jockeying for position to take over the bek'hai when the Domo'dahm's years were up. This would be the best chance either of them had to make a lasting impression that could bring the bek'hai under their control. Not only would he have to outmaneuver the humans, he would need to outmatch Gr'el as well.

He was certain the Domo'dahm was fully aware of this. Rorn'el was affording him the chance to either prove himself or die.

He would make sure he wasn't the one who died.

He scowled at the thought, the expression forcing his crooked lips open, allowing the gel to seep in through the cracks. He sputtered, forcing it back out and refocusing his efforts to keep his mouth on the breathing apparatus.

Disgusting.

He shifted his attention back to the approaching hangar. The white lights had expanded, showing a depth to the space as it sank back into the fortress. It took little effort for him to line the gi'shah up with the pattern, and even less for him to guide the fighter through an atmospheric filter and into the cavernous space. Dozens of gi'shah rested in organized patterns along the floor of the hangar, along with a few of the larger ek'shah, more heavily armored and less maneuverable craft that were intended primarily for close combat. They had been sent out sparingly in the years since they had arrived on Earth.

The lights directed him to the proper position on the hangar floor. Tea'va turned the gi'shah sharply as it sank in the artificial gravity, bringing it to the ground with a soft thud. He watched through the viewport as a team of five human clones rushed over, pushing an apparatus with a large, empty bin ahead of them. They reached the fighter, and a moment later he heard a thud and pop, and then the gel began to drain from the cockpit.

Tea'va shivered slightly as it was released, though the gori'shah suit helped keep his thinner skin warmer. As soon as the gel was down to his ankles, he removed the cap, signaling the cockpit hatch to open. It rotated up on a hinge, revealing the rest of the hangar to him. A smaller pur'dahm was waiting nearby, his long fingers, thicker, scalier skin, and lack of expression showing him as a less successful splice.

"Pur'dahm Tea'va," the bek'hai said, lowering his head in submission. "The crew of the Ishur is prepared to enter your servitude."

Tea'va could imagine how difficult the statement was for the pur'-dahm. As the now former commander of the Ishur, Ilk'ash had not only been demoted but also relegated to the third position in the command cell.

"Authority accepted," Tea'va said, raising his head in response. The body language was more important than the words. He took three steps toward the other pur'dahm before turning to wait for Gr'el.

He was already approaching. He lowered his head to Tea'va, just enough to be proper. "Gr'el dur Lok'ash is prepared to enter your servitude."

"Authority accepted," Tea'va repeated, raising his head. He was more careful this time, adjusting only enough to finish the ritual but not embarrass the pur'dahm. "Ilk'ash, take us to the bridge."

"Of course, Dahm Tea'va. Follow me."

Tea'va fell in line behind Ilk'ash and Gr'el, forcing himself to hold his mouth closed, or else risk upsetting Gr'el with a satisfied smirk. He was almost happy the Heil'shur had gotten away.

With greater risk came greater reward.

[12]

"Tell me about your pursuit of the human starship," Tea'va said.

He had positioned himself in the center of the bridge, in a seat on a pedestal intended for something much larger than he was. While many aspects of the bek'hai fortresses had been adjusted for the drumhr, there were reminders of their prior evolution still mingled in the details.

Tea'va didn't know why this seat had yet to be replaced. He didn't care. It was comfortable enough, even if it did make him look small.

Ilk'ash was at the command station below and to his left, his hands resting in more of the koo'lek gel so that he could monitor the ship's systems. He looked uncomfortable in the spot, unused to being forced into such activity. As a commander, he would never have been involved with managing the fortress himself.

The bek'hai withdrew his hands, the gel slipping off and back into the semi-circular receptacle in front of him. He then stood and turned to face Tea'va. Even standing, his head barely reached up to Tea'va's feet.

"The Domo'dahm ordered us to prepare the Ishur for launch immediately after the starship arrived inside of our domain," Ilk'ash said. "Most of the lor'hai were already present and carrying about their tasks. Many of the drumhr were not in a stage of warning. Why would they be, when there has been no outside threat for over fifty cycles? Under these circumstances, I am proud of how quickly we were able to put the Ishur into space."

"You should be proud," Gr'el said. "I am willing to wager that the Un fortress is not as well-prepared to launch."

"Go on," Tea'va said. "I'm more interested in how a human ship with no weapons managed to get away from you."

Ilk'ash's head snapped up, his eyes angry. He immediately lowered it again, though Tea'va could picture him glowering into the floor. He had to be careful with Gr'el. He didn't care what Ilk'ash thought of him.

"Their armor absorbed a number of direct plasma hits," Ilk'ash said. "It is thicker than the others we destroyed during the invasion. At least, that is what my science team tells me."

"Why didn't you fire any missiles at them?" Tea'va said.

"The Domo'dahm ordered me not to. He didn't want to waste them. He didn't know they had bolstered their armor either."

"And how did they escape?" Tea'va asked. He didn't need to. He already knew the answer. He had seen the human starship plummeting toward the planet. He had seen the way it shimmered and shifted, trying to gain purchase in the slipstream.

Then he had seen it disappear.

"It entered the slipstream, Domo Tea'va," Ilk'ash replied softly.

"Inside of the defenses?"

"Yes, Domo."

"I have never heard of such a thing."

"Neither had I," Ilk'ash said, looking up again. "If I had not seen it, I wouldn't believe it. They used the slipstream to escape."

"Why didn't you follow?"

"We couldn't."

"Why not?"

"We could not calculate the slipstream coordinates in time. We also-"

"You couldn't calculate the coordinates? A human calculated the coordinates."

Ilk'ash's head lowered a second time, dropping almost to his shoulders. "The humans had time to prepare-"

"I saw the ship come down," Tea'va said, interrupting a second time. "They did not prepare to join the slipstream. I am certain of it. Who is the dahm in charge of the science team on the Ishur?"

"Lor'dahm Zoelle, Dahm Tea'va."

Tea'va felt his anger growing hotter. "A clone?"

"Yes, Dahm."

"One of the un'hai?"

"Yes, Dahm. Shall I call her to the bridge?"

"No. I will deal with that one later."

He paused, thinking. Should he be so bold, so soon? He glanced down at Gr'el. The pur'dahm was looking straight ahead, maintaining decorum. What would the Domo'dahm think if he followed his instinct?

"What did the Domo'dahm think of your failure?" he asked.

"Failure? Dahm, it wasn't my fault. My crew did the best they could. Lor'dahm Zoelle is an accomplished mathematician and astronomer."

"You didn't answer my question."

"He gave the Ishur to you, Tea'va," Ilk'ash said, dropping his title. "That is the answer."

"Your level of respect is even with your level of preparedness, Ilk'ash," Tea'va said. "I don't know how you managed to earn command of the Ishur in the first place, but it is clear to me that your usefulness has come to an end. If you have any pride in you at all, you will turn yourself in for retirement immediately."

Ilk'ash looked up again, angrier than before. Gr'el turned slightly, just enough that he could see Tea'va, but he didn't speak.

Tea'va knew the Domo'dahm would hear of this. He welcomed it.

"Do you have something to say?" he asked.

"Drek. Druk'shur," Ilk'ash cursed. "I will kill you."

He reached out, ready to climb the pedestal to attack. Tea'va didn't move. He didn't give up the exterior of calm. He had to make a statement immediately.

"Gr'el," he said.

The pur'dahm stood, drawing a plasma knife from his uniform and shoving it into Ilk'ash's side with one quick, smooth motion. The drumhr gurgled, still reaching up. Gr'el stabbed him again. He stopped the advance, falling first to his knees, and then onto his side, dead.

Tea'va locked eyes with Gr'el. Neither was surprised by the actions of the other. Both knew that Tea'va couldn't just assume control.

He had to take it.

[13]

They barely spoke for another hour as they fled downriver, away from the carnage and the destroyed mech. Of course, Donovan had questions. So many questions. How the hell had Ehri gotten to the other side of the river bank? How had she gained control of the mech? How did she even know how to pilot the thing?

She was supposed to be a scientist. Maybe she had trained with a pur'dahm hunter. Maybe she knew how to fight. This was more than knowing how to fight. It seemed like there was nothing she couldn't do.

Had Juliet St. Martin been the same way? It was her husband who had gotten the colony ship away from Earth during the invasion, somehow managing to avoid the plasma fire of the bek'hai's massive fortresses.

Were the other clones like Ehri just as gifted? Was the difference that they didn't know it?

"We should stop here," Donovan said.

They were in the midst of some thick vegetation that offered strong cover from all directions. The river was rough beside them, pouring over a patch of rocks and debris that kicked a fine mist over the area, keeping it damp.

"Diaz, can you help me with him?" He was too tired to lower the pilot to the ground without the risk of dropping him.

"I can help you," Ehri said.

"I've got it, Mary Sue," Diaz said, moving in front of her. "You don't have to do everything for us."

Donovan opened his mouth to rebut her and then decided against it. They could handle their differences themselves, and if Diaz was pissed and jealous, that was her own problem.

She helped him lower the pilot to the ground. Donovan reached down and felt his pulse. It was still steady.

"I don't know why he's been out for so long," Diaz said quietly. "I thought the bek'hai magic band-aid was supposed to heal him?"

Donovan smiled at that one. "Are you okay, Lieutenant?" he said, reminding her they still had a job to do.

"I'm feeling a little uncertain about Ehri. Every time we think we know her, she makes us look stupid again."

"I can hear you, Lieutenant Diaz," Ehri said.

"See," Diaz whispered.

Donovan stood, surveying both of them. "I think we're all exhausted and on edge, and it's getting the best of us. Before we wind up ripping one another's throats out, maybe you can debrief us on exactly what happened back there?"

"Of course, Major," Ehri said. "There isn't much to tell. I heard the mech approaching across the river, so I broke off from you, crossed at a ford a few hundred meters further upstream, and came at the mech from behind."

"If there was a ford so close, why weren't you directing us to it?" Diaz asked.

"Because of the mech. If it had reached us together, we would all be dead right now."

Donovan couldn't argue with that. "You made it ahead of us in a hurry."

"As with my hearing, most of my abilities are augmented. As you know, the bek'hai have a long history of genetic manipulation.

Consider that they have been able to combine human DNA with their own in only fifty years. There are thousands of years of study and science behind those capabilities."

"Yet they couldn't prevent themselves from almost going extinct?"

"A series of tragic mistakes. Humans are not immune to the same."

"Why aren't the soldier clones powered up like you are?" Diaz asked.

"The Children of the Un'hai are special. You could say favored."

"Un'hai?" Donovan said. "Juliet St. Martin?"

"Yes."

"Your Domo'dahm must have been seriously in love with Juliet," Diaz said.

"He was. As much as any bek'hai is capable of love."

"What about the mech? You never told me you could pilot one of those things."

"I told you I know how to fight. That includes usage of all of the bek'hai weapons of war. I know the workings of the gi'shah, though they are not equipped to be piloted by clones."

"Gi'shah?"

"The starfighters. Your forces call them Bats. They currently require a symbiotic interface which makes them incompatible with the lor'hai. The mechs; however, were created for this planet, and with both clone and drumhr usage in mind."

"What about real human usage?" Diaz asked.

"It is likely that you could be taught, but the controls have the same lockout as the rifles normally do."

"We've gotten around that problem once," Donovan said. "Maybe we can do it again?"

"Getting ahead of yourself a bit, Major?" Diaz said. "We've got bigger problems right now."

"Affirmative," Donovan said. "How far off course are we from returning to base?"

"Forty kilometers or so," Ehri said. "It will be dangerous to go back there."

"I know, but we have to. If any of the children survived, if my mother survived. They're going to need someone to try to get them out." He held up the bek'hai rifle. "We're the best chance they've got."

"We may be the only chance they've got," Diaz said. "We don't leave people behind. We can't just make new ones."

Ehri didn't react to the barb. She shifted her attention to the pilot at their feet. His eyes had opened at some point during the conversation.

"He's awake," she said.

Donovan looked down at the pilot. He was staring at them, watching them. His breathing was calm.

"My name is Major Donovan Peters," Donovan said, leaning down to greet him. "I'm glad you're finally awake. Welcome to Earth."

[14]

"Captain Soon Kim," the pilot said. His voice was soft. Tired. "New Earth Alliance." He smiled weakly, lifting his arm to salute. "I've never been to Earth before." He breathed in. "I've never breathed fresh air. I've never been outside! It's incredible."

Donovan still felt odd returning the Captain's salute. His own rank wasn't a real thing. Not compared to a man who had spent his whole life training to be a soldier. At the same time, he knew the planet. Captain Soon didn't.

"I wish we were meeting under better circumstances, Captain," Donovan said. "I wish I was welcoming you home. You and all of your people."

"Me, too. Do you know? Did Captain St. Martin make it out?"

"He did," Ehri said.

Soon smiled. "We did it. I can't believe we did it." He tried to push himself up, groaning and laying back down. "Must have hit my head. Hard."

"You have a wound to your abdomen as well," Ehri said. "It will heal quickly, but it will help if you stay still."

"We had to carry you quite a way," Donovan said. "It didn't help. We didn't have a choice."

"I'm sure you didn't."

"Diaz, can you get Captain Kim some water?"

"Yes, sir," Diaz replied, heading off toward the river.

"That's Lieutenant Renata Diaz," Donovan said. "This is Ehri."

"Just Ehri?" Soon said.

"I'm a lor'hai," Ehri replied. "A bek'hai clone."

"Bek'hai? You mean the enemy?"

Donovan expected Soon would be afraid. He wasn't.

"She helped us get the weapons," Donovan said. "She's on our side."

Soon stared at her in silence for a moment. "You look familiar." His face changed when he placed her. "General St. Martin has a picture of his wife, Juliet. I've seen it a thousand times. Even with the grime on your face, I would know it anywhere."

"Yes," Ehri said. "I am aware of Juliet St. Martin."

"Did Gabriel see you?"

"He did," Donovan said, remembering the look on Captain St. Martin's face when he saw the spitting image of his mother. "He was shocked, to say the least."

"I can imagine."

Diaz returned with the water, held in a large leaf. She kneeled next to Soon, helping him drink.

"Thank you," Soon said. "I've never tasted anything like it."

"You're welcome, Captain."

"We have a lot of catching up to do," Soon said. "A lot you need to tell me. A lot I need to tell you."

"You should rest, Captain," Ehri said. "You likely have a concussion. We're fortunate you didn't die with as much as we put you through."

"There's no time to rest," Soon said. "Not now. If the enemy wasn't taking us seriously before, we both know they are now, or they wouldn't have launched a ship to chase the Magellan."

"I can't argue with that," Donovan said. "We're headed back to the rebel base. It was attacked by the bek'hai, but there's a chance there may be some survivors."

"How have you managed it all these years, Major?" Soon said. "Being down here with them? Being hunted?"

Donovan remembered what it had taken for him and his mother to get to Mexico. To make it to the missile silo they had called home up until yesterday. "As much as you're enjoying the taste of the water and the smell of the air, I think we'd feel equally grateful to be at peace, to have some measure of safety and security. To be out there, instead of down here."

"Not me," Diaz said. "Somebody has to fight. Somebody has to keep it all going."

"You don't want peace?" Ehri asked.

"Of course, I do. Peace on Earth. No more bek'hai. That's why we're all here, right?"

"General St. Martin swore he would come back," Soon said. "For as long as I've been alive, he promised we would find a way to fight the enemy, and when we did, we would. He's an incredible man, the General. You're right, Lieutenant. Somebody has to keep it all going. We have a key. We just need to figure out how to use it. Our scientist, Reza, he's a genius. If anyone can reverse-engineer the enemy tech, it's him. The Magellan will be back. I can promise you that. If we can keep the enemy on their toes, if we can soften them up until the General returns, that's what we need to do."

"That's what we will do," Donovan said. "We already sent a message to our headquarters in New York, to General Parker. The rest of the resistance will be organizing as we speak, preparing to fight back. Some of our people must have escaped. Once we regroup, we can make plans to begin to counter the bek'hai."

Soon grunted in agreement, his eyes shifting over to Ehri. "Where do you fit into all of this?"

"I convinced my Domo'dahm, my leader, to allow me to study humans up close. To join them before he completed his goal of ending the resistance. I learned of your ways. Your freedoms. Your ability to choose. I don't want to destroy my people. The lor'hai, the clones, are all like you. We are fully human, even if we are copies. The others don't choose freedom because they don't know what it is.

They don't know it is a choice. I hope that by helping you, I will be able to give them a choice, and in doing so, will force the Domo'dahm and the drumhr to make a choice before all of our blood is shed."

"I appreciate the idealism," Soon said. "I hope you have a chance to practice it. For my part, I'm not keen on letting the aliens off the hook so easily. Not the ones who are in charge, anyway."

"I understand," Ehri said. "I have pledged my loyalty to Major Peters. I will follow his orders as they are given. At the same time, I trust in the compassion of humanity, as much as anything else."

"You should try to rest a little," Diaz said. "We need to keep quiet, anyway. The bek'hai have excellent hearing." She looked over at Ehri when she said it.

"Sensors," Donovan said. "Heat. Motion. Sound. There are ways to avoid all of them, and we'll teach you. For now, enjoy the chance to sleep under the stars for once, instead of among them. Enjoy the sound of flowing water. Wind. Air."

Soon grunted again. "I'd rather be back up there with my wife, to be honest. But I'll take what I can get. I hope I get to share this with her one day."

"I hope so too, Captain. I hope so, too."

[15]

GABRIEL WAS ON HIS WAY TO THE BRIDGE WHEN HE NEARLY collided with Guy Larone. The astronomer was on his way out of the main conference room, a concerned look crossing his otherwise sour expression.

"Pardon me, Captain," he said, his eyes betraying his almost cordial words.

Gabriel didn't have a chance to reply. The scientist continued past him, storming down the corridor.

Reza, Sarah, and Colonel Choi followed close behind, more calm in their demeanor. More focused. Reza smiled when he saw Gabriel.

"Captain St. Martin," he said. "How is your father?"

"I don't know," Gabriel lied. "He won't let anyone in to see him."

"Not even you?" Sarah asked.

"No. Believe me, I tried."

He glanced at Colonel Choi. Her face suggested she didn't quite believe him. That was okay. As long as he didn't say anything, he was keeping his father's promise.

It had been nearly twenty-four hours since he had spoken to Theodore. He had done as his old man had asked, retreating to his own concerns while his father succumbed to the pains of withdrawal from the meds. He could picture Theodore in the bathroom, spitting up everything he tried to put down, cursing against the agony he was surely feeling in the stumps of his legs by now. The thought made him want to rush to his father's side, to do something for him.

Instead, he had been headed up to the bridge to take a shift. The Magellan was doing little more than traveling in the general direction of home at STL speed, balancing her acceleration with the overall load on the reactors. That didn't mean he couldn't give Lieutenant Bale a little R&R time.

"What happened to Guy?" he asked, pointing at the man's back, nearly vanished in the dimness of the ship's lighting. Repair crews were still working on getting power regulation back up to spec.

"He's unhappy," Sarah said. "What else is new."

"About being stuck out here?" Gabriel asked.

Guy's wife rolled her eyes. "About pretty much everything. I've tried to get him to see the light in all of this, but all he wants to do is complain about how we could have been on our way to the New Earth by now."

"The one that only half of us would have reached?" Choi said.

Sarah looked at the floor. "Yes, ma'am. We were all trying to find a viable solution for our future. It was never personal."

"When you're intentionally letting people die, it's always personal," Choi said. "But personal feelings aren't what's important right now. Captain, Reza and Sarah have been working on the slipstream problem."

"And?" Gabriel asked.

"We've calculated that the stream that brought us here is likely still active," Reza said. "What we think happened is that the gravitational field of the Earth pushed us forward on it, onto the leading edge."

"Normally, a starship can't join the edge of a stream because the nacelles need more purchase in subspace," Sarah said. "The result is that we were cast off by the stream when it reached its terminus."

"Cast off?"

"Like the ocean tides on Earth," Colonel Choi said. "We washed up on the shore."

"I don't completely understand that," Gabriel said.

"The important part is that we've been able to reconcile our position with the edge of the slipstream," Reza said. "We're outside of mapped space, but our sensors have picked up a solar system approximately two thousand AU from here. We believe we can pick up a slipstream there."

"That's good news," Gabriel said, doing the math in his head. Somewhere between twenty and thirty days. It was more than he had hoped for, but it was better than being stuck for months. "I would think Guy would have been excited about getting out of here."

"You would think that, wouldn't you?" Sarah said.

"He thinks we've doomed the entire colony," Choi said. "We showed the Dread that we're willing to fight back and made them angry, and now they're going to come looking for us."

"That part is probably true," Gabriel said. "He does realize the Dread don't know where the colony is, and that space is a big place? Plus, we have the plasma rifle."

"We've been tied up figuring out where the Magellan is," Reza said. "Now that we have a course to set, we'll start working on the rifle."

"That's where Guy was headed," Sarah said. "He wanted to examine the device before Reza got to it. I think he's feeling a little jealous."

Gabriel noticed the way Sarah looked at Reza when she said it. It wasn't any of his business, but it appeared that Guy might have a reason to be angry.

Reza seemed oblivious to the older woman's attention. "Colonel, Captain, even if we do discover the method the Dread use to defeat their own shields, how are we going to weaponize it? The Magellan doesn't have any offensive capability."

"We'll get to that when we have to," Colonel Choi replied. "With any luck, we'll have to figure that out very soon."

"Yes, ma'am," Reza said. "If you'll excuse me, I'm going to head down to the mess, and then join Guy in the hold."

"Reza, do you mind if I join you?" Sarah asked.

He shrugged. "Sure, if you want."

"Colonel," Sarah said. "Captain." She smiled at them both, and then headed off alongside Reza.

Both Gabriel and Colonel Choi watched them depart for a moment. Then Choi turned to him.

"You saw your father, didn't you?"

"No," Gabriel said.

"You can't lie to me," Choi said. "You spent nine months in my womb, remember?"

"Then don't push," Gabriel said.

Choi nodded. "Understood. Should I be worried?"

"About my father? No. About Guy Larone? Maybe. Did you see the way Sarah was making eyes at Reza?"

"I did. She's old enough to be his mother."

"Thankfully, Reza is too focused on his work to notice. For now. I'm willing to bet Guy has noticed."

"You think he'll do something irrational?"

"If his wife starts cheating on him on top of all of the other embarrassments he's already endured? His ego is getting crushed. I don't know if he can take it."

"Those embarrassments are of his own doing."

"I know. You're in charge while Theodore is missing in action, Colonel, but I recommend not giving him unfettered access to the most powerful weapon on the ship."

"Agreed. I'll send Hafizi down to the hold, ostensibly to keep an eye on the weapon, not on Guy."

"Yes, ma'am."

"Where are you headed, Captain?"

"I was going to relieve Lieutenant Bale. I've had time to rest and recover. She hasn't."

"Bale is off-duty," Choi said. "Maggie is handling flight control at the moment. It isn't as if we're in any imminent danger."

"There's no chance the Dread fortress followed us?"

"No. According to Reza, their ship's design would make it unable to reach slip speed inside of the atmosphere. Even if they followed the same stream, their wave calculations would be completely different, as would their speed. They would be weeks out of sync, and considering how much there is out there, the odds of crossing paths with them are infinitesimally low."

Gabriel smiled. "You sound just like Reza."

"I'm not surprised. I was quoting him. In any case, Captain, take advantage of the time you have. I suspect we'll all have plenty to do soon enough."

[16]

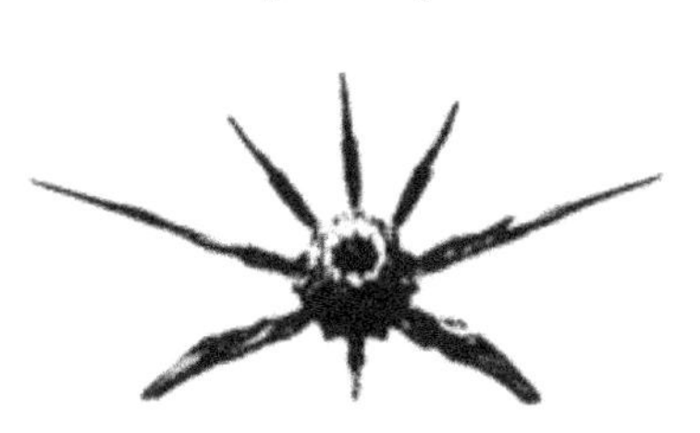

THEODORE ST. MARTIN CLUNG TO THE EDGE OF THE SINK, dropping his head over the waste disposal. His stomach gurgled, and then he coughed, choking up small amounts of bile. It was all that was left in his system, ravaged and purged over the last twenty-four hours at his cold stop of the pain meds that had made him weak.

It was nothing compared to the pain in his legs. Without the chemicals coursing through his bloodstream, the burning and itching sensations had returned with full force, leaving him barely able to prop himself up to vomit. He had never felt physical pain like it before.

At the same time, he had known mental anguish ten times worse. He could recall it like it was yesterday. The day they reached Ursa Majoris. The first time he had a minute to himself, time to think about his Juliet.

It was another pain to add to the rest of the stack. Juliet had been captured and cloned. His Juliet, his love, his angel. She was dead, sure as shit. She was gone. But her face would always be there to remind him. To distract him. He accepted that she was with God. That didn't make it hurt less. Everybody had a degree of selfishness in him. That was his.

There were strategic implications, too. Could he fire on an enemy position when he knew he would be destroying her likeness, enemy or not? Could he do harm to a creature made from her DNA, who might share some of the qualities and quirks that he had loved so much?

He knew he might have to. He knew he had to be ready for that.

One thing at a time. The withdrawal was kicking his ass right now. There would be time for the tough choices to do that later.

He coughed again, his hand slipping on the edge of the sink. He cursed, turning his shoulder so it would hit the shelf, cursing again at another new pain, and falling onto the floor.

"General, are you okay?" he heard Diallo say. He appreciated the loyalty of the damnable woman, but she made him feel like an infant sometimes.

"Just dandy, Sergeant," he replied. "Fell on my ass again. At least it makes it harder for it to get kicked."

He rolled over and leaned back against the metal cabinet, gritting his teeth. The pain was intense. He wondered if Vivian had felt this way when she delivered Gabriel? He had been there with her. He had watched it happen. She was a trooper. The most loyal friend he had. Only Gabriel was more loyal.

He reached up, wiping some cold sweat from his forehead. He had refused medical attention, but Diallo said stopping the medication the way he did would leave him this way for forty-eight hours. Two days. He could manage two days. It was a small price to pay for almost killing everyone on board, and ending their side of the war. A small absolution. He had been stupid for taking the pills in the first place.

Forty-eight hours. It was making him feel old. Hell, he was old. He had no business still being alive, and he knew it. Stupidity had caused him to crash into that BIS. Arrogance. Maybe there had been a systems failure, but he shouldn't have been out there to begin with. He should have been above such things. Getting older was hard. To lose your reflexes, your eyesight, your legs. Getting older meant more and more loss, either within you, around you, or yourself altogether. He was the Old Gator. He had a responsibility.

He closed his eyes, focusing on his breathing. Medication or meditation. That was the only way forward. He couldn't command with the full brunt of the pain, no matter how tough he tried to be. The nerves were damaged, sending constant signals of panic and fury to his brain.

Minutes passed. Tears began to roll from his eyes. He couldn't do it. He couldn't conquer this demon. No matter how much he wanted to. Its pull was too strong.

He took the bottle of pills from his pocket and looked at it. His lip curled in pathetic sadness, his heart thumping rapidly. Why did things have to be so hard for him? Why did God challenge him this way? He had played it strong for Gabriel. Didn't let him see how hard this really was, and how hard he knew it would be.

He opened the top and looked into the bottle. His legs were throbbing. Burning. Stabbing. He thought of Juliet. She would have been so calm, so cool and collected. She would have helped him through the meditation. She would have been patient.

He shifted, turning the bottle over into the waste disposal, taking away his choices. He had to do it. For her memory. For Gabriel. For all of the souls on his ship.

For himself.

He heard her voice in his head as he focused on his breath again. "In through the nose. Hold. Out through the mouth. Five. Seven. Five."

He repeated it over and over as he did it. He didn't know for how long. He only knew there was a point that he stopped thinking about his legs. He stopped thinking about the pain. He stopped thinking about everything.

Everything except Juliet. What would she want him to do about the clones? About the Dread?

Save the planet. Be compassionate. He was a military man. Compassion was hard to do.

If he had the chance, he would try.

For her.

First, he needed the chance. He needed to survive this.

Forty-eight hours.

He opened his eyes, pulling out his watch. An hour had passed.

Only twenty-two to go.

[17]

"How could anyone be alive out there?" Diaz said.

Donovan peered across the remains of the city from their vantage point at the base of the mountain. There had been few enough buildings still upright, and many had been brought to the ground by Dread mech and fighter attacks. Some of the areas were still smoldering, sending plumes of smoke into the sky. There were bodies visible on the ground, soldiers mostly, men and women who Donovan had served with and in some cases called friends.

"I'm sorry," Soon said, standing beside him. The bek'hai bandage had served its purpose, healing the gash in his side fast and well. His head was better but not perfect. He refused Donovan's offer of a rifle they had captured, telling him that he wouldn't know which of the three duplicates he should shoot at.

"The children were hidden," Donovan said, refusing to give up on their people. "They could still be down there. Others might have come back, too."

"We should be quick," Diaz said. "Get in, look for survivors, get out."

"Agreed," Donovan said. "Soon, can you handle it?"

"Don't worry about me, Major. Take care of yourself and your people."

Donovan pointed to the mass of mud they had carried from the river. It was a heavy burden to manage, but he knew they would need it. They set about covering themselves in the mud.

"You have the signals down?" Donovan asked.

"Yes, sir," Soon replied.

Donovan slopped the wet earth into his hair and over his face. The others did the same. Once they were damp, he led them down and out to the open road. There was no sign of Dread soldiers, mechs, or fighters, though they had heard them flying overhead overnight.

"Have they stopped giving chase?" Donovan asked.

They had seen the fortress floating in orbit when daylight had come. They had watched two of the starfighters fly up to it, and a short time later it had left. They all knew it was following the Magellan.

"A trap?" Soon asked. "Maybe they're waiting for us in the base?"

"No," Ehri said. "The bek'hai don't fight like that. They won't hide underground. I believe this is a sign of respect. The Domo'dahm is allowing you to return to your home."

"How nice of him," Diaz said.

"Of course, they will be monitoring the area. He'll want to know when you do return. They will probably give you a small head start before following."

"Is it us he respects?" Donovan asked. "Or you?"

"We destroyed a mechanized armor and a fighter, as well as a squad of hunters. It is all of us, Major. We have earned our way here."

"Do you think he'd be willing to give me my brother back?" Diaz asked.

"Your brother is very intelligent and very handsome. I believe he will become a pur'hai."

"Pur'hai?"

"A template for cloning. It is the easiest life a human can have among the bek'hai if that is any consolation."

"It isn't," Diaz said.

"Okay, quiet time," Donovan said. "We need to get across the open area to that rubble as fast as possible. Soon, if you want to stay here, we can rendezvous back at this spot."

"I can run. My head can wait."

Donovan nodded. "Let's move."

They charged across the field at a sprint. Donovan kept his eyes on the sky, watching for signs of incoming fighters. Diaz scanned the ground, while Ehri and Soon took up the rear. Soon was slower than Donovan would have liked, but he managed to stay on his feet and running until he caught up to them at a blown-out wall.

"I should have spent more time in the gym," Soon whispered, breathing hard.

"You made it; that's all that matters," Ehri replied, also keeping her voice low.

Donovan put his finger to his lips. Then he moved to the corner of the building and tracked his vision across the street. He knew Wilcox as soon as he saw her, laying on her back with a gaping wound in her chest.

He felt a pang of sadness and forced himself to swallow it. He had to worry about the ones who might still be alive. He used hand gestures to lead them around the corner, making a zig-zag pattern from cover to cover through the city.

They paused when a distant rumble sounded.

"Diaz, can you get eyes on whatever is making that noise?" Donovan said.

Diaz nodded, running across the street and scaling a pile of debris. The rumbling remained distant until it faded completely. Diaz returned a moment later.

"Some kind of Dread ship," she said.

"What did it look like?" Ehri asked.

"Long, narrow. Lots of spikes or points or something."

"A transport. Which direction was it headed?"

"Northeast."

"What does it mean?" Donovan asked.

"I'm not sure," Ehri said. "The transport can hold up to one thousand soldiers, both clones and drumhr. The Domo'dahm may be seeking to accelerate his conquest of the resistance now that we have threatened the status quo."

Donovan tried not to think about how many humans that single ship was going to be responsible for killing. It was harder to do when a second rumble echoed across the sky, matching the first. A third followed a moment later.

"I'm afraid that escalation is the most likely cause," Ehri said.

"There's nothing we can about that right now," Donovan said.

He brought them the remaining distance to the pile of rubble that had once hidden the silo. It had been blasted aside, leaving a gaping hole that revealed the depth of the missile tube. There were no bodies at the bottom. He hoped that meant the Dread had decided not to go down.

"Diaz, I need you stay up here to keep watch."

"Me?" Diaz said, reacting to the request. "Why me? Why not Ehri?"

"Diaz," Donovan barked softly. "That's an order, Lieutenant."

She stared at him for a moment before shaking her head. "Order? The military is gone, amigo. We're nothing but a pair of kids who are in way over our heads. That was my home, too."

Donovan felt himself getting angry. She was choosing a lousy time to be difficult. "Ehri, stay and keep watch with Diaz. Soon and I will go down."

"Yes, Major," Ehri said. Diaz scowled but knew better than to complain again.

"What do you say, Captain?" Donovan asked.

"Lead the way," Soon replied.

[18]

"Your Lieutenant seems to be a bit of a spitfire," Soon said as they descended the silo.

"Renata? She wears her heart on her sleeve. Sometimes that's a good thing. Sometimes it isn't. That's why I left her up there. After losing her brother, she might not react well to finding everyone else dead or gone. I need her rational."

"A good assessment of the situation. You trust her to be alone with the clone?"

"Ehri can take care of herself."

"I meant, do you trust the clone?"

"Yes. With my life." He remembered the kiss he had shared with Ehri. There hadn't been any time to explore that any further. Maybe one day. "She saved our lives, and yours."

"I don't mean to be ungrateful, Major. We know so little about the situation down here. So little about them. We're raised knowing that they stole our home and killed billions of our people. That alone is enough to inspire hate and mistrust."

"It isn't any different down here. But it's harder to hate something once you know it personally. Once you can relate to it."

"That is true."

"And believe me, I won't hesitate to kill any of the Dread that I have to in order to get our planet back. What Ehri says about freeing the clones is all well and good, but it isn't my top priority."

"I'm glad to hear that, Major."

They reached the base of the silo. The heavy lead door that was supposed to protect them was hanging open; the locks sawed off by a plasma beam.

"So much for them not coming down here," Donovan said, feeling his stomach drop. He didn't want to lose his mother. Not after everything they had endured.

He had a second Dread rifle slung over his shoulder. He lifted it and handed it to Soon. "Ehri said they won't ambush us down here, but just in case she's wrong. Shoot at all of them if you have to."

Soon took the rifle, running his hand along it. "I can't believe I can kill them with this. I've never killed anything before."

"Remember that it's them or us. Don't let it be us."

"Yes, sir."

Donovan stared at the half-open doorway for a moment. His heart was racing, his nerves tense. He breathed out heavily and then made his way into the base.

He clenched his teeth at the sight of Captain Reyes crumpled in the corner, his neck clearly broken. A woman's body was a few feet back, her neck bruised. Choked to death. She looked like she had been trying to run.

"Brutal," Soon said, the sadness in his voice tangible.

"More than it had to be," Donovan agreed.

They kept going, moving through the long corridor that connected the silo with the living area. There were no other bodies in it. There were also no scorch marks or bullet fragments. He realized why when he reached the end.

The few who had remained inside the base had barricaded the door. Then they had tried to escape through it. The Dread had come at them from behind, somehow finding another way in. Had the bek'hai discovered the path they had taken out?

He felt his heart jump. His mother was supposed to take the children that way. Had she tried? Had they found her? He was tempted to rush to the hidden passage behind General Rodriguez's office. He didn't. He had to be careful and do things right.

There were six corpses right at the barricade, all of them killed with blunt force trauma, thrown or crushed or beaten. It was an ugly way to die. An unnecessary way to die. Why had the Dread done it? What did they have to gain through the violence?

Ehri said the Domo'dahm respected them, but he didn't see that. He saw the Dread Leader taunting them, teasing them, showing them how weak and small and unimportant humans were. Not even important enough to waste plasma energy on.

They worked their way through the halls. Donovan kept his ears open for signs of activity. There was no sound. The silo was a tomb.

He finally reached the General's office. The door was hanging open slightly, the base's lights revealing little. Donovan could barely breathe, his body was so tense, his heart racing so fast. In the back of his mind, he knew what he was going to find. He knew she was going to be dead. That they were all going to be dead.

"I can check it if you want," Soon whispered.

Donovan was tempted. He shook his head. "I have to."

"Okay."

He led with the front of the rifle, using it to push the door open the rest of the way. His heart sunk to see that the door to the passage was open, though there were no bodies directly inside. He started toward it.

A gunshot sounded from somewhere deeper inside the base.

It was followed by three more.

[19]

DONOVAN STARED AT THE OPENING TO THE PASSAGE FOR A FEW seconds before turning. Someone was in here, alive, and they were shooting at something.

"Come on," he said, rushing past Soon and down the corridor.

"Where?" Soon said.

Donovan wasn't sure. The shots were muffled, only obvious because of the overall silence of the base. It had sounded like they came from further down.

He reached the steps, pausing before opening the door. He needed more. Another sound. The base was too big to find the source quickly without it.

It was probably too late already.

He closed his eyes. Silence. He would have to guess. Someone had been alive in here. Who might it be?

He entered the stairwell, descending as fast as he could, Soon close behind him. He reached the second floor, stopping at the nursery and peering in through the small window. Empty. He hurried down the hallway, heading for the infirmary.

A large shape turned the corner ahead of him. For a split-second, he thought it was a bek'hai hunter in powered armor, it was so big. He almost fired without thinking.

The shape gained focus. A man, muscular, with dark skin and big eyes. He was bleeding from his shoulder, and had a pistol in his hand.

A Dread weapon.

Donovan threw himself to the side, shoving Soon with his shoulder at the same time. The clone's attack missed, the plasma strike going wide. Donovan stumbled back the other direction, keeping the clone's attention. It tracked him calmly, taking the time to aim.

A bolt from the other side of the corridor caught it in the chest. It grunted but didn't fall, finally taking the shot.

It hit the wall right next to Donovan's head, the aim thrown just enough by Soon's attack. That was the only shot it was able to fire, as four more bolts burned into it in rapid succession. The clone fell face down and didn't move.

"Thanks," Donovan said, looking over at Soon.

The pilot was shaking, his eyes stuck on the dead clone, his weapon still raised and ready to shoot again.

"Damn," Soon said, swallowing hard. He lowered the rifle. "They look just like us."

"They are us. Copies of us. Stay alert. There may be more." Donovan approached the clone.

It was wearing a rough spun green shirt and pants, similar to the simple fatigues the resistance soldiers usually wore. It was barefoot too, intended to look like a rebel fighter. It was no one that Donovan recognized.

"So much for not ambushing us down here," he said. Ehri had been wrong about the Domo'dahm's intentions.

Soon scanned the corridor, keeping the rifle ready. He had passed the most important test with flying colors, even if it had left him unsteady.

Donovan reached under the clone, grabbing the pistol and examining it. He hadn't seen such a small plasma weapon before. It didn't seem as powerful as the rifle, but it was more than enough to kill a human, and likely easy to conceal. Of course, it was locked.

"Somebody shot him," Soon said.

"It was coming from the infirmary," Donovan said. It was leaving, which meant whoever had shot it was most likely dead. He hoped not.

They hurried to the area, finding the medical equipment in disarray, the exam table on its side. There was blood on the ground, the clone's fresh blood. There was a second spread of still wet blood on the back wall, the pattern disrupted by a now-closed door.

"Who's in there?" Donovan said, trying to keep his voice low. He approached the door cautiously. "Doctor Iwu?"

He heard motion behind the door. He knocked softly.

"Doctor Iwu? Is that you? It's Donovan Peters."

The door clicked and opened. Doctor Iwu was standing behind it, holding General Rodriguez's gun in her hand.

"Donovan? You're alive." Her face hardened. "I need your help."

She lowered the gun, turning on her heel and heading back. Donovan followed behind her.

General Rodriguez was laying across her desk, his shirt torn off, his stomach bleeding beneath a heavy bandage.

"General?" Donovan said.

Rodriguez's head turned slowly. He smiled when he saw Donovan. "Donovan. Thank God."

"Donovan, I need you to keep pressure on the wound," Iwu said, pushing past him. "Excuse me," she said to Soon, who filed into the room.

"What's going on?" Donovan said. He turned around, watching Iwu search the cabinets for tools.

"The plasma bolt tore through his internals," Iwu said. "Either we sew them back together and pray, or he dies." She found what she was looking for and headed back into the room. "Did you kill the Dread soldier?"

"Yes," Donovan said. "General, where's everyone else?"

"I don't know," Rodriguez said, his voice barely more than a whisper. It was obvious he was having trouble breathing.

"Keep pressure here," Iwu said, pointing. She laid the tools out on the desk next to the General. Donovan did as she said. "You." Iwu looked at Soon. "When I ask for bandages, they're over there."

Soon found them. "Yes, ma'am."

"They were supposed to double back," Rodriguez continued. "Nobody came."

"I came," Iwu said.

"How long?" Donovan asked.

"Three hours. After the Dread cleared out."

"Except it wasn't clear," Donovan said. "The clone."

"It was clear," Iwu said, taking one of the tools and lifting the bandage. "There's too much blood." She was angry.

"It followed me back here," Rodriguez said. "I thought I had lost them. An entire squad of clones, plus that one. I've never seen a clone like that before." It took him ten breaths to say it, and he growled in pain when he was done.

"Me neither," Donovan said.

"Can you stop talking?" Iwu said to Rodriguez. "It makes it worse."

"It thought I was dead," Rodriguez said. "That's why it left. It didn't know the Doc was here."

"I said shut up," Iwu said. "You're going to die."

"Where's the rest of the squad?" Donovan asked.

"Don't know. You didn't see them?"

Donovan glanced over at Soon, who nodded and left the room.

"Who is that?" Rodriguez said. Iwu had moved back into the exam room, searching for something.

"Captain Soon Kim. He's a pilot from the space force. His fighter crashed. We saved him."

"You accomplished your mission?"

"Yes, sir."

"Suction. I need suction, damn it," Iwu said from the other room.

"I'm going to die, Major. There's nothing she can do about it now, even if she's too pig-headed not to try."

"Are they all dead?" Donovan asked. "The other resistance soldiers?"

"They didn't come back, except for you. They better be." He tried to laugh. It turned into a gurgling cough. Iwu came back into the room.

"Christian, you need to stop talking," Iwu said.

"Forget it, Nailah," Rodriguez said. "Even if you patch me, I can't move like this. You need to get out of here."

"I can't just leave you."

"You have to. It isn't safe. Donovan, I'm sorry. Your mom is probably dead. It's my fault. It was a bad plan."

Donovan ignored the pang of sadness. He didn't want to hear Rodriguez tell him what he already knew. "It wasn't, General. We did the best we could. We got the weapon to General St. Martin. That's the best we could have hoped for."

"It is. Thanks to you, Diaz, and Matteo. Thank you, Donovan."

"Major," Soon said, rushing into the room. "We've got company."

"Nailah, you have to go with them."

Doc Iwu looked pained, but she nodded. "You're a good man, Christian."

"You're a good woman. That's why I want you to stay alive."

She leaned down, kissing him on the mouth. "I always wanted to do that," she said.

"You should have said so sooner. Give me my gun."

She handed him his gun. He lifted himself to his feet, using the desk to stay up.

"Go. Donovan, try to make your way back to the States. There's a resistance base in Texas. At least, there was as of a few weeks ago. Austin. Look for the broken angel. The access code is one forty-three, twelve. It's a long way, but I know you can make it. Get the weapon to them in case the Gator doesn't make it back."

"Yes, sir," Donovan said.

"Major," Soon said.

"Goodbye, General," Donovan said.

"Adios, Donovan," Rodriguez replied. "Take care of yourself."

Donovan took Iwu's arm, pulling her gently out of the room, joining Soon and heading out into the hallway. He could hear the motion now. It sounded like the soldiers were headed their way.

"Go that way," Rodriguez said, stumbling through the door behind them, barely able to stand. "I'll keep them busy."

Donovan didn't argue. He kept moving. He heard Rodriguez speaking behind him as he turned the corner.

"In your unfailing love, silence my enemies; destroy all my foes, for I am your servant."

They were on the stairs when the gunshots sounded again.

[20]

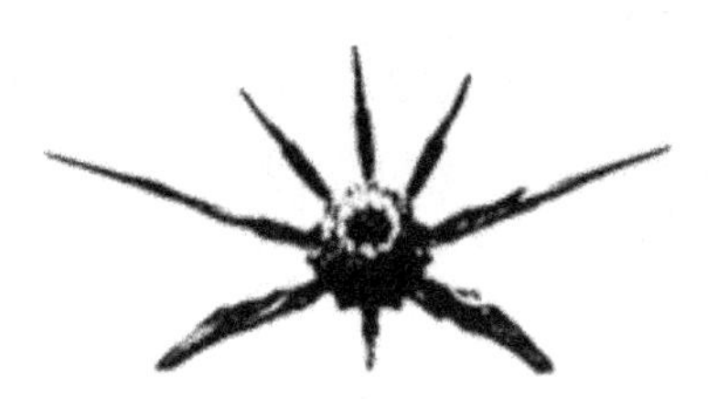

THEY RETURNED TO THE FIRST LEVEL OF THE BASE. THE shooting stopped by the time they reached the stairs, and they paused to listen. It was silent for a few moments before the enemy footsteps could be heard once more.

"He didn't get all of them," Soon said.

"We should get out of here," Iwu said. "That's what he wanted."

"Did you check the passage?" Donovan asked her.

"What passage?"

"The one in the General's office."

"No. I didn't know there was one."

"Then I'm not leaving. I need to know."

Rodriguez told him his mother was likely dead, and he knew it was true. Why did he have to go back to look for himself? What was the reason?

He had already lost Matteo. He wouldn't abandon her. Not if there was any chance she was alive. That was the reason. That was what he told himself.

"He died to get us out," Iwu said.

"He was going to die anyway," Donovan said. "We'll have a better defensive position from the General's office. And an escape route."

"Donovan," Diaz said, appearing from the corridor on their left.

He whipped his head around, his heart jumping. He had been so focused on listening to the Dread on the stairs he hadn't heard her coming. Stupid.

Ehri appeared beside her a moment later.

"We destroyed a squad of clone soldiers trying to get into the base," Ehri said. She froze for a second. "There are more already here?"

"Yes. They followed General Rodriguez back. I guess the Domo'-dahm didn't want him to get away."

"Where is the General?"

"Dead," Iwu said.

"The Domo'dahm isn't behind this. One of the pur'dahm perhaps, trying to make a good impression. Ulr'ek or Dur'rek, I bet. If the pur'-dahm could capture the General and interrogate him for information about the other resistance leaders, it would allow him to move up a cell."

"So it was a trap?" Soon said.

"Yes, but not for us. Even so, we must leave this area."

"We will. I need to finish what I started here. I need to know if she's dead or not."

"I understand."

"We've got the numbers. We should take care of this group. Soon, you and Diaz take position over there. Ehri, Doc Iwu, and I will wait there. We'll catch them in a crossfire when they come out of the stairwell."

"Yes, sir," Soon and Diaz said, backing up into the corridor.

Donovan retreated to the side, along the same wall as the stairs, positioning himself in front of Doctor Iwu.

Then they waited.

The three remaining Dread clones reached the top of the stair-well a minute later, moving out onto the floor without noticing the gathered rebel soldiers right away. By the time they did, it was too late. Bolts from both sides tore into them, dropping them in the space of a single breath.

"Nice work," Donovan said, stepping over the dead clones. "I guess it would have been too much to ask for the pur'dahm behind this to do the dirty work."

"Neither of those pur'dahm are hunters," Ehri said. "They are strategists. Politicians."

"This is a game to them?"

"In the sense that they are jockeying for position within a traditional ranking system, perhaps. There is nothing jovial about it."

They returned to Rodriguez's office. Donovan felt the same fear and anxiety bubbling up a second time as he entered the room. Until he saw her, there was a chance she had gotten away. He needed to know.

He circled the desk, reaching the open passage. He didn't hesitate, pushing it open wider so he could fit through and allow more light to filter in.

Nothing. There was nothing. Where were they?

He looked back at the others. They were waiting for him to make a decision. Should they follow the passage and keep seeking his mother and the children, or should they head back out through the silo? There were no guarantees either way, but the silo was definitely the shorter escape route.

Diaz had lost Matteo and kept going. She hadn't insisted that they find him, as much as he was sure she wanted to. She knew that wasn't the world they lived in. He knew it, too. He didn't have to like it.

He did have to accept it.

All of these people were looking for him to lead them and to keep their small part of the resistance going. They had gotten the weapon to General St. Martin. Now their job was to get the ground forces ready. They had to rendezvous with the rebels in Austin and reconnect with the larger forces, before the bek'hai turned those forces into scattered remains like they had done here.

Maybe Ehri understood why he wanted to find his mother. That didn't mean it was the right decision. Not now.

"It's time to go," he said, leaving the passage and heading back the way they had come.

[21]

"Lor'dahm Zoelle," Te'ave said, looking down at the clone from his position on the command dais.

"Dahm Tea'va," Zoelle said, lowering her head to her chest. "I am at your service."

"Ilk'ash spoke very highly of you before I had him retired."

Tea'va watched the clone carefully, studying her reaction to the news. She flinched slightly but otherwise remained in place.

"I would be honored to prove my worth to you, Dahm."

Tea'va almost smiled at the response. It nearly sounded sincere.

"Tell me, Lor'dahm. Were you practicing copulation with Ilk'ash?"

"Dahm?" she raised her head only slightly, maintaining respect. "I do not know what this means?"

"Were you ever unclothed with him?"

"No, Dahm. Why would I do such a thing?"

Tea'va stood. He was pleased with her response. She didn't know that had she answered differently, he would have killed her as well. "Why, indeed?" He made his way from the dais, reaching the level of the deck and standing in front of her. "Look at my face."

Zoelle raised her head, looking up at him. Tea'va had never been this close to an un'hai before. He stared at her features. Her soft, pale skin, her blue eyes. She had a smell of Earth. Flowers and spices. Did the humans think she was a pretty thing?

He didn't.

"Ilk'ash also told me that you were unable to calculate the human starship's slip trajectory in time to follow. You and your team. Is this correct?"

She didn't buckle under the statement. "Yes, Dahm."

"Why not?"

"We failed, Dahm. We were not prepared."

Tea'va smiled. She didn't react to his crooked grin either. "Your honesty is refreshing."

"The Lore of the Bek'hai demands honesty from a lor'hai, Dahm."

It was true that their laws put this burden on clones. It was also true that few enough of them followed it. Especially the un'hai. Even after fifty years of modification, they remained willful.

"Have you since calculated the trajectory?" Tea'va asked. It was intended to be the last question he had that would decide whether or not he replaced her, but he had already decided. He would keep this one. She was properly obedient, even if her team was not adequately intelligent.

"We have, Dahm. The slipstream has a powerful course through the planet. Once the gravitational effects are factored in, the wave will have carried them approximately six hundred light years from this location, if they rode it to its terminus. Based on the calculated wave velocity and the distortion of the accelerated stream, there is a ninety-eight percent likelihood that they did."

"They will have gone beyond the limits of the stream's ability to carry them. Are there other streams they can join to vector away, or can we follow?"

"We can follow, Dahm Tea'va. Most of the way."

"Most?" he shouted, losing control of his temper. He clenched his jaw. "Most?" he repeated more quietly. He noticed Gr'el was watching him with intense interest. Tea'va knew the pur'dahm would seize any sign of weakness he could find. He had to get his emotions under control.

"As you know, the slipstream wave strength is variable. We would be required to remain stationary for six Earth days to join a stream that is of equivalent power."

"We can't afford to wait six days," Tea'va said. "How close can we get?"

"Within one hundred light years, Dahm," Zoelle said, remaining calm.

Tea'va nearly shouted again. He held his tongue.

"That distance might as well be six hundred light years," he said.

"Perhaps we should consider a different approach?" Gr'el said.

Tea'va didn't want to listen to his Si'dahm. It would look bad to the Domo'dahm if he didn't entertain the pur'dahm's words.

"What do you suggest?"

"We seek out the human settlement," Gr'el said. "We know from our scans of the smaller craft we destroyed that they have a limited range. I am certain with the help of the complete science cell we can limit the possible locations. We can destroy the remaining colony, and then wait for the starship to return."

"And what if they don't return?" Tea'va asked. "What if they choose to go back to Earth?"

"Why would they do that? They may have escaped with our technology, but they would still need to be able to integrate it with their ship. One ship, against all of ours."

"One ship that has escaped us twice already. The Heil'shur, who has evaded our defenses over fifty times. Do not underestimate them, Gr'el. That is why they got away to begin with."

"One hundred light years, Tea'va. You cannot argue with pure mathematics."

"If I might, Si'dahm," Zoelle said.

"Go ahead," Tea'va said, not waiting for Gr'el to answer her.

"I have already plotted a course that will bring us close to our most accurate estimate of their position, a system we have charted as Pol'tik. We believe this is where their slipstream typically fades."

"How many streams?" Gr'el asked.

"Fourteen."

"Fourteen?" the pur'dahm replied in disbelief. "It isn't possible for you to accurately calculate the relative positions of fourteen streams."

"Of course, the timing is not perfect, Si'dahm, due to the variable nature of the waves, but I have chosen a course that remains highly stable. The risk is minimal."

"Would you be willing to put your life on it?" Gr'el asked.

Zoelle didn't look at him. She looked at Tea'va instead, keeping her eyes locked on his. There was no fear in them, only confidence.

"We were not prepared before, Dahm. We are prepared now."

"What is the time in slipspace?"

"Four hundred thirty-two to four-hundred eighty hours."

"Dahm Tea'va, you can't," Gr'el said. "Both the lor'hai and the drumhr will become sick."

"Do you want to advance in the cell, Gr'el?"

"Yes."

"With risk comes reward. We will either return to the Domo'-dahm as victors, or we will not return at all."

Gr'el lowered his head, surprising Tea'va with the strength of his submission. The pur'dahm understood the game better than he had even thought. "Yes, Dahm."

"Enter the calculations, Lor'dahm Zoelle. We will depart as soon as they are verified."

"Yes, Dahm Tea'va."

"You are dismissed."

Zoelle lowered her head to him, spinning on her heel at the same time and heading for the exit. The lor'hai that composed the rest of the bridge crew watched her from the corner of their eyes. Tea'va could see their interest there. Their longing. It was revolting. He decided he would meet her in private next time, so he wouldn't have to look at it. Nor would he have to deal with Gr'el's opinions.

"Dahm Tea'va," Gr'el said. "A word?"

"Yes, Si'dahm?" Tea'va said.

"I too would like to move up in the cell, and destroying the humans will be the impetus that will allow this to occur. As you are well aware, I am currently behind Orish'ek to replace Rorn'el on his retirement. I'm certain you also understand what that makes you and me."

Tea'va did understand. It was a delicate game they played. If they succeeded, Orish'ek would be out of the picture, but as commander of the Ishur, it would be Tea'va who took his place, leaving Gr'el still in the second position. At the same time, Gr'el couldn't sabotage the mission, or he would lose his place altogether. It meant that his Si'dahm would be plotting against him, even as they were working together. The pur'dahm was being gracious in warning him of his intentions, though Tea'va didn't need the warning.

"As I said, Gr'el. With risk comes reward. One of us will gain Rorn'el's position when he retires. The other will be dead."

[22]

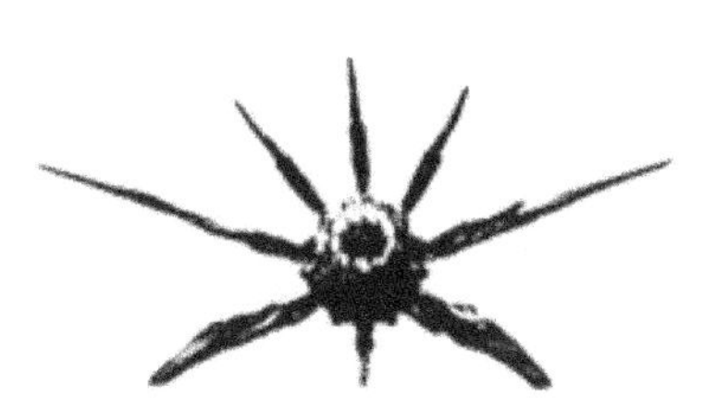

"MY GREAT-GRANDFATHER GREW UP HERE," DIAZ SAID, HER EYES scanning the scattered ruins of the city.

"San Luis Potosi," Ehri said. "Population four million at the time of the invasion."

"Your invasion," Diaz said.

"Not hers," Donovan replied. "The bek'hai. Ehri didn't exist before they arrived. It's ignorant to blame someone for something they didn't do."

Diaz glared at Donovan. Ehri raised her hand, playing peacemaker. "It is human nature, Major. Racial inequality persisted for centuries because of the sins of your forefathers. Besides, I'm willing to accept the derision."

"You shouldn't have to deal with derision," Donovan said, glaring back at Diaz. "Especially from your allies."

He didn't blame Diaz for her mood. They were all in poor spirits, after having spent the last twenty days on the road from Mexico. It was a grueling journey, slowed by their need to travel on foot, slowed even more by the frequent flyovers the Dread were making in an attempt to locate them. They had covered a little over four hundred kilometers in that time. It was a snail's pace as far as a Donovan was concerned, and it left him worried on a daily basis that the war would be over and lost before they ever arrived at the resistance base in Austin.

If there was still a resistance base to arrive at.

The pace was only one of their problems. The weather hadn't been favorable, the onset of summer leading into rising temperatures, high humidity, and an overabundance of mosquitos. They were fortunate malaria, and other insect-borne illnesses had been stamped out years ago. The loss of so many humans had given nature a chance to rebound, and the mosquito population was no different. While the Dread clothing made most of their bodies immune, their hands, necks, and faces were still exposed and had been fed upon freely. The summer weather had also brought the rain, daily thunderstorms and downpours that benefitted them by making them difficult for the Dread to track, but also left them constantly damp.

They had reached the outskirts of the city the night before, waiting until the sun had ridden high before moving into the ruins. It meant dealing with the heat, but that was better than dealing with the Dread, who they had found tended to avoid the direct sunlight when they could. Ehri had said the intensity would degrade their armor faster, reducing its effective lifespan from two thousand years to closer to eighteen hundred. Donovan had thought she was joking at first. She had reminded him to try not to think like a human. For a race the age of the bek'hai, such things were worth consideration.

While potable water had been easy to capture thanks to the heavy rains, food had been a different story. They had hurried away from the silo without pausing to take any of the stockpiled food, though Diaz had insisted on pausing at the Collection to locate the teddy bear her father had given her when she was only three years old. The plasma rifles they carried were useless for hunting, which had meant spending time every day foraging as best they could, or in some cases going hungry. None of them had been carrying a lot of extra weight when they had started the walk. Now they were all as lean as they could be.

"Where did he live?" Soon asked.

"My great-grandfather?" Diaz replied.

"Yes."

"Near the city center, close to the Barrio de San Sebastian. He died in the invasion. My mother told me he urged her father to get her away from the city when the news reports of the Dread ships started coming in. He practically threw them out himself." She smiled at the memory. "I wouldn't be here today if it weren't for him."

"It's still hard to look at," Soon said.

"It doesn't get easier," Donovan replied. "You tell yourself that you get used to it, but you don't. Our world isn't supposed to look like this."

Soon stared at the city. His initial wonder and intrigue over the planet had faded within the first few days, replaced with the cold, hard reality of not only what had occurred, but also how it was still affecting them all today. He had nearly come to tears as they had walked along the side of the highway, where hundreds of old cars had come to a final rest and the wild around them had started to cover it over. Some of the cars had bodies in them. Few carried any food. There had been so little time to try to escape, and the Dread had seen to it that they hadn't.

Donovan had talked to the pilot at length about that reality and how it compared to life at the human settlement on Calawan. They had wound up both agreeing they would rather be there than here, where freedom was a constant, daily battle, and usually meant little more than bare survival.

They had talked about other things as well, and most importantly about General St. Martin and his son, Gabriel. Soon had nothing but praises for both of the men, and firm conviction that not only would they return, but when they did the Dread would be truly challenged for the first time since their arrival. Soon had told him that the New Earth Alliance had a fighting force at their settlement, one that had been raised to wage war against the Dread. Once they could arm them properly, it would only be a matter of time.

"There's no use crying about it," Diaz said, moving ahead of them. "Don't get sad. Get even."

She hopped over a small, half crumbled wall, vanishing behind the uneven ground. The tip of her rifle appeared a moment later, signaling that she had expected the drop.

"This way," she said.

Donovan motioned for the rest of them to follow. For all Diaz's talk, she seemed to be taking their current situation the hardest. She had always been tough, but she had also managed to maintain some edge of softness, a genuine heart that beamed through the hardened exterior. Donovan had watched that light fade into a constant, desperate anger. She wanted to reach Austin. She wanted to get the weapons in the hands of someone who might be able to decipher them from the ground. She didn't want to depend on anyone else. Not General St. Martin, and not even him.

She had lost too much and was hurting too much. The more he tried to get her alone, to get her to open up, the more she withdrew. She said she didn't blame him for Matteo. That might have been true in the first few days. He knew that was bullshit, now. They had known one another all of their lives and had always shared a connection through her brother. Now that he was gone, the connection was gone.

It would have been harder to take if he didn't have Ehri.

As much as he tried to deny it, as much as he wanted to make it about the mission, and about the war, he couldn't help the feelings that were prompted whenever he was near her. Whether they were talking about human or bek'hai society, or simply sitting in silence, her very existence grew more important to him every day. He often found himself ruminating on the kiss they had shared back in the silo. When he had done it, he had thought that it was because he wanted to win her over to their side, and maybe he had. Now he wanted to do it again for the emotional value and connection. To show her how he felt.

Love? That might have been taking things a little too far. He had a definite crush on her. It was a strange feeling, one that made him both excited and uncomfortable. She was a replica of General St. Martin's wife. That fact alone made it strange. He also didn't know if she felt the same way. He was certain they were friends, but beyond that? She had never treated him in a way that suggested anything more. Was it because she didn't know anything about it? Or was it because those feelings just weren't there? It was maddening for him to think about, and at the same time, he wasn't going to make any romantic move on her.

They had enough problems.

They scaled the wall, dropping down into a narrow alley. Donovan turned when he reached the bottom, reaching back and helping Doc Iwu down. She was doing her best to hold her own, but she was older than the rest of them by at least twenty years, a child during the invasion. She struggled to keep up at times, though she had done so with the same poise and dignity that came so naturally to her.

"Thank you," she said, reaching the ground.

"Of course," Donovan replied.

Diaz was on point, her hand up to keep them stationary in the alley. Donovan could see by the way her head was darting back and forth that she was trying to find a route through the rubble. Their goal was to locate a market or a shelter, or some other building that may have been holding canned food and hope that it hadn't already been picked clean.

They had to be careful. The Dread weren't the only concern. There were plenty of random groups of humans who would rather prey on one another than wage war against the common enemy. General Rodriguez had always referred to them as jackals.

Diaz signaled for them to wait and then took off at a run, crossing an open area and ducking back into another narrow alley. She turned around when she reached it, looking back at them. Then she motioned them to get down.

Donovan dropped with the others, ducking into the shadows as a Dread fighter streaked over the position. The flybys were common in the morning and evening. They had been rare at this time of day.

It wasn't a good sign.

Seconds passed. Donovan finally stood and motioned to the

others to do the same. Diaz was on her feet on the other side. She waited a few seconds before signaling them to cross.

Donovan stayed in the rear, covering them as they passed the wider passage. They made it across without incident and then ducked a minute later when another Dread fighter went over.

"Do you think they spotted us?" he whispered to Ehri.

"I don't think so. They're moving too fast."

"D, look," Diaz said, pointing toward the sky.

A Dread transport had appeared behind the fighters. It was moving much slower, and coming in low enough that Donovan could make out the ripples of the armor that covered it.

"You're sure they haven't seen us?" Donovan asked.

"As sure as I can be," Ehri replied.

"Major," Iwu said. "Something's moving over there."

Donovan crawled to Iwu. She was near the corner of the rubble, also on her stomach. He watched as two people ran across the open area. They were dressed in rags and filthy. Scavengers.

The transport shifted direction, turning slightly toward them. Plasma cannons released rounds of bolts that decimated the area, raising a cloud of smoke, dust, and debris. The transport continued, disrupting the rising cloud as it passed and allowing Donovan to catch a glimpse of the scavengers.

They were both dead.

"There must be a small settlement here," Diaz said, joining him. "They'll have already picked the markets and pantries clean, but at least we can use the cover to get through the city."

Donovan looked back at her. "We should help them."

"Are you loco? There's five of us against an entire transport of them, plus two fighters."

Donovan considered, and then slid back to where Ehri was positioned. "If we can get to that transport, would you be able to fly it?"

"If it has been modified for lor'hai use, yes. Not all of the transports have."

"How can you tell?"

"If the transport only contains clones, it is likely that I can fly it. Otherwise, there is a good chance it has a drumhr pilot."

Shouts echoed in the distance, along with sporadic gunfire. Donovan had to make a decision. Escape the city on foot, knowing it would take them at least another sixty days to reach Austin, or make a play for the transport.

"I say we go for it," Soon said, unprompted. "We're already beaten and hungry, and if we manage to win?"

"If we manage to win, we'll piss off the Domo'dahm more than he is already," Donovan said. "That might be a mistake."

"He sent an entire transport to kill the people here," Ehri said. "Listen."

Donovan did. The gunfire was random, and already decreasing in volume.

"They aren't soldiers. They aren't fighters. He's destroying them anyway. He wants to kill every last one of us."

"Us?" Donovan said, surprised by the remarks.

Ehri froze for a moment, having surprised herself. Then she nodded.

"This is our war, Major. Let us fight."

[23]

Donovan crossed over a smaller pile of debris, turning the corner, leading with the end of the Dread rifle. The shouting and screams were louder now. Closer. They had closed the gap between the fighting and their original position, though the Dread transport was still out of sight.

He looked back at Soon, using the hand gestures he had taught the pilot to direct him around a separate pile of rubble. Then he glanced over at Ehri, pressed against a solitary standing wall to his left. He saw a Dread clone ahead of her, facing away from them. He signaled her a warning.

A soft whistle beyond his line of sight gave him Diaz's position. He had sent her to find the transport and report back if she saw any of the bek'hai, an indication that they might not be able to use the vehicle. Not that it would stop them from attacking. It was almost too late for that.

A clone came around the corner, shooting at something Donovan couldn't see. He was cautious with his power levels, taking the few seconds to aim before pulling the trigger and sending a bolt into the clone's abdomen. The enemy soldier fell.

Now it was too late.

Ehri broke around the corner, taking the clone by surprise. She didn't shoot him, using the rifle as a club instead. She hit him hard in the jaw, knocking him over. She fell on top of him, letting her weapon fall to her side and freeing her hands. She shifted on him, twisting his head with enough force that Donovan heard the crack of his neck. She grabbed her rifle and sprang back to her feet, signaling the all clear to him a second later.

It wasn't clear on the other side. An entire squad of clones had appeared ahead of Soon. One of them must have spotted him, because he was crouched behind the rubble, staying clear of the incoming plasma fire.

Donovan gestured to Ehri, and they made their way around the position, getting a better angle of attack on the soldiers. They fired in tandem, efficiently dropping them one at a time. Soon stood when the shooting stopped, giving them the thumbs up.

Diaz whistled again. Donovan ran to Soon's side.

"Head back to Doc Iwu, help her through this mess," he said.

"Yes, sir," Soon replied, falling back. "Thanks for the save."

"Anytime."

Donovan and Ehri went forward in the direction of Diaz's signal. He didn't know how she managed to evade the enemy so well, but he was glad for it.

A scream close to their left forced them off course. Donovan made his way past a somewhat intact building, spotting the scavengers before he saw the soldiers. They were trying to hide between two old cars, the plasma fire keeping them pinned down and frightened.

The soldiers never saw him or Ehri coming. Two plasma bolts dropped them, freeing the scavengers.

One of them was too scared to move right away. The other stood.

"Who are you?" she asked.

"The resistance," Donovan replied.

"The resistance is gone," the woman said.

"Who told you that?"

"Our leader, Murphy. He said that the base in Mexico City was wiped out and that the Dread are sending their armies after the rest. He said even the peaceful settlements and the jackals weren't safe. That's why we were trying to hide here. We thought we could escape their attention." The woman paused. "That's one of their weapons, isn't it?"

"Yes. Whatever you heard, it's wrong. The resistance isn't over."

"There were rumors someone had gotten their hands on Dread weapons, and that they were killing the bastards. I guess that's you." She smiled. "It may be too little, too late, I'm afraid."

"We're not going to let it be. Do you know where the rest of your people are?"

"That way," she said, pointing in the same direction as Diaz. "We had a few guns; maybe we'll take some of the clones with us. We can't do anything about the others, though."

"Others? Did you see the Dread?"

"I saw one. He killed my husband. He went that way."

"You might be safest to stay here for a while."

"What's your name, son?"

"Major Donovan Peters, ma'am."

"I'll pray for you, Major Peters. For as much time as I have left on this Earth. God bless you."

Donovan nodded, breaking off to join Ehri. She was standing behind another building, watching the field ahead of them.

"It looks like they've pinned down a small force over there," she said, pointing at a small zone where a group of scavengers and clones were trading fire. "Diaz is positioned over there." She pointed behind the clones, toward a thirty-foot pile of debris that had once been a skyscraper. "I think the transport is behind it."

"The woman told me she saw a bek'hai. We might be out of luck."

"What do you want to do?"

"What can we do? We've already committed. We'll try to make it to the transport and hope for the best."

"What about the others?"

Donovan knew she meant the scavengers. There was a good

chance that helping them would bring the remaining bulk of the bek'hai clones to their position.

Donovan shifted as Soon and Iwu came up behind them, joining them at the wall.

"We got three of them," Soon said.

"Not before they killed two more civilians," Iwu said.

"They're all going to die like that," Soon said, noticing the firefight.

"You want to stop it, Captain?" Donovan asked.

"Yes, sir."

"Okay. Circle to that corner. Ehri, wait here with Doc Iwu. I'll head to the left and try to get to their flank."

Diaz whistled again. It was a sharper tone. She was asking them to hurry.

"Forget that," he said. "There's no time to get fancy. Conserve your ammo, watch out for friendlies. Follow my lead."

Donovan closed his eyes for a moment. The woman had blessed him.

He hoped it helped.

[24]

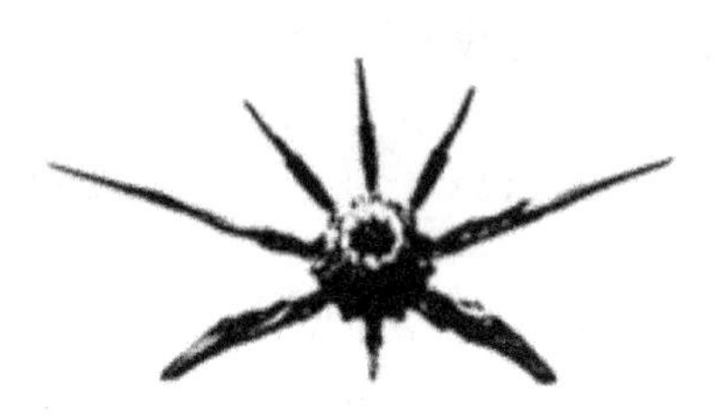

He moved out from behind the wall, sprinting towards an old car thirty meters away. The others followed behind him, joining him in the race.

One of the Dread clones must have noticed them, because a plasma bolt burned past his head a moment later, followed by two more. Then the return volleys began, Soon and Ehri returning fire, disrupting the attack and giving him a chance to reach cover.

They crouched behind it, the Dread offensive now split between them and the scavengers.

"I think I hit one," Soon said, pressed against the car beside him.

"We can't stay here," Ehri said. "Move."

She grabbed Donovan's arm, pulling him away from the car. Why? They would die as soon as they left cover.

Soon and Iwu followed them without question. Bolts cut the air around them, and then a heavy stream of burning energy blasted into the car, the Dread fighter streaking past as it finished its run, leaving the wreck in smoldering slag. Donovan looked back to the clones. One fell. Then another. To his left, the scavengers were breaking cover, going on the offensive.

"They're rallying," he said, stopping his retreat. They were open, too open, but they might not get another chance. He started shooting back at the Dread, careful not to waste the bolts he had remaining. He hit one, and then a second. He looked up. The fighter was circling back, coming in for another run. It would cut them apart.

"We need cover," he said.

Ehri noticed the fighter. "There isn't any."

"Back toward the scavengers."

He led them toward the human position, tracing the outskirts of the battlefield. Bullets and plasma bolts were filling the air with obstacles. There was nothing they could do but run.

They reached the line, where dirty men and women fired at the Dread with century-old pistols and rifles. They were surprised by the newcomers, but they didn't stop attacking.

The fighter streaked over, plasma cannon firing and slamming into the center of the human militia. Screams and shouts followed, along with smoke and debris.

"This isn't working out for us," Donovan said.

"I need to reach the transport," Ehri said.

"What if you can't fly it?"

"Then we're dead anyway."

Donovan frantically scanned the line of scavengers. There were only a dozen of them left, standing resolved in front of a stairwell.

That was why they hadn't run. They were defending something. Children, if he had to guess.

"Murphy," he shouted. "I'm looking for Murphy."

One of the men turned his haggard face in Donovan's direction. Donovan ran over to him.

"I need cover fire. A lot of it. From here to that corridor over there. Can you do it?"

"Who the hell do you think you are?" Murphy asked. He was a big man with tattooed arms and a thick beard.

"I know you have children down there," Donovan said. "Maybe women, too. Lay down some cover fire, and we may all be able to survive this."

Murphy didn't look convinced. He shouted to the scavengers anyway.

"Keep them covered. Keep it clear."

Donovan retreated to the others. "Ehri, let's go."

She stood, following him as he ran across the open field.

Bolts whizzed past them once more, diminishing as Murphy and the scavengers organized their fire. Soon joined them, sending plasma digging into the enemy position.

Donovan's heart was racing, his legs burning as he streaked across the field with Ehri beside him. The sprint seemed effortless to her, legs moving steady and strong to keep pace.

He heard the fighter coming, swooping in behind them. Ehri heard it too. They fell forward, pausing their run, tumbling on the ground as the plasma beam slammed into the ground ahead of them, close enough that he could feel the ionized heat of it. He rolled to a stop, wasting no time pushing himself up. Ehri did the same, falling in beside him. They were almost to the narrow corridor between the buildings.

Somehow, they were still alive.

They reached the wall, breaking free of the firefight, hurrying to the other end of the decimated building. The front of the transport became visible as they did, angled slightly toward them. It reminded him of a hornet with its sleek, angry face.

There were no soldiers near the transport that he could see. It looked as if it had been landed and abandoned, the entire contingent of the soldiers disembarking into the fray.

"We made it," he said through heavy breath, too excited about the outcome to stay silent. Ehri was pacing ahead of him, rushing to the open platform into the vehicle with an abandon that surprised him.

Humans were dying, and she wanted to stop it.

"Lor'el shur!"

The shout from behind them broke Donovan's train of thought, and caused Ehri to pull up to a fast stop in front of him.

They turned to face the source at the same time.

An armored pur'dahm, cradling something in his arms. He threw it to the ground as they looked his way.

Donovan couldn't breathe.

It was Diaz.

[25]

"LOR'EL SHUR," THE BEK'HAI REPEATED, HIS HELMETED HEAD turning from Ehri to Donovan. "Come back with me, un'hai," he said to Ehri in thick, growling English. "No more humans have to die today."

Donovan stared at the body on the ground in front of the pur'-dahm. Diaz's limbs were twisted unnaturally; her head limp on a broken neck. His entire body was numb and tingling. His mind was nearly blank.

He had known Diaz almost their entire lives. She had gone from annoying kid sister, to valued Lieutenant, to what, exactly? He didn't know. Ehri had come along, and everything had been happening so fast.

It didn't matter now. She wasn't just dead. She was broken. Treated like a toy and used as an example by the Dread Warrior.

Ehri was making her way back toward the bek'hai. Her face was stone, but her eyes betrayed her anger. She and Diaz had never gotten along, but to Donovan they had been more like bickering sisters. They shared a level of respect if nothing else.

"Come with you? I'll kill you, Til'ek," she said.

"Ehri, no," Donovan said.

She froze next to him. "What?"

Donovan swallowed his nerves, taking a few steps in the pur'-dahm's direction. He hoped he understood the customs.

"Call off your soldiers, Til'ek," he said. "We can settle this here and now."

The bek'hai seemed amused. "Hesh dur bek?"

Ehri had taught him those words. An honor fight. A duel.

"Yes."

"I will crush you."

"Hand to hand in your armor, you will. Will you fight on my terms?"

"Name them."

"Ehri, did you ever watch streams from the twentieth century? Westerns?"

"Westerns?"

"Gunfights? Two people at opposite ends of a street, ready to draw their weapons?" He had seen an old stream of it once. He knew people settled their differences that way centuries ago. It was the most fair fight he could have with the Dread pur'dahm.

She considered for a moment and then nodded. "Yes, I do remember something like that, once."

"Can you describe it to that asshole in his language, so we're clear?"

"Of course."

Ehri barked at the pur'dahm in the bek'hai's guttural language, describing how it worked. Donovan noticed that the sounds of violence had paused in the distance. Til'ek must have ordered his troops to stand down.

Donovan's eyes fell back to Diaz's body. He felt the anger welling up. It was his fault she was dead. He shouldn't have let her go off on her own, but she had always been so good at evading the enemy. He wouldn't fail again.

"When I am victorious, your people will be forfeit to me," Til'ek said. "And you will return to the Domo'dahm and explain yourself."

"If I win, your forces will retreat from this area," Donovan said. "On foot."

"You want the ship? I piloted it here, lor'hai. You cannot use it."

The words were a blow. Ehri's face showed her frustration for an instant before returning to calm. Donovan fought hard to keep his emotions from becoming apparent. Even if he won, they were still going to be on foot. Maybe they could at least salvage something from the vehicle.

"On foot," he repeated. "And these people are to be spared."

"I do not have the power to promise that. Only the Domo'dahm can spare your people, and he chooses not to. I can offer three days."

Donovan glanced at Ehri. She nodded. He was telling the truth.

"Agreed."

The pur'dahm bowed his head slightly. Donovan knew it was a show of respect. He did the same. Then they approached one another, for a moment standing face to face. The bek'hai was shorter than him without the armor, slightly taller with it.

They didn't speak, turning back-to-back. Then they walked away from one another, fifty steps each before turning around again.

Donovan held the Dread rifle at his side, staring across the distance to Til'ek. The Dread was holding his weapon almost casually. He was arrogant. He didn't believe a human could outmatch him at anything.

Donovan would make sure it was his undoing.

They faced off, motionless and silent. Donovan caught movement in the corner of his eye. The Dread clones, the scavengers, Soon and Doc Iwu had all come to witness this. He couldn't see Iwu's face when she noticed Diaz's body. He didn't dare lose his concentration.

Til'ek twitched, his rifle rising from his hip.

Time seemed to stop.

Donovan began lifting his weapon. He could hear every heartbeat in his ears, sense every molecule of air against his face, smell every scent of death and blood and burning. It all happened so fast, and yet so slow. He got the rifle up in one hand. The pur'dahm did the same.

He squeezed the trigger, the plasma bolt rocketing across the distance. Til'ek had yet to take his shot.

The Dread saw the bolt coming. He fired back in desperation, his bolt going wide as Donovan's blast hit him square in the chest. The plasma pierced his armor, burning a hole through it and his flesh. He didn't seem to understand the rules. He stumbled, trying to get his rifle up and shoot again, sending a bolt into the ground ahead of Donovan. A second bolt from Donovan's right it the pur'dahm in the face. Ehri. The body tumbled to the dirt.

Silence. Til'ek's corpse rested a few meters from Diaz. Donovan let himself breathe, the tears springing up as soon as the moment had passed. The scavengers and the bek'hai clones all remained in place, shocked and confused.

"Yes," he heard Soon shout from his left.

The pilot's voice shattered the tense aftermath. The scavengers raised their rifles, aiming them at the clones. The clones didn't fight back.

At once, they all turned and began to walk away.

Donovan ran to Diaz, crouching down next to her. The teddy bear she had salvaged from the silo was hanging by its neck from her belt. He reached down and took it, holding it tight in his hand while he let the tears come. He hadn't cried for his mother like this, but then, he had never seen her body.

Ehri stepped up next to him, putting her hand on his shoulder.

"The bek'hai have no death rituals," she said awkwardly. "Death just is. I'm sorry."

"We'll help you bury her," Murphy said. "It's the least we can do."

"You have three days," Donovan said, looking up at him. "That's all I could get you."

"It will have to be enough. We've been running from them for years. It's getting harder, but we do what we have to. You saved our lives here. You saved my daughter's life."

"And my son's," one of the other scavenger said.

"And ours." Donovan recognized the woman that had been trapped behind the car.

"Ehri, check the transport," Donovan said. "See if there's anything we can use. Unsecured weapons, hopefully."

"Yes, sir," Ehri said, moving away.

Soon and Iwu made their way to him.

"I'm sorry," Soon said.

"So am I," Iwu said.

"We won today," Soon added. "Thanks to you, and to her. These people are alive because of us."

Donovan smiled. In this world, the best any of them could hope for was not to die for nothing.

Diaz hadn't.

[26]

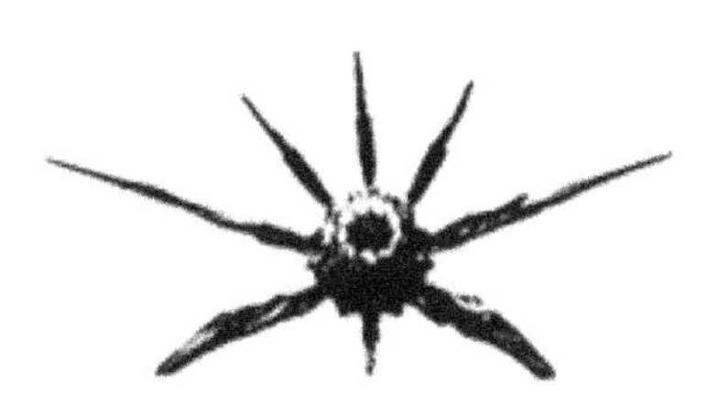

Tea'va shuddered slightly as the *Ishur* came off of the last of the fourteen slipspace waves, the universe coming back into focus through the viewport. At first, all he saw was empty space and a few stars through eyes blurred by too much time in the void. They regained themselves within seconds, and he turned his head to survey the crew beneath him.

Gr'el seemed to be the next least affected. He leaned forward at his station, shaking slightly, before sitting back and looking around. The clones were faring the worst. Some sat motionless. Others vomited onto the floor.

One fell from his chair, dead.

Fourteen. It had to be a record. Just remembering the sequence of returning to realspace, accelerating to the next point, and joining the slipstream again made Tea'va feel dizzy once more.

He had to stop thinking about it.

He stood up, fighting off the instability of his legs. It was as if his body had yet to return to the same spacetime, and was moving out of sync with his mind. He leaned against the side of the dais as he descended.

"Gr'el, you have the bridge," he said as he passed the pur'dahm.

"Yes, Dahm," Gr'el replied.

"Get a report on the health of the lor'hai. Begin scanning the system for signs of the human ship."

"Yes, Dahm."

Tea'va made his way from the bridge. The days in slipspace had given him an appropriate amount of time to adapt to being in command. He had calmed a bit as a result, feeling more confident and less defensive. The crew knew who was in charge. Even Gr'el grudgingly accepted it for now. He was certain his Si'dahm was plotting against him, but Gr'el had not even tried to be subtle about that. It was all part of the game, and his responsibility to see it coming.

Zoelle had been valuable in that regard. He had found an ally in the un'hai, one who was eager to please him. He had confided in her about Gr'el's position, and she had quietly organized a network of spies to watch the Si'dahm and ensure he was not creating a faction of his own. So far he wasn't, but it was still early.

As much as he had wanted to hate the clone before they had met, he had become quite fond of her. He had no interest in her body, or in trying to breed with her. Rather, he appreciated her analytical mind and her genuine intellect and ability to reason through challenging problems. He had gone to her to discuss his position in the cell on more than one occasion, and she had provided discourse that he had always been lacking.

When the human ship was destroyed, and he returned to Earth to take the bek'hai from the Domo'dahm, he would do it with Zoelle as his heil'bek. He was certain that with her input, there was nothing that he couldn't accomplish.

At the same time, there was a part of him that was disgusted with the thought. He had come into being with the idea that he didn't need anybody to help him do anything. He would rise to power on his own, under his own strength, and when he ruled the bek'hai he would do it his way and his way only.

How had this creature, a lor'hai, changed his perspective so quickly?

Had this same fate befallen the Domo'dahm? Was that why the original un'hai had become so revered?

He would have to be careful, and work harder to keep his emotions in check. It was one thing to value the opinion of the un'hai. It was another to rush into giving her such control.

She was waiting for him in his quarters when he reached them. He hadn't requested her presence, and for a moment he was angry that she had been so presumptuous. Maybe it was better to retire her now and avoid complications later? But she had plotted this course, a complex masterpiece of mathematics, and gotten them to the Pol'tik system ahead of the human ship. Surely, that kind of performance deserved a little forgiveness.

"Zoelle," Tea'va said, remaining calm. "Why have you come to see me?"

She was standing near the viewport, looking out at the newly refocused stars. Her gori'shah covered the length of her arms and neck and fell to the heels of her feet. It was also loose around her chest, making her gender less apparent. It was a more conservative look than the last time he had seen her. He approved.

"Dahm Tea'va," she said, turning and sweeping her head low in a strong sign of servitude. "My apologies for intruding. I would not if it were not important."

"What is your concern?" Tea'va asked.

"I have been studying the effects of the compounded slipspace maneuvers on the health of the crew, both drumhr and lor'hai, to help educate future needs to follow a similar trajectory."

"And what did you discover?"

"Forty percent of the drumhr are sick beyond operating capacity. It is a higher number than I had hoped, but it is still within range of my calculations. Interestingly, Var'ek, like yourself, did not suffer any ill effect from the travel."

"I would not say that I have not felt unwell. You also appear to have escaped unharmed."

"I have been too consumed with my work to tell one spacetime from another." She smiled at that. Tea'va cocked his head in curiosity, and the smile vanished. "The lor'hai did not fare as well, Dahm. Ninety-five percent are unable to perform their duties, and two percent of them did not survive the trip. By my estimates, it will take four days before the crew is well enough to be back at full operational capability."

"I already know the lor'hai are weak," Tea'va said. "While you overassessed their capability, I assumed what you have just stated as true. I am not surprised."

"With your permission, Dahm, I urge caution in the next few days. With our numbers at their current levels, we would be hard-pressed to mount a serious offensive should the human starship arrive."

"Caution?" Tea'va said. That statement started to make him angry. "Their ship has no weapons. Once we have caught up to them, we can destroy them at our leisure. I trust you won't let them slip away again?"

"No, Dahm. I will not. Even so, I ask that you consider that the humans may have succeeded in reverse-engineering our technology and that they may have already produced one or more weapons capable of damaging the lek'shah. Also, there is the matter of the slip-space variability in this system that could become a detriment, for as much as we have used it as an asset."

"You overestimate them as you overestimated the lor'hai. They have not had enough time to determine the properties of the weapon so soon. In fact, I don't believe they will ever comprehend the nature of the technology. Their methods and understanding are too primitive to make the proper logical assumptions."

"I disagree, Dahm Tea'va," Zoelle said, keeping her head low as she did. "The humans caught us off-guard, both in their ability to escape with the weapon and in their ability to escape from Earth. They have proven to be unpredictable and resourceful, and I believe that makes them dangerous."

Tea'va stared at Zoelle. "You almost sound as though you admire them."

"I am intrigued by their actions, as any scientifically minded clone would be. I wish only to serve you, Dahm, and offer you my opinion, as you have specifically requested it in the past. You have shared your political ambitions with me, and I would like to see you achieve them."

"Those are the right words. I am curious about your motivation."

"When you have power, I will have power. It is as simple as that."

"I did not believe the lor'hai hungered for such things. You are less. You will always be less."

They were sharp words, but they drew no reaction from her. "Within the right contexts, with the right pur'dahm as Domo'dahm, I believe I can be more."

They were both silent for a moment while Tea'va considered her words. If she had been any other lor'hai, he would have dismissed them already. He did value her opinions, her honesty, and her subservience.

"I will think on what you have said. Go now. I require time in the regeneration chamber."

Zoelle swept herself low again. "Yes, Dahm. Thank you, Dahm."

She was heading for the exit when Gr'el's voice pierced the room.

"Dahm Tea'va, my apologies for the disruption, but our scans have returned an anomaly near the edge of the system. I believe we have found them."

[27]

Tea'va hurried from his quarters with Zoelle trailing a few meters behind him. His legs were still unsteady from the slip-space travel, his excitement growing at their immediate success. The un'hai behind him had made it possible, and if power were what she was after, he would be sure to reward her for that.

"Where are they?" he asked as he gained the bridge. The crew was supposed to stand and lower their heads in deference, and some tried, but many were too unwell to react quickly enough.

Gr'el brought up a star map, a holographic view of the system that hung in the center of the bridge. The Ishur was obvious near one side of the system. A purple shape hung at the other side. The anomaly.

"It may not be the humans, Dahm," Zoelle said. "Only an unexpected mass within the system, based on our prior mappings and projections."

"What else would it be?" Gr'el asked. "The Azera?"

"Not this far from their home world," Tea'va said. "It has to be the humans." He glanced at Zoelle. "Or do you have another guess?"

"No, Dahm."

She wouldn't dare repeat what she had said to him in his quarters in front of Gr'el and the crew. Even so, her reaction forced him to consider it. The lor'hai were sick and even the drumhr were at half-strength. At the moment the Ishur was barely able to stay operational. If the enemy had managed to harness the technology to damage the ship's armor, they would be on much more equal footing in a fight.

If they had conquered the technology. The plasma weapons were deceptively simple things, and the most important components were at nano-scale. Did the human ship even possess the means to see that deeply into the internals?

He doubted it.

"How quickly can we intercept?"

"Six hours, Dahm," Gr'el said.

"Zoelle, what will the state of the crew be in that time?"

"Not optimal, Dahm. A ten percent improvement, if that."

Tea'va could tell by her expression that she was trying to warn him subtly against moving forward once more. Some part of her believed the humans were capable of creating a weapon, and that the Heil'shur would be skilled enough to use it to destroy them. He didn't understand how that could be.

"We cannot let them slip away again," Gr'el said. "We must move forward now before they can reach a stream."

"If they run, we can follow," Zoelle said.

"Why is this lor'hai on the bridge, Tea'va?" Gr'el replied. "I do not recall you requesting her here, and I certainly did not."

Tea'va felt the fury rising within him. Gr'el wanted to make him look like a fool.

"If I did not want her here, she would not be here," he growled.

He didn't have the option of heeding her words now. It would make him look weak. Not that he was going to, anyway.

"Set a course for the anomaly at full thrust. Gr'el, order the Gi'shah Dahm to assess his drumhr and prepare the combat ready. Also, get an assessment of how many plasma batteries we have the crew to operate. We will devise our strategy based on our operational efficiencies."

"Yes, Dahm" Gr'el said.

"Zoelle, you are dismissed. Scientists have no place in war."

She bowed low, the subtle change in her face telling him she didn't approve.

Fortunately, the decision wasn't hers.

He stared at the purple blob in the middle of the display. His crew was sick from the many slips it had taken to reach the system, but it was a risk that was already bearing results. He hadn't come this far to back away once the humans came into his sights.

"Prepare for battle."

[28]

Gabriel was getting worried.

Twenty days had passed since the Magellan had dropped back into realspace.

Twenty days since his father had vanished from the bridge, retreating to his quarters to battle his addiction to the pain medication and to battle his ability to handle the pain.

Twenty days out of twenty-two that would see them reaching the planetary system where they could finally rejoin a slipstream and make their way back home.

His father had yet to make a public appearance. He had remained in hiding, secured behind the barrier of Diallo and Hafizi, who refused to let anyone into the quarters, not even to make sure Theodore was still alive. They insisted that he was. That was all the information they would give, even to him.

He had made a promise to his father that he would keep quiet, but it was getting harder to do with each passing day. There were whispers among the crew that his father had lost his mind, deteriorated to the point that he couldn't lead them, or had flat-out given up on the mission and abandoned them completely. Fortunately, that was the rumor that was least believed. Most felt he was in bad shape, an unfortunate casualty of war.

Even Gabriel was beginning to think that way.

The other thing that had him worried was Guy and Reza's lack of progress on the weapon they had recovered. In the first week, the pair had spent eighteen out of every twenty-four hours down in the laboratory, trying to crack the mystery of the device. It had proven to be harder than they had expected. By the second week, that time had been reduced to twelve hours. Now nearing the end of their third week, Colonel Choi had sent Gabriel to find Reza, who hadn't made an appearance in the lab in three days.

Gabriel wished General St. Martin would return to the bridge to pull them together. Sometimes, he even prayed that he would. A pall was being cast over the ship, despite the repair crews getting most of the damage shored up, despite their proximity to a slipstream that would finally get them back into the fight. The entire mission, the entire war, was beginning to come unglued by inaction, the cracks forming at the seams. He knew Theodore could fix them with one round of sharp commands cracked off in his signature Cajun accent.

But he also couldn't rely on it.

It was a hard thing for him to accept. His father had always been so dependable. He felt sick at the idea that this was a fight the General couldn't win. That after years of promises that he would get the planet back, he would fall apart over something as small as a pill. It was such a human thing, and he had never seen his father as human.

Reza's quarters weren't far from the central hub. He had been given a larger berthing than some of the other crew members, to allow him space and privacy and the ability to think without distraction. Gabriel had spoken to Miranda before heading down, trying to determine where Reza had been for the last three days. As part of operations, she was supposed to know where every crew member was when they were on duty. She had told him that the scientist had been spotted in the mess a few times each day, often with Sarah Larone at the table with him.

It was a worrying development for Gabriel. Guy was smart, but he was also a hothead, and if anything was happening between Reza and Sarah, it had the potential to explode. In a closed environment like theirs, it only took one detonation to cause a chain reaction of bad morale.

And morale was already down. They couldn't afford to let it get any worse.

He reached the scientist's door and banged the side of his fist against it. He knew the control pad was non-functional. Reza had rigged something to get himself in and out, and most of the time that was good enough.

Nobody answered.

"Maggie, connect me to Spaceman Locke," Gabriel said, asking the ship's computer to patch him into her station.

"Yes, Captain," it replied, the voice seeming to come from everywhere.

"Captain St. Martin," Miranda said. "How can I help you?"

"I'm at Reza's door, but nobody is answering. Can you verify he's in there?"

"Give me a minute, sir," Miranda replied.

He knocked again while he waited for her to get back to him, again receiving no response.

"I asked around. He isn't in the mess or the lab. Nobody has seen him in a while."

Gabriel wished the doors on the Magellan were a little less thick. "What about Sarah?" he asked, unhappy that he even needed to question.

"One minute, sir."

Gabriel waited again while she pinged the senior officers, asking after Sarah Larone's whereabouts.

"She hasn't been seen in awhile either, sir," Miranda said. "Guy said that if you do find her, he would appreciate a minute alone with his wife so they can talk."

"How did he sound when he said that?"

"Angrier than usual."

"I don't have a good feeling about this."

"No, sir."

"Have you tried to contact Reza?"

"Yes, sir. His comm is set to private."

"Sarah?"

"The same."

"Bad to worse."

"Do you think they're messing around behind Guy's back, sir?"

"Messing around? Yes. Behind his back? Not nearly far enough."

Gabriel sighed. Colonel Choi was doing the best she could, but she didn't want to get involved in people's private lives. His father would have never let this become an issue. He blamed himself for not doing more himself. Reza and Sarah were civilians, but they were on a ship at war, and they had a duty to conduct themselves with more tact.

"Maggie, connect me to Reza Mokri, please," Gabriel said.

"Reza Mokri has set his communication status to private," Maggie said.

"Command override," Gabriel said. "Captain Gabriel St. Martin. Reason: mission critical communication."

"Override accepted."

"Reza," Gabriel said. "It's Gabriel. I'm standing outside your door. You have ten seconds to open it before I get a tech to open it for me. I'm not usually a violent man, but if I have to do that, I will be."

[29]

He stood facing the door, tapping his foot to count off the seconds. He had reached five when the door slid open.

Reza had a pair of pants on without a shirt. His wild hair was even more wild than usual. He caught a glimpse of Sarah Larone in the background, sitting in bed with the blankets covering her.

"Gabriel," Reza said.

Gabriel grabbed him by the arm, tugging him from the room.

Reza hit hard against the bulkhead, his door closing behind him. Gabriel didn't want to be violent. He didn't want to be angry. He was angrier because of that.

"You do recall that we're at war, do you not Mr. Mokri?" he said, getting up in Reza's face.

"Gabriel? I... uh..."

"It's Captain St. Martin," Gabriel snapped.

"Uh... Yes, okay," Reza replied, still stunned.

"Yes, what?" Gabriel shouted.

"Yes, sir," Reza said.

Gabriel let him go, backing up a step and pointing a finger at him. "I don't want you to say a damn thing. I don't want to hear any excuses. What you do with your free time is your own business, as long as it doesn't impact the operations of this ship."

He paused, giving Reza a chance to try to speak. The scientist remained pressed against the wall, his eyes frightened.

"Number one, you don't have any free time on this ship. Number two, what you're doing with what you don't have is impacting our operations beyond my capacity to understand how you think it could possibly be acceptable."

"Colonel Choi," Reza started to say.

"Colonel Choi was giving you a chance to use some of your intelligence to figure things out for yourself. Apparently, you're incapable of doing that when there's a woman added to the equation. A woman who is married, I might add. A woman who also helped get you tossed into prison, by the way."

"Sarah's not like that. She was just trying to-"

"Trying to what? Save half the settlement? And suddenly that's okay for you, too?"

"Uh... No... Gab- Captain St. Martin, sir. Please. I can explain."

"I don't want you to explain. I don't want either of you to explain. I don't care if she came on to you, or you came on to her. I don't care if she's misunderstood, or you're misunderstood. I don't care if the two of you having sex with one another helps one, or the both of you think better." He paused. "Unless you can tell me that you have a solution to our problem with the Dread weapon that resulted from your romantic interlude?"

"Uh." Reza looked at the floor. "No, sir."

"Do you think that Guy is stupid? Do you think he has no idea what's going on with you two? I have three scientists on this ship. Three scientists that are supposed to be reverse-engineering an enemy weapon so that we can get our planet back from the Dread, which in my estimation is a little more important than a few minutes, hours, or days of physical pleasure. Now those three scientists are going to be impossible to get to work together with any kind of cohesive effectiveness. Do you get where I'm going, Mr. Mokri?"

"Yes, sir. I wasn't thinking-"

"I know you weren't thinking. Neither of you were thinking. If you were thinking, maybe you would have solved the damn problem already, instead of making a bigger one."

Reza swallowed hard. "I'll get back to the lab. I'll put in extra time. I promise."

"I'm not about to work with this little piece of shit," Guy said.

Gabriel turned to look at Guy, who had approached unnoticed in the middle of his tirade. Guy looked almost as haggard as Reza, though it was likely from stress and lack of sleep. The scientist's hands were balled into fists, his face beet red.

"I'd like nothing more than to beat the living snot out of him and you, Captain St. Martin. This is your fault. You and your father. We don't belong out here, trying to win an unwinnable war. The weapon? All it has served to do is prove it. I've scanned the entire thing in and virtually disassembled every component. There is nothing about it that offers any clue as to why it can defeat the Dread armor when nothing else can. You've hindered our chances to reach the New Earth with this folly, and if that wasn't enough, you've destroyed my marriage as well."

Gabriel barely heard any of the other words that Guy had spewed. Nothing? There was nothing? He had seen the Dread plasma rifle pierce the Dread armor. There was something. There had to be. Why had the scientist been unable to find it?

"There has to be a difference," Reza said. "You aren't looking at it right. But then, you don't look at anything right, do you? You think everything and everyone is against you. Even your wife."

Guy's face contorted in anger, and he lunged for Reza. "Don't you dare say a thing about my wife," he snarled.

Gabriel stepped between them, pushing Guy back. He ducked aside as Guy took a swing at him, dodging it before punching the scientist hard in the gut.

Guy doubled over; the wind knocked out of him. Then he started to sob.

"I wanted to get us off that damned rock," he said. "To give humankind a chance to start over, to grow and expand. Why does that make me the bad guy? I don't want others to die, but there was no other way to make it work. Sarah said she understood. She supported me. And then we came here, and she turned on me so quickly. She came over to that crusty old man's side without a second thought. She betrayed me once, and now she's betrayed me again. What did I do to deserve that?"

Gabriel looked at Guy, finding himself almost sympathizing with him. The anger was fading from him quickly. He needed to get both Guy and Reza back on track, their attention refocused on the Dread technology.

Reza's door opened again, and Sarah came out, fully dressed. She glanced at Gabriel and then looked away, embarrassed.

Guy looked up at her, his eyes red, tears on his face. Her expression turned more distraught when she saw it.

"The weapon is useless, Captain," Guy said softly. "The Dread are too advanced. We don't have the means to break down what they've done into something we can use. I'm sorry. I've tried to play along, to be part of the solution. I tried to work it out. I failed. I'm sorry I failed."

Gabriel realized Guy was speaking to Sarah when he said that. Tears were beginning to flow from her eyes as well. He looked at Reza, who was slouched against the bulkhead, looking small.

"What do we do now?" Reza asked.

"You get dressed and get your ass down to the lab," Gabriel said. "I need to know if what Guy is saying is true. Guy, Sarah, whatever you need to figure out, figure it out. I need everyone operating-"

Gabriel was cut off as the lights began flashing around them, and a voice sounded from the speakers.

"Captain St. Martin to the bridge," Colonel Choi said. "All other crew to your stations immediately. This a red alert. I repeat, this is a red alert."

"What's happening?" Reza said.

Gabriel did his best to keep himself from tensing. "It means the enemy has been spotted."

[30]

"CAPTAIN, TAKE THE PILOT STATION PLEASE," COLONEL CHOI said, the moment Gabriel arrived on the bridge. Sarah and Guy weren't far behind, taking their places at their station without comment.

Reza had returned to his quarters to find some clothes.

"What's the situation, ma'am?" Gabriel asked on his way.

"Maggie, release steering controls," Choi said.

"Releasing," the computer replied.

"You know what Red Alert means, Captain," Choi said, glancing over at the Larones. She didn't look happy.

"Yes, ma'am."

Gabriel took his seat, bringing up the sensor view to see for himself. The shape of the Dread fortress was unmistakable. He checked the distance. It was still a good ten minutes away from their position. At least they had a little time to prepare.

"How did they find us?" Guy asked. His eyes were still red, but he had regained his composure and was pointedly ignoring his wife. He didn't even flinch when Reza finally made it to the bridge and joined them.

"They must have followed the stream," Reza said. "They knew

which one we took, and they would have understood the likelihood that we were dropped at the terminus. The real question is, how did they get here so fast?"

"There were no streams from Earth to here," Sarah said. "They would have had to make multiple slips."

"That would make humans ill," Choi said. "Do you think it affects them the same way?"

"I don't know," Reza said.

"What should we do, Colonel?" Gabriel asked. He had control of the Magellan, but no idea what to do with it. He checked their surroundings. There was a small planet not far from them, but it would offer limited cover.

Then again, limited was better than none.

"Head for that planet," Choi said, sharing his thought. "We'll figure the rest out when we get there."

Gabriel took the controls, adjusting the main thrusters and vectoring thrust to begin to bring the Magellan around. He tensed when the Dread fortress released the first volley from its main plasma cannon, sending a huge stream of molten energy spewing toward them.

Gabriel deftly adjusted course and speed, rotating the Magellan and turning it belly up. The plasma continued past them, missing by a wide margin.

"They're trying to keep us from the planet," Miranda said from her station.

"Clearly," Choi agreed. "Captain St. Martin, we need to make it to the other side. It's our only chance to delay them."

"Yes, ma'am," Gabriel said. He was surprisingly calm, despite the fact that the Dread were closing in, and they still had no means to fight them.

He got the bow of the Magellan pointed toward the planet and drove the mains to full thrust. The direction put them moving away from the Dread fortress, exposing their rear and their engines. It was a dangerous thing to do, but they didn't have a choice. He put a hand to his chest, whispering a prayer and tapping the crucifix beneath his shirt. He needed his mother's divine intercession now more than ever.

A second plasma blast launched from the Dread ship. Gabriel followed it closely on his screen. He shifted the Magellan, rolling it and dipping like he would if he were in a fighter. The larger ship was slower to respond, the size making it less maneuverable. He cursed at it for being slow before breathing a sigh of relief as the plasma cleared the top of the ship by meters.

"Too close," he said.

"They're closing the distance," Reza said. "We can't outrun them."

"We'll make it," Gabriel said, monitoring the two distances.

A third plasma stream streaked toward them. Gabriel adjusted course, making every effort to avoid the attack. The Dread fortress was closer, the Magellan too slow to change position, or maybe the enemy had guessed their direction. The plasma skimmed the edge of the left QPG nacelle, tearing the side of it away in a shower of quickly snuffed out sparks.

"Damn it," Gabriel said out loud. He wasn't used to piloting a ship like this, and they were going to die because of it. He knew it, and by the hushed silence around him, he was sure the rest of them knew it too. "Where the hell is my father?"

"Locked and loaded, my boy," Theodore said, rolling onto the bridge. "Sorry I'm late, but I needed to pee first."

Gabriel felt the change in the air the moment he did, the feeling of tense desperation turning in an instant to one of true hope. He was amazed by the effect his father had with nothing more than his calm, confident presence.

"Colonel Choi, you are relieved of command," Theodore said. "If you don't mind stepping away from my chair?"

"Of course not, General," Choi said.

"Captain St. Martin, head on down to the hangar and get your fighter crew ready for launch. I'll take the reins from here."

Gabriel stood and turned around, setting his eyes on his father for the first time in three weeks. General St. Martin had done more than clean himself up. He had transformed himself. He was freshly washed and shaved, his hair tight against his scalp, his uniform crisp. There was no sign of pain as he lifted himself into the command chair. There was no sign of weakness.

"Don't just stand there staring at me like you see a ghost, Captain," Theodore said. "We've got couillons to confuse."

"Sir?" Gabriel said. "You want to launch the fighters?"

"Are you questioning my command?" Theodore yelled. "I know we can't hurt them, but that don't mean we ain't going to try. I bet it's the last thing in the world they expect."

"Yes, sir," Gabriel said, reaching the command chair. His father didn't look at him; his focus was already dedicated to evading the Dread attack. "It's good to have you back, sir."

He couldn't resist the urge to put his hand on his father's shoulder as he said it.

Theodore risked a glance over, a small smile creasing his face. "Thank you, Gabriel. It's good to see you, too. Now, let's show them what we're made of."

"Yes, sir."

[31]

"THIS IS CRAZY," LIEUTENANT BALE SAID OVER THE COMM. "Completely crazy. The General is missing for three weeks, and then he just shows up at the eleventh hour and takes command, and we follow him like he was never gone?"

Gabriel adjusted his seat in his fighter, flipping the switch to prep the thrusters. "Yes."

"And nobody is worried that maybe he's not all there?"

"I'll take my father flying the Magellan not all there over myself any day. Besides, did you get a look at him? I haven't seen him that fit in twenty years."

"Okay, but he's going to send us out there. That doesn't worry you? We can't hurt the Dread, Captain. What are we supposed to do? Wave at them as they blow us into space junk?"

"We're supposed to do whatever the General says. Are you going to stop whining, Bale, or are you going to mutiny? One way maybe you die a hero. The other way, you just die."

Bale fell silent. Gabriel could hear the snickers of the other two pilots on the comm. Gerhardt and Celia. They were both as green as any pilot could be, greener even then Lieutenant Bale. At least she had flown a combat mission before.

He was leading a squad of children on a suicide mission and asking them to be happy about it. The crazy thing was that he was happy about it. Happy to have his father back on the bridge. Happy to be doing something against the Dread.

"This is General St. Martin." Theodore's voice cut across their comm. "Get ready to launch on my mark. Timing is everything here, boys and girls, so don't dilly-dally."

"Yes, sir," Gabriel replied for them.

"What do you think he's doing?" Bale asked.

"We won't know until we get out there," Gabriel replied. "What I do know is that we aren't dead yet. That's a positive sign."

"Looks like your squadron's going to have some company out there, Captain," Miranda said. "Half a dozen Dread Bats are incoming. Watch your six."

Gabriel closed his eyes to calm the sudden rush of fear. They could avoid the Dread fortress' plasma fire as long as they didn't center themselves on the main cannon. Their fighters were another story.

What the heck was his father doing?

He jumped when the hangar began to open, individual bay doors moving aside at the same time. The oxygen had already been pumped out, and on his father's command, they would release the clamps holding them to Magellan and join the fray.

Gabriel's heart rate spiked. He had never been in combat in space before. Sure, he had trained for it, but this was the real thing.

He had survived on Earth. He would survive here.

"Stay tight," he said. "Cover each other out there."

"Yes, sir," his pilots replied.

He felt the fighter shift slightly as the clamps release.

"Now," Theodore shouted.

Gabriel fired his thrusters, launching from the hangar ahead of the others. He didn't check to see if they had followed. He was certain they had.

The fighter moved out into space. He found the Bats immediately, strafing the left side of the Magellan with their smaller plasma weapons, hitting the same nacelle that had been grazed by the fortress' plasma cannon.

Gabriel's heart sank when he realized why.

Without the nacelle, they couldn't escape.

He cursed himself silently for letting the enemy hit one of the most vulnerable parts of the ship. His father would never have made that mistake. Why couldn't he have shown up a little earlier? A minute, an hour, a day. Theodore had shown too much confidence in him.

It wasn't over yet.

He tracked the other targets. The Dread fortress was still behind the Magellan, but it was drawing closer. The Magellan was still moving toward the planet, vectoring in a random pattern to throw the enemy cannons.

He had to do something about the Bats.

"Form up, we need to hit them hard," he said.

"Sir?" Bale replied. "You want to attack?"

"We still have power left, and if they destroy the nacelle, we'll be trapped out here forever."

"Our weapons are useless," Gerhardt said.

"Are you questioning me, son?" Gabriel replied, barking like his old man.

"No, sir," the pilot replied meekly.

"Stay tight, concentrate your fire. The rounds still have force. At the very least we can push them off target and try to buy the General time for him to create a miracle."

"Yes, sir," they replied.

Gabriel led them back toward the nacelle, checking his levels. Each shot drained the battery that powered the starfighter. Would there be anywhere near enough available energy to do much of anything against the Dread?

He was going to find out.

A flash of light blinded him for a moment, the fortress' main cannon sending a burst of energy over the top of the Magellan.

Gabriel would never know how his father did it, but he was thankful that he could.

"You need to get those sons of bitches off my shoulder," Theodore said. "Maggie's chewing my ear about critical damage."

"Yes, sir," Gabriel replied. "I'm about to engage."

"Good man."

Gabriel focused his eyes forward, tracking the closest of the Bats. Like the fortress, they were struggling to keep up with the many changes in direction Theodore was expertly affecting on the starship, their aim not always centered on the weakened area of the nacelle. Taking fire might not hurt them, but it would give them more of a distraction.

Was that his father's plan? Buy time to reach the planet, use it as a shield to swing around and escape to a stream? The Dread might be able to follow, but it would be difficult for them to know where the Magellan had dropped back into realspace. Or at least, they had to hope it would be. They had no idea of the extent of the enemy's capabilities when it came to space travel. The fact that they were hitting the nacelle suggested that even if they could track the ship, they didn't want to.

"Target the closest enemy ship, prepare to fire."

"Roger," the pilots replied.

Gabriel and his squadron swooped down on the Bats, coming at them from an off angle to try to evade detection. He was about to give the order to shoot when they suddenly veered away, breaking off the attack on the Magellan, spinning back to face the fighters.

"Break away, spread out," Gabriel said, caught by surprise as lances of plasma punctuated the space around him.

He rolled the fighter, adding a little extra to the underside vectoring thruster and pushing it out of plane from the incoming attack before streaking past. He flipped the fighter back when he neared the nacelle, returning to the fight.

"Sir, they broke off the attack," Gabriel said. "They're targeting the squadron."

"Ha! Better than I hoped," Theodore replied. "Keep them busy, Captain, we're almost there."

Gabriel looked out at the planet. They weren't that close to it yet. Almost where?

He didn't have any more time to think about it. He threw the fighter into a wild swerve as one of the Bats dove in at him, plasma cannons sending bolts flying past him. He scanned for the rest of the squadron. They were outnumbered, but their fighters were smaller and more nimble. For the moment, they were managing to keep the Dread off them.

He knew from Earth that it wouldn't last. The pilots would adjust to their tactics and then begin to pick them apart.

"Bale, watch your tail," he said, avoiding the fire from the Bat behind him and coming up on Bale's position. "Bring him over to me; I'll try to knock him off course."

"Yes, sir," Bale replied, her voice calm. Regardless of how she had gotten into and through the Academy, she was proving to be a solid performer.

She shifted her vectors, rolling her fighter over and coming back his way. Her ship was a blur rocketing past him, and he opened fire, sending hundreds of ion blasts out at the chasing Bat.

He expected that the Bat would take the hit, lose its concentration, and break off for another approach.

Instead, he watched as his rounds tore into the dark skin of the alien craft, ripping through in a way he had never seen before. The shots pierced the hide, one of them hitting something that must have been important. A brief flash of a small internal explosion, and then the Bat went dark, floating away from the battle on its final trajectory.

Gabriel blasted past the dead ship, his mouth hanging open in silent shock. What the? It couldn't be, could it? Had Reza secretly solved the riddle and augmented the fighters to be able to defeat the Dread armor? And not tell anyone? That didn't make any sense.

Nothing else did either, but somehow it was true.

"Alpha Squadron, the Bats are vulnerable," Gabriel said, still in disbelief. "I repeat, they're vulnerable. If you can hit them, hit them hard."

"Captain, I hope you ain't playing a nasty trick on an Old Gator," Theodore said, hearing the report.

"No, sir," Gabriel replied. "I just disabled one of them. I'm as surprised as you."

"Well, this don't change my plans too much, but maybe just enough. Keep those couillons distracted; I'm about to put the fear of God into these bastards."

"Sir? Do you feel okay?"

"Trust me, Gabe. I feel better than I have in years. Mind over matter. Hang tight."

"Yes, sir."

Gabriel let himself smile as he shifted direction, heading back at one of the enemy fighters. They were more cautious now, backing further away from the Magellan and his squadron, spending more time on the defensive. Were they surprised by their vulnerability too?

He watched as Bale lit up, sending a stream of ions into a second Bat. He almost laughed when the rounds poured into the ship, creating the same scene as he had. A small flash and then it stopped reacting, floating away on a straight path.

"Try to keep up with me now, Captain," Theodore said.

Gabriel swung around the Bats, watching as the Magellan's main thrusters burned out. A moment later, vectoring thrusters fired from the bottom and the left of the ship, pushing it up and over. A moment after that he noticed that the hangar doors had sealed, and now were re-opening. Oxygen vented out as they did, adding a little more thrust.

The Magellan rose up, vertical to the fortress within seconds. It looked vulnerable, and the Dread believed it had to be. The main cannon belched plasma, spewing it forth in a stream that should have cut right through the center of the Magellan.

Except she was still rolling up and over, the rear rising and swinging out behind her. The plasma blast passed harmlessly beneath, and the ship came about, the bow facing directly toward the Dread starship.

Then the mains reignited, a ring of heat forming around each of the outputs, a jet of energy forming behind it. The engines could output massive thrust for a short amount of time to escape atmosphere and gravity. It would put a strain on the systems and drain their reserve energy stores almost completely. It was a desperate maneuver, but also a brilliant one.

"Form up," Gabriel said to his squadron. "We don't want to fall out of range."

"Roger."

They only had so much power themselves, and would need to use all of it to keep pace with the Magellan.

They streaked alongside the main action. Gabriel's eyes were peeled to the starship as it pointed itself directly at the fortress. Was his father planning to ram them? He might hurt the Dread ship, but he would kill himself and everyone around him at the same time.

Or was he daring the Dread to let him strike them? Was he testing their mettle and motivations?

The Magellan leaped at the Dread fortress, the long bow like a spear ahead of it. The Fortress responded immediately, changing direction, dropping down, not wasting any time trying to avoid it. Gabriel increased his thrust, accelerating ahead of the Magellan as the secondary burn faded out.

The Magellan crossed over the top of the fortress, shooting past it and heading toward the inner portion of the system. The Fortress remained behind it, working to change course, its forward velocity carrying it further and further away as it did. The Dread Bats peeled off, ceasing the chase and heading back to their ship.

"Score one for the Old Gator," Bale said, her voice bubbling through the comm.

"Roger that," Gabriel replied. "Let's head home."

[32]

Gabriel opened the fighter's cockpit, climbing out and standing on the floor of the hangar. The air was harder to breathe than before, the oxygen levels limited after Theodore's maneuver to get them past the Dread.

He had never been happier to be short of breath.

He left his bay, heading through the interlocks and into the connecting corridor, where Captain Sturges was already waiting for him, a big smile on his grizzled face.

"Nice flying, Captain," Sturges said.

"Maybe I'll see you out there next time?" Gabriel replied.

"Me? I'm old and slow. The BIS is more my speed." He clapped Gabriel on the shoulder. "Truly well done, Gabe."

Lieutenant Bale was the next pilot to appear in the corridor. She rushed over to Gabriel, wrapping her arms around him. "He did it. He really did it."

"I told you to have faith," Gabriel said, returning the embrace. He released her as Gerhardt and Celia joined them.

"Mission accomplished, sir," Celia said. Her hair was matted with her cold sweat.

"You both did well," Gabriel said. "You survived your first mission. I'm proud of you both."

"Thank you, sir," they replied.

"I'm heading up to the bridge," Gabriel said. "Captain Sturges, can you take care of these brave souls for me?"

"Yes, sir," Sturges said. "Thank your father for me."

"Will do."

Gabriel hurried to the bridge, leaving his flight suit on and zipped. They might have escaped the Dread this time, but he was certain the enemy wasn't about to give up its pursuit. They had bought themselves some time, that was all.

It was as much as they could hope for.

"Hull integrity is good," Sergeant Abdullah was saying as Gabriel reached the bridge. "Decks are sealed and stable. All of the damage was isolated to the port-side QPG nacelle. I'm still collating the sensor readings and data outputs from the nacelle to get a full understanding of the damage."

"How does the old girl look from the outside, Captain?" Theodore asked without looking.

Gabriel moved to stand beside the General. "The plasma grazed the side of her, sir," he said. "There was quite a bit of visible damage, and the fighters were doing their best to add to it. It's my fault she got hit, sir."

"Nonsense," Theodore said. "You're the best damn pilot I've ever seen. Half this game is luck, and you got a little bit unlucky. It could just as easily have been me at the wheel."

Gabriel remained silent, not quite willing to accept Theodore's excuse.

"The important part is that we're still alive. We can still fight. Even better, you managed to shoot down one of their fighters."

"So did Bale, sir," Gabriel said.

"A damn fine job, Captain. The point being, they were vulnerable. That's data we can use, ain't that right, Mr. Mokri?"

"Yes, sir," Reza replied.

"Maggie, how's our distance from that big turd out there?"

"Ten thousand kilometers and holding," Maggie replied.

"Seems like they're backing off to regroup," Theodore said. "Ha! I don't think they were expecting that little game of chicken."

"We're lucky you didn't kill us all," Guy said.

"Damn right, Mr. Larone," Theodore replied. "Sometimes luck is all we have left to lean on. By the by, you've had three weeks with the Dread rifle. What have you got?"

Colonel Choi interrupted before Guy could respond. "Pardon me, sir, but I recommend tabling that discussion in the immediate. I think the entire crew might appreciate a word from you. We've been worried about you, General."

"I was worried about myself for a while there," Theodore said softly, his expression changing. He recovered a moment later. "Quite right, Colonel. Quite right." He leaned forward to tap his control pad.

"Sir," Abdullah said before he could. "The preliminary report is in. Maggie's initial assessment was accurate. The main power conduit to the nacelle is offline, and we lost thirty percent of the phase surface."

"That sounds bad," Reza said.

"It means we can't slip," Theodore replied. He paused while he considered. "Can we repair it?"

"The conduit if we can get a crew out to it. The phase surface is going to be a little more challenging. We don't have any paint on board."

"Can we slip without it?" Choi asked.

"Good question," Theodore said. "Mr. Mokri? Mrs. Larone?"

They glanced over at one another, clearly uncomfortable to be grouped together. Gabriel noticed his father's eyebrow raising as they did.

"Hmmm," he said, coughing lightly. "What do we have here?"

"Uh. It's. Uh. It's nothing, General," Reza said, looking at the floor, his face turning red.

"Ha! Funniest nothing I ever did see. I wasn't born yesterday, Mr. Mokri. We can deal with that later. Can one of you answer my question? Mr. Larone, do you want to take a stab at it?"

"Slipping a starship is usually based on a percentage of phase surface in comparison to overall size," Guy said before Reza could respond. "We would need to know the overall cubic size of the Magellan as well as the size of the QPG prepared surfaces. If she were constructed with some buffer, it's quite possible getting the conduit back online would be good enough."

"What if it's close?" Theodore said.

"What do you mean, General?" Guy replied.

"The math. What if it's close? What if we try to slip without enough surface?"

"Part of the ship will make it into slipspace," Reza said. "The other part won't."

"You'll tear the Magellan into pieces," Guy said.

"The surface damage is an estimate, sir," Sergeant Abdullah said. "We'd need a team to go out there and measure."

Theodore sat back in the command chair. He ran a hand across a clean-shaven chin. "Seems we're in a bit of a pickle then, don't it? I doubt that Dread ship out there is going to wait for us to make a few spacewalks and fix our nacelle. In fact, I suppose they're going to do whatever they can to prevent it."

He leaned forward on his arms, looking the crew over. He turned his head and looked at Gabriel before speaking again.

"Here's what we're going to do. I'm going to make a rousing speech ship-wide to get morale back under its own power. Then I'm going to pull Mr. Mokri, Mrs. Larone, Vivian, and Gabriel aside so someone can tell me what all is with the weird tension on my bridge. I have to tell you, I don't like it, and I ain't in favor. Mr. Larone, I expect to find you with the alien rifle after that. I want a full report on what you've learned about the thing, and I want you to give a bit of thought to why the Dread fighters might have been vulnerable right here when they have never been before. I feel like there's an obvious clue staring us in the face, and we're too trained to feel powerless to notice.

"Sergeant Abdullah, get me a plan on how we can get the team out to the nacelle for repairs without slowing down, and with the understanding that we may come under enemy attack at any moment."

"Yes, sir," Abdullah said.

"Gabriel, while I'm yapping, get a message down to Lieutenant Bale. I want two pilots riding the hot seat at all times, and since we're low on trained bodies, she's up first with Lieutenant Celia."

"Yes, sir," Gabriel said.

"Oh, and tell her she's promoted to First Lieutenant."

"Yes, sir."

"While I'm at it, congratulations, Major St. Martin."

Gabriel froze. "What?"

"You've earned it, Major."

"Sir, I appreciate it, but I can't."

"Why not? You worried about nepotism? Nobody's going to question you. You're the best damned pilot we've ever had. Besides, it's all academic at this point. You aren't getting paid, anyhow."

"The Magellan was hit under my stick," Gabriel argued.

"Blah, blah, Major. Remember what I said about luck? You ain't happy with that?"

Gabriel didn't answer fast enough.

"All in favor of Captain St. Martin's promotion, say 'aye,'" Theodore said.

"Aye," the bridge crew replied. Everyone except Guy Larone.

"Maggie, note it in the record. Second Lieutenant Sandra Bale is promoted to First Lieutenant. Captain Gabriel St. Martin is promoted to Major."

"Data recorded," the computer replied.

"There you go. It's done. Now skedaddle so we can get on with the important business."

Gabriel saluted. Theodore saluted back. Then Gabriel left the bridge. He considered contacting Bale through the comm but decided to go and find her instead. Why not break the news to her in person?

His father's voice boomed through the ship while he walked.

"This is General Theodore St. Martin. As you may or may not

know, I was incapacitated up until recently. The loss of my legs was causing me a great deal of pain, and to help deal with that pain, I was taking medicine prescribed by the doctors back home.

That medicine was affecting my operational abilities, and in one instance affected my ability to make an important decision that almost cost the lives of each and every one of you. It was a failure that struck me right down to the core. A failure that I've sworn to myself to never be in the position to repeat.

I've been to hell and back over the last few weeks. The withdrawal from the pain medication was a challenge on its own, and damn near murderous in conjunction with the continuing pain in my limbs. There were times when I believed it was a fight I couldn't win."

Silence fell in the corridor. Gabriel could tell his father was choking up.

"I know there have been rumors that I've lost my touch and that I'm not the man I used to be. I'm gonna put those rumors to rest right now. I ain't the man I used to be. I've been to hell and back, and I'm better for it. I'm stronger; I'm smarter, and I'm more resolved than ever to see this thing through. We survived the first round against the Dread; and I know that together we'll survive the next round too.

"I know that I let you down, and I'm sorry. It ain't often a General apologizes to his troops, but I know there's power in humility. I know that we ain't just a collection of soldiers. We're a family, and we owe it to one another to do right and to be man enough to admit when we've done wrong. Again, to each and every one of you, I'm sorry.

"The enemy is at our door. They came knocking, and not only did we slam that door in their face, but we also broke their nose to boot. We showed them that just because we don't have any big, bad guns, that don't mean we're going to roll over and die. We showed them that we're made of tougher stuff, and if they want to wipe us out of the universe, they're going to have to earn it.

"I went to hell and back, and I was afraid. But I tell you, I ain't afraid anymore. Not with you, the good men and women who have joined me on this ship, on this mission to free our brothers and sisters back on Earth. I believe in you. I trust in you. I'm proud to have you with me. Let the Dread come. Let them try to break us, to destroy us, to knock our door down and finish us once and for all.

"I'll be here to stop them, and I know you'll be here with me. Together, we'll show these yellow-bellied couillons who we are. Together, we'll show them that they messed with the wrong damn race, and the wrong damn planet. Together, we'll break their armor, and then we'll break their spirits.

"Thank you, and God bless."

[33]

Tea'va stared silently through the viewport of his bridge. The expansive outer edge of the Pol'tik system was spread out ahead of him.

The human starship wasn't there.

It was behind them, having executed a maneuver he wasn't expecting, a maneuver made possible by the druk Heil'shur.

He knew that it had been him out there, leading a squadron of the small human fighters against his gi'shah. He recognized the markings of the fighter, including the dark splotches where his plasma had singed the frame. How he wished he could have been out there with his pilots, hunting down the human who was causing him so much grief.

How he wished he had been able to send more than six of the gi'shah into the battle.

Zoelle had warned him against committing to a battle so soon after arriving in the system. She had tried to tell him that his ranks were too thin, his forces too weak from the travel. He had chosen to listen to Gr'el instead and push the attack. Despite his inability to field a full complement of fighters. Despite his inability to operate more than the main plasma cannon. Despite being beyond the flow of slipspace, and despite the weakened state of his crew slowing their reflexes and hurting their effectiveness.

She had tried to tell him not to underestimate the humans. He should have been more considerate. He should have remembered that they had the Heil'shur, instead of rushing to make a decision.

He looked down at Gr'el. His Si'dahm was setting navigation to get the ship turned around and back in pursuit of the humans. It was his fault this had happened, but Tea'va knew he would report back to the Domo'dahm and shift the blame to make him look weak and foolish.

Thanks to Gr'el, the humans had discovered that the lek'shah had a vulnerability. It would only be a matter of time before they realized what it was, and from there made the correct logical assumptions to form a theoretical basis on how the bek'hai armor was so impervious to their weapons. After that, it would only be a matter of time before they were able to duplicate the feat. He didn't need to hold humans in high regard to accept that they could figure out that much, at least. It was an elementary level of deductive reasoning.

He slammed his hand down on the side of his chair, causing a few of the lor'hai to jump. And it was all because of Gr'el and the Heil'shur. If the Heil'shur hadn't shot down one of the gi'shah, if Gr'el hadn't convinced him to attack straight away, they would be in a different situation now.

He wanted to end his Si'dahm, to retire him here and now. He knew he couldn't. The only way he could be rid of Gr'el was if he died in battle and the right evidence was available to prove as much. It would be a difficult scenario to orchestrate, but he decided that he would find a way, no matter what it took. Certainly, Zoelle would help him, and use her connections among the lor'hai to make it so. As Domo'dahm, he could reward all of them handsomely for their loyalty.

He got to his feet and began descending the command dais. At least the attack hadn't been a total failure. They had damaged the human starship's slip nacelle. He was certain it would be enough to keep them from leaving the Pol'tik system any time soon. It meant that he could afford to be patient for now, to give chase to the fleeing ship but keep his distance, to allow his crew to regain their strength before making a second attempt.

He would have to make that attempt before the humans could solve the equation, but he had time. A day or two at least to let his lor'hai and the drumhr recover their strength. The human ship had survived this time.

It wouldn't survive the next.

He left the bridge without a word. Gr'el was at least capable of staying behind the human ship, and he had delayed his time in the regeneration chamber for as long as he dared. He could feel his muscles weakening, his body beginning to reject itself. It had been weeks since he had used the chamber, a vast improvement over other drumhr who had to use it every few days.

He expected Zoelle to be waiting in his quarters again when he reached them. She wasn't. Instead, a plump Mother was standing at the door, clothed in a simple white dress that hung to her knees.

He was tempted to return to the bridge and stab Gr'el right then and there. He was taunting him, trying to get under his skin. Who else might have sent this creature to him?

"Dahm Tea'va," she said, lowering herself to her knees and bowing before him.

"Who sent you here?" Tea'va asked.

"Si'dahm Gr'el," she replied. "On behalf of Domo'dahm Rorn'el."

He was about to tell her to leave. The Domo'dahm? That gave him pause.

"Is that what Gr'el told you?"

"Yes, Dahm."

"How do you know he isn't lying?"

"It is not my place to judge the words of the Si'dahm, Dahm."

Tea'va paused. What if Gr'el wasn't lying? Certainly, he had sent a report to Rorn'el before the battle, and would send another soon.

Had the Domo'dahm ordered this? Was he trying to ruin him and keep him from power?

No. The Domo'dahm had always supported him. Rorn'el knew that he was the superior pur'dahm. It was up to him to prove it.

Still, it was possible the Domo'dahm was trying to entice him with this thing. To test his willingness to please him by breeding.

He had no desire to please him.

"Stand up, Mother," Tea'va said.

The clone stood.

"Follow me."

The hatch to Tea'va's quarters slid open. He allowed the Mother to enter behind him as he approached his regeneration chamber and began tapping on the surface to program it.

He could see the Mother in the reflection as he did. One hand was reaching for the strap of her dress because she thought that was why he had brought her in. The other was reaching beneath. Disgusting.

He didn't want to see her human flesh or the ways she might try to entice him. He turned quickly, reaching out and grabbing her hand. She screeched in fear as he tightened his grip on her wrist, pulling her arms away from her body.

A plasma knife fell from her grip and clattered onto the floor.

Tea'va's eyes narrowed. What was this?

She lashed out at him, her foot catching him in the knee, buckling it and forcing him to fall. He loosened his grip on her to catch himself, and she slipped back, ducking down to grab the knife.

"Did Gr'el send you to kill me?" he asked, recovering and moving out of range of her reach. He didn't fear the clone now that the element of surprise had been lost. He was a pur'dahm, the ability to defend himself part of the implanted knowledge that he had been created with.

She didn't speak. She lunged forward with surprising speed, picking up the knife on the way. She swung it at him, forcing him to move to the side, nearly killed because he wasn't taking the threat seriously enough.

Why would he? Mothers weren't programmed to fight. They held only one purpose for being, one that had yet to be fulfilled.

At least, that was how it was supposed to be.

He got his arms up in time to block her next attack, batting the hand with the knife aside. She came at him ferociously; her lips split into a mad grin. He moved backward, circling the regeneration chamber.

"How did Gr'el do this?" Tea'va asked out loud. It was more than her ability to fight. She wasn't sick either. Unless...

She rushed him again, the knife darting toward his throat, his chest, his gut. He slapped each attack aside, a greater concern rising in the back of his mind.

Could it be? Was it possible? And right under his view?

The Mother lurched forward again. He caught her wrist this time, holding on and pushing her back. The force sent her to the floor, and he fell on top of her, the knife positioned between them.

If it were true, it wasn't a new plan. Perhaps he wasn't even the original target. If not, then who?

The Domo'dahm, of course. Tea'va almost laughed at the thought. He wasn't the only one with designs on breaking tradition, on stealing rulership instead of earning it through succession.

The Mother's arms were more powerful than normal, and in his weakened state, he found her strength almost equal to his. He struggled against her, pushing the knife down toward her ever so slowly. She didn't lose the grin while he did.

His anger flowed, and with one last burst of fury, he sank the plasma knife into her chest. The force buried it so deep his hand began to press into the wound. He released the knife, staring down at her while she died.

He got to his feet, still shaking with anger. Gr'el had forfeited his life by sending an assassin to kill him. He didn't care if the Domo'-dahm found out. He didn't care if all of the bek'hai armies came to capture him. He had taken the game and made it personal. Was his disdain so great?

He stumbled away from the body toward the wall, opening the

compartment that held his plasma gun. He needed to calm himself and be careful. If his hypothesis was correct, Gr'el had done more than betray him.

He had betrayed the Domo'dahm as well and created his own army of clones.

[34]

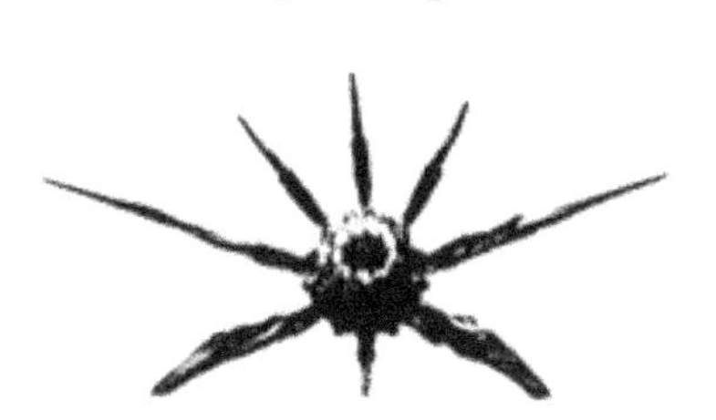

Tea'va didn't rush right to the bridge to confront his Si'dahm. He also didn't report anything out of the ordinary regarding the Mother. Instead, he dressed her wound to prevent her from bleeding and then moved her body to his bed. He considered removing her clothing before positioning her to look as if she were sleeping, but couldn't bring himself to do it. He hated the thought that anyone should come upon her like this and guess at what he had done.

As if he were so weak.

When that was done, he dressed in a skin-tight gori'shah suit beneath his official robes, mounting the plasma gun in a holster there, within easy reach of his hand. He looked longingly at the regeneration chamber before leaving his quarters. He could survive a few more days without. The risk was too great to ignore.

Then he moved out into the corridor, scanning for others as he did. He didn't want to be seen if he could avoid it, especially by the lor'hai. He was no longer sure who he could trust.

Could he trust anyone?

He considered Zoelle. She had tried to help him. She had tried to warn him. If he hadn't pressed the attack, it would have been more difficult for Gr'el to move forward with his plan. At the same time, he had entrusted her with relaying anything she heard about Gr'el's designs to him, and she had said nothing.

Did that make her a friend or a foe?

He couldn't assume anyone was a friend. He had been foolish enough already. He had to stop looking to others and tackle this concern on his own. First, he had to know if his theory was correct.

He made his way down the corridor to the nearest transport beam. Each of the massive Fortresses was a self-sufficient city unto itself, and as a result, the Ishur held a cloning factory buried deep within its bowels. Tea'va was headed there, entering the green light of the beam and sending himself almost instantly down to the lowest part of the vessel.

He stepped out and walked down one of the corridors leading out of the transport hub. He was cautious as he did, taking care to keep his steps soft, his attention on all of his surroundings. He was the Dahm of the ship, and would have command over anyone who saw him, but only if they were loyal.

Was anyone on the ship loyal?

He had always been mistrustful of the other drumhr. He knew they envied him for his ability to breathe freely in Earth's atmosphere, and for his greater ratio of flesh to bone. He knew they saw him as the future, a future the Domo'dahm claimed to support, even as they vied for the same scraps of power.

He had always hated the lor'hai as well. Especially the un'hai, until Zoelle. She was the first clone he had ever cared for at all. Now he couldn't help but wonder if she had been dishonest with him from the beginning. She had admitted her desire for power to him. Power she had claimed to want to earn from him. What if she were seeking the same from Gr'el instead? Or worse, at the same time? What if she were using them both?

It was as appealing in its deviousness as it was repulsive in its potential. Was a clone capable of such things? If any were, it would be her.

He hated the thought. He hated himself for thinking it, and her for being who and what she was. His anger continued to simmer as he crossed the expanse of the ship.

A group of lor'hai turned the corner ahead of him. He didn't react immediately but then ducked to the side, standing in the shadows along the wall with his head down, looking at his hands as if he were carrying something interesting. He kept his eyes high enough that he could watch the clones as they passed. They didn't so much as look at him. It was the proper action, as he had not addressed them either.

He continued once they were gone, increasing his pace. Gr'el would surely be questioning the fate of his assassin by now. He would likely be seeking a reason to visit Tea'va in his quarters. A reason to find him dead. A task from the Domo'dahm, perhaps? He would not expect that his Mother was still missing, and no answer was forthcoming from Tea'va, the entry to his space barred to the pur'dahm.

He neared the entrance to the facility. It was located in a tall, cavernous space within the ship, adjacent to the laboratories where drumhr and lor'hai science teams worked to improve the compatibility of the genetic splice and to improve the health of the bek'hai. As a starship at war, the Ishur's geneticist population was only a handful, and the cloning facility should have been in hibernation until they needed to bolster their numbers.

He could tell right away that it wasn't sleeping. The facility rose along the frame of the room like a rounded honeycomb, and light was escaping through the thinner areas in the flesh-like wall. The floor vibrated softly from the operation of a segregated power supply. Tea'va hadn't known the Ishur's cloning facility was on separate power. No wonder there had been no noticeable strain on their overall output.

A clone soldier was standing guard near the entrance. There would be no way for Tea'va to enter without passing him. It didn't matter. Now that he had confirmed his suspicion, he needed to shift his focus to the truth that was coming further into clarity.

Gr'el was creating clones behind his back. Zoelle had to know about it and had lied to him. His command and his life were both under threat.

He cursed his blindness to the whole thing as he turned around and headed back to the upper part of the ship. He had to hurry and rally the lor'hai and drumhr who would be loyal to their Dahm. He had to stop Gr'el before his was able to solidify his plans. The first wave of clones had no doubt been released after the Ishur had arrived in the Pol'tik system. That was why the Mother had been unaffected by the travel. It meant there were as many as two hundred of them on board, fresh and healthy and under Gr'el's control.

He growled under his breath. It was all falling apart so quickly, so easily. All of his plans were unraveling before he ever had the chance to execute them. Druk to the humans. Druk to Gr'el. Druk to the un'hai, to Zoelle, and to all of the lor'hai.

He touched the pin on his chest, opening a comm channel. The drumhr would be loyal to their Dahm. No amount of empty promises could buy their loyalty.

"This is Dahm Tea'va," he said. "Gi'shah Dahm Vel'ik, what is your status?"

He waited through the silence.

"Gi'shah Dahm Vel'ik, status report," he said.

Again, only silence.

He growled again as he reached the transport hub. He turned the corner, heading for the beam and the upper decks of the fortress. He froze when he saw two lor'hai soldiers standing over the body of a third clone. He recognized the dead one as a member of the original crew.

Was he too late?

He grabbed the weapon from beneath his robes, holding it behind him as he approached the clones.

"What is the meaning of this?" he asked.

The two clones didn't speak. They each raised a plasma gun toward him and then tumbled over as he shot them in the head.

He didn't step into the beam. He knew now that he was too late.

Gr'el had likely made his move at the same time the Mother was attacking him. There was some small satisfaction that his traitorous commander would soon discover that he was still alive, but it was only a small sense.

Just like that, he had lost control of the Ishur.

[35]

Donovan didn't bury Diaz, despite Murphy's offer of help from the scavengers they had saved. He burned her instead, building a massive funeral pyre in the center of the destroyed city, right near the church, close to where her grandfather had once lived. He had a feeling she would want it that way, especially knowing that there was no way the bek'hai wouldn't see the smoke. He pictured the rising pillar as a gigantic middle finger, casting its opinion back toward the dark spots in the distance. Diaz would have approved of that.

The pur'dahm had promised three days, and Ehri had affirmed that the Dread would keep the promise. For whatever else they were or weren't, they did have an honor system that they held to, one that had survived tens of thousands of years.

He hadn't said anything when he lit the pyre. He simply stood and watched the flames rise up the vegetation until they had enveloped Diaz and started to burn her flesh. He had wanted to turn away then, but he didn't. She was more than Renata Diaz. She was all of the people who had died for their cause, and he wasn't going to disrespect them by looking away.

Ehri, Soon, and Iwu remained close for a long time. Soon took a seat on the ground after a while, his head beginning to bother him. The others helped him maintain the vigil for the three hours it took to begin to die down. Murphy joined them an hour in, trailed by his wife and daughter.

"What do we do now?" the leader of the scavengers asked him. Murphy couldn't have been more than a few years older than Donovan, but he looked so much older.

"Why are you asking me?" Donovan replied. He couldn't even keep his friends alive.

"You're with the resistance. I thought that you might have a plan."

"I had the beginning of a plan. It fell apart."

Murphy looked at the pyre. "Was she your wife?"

"A friend. Maybe she would have wanted to be if it weren't for the Dread."

"Do you think she would have been?"

"I don't know. It doesn't matter now."

"It always matters. It's the possibility that motivates us. The potential that keeps us going. If you cared about her, it will motivate you more to make the Dread pay."

Donovan let himself smile. "I already have more than enough for them to pay for. What about you?"

"Everyone here has lost something. It might surprise you to hear that some of the worst stories come from people who have had run-ins with jackals. They say they make the Dread look downright friendly sometimes."

"Is it that bad?"

"I don't know. What I do know is that it isn't safe out there. Not for anyone. We came this way hoping to steer clear of it. We thought this city would stay abandoned. We've only been here a week. The Dread didn't waste any time coming after us."

"They have orders to kill everyone who's left," Donovan said.

"I've heard Washington State. Well, what used to be Washington State, is getting hit hard. There was a pretty large settlement building up there. A peaceful settlement. I heard they had been bribing the local bek'hai contingent to let them alone."

"Bribing them with what?"

"Booze? Women? Who knows. I heard they don't like any of that stuff. I have no idea what could convince them to be compassionate."

Donovan glanced over at Ehri, who shrugged.

"Yeah, anyway," Murphy continued. "Like I said, it isn't safe out there. For anybody. Then you come along. You're fighting the bek'hai. You have their weapons. You killed that one as easy and cold as I've seen a man kill any living thing. There's safety in numbers, mister." He paused. "Where the hell are my manners? I don't even know your name." He stuck out his hand. "Murphy O'Han. This is my wife Linda, and our daughter Shea."

Donovan took it. "Major Donovan Peters. This is Ehri. Captain Soon Kim is sitting over there with Doctor Nailah Iwu."

"A doctor?" Linda said. "For real?"

"Yes. Why?"

"Linda's sister is back in the underground. She's got an infection."

"Do you think she can help?"

"She will if she can," Donovan said.

Linda took Shea by the hand and guided her away from them and to Doc Iwu.

"So I was saying," Murphy said. "It's clearly not safe for us here. Maybe not anywhere. If we want to survive, we have to stick together, right?"

"Or scatter too far apart to get caught," Donovan replied.

"Workable in theory, but impossible in practice. Us humans are too social. We'll bunch up again sooner or later."

Donovan knew that was true. "So you want to travel with us?"

"I don't know where you're going, but it has to be better than here."

"I can't guarantee that."

"I'm not looking for a guarantee. Look, I've got fifty people down in the underground, and another fifteen left that are willing and able to hold a firearm and stand and fight against the Dread. That's sixty-six of us that I'm doing my best to keep alive. I didn't ask for the position, but it's mine."

"I understand how that is."

"Then you know I have a responsibility to do what I think is best for these people. Judging by the fact that you bought us three days of peace by killing that ugly bastard, I think our best chance is with you."

Donovan stared at the flames while he thought about it. "The problem is that if I accept you, they become my responsibility. I have a war to fight. I can't afford to be tied down by civilians."

"I get that, Major," Murphy said. "I respect that. If you say yes, they stay my responsibility. I take care of them; you take care of yourself. Well, maybe you send a few shots our way if the Dread attack. I want to help you fight your war, not hurt it. Believe me; even you'll be safer with some more bodies around you. The Dread purge is making the jackals more desperate. They think stockpiling weapons and food and slaves is going to save them in the end. Idiots."

"Did you say slaves?"

Murphy shook his head. "You think the Dread are the only ones keeping slaves these days? Not so, Major. I've heard stories. The jackals are taking servants of their own, women and children mainly. You can guess what they're using them for."

"Even if we win the war, will there be anything left to salvage?" Donovan asked.

"There's a lot of good people out there, too. It's just that they're running scared, hiding most of the time. You have the training. You have the weapons. Maybe you can do something about it."

"We're trying," Donovan said. "It isn't easy."

"Nothing worth doing ever is. What do you say, Major? Let us tag along. We'll give you safety in numbers; you'll give us safety in your experience. It's a good deal for both of us."

Donovan looked at Ehri. She didn't say anything. This was his decision to make. Like Murphy, he had somehow wound up in charge.

"Do you promise to follow my orders?" Donovan asked.

"Yes, sir," Murphy replied. "I'll make sure the others do, too."

Donovan wasn't confident he was doing the right thing, but he put his hand out anyway. He couldn't abandon these people after he had managed to save them.

"Deal."

[36]

It was early morning when Donovan finally left the pyre to smolder. Diaz's corpse was no longer visible beneath the ashen remains of the fuel that consumed it. Murphy had agreed to take care of the bones, and he and a few of his men had been busy digging the grave nearby.

"Major," Ehri said. She had remained by his side for hours, standing with him in silent support, though she had left a few times to check on the others.

"What is it?" Donovan asked.

"We should go and examine the transport. Til'ik honored your request and ordered his troops to abandon it as it was."

"Not the smartest idea, was it?"

"He didn't expect you to defeat him. I can only imagine the Domo'dahm's reaction when he learns what happened. He will probably end Til'ik's splice line completely."

"Have you seen Soon and Nailah?" Donovan asked.

"They're with the people in the underground. Doctor Iwu is treating whoever she can, and Soon is playing with the children."

"With his injury?"

"He's mostly telling them stories about space."

"Maybe we should go down there instead?"

Ehri smiled. "It is good you haven't lost your spirit, Major."

"I won't let them take everything from me," he replied. "Let's go see the transport."

They crossed the open area, back to where the Dread ship was still resting. Murphy's people had stayed away from it at his request, looking relieved that they didn't have to get too close. Donovan had become so accustomed to the enemy he had forgotten how most people feared them.

The transport was large, nearly twenty meters long and five meters wide, with an angry face and the scaly, irregular shape created by the armored shell. There was a ramp leading up to the side of the vessel, and Donovan and Ehri climbed it to make their way inside.

There were no seats in the vehicle, but there were ripples in the floor where the clones could place their feet. The front of the ship was open, the outside visible through a clear viewport.

"A restraining field holds the soldiers in place," Ehri said, pointing at the ripples. "It is the same field that prevents the vacuum of space from entering the bek'hai ships beyond the atmosphere. It also provides artificial gravity to the fortress, and allows a vessel like this to fly."

"How does it work?"

"Microburst Gravitomagnetism. A type of magnetic field. It is similar to the process used on human starships, only more refined."

"You mean more advanced?"

"The bek'hai are thousands of years older than the human race. There's nothing shameful about what your kind has accomplished."

"I never said I was ashamed."

Ehri brought him to the front of the ship. The pilot seat was human-scale and looked rather comfortable. It was the controls that gave Donovan pause.

"How does it work?" he asked, staring down at the two pools of blue gel positioned on either side of the chair. They were resting in cutouts of four-fingered hands that were twice the size of a human's.

"It is called Kool'ek. It is an organic, conductive gel that is used for direct communication from the nervous system of a bek'hai to the ship's control system. The pilot places their hands in the gel, and the link allows instantaneous bi-directional feedback. In a sense, the bek'hai becomes the ship."

"It doesn't work for humans?"

"No. We lack the chemistry to create the proper signals, as do the more advanced drumhr splices. There are workarounds that utilize the gori'shah as a go-between, but they reduce the overall effectiveness of the system. The kool'ek is being phased out as the bek'hai move closer to maintaining a balance of derived genetics, but until the majority of drumhr are converted, such technology will remain. It is unfortunate. If we could fly the transport, we would be at the resistance base within a few hours."

"Very unfortunate," Donovan said. "Can we do anything with the transport?"

"That is what we came to find out."

She headed to the rear of the ship again, finding a blank space on the rear wall and putting her hand to it. A seam appeared on the wall, and then it slid aside, revealing a storage compartment.

Donovan peered into the space. It was large enough for a person to stand in or pass through. There was a visible hatch at the rear, and storage racks aligned on either side. The racks were mostly empty, but not completely. Four plasma rifles remained, standing upright in a simple receptacle.

Ehri entered the compartment and lifted one of them. She smiled and passed it to Donovan. "Unsecured."

He took it and turned it on, and then nodded. "What's back there?" he asked.

"The power generators."

"How do they work?"

"You are very curious today."

"I'm being exposed to more and more of the bek'hai technology. I want to understand it."

"The generators on the transports are a simplified version of the system you saw inside the capital fortress. It is like your quantum phase generators in that it creates a pathway into slipspace, though in this case, it is the size of a pinhole. The system extracts the zero-point energy from the quantum state."

"Won't that cause problems with slipspace? Instability or something?"

"No. The amount of zero-point energy available is large enough to be considered infinite. The difficult part is in the extraction. The fortresses increase the size and output of the generators, and pair them with secondary systems that store excess energy for use when a slipspace link is unavailable."

"I always heard that slipspace is everywhere."

"Almost, but not quite. There are a number of dead zones throughout the universe. Most occur near supermassive black holes, but they aren't unheard of in random places. Even the bek'hai don't understand the exact nature of these regions."

"It's a hard concept for me to get my head around," Donovan said.

"It can be challenging," Ehri agreed. "The fact that you asked at all is an important first step."

Donovan smiled. "Thanks." He pointed at the rifles in the rack. "This gives us seven. I'll have Murphy hand out the extras to the most skilled shooters in his group."

"I think that's a good idea."

Donovan backed up into the center of the transport again, looking around at the inner part of the ship. Ehri joined him there a moment later.

"I noticed how angry you became when you saw the soldiers killing the scavengers," he said. "And how angry you became at Til'ik for what he did."

"Every moment of freedom brings me further from my life as a slave," Ehri said. "Every moment with you and the others helps me feel more human. I want to be accepted by you. To be one of you. I want to show the other lor'hai that they can be, too. I'm genetically human. My loyalty is to my kind. Humankind. The bek'hai made me, but that does not give them the right to own me."

"You are accepted and valued. I'm happy that you're with us. With me."

Donovan stood facing her, looking into her eyes. A brief thought crossed his mind that he should kiss her, but he dismissed it as an image of Diaz's lifeless body followed. He broke her gaze, looking around at the transport again.

"I have an idea," he said a moment later. "Tell me if you think this will work."

[37]

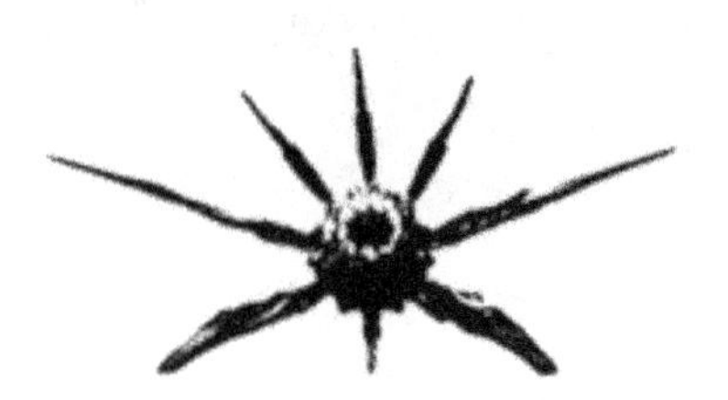

THEODORE AND COLONEL CHOI WERE ALREADY IN THE conference room when Gabriel arrived. They were talking softly to one another and fell silent when he entered the room.

"Captain St. Martin reporting, sir," Gabriel said.

Theodore raised his eyebrow.

"Major St. Martin, reporting," Gabriel corrected.

"That's better. At ease, Major. The rest of the required participants will be along in a moment."

Gabriel took a seat next to Colonel Choi.

"Did you give Lieutenant Bale the news?"

"Yes, sir. She said she promises she won't let you down."

"I'm not completely sure about that, but I guess we'll see how the stump shakes."

"Sir?"

"She's impulsive, and her moral character is weak. She's either going to clean up her act, or she's going to get herself killed, maybe along with us."

"Isn't that a bit of a risk?" Choi asked.

"Yup. Sometimes it's necessary. She has potential if she can grow up a little. Anyway, that's small potatoes compared to what all else is going on around this neck of the bayou. Vivian here's been filling me in on everything. I'm about as angry as a rattlesnake in an alligator's gullet."

"You look great, though," Gabriel said.

Theodore smiled. "I've been out of action too long. Way too long. Casting off that demon was something else. I spent three days in bed, barely able to move, it all hurt so much. Then I woke up on the fourth day and knew I had to make a decision to live or die. I promised your mother I would live a long time ago, so it wasn't really much of a decision."

"Yes, sir."

Sergeant Diallo entered the room, with Guy Larone behind him.

"Guy. Thanks for coming," Theodore said.

"I don't recall having a choice, General," Guy replied.

"But you didn't bitch too much. I'll take whatever victory I can get."

Guy surprised Gabriel, sitting down next to him. Diallo left the room, and Hafizi entered a moment later with Sarah Larone.

"General," she said, sitting opposite her husband.

"Where's Reza?" Gabriel asked.

"He'll be along shortly," Theodore replied. "I wanted to talk to Guy and Sarah without him first. Sergeant Hafizi, can you wait outside with Diallo, and keep anyone from getting too close."

"Yes, sir," Hafizi said, leaving the room.

Gabriel looked at his father. He knew what his request meant.

Theodore cleared his throat, rolled his chair back, and leaned up on his arms. He looked at Guy, and then at Sarah.

"I already chewed out Mr. Mokri," he said. "Be glad you didn't decide to sit in that chair. He had to go back to his quarters to get a new pair of pants. Thing is, Reza's just a kid. Responsible for his own actions, yes, which is why he got chewed, but still a kid. Mrs. Larone, you should have known better."

Sarah looked down at the table. "Yes, sir. I'm sorry-"

"Sorry?" Theodore said.

Gabriel cringed, knowing it was the wrong thing to say.

"You're sorry?"

"It was a mistake," she said.

"Are you taking powerful narcotics that affect your judgment, Mrs. Larone?" Theodore said.

"What? No, sir."

"Then how the hell do you get away with categorizing putting the integrity of this team and the overall chance of the mission's success as a damned mistake?" Theodore roared, so loudly even Colonel Choi flinched. "That weapon is the key to this war. This entire damned war, Mrs. Larone, but for some reason, you decided that playing house with a man half your age was more important. Somehow, you thought that was some kind of acceptable. Do you even have the smallest understanding of the effects your shortsighted, ill-advised actions have already had on our chances?"

"General, I-"

"It is well within my rights as the commander of this starship to have you tried and convicted of treason, Mrs. Larone. You and Mr. Mokri both. I don't want your damned reasons, and I don't want your damned excuses. It wasn't a mistake. It was stupid. Pure, unfiltered, unadulterated stupid."

Sarah kept her head down, staying silent.

"General," Guy said.

"Hold on a second, Mr. Larone. I'm not quite done."

"General, wait," Guy said again.

Theodore looked at him without speaking.

"I don't want you to yell at her," Guy said. "What's done is done. It won't change her decision, or put things back together."

"Entirely my point," Theodore said.

"It won't help, either. It isn't her fault, General. It's mine."

"Oh? How so?"

"I've spent the last few weeks acting like a child. Pouting at the situation we're in, instead of doing my part. I closed myself off, made myself unavailable." He looked at Sarah. "What else were you going to do?"

"Not be unfaithful," Theodore said. "That's the coward's way out."

"I don't want us to fight, General," Guy said. "What you said is right. The enemy is behind us, and we don't have a way to defend ourselves. That first attack, that was nothing. It was a test."

"My thoughts, exactly. Do you have a theory as to why?"

"Slipspace sickness," Guy said. "Their human clones would have the same response to long slipstream travel as we do if we aren't careful."

"I like the way you're thinking right now, Mr. Larone. If your hypothesis is right, we probably have two, maybe three days to figure out how to either stop their next attack or escape before they can hit us."

"We can't fix the nacelle in three days," Colonel Choi said. "There is no escape."

"Then we need to figure out how to repel them," Theodore said. "I need your heads in the game. All three of you. Together."

Guy's jaw tensed. Gabriel waited for him to rebuff the request. He nodded instead. "This isn't about me, or Reza, or Sarah. I understand that now. I'm sorry, General. I'm sorry, Sarah. I won't cause any more grief. What I want won't matter if we're dead. What any of us want won't matter if we're dead."

"I'm glad you see it my way, Mr. Larone. To be frank, I don't care about your individual personal lives. I do care about this mission and the integrity of it. We need to put our heads down and worry about surviving the Dread, not acting like a bunch of children. Do you think you can do that? Mr. Larone? Mrs. Larone?"

"Yes, sir," Guy said.

"Yes, sir," Sarah said. Her cheeks were wet with her tears.

"Good. Gabriel, go tell Diallo to fetch Mr. Mokri for me."

"Yes, sir."

"Mr. Larone, I want you to show us everything you've got. Let's put our heads together and solve this thing."

[38]

Reza entered the meeting room with Sergeant Diallo. Diallo was holding the Dread rifle, while Reza was carrying his tablet, the same one that Gabriel had often seen him absorbed by back on Alpha Settlement. He was staring at it even now, a look of interested curiosity drawn across his face.

"Mr. Mokri," Theodore said loudly.

The scientist shuddered slightly at the sound of the General's voice, looking up from the screen while his face turned red.

"Uh. Yes. Yes, sir," he said. He surveyed the room, his eyes purposely passing over Sarah Larone faster than the others.

Gabriel watched Guy's face. The older man held it tight and expressionless. There was no doubt he was angry at Reza, but he was doing a good job sticking to his promise and keeping his emotions to himself.

"Do you have everything I requested, son?"

"Yes, sir," Reza said, a little more comfortably the second time.

He approached the table, sitting at the end of it away from everyone else. He placed his tablet on the counter, tapping it a few times to switch the display. A three-dimensional image of the Dread plasma rifle appeared suspended in the center of them.

"I think Guy should be the first one to go over this," Reza said. "He's done the most work on the weapon."

"Agreed," Theodore said. "Mr. Larone? You're up."

"Yes, General," Guy said, getting to his feet. "You didn't want to risk damaging the rifle, so we did the highest resolution three-dimensional scan and composition analysis possible with the equipment we have on board. It isn't quite to the level of what we can achieve back home, but as you can see we were able to get a decent visual composite breakdown of the weapon into the system. From this, I was able to learn to take the real weapon apart and put it back together in working order."

"Have you?" Colonel Choi asked.

"No, ma'am," Guy replied. "I didn't want to be solely responsible for it, and Reza has better eyes than I do. In any case, I have been working with the model since we began heading for this system." He leaned forward, expertly manipulating the image, breaking it apart into its component parts. "I've identified one hundred percent of the parts used in the manufacture of the weapon, and matched them up with equivalent human technology. While some of the Dread's manufacturing processes and production compounds are more advanced than our own, the basic function of the rifle is in line with our science."

"What does that mean in English, Mr. Larone?" Theodore asked.

"It means that I believe I understand exactly how the weapon works, based on what we've derived from the imaging. Except, clearly I don't understand how it works, because I have no idea how it can penetrate their armor, while our own weapons can't. There's nothing in the composition of the weapon that suggests it has any special properties that we can't replicate."

"So you don't know how it works?" Gabriel asked.

"I know exactly how it works, up to that point. But I have identified all of the components. There is nothing out of the ordinary that I can see."

"There has to be something, Mr. Larone," Theodore said.

"Yes, General. And it is that truth that has me frustrated. I know there must be something different about it, and yet I can't discern that difference."

"It might help to take the weapon apart, sir," Reza said.

"Is that right, Mr. Larone?"

"Yes, General. As I said, I did the best I could with the equipment we have. Seeing the real thing may reveal something I missed."

"Mr. Mokri, do you understand how to deconstruct the weapon?"

"I've been reviewing Guy's scans," Reza said. "I believe so."

"You ought to be certain, son. We only get one shot at this."

Reza bit his lower lip and then nodded. "I can do it, General."

"Good man," Theodore said. "What do you need?"

"My tools from the lab. I can go and get them."

"No. Stay put. Sergeant Diallo, would you mind?"

"Yes, sir," Diallo replied.

"They're on the bench," Reza said. "Just grab all of them."

"Of course, Mr. Mokri," Diallo said. He handed Reza the rifle and headed from the room.

Reza placed the weapon on the table, looking uncomfortable to touch it. "I don't like guns," he said.

"The reason I wanted you to stay was so that we could talk things through a little bit. The fact is, we got a big fat clue as to what all we should be looking for from our encounter with that Dread fortress that's hugging our ass back there."

"Their armor was vulnerable to our weapons," Gabriel said.

"Yes," Guy said. "I have been giving it some thought, as you requested General."

"And?" Theodore asked.

"There is one thing that is different from this encounter with the Dread, and all of our prior encounters with the Dread." He pointed at the schematic of the rifle. "Do you mind if I replace this for a moment?"

"Go on, Mr. Larone."

Guy put his tablet on the table, replacing the image of the gun with one of his own.

"This is a star map of the system we are currently skirting the edge of," he said. "It happens to be right on the corner of a slipspace dead zone, which is where we've been trapped for the last three weeks."

He tapped his pad, and a field of red mist appeared throughout the system beyond the Magellan.

"These are the slipstreams we've detected within the system. There are two dozen of them crisscrossing one another, but as you can see they all reach their terminus at an eerily similar location."

"Any idea why?" Gabriel asked.

"No. We don't understand what causes slipstreams to end, or slipspace to have what seem to be holes throughout. It could be caused by dimensional tears, but to be honest, we don't have the technology to make more than a random guess. What we do know is that slipspace is a dimension that runs parallel to our own, and it is filled with ripples in spacetime. Streams. Riding these streams allow us to travel faster than light by using quantum phasing to cross the boundary between dimensions and take advantage of these distortions."

"Astrophysics one-oh-three," Reza said. Guy almost glared at him but stopped himself short. Reza's face reddened again as he prepared for Theodore to bawl him out again.

"Go on," Theodore said, glaring at Reza.

"Those are the slipstreams," Guy said, pointing at the mist. Then he pointed at the green dot some distance away from it. "That's us."

"We're still in the dead zone," Choi said. "You're suggesting that the Dread armor uses slipspace?"

"I believe it is so, yes."

"You mean it's phased?" Gabriel asked, not quite believing it. "How can something static like metal rest permanently in another dimension?"

"I didn't say it was," Guy replied.

"The Dread armor is coated in phase paint," Reza said. "Yes. It could be. It doesn't have to be phased all the time, only when it detects something is about to strike it. It enters phase, and the threat is avoided."

"No," Theodore said. "Missiles would go right through if that were the case. They don't. They hit the armor, explode, and don't leave a scratch."

"And shooting it still exerts a force on the armor," Gabriel said. "That wouldn't happen if the ions were being phased into slipspace."

"True," Reza said, pausing to think.

"What if the phase were partial?" Sarah said, speaking for the first time.

"What do you mean?" Guy asked.

"Well, instead of trying to stop the entire attack, only part of it is deflected. For instance, a missile strikes the armor and detonates. The force still exists, but enough of it is absorbed into phase that it doesn't cause any damage. It just kind of pushes against the armor."

"An interesting thought," Guy said. "To take it one step further, what if there is another type of phase, or use for the properties of quantum phasing that humans have yet to discover? What if slipspace can be manipulated into realspace, similarly to how we manipulate this dimension into that one."

"You mean pull slipspace in?" Reza said. "Impossible."

"Is it?" Guy asked.

"There's no viable theory to suggest it. No math that can prove it, or an experiment that has shown it."

"They used to say the same damn thing about slipspace," Theodore said. "They said it didn't exist, and even if it did, we could never use it to go faster than light. They said it was all just made up sci-fi bullshit. Until it wasn't."

"The Dread are an advanced race," Gabriel said. "I don't think it's safe to dismiss the potential for them to do anything just because we haven't done it yet."

"Especially because we haven't done it yet," Choi agreed. "I'm sure many geneticists would have thought the cloning and gene manipulation the Dread use was also impossible. When we limit the capabilities of the universe to what we currently understand, we undermine the potential of it."

Diallo re-appeared in the room, holding a bag full of small tools. He dropped it on the table in front of Reza.

"Thank you, Sergeant," Theodore said.

"Yes, sir."

"As I was saying, General," Guy said. "What if slipspace could be pulled into this dimension? How would it work? What effects would it have? I don't know the answer, but what we do know is that the Dread armor absorbs damage without the kinetic force of the blow being deleted. Reduced perhaps, but not removed. We also know that it is dependent on slipspace to operate. Without it, the armor is still solid, but it is not even as solid as the metal plating on the Magellan's hull. Finally, we know that whatever allows the weapon to bypass the defenses operates at a scale we weren't able to pick up with our scanning equipment."

"It may be nano-scale," Sarah said.

"Well, then, what are you waiting for, Mr. Mokri?" Theodore asked. "Open her up and let's see what we can see."

[39]

"What's the word from the science team?" Miranda asked.

Gabriel stood just inside the doorway to her quarters, stroking Wallace's head. His father had ordered him to take a break from the research that was ongoing in the meeting room since he would need to relieve Lieutenant Bale from her shift on the hot seat within the next few hours. He was supposed to hit the sack, but the whole thing had left his mind whirling and unable to calm enough to fall asleep.

He had decided to find Wallace instead, heading first to Daphne's quarters, and then to Miranda's, which was where he had found the dog.

"They're picking the Dread weapon apart a piece at a time, and then running everything through a microscope. It's slow going."

"What about your father?"

Gabriel smiled. "You saw him on the bridge. When I went to see him, and he popped up and told me he wanted to steal the Magellan, I thought I was seeing the old Old Gator. Now I know I wasn't. The real General St. Martin is the one we saw a few hours ago."

"He's changed the entire complexion of the ship. The crew is working with purpose and energy again. Of course, surviving a skirmish with the Dread didn't hurt."

"No. It felt pretty good."

"I'm glad you're not still beating yourself up about the nacelle."

Gabriel grimaced. "Oh. Thanks for reminding me."

"Come on, Captain, you know I'm always on your side."

She was. She always had been. "Don't you mean Major?"

She laughed. "I'm teasing you again. Seriously, Gabriel, I'm glad you made it back in one piece. I was worried about you."

"I don't know what would have happened if the Dread hadn't been vulnerable. Bale was real close to getting cut down, and if one of us had gone down, I think the others would have followed pretty soon after."

"But they were vulnerable, she didn't get shot down, and you're all still here. That's the important thing."

"I know. It's hard not to worry sometimes. It's hard to stop thinking in general. The Dread fortress is still behind us, and we can't get away. It's not a question of if they'll try again, it's when. My father looks great, and he sounds great, but I'm still worried about him. When I saw that clone of my mother on Earth, I could barely breathe. I could barely think. It hit me like a meteor. How is he going to react if he ever comes face to face with one?"

"Do you think he'll fall apart?"

"No. But what if they're not friendly? What if it's trying to kill him? He might just stand there and take it."

"And risk all of our lives again? I doubt that."

"Maybe you're right. I hope you're right."

"What else is bothering you?"

He shook his head. He had been feeling the doubts for a while, but it was hard to admit to them. "What if it's all for nothing?" he asked, throwing it out there. If he couldn't tell Miranda about it, he couldn't tell anyone. "What if we got the weapon back, but we can't figure out how to use it? Everyone on Earth will die. Everyone in the settlement will die. We'll die. We're responsible for the continuation of the entire human race."

"And everyone on this ship is doing the best they can. It's the only thing we can do, right?"

"That doesn't make it easier to stop thinking about it. I feel responsible for these people. As much as my father does. Maybe more, since I'm the one who got us stuck here."

"Gabe-" Miranda started to say.

"I know, I know. I did my best. Anyway, I have to go try to get some rest, or I'm going to be running on fumes if the Dread attack. Thanks for listening, Randa."

"You know I always will."

Gabriel smiled. He didn't think about it much, but she was his best friend. Always there for him. Always loyal. When he had lost Jessica, he had felt like she had lost her, too. "I can't tell you how much I appreciate that, or how much I appreciate you."

"You just did."

She reached out for him. He stepped forward into her embrace, holding her for a minute before letting go. They stared at one another for a long moment.

"Look, I don't want to be overly forward, and I don't want you to get the wrong idea," Miranda said. "Maybe you just need some company to help you relax."

"You mean Wallace? I think he's happier with you."

"I mean human company," she replied. "Why don't you hang out here? We can watch a stream, and maybe having someone else around will help you stop thinking so much."

Gabriel considered for a moment. He couldn't think of a reason why he shouldn't.

"It's worth a shot," he said. "If you don't mind."

"I don't mind at all. I like having you around."

"In that case, what do you want to watch?"

"The selection is pretty slim, but there has to be something in there we've seen less than a thousand times."

Gabriel stepped away from the door, giving himself permission to smile. He had no idea what the future was going to bring, but for right now he would just relax and let it go. His father was back and better than ever, Reza and the Larones were working on deciphering the mystery of the Dread technology, and Miranda was, well, he wasn't completely certain what Miranda was. A friend for sure, but there was something else there, a new sensation tugging at his emotions and whispering that maybe she could be something more.

He let that thought fade away and took his position beside her on her bunk, facing her comm station. For now, he was content enough to share her presence.

Besides, they had a war to win.

[40]

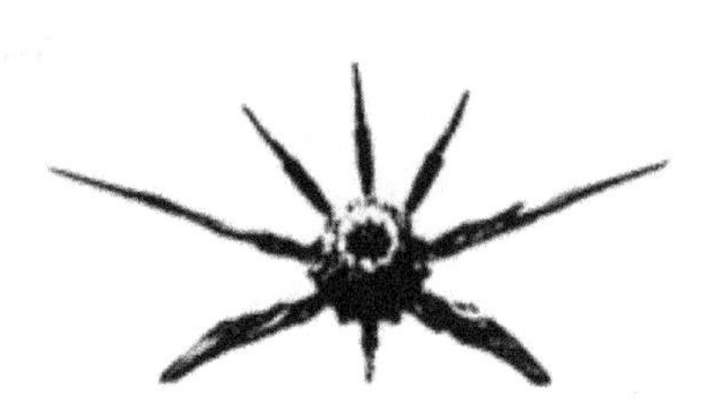

"THERE," DONOVAN SHOUTED, POINTING AT A SPOT BENEATH the Dread transport. "That's where it's stuck."

Murphy ran back to where he was standing, coming up beside him and leaning over. "Damn it. I told Rosa to guide us further to the right. It's going to take time to get free."

Donovan surveyed the area around them. There was a line of brush ten meters deep on both sides of the road, along with a large old building set back a few hundred meters on their left. A side road led up to it, and a sign rested against a worn facade. "Parada de descanso," it read in faded white lettering on an orange background. Rest stop.

Ehri approached a moment later, running back from her position at the front of the group. She also dipped down to see what had happened.

"We'll need something to dig it out with," she said.

"Do you have a shovel?" Donovan asked.

"No," Murphy replied. "We were too busy collecting food, clothes, guns and ammunition. I never thought we would need a shovel."

"Ehri, how much time do we have left?" Soon said, circling from the other side of the transport.

"Approximately eight hours, Captain."

"We aren't going to make it to Monterrey before then."

Donovan stared down the length of the roadway at the tractor ahead of them, vibrating softly as it sat idle, its driver waiting for him to pass along his orders.

His original idea had been to try to rig the anti-gravity controller on the Dread transport such that they could get it to sit a few inches off the ground. At that point, it would offer little to no friction, and they would be able to attach a few ropes to it and pull it along, like a covered wagon from that same old western he had seen. Most of the group could be piled inside to ride in comfort while a few pulled and a few guarded, taking turns as needed throughout the day and night to make it as far as possible in relative safety before the hard-won days of peace came to an abrupt end.

Ehri thought it was a great idea, and had immediately gone to the rear of the vehicle to begin working with the zero point engine that powered it while he returned to Murphy to inform him of his plan. Within an hour, Ehri had come running to show him that she had gotten the transport jury-rigged to the point that the engine was running, and power had been diverted to the plates on the bottom of the craft. He and Murphy had watched as she got it floating nearly a foot off the ground. Then they had watched as it tumbled back to earth a few seconds later, victim of a secondary security system that prevented it from changing coordinates without a pilot at the helm.

Donovan had been discouraged and ready to give up. Murphy hadn't. He quickly organized the scavengers to find an alternative means of enacting a similar plan. It had taken nearly a full day to get all of the pieces in place, but by the end they had managed to slip the frame of an old semi-trailer beneath the transport, letting it bear the weight of the ship and giving it a line of wheels to roll on. They had also somehow located a huge farming machine an hour outside of the city, a behemoth of rolling alloy that was almost wider than the transport itself. It had been lost for years beneath the crops it had been built to collect, a buried treasure that the scavengers had been lucky to come across. It had taken a little engineering know-how to get the long-dead battery feeding from the transport's generator, but Ehri and Rosa, a seventy-eight-year-old survivor of the Dread invasion, had managed to get it done.

They had been making good time since then, covering more ground in the hours that followed than any of them could have managed in a week on foot. The travel had been easy once they reached the wider road, with the tractor able to roll down the center of the highway, pushing most of the remaining derelict cars out of its path with ease and trailing the transport behind it.

Then they had come across deep scars in the road left by the Dread attack decades earlier. The tractor had gone over them without a problem. The transport hadn't been as fortunate, the rear-most axle getting hung up on a thick pile of rubble. The obstruction hadn't immediately overloaded the cab, but they all knew it would thicken and multiply if they continued to push it until it both bogged down their makeshift wagon and left it impossible to dig out.

"What do you want to do?" Murphy asked. "We came down through Monterrey. I remember that rest stop. It's a good two hundred kilometers to decent protection from here."

"We can cover that ground easily in the Monster," Soon said, using the nickname for the machine they had created. "Once we get it unstuck."

"It will take five hours to reach Monterrey," Ehri said. "We have less than three to get it loose."

"Can you levitate the transport again?" Donovan asked.

"No, Major. As soon as we moved it away from its landing position, the security systems shut down access to the anti-gravity functions."

Donovan considered the situation. Their agreement would expire soon, and he was sure the Dread wouldn't waste any time sending a force to deal with them. The goal was to be out of sight when that happened, preferably somewhere underground with the transport safely hidden away. They were hopeful the Dread would sweep the area, find nothing, and then decide to pass them over. That would give them an opportunity to bring the Monster back out and make a run for the border, crossing over into what had once been the United States of America and making a beeline for Austin before they were discovered.

It wasn't a great plan, but it was the only thing they had. Except now a simple error in judgment had left them stuck, and he had to make a decision: Try to get the Monster moving again or abandon it and take their chances on foot.

It wasn't much of a decision. He didn't like their chances on foot, which was why they had gone through so much trouble to create the Monster in the first place. He knew there were jackals out there, and while they had recovered more of the alien rifles it wouldn't help them if they were ambushed or attacked by a human force with greater numbers. It gnawed at him that they even had to worry about it. Didn't humankind have enough to deal with? He hated that some people would rather sew chaos than save one another from it.

"You said you passed that building before," he said. "Did you go inside?"

"No, sir. We went past it in the middle of the night, as quick and quiet as we could. For all we know, that place is already occupied."

"Jackals?"

"Maybe. Or anyone else who might shoot first and ask questions later. We were trying not to lose anyone. The Dread didn't let that happen."

"We need to make an attempt to excavate the transport. Our only choice is to see if there's anything we can salvage inside that building that might help us dig out the wheels."

"Understood. I don't have a problem with that, Major. Not when I know Linda and Shea and the others can stay safe inside the Monster while we explore."

"We'll leave the Dread weapons with them. If there's any trouble, it won't help to give up the means to get to the others."

"Agreed," Murphy said.

Donovan turned to Ehri and Soon. "We'll exchange our rifles for traditional guns, and then go search that old building over there. We have one hour, and then we have to consider abandoning the Monster and going ahead on foot."

"Yes, sir," both Soon and Ehri said.

"What if we find other people in there?" Soon asked a moment later.

Donovan glanced at Murphy, who shrugged. It seemed like his group went through a lot of trouble to intentionally not find other people. He couldn't question the practice when they had managed to survive.

"If they're friendly, we give them a chance to join us. If they're hostile, we take them out."

Soon's face blanched at the idea, but he nodded. "I hope it doesn't come to that."

Donovan looked over at the building. It certainly appeared abandoned. "Me, too, Captain. Me, too."

[41]

THEY APPROACHED THE BUILDING CAUTIOUSLY, STAYING LOW IN the surrounding brush for as long as they could before breaking the cover and running full-speed to the smooth metal wall closest to the entrance.

Donovan smiled when Soon reached the wall first, barely a step ahead of Ehri. A chance to rest in the Monster for a day had helped the pilot regain most of his former health, and he was showing himself to be a capable soldier.

Murphy reached the wall after Donovan, pausing against it and breathing hard. The leader of the scavengers had proven that he and his people were incredibly resourceful, but also not accustomed to fighting. They had always preferred to run and hide than to take a stand, though Donovan's growing reputation seemed to have emboldened them. He had insisted on coming along, certain that he could help them find something they could use to get the transport unstuck. Even so, his nerves were obviously frayed, his eyes wide and body shaking.

Donovan pushed back the thought of Diaz. She loved these kinds of missions and had always been at home exploring potentially dangerous areas. He wished they didn't have to do it without her.

"Ehri," he whispered, pointing to the wall on the other side of the entry.

It had been a pair of sliding glass doors once. Those doors were long shattered, replaced by piles of debris that siphoned anyone who wanted through to a tight spot in the center. There was no question someone had lived there at one time. The question was whether or not anyone was still inside.

She darted across the open space, coming to rest against the wall once more. The activity didn't draw any attention from inside.

"Cover me," Donovan said, slipping away from the wall and approaching the bottleneck. Dirty food containers rested on the floor at the base of the entrance, abandoned months, if not years, earlier.

He led with the antique handgun Murphy had provided him. It was sleek in appearance and fairly heavy, with a fourteen round magazine loaded and ready and two more in his pockets. It was the kind of weapon a Dread would laugh at. It could still kill a human without much effort.

He hoped it didn't come to that. He had killed Dread clones that were essentially human, but he had never hurt another free human being, and he had no desire to start.

He was halfway across the barrier when a noise to his left caused him to pause, dropping to a knee and aiming the weapon. Ehri appeared behind him a moment later, keeping him covered. A cat appeared in the darkness, hissing and running from them, out into the brush.

"Damn cat," Donovan said. "Scared the crap out of me."

"My apologies, Major, I should have warned you. I saw it from back there."

Donovan glanced back at Ehri. Her enhanced capabilities continued to surprise him. "Anything else up there I should know about?"

She smiled. "No, Major."

Donovan waved Murphy and Soon forward, and they finished passing through the barrier and into the building. It had originally been designed as a place for travelers to pause and eat, use the restroom, and maybe buy something. As a result, it was organized into corridors with storefronts lining them, selling everything from hats to t-shirts to medicine.

Moving through the space, they quickly discovered that most of it had already been picked clean by earlier passers-by. Even the cleaning robots had been disassembled, their interior parts salvaged for use in more valuable tools.

"I was hopeful," Donovan said as they walked along the final line of stores. "But this place is too close to the road to have stayed pristine."

"It was worth a shot," Murphy said. "We've only lost twenty minutes, and now we know for sure our ride is done. We'll have to go on foot from here on out."

"We'll never make it to Monterrey on foot before the treaty ends," Soon said. "We have eight hours."

"We'll think of something," Donovan said. If he had learned anything, it was never to give up. He looked at Ehri. "How far can the tractor take us once we disconnect the generator?"

"With everyone weighing it down? Twenty kilometers at most."

"That's twenty more than we'll cover otherwise. I hate to lose the security the transport offers, but we knew we might not be able to hold onto it forever."

"We're lucky we made it as far as we have," Murphy said. "It took us weeks to get down to San Luis, and we made it back here in one tenth of the time. Then again, I know for a fact there's a gang of jackals in Monterrey. We managed to slip past, but all the signs were there. It would have been nice to have some protection."

"If that's true, the Dread have probably attacked them by now," Donovan said. "They may be helping us by clearing the cities before we get to them."

"Wouldn't that be something?" Murphy said.

"In any case, standing here isn't going to get anything done," Donovan said. "Let's head back to the others. We need to get them ready to move on foot again. Can Jane walk?"

"Thanks to Doctor Iwu she can," Murphy said.

"Good." Donovan took two steps before pausing. "Where's Soon?"

Ehri and Murphy looked at one another, and then scanned the corridor.

"There," Ehri said a moment later. Soon had gone into one of the stores and was standing motionless in front of something.

"What's he doing?" Murphy asked.

Donovan couldn't tell. He headed over to the pilot, finding him flipping through a line of clothes sized for an infant.

"Captain?" Donovan said.

"What do you think of this, Major?" Soon asked, lifting one of the tiny outfits from the rack. It was green and black, with a small patch across the chest that said "Federacion Mexicana De Futbol Asoc., A.C."

"I don't think it will fit you," Donovan replied.

Soon smiled. "Sorry for wandering away, Major. It's just that my wife Daphne and I really want to have a baby. It's a little more complicated than that up there because we only have resources to support a limited population. We have to wait our turn. Down here? There's enough for everybody. I can't even tell you how much I'd love to have Daphne here with me, and to dress the future Soon Junior in this thing."

Donovan put his hand on Soon's shoulder. "Then we need to do everything in our power to make it happen."

"Do you think we can, Major? The Monster was genius, but our luck seems to be out. We're stranded, and our position is way too open. I came in here, and now I'm hoping Daphne knows how much I miss her, and how much I want to give this outfit to her, even if I have no idea what it says on it. Even if the odds of that happening are getting lower by the minute."

Donovan dug his fingers into Soon's arm, turning the pilot toward him. A wave of anger bubbled up, pouring from the wounds he had buried.

"We aren't going to die here, Captain. You hear me? Not you. Not me. Not anyone else. We got you away from the Dread; we escaped Mexico City and San Luis, and we made it all the way here. Nobody said it would be easy, but we're going to survive this thing. We're going to topple the Dread, and we're going to bring your wife home. Do you get that, Captain? She's going to come home to you, right here on Earth."

Soon stood in front of him, shocked into silence for a moment. Then he nodded, clutching the cloth he had picked up tightly in a fist.

"Yes, sir," he said.

"Come on," Donovan said, turning back to where he had left Ehri and Murphy.

He looked just in time to see Ehri running toward him, her mouth opening in a scream, her arms waving at them to get down.

Then the gunfire started, bullets hitting her body and throwing her to the ground. He felt his heart jump again as Murphy fell to the ground behind her, his body riddled with holes, his face vanishing under the barrage.

[42]

DONOVAN HIT THE GROUND BESIDE SOON, LYING PRONE AS THE bullets continued to pass over them for a few more seconds.

Then it stopped as quickly as it had started. The world fell silent again, the smell of blood and metal leaving a thick taste in the air. Donovan looked up, trying to find the attackers and trying to find Ehri. How could he have just lost her like that? She had enhanced senses, and she hadn't heard them coming. He still didn't see anyone in the hallway. Where the hell were they?

"Get up," a voice said. It came from all around them. From the building's comm system.

Donovan remained on the floor. He looked over at Soon. He was unharmed.

"Look in front of you," the voice said.

Donovan did. The red point of a laser was hitting the floor there. He followed it to the source, an opening in the ceiling ductwork that he had failed to notice earlier. The building had been occupied the entire time. They just hadn't known it, and now Murphy and Ehri were dead.

"We could have killed you already if we wanted to, Major," the voice said. "Lucky for you, we have a soft spot for the military. That was a pretty killer pep-talk you were giving, by the way. I couldn't have done it better myself. Oh, and you, Captain. Oh, my. So emotional. So sweet. I cried a little bit." A moment of silence was followed by a sharp command. "Get up."

Donovan pulled himself to his feet, staring up at the laser. Soon stood beside him. "Who are you?" he asked.

"My name is Kraeger. Welcome to my honeypot."

"What do you want with us?" Donovan looked over to where Ehri was laying on the ground. She wasn't moving.

"Honeypot, Major. Do you know what that is?"

"A trap," Donovan said.

"Exactly. One that you and your friends walked right into."

"You didn't have to kill them," Soon said.

"That's a matter of opinion," Kraeger replied. "I needed you to know I mean business. Like I said, the only reason I didn't kill you is because I have a soft spot for the resistance. Step forward, to the center of the corridor. Oh, and lose the guns."

Soon looked at Donovan, who nodded. They both dropped their guns and moved to the center of the space.

The laser remained in front of them. Donovan heard footsteps in the building, and a minute later a muscular older man in a white t-shirt and stained jeans appeared, flanked by a dozen other men and women. They were all heavily armed with weapons that looked much more modern than anything Donovan had seen before. Somehow, these jackals were better armed than the resistance.

"Major," the man said, stepping ahead of the others and putting out his hand. "Kraeger."

Donovan didn't take the hand. Kraeger smiled at that.

"I could kill you for being rude."

"You won't," Donovan said. "You want something from me."

"I want a few things from you. Seeing that I've got you by the balls, I think you're going to give them to me, too."

"What makes you say that?"

"Grab him," Kraeger said.

Three of the men broke off from the others, approaching Soon.

One took each of his arms, holding him tight. The other produced a knife, moving to Soon's left hand.

"How many fingers will it take, Major?" Kraeger asked. "Two? Three?" He nodded, and the man grabbed Soon's hand.

"Wait," Donovan said. "What do you want from me?"

Kraeger put up his hand. His lackey let go of Soon's.

"I knew you would be reasonable. I don't want to hurt you or the Captain here. What I do want is to know how you managed to capture a Dread transport? That is beyond impressive, Major."

"I took it," Donovan said.

"From the Dread?" one of Kraeger's people said. "Not likely."

"From the Dread," Donovan said. "Look, I don't know you, and you don't know me, but we don't have to be enemies. The Dread can be fought. They can be hurt. They can even be killed."

"With their own weapons. Yes, Major, we intercepted that message."

"What do you mean, intercepted?" Donovan asked.

"We've been tapping into resistance channels for years, Major. Not always from here, we've only been here two or three, but out there. Following the tides, waiting for some kind of hope."

"Then you know there is hope. We've been in contact with the space forces. We got one of the weapons to them, to learn how to defeat their armor. We're working together to stop the Dread. You could have helped us, instead of shooting first."

Kraeger laughed. "Help you? You're lucky I haven't killed you already. Do you know what your little victory did, Major? You haven't been listening to the chatter, so let me tell you. A month ago, there were twenty-two free settlements positioned around North America. These are civilians, regular men, women, and children, not murderous assholes like me and mine. Do you know how many are left?"

Donovan knew what Murphy had told him about Washington. He felt a cold chill settle over him. "No."

"Six," Kraeger said. "Feel proud of yourself? Feel like you're winning?"

"At least I'm trying instead of luring innocent people in and killing them for what they have."

"Careful, Major," Kraeger said. "It is possible for my good will to run out. You don't know enough about what we do here to make statements like that."

"The Dread were coming before I did anything. You know it was only a matter of time."

"Maybe." Kraeger shrugged. "It doesn't matter now, does it. The resistance is falling apart, Major. You've seen it yourself. It's too little, too late, which means it's more important than ever for those of us who want to survive to do whatever it takes. Whatever. It. Takes. Do you hear me?"

Donovan glanced over at Soon. "Yes, sir," he said.

"Sir?" Kraeger replied, laughing. "I like that. We've been watching you since your rig got stuck outside. I know you have people and equipment inside that transport. I want it."

"The equipment?"

"And the people."

"What for?"

"They managed to create that monster out there. It looks like they got the Dread power source hooked up to the tractor's battery. We need people with skills like that. The ones who don't have any? We'll find a use for them, too."

"I can't turn them over to you."

"Yes, Major. You can. And why not? We don't have to be enemies. I'd be happy to bring you and the Captain on. Like I said, I need people with skills."

"How do you know you can trust us?"

"Because you have morals. You won't say yes unless you mean it. You'd rather die."

"I'd say yes to keep you from torturing my friend."

"Fair enough. I'll tell you what. I'm going to take torture off the table. Let him go."

The men dropped Soon's arms and backed off.

"There. You see? We can be civilized. The Dread are coming for us, Major. They want to wipe humankind off the Earth. I'm not like the other assholes out there. I know what's going down. The difference is, I want to save what I can, and I have a plan to do it."

"Which is?"

"I've been here for almost three years. The Dread have been in this building four times already, searching. They haven't found us yet. Do you know why not?"

"You hide?"

"Yes, we hide. But the answer isn't that we hide. It's how we hide. It's where we hide."

"And where is that?"

"I want to show you, Major. I do. I can't unless you join up."

"You killed my people."

Kraeger sighed in frustration. "Yes, I killed two of your people. We kill people all the time. So do the Dread. That's the way the world works now. You give something to get something. In this case, your people gave up two of their own in exchange for a chance at something better. I'm not saying it will be an easy life for them, but at least they'll be alive and contributing, and who knows? If the space forces do come back, maybe we'll all survive."

"Have all the people who came here gotten this offer?" Donovan asked.

"Not even half," Kraeger said. "We take people who can help us. We kill the ones who can't. We can't risk word of our community getting out. We can't take the chance that the Dread will discover us."

"What are the Dread going to think when they find our rig right outside your front door?" Donovan said.

"They'll search the building again. They'll find nothing, again. No bodies, no blood. We've been doing this long enough to get it right."

"And if I say no, you kill me?"

"And everyone with you."

"You can't get into the transport."

"Then the Dread will kill them when they show up. How did you make it this far without them stopping you, anyway, Major?"

"I got into an Honor Fight with one of them. I won three days of peace."

"Well hell, I'm even more impressed. You should join up, Major. I know it wasn't the plan when you showed up here, but I think you'll be glad you did. A guy like you can get ahead in a hurry."

"I'm with the resistance," Donovan said. "I want to stay with the resistance. What if I give you the others and walk away?"

Kraeger laughed. "See? That's what I mean. We get to talking, and things change. But what if I had talked first, instead of killing your friends? You wouldn't be taking me seriously right now. You wouldn't be so willing to negotiate. I can't let you walk, Major. You know we're here, and I don't take risks."

"No exceptions? I promise I won't talk."

"Sorry, Major. No exceptions."

Donovan glanced over at Soon, and then back to Kraeger. He wasn't ready to give up his mission to reach Austin, but what choice did he have? The man had him by the throat and was offering him and the scavengers a chance to live. It was more than most got.

He glanced over Kraeger's shoulder again, to where Ehri had fallen. He had murdered her in cold blood to make a statement. Could he live with a man like that? Could he turn the scavengers over to a man like that? It didn't matter what his reasons were. The fact that he was even capable of the act spoke volumes.

He bit his lip, casting his eyes to the ground and putting his hand to his head like he was considering. He fought to keep himself calm and not give anything away.

Ehri was gone.

[43]

"ANYTHING NEW TO REPORT?" THEODORE ASKED, ROLLING smoothly onto the bridge.

Colonel Choi stood as he entered. "General on the bridge," she said.

The rest of the crew stood to face him.

"At ease," Theodore said.

The crew returned to their positions, Gabriel included. He had spent the last forty-eight hours splitting time between resting in the cockpit of his starfighter, running through the corridors of the Magellan with Wallace and Miranda in an effort to get some exercise, and manning the pilot station on the bridge. He wasn't required to be there, and Maggie could handle the flying duties while they continued on their course along the edge of the star system, but he didn't want to miss anything.

"Colonel, what's the status of the Dread fortress?" Theodore asked.

"They're remaining in position behind us, General," Choi replied. "I don't think they're near full thrust."

"Me neither. It's been a couple of days, which means if Guy was right about them being slipsick, all but the weakest will be recovering, and the rest will be dead." Theodore looked over at where Sarah Larone was sitting by herself. "Mrs. Larone, why are you on the bridge?"

She stood and faced him. "Sir, Guy and Reza asked me to be here to liaise with you."

Theodore's brow creased. "How do you mean?"

She smiled. "They're onto something sir, the two of them. They have a new theory regarding slipspace, based on the ideas we've come up with on the Dread technology. They asked me to be here when you arrived, to keep you updated on their progress."

"I see. In that case, Mrs. Larone, update me."

"Yes, sir. Can we go to the conference room? I have a sim I can show you."

"Of course. "Major St. Martin, can you please attend? You too, Colonel. Sergeant Abdullah, you have the bridge. Don't let Maggie do anything I wouldn't do."

"Yes, sir," Abdullah said, standing to take the command chair.

Gabriel retreated to the rear of the bridge to stand beside Theodore as he swung himself easily into his chair. He was still amazed at how much stronger and healthier his father looked, though he did notice a wince as Theodore settled himself in his seat. How much pain was the General masking?

They crossed the corridor into the conference room, the four of them sitting in a semi-circle around the end. Sarah withdrew her tablet and placed it on the table. It projected the Dread rifle in front of them.

"As you know, we had to bring the rifle back down to the lab after Reza began disassembling it. Once we started opening it up, we realized what a poor job our scanners did in picking up some of the components."

"Because they're organic in nature," Theodore said.

Sarah seemed surprised. "You spoke to Guy already?"

"Yesterday. It seems like you have more for me today."

"Yes, sir. As you said, we discovered that some of the internals are made of organic compounds. Some further studies I've done have proven that these compounds are basic in nature, but by our standards, they can be considered living organisms."

"You're saying the gun is alive?" Gabriel asked.

"Yes, Major. In a sense. The organisms are fueled by the same electrical supply that powers the weapon. They take the energy and excrete trace elements of waste that we believe get burned off when the weapon is fired. That's not too important in itself. We believe the Dread have found a way to use organic compounds to replace common minerals used by humans. Copper, for example. It is likely they didn't have these minerals on their homeworld, and so their technology emerged differently than ours."

"But it isn't related to how the weapon functions overall?" Choi asked.

"We don't believe so."

"How does the weapon work, Mrs. Larone?" Theodore asked.

She waved her hand over the projection, pulling it apart the way Reza had done earlier. Except now there were at least three dozen more parts.

"There are two parts to this equation, General," Sarah said. "The first is the weapon itself, able to pierce the Dread armor. The second is the armor, able to deflect pretty much anything without taking noticeable damage."

"Sounds about right."

Sarah manipulated the weapon, turning it so that the center was right in front of them. She pushed the rest of it aside, leaving what appeared to be a simple, rippled ring in the view.

"We're calling this a phase modulator. This is the visible part of it, but once we took the weapon part we were able to examine it under magnification." She reached for a piece of the image and blew it up, expanding it until a web of circuitry became visible. "Everything here is nano-scale. There are almost two billion of what we're calling 'phase points' embedded into the ring. Each phase point is connected to a small node that we think is a controller that manages the point."

"I'm an old gator, Mrs. Larone," Theodore said. "Keep the next part simple for me."

"Essentially, when the weapon is triggered and the phase modulator is engaged, it puts whatever passes through it into what Guy is calling a quantum vortex." She paused, the excitement of her next statement clear on her face. "His new theory is that it phases the plasma through another dimension of spacetime. One that humankind hasn't discovered yet."

"A third dimension?" Choi said.

"Yes," she replied, almost giggling. "One with properties we don't completely understand. What we do know is that it allows the plasma to pass through the enemies' shielding. We believe that the enemy shields may also be utilizing this dark energy as part of their function. Guy and Reza are exploring that concept right now."

"How is that possible?" Gabriel said. "I mean, slipspace is composed of ripples in space and time. This other dimension is composed of what?"

"Matter and energy. Like realspace, but different. Reza thinks this new dimension may be the source of dark matter. In fact, he's taken to calling it darkspace. His idea is that it leaks through into our space because darkspace is so dense that it can't contain it."

"The majority of the universe is made up of dark matter," Choi said.

"Yes, Colonel. If he's right, we may have found a clue to the origin of our universe itself."

"For all we know, the Dread already understand the origin of the universe," Gabriel said.

"It is possible," Sarah agreed.

"You got all that from looking at the gun under a microscope?" Theodore asked.

"No, sir. To be honest, it's all theoretical, based on one observable calculation. Reza isolated one of the phase points and was able to trigger it. It broke our sensors, but not before he was able to take measurements."

"What do you mean, broke?"

"They were too close to it, I guess. Without being inside the weapon's shielding, it caused a small electromagnetic pulse that killed the equipment."

Theodore smiled. "You're saying you could have shorted out the entire ship and killed every last one of us?"

Sarah's face turned red. "Uh. I suppose I am, sir."

"Ha! Wouldn't that have been a real kick in the pants?"

"I don't understand," Gabriel said. "If this isn't related to slipspace, why are the Dread ships vulnerable in slipspace dead zones?"

"It is related to slipspace," Sarah said. "Directly related. Think of it like a ligament holding muscle to bone. Darkspace is a thin layer that sits between realspace and slipspace. In fact, it's quite possible that we pass through it every time we slip, it's just that it's so narrow that our equipment can't detect it. In fact, we think the slipspace dead zones aren't caused by a lack of waves, but a detachment between darkspace and slipspace within them."

Gabriel waved his hands in the air. "You're saying it's the stuff that holds all of this together?"

"It may be, Major. We also now think the reason that slipspace is black instead of white is because the density of darkspace is keeping the light in realspace from penetrating through."

Theodore whistled. "Mrs. Larone, I have to say that you and your husband and Reza have done fantastic work here. Simply fantastic. I'm happy to hear we may be breaking new ground on our understanding of the universe, and I hate to spoil the fun, but what does it mean for us today? We've still got a Dread fortress on our tail, and they ain't going to stay back there forever."

[44]

"AH, GENERAL," GUY SAID, LOOKING UP AS THEODORE ENTERED the makeshift lab with Gabriel, Sarah, and Colonel Choi. He was hunched over his tablet, his hair messy and his eyes red from lack of sleep. "I assume you spoke to Sarah." He stumbled to his feet.

"That's why we're here, Mr. Larone," Theodore said. "She gave me the rundown on this so-called darkspace. Where is Mr. Mokri?"

"He went to retrieve some of the phase paint from inventory," Guy said. "We were about to test my theory."

"Which one?" Theodore asked. "You seem to have come up with a whole barrel of them."

"It's amazing what you can do with the right motivation, and with a little push from alien technology. I haven't been this excited about anything since I met Sarah." He looked at her. "You're still more exciting, darling."

She blushed and smiled in response, acting demure. Gabriel didn't know what the current situation was between the three scientists, and he didn't care. At least they were working together on the problem.

Reza approached behind them, holding a container of the paint.

"Oh. Uh. General." He put the paint on the floor and saluted. "Sir. You're just in time to see if we're onto something."

"I hope for all our sakes you are, Mr. Mokri," Theodore replied.

"Yes, sir." He picked up the paint and carried it across the lab.

They had taken root in a large space deep inside the Magellan. They had moved a ton of equipment from its original place on the ship into a corner of it, along with a simple workbench and stools, tablets and projectors. It was an organized chaos of tools and devices that Gabriel didn't recognize or understand the purpose for.

Reza walked to the far end of the space, a hundred meters distant from them. He lifted the paint container and began spraying it against the inner bulkhead. It dried nearly instantly, leaving a dark, uneven film across the area.

He came back to them. A battery was resting in a cart nearby, attached to his tablet and connected to the Dread rifle, which was protruding a thick wire. He grabbed it and began pushing it toward the painted wall.

"Mr. Mokri," Theodore said. "Would you mind telling me what you're doing? We don't have much of that paint as it is, and last I heard we needed it to repair the nacelle."

"We would have to be able to get someone outside to repair the nacelle, sir," Reza said. "Which we can't do as long as they're vulnerable to attack."

"Gabriel can keep the Dread away from the repair team."

"Maybe. Maybe not. You may not have to take that risk if our theory holds up."

"My theory," Guy said.

"Whatever," Reza replied. He kept walking back to the paint, kneeling beside it and rigging the wire against the surface of it. "The paint is conductive," he shouted back, his voice echoing in the chamber. "In simple terms, the quantum phase generators pass energy into it in a defined frequency, which causes the nanoparticles within the material to accelerate and spin. The spin creates a bond between the material here and sibling particles in slipspace, which drags the Magellan out of this spacetime and into that one. These particles travel through slipspace in various densities, always moving and spinning. It is these densities that make up the waves. When we create a strong enough bond, we join the wave, and move from our space into that one."

"I'm a soldier, not a scientist. I'll take your word for it, son," Theodore said.

"Uh. Right. Anyway, the theory-"

"My theory," Guy said again, interrupting. "Is that we can use the phase modulator on the Dread rifle to alter the spin of the particles, so that instead of pushing us toward slipspace, we pull slipspace to us."

"And how is that going to help?"

"My dearest Sarah explained the concept of Laronespace to you?"

"Darkspace," Reza said.

Guy looked back at him.

"Darkspace," Theodore said, confirming Reza's naming. "Yes, she did. Go on."

"To pull slipspace to us, we have to lift Laronespace with it. How do I explain simply?" He paused, considering. "You were born on Earth before the invasion, so you'll understand this simile. It is like swimming instead of sinking. We want to skim the surface, to bring the Magellan into phase with Laronespace instead of slipspace. But, as you know, it's a lot easier to sink than swim."

"Not if you just relax and let yourself float," Theodore said.

Guy paused. "Not exactly like swimming, then."

"You said darkspace is dense," Gabriel said. "Wouldn't that make it easier to sit on top of it, not harder?"

Guy's face tightened. "I'm trying to put things in layman's terms so that you all understand. Density is a relative analogous synonym, in this case. I can show you the calculation that describes the properties we have theorized, but that will be even less meaningful to you.

Gabriel opened his mouth to reply. Theodore interrupted him. "I get the point, Mr. Larone. What exactly are you preparing to do?"

"We've been skirting the edge of the dead zone for the last two days. We're going to cross a short break in it in about a minute. Ten seconds at most, but that's all the time we need."

"Mmm. What exactly are you going to do?" Theodore asked again.

"You might want to roll back, General," Sarah said, putting her hand on his shoulder. "We aren't completely sure about the results."

"Are you telling me you're putting my ship at risk again?" Theodore barked.

"No risk, no reward, General," Guy said. "My calculations are good. Sarah checked them. So did Reza. Besides, I don't think it will damage the ship if it doesn't work."

"Let's hope not."

Guy watched his tablet as the seconds passed. Gabriel, Theodore, and Colonel Choi stood behind them, waiting to see what they were going to do. Gabriel glanced down at his father at the same time Theodore looked up at him. His face hopeful and doubting. This was the culmination of the effort Major Peters and his team had made to get the weapon to them in the first place. It was what Soon had sacrificed himself for. What so many had sacrificed themselves for.

Gabriel felt his heartbeat increasing, his body tensing as the seconds ticked away. He put his hand on his father's shoulder, squeezing it lightly. His other hand landed on his mother's crucifix. Would this work? Would they finally have a way to fight back against the Dread?

A small chime sounded from Guy's tablet. He bent over, retrieving a standard issue assault rifle from beneath the workbench. He held it out to Gabriel. "Major, if you would shoot the wall." Then he turned to Reza and shouted, "Turn it on."

Reza responded by tapping something on his own tablet. There was no change in sound, no difference in the before or after, but the scientist gave them the thumbs-up and then backed away from the area.

Gabriel approached Guy, taking the rifle from him. He pointed it at the bulkhead. He had no idea what was supposed to happen.

He pulled the trigger.

The noise of it echoed across the room. At the far end of the wall, an inky blackness appeared around wherever the bullets struck, flashing for the briefest of instants before vanishing again.

Reza stood at the end of the space near the wall, his fists up in triumph as he whooped and cheered. "Yes. Yes. It works. I don't believe it. It works."

[45]

He turned to face them, a huge smile on his face. A moment later, smoke began pouring from the battery.

His smile vanished, and he ran to the cart, grabbing the Dread rifle and running back toward them. "Watch out," he shouted. He threw himself to the ground as a small flame erupted from the battery and then went out, leaving the entire chamber in silence.

Reza pulled himself to his knees, looking back at the smoldering, half-melted battery, and then at them. "I think we were a little off on the power requirements," he said. "We can work on that."

"Did you see it, General?" Guy said, smiling.

Gabriel thought it might be the first time he had ever seen the man smile.

"I saw something," Theodore said. "Now tell me what it was."

"Darkspace," Guy said, forgetting to use his name for it in his excitement. "We modulated the phase of the paint at the point of impact to bring it into this spacetime, using it as a shield against the Major's projectiles. Because the impact occurs, it still exerts a force on the surface, but the interceding layer of darkspace absorbs most of the energy, limiting its penetrating effects."

"In other words?"

"In other words, we just replicated the Dread's shields."

Theodore smiled. "That's a fine step forward, Mr. Larone. I assume that since you now know how the shields work, you can find a way to defeat them?"

Guy's smile vanished. It was as if Theodore had punched him in the gut.

"What is it?" Theodore asked.

"General, the Dread plasma rifle has two billion phase modulators in an area the size of your first. That's billion, with a 'b.' We don't have anything that can come close to replicating that kind of nano scale construction, and even if we did, it might take months to design a template."

"The other problem is power," Reza said, joining them. He handed the Dread rifle to Gabriel. "That was the largest battery we had in inventory, and it was enough to power the system across a two-meter square section of the wall for about five seconds. Based on that, the power supply in the Dread weapon contains fifty to sixty times more energy. Our battery might be able to fire ten to twenty rounds, and that was the only one we had."

Theodore stared at them. Gabriel could tell his mind was working, taking in the cold facts and trying to adjust strategy around them.

"You said if it worked we might be able to get the nacelle repaired without risking our people."

"Yes, sir. We could theoretically create a shield that would cover the team as they worked on the repairs. If we hook into the Magellan's power supply, it should be enough to protect them from attack."

"Except the Dread can shoot right through their own shields," Gabriel said. "Remember? How would that help?"

"On its own, it wouldn't," Guy said.

"We have another theory," Reza said. "But it's a little harder to test out."

"Which is?" Theodore asked.

"Phase modulation," Guy said. "We think we can alter the phase such that it cancels out the ability of the Dread's weapons to bypass it. Or at a minimum reduces the impact."

"You mean to create a shield against their weapons?" Theodore said.

"Yes, sir. If we had two of the Dread rifles, we could use one to power the shields, and another to test the theory, but-"

"But you don't have two weapons," Theodore said. "And I don't think we'll be getting another anytime soon. There's no way to prove your theory without them?"

"The math seems to be holding up," Reza said. "But without a real test, there's no way to be completely confident."

"Sir," Colonel Choi said. "We need to repair the nacelle if we're going to get out of the system and back home. If we put our fighters out there at the same time, we can minimize the risk."

"Understood, Colonel," Theodore said. He shifted his attention to the wall at the end of the space, staring at it in silence.

To Gabriel, it seemed like the decision was cut and dry. Like the Colonel had said, they had to fix the nacelle, and this was a chance for them to do it. The Dread would undoubtedly target the nacelle, knowing that destroying it would keep the Magellan stranded here forever. They wouldn't even need to do any further damage at that point. They could just leave them here to drift and starve to death.

Wouldn't it be a shock when their attack proved ineffective?

"No," Theodore said a moment later. "I'm not going to do that."

"Sir?" Gabriel said, surprised by the response. "What do you mean?"

"Am I speaking another language, because that sure sounded like English to me? I said I'm not going to do it. Maybe it will work, maybe it won't. It don't matter because either way, it's short-sighted, plain and simple."

"Short-sighted?" Sarah asked.

"Yes, Mrs. Larone. Short-sighted. As in, it ain't going to solve our bigger problem."

"Which is what?" Gabriel asked.

"Power, son. Energy. According to our resident geniuses, we need a pool of it the size of a bayou to feed the tech the Dread are using.

What we've got on board is more like a single drop on the head of a pin."

"We can work on the power problem, General," Reza said. "I'm sure we can reduce the overall requirements."

"Can you?" Theodore asked. "The Dread haven't been able to, and I bet they've had a long time to do it."

"We have different materials to work with. There may be limitations to their organic compounds that we can avoid with minerals."

"How soon?"

None of the scientists replied.

"My point exactly."

"Do you have another idea, General?" Choi asked.

"As a matter of fact, I think I do."

[46]

THE REPORT OF A SINGLE ROUND ECHOED IN THE HALLWAY. A soft grunt, and then a rifle fell from the open space in the ductwork, clattering on the floor.

"What the?" Kraeger started to say.

Donovan threw himself forward at the man, grabbing him around the waist and pushing him to the ground. There was no time for him to worry about what was going to happen next, or if Soon had caught on quickly enough to survive. They had one chance to try to get out of this, and he had to take it.

A second report sounded. Then a third and a fourth. Donovan felt blood land on him as he fell to the ground on top of a surprised Kraeger, whose face curled into a snarl as he punched Donovan in the ribs. He couldn't see the Dread cloth beneath the other clothes. He didn't know the punches barely had an effect.

"You son of a bitch," Kraeger cursed, still hitting him. Donovan punched back, hitting him in the jaw and then the eye. The older man shouted, using all of his force to turn himself over and push Donovan off.

Donovan rolled away to his feet. One of Kraeger's men was there, raising his rifle to shoot him point blank. Then the butt of a second rifle cracked against the man's head, dropping him and leaving Soon standing behind him.

"Watch out," Donovan said. Another jackal was coming at Soon with a knife. He went down as a fifth shot sounded, hitting him square on the side of the head.

Donovan started to turn back to Kraeger, suddenly pulled off balance as the man tackled him from behind. They sprawled on the floor, but Donovan managed to get his balance and roll his assailant off again. They both got to their feet facing one another.

A gun appeared against Kraeger's head.

"Don't move," Ehri said, holding the pistol against his temple.

Donovan looked at her. Her arm had been bleeding, leaving a stain around the wound. There was another stain on her leg.

"Tell your people to back off," Donovan said, noticing the four jackals still standing were regrouping.

Kraeger looked defiant. Ehri pushed the gun harder against his head.

"Do it," she said.

"Okay. Okay. Back off," he said. He glared at Donovan. "I'm sure we can work something out."

"Are you okay?" Donovan asked Ehri.

"Yes. The gori'shah reduced the impact sufficiently. The wounds are healing. I didn't think it was wise to give myself away."

"Good call."

"Gori'shah?" Kraeger said. "You sound like one of them. You should have been dead."

"You should have checked the bodies instead of assuming," Donovan said. "She sounds like one of them because she is one of them. The clones are turning on their masters. We have their weapons. We're killing their pur'dahm, and stealing their transports. Don't you get it? Whatever you think you're trying to do, you're wrong. The tide is turning. We have a chance to fight back. To really fight back. I don't like what is happening to the civilian settlements, and I don't feel like a hero. But I do think we can win."

Kraeger laughed at that. "You're crazier than I am if you think you can win. One Dread warrior. One transport. Big deal. They have hundreds of both."

"Everything starts with one," Ehri said. "One escaped starship. One unsecured rifle. One clone who wants to choose for themselves."

"Whatever. It looks like you've got me by the balls now, Major. You're right. I screwed up. Now I've got to face the consequences. If I were you, I would kill me. I would kill every last one of us. We've done things, Major. Terrible things. Torture. Murder. I even ate human flesh once. I don't regret it, either. I survived the way I had to. We all survive the way we have to."

Donovan looked at Kraeger. As much as he wanted to despise him, he found that he couldn't. He could have just as easily ended up like him if his situation had been different. All of humanity was doing what it could to survive. It didn't mean fighting with one another was the right thing, but what if there was no other choice? What if it meant living or dying? At least Kraeger was trying to put something together, to build some kind of community, even if he didn't understand how it worked yet. The man wasn't killing for sport.

At least, Donovan didn't think he was.

"Where did you get these weapons?" he asked, taking the rifle Soon was carrying and holding it up to Kraeger. "These are newer than anything I've seen."

"This is the honeypot, Major," Kraeger replied. "Not home base."

"Where's home base?"

"Kraeger," one of his followers said. "Don't."

Kraeger looked at him. "It's over, Julio. Can't you see that? We lost. Besides, the Major here isn't going to hurt anybody. Are you?"

"Not unless they try to hurt us," Donovan replied.

"Yeah, but-"

"Am I in charge?" Kraeger shouted.

Julio backed down without another word.

"I'll take you there. Maybe once you've seen it, you'll change your mind about joining us."

"Are you planning to become part of the rebellion?" Donovan asked.

"Not if I can help it."

Donovan smiled. "What if you can't?"

[47]

Donovan trailed behind Kraeger, while Soon and Ehri covered the rest of his remaining followers, keeping them at gunpoint while they traversed the building. Kraeger hadn't stopped talking the entire time, keeping up a litany of chatter about how he wound up first in Mexico, and then at the rest stop between San Luis and Monterrey.

"I almost died five, six times on the way down," he was saying as they reached the small security room in the back corner of the structure. "Not Dread, mind you. Jackals. It isn't just the innocents they go after, you know. Anybody who looks weak is fair game, and I was pretty weak at the time. Not by choice. Just a series of bad decisions that didn't pan out in my favor." He laughed. "All because of a girl, believe it or not."

Donovan didn't answer. He kept hoping that not engaging would get the man to quiet down. It didn't seem to be working.

"So, I came into this place, and there was just blood and guts and death everywhere. At first, I thought it was more jackals, and I was ready to get the hell out, but then I came across the dead clone. The Dread had cleaned this place out maybe a day or two before I got here. Just wiped everyone out. They had used small arms, though, not heavy slugs like their mechs fire. They wanted this place intact. They wanted to use it to bring people in. Their honeypot."

They filed into the space. There was power being fed to the equipment, and screens displayed the inside of the building from almost every angle. There were even cameras on the outside of the space, and Donovan could see the Monster clearly through one of them.

"Standard security," Kraeger said. "Low cost, easy to maintain. Nothing fancy like they had up in the States. It was out of order when I got here. Like I was saying, the Dread were using this place to bait humans. It got me thinking about the idea as I explored. What if I could do the same? What if I could start rebuilding my resources, start a new community, do my part to save humankind? It was all wishful thinking at the time. I knew if enough people showed up here the Dread would come back and wipe them out again. I'm sure you've heard of it happening before?"

"Too often," Donovan said.

"Yeah. So I was just daydreaming about it. I didn't think it would ever work. Then I came in here, and I learned the most important lesson of my life."

Kraeger paused and looked at Donovan, waiting for him to ask.

"Which was?"

He smiled and reached under the security desk, feeling the bottom. He did something, and a piece of the floor slid aside, revealing a ladder the descended into darkness.

"Always be on the lookout for narcotics trafficking tunnels," he said.

"Narcotics?" Donovan said. "As in, illegal drugs?"

"Yup. I came in here and looked around a little bit. I found a frayed wire leading into the floor, and that made me curious. So I ended up on my hands and knees below the desk until a cat or something made noise and I tried to jump up." He laughed. "I hit my head on the switch to activate the hidden door. It was a total accident, can you believe that? Anyway, I followed the rabbit hole. The tunnel to the drop point is about a kilometer long. That was where I found a stash of drugs and guns. There's another tunnel that goes five kilometers out that way, toward the mountains. That's where the bunker is."

He moved to the ladder, turning around to climb down.

"From what I've been able to learn, it used to belong to a guy named 'El Diablo.' The Devil. He was a pretty high and mighty drug kingpin until the day the Dread attacked. The bunker was his hiding place away from all the rivals and government agencies that wanted to take him down. It was like his own private estate, tucked away from prying eyes and offering a level of comfort and security that should have carried him through a pretty peaceful life hiding from the aliens."

"Should have?"

"When I found the place, the generator was running, and the power was on, but nobody was home. It seemed that El Diablo and his entourage never made it to the bunker to hide. They probably got blasted on the way here."

Kraeger started climbing down the ladder. Donovan followed after, careful to keep him in view. They descended twenty meters until the walls around them opened up into a fairly large tunnel.

"I always guessed that he owned the building through some shell corporation or something and that the whole thing was a front for his real operations. It's easy to access from the highway, but also pretty nondescript and utilitarian. Who would ever have thought it was a facade?"

"How many people are down here?" Donovan asked, staring past Kraeger and into the long corridor. He couldn't believe a place like this had been so close to the resistance base the entire time, and he had never known about it. Then again, wasn't that the point?

"Four hundred," Kraeger replied.

"How do you keep that many people fed down here? There's nothing to forage nearby." He remembered that Kraeger had mentioned eating human flesh, and he began to feel sick.

"That was a part of a darker past," Kraeger said, noticing his discomfort. "The bunker is self-sufficient, Major. Indoor farms provide more than enough veggies to keep everyone healthy without resorting to cannibalism. It's funny when you think about it. El Diablo must have spent billions to get it assembled, and then he got offed before he ever got to use it. But now we have a growing community here. A thriving community. It's like a fairy-tale."

"Except for the part where you kill people," Donovan said.

"I won't lie and tell you I never enjoy killing. But the difference between me and some random asshole is that I have a reason for it. You come into my house looking for food or shelter; I'm happy to oblige if you can be of service to me. If you have skills. If you've been out there too long, if you're rabid, or if you're too damn weak and useless, then I don't have a use for you and the rest of the world doesn't either. You're Dread fodder regardless, so is it a big deal if I keep you from grabbing that last candy bar that might keep someone strong alive for another day? If that little bit of sustenance can get them to me?"

Kraeger stopped walking, turning and facing Donovan. He raised his gun in response, uncertain about the man's intentions.

"Answer that for me, Major. Should I let weak people live and risk that the strong people will die? Do you think there's a place for that kind of charity in the world today?"

Donovan would have known the answer to that a month ago. The world they lived in had always been dangerous, but there had been room for everyone in the security of the silo. But now the resistance base was gone. Matteo was gone. His mother and Diaz were gone. Thousands of people were dying every day at the hands of the Dread. Maybe there was some truth to Kraeger's words, even if it was a truth he didn't want to see.

"I can tell you're not as sure as you were an hour ago," Kraeger said. "I call that progress. I can show you more, Major, but I know you have somewhere else you want to be. So what do you want to do with me? With us? I can't stop you from taking your people and leaving, or from killing me and claiming this place for yourself. So the question is: now what?"

[48]

"How long?" Donovan asked.

Kraeger turned his wrist, checking a heavy, antique gold watch he had recovered from his quarters in the bunker the residents affectionately referred to as Hell.

"The situation's a little different this time, Major," Kraeger said. "Usually, they come to check their trap, find nothing, and head out. You left their transport sitting out there on the back of a big-rig. Not to mention, they appear to be more than a little worried about you."

They were inside what Kraeger had called the Ready Room, a secondary, heavily fortified space inside Hell that contained remote links to the cameras positioned throughout the external complex. Through them, Donovan could see the new Dread troop transport that had arrived. Clone soldiers were crawling all over the interior of the former shopping area, examining every nook and cranny for evidence that Donovan, Ehri, and the rest of the scavengers were hiding inside.

According to Kraeger, that was the typical Dread deployment. In this case, their forces had been bolstered by a pair of mechs and the presence of a squad of fully armored pur'dahm. Ehri had identified them as more hunters.

"But we're safe down here, right?" Donovan said.

"So far, so good," Kraeger replied. "But we left your people out by the tunnel armed to the teeth for a reason."

Donovan checked the camera feed that showed the scene by the heavy steel door that could seal the bunker off from the tunnel. Soon was leading a group composed of both scavengers and jackals there, the men and women who had agreed to be part of their overall defenses. They had ten of the enemy plasma rifles in all, enough to put up a pretty good fight if the Dread found the tunnel and entered it.

It had taken Donovan nearly the entire remainder of the hour he had had given them to free the Monster to come to the decision to work with Kraeger. Then it took almost another hour to forge an agreement with him to allow any scavengers who wanted to stay to stay, and to swear to let them become part of the community regardless of their skills. Donovan hadn't known exactly what he was bargaining for until he returned to the scavengers, explained Murphy's death, and led them down into the tunnels and to the bunker.

Hell wasn't a bad place overall, but it did come with a well-defined hierarchy of status based on usefulness. Women were valued for one of two things. Either you had a trade the community could use, or you had a body the community could use. It was a hard idea to accept, but the cold truth was that humankind needed more humans, and there was only one way to get them. At the same time, the pregnant women Donovan had seen were treated like royalty, given every comfort they could want as well as the best pick of the available food.

The process was similar for the men, though they were typically culled based on age, physical health, and personality along with skill set. And when Kraeger said culled, he meant culled. The majority of the travelers they killed were men who didn't fit into the community; the decision made after an ambush and a quick interview. While Donovan had made Kraeger promise to spare the scavengers, he had a feeling that treaty was only going to be good for as long as Donovan was in the bunker. Kraeger claimed to be an honorable man, but he was also a pragmatist, and those two things didn't always mesh.

"They're in the control room," Donovan said, watching one of the pur'dahm hunters move in. The armored bek'hai stared at the equipment, tapping on the panel to see if it was functional before turning and running his eyes across the room. He walked out a moment later.

"A good sign," Kraeger said.

"Where do you think they're going to think we are when they can't find us?" Donovan asked.

"Scattered into the brush, most like," Kraeger said. "That's what usually happens. They'll try to track you down, find a few stragglers out there, and then kill them and call it a day."

"You've seen it happen?"

"Plenty of times. I spent twenty years out there before I came here."

"Before or after the woman was involved?"

He laughed. "Both. I had a couple of years in the middle that were damn good. A few on either end that made me question my sanity." His face suddenly turned dark, and he cast his eyes to the floor. "You have to learn to accept who you become, or you can't ever come back."

"I've only ever been one thing, and I plan to keep it that way. A soldier."

"I wish you the best of luck with that, Major."

They sat silently for a minute, watching the Dread. It was obvious when they finished the sweep because they retreated as one back to the transports. The hunters loaded themselves into the one Donovan had taken, and it lifted off with the others, heading out toward the brush. The two mechs abandoned the facility as well, moving west.

"Looks like they gave up."

"They never see us coming or going because we hardly ever go outside. They have no reason to think there's anything hidden in here. Wasn't that the reason El Diablo built the bunker here to begin with?" Kraeger was silent for a moment before he looked at Donovan. "You know, Major, I've been thinking about what you said earlier. About bringing the fight to the enemy. Were you serious about that?"

"We're on our way to join the resistance in Austin," Donovan said. "General Rodriguez told me there's a force massing there, one that's still hidden from the Dread."

"You mean you hope it's still hidden from the Dread."

"There's no way to know for sure until we get there. Unless you've heard otherwise?"

Kraeger had shown him the equipment they used to sniff packets out of the hard-wired network the resistance was utilizing to communicate with one another. He had been eavesdropping on the rebels for some time, keeping up with their messages back and forth.

"Not so far, but things can change in a hurry, and they don't always get a message out. With all the activity out here, the odds are that the enemy is hitting Austin hard, or at least has the potential to. So I was thinking about what you and the clone said. There always has to be a first, right?"

"Right. You have something in mind?"

"I think we should hit them back."

"We? You said you didn't want to be part of the resistance."

"I don't, especially. But I also told you I have a soft spot for the military. The thing is, there's a Dread base not too far from here. It's not a fortress or anything. It's a smaller outpost. I think the mechs are headed back there. Anyway, with the contingent out searching for you, I have a feeling the defenses are going to be relatively light. A quick, coordinated strike could net you a solid victory against the enemy, a victory that we can broadcast out to the rest of the world. It's just the kind of thing you need if you want humans to stop being so helpless, stop killing each other, and maybe get them to seek out the rebellion."

"You almost sound like you're feeling a little more hopeful already," Donovan said.

Kraeger smiled. "I see that they're worried about you. I like that. Besides, you seem hell-bent on going forward no matter what I do.

You may not be a hero, but you're a stubborn son of a bitch, and I admire that just as much. Even if you are just a kid."

"Thanks, I think."

"Yeah, so this base I'm talking about is about ten klicks west of here. They'll probably have left a couple dozen clones behind, and those mechs, but that's about it. I found some explosives in the armory here when I moved in. It won't do shit to the outside of their structures, but maybe we can wreak some havoc on the inside."

Donovan considered it. The whole reason to head to Austin was to join the resistance there and to tell them how they could get ready to fight back. There was a certain appeal to being able to show them, and to lead by example.

"If we attack their base they're going to come back at us even harder than before," he said. "They might not give up on this place so easily."

"Yeah. That's the rub, Major. If you do this, you and whoever decides to come with you can't come back here. You hit the base, and you vanish into the night. Head to Austin, go back to Mexico City, whatever you want, just not this place."

They shared another moment of silence. Donovan wanted to pretend he had a choice when he already knew he didn't.

"I guess you're going to get rid of me a lot sooner than you were expecting," he said.

Kraeger laughed. "I guess you're going to be stuck with me a little longer than you were expecting, Major. I'm getting old, and while I'm proud of what I've done here, I know that nothing stays the same. I can try to hold onto it, or I can accept it. You're exactly the sign I didn't know I was looking for.

"In other words, I'm coming with you."

[49]

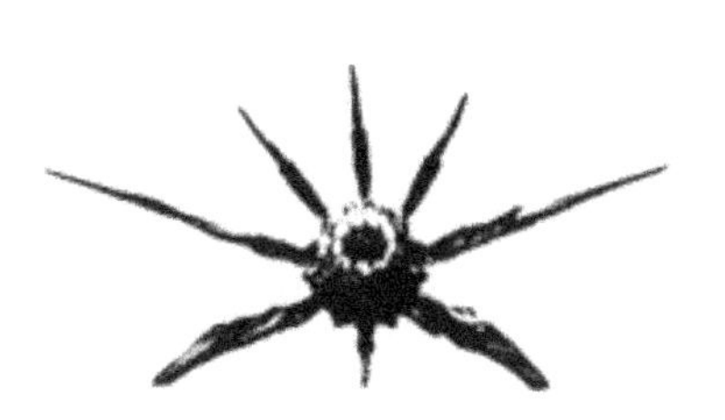

"How's the patient," Donovan asked, entering the bunker's medical facilities.

He paused to take them in as he did, impressed with the space. The equipment was the latest humankind had produced before the invasion, and the room was spotless and sterile. El Diablo had spared no expense on the place, prepared for the worst in the event of an emergency. For criminals, emergencies probably weren't that out of the ordinary.

"Her recovery is not human," Doc Iwu said, turning to face Donovan as he entered. She looked more relaxed and at peace now that she was back in a room filled with stainless steel and gauze.

Ehri was sitting on the edge of the exam table, her gori'shah in a pile behind her. She was dressed in her underwear and a tank top, with one bandage wrapped around her shoulder and another around her leg. She smiled when she saw Donovan.

"Another genetic enhancement?" Donovan asked.

"Partially," she replied. "The gori'shah also assists in healing underlying wounds. If the bullet had not gone through, the symbiotes would have worked to remove it. They also leave their saliva on the damage itself, which promotes healing. I tried to convince Nailah to leave it alone and let them do their work, but she wouldn't have it."

"I'm not about to trust something I can't see," Iwu replied. "Especially not microscopic worms."

"They aren't worms," Ehri said. "They're larvae."

"For what?" Donovan asked. "You've never answered that."

"I don't know what they become," she replied. "The gori'shah are replaced on a regular basis, cycled through by the ones we call the lek'hai. The Keepers. It is said that the gori'shah are the backbone of our technology, much of which is, or was at some point, organic."

"So it's like raising cattle for meat?"

"Not exactly, but an adequate simile. I trust that since you are here the bek'hai have gone?"

"Yeah. They didn't find anything, and they headed off to the east to search the wilderness. Kraeger is convinced they'll find a few random humans out there and slaughter them before giving up."

"I don't think they're going to give up that easily. Not on finding us."

"Me neither, but Kraeger put me onto something. He said the Dread have a base not too far from here. An outpost. He thinks the mechs came from there. He suggested that we attack it."

"What?" Iwu said. "Donovan, I don't think that's a good idea."

"Why not?"

"You're going to bring the entire Dread army down on you if you go after them like that. You've been lucky so far, but that's asking for a little too much trouble."

"I've been thinking about that. I don't disagree with you, but the truth is that we need to do something. We don't know Austin will still be viable by the time we reach it, and based on what we know there's a good chance it won't be. If that turns out to be the case, we'll have wasted an opportunity to make a statement that we can fight back, really fight back, against the Dread. To rally the resistance everywhere by hitting them directly and doing some real damage. We've got a tiny bit of momentum here, and I'm worried about losing it by playing it too safe."

"Play it too reckless, and you'll lose everything for everyone."

"You mean this place?"

She nodded. "There are sixty pregnant women here. Forty-six children. I don't want them to die the way they did back at the silo."

"Neither do I. When we go, we won't be coming back." He looked at Ehri. "What do you think?"

"This isn't my decision to make, Major. It is yours."

"I'm asking for your opinion."

"I pledged my loyalty to you. I'll follow wherever you go, and fight as hard as any other human. Kraeger is an interesting man, an odd mix of selfishness and patriotism. He's based his community on keeping only the strong, and yet he weakens its ability to survive and adapt by anchoring it with the young. I think his motives are also mixed. He knows the bek'hai want you, or me through you, and so he wants you gone from here. At the same time, he wants you to succeed."

"He's decided he wants to come with us."

"Interesting. He understands what he has created here. For as much as he has said we can't defeat the bek'hai, deeper down I think he knows the only chance this community has is for us to fight, and to win."

"And you think we should fight?"

"Yes."

"Me, too. After everything that's happened, I wasn't sure if I should trust my instincts."

"They've carried us this far, Major."

"And gotten a lot of people I cared about killed."

"No. They have always been dying. Now they are dying for something."

Donovan couldn't argue with that. It was the one thought that helped ease the guilt. It slipped away from him sometimes, but Ehri was always there to bring him back in line. He caught her eyes with his own, holding them for a minute. He couldn't imagine where he would be if Kraeger had been successful in his efforts to kill her. He wasn't sure he could take one more loss like that.

"When are you leaving?" Iwu asked. "The wounds are in good shape, but it would be better for her to rest a day or two."

"Within the hour," Donovan said, breaking eye contact with Ehri. "I assume you're staying here?"

"There aren't many doctors left in this world," she replied. "The mortality rate for the women here is over fifty percent. They have the right tools, but they didn't have anyone with a medical background to teach them. I think I can bring that down to near zero, and train some of the people we saved. I can give them a skill that will make them valuable, not only here and now, but after you get the Dread off the planet once and for all. Besides, I'm an old woman, Donovan. We both know I've been slowing you down. I do appreciate you looking out for me."

"I'm glad you made it out," Donovan said. "The world does need people like you. Not just your medical skills, but your compassion and spirit."

Doc Iwu surprised him, approaching and wrapping her arms around him. He returned the embrace once he got over his shock. He had never known her to be affectionate. Her care was business-like and rational, not emotional. At least not until now.

"Take care of yourself, Major," she said. "I know you'll make the General proud."

"Yes, ma'am," Donovan said. He looked at Ehri again. "We'll be meeting near the entrance in forty minutes."

"I'll be there."

Donovan turned to leave. He paused there, a sudden thought creeping into his head. Kraeger had given him the idea that they should go in and do as much damage as they could, but maybe that wasn't the only option.

"Ehri, how much can you teach Soon and me about piloting a bek'hai mech in thirty minutes or less?"

[50]

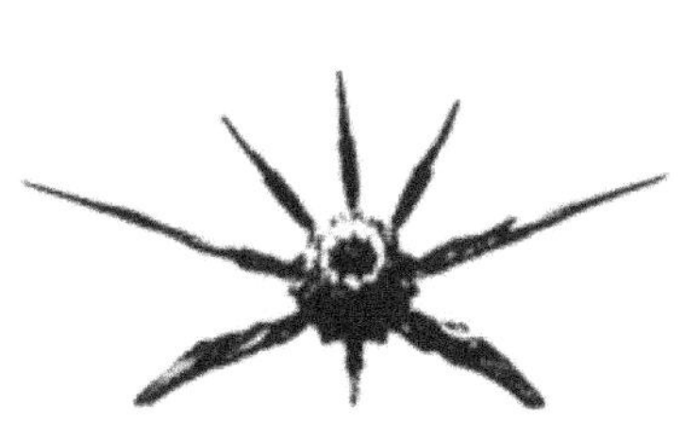

Tea'va peered around the corner, taking extra care that the corridor was clear before darting across it to the other side. He pressed the panel to his right, and a small hatch opened beside him. He crossed into it, leaning back against the wall as the hatch slid closed and left him in near total darkness.

Two shifts. That was how long it had taken for him to navigate from the bowels of the Ishur up three decks. It was impossibly slow, every step made challenging by the arrival of another batch of clones, and by Gr'el's sudden domination of the ship. His Si'dahm had managed to tear him from power with almost zero resistance, and in a way that made the failure look like Tea'va's alone. Did the Domo'-dahm know what Gr'el had done? Did he approve?

It didn't matter. Gr'el's worst mistake was that he had failed in his initial assassination attempt, and he had failed to capture Tea'va since. Tea'va was certain it was because the pur'dahm had underestimated him and his deep knowledge of the fortress. The ships were so large that few beyond the clones made to care for them knew every service tunnel and access point, every ingress and egress.

But he knew. He knew because he had never trusted. Because he had never believed that any would seek to aid him in his mission of conquest. Why would they, when they all sought the same station? If he were going to rise to power, he needed to not only be stronger, not only be smarter, but also be more tolerant to change and more able to adjust. Knowledge was power.

It had allowed him to hide from Gr'el's patrols as they began to hunt him. It had allowed him to drop down on them unaware, to destroy an entire squad of clones and vanish back into the dark. It had permitted him to put fear into the pur'dahm traitor, to show him that he would not be an easy kill and that if he wanted to maintain control of the Ishur he would need to earn it.

Of course, the odds were still against him. Every drumhr who may have been loyal to him had been retired and almost every clone that had lived before they arrived in Pol'tik had been destroyed.

Almost every clone.

He had seen Zoelle earlier, walking the corridors from her lab with her two assistants, who were also Children of the Un'hai. She had passed one of Gr'el's patrols unharmed, an act that proved to him beyond all doubt that she had betrayed him, earning his trust and then turning on him at her convenience. She had helped Gr'el make his new clones in secret, knowing what the Si'dahm planned. He didn't know how they had managed to make this alliance ahead of time before he had even been assigned to the Ishur in the first place.

He was about to find out.

The back routes of the fortress were narrow and normally occupied by drek'er, Cleaners, small-statured clones who were in charge of maintaining the inner workings of the ship. They would skitter about from one location to another in a constant cycle, testing power outputs, optimizing flow, and ensuring that the millions of components remained in working order. The fortresses didn't require much maintenance, but constant monitoring was what kept them that way.

The Cleaners were in another part of the ship, and so their passages were barren. Tea'va was able to move through them unhindered, without worry of being captured. While he was sure Gr'el knew the corridors existed, he also doubted the pur'dahm had any idea where they were or how to reach them. His rival also probably couldn't conceive of traveling like this. It was an affront to their ideas of honor. One that had allowed humankind to survive far too long.

It was a weakness he was not afraid to exploit.

The passage took him behind the private cells assigned to each member of the crew. This deck was for the scientists, Zoelle and her lor'hai. He had seen her return here earlier. He knew she would be inside, likely asleep.

From that passage, there was a small crawlspace that went up and over the top of the cells, an area purposely left open for ventilation. Tea'va pulled himself up into the narrow space, for a moment frightened that he would get stuck there as the floor and ceiling pressed against him. He pulled himself along on his elbows; his head cocked to the side to fit it through the passage, stopping as he reached the center of one of the cells. A thin screen separated him from it, one that he could peer down through at the occupant. An un'hai, but not Zoelle. While they were identical in appearance, he was certain he would know her when he saw her. This one was asleep in her bed, mouth open and head lolled to the side.

He continued, dragging his body through the tight confines to the next cell. He looked down into it. The un'hai inside was sitting up in bed, staring at the wall.

"I knew you would come," Zoelle said without shifting her gaze.

How did she know he was there?

He held back the sudden rage he felt at her betrayal. She was calm and collected. He had to be the same.

"Why?" he said. It was the only word he could manage without his voice shaking.

"I told you why," she replied. "Power."

He clenched his fists; his knuckles white around the grip of his weapon. "I offered you power."

"You offered me something you don't yet have. Gr'el offered me something he already controls. It is not personal, Tea'va."

She didn't use his title. He bristled at that while he angled his plasma pistol, getting it into position to end her life.

"I trusted you."

"That was the idea. You are so aloof from the others, and you are so suspicious. It makes you easier to manipulate, not harder."

"What did he promise you? To be his heil'bek? To overthrow the Domo'dahm with him, as I did?"

There was so little space; it was hard to get a bead on her from where he was. He could spray the room with plasma. It would have to be enough.

"Yes. And he has already delivered the first of those. He has named me his heil'bek and afforded me Si'dahm status on the Ishur. A clone as a Si'dahm, Tea'va. It is the first time." She looked up at the screen now, though she couldn't see him through it. "You disregarded me. You removed me from the bridge before the battle. That was one of your mistakes."

"If you are Si'dahm, why are you still down here?"

"Because I knew you would come. Of the things you are and are not, Tea'va, I will agree that you are resourceful; however, I would not judge you intelligent."

Tea'va felt his heart pulse. He knew what she was saying, and she was right. He shouldn't have lingered when he saw that she was waiting. What was he thinking?

He didn't waste time shooting. There was no point to it now. He should never have been there at all. Why had he come?

He began to push himself back, fighting against the friction of the small space to return to the corridor. He could hear the sounds now. The soldiers were coming for him.

Fool. He was a fool. All of that time and energy wasted, and for what? A word with a traitor? He had gained little from her. Only that he now knew Gr'el also intended to kill the Domo'dahm. Was that something he would survive long enough to use?

He slid along the top of the passage, feeling a bit of relief as his legs came clear of the floor and dangled down. One last push and he was free, back upright and clear.

He looked to his left. A squad of soldiers was approaching.

He looked to his right. Another squad.

He held up his weapon. He was going to die in here if he didn't do something.

He looked both ways once more. Then he dropped the weapon and put his hands out.

"I submit," he shouted, the taste of it like acid on this tongue. "I submit."

[51]

THEY DIDN'T KILL HIM RIGHT AWAY. IT WOULD HAVE BEEN against their laws to do so. A pur'dahm who surrendered had the right to retire themselves after a suitable time for preparation that usually consisted of composing a history of their life and accomplishments.

As the soldiers led him from the back routes to the main corridor, Tea'va thought about how little he had accomplished and how many of his deeds had ended in failure. For all of his goals and plans, was Zoelle right about him? Was he simply not very intelligent?

It was an idea that was difficult for him to accept. An idea that he refused to give in to. Bad luck, that's all that it was. A history of close calls and late decisions. He had been so close to shooting down the Heil'shur. He had almost been a hero before this journey. Before the opportunity had arisen for it to all fall apart.

Zoelle met the soldiers in the corridor; her head held high as she reached them. They bowed before her, causing her to smile.

"I see you surrendered," she said. "It won't save your life."

He looked at her without speaking. He was done with her. With all of them. He was the future of the bek'hai. His story was not fully written yet.

"Do you have anything you want to say?" she asked.

He didn't respond.

"Very well. You will be returned to your room and allowed one day to prepare, in accordance with our laws. Don't think to delay your retirement somehow. Gr'el will not allow it."

She turned on her heel, heading away from him. He watched her go. He hadn't bothered to kill her before. When he did, he would make sure she looked him in the eye.

The lead soldier pointed him in the opposite direction. He walked ahead of them, unencumbered. He was still a pur'dahm. He still commanded respect.

He led his captors through the hallway toward a transport beam. The squad leader took his arm when they reached it, a precaution against him trying to escape. He clenched his teeth at the touch. It was demeaning to be handled by a lor'hai. It had been demeaning to surrender to one.

He stepped into the beam, transporting himself up to the officer's quarters. One of the bridge crew was there, and he looked away as Tea'va passed. Another traitor to his Dahm. Tea'va wanted to destroy him. He glared at the drumhr as he passed, but still didn't speak. He decided he would not speak again. Not to traitors. Not to lor'hai. He was done with words. He needed a way out.

He expected that Gr'el would be in his quarters when he arrived. He assumed the pur'dahm would come to gloat and to mock. He had done so little to succeed in outmaneuvering the most advanced drumhr bek'hai science had produced. All it had taken was a single un'hai to disarm the one who claimed not to be taken with them.

Gr'el wasn't there. Neither was the Mother he had killed. His room was empty and clean, as though he still owned it. As though he was still commanding the Ishur.

It was a greater statement than anything the pur'dahm could have said in person, and it drove Tea'va to slam his fists against the walls in anger.

He caught himself a moment later. He had been foolish, and displaying his anger would only make him more so. He needed to be calm and think clearly. He was still growing weaker from his time outside of the regeneration chamber. He could spend some time in it, heal his body and his mind and still be able to... To what? He had surrendered. It was on his honor to retire himself. What use would healing be for that?

He crossed the room to his terminal. Surely he had done something in his life worth recording? Surely not all of it could be a failure? He had risen to the Second Cell after all. He had convinced the Domo'dahm to give him command of the Ishur.

Or had he? Did the Domo'dahm really want him as a successor? He was more human than any of the other drumhr.

Was he too human?

He glanced out of the viewport at the end of his quarters, staring into space. He had never considered that possibility before. His functional sex organs and his ability to breathe Earth's atmosphere freely were supposed to be the herald of bek'hai resurgence, but what if everything else about him was loathsome? His skin. His lips. The smoothness of his skull. What if his refusal to breed had made him expendable? Had given the Domo'dahm cause to want to displace him or at least to allow it?

His anger flared again. He was a bigger fool than he had even realized. The Domo'dahm hadn't given him command of the Ishur as an opportunity to earn his place. He had set him up to fail. He had set him up to die.

There had to be a way out. He would think of something. He approached the viewport, still looking out into space. He could see the light from the human starship's main thrusters ahead of them. All he wanted was one more chance at the Heil'shur. One more battle to decide who was the superior pilot.

He felt something wet on his eye, and he reached up and lifted it with his finger. He stared at it for a moment. A tear? Was he crying? Bek'hai didn't cry. Drumhr couldn't cry. None, except for him.

He blinked a few times, and then wiped the tears away with the sleeve of his gori'shah. He was pathetic. Simply pathetic.

He looked out the viewport again. He let his eyes trail along the space ahead of him, expecting them to come to rest on the glow of the thrusters once more.

He froze when he didn't see them, squinting his eyes and leaning closer to the clear lek'shah until his head was pressed against it. He found the human ship a moment later.

It was coming about, and heading straight for them.

[52]

"Alpha Squadron, report," Gabriel said as he slid down into the seat of his starfighter.

"First Lieutenant Bale, ready."

"Second Lieutenant Celia, ready."

"Second Lieutenant Gerhardt, ready."

"Captain Sturges, ready."

Gabriel smiled when he heard the older officer's voice. They had scrambled to get one more of the fighters online and then scrambled again to find a pilot to fly it. Sturges was past his prime, and hadn't flown a fighter in years, but they needed every extra hand they could get.

The General had a plan, and it was a doozy.

It was also already underway. Theodore had taken them all by surprise, barking orders from his wheelchair down in the science lab. He knew exactly what he wanted to do, as crazy as it was, and there was no time to waste in doing it. They had a small window of opportunity to get this right.

"Alpha Squadron, prepare to launch." Theodore's voice cut across the comm channel. Gabriel had never heard his father so determined.

The main hangar door began sliding open.

"Roger," Gabriel said. "Alpha Squadron is loaded and ready."

"Good hunting, Major," Miranda said through his channel.

"Remember," Gabriel said, taking the fighter's controls in his hands. "We're going to be moving out of the dead zone. Once we do, they'll be invulnerable."

"Yes, sir," the other pilots replied.

"Alpha Squadron, you are go," Miranda said.

"Roger," Gabriel said. "Let's do this." He reached up and squeezed the crucifix below his flight suit. "Give me strength."

The fighters added thrust as one, bursting from the hangar in the Magellan's side and making a quick right turn. They spread apart, taking up a large diamond formation above the starship as the General cut the main engines and fired the vectoring thrusters, rolling her over at the same time. The turn wasn't quite as tight as it had been the last time, but the result was identical.

It left the Magellan pointing straight at the Dread fortress.

Gabriel watched as a stream of superheated plasma poured out from the rear of the starship, the mains firing at full thrust. It pushed the craft forward once more.

"Let's stay ahead of her," Gabriel said, pushing his thrusters.

The fighters shot forward, swooping down in front of the Magellan and continuing to add velocity.

Five seconds passed. Then ten. They rocketed toward the fortress without a response, the fighters closing the gap much faster than the Magellan.

Gabriel's fighter beeped, the targeting computer picking up new obstacles. A dozen bolts of plasma suddenly lanced the sky, streaking past a little too close.

"Here we go," Gabriel said. "Stay alert."

The Dread fighters came into view a moment later, a dozen in all. It was a much smaller number than Gabriel had been expecting.

He didn't want to be ungrateful, but why?

There was no more time to think about it. The first of the Bats began shooting at them.

"Take evasive. Celia, Gerhardt, Bale, you're on the fighters. Keep them off the Magellan." His father was going to have a hard enough time evading the fortress' plasma without having to worry about them, too. "Sturges, you're with me."

"Roger," Captain Sturges replied.

Gabriel opened fire as the Dread Bats approached, sending his fighter into a sine-wave flight pattern and adding a bit of spin. Plasma streaked around him, the flashes bright enough to be blinding if he wasn't careful. He blew past one of the fighters, throwing his craft into a tight flip and triggering his guns. His rounds caught the Dread Bat in the tail, the dead zone stealing its shields and allowing the energy to penetrate. It exploded a moment later in a short fireball that Gabriel didn't see. He had already flipped his fighter back toward the fortress.

"We're coming up too slow," Sturges said.

Gabriel checked his screen. He was sure his father saw the same thing. "We're almost there. Stay alert."

The fortress drew closer, looming over them within seconds. It was even larger in space than it had been on the ground, a large part of it having been settled within the earth. Gabriel gasped at the sheer immensity as his fighter came within a few kilometers of the side and he adjusted his thrust to keep from crashing into it.

"How do we fight this?" Sturges said.

"We are fighting this," Gabriel replied.

"Bale, I need assistance," Celia said through the comm. "I've got two Bats on my tail."

"I'm coming," Bale said. "Hard port, drop ninety degrees."

"Roger."

Gabriel's computer beeped again. He looked ahead as another squadron of bats appeared ahead of them, launching from the fortress. They cut immediately, vectoring right toward them.

"Major," Sturges said.

"These are ours," Gabriel replied. "Keep them busy." He checked his screen. "We've got thirty seconds."

"I can't get them off me," Gerhardt said. "Celia. Bale. They've got me in a cross-"

His signal vanished.

Gabriel cursed under his breath, hitting the trigger on his cannons as they swept past the incoming Dread bats, keeping his starfighter rotating and vectoring as he did. A plasma blast scorched the side of his cockpit, leaving a dark stain to his left. It had missed by centimeters at best. He had to focus. Forget about the others. His mission was to clear the way here.

He dropped his thrust, rolling the fighter over again. Sturges had turned around ahead of him and was shooting away, putting distance between them while the Bats gave chase. Gabriel slammed on the thrusters, watching his power levels drop as he moved up on the enemy. One of them slotted in behind him at the same time, and he zigged and zagged to stay out of its crosshairs.

Plasma bolts took aim at Sturges' craft, dozens of them bypassing the fighter as the old Captain showed himself to be closer to his prime than anyone had thought. He maneuvered like a pro, moving across every plane to keep the Dread fighters close.

"We're running out of time," Sturges said. "I'm going to bring them to you. You hit these; I'll get the one on your tail."

Gabriel checked his screen. "Negative. You can't make that pattern without leaving yourself wide open."

"Already doing it, son," Sturges said. "Be ready."

Gabriel felt his heart lurch. Damn it.

Sturges' fighter rolled and flipped, a burst of the rear thrusters sending him on a collision course with Gabriel. Gabriel stopped watching the screen, scanning the field ahead of him for the enemy fighters. It wasn't his decision to make. Not now. It was his job to ensure it wasn't for nothing.

The two human fighters closed within seconds of one another.

"Now," Sturges said.

Gabriel bounced his fighter up as the older pilot's fire trailed below, slamming hard into the oncoming Dread Bat. Gabriel tracked the three Bats on Sturges' tail, trying hard to ignore their fire as the straight line allowed them an easier target. He held the trigger down while he rocked his starfighter, sending a stream of ion blasts on a collision course with them.

Sturges' starfighter exploded.

His rounds hit the Bats. One of them exploded while the other two lost power. The path was as clear as he could make it.

Gabriel checked his screen.

Time was up.

Where was his father?

[53]

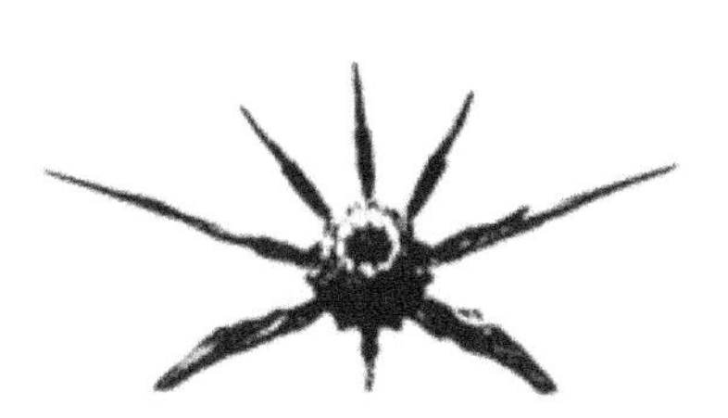

THEODORE SHIFTED IN THE COMMAND CHAIR OF THE Magellan's bridge. "Colonel, get me a status from Guy and Reza."

"Yes, sir," Choi replied.

He returned his attention to the view ahead. The Dread fortress was growing larger and larger, its defensive plasma fire growing more intense.

"Come on, Maggie," he whispered. "We made it off Earth; we can make it through this. For her sake."

The starship shook slightly as it took another hit.

"Deck L," Abdullah said. "It pierced the armor. Emergency bulkheads are sealing."

Theodore cursed to himself and renewed his focus on the controls. He fired starboard vectoring thrusters six and nine, then port four and eight, then hull number seven, his fingers working an intricate pattern across the controls. Flying a starship like the Magellan was supposed to be easy. The vectoring thrusters had always been intended for docking, not for war, and using them this way was akin to playing a musical instrument. Some people couldn't play a note. Some were adequate amateurs. Some were cool and professional.

He was a virtuoso.

Gabriel would be too, he knew, with more experience. He had done well the first time, managing to handle the ship with one hand tied behind his back because he didn't know the intricacies of managing the separate thrusters, or how they would affect the ship's overall vectors and profile. Gabriel could be better than him if they survived long enough.

Hell, he was sure Gabriel was already better than him. He felt a sense of pride in that. The pride helped him focus.

His boy was out there, and he wasn't about to let him down.

He triggered more of the thrusters in an uneven sequence, kicked the Magellan's stern out to the left, then up, bringing it around and down. Plasma bolts streamed around her, most passing in the spaces left behind by the evasive maneuvers, some striking the heavy armor plating.

"Colonel," he snapped, still waiting for an answer.

He hadn't given the scientists much time to prepare, but he also had a feeling they would work better under pressure. They had already accomplished so much in so little time after he had set them straight. He didn't fault people for occasional weakness. He had been forced to deal with his own, and nobody was perfect. Infidelity? That was one flaw he couldn't stomach. It had made even looking at the Larones and Reza difficult.

"They're hooking everything up now, sir. Guy wants you to know that none of this has been tested, and the odds of success are relatively low."

"Not what I want to hear, Colonel," Theodore said. "Tell him he has to make it work, or we're all gonna die."

"Yes, sir."

There was a chance they would all die anyway. Their part of the plan was only the first part. But what a victory it would be in itself to make it that far.

"We just lost Gerhardt," he heard Bale say over Alpha Squadron's comm. "We can't keep this up for long."

"You don't need to keep it up for long," Gabriel replied. "General, the path is clear. Passing coordinates."

"You got that, Maggie?" Theodore asked.

"Data received," Maggie said.

Theodore looked down at his screen. The Dread fortress was covering most of it, but now a red target had appeared against it.

The Magellan shook again. A warning tone sounded.

"Life support systems were hit," Abdullah said. "Main control is down."

"Initiating emergency support systems," Maggie said.

Theodore forced himself to stay calm. Even a virtuoso couldn't get through the fire they were taking without a scratch. He knew his plan was a risk, a Hail Mary chance to get them out of the situation they were in. He had to trust in himself, and in God.

The way he saw it, the Man Upstairs owed him for taking Juliet away, and this was his moment to cash in.

"Time?" he shouted.

"Ten seconds, General," Spaceman Locke replied.

He smiled to hear her voice. Gabriel had been spending more time with her lately. That was good. They had been friends for a long time, but Jessica's death had hit his son hard and kept him away from romance all of these years. He trusted Gabe not to get involved in anything that would diminish his capacity as a soldier. He also knew from experience that the love of a good woman could be the difference between being mediocre and being exceptional.

"Mr. Larone," he said, opening a channel and communicating with the scientist directly. "You have ten seconds."

"Ten seconds?" Guy replied. "General-"

"Do it," Theodore shouted.

The fire was getting more intense. The Magellan shook again. The closer they came to the fortress, the larger their profile, and the less time they had to avoid the attack.

"Five seconds," Spaceman Locke said. "Four seconds. Three seconds."

"Got it," Guy shouted over the comm. "We're active. I hope this works."

"Two seconds."

The main plasma cannon on the Dread fortress lit up, a bright blue light way too close for comfort. Secondary plasma peppered the hull, and a second warning began sounding.

"We're not going to make it," Choi whispered.

"Yes we are, damn it," Theodore growled.

The Dread cannon erupted, a bright beam of energy only a thousand kilometers away. It arced toward the Magellan in a path that made it unavoidable, the light of it becoming blinding as it reached them.

There was no sound. There was no impact. There was no explosion. The plasma struck the front of the Magellan, vanishing into a black void that appeared along the surface of the bow. The force of it slowed their velocity, pushing against them, but the energy, the destructive power, disappeared beneath the darkspace shield.

It was over within a second, the main cannon's fury absorbed. Secondary fire was caught along the other painted edges of the Magellan, the hull, and the nacelles.

Nobody cheered. Nobody even breathed. The tech worked, but they weren't safe yet.

"Power levels critical," Maggie said

Power. It was all about power. The Dread fortress was huge in front of them. For all the size of the Magellan, it was nothing in comparison.

"The left nacelle is gone," Abdullah said.

Theodore nodded. He knew they weren't getting home that way.

"Gabriel, what's our status?" Theodore said.

"Still clear, General," Gabriel replied. "Follow the target. I'm holding them off."

He fired the vectoring thrusters, managing the distance between the Dread fortress and the Magellan. The enemy plasma stopped coming as they moved in too close to be targeted.

It was working. As impossible as it was. As impossible as it seemed. His plan was working.

The Magellan continued to drop as the fortress moved closer, from hundreds of kilometers to less than a dozen within seconds.

"Let's hope we have enough power for one last push," he said. "Gabriel, clear out."

"Yes, sir," Gabriel said.

The hangar appeared in front of them a moment later, as Theodore aligned the Magellan with the target. They were close now, so close they had no other options. As if they did before.

A single starfighter streaked out of the hangar, whipping past the viewport. Theodore cringed when he saw the number of plasma burns across the fuselage, and against the cockpit. It made him as sure as anything that his son was blessed.

"Power levels at ten percent, General," Maggie said.

"Brace for impact," Theodore said.

The fortress' hangar was big. So was the Magellan, and it was coming in hard. He had no idea what would happen when their shields struck the enemy's shields.

They were about to find out.

He fired reverse thrusters, pushing them to full. It would help, but it wouldn't be enough. The fortress vanished into nothing but a solid line of black with a giant open mouth. He could see the inside of the hangar now, the Dread tech keeping the atmosphere contained and gravity in place. He could see the soldiers that Gabriel had killed, the unpiloted ships he had destroyed.

The Magellan passed into the hangar, the gravity instantly pulling it to the floor. It hit with a deafening, grinding whoomp, pulling them hard in their seats, the din continuing as momentum dragged the starship across. The rear of the hangar approached in a hurry, and Theodore couldn't help but close his eyes as the impact grew imminent.

He felt and heard the crash as the shielded bow of the Magellan struck the shielded interior of the fortress. The noise was louder than anything he had ever experienced, the forces involved threatening to break every bone in his body. If the seeming magic of the dark shields hadn't reduced the overall impact, he was sure it would have.

He opened his eyes. The black material ahead of him rippled outward, the shockwave of force spreading across the fortress, being distributed throughout the alien ship like an earthquake. The rumbling continued for another ten seconds as if they were sitting in the center of a volcano.

And then everything was silent.

[54]

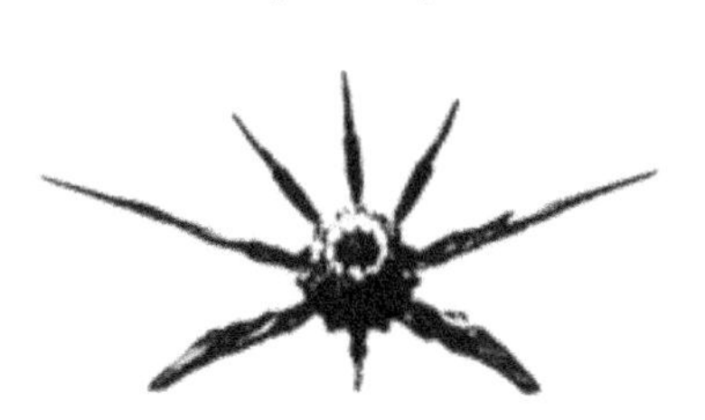

They left an hour later without much fanfare, and with a surprising ambivalence from the residents of Hell at the idea of losing their leader.

"I took them in and made them tough," Kraeger said. "They're too strong to give a shit about me, and Fox will do a better job than I ever did."

They numbered nearly three-dozen, having accepted over forty volunteers from the ranks of both the community and the scavengers and cutting some back out after a rudimentary examination of their overall health. Just because someone wanted to fight didn't mean they would be an asset over a liability, and Donovan discovered that Kraeger did have a sharp mind for making that determination. They were fewer in quantity because of it, but greater in operational efficiency and strength.

They were also greater in overall firepower. Beyond the bek'hai plasma rifles, the community had access to a massive supply of guns, ammunition, and explosives. It was all military grade, the type of equipment the resistance had run out of or lost control of a long time ago. It was nothing that could damage the enemy's armor, but it would be effective against clones.

They were careful up until the point they left the base, filing out into the night, making a quick, concerted dash across the open highway to the tractor cab of the now defunct Monster. A lookout was keeping a close eye on the cameras back in the bunker, ready to transmit a signal to Kraeger in the event of an emergency.

They scaled the industrial machine, taking position along its sides and top, dropping prone and keeping their rifles aimed out into the night. If the Dread were close enough they would be sure to take notice as soon as the rebels powered on the machine and heated it up, but there was no sign of them anywhere nearby. The brush was thick but relatively flat, giving them a long line of sight in every direction.

There was nothing. At least not yet.

"Start it up," Donovan said.

Ehri pressed the button to begin sending power from the battery to the huge, studded wheels. She tapped another button to release the brakes and allow the tractor to move again. It went forward, accelerating smoothly as she increased the throttle and began turning it to the west.

"Here we go," Donovan said.

His heart was racing, but his nerves were calm. He was excited about this, more excited than he had expected. The Dread had taken so much from him and from humankind. He was eager to take something back.

The tractor angled toward the building, picking up speed as it left the roadway and jostled onto the dirt and vegetation. It rolled over it all with ease, gaining momentum and sliding deeper into the wilderness. Within minutes the road was hazy behind them, and a small incline began to appear on the horizon.

"It's right over that hill," Kraeger said. "Eight minutes out."

The tractor was surprisingly fast with the transport unhitched from it and Ehri pushing it to full throttle. It wasn't long before Donovan could feel the heat of the vehicle's exertion begin filtering into the cabin, leaving him sweating.

"There's no way they aren't going to spot us like this," Soon said.

"It's okay if they see us," Donovan said. "They just need to see us too late."

It was Kraeger who had presented the haphazard plan. It was Donovan who agreed with the logic of it. They would lose a lot of time going to the Dread facility on foot, time that would allow the larger force to return. By charging in the tractor, they might be able to catch the Dread off-guard in more ways than one.

They reached the hill in no time, coming upon the incline and rumbling up it with only a minor slowdown. Donovan leaned out the door of the cab, looking behind them. There was a light in the distant sky. A Dread fighter, or the transport heading back to base?

He grabbed Kraeger's shoulder and pointed to it.

"It's going to be close," Kraeger said.

"We have to reach the mechs before the reinforcements get here," Donovan said.

"I'm going as fast as I can, Major," Ehri replied.

The tractor trundled up the hill, slowing to almost half the speed as it neared the crest.

"That's it," Ehri said.

"Kraeger, you know what to do," Donovan said.

"See you in Hell, Major," Kraeger said. "The real one." Then he moved to the side of the vehicle and jumped off.

The rest of their small army jumped with him, abandoning the tractor to make the remainder of the trip on foot. They rolled beside and then behind the vehicle as it reached the apex of the incline, giving them a view of the Dread base a moment before they started dropping toward it.

It was a more open facility than the much larger city, with four roundish main buildings and a few smaller outbuildings all connected by narrow corridors. It gave the outpost an almost insectoid appearance, one that loosely resembled an asymmetrical wheel and spokes.

Donovan quickly spotted the two mechs he had seen earlier. They were moving to the front of the outpost, directly ahead of them.

"They saw us," Soon said, reaching up and pulling the safety restraints over his chest.

Donovan found his seat and did the same. "Let's hope their aim is off."

The tractor shook as it began to roll down the other side of the hill. Ehri kept the throttle all the way forward and began rocking the machine from side to side while it charged ahead. The mechs raised their weapons in unison, sending a spew of heavy slugs at them.

The projectiles slammed into the heavy metal shell of the vehicle, creating a din of clanks and thunks as they tore into to machine. Sparks skittered off the plating in front of the cabin as rounds nearly found them and the entire night sky grew bright white at the onslaught.

Plasma fire began streaking past them, the shots coming close to the mechs but intentionally not hitting them. Kraeger and his team were attempting to distract the pilots, to give them something else to think about and throw their aim.

The tractor continued on its course, racing down the hill toward the mechanized armors. Slugs continued to tear it apart, and Donovan watched chunks of iron explode from the machine, leaving a trail of debris along the sides. Something popped near the back, and a huge plume of smoke appeared in front of them. He expected that any moment one of the projectiles would find its way into the cabin and kill them all. One came close, catching the edge of the cage and tearing a huge hole in the side, taking the door with it.

It didn't matter. They had reached the point of no return. The mechs had also failed to adjust to their tactic. Was it because they didn't think the machine was a threat or was it because they just weren't accustomed to playing defense?

Whatever the reason, the tractor continued its approach, growing ever closer to the mechs until it was right on top of them, nearly as tall as they were and much, much heavier.

The Dread pilots finally realized what was about to happen, and they concentrated their fire on the front of the tractor, trying to slow its momentum.

Of course, they couldn't. Of course, it was too late.

The massive vehicle slammed hard into the mechs, catching one full on and clipping the other. That one spun and tumbled to the ground with a jolt, while the first was pushed backward, sinking into the front of the machine and finding itself pinned. Donovan braced himself as the tractor sandwiched the mech between itself and the wall of one of the outbuildings, slamming into it and coming to a sudden, complete stop.

"Come on," Donovan said

He removed the restraints and got to his feet. They had been hoping they would be able to catch both of the machines with the tractor. They would have to settle for the one. He could see the upper part of it ahead of him. It was struggling to get free, pressing against the weight of the truck.

Soon threw off his restraints, as did Ehri. They had an easy exit from the torn cage, and they made their way out of the hole and into the open air. Donovan found the first mech getting back to its feet, recovering from the glancing blow it had taken.

They were running out of time.

"Ehri, go," Donovan said. She was already moving, rushing toward the mech. He hoped they hadn't hit it too hard. They needed it to get loose.

"This is even crazier now that we're here," Soon said, watching along with him. Ehri jumped from the front of the tractor to the shoulders of the mech, a fifteen-foot leap that she made look easy.

"We're just getting started, Captain," Donovan replied.

The Dread forces were beginning to pour out of the buildings, getting mixed up with heavy fire from Kraeger and his approaching force. Clones were already falling nearby, hit by both plasma and traditional rounds, clearly caught unready for the assault.

Donovan almost fell as the trapped mech managed to get enough force behind it to shake the tractor. He leaned down, putting a hand on the scored metal, looking back to see that it was getting loose. Ehri had scaled the front of it, and he saw her put her hand to a spot on the chest and open a small access panel. She moved her hand across that, and the side of the mech's chest cavity parted, revealing the pilot inside. He could see the surprise on the pilot's face as Ehri shot him.

"What about that guy?" Soon said, pointing at the second mech. It was back on its feet, and facing their way.

"Run," Donovan said, turning and dashing across the top of the tractor. Projectiles dug into the metal behind them as he crossed to the other side. He reached the edge without pausing, jumping without a second thought.

He tucked his shoulder, hitting the ground in a hard roll. Soon was right behind him, trying to copy the move and coming up a little short. He landed hard on his side and didn't get up right away, stunned by the impact.

Donovan rushed back to him. A Dread soldier appeared in the doorway of the building they crashed against, and he got his rifle up in time to bring the clone down. He reached Soon, leaning next to him.

"Captain?"

Soon groaned and pushed himself up. His clothes were torn, but Diaz's gori'shah had survived beneath it, helping absorb some of the fall.

"I'm not dead yet," Soon said.

Donovan helped him up, and they both looked over in surprise as the tractor was shoved back, Ehri working the mech completely free.

"We're going to have company," Donovan said, pointing at the light that had been following them in. It was the transport the hunters had taken out into the wild. "Bad company. Hurry."

Donovan led Soon toward the doorway. The clone he had shot was slumped there, along with another that had been hit by Kraeger's more distant fire. They stepped over it, moving into the structure. They could hear Ehri's mech join the attack behind them, the whine of the powerful guns and the hard echoes of the slugs pouring into the second armor. Donovan turned his head right before rounding the corner, seeing Ehri's mech ducking around the tractor, using it as cover while she rained fire on the opposition.

"We need to clear the way for Kraeger," Donovan said.

They raced through the structure, catching the clone soldiers by surprise, hitting them with conventional fire before they could make it out the door. Only a few appeared by the time they had reached the first connecting corridor, proving Kraeger's hunch right. The base wasn't heavily defended.

"Honey, I'm hoooommmmeee," he heard Kraeger shout from somewhere behind him. "Get those charges down boys and girls. I'm expecting fireworks."

"Where to?" Soon asked.

Donovan paused. "Command is that way," Donovan said, following the layout Ehri had given them in his head. "There should be a hangar that way. I don't know if they have any equipment we can use in there, but it's worth trying to take what we can. Let's wait here for the others to catch up."

"Yes, sir," Soon said.

Kraeger appeared at the end of the corridor a moment later, flanked by ten men.

"How are we doing?" Donovan asked.

"It's fifteen to six in our favor, Major," Kraeger said. "And I think the odds are going to get better. Your alien girlfriend beat the hell out of that other mech. I'm glad she's on our side."

"Me too," Donovan said, relieved to know Ehri was okay. "We need to split up. Half to the Command Center, the other half to the hangar."

"You heard the man," Kraeger said. "I assume you want the charges in the Command Center?"

"Absolutely."

Soon put his hand on Donovan's shoulder. "If I don't see you again, Major, it was an honor."

"For me, too, Captain," Donovan said.

"Aww. You two are going to make me cry again. I think we should get moving."

Soon saluted, and then started running down the corridor toward the hangar, half of the other rebels following behind him.

"Well, you were right, Major," Kraeger said. "We can fight back. Are you ready to blow the insides of this place to mush?"

[55]

The resistance in the hallways was light, the majority of it coming from a single squad of clone soldiers being led by an armored bek'hai in the corridor right outside the Command Center. Donovan and the others were pinned down there for a few minutes while they traded fire, the battle ending quickly when Kraeger threw a well-placed explosive into the center of them. The blast shredded the clones and left the Dread dazed long enough to get shot.

They filed into the Center. It was similar to the room that Donovan and Diaz had met Ehri in. Sparse and solid and cold. Simple slabs of metal rose up throughout the room, trailing back into the dark, uneven walls and flooring. A raised dais with a single chair resting on it sat in the center, ringed by three more levels of what appeared to be workstations of some kind.

The stations were all deserted, except for the chair in the center. A bek'hai in a flowing gori'shah was sitting there, looking ahead to a feed of the battle continuing outside.

Donovan let his eyes wander to the feed. He saw the tractor first and shuddered at the amount of damage it had sustained. It was a miracle they had survived their initial attack. He found Ehri's mech ducked behind it with the remainder of the rebel soldiers. The transport carrying the hunters was further afield, on its side against the ground and smoking.

Three more Dread mechs had appeared in the distance and were peppering the tractor with fire, trying to get it out of the way once and for all. Two Dread fighters were circling, staying at a safe distance.

Donovan's heart sank. Either the forces hadn't been as light as Kraeger assumed, or reinforcements were already on the way before the battle started. Whatever the reason, it looked like it was only a matter of time before they were overwhelmed.

"Screw it, Major," Kraeger said. "Let's finish the job and go out as heroes."

"Funny thing for you to say," Donovan replied.

"What can I say? I'm fickle."

The pur'dahm reacted at the sound of their voices, turning his head to look at them. He was uglier than some of the others Donovan had seen, the ridges of bone on his head protruding in odd, asymmetrical angles, his skin thicker and more gray. He looked old.

"Druk'shur," he said calmly. "The resistance ends tonight."

"Maybe," Kraeger said. "You first."

He fired his rifle. The plasma caught the bek'hai between the eyes, sending him tumbling from the dais.

"Set the charges," Kraeger roared. "We aren't dead until we're dead."

The others set about spreading the explosives while Donovan watched the action unfolding outside. Smoke was pouring from the tractor, and Ehri had turned the mech to get it in front of as many of the rebels as she could. He could see some of the slugs were getting through now, digging into the mech's armor, the enemy drawing nearer.

They had tried to do something special. They had tried to claim the first real victory in the war against the Dread. If he was going to die, at least he could find comfort in the fact that he had died doing something, the same way his mother, Matteo, Diaz, and all of the others had. His life was only a waste if he died for nothing.

"Charges are set, Major," Kraeger said. "Let's see if we can get out of here."

Donovan kept his eyes on the feed. Everything seemed to be moving in slow motion out there as the fighters swooped down, unleashing heavy plasma on Ehri's position. The shots hit the tractor, and one of them struck something important. He felt like his heart stopped beating as he witnessed the growing flume of the explosion, the battery detonating, its secure containment structure already turned to slag.

The mech was thrown backward, the rebels incinerated. The building shook from the shockwave, and again when the mech slammed into it once more.

"I don't think we're getting out of here," Donovan said, stunned.

"You don't survive by giving up, Major," Kraeger replied. "No matter how bad it looks. No matter how futile it seems. I know. I've been as low as any man can be."

Donovan nodded. Kraeger was right. He had to keep fighting.

He started toward the doorway.

An armored pur'dahm stepped into it.

Donovan couldn't see the hunter's face. It was hidden behind a dark mask, still connected to the tanks that allowed the drumhr to breathe more easily outside. He entered wordlessly, rifle shouldered, replaced with an odd, dark blade that was sweating plasma.

"What the?" Kraeger said, raising his weapon to attack.

The hunter burst forward, crossing the room in three steps, the rebel's defenses too slow. Plasma bolts hit the wall around him as he reached their forces, decapitating the first of them, then the second, and the third.

Donovan and Kraeger backed away, both shooting at the bek'hai. Donovan didn't have a Dread weapon, and his bullets pinged harmlessly against the armor. Kraeger's shots came close, but somehow the hunter was avoiding them.

"Druk'shur," a voice said from the doorway.

A second hunter was there, also carrying a blade. He spun it casually in his grip as he entered the room.

"Druk this," Kraeger said, turning to shoot.

Then the first hunter was on top of him, grabbing the weapon from his hands and throwing it aside. He didn't kill Kraeger right away. Donovan knew why.

"Where is your base?" the second hunter said in thick English.

"Go to Hell," Kraeger said, smiling.

The first grabbed him by the head and threw him forcefully to the ground.

"There are two ways to die, human. You choose."

Kraeger moved to his hands and knees. He looked a little dazed, but he was trying to get up again.

Donovan stood behind them. They didn't care if he was armed, they knew he couldn't hurt them. They also knew he couldn't escape. He looked around the room, searching for something he could use. A plasma rifle was on the floor a few meters away. Could he reach it in time? He had seen how the hunters moved. He doubted it.

"How about instead of giving up my people, I give you this?" Kraeger said, raising his middle finger. The hunter hit him again, the force putting him back on the floor. He didn't get up as quickly.

"You," the second said, turning to Donovan. "You started this with the un'hai traitor. Where is your base?"

Donovan smiled. "Go to Hell," he said, mimicking Kraeger. He gave them the finger for good measure. He was about to die. Why not?

"I did not expect you to reveal your base, Heil'drek," the hunter said. "You have great honor as a warrior and my respect. For that, I will retire you without pain."

He raised the plasma sword.

The building quaked, rocking so hard it knocked both Donovan and the hunter from their feet as something large smashed against it.

Donovan didn't get back up. Instead, he scrambled for the plasma rifle, crawling toward it on his hands and knees, not even daring to look back. He had one chance to reach it before the pur'dahm cut him in half.

He almost had it in hand when he sensed the hunter's presence behind him. He rolled to the side as the blade came down, sinking slightly into the floor and then lifting away. He looked up at the hunter, knowing he wouldn't be able to avoid a second strike.

A muffled whine interrupted everything, and a split-second later the entire room began to blow apart under the force of slugs coming in from outside. Donovan looked over at the feed just in time to see the front of a mech nearly butted up against it, too clean and fresh to be Ehri.

The hunter turned to face the new attack at the same time the bullets began ripping into him, hitting him hard enough that his body was sent across the room and into the wall. The other hunter was down as well, while Kraeger was lying prostrate on the floor, his hands over his head.

The shooting stopped. The wall was in pieces ahead of them, revealing the front of the mech. The feed was destroyed, as was most of the interior of the room.

The front of the mech shifted, the cockpit opening. Soon's head appeared a moment later.

"Sorry I'm late, Major. Ehri made these things sound like they were easy to use."

Donovan stared at the pilot, the shock of the turn of events keeping him speechless.

"I didn't hit you, did I?"

Donovan pointed past the mech. Soon was leaving himself vulnerable, and there was still a battle going on. Or was there? He didn't hear any gunfire.

"It's okay, Major. We won."

[56]

Donovan and Kraeger met Soon and Ehri outside, along with the remaining rebels, six in all. They had lost over two-thirds of their forces.

They had killed a lot more of the enemy than that.

Ehri's mech was a mangled mess, one of the arms missing, the other twisted into an ugly shape. The legs were badly damaged, and there were score marks across every inch of the armor. Somehow, she had kept herself facing the onslaught and prevented the cockpit from being hit. She had jumped out of the machine sweaty but unharmed.

Smoke rose all around them, the field outside littered with dead clones, a downed transport, four destroyed mechs, and even a crashed Dread fighter. It was an unexpected and impressive victory. One that Donovan had never imagined he would live to see.

"We can't linger here long," Ehri said. "The Domo'dahm will be furious at the losses."

"Good," Kraeger said. "It's about time he's the one upset about losing. I'm willing to wait for round two."

"I'm not," Donovan said. "What we did here was a start. Our first victory. Now our job is to make sure it isn't our last."

"It won't be," Soon said. "There's another mech inside the hangar with your name on it, Major."

Donovan considered for a moment before shaking his head. "It'll make us too easy to track. We should go on foot."

"It will shorten the time to Austin considerably, Major," Ehri said. "And will not reduce the fury of the Domo'dahm's retaliation. Besides, the resistance may need the relief these weapons can provide."

"What about the rest of us?" Kraeger asked. "We're supposed to walk?"

"There's a slug looking thing in the hangar, too," Soon said. "Ehri says it's ground transportation."

"A ped'ek. An armored carrier," Ehri said. "Once used to collect humans for processing. It has been dormant for some time, but it should still be functional."

"Processing?"

"In the early days of the invasion humans were collected for testing, to determine the proper genetics for splicing. This went on for twenty years or so until enough positive samples had been collected. The transports were used to ferry the prisoners to the testing facility."

"Why not put them on a regular transport?" Donovan asked.

"They didn't want to soil the ships by allowing contact with human flesh."

"What?" Soon said. "I don't get it. The Dread are mixing genes with us."

"By necessity, Captain. Not choice. Make no mistake, the Domo'dahm and many of the drumhr are disgusted by humankind. The clones are tolerated because they are clones and as such considered clean. Some of your ways are being adopted because they will prolong the race. It is all out of need, not desire."

"Okay, but then it won't be equipped to be driven by a human, will it?"

"A mech should be able to pull it quite easily."

"Monster two-oh?" Soon said. "It's a decent upgrade."

"That tractor saved our lives," Donovan said.

"May she rest in peace," Kraeger said, making the sign of the cross toward the remains of the vehicle. "Let's not dally, Major. We've got a war to win."

Kraeger headed off toward the hangar, leaving the others to watch him go.

"He killed Murphy," Donovan said.

"And countless others," Ehri replied.

"He's also a good fighter," Soon said. "I don't know what his background is, but I think he was trained by the military."

"He might have grown up as part of the resistance. That would explain his self-proclaimed soft spot. You're a pretty good fighter yourself, Captain."

"I have a lot to live for," Soon replied.

"We all do," Donovan replied. He stepped over to the remaining rebels. "Good work, all of you. I'm sorry I don't know you very well, but I hope to get the chance to. We're going to be heading to Austin, Texas. There's a resistance base there. Will you be coming?"

"I wouldn't miss it for anything, sir," a woman with short hair and a scar on her cheek said.

"Me neither," one of the others said.

"Let's give them Hell, Major," a third replied.

"Absolutely."

[57]

THE HUNTER REMAINED OUT OF SIGHT.

Watching.

Waiting.

He had seen the battle. He had followed from the tomb of his brothers, beneath the crashed ship where he continued to observe. The druk'shur had captured their equipment. Their weapons. Their armors. They had done what none of the pur'dahm ever believed possible.

They had challenged the might of the bek'hai, and they had survived.

It was a difficult outcome for him to accept. He knew without question that the bek'hai were the superior race and that the pur'-dahm were the most superior of the species. And yet, his two surviving brothers had chosen to chase after the Heil'drek while he had chosen to remain. Was it truly cowardice, as his brother had claimed? Was it caution?

Or was it something else? Something more visceral, more powerful? He was Lex'el dur Rorn'el. A splice from the line of the Domo'-dahm himself. He had more reason than most to want to prove his line. More reason than most to want to quell the spreading infection of humankind, to stop the return of their cancerous grip on the planet.

Had he stayed behind because he was afraid, or had he remained because the challenge was not great enough?

He knew the answer for himself, and his brothers had failed to survive to question it. That was just as well. They had always been inferior. Weaker. Slower. Less skilled. None of them could question that. Not when he was the champion of the Cruhr dur bek. Not when he had been undefeated for over two years.

He wasn't *a* hunter.

He was *the* hunter, and he had chosen to allow the humans their victory. He knew that it would be short-lived, and when he returned to the Domo'dahm with the Heil'drek's head, and with Ehri dur Tuhrik's head, he would be the one to claim his rightful position in the Domo'dahm's cell.

To the victor went the spoils.

The hunter remained out of sight as the humans emerged, no longer exposed but within the armored safety of a pair of gur'shah and humorously trailing a ped'ek. He tightened his uneven lips to prevent himself from laughing at the absurdity, and then opened his mouth in surprise as the mechs stopped walking and the people in the ped'ek disembarked, turning to face the facility.

Then the larger human took something in his hand and held it up toward the base. He flicked his finger, and the ground began to shake. Flames and debris spewed from the open areas followed by billowing smoke, and the humans shouted and cheered.

Then they returned to the vehicle and resumed their motion away from the base.

The hunter shifted his position beneath the ruined transport to watch them, tracking their direction and velocity.

When they had passed, he pulled himself from beneath the wreckage, climbing to his feet and adjusting the feed to his oxygen tanks. He would have to risk breathing the heavier outside air, or he wouldn't have a large enough supply to follow.

He bent down and retrieved his two lek'sai from the dirt, carefully rubbing them clean on the corpse of a nearby human before returning them to their sleeves on his back. His rifle had been damaged in the crash, but that was well and good.

He preferred to get close to his prey.

He looked to the north, where the humans were quickly vanishing over the horizon. He couldn't match their pace on foot, but that too was well and good.

He was the hunter.

He could be patient.

[58]

Tea'va stared out of the viewport, his emotions crossing between surprised confusion and impressed respect. The human ship had definitely turned to face the fortress, and now he could see that they had launched their starfighters, the intent of their actions clear.

The Heil'shur and his allies intended to attack. It seemed ridiculous and impossible. What could they be thinking? Gr'el would surely chew them apart.

Tea'va paused to reconsider. Maybe not. Gr'el had been forced to kill a large number of the drumhr on the ship to cement his rise to command. He had also been required to destroy all of the original lor'hai, save for Zoelle and her scientists. While the cloning facility had turned out two replacement batches so far, it was still a number fewer than the ship originally carried.

If the humans had discovered how their technology worked, was it possible they would be able to mount an effective attack? Clearly, they were going to try.

A warning tone began to sound from his terminal as it would at every terminal across the ship, calling all available soldiers to battle. His lips parted in a crooked smile at the sudden turn of events. If the humans managed to cause enough of a diversion, there was a chance he could recover after all.

He kept watching the viewport while the first two squadrons of gi'shah launch away from the ship toward the interlopers. His gaze was intense as the two sides closed the distance between one another. He was sure the Heil'shur was out there. Which one was he?

Three of the ships turned back, giving chase to the gi'shah who were targeting the starship. Two continued forward, dodging the plasma defenses and drawing nearer to the fortress. He saw one of them nearly collide with a gi'shah and then make a smooth flip, let loose a stream of fire, flip and continue again. The Heil'shur! It was him. He was certain of it. Instead of feeling angry, he was nearly gleeful. Let Gr'el deal with that!

He tore himself away from the viewport. It wouldn't serve to linger here. He moved to the door and opened it.

Two soldiers remained outside his quarters. The others had gone running to their battle stations. They turned to face Tea'va, raising their weapons toward him to threaten him back inside.

"You are to be retired," one of them said. "Uphold your honor."

"Honor?" Tea'va said.

He pushed himself forward like a dart, using his hands to slap the soldier's rifles aside. He punched the first in the face, his palm up and out, shoving into the clone's nose. He heard the wet crack of cartilage and the soldier fell to the ground. He spun on his heel, his opposite leg sweeping up, slamming the second soldier's rifle again with enough force that it nearly turned the clone around. He stepped forward, grabbing the soldier's head and twisting until his neck broke.

"That is what I think of Gr'el's honor," he said, bending down to pick up one of the rifles.

He headed across the corridor. The fortress was still fairly quiet, the rush of its personnel already finished. They had gone to their stations to help in the fight and left him alone to move as he wished. Gr'el was a fool to leave him with only two guards. He was being treated like a failed drumhr, not a pur'dahm of the Second Cell. It was insulting, and he was sure his rival intended it to be that way.

It didn't matter now. The humans had given him the distraction he needed to get free. Now that he was out, he could make his way to the bridge, kill Gr'el, and regain control of the Ishur.

He stopped himself a few steps later. What if the humans had figured out how their technology worked? What if they had a plan? What if the infighting between himself and Gr'el had given them the opening they needed to win the battle?

It continued to seem impossible. The firepower of a bek'hai fortress against a ship without any offensive capabilities? How could the humans possibly win against that? Except Gr'el wouldn't be able to field half of the starfighters, or control half of the gun batteries.

Maybe it wasn't completely impossible after all.

He ran along the corridor until he reached another viewport. He looked out in time to see two of the human starfighters rush past, tracking down the side of the ship and out of view. He found the larger starship, taking heavy fire but still vectoring toward them.

The ship had evaded them the first time, sneaking around the fortress to get ahead and begin the chase. He knew Gr'el wouldn't allow that to happen again. The pur'dahm would stand his ground, positioning the fortress so that the human ship would have no choice but to smash right into it.

The ship's commander was smart. He had escaped them twice already. He had to be expecting that this was the case.

Tea'va stared out at the scene, trying to think like the humans. A starship with no weapons and no ability to slip, being chased by an enemy with superior numbers and firepower. A decision to turn around and head directly into the jaws of the gur'uhm. If he assumed that the commander knew he would not be able to circumvent the fortress again, what could he guess that such a commander would do?

A human starfighter rocketed past his viewport again, trailing three gi'shah. The second starfighter was coming up with another gi'shah behind him. They were so close that Tea'va could see the pilots of the human ships. One was old, the other young. They approached one another, the older one shooting at the younger one. Not at. Below. The gi'shah giving chase was hit. So was the older human, his ship vanishing in a small fireball and spitting debris away. The younger pilot followed up the attack by turning his starfighter in an unbelievable maneuver, spraying each of the gi'shah, destroying one and disabling the others.

That one had to be the Heil'shur.

Tea'va ran along the corridor, heading for the nearest transport beam while keeping an eye on the battle. The young human's fighter burst away again, and this time, there were no gi'shah to follow.

Why had he come to engage them so close to the fortress, while the others were staying back to protect the larger ship?

He had a feeling he knew. But could the human starship survive the journey?

He made it to the transport beam, taking it down to one of the decks that adjoined the hangar. Immediately, he could hear the sound of gunfire coming from inside. The Heil'shur was in the fortress, using the fighter's cannons on any of the clones that remained in the hangar.

That was where he decided to go. He turned the corner at the same time a squad of clones did. They stood only a meter apart for a moment, both taken by surprise. Tea'va recovered first, his plasma quickly dispatching the unprepared group of clones. He continued down the corridor, over the top of the hangar and to the control pod that hung above the space. He opened the hatch, shooting the drumhr he caught trying to escape and then descending into the pod. He could see the Heil'shur's fighter clearly now, on the ground and facing away from him.

He looked out past the hangar and into space. He could see the starship from his position. It was beaten and battered. One of the nacelles had already been destroyed. It was coming this way. He was sure of it. The hangar was large enough to house the human ship but just barely. There would be no way to stop the momentum in time, no way to come to a smooth stop. If the ship did enter, it was going to collide. The shielded lek'shah could survive a blow like that. Unless the human ship had a similar shield to absorb some of the force, there was no way that it could.

He glanced down at the Heil'shur's fighter, resting on the floor of the abandoned hangar. He could almost see the top of the pilot's head clearly from his position. He was a human. A regular human. Nothing exceptional. And yet, he was a worthy adversary. A human who had proven he was as skilled as a bek'hai. Most of the pur'dahm believed it impossible; that it wasn't the skill of the Heil'shur, but the failure of those that had faced him. Tea'va had seen him more than any of the others. He knew they were wrong.

The fighter's thrusters fired, and it began to slide along the floor on a small set of skids, headed back to space. Tea'va looked down at the controls. An electromagnetic shield kept the atmosphere out, but the hangar also had lek'shah doors that were normally closed for slip-space travel. He could trigger the command to close the doors. He could seal the Heil'shur in and the human starship out. He could effectively end the resistance for good.

He hesitated, finding the human starship once more. He was caught by surprise when the fortress' main plasma cannon fired, bathing the ship in bright light.

The plasma paused, a sudden impenetrable darkness spreading from the bow. Tea'va watched in amazement, his mouth dropping open as the plasma poured into the darkness and disappeared. Then the light grew too bright to see beyond, the plasma washing over the human ship. Tea'va couldn't breathe. He couldn't move.

The remains of the attack passed over the ship.

It was still coming his way.

It was impossible. Completely impossible. The plasma beam was phase modulated. It would have torn a hole into a fortress if it had struck one. Not only were the humans alive, they weren't even hit.

They hadn't just reverse-engineered the technology. They had improved it.

He put his hand over the terminal, ready to close the hangar doors. It would be so easy to shut them out. To let them slap harmlessly against the outside of the ship. Shields or no shields, they would never get in that way.

Gr'el had turned on him. Zoelle had turned on him. Even the

Domo'dahm had turned on him, shunning him for being too human while at the same time asking the bek'hai to accept their evolution and the inclusion of human traits. He owed them nothing. He owed the bek'hai nothing. They had made him into a hybrid freak and then disregarded him for his advancements. They had used him and then cast him aside.

The humans were a different story. If they made it onto the ship, they would need help to control it. They would need help to understand it and to make it function. They would come to depend on him, and that was something that he could use. Not only to get revenge on Gr'el but to strike back at the Domo'dahm and turn the course of his misfortune.

He lifted his hand away, watching as the fighter slid out of the hangar, through the shield and into space. The starship was drawing near, coming right at him, ready to force its way into the fortress. He scrambled from the control room, climbing out and running back toward the transport beam. He needed to get down to the base level. He would have one good opportunity to make this work.

He was halfway there when the impact came. He could sense it before he felt it, the lek'shah phasing as it was struck. Then the shockwave came, powerful enough that the entire fortress groaned in pain, substantial enough that it knocked him off his feet. He stayed on his hands and knees for a moment, waiting to see if the blow was enough to destroy them. When there was no sign of critical failure, when the ship maintained both power and life support, he rose once more and continued his run.

The bek'hai had used him. He would use the humans, first for revenge, and then to regain control.

Then he would end them all for good.

[59]

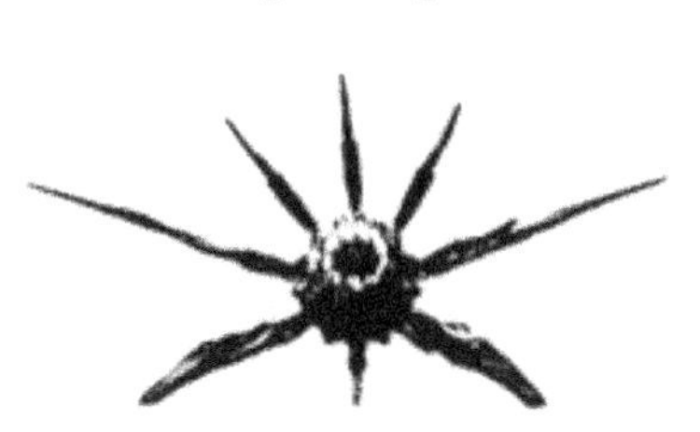

Theodore looked up. Smoke was filling the bridge, the equipment sparking and shorting, strained beyond its limits at the impact. His chest hurt where the emergency straps had dug into it, reminding him that he had nearly been strained beyond his limit.

Nearly, but not quite.

The ship still had emergency power. He had no idea how. It was some kind of miracle in itself.

"Maggie, you there?" he said, coughing.

"Yes, General," the computer replied, oblivious to their state.

"How's the atmosphere outside?"

"Eighty percent oxygen, fifteen percent nitrogen. Other components include water vapor, argon, helium, and an unidentified gas."

It was breathable, as he suspected. That was good enough. "Patch me in with Colonel Graham."

"Yes, General."

"Colonel," Theodore said. "Status report."

"A little shaken, General," Graham replied. "We're ready to move."

"Do it. Secure the perimeter. We'll meet you outside."

"Maggie, sound the evac." He paused to cough again. "Everybody okay up there?"

A round of affirmatives greeted him.

"We need to get off this thing. Follow along behind me, make sure you grab a gun on the way out. If they're gone before you get there, stay with the people who are armed."

"Yes, sir," the crew replied.

Theodore unstrapped himself, and then transferred into his chair. Colonel Choi appeared beside it.

"Can you get the locks for me, Colonel?" he asked.

She bent down to release the chair from the floor. The rest of the bridge crew was assembling in front of them. He counted heads, happy to see they were all up and about.

"Stay alert. We made it this far, but we haven't won a damn thing yet."

He turned the chair, rolling it from the bridge and out into the corridor. This part of the ship was vacant; the personnel already shuffled to prepare for the incursion. They had managed to survive the crash landing on the alien ship; now they needed to find a way to gain control of it. The Dread used clones for everything, so there had to be a means for a human to pilot it.

And if a human could pilot it, then he damn well could.

The corridors were hazy, and the smell of burning wires and metal was thick in the air. The emergency lighting cast a shadow of light along the haze, which would have made the Magellan eerie if it weren't so familiar. Theodore cursed as they came across the body of one of the crew, who hadn't managed to buckle up in time.

Someone behind him cried out at the sight. Someone else vomited. He couldn't blame them. He tensed his own stomach to keep his emotions in check. This was war. Casualties happened. May God have mercy on their souls.

They kept going, moving at a light run. Theodore had no idea what kind of defenses the Dread were going to have. Unless they had brought the ship full-stop in a hurry, they had a limited amount of time before they could back up into the crease through the dead zone, or move the ship out of it completely. The only shot they had was to hit the enemy while they were still vulnerable.

"General, this is Sergeant Hafizi. Delta Squad is on the ground outside. The area is clear and secure."

His voice was choppy through the damaged comm system.

"This is Graham. Beta squad is out and clear."

"General, this is Alpha Squadron Leader. There's no activity outside the fortress. I don't think they have any other fighters."

Theodore looked over at Choi. "No more pilots, more like," he said. "Something fishy's going on here. I'm not complaining, but I expected this to be a little harder."

"Me, too," Choi replied.

"Maggie, pass a message to Gabriel to bring his squad in. If they had more Bats to send at us, they would have done it already, and we may need the extra hands on the ground."

"Yes, General."

"Send a message to Hafizi, too. Get his team moving into position to cover wherever Beta ain't."

"Yes, General."

They reached the emergency stairwell. Choi, Abdullah, and Locke all helped lift his chair, carrying him down the steps. He hated that they had to do it, but he stayed silent. Now wasn't the time to complain about being independent.

"General, Alpha Squadron is home," Gabriel said through the comm.

"Heh. Home? We'll see about that. Vacation rental, more like."

It took almost five minutes for them to get down the stairwell to the belly of the ship, where the emergency ground access was located. For each second of each minute, Theodore waited to hear from Hafizi that they were taking heavy fire, or from Graham that they were under attack. No such messages came. It was almost as if the Dread were hiding.

Or waiting.

Whichever it was, he didn't like it.

Sergeant Diallo was waiting at the exit with Guy, Sarah, and Reza. She was holding their single Dread weapon.

"General," she said, saluting as he approached.

"Sergeant. That thing still work?"

"Yes, sir," Reza said.

Theodore spun his chair to face them. "I don't have the words to express my gratitude over what you three have accomplished here. I'm proud as heck of each and every one of you, and grateful to have you on my ship. Let's not get too comfy, though; we're not of the swamp just yet."

"Yes, sir," they replied.

"The others are already on the ground, sir," Diallo said.

"No sign of the enemy?"

"Not yet. I think they're afraid of us."

"I think they're working out a nice, proper welcome. And I don't mean good old-fashioned southern hospitality. Maggie, how long until we clear the dead zone?"

"Three minutes, General."

"That's about how long I think we have. Maggie, set yourself to secure standby and power down. Unlock only by command of myself, Colonel Choi, or Major St. Martin."

"Yes, General. It was nice to see you again, General. Farewell."

"Farewell, Maggie."

The emergency lighting dimmed further as the Magellan began to shut down. Theodore stayed behind Diallo as they moved down the ramp to the floor of the Dread fortress. He could see most of the crew assembled beneath them, many of them armed and all of them organized and alert, taking cover behind whatever they could find, their weapons trained on the apparent exits to the hangar.

He saw Gabriel and his dog crouched next to Lieutenant Bale, unarmed but still watching the ingress points. He was alive and unharmed. He could only hope he would stay that way.

"General," Colonel Graham said when he reached the ground. "I've got everyone organized. How do you want to do this?"

"These couillons must have a bridge or a control room or something somewhere in here. We move together, one unit until we find it. We've got one gun that can hurt them, and it needs to go to the best shot." He turned to Sergeant Diallo. "Is that you, Sergeant?"

"Yes, sir," Diallo replied.

"Good woman." Theodore coughed slightly before raising his voice. "All right boys and girls, this is it. I think the fact that we're being ignored in here is a good start. We're still alive, and I plan for us to stay that way. We've got the Dread rifle; now the mission is to find whatever passes for a CIC around here and take control of it. We cut off the head, the rest of the snake will be left flopping around. Any questions?"

Nobody said anything, though they all turned his way, their expressions clearly reflecting the respect they had for him. Even Gabriel. Especially Gabriel. He wanted to go over to his boy, but he wasn't his son right now. He was just another soldier.

"In that case, let's-"

One of the doors to their right slid open, cutting him off. Diallo ducked in front of him, protecting him while raising the Dread rifle to fire back at the incoming soldiers. The rest of his crew reacted in kind, those with weapons training them on the door, the remainder taking cover.

Except there were no incoming soldiers. At first, nothing came through the door. It sat open, the corridor behind it vacant.

Then a single form appeared from the shadows. It was taller and leaner than an average human, with long fingers and small ridges on the sides of its head. It was wearing a skintight suit of some kind and was holding a rifle by the barrel, hands up and out in a submissive posture. It smiled at them as it entered the hangar, a crooked smile that revealed white human teeth.

It scanned the line, starting with Theodore and sweeping across their defensive positions. It stopped when its eyes fell on Gabriel.

"There you are," it said. "The Heil'shur. Much honor and respect to you. My name is Tea'va dur Orin'ek." It bowed low before them. "I am humbly indebted to you for your intercession, and wish to offer myself to you in service."

[60]

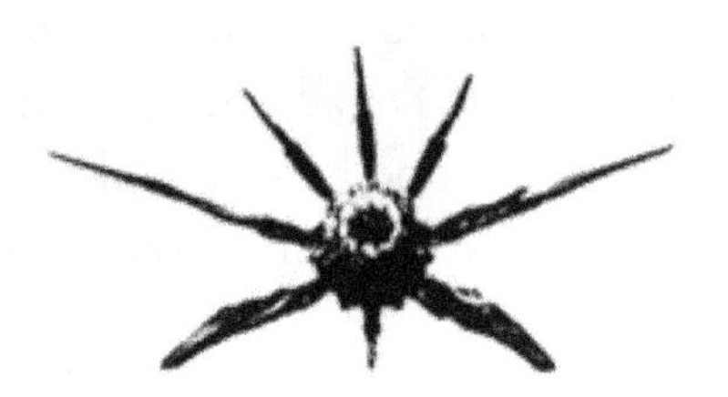

GABRIEL STARED AT THE DREAD STANDING IN FRONT OF HIM along with the rest of the crew. Most of them had never seen the enemy who stole their home world at all. Gabriel had never seen one outside of their impenetrable armor.

Seconds passed in tense silence. The alien, Tea'va, waited motionless for Gabriel to respond to his offer. To respond at all. Gabriel was too stunned to speak. The fact that their opponent looked so human was one shock. That Tea'va had offered to help them was another. This whole mission had felt as if it were being guided by an invisible hand. His mother's, maybe? But this?

This was something else entirely.

He dared a quick glance over to his father, who was already looking back at him. The General nodded shortly, giving him permission to interact.

"Heil'shur?" he said.

"It means honored adversary," Tea'va replied. "We have met before. In the dark above the planet called Earth."

"We've met before? You mean you're a pilot?"

"Yes. You have escaped from me many times. Your skill is unmatched among both our races."

Gabriel wasn't so sure about that. He had seen the damage to his fighter when he climbed out of it. It was luck, not skill.

"Why are you here? Why offer us your help? What are you hoping to achieve?"

"As I said, I wish to offer my services. I am lor'el on this ship. An outcast. Mistreated and dishonored for my appearance. I have done all that they ask, and yet they say I am too human. If I am too human, if I am a failure for that, then I shall become a human." He laughed in a shrill cackle. "Revenge, Heil'shur. That is what I hope to achieve. Revenge against the bek'hai who have stolen your world, and betrayed me."

"And we're just supposed to believe that?" Gabriel asked. He had no idea what the enemy's tactics looked like. Would they send a single combatant in to distract them?

"No. Only a gruk would do so," Tea'va said. "I've brought you something. Two things."

He raised his hands a little higher and then threw his rifle toward Gabriel. Gabriel reached up and caught it, lowering it and checking it. It was active.

"I can take you to more," Tea'va said. "I also have this."

He backed away again, beyond the entrance to the hangar. The movement caused the other members of the crew to tense.

"Easy," Gabriel said to those around him. "Take it easy."

Tea'va dragged something into view. A dead Dread. He held it up to them so they could see he had shot it in the head. Then he dropped it unceremoniously to the floor.

"This one and five others were on their way here, to fortify this position and prepare for the ambush. I destroyed them for you, as a sign of my loyalty if you will have it."

Gabriel looked to his father again. This wasn't his decision to make. It was Theodore's.

His father tapped his wrist. They didn't have a lot of time.

That was all he did. He didn't provide a yes or a no. He was leaving Gabriel to make the decision for them. Trusting his instincts.

They didn't have many options. They had managed to get on

board the ship, which was a miracle in itself. But they still didn't know where to go, what kind of opposition they would run into, nothing. What were their chances if they went in blind? Minimal, and they all knew it. They had done it because they were desperate, not because it was ideal. If this Dread, this Tea'va, was leading them into a trap, they were goners, but they would have likely been goners anyway. If he really did intend to help them? They might be able to pull off one of the greatest military victories of all time.

"Very well, Tea'va. I accept your offer. If revenge is what you're after, then there will be plenty of opportunities for you to get it."

The Dread smiled again. Gabriel couldn't help but recoil slightly at the sight of it. It was so close to human, and yet alien enough that his mind couldn't quite accept it.

"They will be coming when the Ishur exits the void," Tea'va said. "When your weapons will be ineffective against them once more. Your tactics and timing were impressive. Was it your idea?"

"My father's," Gabriel said.

"Father?" Tea'va replied. "I have heard of this thing. Bek'hai have no fathers. What you did with your shields, I did not believe it was possible." He made a clicking noise that seemed impressed. "Come. We must reach the armory before Gr'el can adjust to my treachery. He will be reinforcing this position with the few units he has to spare."

Few units to spare? That sounded promising. Gabriel glanced over at Theodore again. The General smiled.

"You heard the Dread," his father said. "Form up and move out. O'Dea, run on over to the other side of Maggie and get Hafizi and Beta in line behind us."

"Yes, sir," Daphne said, rushing away from the scene.

"According to my watch we've got less than a minute," Theodore said.

"Is this your Si'dahm?" Tea'va asked. "Your second in command?"

"No," Gabriel replied. "General St. Martin is the leader of our forces."

Tea'va faced Theodore, sweeping low again, his head down in a submissive pose. "My apologies, Dahm St. Martin."

"Don't worry about it," Theodore said. "Just get us some guns, and you and me will be best friends forever."

"As you command, Dahm St. Martin. This way."

Tea'va moved back across the threshold, out of the hangar. The entire crew of the Magellan hesitated to follow, Gabriel included. It was one thing to verbally accept this apparently traitorous enemy's help. It was another to follow him into the unknown.

"Don't just stand there lallygagging," Theodore said. "We doubled down; now it's time to show our hand." He began rolling forward ahead of them. Sergeant Diallo was caught off guard, but she hurried to catch up.

Gabriel got in motion as well, moving from his cover behind a Dread starfighter. Colonel Graham fell in beside him, along with Bale and Celia.

The Dread stood a dozen meters ahead of them, at the intersection of another corridor. He waited for Theodore and Gabriel to reach him before pointing out the others he had killed, all with a single wound to the head.

Gabriel was as impressed with Tea'va as Tea'va had seemed to be with him. The Dread was not only a pilot, but he was also a crack shot. Gabriel wished he could say the same about his ground combat skills.

"We go that way. We will cross three more corridors to reach the hub. There will be a green light in the center. It is a transport beam. Lower your hands to go down. This one will take you to the lowest deck, where the main armory is located. Pass word to the others in your cell. Once we have taken the weapons, I will lead you to the bridge. Expect strong resistance there."

"How many soldiers does this Gr'el fellow have?" Theodore asked.

"Fortunately for you, not anywhere near as many as he had before. He seized control of this ship from its original commander and destroyed every drumhr and lor'hai whose loyalty was questionable. That is why he is holding back. He won't risk what he has remaining when he can hold out for a better overall position."

"I would do the same thing," Theodore said.

"Gr'el didn't question your loyalty?" Gabriel asked.

"Of course, he did. I was this ship's original commander. He betrayed me with the blessing of the Domo'dahm, our leader, because of my humanity. Your attack allowed me to break free. That is why I owe you a debt of gratitude. Your numbers are nearly equal to his. If we can reach the armory, you will almost be on even-"

Tea'va stopped speaking, darting forward and shoving Gabriel back against the wall. Gabriel felt his stomach clench, waiting for the killing blow. A plasma bolt whizzed past him, right where he had been standing a moment before. Another followed, striking the corner of the intersection as Tea'va released him and urged them back.

Shouts went up from the rear of the rebel forces, followed by opposing bursts of plasma and heavy ions.

The Dread starship was out of the dead zone, and the reinforcements had arrived.

[61]

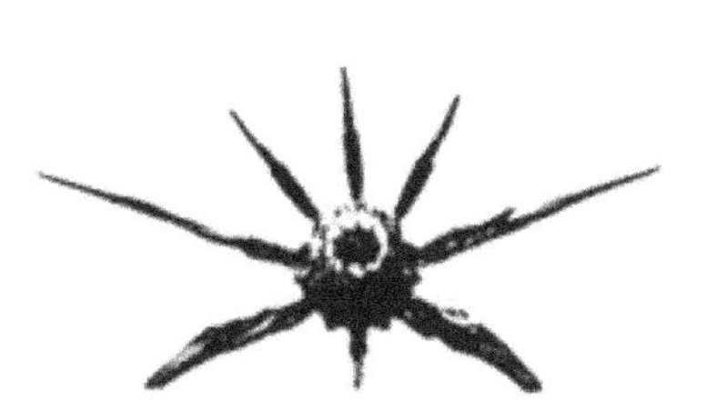

"Damn it," Theodore said, throwing his chair back against the wall and turning his head toward the rear of their column. "We need one of those guns back there. Diallo, make it happen."

Sergeant Diallo was crouched beside Theodore, positioned in front of him to take any wayward shots that managed to come near.

"Sir, I should stay with you," she said.

"Are you questioning me during a firefight, Sergeant?" Theodore roared. "I'll court martial you right here."

Diallo headed away at a run, carrying the Dread rifle toward the rear. Gabriel glanced back at her before returning his attention to the incoming forces.

The attack had come from both ends at once, the enemy clones moving in from the intersecting corridors. There was little cover. Nowhere to hide. The area was filled with shouts and cries and screams, with red and blue bolts of energy. The clones weren't wearing armor, but the front line was carrying shields made of the same impenetrable black material and using them to absorb the human counterattack.

Gabriel fired the Dread rifle, impressed by the lack of kick and the ease of use. His bolt struck one of the shields, leaving a score mark in it but not piercing through in one blast. He fired three more times with similar results. A return bolt flashed past him, and one of the crew members cried out a few feet away.

"We're getting chewed apart out here," Theodore said. "We need to retreat and get some cover." He spun on one wheel. "Graham," he bellowed. "Get everybody moving back to the hangar."

"Yes, sir," Graham shouted. The Colonel was pressed against the wall, firing ahead at the clones.

"So much for reaching the armory," Theodore said. "You were too slow getting to us."

Tea'va made a face. Gabriel thought he saw a hint of anger, but it was gone in an instant. "You were too slow in your landing, Dahm St. Martin," the Dread replied calmly. "We must change our tactics if you want your people to live. Send them back. We will go forward."

Gabriel looked back over his shoulder. Diallo was positioned in the intersection, putting down cover fire across the corridor with the Dread rifle and keeping the enemy fire somewhat suppressed. He could see most of the crew retreating, but also dozens of men and women already motionless on the ground. He had known each and every one of them by name. Now they were gone, just like that. He felt a pain in his chest. Where was Miranda? A spike of fear threatened his composure. He couldn't worry about her now.

A squad of soldiers was moving in their direction. Delta.

"Sir," Sergeant Hafizi said, saluting as he reached them. "Diallo sent me to help get you out safe."

"We aren't going out," Theodore replied. "We're going ahead."

"Sir, I don't think-"

"Am I the General here?" Theodore snapped. "Get in line, soldier."

"Yes, sir," Hafizi replied.

Gabriel saw Tea'va smile. The Dread was amused.

"So how do we get out of this?" Gabriel asked.

"Back away down the corridor," Tea'va replied.

"We'll get caught in the center. Boxed in."

"You can trust me and live, or question and die."

"Do it," Theodore said. "Our fate is in God's hands now."

They began backing up, clearing the intersection and avoiding further fire. Gabriel noticed Reza was with them as they did. How did the scientist end up at the front of the line? There was no time to ask him.

"Cover the rear," Tea'va said. He flexed his hands and began moving forward.

"You're going after them unarmed?" Gabriel asked.

"They are lor'hai. I am pur'dahm."

It was the only explanation he gave. Then he rushed forward, leaping across the corridor, hitting the wall with his feet and springing back out of sight. A rush of plasma crossed the hallway, followed by screams.

Gabriel turned to face the second intersection. The enemy was drawing closer, leaving Diallo on the opposite side, trying to keep them at bay. Too many of their crew were on the ground in the middle of it all. He didn't want to look at them, terrified of who he would find in the mix. Miranda? Daphne? Colonel Choi?

He made it to the intersection and began shooting in the opposite direction as the Sergeant. The combined force was enough to temporarily halt the attack, the incoming enemy clones remaining cautious. They could afford to be patient.

"Heil'shur," he heard Tea'va say a few seconds later. He turned to the Dread, who was holding one of the shields in one hand, a plasma rifle in the other. His clothing was burned, but he appeared unharmed.

"Diallo," Theodore said. "Take that thing and get it back to the others. Bar the door to the Magellan with it if you have to."

"Sir?"

"If we can take the ship, we can stop the attack. Ain't that right?"

Tea'va nodded, throwing both the shield and the rifle across the intersection. Diallo scooped up both and began retreating to the hangar. Gabriel could hear more screams from back there, as the Dread forces began closing in around them. He hoped it would be enough to save them.

"This way," Tea'va said, leading them forward again. He ran ahead, his long legs carrying him quickly. He paused at the intersection, checked it, and burst forward again.

Gabriel ran behind the Dread, while the soldiers of Delta Squad kept his father surrounded. Reza stayed close to them, keeping pace.

They crossed the corridors, reaching a longer hallway illuminated by a green beam of light in the center. The transport beam. Tea'va stopped in front of it, waving them past. "The bridge is twenty decks up."

"What about the armory?" Theodore said.

"It will be fortified beyond our capacity to take it. Gr'el reacted more quickly than I estimated. He must have guessed I am helping you."

"Won't the bridge be fortified as well?" Gabriel said.

"Yes. There is another way. One he won't expect. Remember. Raise your hands to go up, try to count the floors. Otherwise, we will be separated."

"Hafizi, here," Gabriel said, handing his rifle to the Sergeant. "Take point."

"Yes, sir," Hafizi replied. He moved toward the transport beam with the squad. They stepped inside, seeming to dematerialize as they did.

"That's some serious voodoo," Theodore said.

"Voodoo?" Tea'va replied.

"I'll explain later." He rolled into the light and vanished.

Gabriel waited for Reza to go through, and then he joined them, stepping into the beam with Tea'va. He looked up, feeling a rush of something for just a second before it all stopped. He stepped forward, coming out into an identical corridor behind Delta Squad and the others. He was nearly hit in the face by an incoming plasma bolt as he did, finding them engaged by another group of clones. The Dread soldiers didn't have a shield to protect them, so they hid around the corners, popping out to attack. Hafizi's team returned fire when they did, keeping them honest. One of Delta's soldiers was down directly in front of Theodore's chair. The unfortunate crewman had likely saved his father's life.

"We must get down this corridor," Tea'va said. "There is a rear access channel to the bridge beyond that point. Even if Gr'el knows about it, which I doubt, it will be difficult to defend in numbers. We can use it to circumvent any defensive positions he has created."

"Maybe we can go another way?" Gabriel said, ducking down as another plasma bolt flew past.

"There is no other way, Heil'shur." The Dread smiled again. It was less alarming now that Gabriel had seen it a few times. "If we die, we die with honor. Yes?"

"Yeah. I guess so."

"You heard him," Theodore said. "We have to push forward and break through the defenses. This ain't no time to be yellow. Let's show these couillons who we are."

"Yes, sir," Hafizi replied. "Delta, we're going in."

The Sergeant took a step forward. A plasma bolt caught him right in the chest, making a sizzling noise as it burned into his flesh. The force of it knocked him to the ground, and he landed dead on his back.

Another soldier was hit a moment later, and he fell with a shout, coming to rest at Gabriel's feet. He heard Tea'va growl beside him, and then the Dread was rushing the enemy position again, pausing momentarily to grab Hafizi's fallen rifle.

"Gabriel," Theodore said. Gabriel looked at his father. He was holding his antique handgun out to him. "I can't roll and shoot at the same time, son. You've already made me prouder than any man has any right to be. Don't be afraid."

He knew what his father was suggesting. He didn't hesitate. There were no other choices left.

He grabbed the pistol, rushing down the hallway behind the Dread warrior.

[62]

THE VOLUME OF FIRE WAS INTENSE. PLASMA BOLTS STREAKED past Gabriel, and he did his best to use his skills as a pilot to try to throw the aim of the enemy soldiers, jerking side to side as he ran, following behind Tea'va. He could feel the heat of the energy going past his face, past his arms and legs. One bolt caught the edge of his shoulder, and he clenched his teeth at the burn of it on his arm. He didn't let it slow him. Somehow, some way, he was going to make it through the barrage. They hadn't come this far to lose now.

Tea'va paced ahead of him, moving so much faster than a human. He dropped as he neared the enemy position, sliding forward on his back toward the thick of it. One of the clones rose to track him, and Gabriel aimed and fired, the kick of the gun nearly pulling it from his hand. The shot hit the clone in the arm, the force enough to spin him around. A second clone broke cover and took aim at Gabriel. Gabriel managed to swing the ancient pistol back toward the enemy, pulling the trigger and watching as the clone's entire chest exploded out from the force of the impact.

The rest of the enemy soldiers were down by the time he reached them, with Tea'va standing in the center.

"Much respect, Heil'shur," Tea'va said.

"Much respect," Gabriel replied.

The others caught up to them a moment later. His father, Reza, and the two remaining soldiers, Corporals Kilani and Bush.

"Nice work, Major," Theodore said.

"Thank you, sir," Gabriel replied.

"This way," Tea'va said. "Do not delay."

They resumed their frantic pace through the fortress, passing a number of empty corridors and sealed doors until they reached what looked to Gabriel to be a solid wall. Tea'va waved his hand in front of it, and a previously invisible hatch slid open.

"In here," he said.

Gabriel leaned in. The passage was small and narrow.

Too narrow for his father to follow.

"That isn't going to work," Gabriel said.

Tea'va moved back out into the corridor, his expression confused at first until his eyes landed on Theodore. Again, Gabriel thought he caught a flash of anger from the Dread, but he wasn't sure.

"Come," he said, quickly crossing to a closed door. It slid open ahead of him, revealing a bare room with only a small bed against the wall. "Your Dahm can wait for us here. It will be safe."

"What?" Gabriel said. "I'm not leaving him behind. Forget it. Find another way, Tea'va."

"There is no other way, Heil'shur. There are only five of us, and still many dozens of soldiers blocking our path to the bridge. Gr'el may know this route, but there is a second further down that I am sure he does not. We must take the first to reach the second, and if your Dahm cannot follow, then he must remain."

"No," Gabriel said. "I'm not leaving him."

"Excuse me, Major," Theodore said. "That isn't your call."

"General," Gabriel said.

"I appreciate that you care, Gabe, but I'm an Old Gator, and not suited for this kind of mission. We both know that. You need to leave me here. If Tea'va says it's safe, then it's safe. I need you to go and get me that bridge. That's an order, Major."

Gabriel gritted his teeth. He didn't like it at all, but orders were orders.

"Yes, sir," he said. He held out the antique pistol. "At least take this."

"No. You might need it. Nobody's going to come and check this little cubby hole of a room for a human with no legs. I'll be perfectly fine. Capture the bridge, and then come back and get me, okay?"

Gabriel withdrew the gun. "Okay." More words flowed to the tip of his tongue, and he was tempted to hold them back. He didn't want any regrets. "I love you, Dad."

Theodore smiled. "I love you too, Gabe. Go and make your mother proud."

"Yes, sir."

"Uh, sir," Reza said. "If you don't mind, I think I'd rather stay here with you."

"Go ahead and take a seat, Mr. Mokri," Theodore replied. "Good hunting, Major. Good hunting all of you."

Gabriel backed out of the room. The hatch slid closed in front of him. He turned to Tea'va. "Okay. Let's go."

Tea'va stared at him for a moment. He seemed confused by the exchange, but he didn't say anything. He brought them back to the hatch, waving them in once more. As soon as they were all inside, the hatch closed, bathing them in near complete darkness.

"I can't see anything," Corporal Kalani said.

"Me neither," Gabriel replied. "Tea'va, how are we supposed to do this blind?"

"I can see, Heil'shur. Put your hand along the wall and follow my voice."

Gabriel put his hand out, touching the side of the passage. The material tingled against his fingertips, as though it were holding an electrical charge. Based on what he had learned of the Dread's shields, maybe it was.

"The wall will curve slightly as we move ahead. Then it will continue straight for some distance. Move as quickly as you can."

Gabriel followed Tea'va's voice, letting the Dread guide them through the passage. They reached the end a few minutes later, with no sign of any opposition.

"Curious," Gabriel thought he heard Tea'va say beneath his breath. It didn't seem that he was expecting to make it this far without being attacked.

A new door slid open and light filtered into the space once more. Gabriel squinted his eyes against it, giving them a moment to adjust. Tea'va's form faded into view beyond the bright light.

"We cross here, to there. This route will evacuate a short distance in front of the bridge. You must adjust to the light quickly."

"We'll do the best we can," Gabriel said.

Tea'va opened the second door and once more directed them in. They followed him, using his voice to make their way through the maintenance corridor. Again, they reached their destination without interruption.

"I do not know what waits beyond this door," Tea'va whispered to him. "The bridge will be on your right. I expect Gr'el's defenses to be organized to the left, most likely clones hiding behind lek'shah shields. Or perhaps he has gathered the few drumhr warriors who were loyal to him here. We will only have a few seconds to use the surprise to our advantage, but they will be vulnerable from behind. Do you understand?"

"Yes," Gabriel said. He tightened his grip on his father's gun. "We're ready."

He could hear Tea'va shift ahead of him. A moment later, the door slid open, and the light began filtering in again. Gabriel squinted his eyes to fight through the blinding glare, moving out into the corridor and turning to the left, aiming the pistol, ready to begin shooting whatever was there in the back.

Except there was nothing there. No fortifications. No soldiers. No shields.

He heard Tea'va mutter something foreign behind him, the Dread's tone of voice surprised and confused. He clearly hadn't been expecting this either.

The door behind them slid open. Gabriel turned toward it just in time to see two plasma bolts fire from behind it, one striking Corporal Kalani, the other hitting Corporal Bush. Both soldiers dropped to the floor.

Then a dozen plasma rifles were trained on them, held not by the clone soldiers Gabriel had seen below, but by two other types of clones. Both were female. One was heavyset, with large breasts and hips and a plump face. The other was like the one he had seen on Earth. The spitting image of his mother.

He felt a chill tingle down his spine at the sight of the four identical copies of Juliet St. Martin. They were each wearing long, dark robes, their hair tied back and up. One of them was wearing a shimmering blue pin, and from the way she stood it was clear she was superior to the others.

He was so surprised by them that he didn't notice the Dread standing in the center of them right away. He was a larger, uglier version of Tea'va, his skin lighter, his hair longer, the bony ridges across his head more prominent. he reminded Gabriel of an image Theodore had shown him once of a real alligator.

"Tea'va," the Dread warrior said in thick English. "I would despise you so much more if you weren't so predictable."

[63]

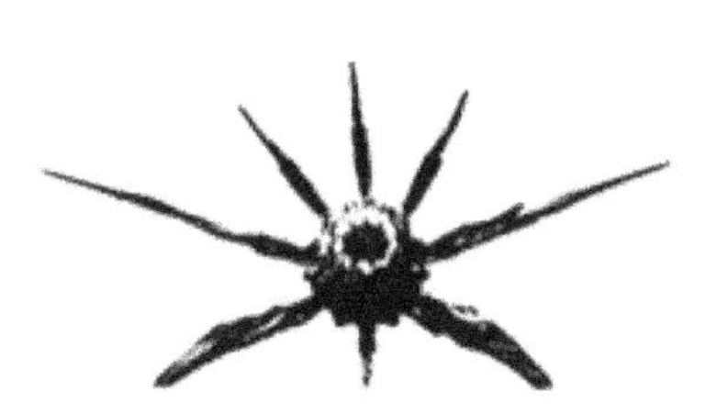

"Gr'el," Tea'va said. "What have you done?"

"What do you mean?" the Dread asked.

"You know what I mean. The Mothers."

"The Mothers are a tool, Tea'va. Like all tools, it only takes a creative mind to find different uses for them. Do you like what I've done with mine?"

"The Domo'dahm-"

"The Domo'dahm has no dominion out here, Tea'va. You know that."

"He trusted you."

"He didn't trust you. He told me that you would plot against him the moment you were out of Earth's orbit. That you were too human, and that humanity would lead you to resent him and the other pur'-dahm for our superiority. He tasked me with removing you quietly, which I have tried to do. Honor and respect for your ability to evade capture, but you are the lowest of the lor'el for running instead of retiring yourself."

"You don't seek to remove me on the wishes of the Domo'dahm. You are plotting to overthrow him yourself, to return with this ship and an army of lor'hai." He thrust his finger out at the Mothers. "Their minds are unfit for the Soldier programming."

"They have taken to it rather well," the Juliet clone with the blue pin said.

"Better than I had hoped," Gr'el said. "In any case, none of that is your concern, Tea'va. You are nothing now. You no longer exist to the bek'hai."

"I am the future of our race," Tea'va said.

"No. You are the mistake of an overzealous scientist who took the human genome too far. Rorn'el allowed you to survive because of your potential to reproduce naturally. But you denied the one thing that set you apart, the one thing that might have put you back into his favor, especially after your repeated failures against the Heil'shur." Gr'el looked at Gabriel for the first time. "Honor and respect to a worthy adversary," he said, bowing. "I am Gr'el, Dahm of the Ishur."

Gabriel didn't respond to the greeting. He was trying to put together the pieces of the Dread's conversation, to understand the complete picture of what was really happening on the fortress. He was starting to feel as though for all of their efforts, and for every member of the crew they had lost, their offensive was inconsequential to the infighting that appeared to be going on. Maybe it was. Gr'el had clearly been expecting Tea'va to lead them here. He had been waiting to get the drop on the traitor.

Tea'va was seething next to him, his teeth bared, his pale face darkened. "Mistake?" he hissed. "You owe me Hesh dur bek for words such as those."

"Honor of battle?" Gr'el said. "You have no honor, Tea'va. You surrendered. You agreed to retirement. You didn't even have the courage to go through with it."

"Who are you to speak of honor and courage? You betrayed me. Worse, you sent a Mother to assassinate me instead of trying to do it yourself. A Mother!"

Tea'va took a step forward. The clones raised their weapons, signaling their warning.

"Careful, Tea'va," Gr'el said. "The only reason I haven't killed you already is because I'm enjoying the embarrassment of your defeat. A Mother is all you are worth. I would never dirty my hands with you."

Tea'va's face gnarled in rage, but he stood his ground, drawing a laugh from the other Dread.

"Even now, you care too much for your life to honor it by attacking me." Gr'el looked over at Gabriel again. "You will make an excellent prize. I have no doubt your genetics are of superior quality. Zoelle, this one should be an improvement for the programming, should it not?"

The Juliet clone with the blue pin nodded. "Yes, my Dahm. The Heil'shur is assuredly of impressive genetic stock."

"You would know," Gabriel said. "Or rather the woman whose life was claimed in your making would know."

"What do you mean?" Gr'el asked.

"My name is Gabriel St. Martin," Gabriel said, feeling his hands clenching into fists. His initial fear of the situation was quickly changing to a cold anger. "My mother was Juliet St. Martin. Does that name mean anything to you?"

The Juliet clones all gasped as one. Gr'el seemed surprised as well, his inhuman smile growing even larger at the news. "You are a child of the un'hai? A natural born child? You are a more valuable prize than I could have ever imagined."

"I don't know what you've done to her," Gabriel said, his sudden anger exploding as he spoke. His hand came up, wrapping around the crucifix below his flight suit, clenching it tightly."You and your Domo'dick, or whatever you call him. My mother was kind and gentle, compassionate and intelligent. She wasn't a traitor. She wasn't a killer. She didn't use humankind like a toy to program to her whims, or anyone else's. She wasn't an inconsequential thing, or a tool to be used as a means to your own ends. You've twisted her memory into something foul. You've soiled everything she stood for. You son of a bitch."

He acted without thinking then, springing forward toward the Dread. Unlike Tea'va, he didn't care if that meant dying. The other clone of her he had met, Ehri, was helping the rebellion. She was fighting for humankind the way Juliet St. Martin would have. He didn't know how or why, but she was.

There had been no one to defend his mother's honor before.

There was now.

He got closer to Gr'el than he expected, almost reaching him before one of the Mothers came from the side, slamming him in the head with the butt of her rifle. He tumbled sideways onto the floor, a sharp pain in his jaw.

"Be careful, druk'shur," Gr'el shouted. "You'll damage him."

"My apologies, Dahm Gr'el," the clone replied, lowering her head.

Gabriel pushed himself into a seated position, clenching his teeth as he did. He looked back at Gr'el, and then beyond him to the Juliet clones. He froze when he noticed that Zoelle was staring right at him, a sudden look of concern on her face. It vanished a moment later.

Was he imagining things?

"And what do you intend to do with me?" Tea'va said.

Gr'el glanced over at Tea'va. "Are you still here?" He reached out, grabbing a rifle from one of the clones. "You've ceased being amusing, lor'el."

He pulled the trigger at the same time Gabriel hit his shoulder, sending the plasma bolt wide. Gr'el pivoted with the blow, swinging the weapon back around and slamming it hard into Gabriel's gut. Gabriel doubled over, the air stolen from his chest. He put his hand on the floor to steady himself. He had to get up. To keep fighting. His mother's memory demanded it.

He felt Gr'el's long fingers wrap around his neck. Then he was lifted off the ground, held by the throat and unable to breathe. It didn't matter what he wanted. His strength was vastly inferior to the Dread's.

"How dare you touch me," Gr'el growled, the pressure from his hands increasing. "I had forgotten how willful the un'hai was rumored to be, and what a poor pur'hai she was. It was only the Domo'dahm's weakness that allowed her to become so revered."

He let go. Gabriel fell to the ground again, gasping for air.

Gr'el aimed his rifle again, this time at Gabriel. "Honor and respect to you for your prowess in battle, Heil'shur. Your courage is commendable. I see now that you will be more trouble than you're worth. I would sooner destroy you and your fellow humans than have your lor'hai aboard my ship, or as part of my bek'hai empire."

"My. Name. Is. Gabriel St. Martin," Gabriel gasped, trying to stand again. "Son of Theodore and Juliet St. Martin. Remember that, asshole."

"Very well, Gabriel-"

A small fist came from Gr'el's left, hitting him square across the jaw with enough force to knock him to the ground. Gabriel's eyes darted to his attacker. The Juliet clone he had called Zoelle.

"You wanted your Hesh dur bek, Tea'va," she said. "Now is your chance."

[64]

"ZOELLE?" GR'EL SAID, HIS WORDS MUFFLED BY HIS BROKEN jaw. "Traitor. Kill her. Kill the Scientists."

The Mothers raised their rifles, turning them toward the Juliets.

Tea'va sprang at Gr'el, kicking him in the face before he could recover and sending him rolling across the floor.

Gabriel pushed aside his shock, forcing himself to his feet.

Zoelle turned on the closest Mother, punching her hard in the stomach, and then in the face, knocking her down.

The plasma followed, Mothers and Scientists shooting at one another at point-blank range. Gabriel didn't know what the difference was between like clones, but Zoelle not only held herself as superior, she clearly was. She danced to the side as a plasma bolt skimmed her robes, twirling and moving forward, grabbing the Mother's arms and lifting them, so the next shot went to the ceiling. She turned again, gathering the Mother's weight and pulling, throwing her over her shoulder while capturing her rifle. The Mother tried to get up, but couldn't before Zoelle shot her.

A second Mother was lining up a shot behind Zoelle. Gabriel stumbled forward, slamming into the clone and falling on top of her. She struggled beneath him while he tried to pin her arms. She pushed back, throwing him aside with a strength he couldn't believe.

It didn't matter. One of the Scientists was over her a moment later, firing down into her chest. She was killed before Gabriel could blink, caught with a plasma blast by a nearby enemy. That Mother went down in a shrill cry, hit by another plasma bolt, this one fired by Zoelle.

Gabriel got back to his feet, finding Gr'el and Tea'va squaring off a few meters away. The two Dread warriors circled one another, their teeth bared like animals, their hands out with fingers curled as if they were claws.

Then Gr'el moved in on Tea'va, his hands a blur as he made a series of quick strikes, slapping and punching at the other Dread. Tea'va moved in time to the attack, shifting his balance and either knocking aside the blows or adjusting to allow them to land harmlessly. He survived the onslaught before countering with a fury of his own, pushing back against Gr'el with a long series of kicks and punches that bore similarity to streams Gabriel had seen of human martial arts. The difference was in the power and quickness of the movements. The Dread were a blur as they attacked and counterattacked one another in near silence.

And then Tea'va seemed to get the better of Gr'el. He slipped behind his rival, locking a hand around his neck and an arm around his chest. The larger Dread writhed beneath the grip, trying to find purchase on the ground, trying to find leverage to turn the hold.

Tea'va grunted as he bent backward, lifting Gr'el from the ground. Gr'el tried to punch him from behind, landing ineffective blows against his sides. Gr'el also attempted to slam him in the face with the back of his head, but it was just out of reach.

"You are a disgrace to the bek'hai," Gr'el said, his voice growing weak. "There is no honor for you in this killing, Tea'va."

"I need no honor from you," Tea'va replied. "All I need is for you to expire. The true betrayal belongs to you and the Domo'dahm."

Gr'el tried to say something else, but couldn't manage it. He gurgled instead, and then shuddered one last time before falling still.

Tea'va dropped his corpse to the floor.

A silence fell over the ship. The battle between the clones was over as well. None of the Mothers were standing. Two of the Scientists remained, including Zoelle. She was walking toward him from his left. Tea'va was coming toward him from his right.

"Zoelle," Tea'va said.

She raised her hand to Tea'va, ignoring the Dread and locking eyes with Gabriel. "Gabriel St. Martin," she said, a tear running from her eye. "I am Zoelle dur Tuhrik, Dahm of the Ishur."

"You are not Dahm," Tea'va said. "Lor'hai cannot be Dahm."

She continued to ignore him. "My ship is yours, Gabriel. As is my life. It is an honor to meet the son of the un'hai."

She fell to her knees in front of him, bowing her head. The other Juliet clone did the same behind her.

Gabriel opened his mouth, catching himself before he called her mother. "I. I need you to call off the attack on my people," he said, finding it hard to breathe.

Zoelle looked back at the other clone, who headed off toward the bridge. "It will be done."

"You have no authority," Tea'va said.

Gabriel turned on the Dread. "What are your intentions, Tea'va?" he snapped. "You pledged yourself to me to help you get revenge, and now you have it. Will you betray me as he betrayed you? If so, do it now."

Once more, Gabriel thought he saw the hint of anger in the Dread's expression. Once more, it faded in an instant. Tea'va didn't attack him. Instead, he lowered his head.

"My apologies, Gabriel St. Martin."

Gabriel turned back to Zoelle. "Please. Stand up. You saved my life. You saved my crew. You saved my father. You never have to lower your head to me."

Zoelle looked up, her eyes moist. "Did you say your father? He is here?"

"Yes."

"I should very much like to meet him."

[65]

"It was simple really, General," Reza said. "The Dread modulation follows a predefined pattern loosely based on rudimentary quantum physics and string theory. Once Guy and I broke down the pattern, we were able to work out an equation to describe how to alter it to defeat the modulation. What I'm not clear about is why the Dread use the technology the way they do. It's as if they figured out the most basic principles of phasing, and decided to stop there. Although, I guess it could have something to do with the resources they have available. The use of organic matter has some clear benefits, but it also has some well-defined drawbacks, especially concerning variability. Do you-"

"Mr. Mokri," Theodore said, glancing over at the scientist. "Can you please pipe it for a minute or two? Gabriel is out there, and so are my people. I'm worried sick about all of them, and I'm too damn old and too damn incapacitated to help out. Do you have any idea what that's like?"

Reza stopped talking. "I'm sorry, General. I talk when I get nervous."

"Understood, but that's the fourth time I've had to ask. The next time, I'm not going to be polite."

"Yes, sir."

Theodore looked away, back toward the door. He knew Reza was going to start up again. It was in the boy's blood. In part it was annoying. In part, it was comforting. At least he wasn't here alone.

It had been nearly an hour since Gabriel had left him in the small room. It was a long time. Too long as far as he was concerned. He was afraid his son was dead, his crew lost. He had been tempted to go out there more times than he could count.

Every part of him wanted to be doing something active, something useful. Every part of him knew it would be a mistake.

His value was in his mind, and in his skill at the command of a starship. His days as a foot soldier had been over long before he had destroyed his legs.

And how the hell would Gabriel find him if he left the room, anyway?

He closed his eyes, his lips moving in another prayer that Gabriel would come through that door again, and sometime soon. He was afraid for him, and at the same time, he had that feeling in his gut that he was still out there. Still alive. He held onto it, refusing to let it go. Gabriel was a better man than he had ever been. He was the best of him and Juliet. He would be okay.

Once they took the ship, once Tea'va showed them how to fly it, he would use it to return to Calawan. Alan couldn't ignore him then. He would have no choice but to organize the troops, and to pour every resource into preparing to return home. They would use what Guy and Sarah and Reza had discovered to build better defenses and better weapons. They would return to Earth as the Dread had arrived.

Completely unstoppable.

He smiled at the thought. He had promised her he would go back. That he would find a way to save them.

The smile vanished. Only if Gabriel survived. Only if they managed to win. Had he saved them by flying the Magellan into the Dread fortress or had he sealed their fate?

He wanted a resolution. An answer to the question.

He wanted Gabriel back.

"It's too quiet in here," he said. "What else you got stewing in that brain of yours, Mr. Mokri?"

"You just told me to shut up, sir."

"And now I'm telling you to talk."

"Okay. Well, I was just thinking a little bit more about the organic compounds we found in the Dread rifle. Of course, the composition is nothing we have on Earth, but the thing is that any organic compound will break down over time. Decompose. The compounds in the rifle looked relatively fresh."

"Meaning what?"

"Meaning that wherever they came from, the Dread must have a source somewhere."

"Like a farm?"

Reza laughed. "Yes, sir. In a sense. Although it is more likely that they grow the organic materials from stem cells. That would be more logical, considering the-"

A knock sounded from the other side of the wall. A simple rhythm that Theodore knew instantly. He was already beaming by the time the door slid open and he saw Gabriel standing there, unharmed and smiling along with him.

"Gabriel," Theodore said. He couldn't remember the last time he had been as excited about anything. Probably the day he had met Juliet. "Thank God."

Gabriel entered the room, leaning down and wrapping his arms around him. "We did it, Dad. The ship is ours."

"I'd say I don't believe it, son, but I always had faith in you."

Gabriel stood up. Theodore could tell right away that there was something off about him.

"What is it?" he asked.

"Uh. Dad, I. I'm not sure about this."

"About what?"

Gabriel's face was flushing. "Just try to stay calm, okay?"

"Damn it, boy, what the hell are you talking about? You want me to stay calm, and you're getting me all worked up with your beating around the bayou."

Gabriel stepped aside.

Everything stopped.

Memories flooded Theodore at the sight of her. So many memories. The day they met. Their first kiss. That day on the beach. The first time they made love. Their first house. The cat she had named Bobo because she thought the way he said it was funny, and it stayed funny that darn kit's entire life. It was as though he relived it all in a single breath.

Juliet. He had spent the last fifty years longing to see her alive one more time. Wanting to look at her face, to see into eyes that could see him back. He felt the tears come, sliding down his cheeks as he stared at the woman in front of him. In the back of his mind, he knew she wasn't the real thing. He knew she was a clone. For a moment, it didn't matter.

"Juliet," he whispered.

She came to him, kneeling beside him with tears on her face, and a smile that he would have known anywhere. A smile he had missed more than anything in the universe.

"Theodore," she said, putting soft hands on his. Hands that tingled at the touch. "It's been so long. I thought I would never see you again."

"What?" he heard Gabriel say behind her.

"It's me," she said, her voice as beautiful and soothing as he remembered. "It's your Juliet. I always knew you would keep your promise. I always knew you would come back. I've prepared them for you.

The Domo'dahm has no idea what he has done."

3. TIDES OF WAR

[1]

Lex'el dur Rorn'el crouched behind an outcropping of broken masonry. He lifted his arm, checking the levels in his oxygen tanks, and then turned his attention to his quarry.

The humans and the un'hai had found a hiding place beneath the twisted metal of one of their simplistic structures, a place marked by a pair of overlapping, symmetrical red lines. It had been destroyed by one of the gur'shah at least a dozen years ago, probably more, the floors collapsed, leaving a small area where the same gur'shah could now remain out of view of the sky.

The Hunter had seen the battle that had won the mechs for the humans. He respected them for their victory, at the same time he despised them for his kind's defeat. It was all well. They would be removed from their so-called rebellion soon.

Today.

Nine days had passed since he had set out to track them. Nine days since he had access to more than a taste of fresh oxygen, as he sought to stretch himself to the limits of his genetic capabilities. Their speed had made following difficult, but their need to hide from passing gi'shah had given him the time he needed to catch up.

And he had caught up. Every daybreak for the last six days. It had meant moving at full speed and barely pausing to rest, but that was the investment required of a Hunter if it wished to catch its prey. It was an investment too few of his pur'dahm brothers were willing to make, choosing the easy kill instead of the true challenge.

It was the reason he was the best of them.

It was the reason he had lived when the others had not.

He moved slowly, methodically, shifting from one position behind the wall to another beside it, peering out at the makeshift camp. Every day had been the same for the humans. They would set up their camp at dawn, finding a place to hide in the ruins of their former civilization. Then they would vanish into the ped'ek, all except a guard, to eat and to sleep. Occasionally, one of them would evacuate the transport to void somewhere nearby, usually before they assumed the guard's duty.

He had never considered attacking them while they did. Perhaps other Hunters might have, but he believed it to be dishonorable. A disgrace. No. He wanted the advantage, as any good Hunter would. But he also needed the humans to have a chance to fight back. There was no glory in killing something that had no means to defend itself.

That was why he had waited so long, watching from a distance for hours as the humans made their camp. He had tracked them hundreds of kilometers as they traveled north. He wasn't completely sure where they were headed, but he had an idea. While the Domo'dahm had been shattering bands of resistance in the north for weeks, there were still reports that a few of the larger groups had managed to evade them, hiding below the ground like druk'kek.

He believed their intent was to rendezvous with these forces, to lend the strength of the bek'hai weaponry to their cause. If the humans were half as intelligent as he was, they would begin attacking other smaller bek'hai outposts from there and work to capture more and more of their technology to use against them.

It was a plan he was going to enjoy ruining. Considering it now, he couldn't help but smile. That was the glory of the Hunter. His glory. The Domo'dahm would surely move him near the front of the cell for singlehandedly ending the largest threat the humans had ever mounted.

His father was certain to be doubly pleased with the death of Ehri dur Tuhrik. The un'hai had always been more willful than the other lor'hai, but her actions were beyond willfulness. It was treachery and disloyalty, with no room for argument. She had betrayed her people, and she was directly responsible for the deaths of his fellow Hunters.

He would be sure to kill her last.

He scanned the camp one last time. The guard posted outside was an older male. Lex'el had seen him during the battle. He had led the charge into the compound, and if his fellow Hunter's deaths were any indication, he had comported himself well. His courage was respectable. Yes. He would be a good one to begin with.

He ducked back behind the wall, reaching down and sliding his lek'sai from his back. He eyed the blades thoughtfully for a moment, before looking out from behind the wall once more. The man was looking away from him, toward another line of destruction, apparently intrigued by something he saw there.

He looked in that direction as well, curious to know what it was.

Then he began running back to the ped'ek, opening the hatch and vanishing inside. Lex'el raised his arm and checked his sensors, hissing as he recognized pur'dahm Fior'el's sigil.

Nine days. That druk'shur had nine days to find the humans and make his attack. He was certain Fior'el's resources must have happened on their position by accident. He had watched how the humans hid from the sortics. It was simple and effective, and no doubt guided by Ehri.

Unless...

He put his other hand on the display, moving his fingers to change the screens, cursing at himself for his stupidity. He tapped the screen violently, shutting down his own transponder.

He hadn't expected any of the pur'dahm would be capable enough to think to track his movements instead of the enemy's.

He leaned back against the wall, closing his eyes. There was nothing for him to do now but wait. He opened a valve on his tank, taking a long breath of pure oxygen, feeling the tingle as it moved through his system. He could only afford to give himself one.

"Do not disappoint me, Ehri dur Tuhrik," he said as he listened for the attack to begin.

It was his glory on the line.

[2]

"GET YOUR LAZY ASSES UP AND MOVING, PEOPLE," KROEGER shouted as he entered the confines of the transport. "We've got not-very-friendlies incoming, and I don't really feel much like dying today."

Major Donovan Peters' eyes snapped open, and he turned his head to where the older man was standing, his neck muscles taut as he released a spew of curses while reaching for one of the bek'hai rifles.

"Don't just lay there like a sack of shit, Major," Kroeger said, noticing him. "Get your tail over to that ugly ass hunk of steel and go kick some tail."

Donovan pushed himself up, shaking the sleep away. He couldn't have been out for more than a few minutes. Had the Dread been following them and waiting for them to settle down for the day?

"Kroeger, take Thompson and Mendez and find some high ground," he said as the rest of his team came alert. Ehri, Soon, you're with me."

"Yes, sir," they all said, gathering themselves.

Kroeger tossed a rifle to both Thompson and Mendez. "Let's go, ladies and gents. We aren't getting paid for this, which means it's our asses on the line."

Then Kroeger was out the door, with the others right behind him.

"They were following us?" Donovan asked as Ehri moved beside him.

"It seems that way," she replied, though something in her expression gave him the feeling she wasn't convinced. "It can't be a large force, or we would have noticed."

"If they call in air support, we're going to be in trouble in a hurry."

"They won't."

Donovan nodded. He had learned a lot about how the bek'hai waged war over the last couple of weeks. Their system was an odd mix of both caste and meritocracy, where the elite caste, the pur'-dahm, fought one another for positioning and power while at the same time seeking to fulfill the Domo'dahm's directives. What that meant for them was that any attacks against them would come from a single pur'dahm looking to gain rank and glory within that system. While the bek'hai elite would use whatever resources he had to achieve the objective, the last thing he would do would be to ask another for assistance. It was a major weakness on the part of the Dread.

A weakness they had exploited during their raid on the smaller bek'hai compound.

A weakness he hoped they could exploit again now.

They spilled out of the transport with Donovan in the lead. A plasma bolt struck the side of the ped'ek a meter from his head when he did, and he turned to see a return bolt vanish into the line of distant rubble as one of their infantry fired back.

"Move faster, Major," Kroeger shouted from somewhere out of sight.

Donovan pushed himself harder, breaking around the back of the transport, using it as cover as he reached the stolen enemy mech. He scaled the side of it, making it to the chest and putting his hand on a small, hidden control there. The cockpit swung open, and he pulled himself inside.

He leaned back, quickly activating the toggles that would start the vehicle's power supply and get it moving. In front of him, alien text surrounded a view of the world outside. He didn't know what most of it meant, and he didn't need to. The important part was universal - a blue reticle in the center of the HUD that showed him where his weapons were going to hit.

He flipped another switch, and a brace dropped over him, securing him to the rear of the cockpit and lowering a pair of joysticks. Each one was attached to rotating joints that mimicked the arms of the mech and provided all the controls for both upper body rotation and offense. His legs were kept free, tracked by sensors that would translate their movement into the bipedal motion of the mechanized armor.

It was all fairly rudimentary; primitive compared to other bek'hai technology. The Dread evolution had forced them to abandon the original control system that utilized a gel-filled capsule and a symbiotic neural network to transfer commands. They had replaced it with manual controls that could be used by the more human drumhr, who had lost the ability to communicate with the symbiotes.

It was nowhere near as efficient, but combined with invincible shields, it was just as effective.

"Rebel One, online," he said, activating the mech's comm system.

He continued to be grateful that the three mechs they had taken from the Dread compound had all been linked together, giving them the ability to coordinate their defense.

"Rebel Two, online," Ehri said a moment later.

"Rebel Three, online," Soon said.

"Let's keep an eye out for targets and stay cautious," Donovan said. "We need to know what we're up against before we do anything stupid."

"Yes, sir," Soon said.

The plasma bolts continued raining in, slipping harmlessly past the mech's shields and burning away at the armor below. Each of the mechs was already pockmarked from what amounted to small arms fire and would be able to take a lot more damage before it succumbed to limited attacks. Donovan knew instinctively that the trailing edge of the offensive would be clone soldiers, heavy in numbers and highly expendable. If the Dread in charge of the attack had any intelligence at all, he would use them as a diversion while he tried to flank their position with his armors.

"Okay, Rebels. We're heading north together. We don't want to get caught in a crossfire."

"Roger," Soon and Ehri replied.

Donovan started moving, walking as though he were standing outside on the ground. The mech began to move the same way, its left shifting and coming down, pressing him forward into an even gait as he moved the machine out from cover and around the hospital, with Ehri and Soon right behind him.

"Rebel Three, rotate right, lay some cover fire for the infantry," he said.

"Roger," Soon replied, turning the top half of his mech and firing a pair of thick plasma bolts into the field. They slammed into the side of a crumbling wall, quieting the smaller attacks.

Donovan looked ahead of them. They were moving deeper into the small town, where more destroyed buildings were waiting. They had chosen the hospital because it was the best cover to be found, and none of the other ruined structures came up higher than the mechs' knees.

It left him uncomfortable as they cleared the safety of the larger building. He didn't see any opposition ahead of them, but he didn't expect that to last.

It didn't.

The enemy forces moved out from behind the more distant buildings, in smaller vehicles Donovan hadn't seen before. They had a loose resemblance to tanks, with angled carapaces and a larger barrel that emerged from it, surrounded by four smaller ones. There were at least a dozen in all, floating slightly above the ground and nearly silent.

"Gel'shah," Ehri said. "The plasma cannon is the most powerful the bek'hai carry on the ground. Do not let it hit you."

No sooner had she spoken than a stream of plasma bolts launched from the tanks, coming toward them in a deadly line.

Donovan watched the trajectory, getting his legs going and moving the mech forward as quickly as he could. He ducked as the screen brightened from the combined firepower, cringing slightly as the blue pulses passed over his head. He hoped Ehri and Soon had managed to evade the assault as well.

The plasma slammed into the hospital behind them a moment later with a burning hiss followed by the crashing of the already damaged floors as they finished giving way.

"I hope Kroeger wasn't in there," Soon said, witnessing the result of the assault.

"It looks like the transport is buried," Ehri replied.

"Damn," Donovan said. "Let's spread out a bit and make it harder for them to concentrate their fire."

"Yes, sir," Soon replied, his mech sidestepping away.

The Dread tanks released a second volley. Again, the mechs ducked beneath it, letting the rounds hit whatever debris was beyond them. It was easier to move aside right now. It wouldn't be once they got closer.

"Rebel Two, Can we take them out from here?" Donovan asked.

"No, Major," Ehri replied. "The armor is too thick. We need to get closer."

"How do you usually take these things on?"

"Gori'shah. Starfighters."

"I knew you were going to say that."

Donovan ducked under the third volley. There was a fifteen-second delay between attacks, presumably while the plasma cannon recharged. The closer they came to the tanks, the better their timing would need to be.

"Keep the rhythm. They need fifteen seconds to recharge. Try to burst forward while they do."

He followed his own advice, sending the mech dashing forward, crashing through damaged mortar and stone before slowing and dropping the mech into a crouch. Ehri and Soon did the same, and the fourth volley passed less than a meter beyond their heads.

"I felt that one," Soon said.

"Rebel Two, are we in range?" Donovan asked.

"Almost, Major," Ehri replied.

He could see the tanks more clearly now. They were backing up and spreading apart, clearly understanding their limitations.

One of the symbols on Donovan's HUD turned red as something hit him from the rear, burning into the mech's armor but not piercing it.

"Gur'shah," Ehri said. "Three of them."

The other side of the pincer. Donovan had been hoping to stay ahead of it, but it wasn't meant to be. "How the hell did they find us?" he hissed. "We managed to avoid them for days." He paused to regain his composure and think. "Rebel Two, can you deal with the rear?"

"I will do my best, Major."

"Rebel Three, break left. I'll go right. Let's see if we can give as good as we're getting."

"Yes, sir," Soon replied.

Donovan steered his mech away from the tanks, using the debris as cover while he tried to flank them and at the same time offering a smaller profile for their plasma bolts to strike. He continued to time the attacks, counting after each blast, using the time as best he could.

He glanced to the corner of his HUD. He knew the larger battle was displayed there, and Ehri's mech was a green shape moving ahead of the three red ones. Smaller dots lined the area to his rear, in the form of the Dread foot soldiers. It took him a few seconds to find Kroeger in the midst of the chaos, three small black dots clustered near the middle of the action. They weren't in a good position, having gotten pinned down there.

"Rebel One, I'm in position," Soon said a moment later, surprising Donovan.

Had he made it around already?

"Prepare to engage," Donovan said.

"Yes, sir."

Donovan ducked the mech behind some rubble, and then rose and faced the tanks.

"Engage," he said, tapping the triggers on the twin joysticks.

Plasma bolts launched from the mech, slamming hard into one of the tanks. The armored side melted, but the armor continued to move, trying to get him in front of its cannon.

He fired again, not wasting any time. He could feel the heat rise in the cockpit as his mech spewed another stream of energy at the tank. It was another direct hit, and it left the tank slagged and silent.

"Rebel Two, how are you holding up back there?" Donovan asked, dropping his mech as another blast passed over him.

"These pilots are druk. I am not surprised. They are carrying the sigil of Fior'el."

"That sounds good for us."

"It is very good for us, Major. Fior'el is from a low cell. This may be his entire militarized pool."

"You're saying he sent his whole army after us?"

"There is a great reward waiting for whichever pur'dahm destroys us. It is a dangerous risk on his part, but worth it, I suppose. I am more concerned with the fact that he knew where we were hiding. It should not have been possible."

"Let's get ourselves safe first, and then we can figure that out."

"Yes, Major."

Donovan unleashed another plasma beam at the scattering tanks, hitting a second as it tried to reverse course. "Take that," he said as it began to smoke. He glanced at his HUD. Soon was holding his own, having already destroyed four of the tanks to his two. Damn, he was good.

He rotated his torso, seeking another target.

A ball of plasma hit his right arm. The impact of it almost

knocked him over, forcing him to scramble to keep the mech upright. The HUD flashed, and a warning tone sounded in the cockpit. Donovan checked the damage by moving the right-hand controls, and finding the arm didn't move with it.

He shook his head, backing away as he counted the seconds. He had gotten too aggressive, and now one of their best assets was damaged. Stupid.

He kept a closer eye on the HUD, watching the movement of the different units his sensors were detecting. He retreated toward Kroeger's position, firing back at the tanks as they also retreated. When Soon's mech passed in front of him, he turned around and unleashed a volley of slugs toward the Dread clones, chewing their front line to pieces.

Kroeger would owe him for saving his life. Again.

"It looks like they're retreating, Major," Soon said, blasting one of the remaining tanks. The others had been backing up, but now they accelerated, trying to escape the battlefield.

"Let them go," Donovan said, releasing his finger from the trigger. He had to continue firing a moment later, as the clones surprised him by pressing their attack. "What the hell? They can't win."

The main forces might have been retreating, but the pur'dahm, Fior'el, continued throwing his clones at them. Donovan felt sick as he kept shooting, cutting them down one after another. There was nothing glorious or honorable about sending these soldiers to slaughter.

"It is the way of the pur'dahm," Ehri said. "Especially Fior'el. Lek'shah resources are limited. Clones are not."

It was disgusting, no matter the reason. He tried to look away as his slugs tore through human bodies, knocking down soldier after soldier until his conscience couldn't take it anymore. He stopped firing, leaving a handful of the clones standing.

"Enough," he said, releasing the controls. He wanted to vomit.

The few remaining clones stopped shooting, standing in the middle of the field, looking at one another, confused. The confusion was interrupted when a series of plasma bolts fired from the ground cut across the field, striking each in turn.

Kroeger stepped out from behind a wall and looked up at him as if he could sense the reluctance to kill. Then he walked over to one of the dead clones and spat on it. He looked back up at Donovan, and sat down on top of the body, waiting.

[3]

"Do you have to sit there like that?" Donovan asked.

"I don't think he minds," Kroeger replied, patting the dead soldier on his bloody rear. "Do you?" He laughed harshly. "Kill or be killed, Major. It's an adage as old as time."

"You could show a little respect."

"For this thing? Why the hell would I? It isn't human. It isn't any different than those machines you blasted. Smaller scale, different materials. That's all."

"They are human," Donovan replied. "They have human DNA. They have individual personalities."

"Well, boo-hoo. If those individual personalities came with the smarts to not walk into the line of fire, maybe you could convince me, and that's a pretty large maybe. Until they stop following every order no matter how asinine it is, not matter how unfair it is, I'm not going to give a shit when they die."

They were standing near the center of the broken city. The smell of blood and burning metal and flesh was thick around them. There was no sign of Fior'el's army. Not any more. The four remaining tanks had retreated along with one badly damaged mech, the pur'd-ham's forces routed in the sneak attack.

Ehri returned from the hospital with Mendez a moment later, her expression dark.

"The collapse damaged the ped'ek, Major," she said. "It is no longer operational."

"What about the contents?"

"We can retrieve them."

"At least it isn't all bad news."

"No, Major."

"Looks like we're humping it the rest of the way," Kroeger said. "That's fine by me. How many kilos until Austin?"

"Three hundred," Ehri said.

"Not bad at all. Hey, what was with that bullshit attack anyway?"

"What do you mean?"

"I mean, they had three mechs to our three, fine. Even Steven. Bastards had a dozen tanks and almost five hundred infantry. You would think that would tip the odds in their favor a little bit. Excuse me if I'm wrong, but we wiped the floor with them." He kicked his chair in the side for emphasis.

"The bek'hai factories are only able to output so much in a given amount of time. The lek'shah especially is very difficult to produce. The lower a pur'dahm is in the cells, the longer he has to wait for these resources."

"Okay, but aren't all clones the same? Equally skilled assholes?"

"If that were true, I would not be standing here. You forget that I am also a clone, Kroeger."

"That's because you've got a mind of your own, and you're easy to look at. Makes it easy to forget. Right, Major?" He gave her a crooked smile, while Donovan felt his face heating up at the comment. "Yeah, so you're saying he gets the rejects?"

"Basically."

Kroeger laughed, patting the corpse on the back. "You hear that, buddy? You're a reject."

"Enough," Donovan said. "Get off him."

Kroeger glanced up at Donovan, raising his eyebrow.

"You wanted to be part of this," Donovan reminded him.

Kroeger stood up. "Yes, sir. I forget myself sometimes."

"The bigger concern is that a pur'dahm with an army of rejects, as you so eloquently put it, was able to track us here while no others, including the Domo'dahm, have. Fior'el is not unintelligent. There is more to this than it seems."

"Like what?" Donovan asked.

"I'm not sure yet," Ehri replied. "It is possible we are being hunted."

"No offense, darling," Kroeger said. "But, duh."

"Hunted, Kroeger. Not chased. By a pur'dahm Hunter."

"Like the ones we encountered at the base? The ones who were about to decapitate you?" Donovan looked right at Kroeger.

"I was setting him up," Kroeger said.

"Yeah, to kill you," Mendez replied.

"If you're right, that means he's out there right now," Donovan said.

Kroeger's eyebrow went up again. "Watching us?"

Ehri nodded. "If I am right."

"We should take him out."

"You are welcome to try. Any Hunter that has been keeping pace with us is no reject. He will be of a high cell, and extremely skilled."

"Yeah? If he's been following us, why hasn't he done us in yet?"

"The time has not been right."

"What the hell does that mean?"

"Does it matter?" Donovan said. "Ehri, what do you suggest we do?"

"When you are the Hunter's prey, there isn't much you can do except defend yourself when he attacks. I will try to bring him out to parlay."

"You want to talk to him?"

"Perhaps I can convince him to give up the hunt."

"You really think so?" Kroeger asked.

"I don't know. What I can tell you is that he was keeping pace with us before we lost the ped'ek. Now he will have time to rest, time to recover and gain strength before he makes his move. We have a slight advantage because we know he is here, and can catch him off guard."

"By talking? Why don't we just scour the earth with our, what do you call them? Grrrr-shah?" He emphasized the first part like a growl. "Plasma talks pretty loud."

"We can't blanket the entire city," Donovan said.

"And we don't have time to sit here all day," Soon said. "I imagine the rest of the bek'hai will figure out what happened here soon enough."

"Soon is right," Ehri said.

"Fine. But I don't see what yapping is going to do for us? He'd be an idiot just to decide to go away if he thinks he can take us out."

"I do not expect him just to go away," Ehri said. She turned to Donovan. "Major? Will you put your faith in me?"

"I have so far."

"I will go out to engage him. He will not dishonor himself by attacking me. Even so, we should be ready to move, in case more pur'-dahm forces are nearby and wish to take advantage of Fior'el's failure."

"Okay," Donovan said. "Mendez, take Ehri's mech. Kroeger, Thompson, these cockpits are tight, but let's head back to the transport and stuff as many weapons into them as we can fit."

"Yes, sir," they said.

He approached Ehri, putting his hand on her shoulder. "Be careful."

She nodded. "I will, Major."

He retreated to his mech, climbing up and into the cockpit. He watched her back through the HUD as she began winding her way through the destruction. Then he got the mech moving again, back to the side of the hospital. The transport was nearly buried beneath a portion that had collapsed across it, leaving only half of the opening into it exposed.

Kroeger paused in front of him to survey it, said something to Thompson that Donovan couldn't hear, and then the two soldiers crawled inside.

"He's a piece of work, isn't he, Major?" Soon said.

"You can say that again."

"You worried about Ehri, Major?"

He rotated the mech's torso back the way she had gone, but she had disappeared from view.

"You can say that again."

[4]

Lex'el dur Rorn'el watched the line of gel'shah retreating from the field. His breathing was sharp and thick as he tried to contain his rage at Fior'el for interrupting his hunt. No. For doing more than interrupting it.

For ruining it.

He had hoped that Ehri and the humans would win the battle because the thought of that pathetic pur'dahm stealing his glory burned him more than anything else could. Even so, the un'hai was smart enough to know that Fior'el would never be able to find them on his own. She would make the connection, and his existence would be revealed.

He slapped his fist on the ground beside him. So close. He had been so close. He took another breath of pure oxygen to comfort himself. There was nothing he could do about it now. A good Hunter knew how to let go of the near misses and refocus.

He stood up, keeping his back pressed against the wall of the shattered building. He wasn't going to give up on his quarry that easily. Not when defeating them would push him so so much closer to succeeding his father as leader of the bek'hai.

He spent the next few minutes watching the remaining gel'shah disappear over the horizon. Then he returned to the corner, peering around it.

Ehri dur Tuhrik was standing only a dozen meters away, her back to him. He swallowed his surprise, resisting the urge to press himself back against the wall. What was she doing here?

He kept his eyes on her as she took a few steps away and then paused, listening. She swiveled her head slightly, and her nostrils flared. She knelt down, putting a finger to the earth and lifting it to her nose before touching it to her tongue.

What was she doing? There was no way she could sense him like that. He hadn't even crossed that area.

Then again, how was she already so close?

He drew further back behind the wall, curious and slightly concerned. Ehri may have been an un'hai, but that didn't explain these actions. It was almost as if -

"Lex'el dur Rorn'el," Ehri said loudly, returning to her feet and pivoting around again.

He ducked back before she could see him there. Did she know for sure he was near or was she guessing? And how did she know it was him out of all of the pur'dahm Hunters.

"Lex'el dur Rorn'el," she repeated. "I know you are here somewhere. I can smell your breath."

His breath? He held it in involuntary response to the statement. How?

"It is a foul thing," she said. "You have been away from the regeneration chamber for some time. Do not tell me that you don't feel it."

He would never admit that he did, even to himself. He remained still, trying to decide what to do.

"The humans don't know where I am, Lex'el. They trust me enough to let me operate on my own."

He made his decision, swinging out from behind the wall.

She was already looking right at him.

"So did the Domo'dahm," he said. "And you betrayed him for it. Do you wish to betray your humans as well?"

"You wouldn't accept that even if I did," Ehri replied.

"No." He took a few steps toward her. "You knew where I was. You could have taken me by surprise."

"I don't desire a war, Lex'el. I believe the bek'hai and the humans can live together."

"Disgusting."

"Why do the bek'hai despise them so, even as they steal their genes?"

"We use their genes by necessity."

"The reason doesn't matter. It is senseless. I was hoping I could open your eyes."

"And what? Get me to side with the humans? To betray my kind? My father?"

"No. You are too honorable to do that. It is one thing that sets you apart from your peers. I was hoping only to convince you to remove yourself from this particular fight."

He laughed. "You don't want me to kill them."

"I won't allow you to kill them."

He laughed harder. "You? You're a scientist, Ehri dur Tuhrik. Your namesake was a pacifist."

"I would rather be a pacifist. I'm going to tell you something I have not told the humans."

He stopped laughing, suddenly intrigued. "Oh?"

"Yes, but this truth cannot reach the Domo'dahm. Once I tell you, I will have no choice but to kill you. Do you understand?"

His eyes narrowed. There was something about the way she said it that gave him pause and sent a slight chill along his arms.

"I can see that you do. You have another choice, Hunter. You can give me your word that you will abandon this hunt. If you want to claim the glory of killing the humans and me, do it in the open, on the field of battle."

"That is not my way, and you know it. I have no armies. I have no gur'shah. I have only myself, and sometimes my brothers. That is the path of the Hunter. You are more than any un'hai I have met before. Only a druk would be unable to see it. Even so, this is my only path to Domo'dahm. Either I kill the humans, or I spend the rest of my life in cruhr dur bek. Those are the only options for me."

"You will never be Domo'dahm, Lex'el. If you know your history, you know the Hunters nearly destroyed the lori'shah, and in doing so nearly destroyed the bek'hai. There has not been a Hunter named Domo'dahm in five thousand years."

"Then my glory will be all the greater," Lex'el said. "I don't know how to exist any other way." He paused, giving one last consideration of her words. "Tell me your secret, Ehri dur Tuhrik."

"I am not a clone. My name is Juliette St. Martin."

She smiled at him. It was not the smile of a scientist.

It was the smile of a Hunter.

[5]

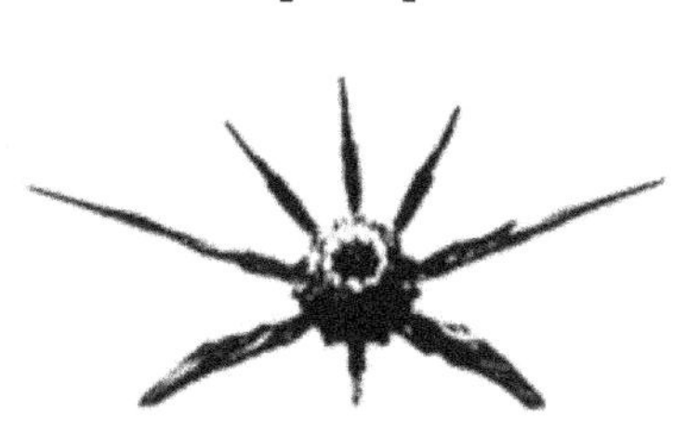

Lex'el dur Rorn'el reached for his lek'sai, giving up on the effort as the un'hai across from him closed the distance between them, faster than he would have ever believed possible.

It took only a single leap forward, nearly five meters from a stand, for her to be on top of him, her foot angling in and hitting him in the chest before he even realized the fight had started. The impact pushed him backward, and he shifted his weight, rolling away on his hands and coming to his feet.

She didn't give him any quarter, coming in hard and fast, throwing quick jabs and hard hooks that he struggled to bring his hands up to block.

"You are a clone, Ehri dur Tuhrik," he hissed, jaw clenched, eyes tight and focused. "No human can do the things you do."

Her smile grew a little wider. She faked a punch to his stomach, and when he moved to block she spun around behind him, grabbing one of his lek'sai and pulling it from him before backing away.

"The bek'hai's advanced command of genetic engineering is useful for more than making twisted monsters or direct copies," she said. "Draw your weapon."

"You want me to believe you are the original pur'hai, from which all of the un'hai were made?" He didn't believe it. Why would he? It sounded ridiculous. And if it were true, why would she hide it from the humans? He drew his lek'sai. It wouldn't matter, once she was dead.

If he could defeat her.

No sooner had he brought the blade into position than she was on him again, her lek'sai flashing, darting in and out as he continued to retreat, barely finding the time to knock the blade aside. It knicked his arm, and then his leg. He growled and clenched his teeth. He was not going to lose like this.

She eased up, stepping back, treating him like a toy.

"I am the original. Juliette St. Martin. I didn't remember. I didn't know it until I saw him. My son, Gabriel. He came to me. He came to Earth to save us."

"Why haven't you told the humans?"

"I have earned their trust as Ehri dur Tuhrik. If I make a claim like that, they will begin to question."

"As they should."

"Yes. So it is better that they do not know." She paused, looking into the distance, in the direction of the humans. "It is better that no one knows." She stared back at him, her expression sending another chill through him. "Make your move, Hunter."

Lex'el was motionless, watching her watching him. Measuring her. Searching for any clue of her planned defense. She was fast. So fast. He didn't want to admit it, but he wasn't sure he could defeat her. He didn't want to admit it, but he was certain that he couldn't. He was going to die today. Within the next few minutes.

He crouched and started to circle. She matched him, following his path, keeping herself balanced. They locked eyes. She smiled. He forced a smile back. He didn't want her to see that for the first time since he had been made, he was truly afraid.

She could see it, though. He could tell. Maybe she could smell it on him. Maybe she could sense his cold sweat, or his ragged breathing. Her senses were enhanced. Her strength enhanced. How had she managed that? Whether or not she was this Juliette St. Martin, how had she altered herself using bek'hai technology and word of it had never reached the Domo'dahm?

She couldn't have done it herself. Who else knew about this? Who had helped her? How? Why?

He wanted to know. He had to survive to learn the fullness of her confession.

He circled her again, looking for an opening, seeking a path to the truth. If there was another traitor within the bek'hai and he discovered them, it could be the final piece he needed to ascend to rule. Unless...

"Who was it?" he asked. "Who helped you?"

"It does not matter. He is dead."

"It was Tuhrik, then?"

"He was obsessed with humans. He was especially obsessed with me. He knew he would have to die to save them, but he also believed their ways are better than our ways. He believed that the bek'hai could only survive in partnership with them, not as conquerors. Fifty years and we have yet to produce a fully viable splice. Fifty years, Lex'el! That should have told the Domo'dahm something. He does not seek viability. Even as the bek'hai are dying, they refuse to accept what they must become." Her smile vanished. "Now, make your move, Hunter. Or I will make it for you."

Lex'el dur Rorn'el opened the path to his oxygen, breathing it in and letting it continue to fuel him. He could feel a small amount of energy return to his body, and he felt a comfort he had nearly forgotten in the nine days he had been tracking them. He watched her for a moment more, no more certain of his odds than when they had started this fight.

Finally, he charged, silent and even, leading with his lek'sai, putting all of his years of training and skill into the approach.

He saw the opening he was looking for then. A slight imbalance on the left side. He adjusted his attack, flipping the blade to his other hand with a deftness and agility few of his brothers could match.

His quarry was still. Motionless. Every part of her, except her foot.

She kicked out, not at him, but at the ground below him.

His foot landed on the chunk of concrete at the same time it slid away. His balance faltered for just an instant.

An instant was all it took to die.

He stumbled, finding his other blade buried in his chest as he tried to recover. He barely felt the pain as he backed away from her, eyes wide in shock. He hadn't seen that coming. He would never have seen that coming.

The strength drained from him along with his life force. He dropped to his knees, looking back at Ehri. There was no hint of glory on her face. No expression of joy or comfort at his defeat. In fact, she looked even sadder than she had moments earlier.

"It is a waste, Lex'el," she said. "It is all such a waste. It never had to be."

He tried to speak. The oxygen was still flowing, but he couldn't get enough of it into his chest to make a sound. He felt hot. Confused. It was getting dark.

"Tuhrik and I tried to change them. To make them see. We failed, and now you are dead. I am sorry, Lex'el dur Rorn'el."

He looked at her but didn't react. His body was unwilling to move at his discretion. He lost his balance, rolling over onto his side.

Two quick gasps, and then the Hunter was gone.

[6]

Domo'dahm Rorn'el peered out from the shadows of his throne, waiting for the messenger to finish the long walk across the antechamber to his position. He could sense Orish'ek shifting in his position beside the throne, eager for whatever news the messenger might bring. Ul'bek was to his left and equally on edge, tapping his sharp fingers against the arm of his seat.

Rorn'el refused to move, though he felt the same unease as his pur'dahm. None of the news they had been receiving recently was to his benefit. It had started with a report from the Ishur that not only was Tea'va planning to use his new position to bring challenge against him but that the pur'dahm he had assigned to watch him, Gr'el, was intending to do the same.

He had known Tea'va couldn't be trusted, which was why he had sent Gr'el with the failure of a pur'dahm. It should have been an easy and clean way to remove the disgusting specimen of a drumhr from his concern. Instead, he had been forced to send two more ships out in pursuit of the Ishur to ensure that whoever was in charge of it by the time they arrived, whether it was Gr'el or Tea'va, would fall back into line or be destroyed.

It was an annoyance, but not a completely unanticipated one. He had been a pur'dahm once himself, fighting with his brothers to gain position within the cells. His victory had come by being aggressive and launching the assault on the planet while the others were still preparing to fulfill Kesh'ek's command. It had been a risky maneuver, as they had not ascertained the humans' technological prowess at that point.

It had been worth the effort.

Still, having three of the domo'shah away from the planet was difficult to accept. The ships were more than transportation. They were home to hundreds of bek'hai, and thousands of lor'hai. They were resources that he hated to part with, especially now.

Ehri dur Tuhrik. He couldn't think of the name without feeling an irrational mix of anger and attraction. She was so much like the human woman, Juliet, that he had become so enamored of. Strong-willed and intelligent, with a streak of compassion that it took him many cycles to come to understand. She had valued life in a way that was still senseless to him sometimes.

He glanced away from the messenger, looking down at the gori'shah cloak he was wearing. He pushed it aside, revealing a simple wooden rosary. He glanced nervously from Orish'ek to Ul'bek, to make sure they couldn't see. It was the only thing he had left of Juliet. A token of her belief in some greater being that controlled the fate of the universe. He had never believed in her Domo'dahm, but lately, he wasn't so sure. When he had ordered the pur'dahm to begin exterminating the remaining humans, he had challenged Him to stop it, if it was not within His will.

That was only days before Ehri dur Tuhrik betrayed him, and now he had lost an outpost worth of resources to her and her small group of human rebels, along with two of his best Hunters. It was an embarrassing defeat, and it had allowed the pur'dahm occasion to begin whispering that he was not up to the task of stopping her and that he still cared too much for the un'hai to approach the problem as he should.

The truth was, they were probably right.

He pushed the cloak back over the rosary as the messenger

neared. He could never say it, but he missed Juliet. He missed her calm, and her kindness. They had destroyed her planet, and she had forgiven them. She had forgiven him. He didn't need her forgiveness and had never asked for it, but he was intrigued by the lack of hate she had always exhibited. How could she be so free of disdain?

There was so much hate silently coursing through the bek'hai, most of it directed at themselves. They had never wanted to leave their homeworld. They had given themselves no choice. After years of warring with one another to stop the murder of the legra'shah and the abandonment of physical reproduction, they had damaged themselves almost beyond repair. If it hadn't been for their chance encounter with a machine the humans had cast out into space, their entire race would have been gone by now, their domo'shah all floating aimlessly throughout the universe, with none alive to guide them.

He forced himself away from those thoughts as the messenger finally reached him. The drumhr was of a low cell. Low enough that Rorn'el didn't recognize him, and had probably never seen him before. He waited while the messenger dropped to a knee, hanging his head low.

"Domo'dahm Rorn'el. Domo'dahm." The drumhr was still while he waited for the Domo'dahm to respond.

"Rise and make your report," Rorn'el said.

The messenger stood. "Domo'dahm, we have received a final communication from the Ishak and the Ishel prior to joining the slipstream. They have charted a course directly to the Pol'tek system, where the Ishur was last reported to be headed."

"When will they arrive?"

"Three days, Domo'dahm."

Three days. Rorn'el smiled. Tea'va had needed much more than that. Whoever his science officer was, they had done a poor job.

"I am pleased," he said.

"Yes, Domo'dahm." The messenger bowed. "Pur'dahm Elsh'ek and Alk'el report that they are continuing the search for Ehri dur Tuhrik and the humans who destroyed Be'kek. They are having difficulty locating them, as the armor they stole allows them movement over any of the terrain moving north, and they do not appear to be following any of the former human paths."

"No doubt she is helping to guide them," Orish'ek said to his right.

"No doubt," Rorn'el agreed. "Are there any other pur'dahm currently tracking the un'hai?"

He could feel Ul'bek's eyes on him immediately, and he hissed softly at his mistake. He shouldn't call her that here.

The messenger continued without pause. It was not his place to judge. "None that have declared themselves, Domo'dahm. As you know, some pur'dahm may seek greater glory by surprising you with her capture."

"Or death," Ul'bek said, perhaps in retaliation for his words.

"Or death," Rorn'el agreed, biting back his anger at the actions that had forced him to agree to allow her to be killed. He still wanted her back. He wanted to know how she could be so like her pur'hai, and yet so different. He leaned forward in his seat, digging his claws into the lek'shah of his chair. "And the location of the human base?"

The messenger dared to let himself smile. It was always better to be the bearer of good news. "Your science team has narrowed the potential systems based on reevaluation of the examination done on the wreckage of similar starships, the most optimal slipstream paths, and the most habitable worlds."

Rorn'el allowed himself to bare his teeth, opening his mouth wide. It was better news than he had expected. He had made a mistake, ignoring the human's surviving off world colony for too long, thinking that the bek'hai would forever be impervious to their efforts of rebellion. It had been a decision made by a Domo'dahm who had been younger, less wise, and too confident.

"I am very, very, pleased," he said.

"Yes, Domo'dahm."

"Orish'ek, prepare a commendation and promotion for the pur'-dahm who owns the science team that completed the analysis."

"Yes, Domo'dahm," Orish'ek replied.

He considered for a moment. "Orish'ek, hold that command. Who is the pur'dahm in question, messenger?"

"Pit'ek," the messenger said.

"Tell Pit'ek he is reassigned to the domo'shah Ishrem. He will be leading the expedition to the systems his scientists have suggested."

The messenger nodded. Orish'ek shifted beside him.

"Are you certain you don't want to tell Pit'ek yourself, Domo'dahm?"

"There is no time," he replied. He raised his voice. "I want that colony destroyed. No survivors. If the human starship tries to return to it, I want them to find it in ruin. This is our world now. Our home. There is no place for humans on it or near it." He lowered his voice again, directing it at the messenger. "Make sure Pit'ek is clear on that. And if he fails to find the colony, tell him that he is to retire himself before he ever returns."

"It will be so, Domo'dahm," the messenger said.

"You are dismissed."

"Yes, Domo'dahm."

Rorn'el leaned back in his throne as the messenger departed. He glanced at Ul'bek and Orish'ek, and then closed his eyes. Juliet had begged him to spare the humans that remained, and swore they were no threat to him. For a short time, he had even believed it, allowing the rebels to plant their seed of discontent.

Fifty cycles later, it was clear to him that their hope of achieving the impossible would only die when they did.

[7]

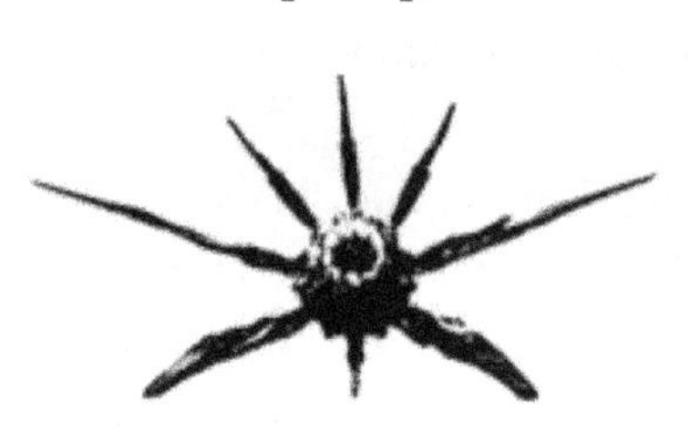

Gabriel St. Martin walked side by side with the bek'hai known as Tea'va. His father, General Theodore St. Martin, rolled a few meters ahead of them, the bek'hai science officer, Zoelle, at his side.

Two days had passed since the crew of the Magellan had successfully, and impossibly, managed to crash their starship aboard a Dread fortress and gain control over it.

Two days had passed since Zoelle had told Theodore that she was his long missing, and previously believed dead wife, Juliet.

Two days had passed since Theodore had believed it.

It was a situation beyond anything Gabriel could ever have imagined. A situation that had left him struggling to come to grips with a weird new order to things. It didn't take much examination to know that this thing was not his mother. Besides the obvious age difference, there was the fact that she was hardly the only clone of Juliet St. Martin the Dread had produced. He had met another just like her on Earth, fighting for the humans with Major Donovan Peters. While he could accept that maybe, just maybe, she was somehow programmed to sympathize with humanity and perhaps even to fight for them, there was something about her that he just didn't trust.

That mistrust was only magnified by the fact that Tea'va didn't have faith in her either, going as far as to find a reason to pull Gabriel aside and explain what the clone had done to him, betraying him to the other pur'dahm, Gr'el, in exchange for a greater position of power.

"Watch her," he had said. "Power is the only thing she truly desires or cares for, and she is willing to do anything, including posturing as Juliet St. Martin, to get it."

While Gabriel didn't know Tea'va well enough to explicitly trust him either, the former commander of the fortress had been proving himself since the moment they met. Not only had he had killed a number of his own in their defense and had directly helped them gain control of the ship, but even now his assistance was invaluable as assisted them in making the most efficient use of the ship they had captured.

The problem was that Theodore was more than willing to accept her account of the truth without any evidence to back the claim. He was smitten with this version of his wife, regardless of how she had come to exist.

It wasn't as though Gabriel couldn't understand why. His father's adoration for his wife was as solid and sure as a steel beam, and the pain he had suffered for all of these years over losing her had been apparent to Gabriel from the time he was old enough to speak. He didn't blame his father for wanting Juliet back so badly that he was willing to disregard logic to make it happen.

But he did blame General St. Martin.

The General had a responsibility to the crew of the Magellan, and as far as Gabriel was concerned, it went above and beyond everything else. Just like Theodore had found the strength to bring the Magellan away from Earth and get the people on board to safety all of those years ago, he had a fresh responsibility to put one hundred percent of his efforts into the war now. While they were still working toward that goal, Gabriel couldn't help but feel like his father's misguided loyalty to the genetic twin of his mother was going to hurt them sooner or later.

"Where are we going?" Gabriel whispered to Tea'va.

His father had asked him to meet near the transport beam and then told him to follow, but hadn't given him any indication of their destination. They had entered the beam and traveled directly to the bottom level of the ship, heading deeper into the heart of the fortress.

The bek'hai glanced over at him, making a face that Gabriel still found difficult to translate. It appeared to him as a mix of amusement and disdain.

"What are the correct words in your language?" Tea'va paused. "The place where we make the clones. Factory, is it? Zoelle wanted to show it to your father."

"Do you know why?"

"Not for certain, but I can guess. I believe she will ask him to make more soldiers."

"Make soldiers?"

"Yes. That is what the factory is for. Not only soldiers. Mothers. Scientists."

Gabriel was only loosely familiar with the different clone types, but he knew there were more than the three Tea'va mentioned. The Cleaners, for example, who moved into the hidden areas of the ship and kept the fortress maintained. He had seen them in the shadows from time to time, going about their business as if nothing was different, seemingly oblivious to the new ownership. It was a sharp contrast to the Mothers, who had refused to serve anyone but Orish'ek. Colonel Graham and his team were still trying to secure the rest of them after they had killed a pair of crew members in an ambush.

The real clone soldiers, on the other hand, were loyal to whoever was Dahm of the fortress. All it had taken to make them stand down and get in line was a word from Tea'va, and now they coexisted with the human crew as though they had always been part of it. It had taken some time for him to sort them out and order each of them to accept a new chain of command, but it was becoming a more common sight to see the strapping, blonde haired doppelgangers working alongside human counterparts.

Still, that was making use of the existing clones that survived the battle.

Making new ones?

That was something else entirely.

"I would say my father would never go for that, but if she's pushing him? I'm not sure."

Tea'va gave him a slight nod of agreement before Gabriel returned his attention forward. He eyed the corner of Zoelle's face, turned slightly in his direction. Had she heard them from that distance?

She didn't react to his stare, continuing ahead with a smooth gait that perfectly matched Theodore's pace in his chair. She had her hand on his shoulder, keeping it there as they walked.

They reached the end of the corridor a few minutes later. Gabriel hadn't seen much of the fortress yet outside of the bridge and some of the living spaces, but he was already impressed with the efficiency of the design. Despite the massive size of the starship, it seemed to him that nothing was ever more than a short walk away.

The sheer volume of the space that opened up ahead of him caused him stare, letting out a small, "wow" as he took in the enormity of it. The fortress had seemed huge from the outside, but whether it was some bend in reality or some trick of the light, it actually seemed bigger on the inside.

"Gabriel, I'm the one without the legs," he heard Theodore say. "Do try to keep up, son."

Gabriel caught himself, taking a few quick steps to catch up. The others were heading toward an illuminated opening in a roundish glob of black carapace, the material Tea'va had told him was called lek'shah. His eyes followed the shape as it flowed upward, spreading out into a larger form that had to be the factory.

He paused once again, impressed with the sight. He would have fallen further behind once more, except Tea'va put a hand on his back and pushed him gently forward.

"It is more impressive on the inside, Heil'bek."

[8]

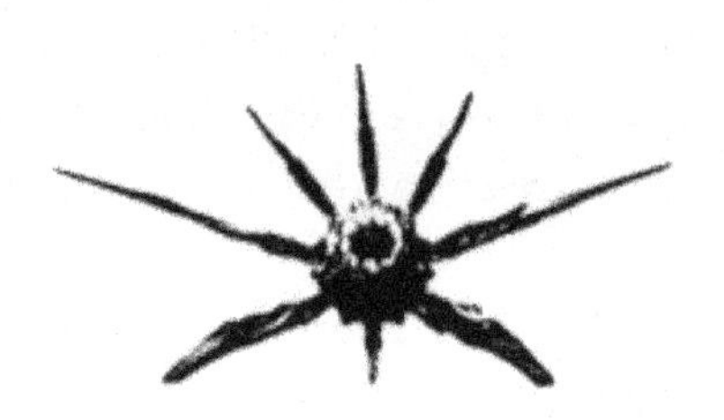

IT DIDN'T TAKE LONG FOR GABRIEL TO DISCOVER THAT TEA'VA was understating the truth. The inside of the clone factory was more impressive than the outside of it. Much more impressive. It was also more than a little disconcerting. He didn't need to ask Theodore directly to know his father felt the same way.

There was a scientist on duty inside the factory, another clone of Juliet St. Martin who didn't seem to bear the same distorted beliefs as Zoelle. She smiled politely at them as they entered, listening attentively as Zoelle ordered her to show the General how the cloning technology operated.

"As you command, Dahm Zoelle," the clone said, bowing to her. Then she looked over at Theodore, bowing to him as well. "Please, follow me, Dahm St. Martin."

Gabriel watched his father's face as he observed the clone. While they had been in control of the ship for two days already, this was the first time they had strayed far from the bridge and was Theodore's first interaction with what Tea'va had named an "un'hai."

He thought he spotted a pained expression on Theodore's face at the sight of the Juliet duplicate, but it was gone within seconds, replaced with a polite, slightly uneasy grin.

"Well, I wouldn't be able to tell the two of you apart, if not for that pin of yours," he said to Zoelle.

"The process creates perfect copies every time," she replied. "You will see."

The clone began walking, taking them deeper into the facility. The entire thing was made of the lek'shah, rounded and shaped and broken up by glowing moss and cutouts that had been replaced with a clear version of the material. Through it, Gabriel could see different parts of the facility. The first looked like a research area, where oddly shaped, alien terminals displayed holographic imagery that reminded him of his chemistry classes growing up. There was a clone laid out on a flat surface there, naked, dead, and cut open. It was one of the mothers.

"What were you doing with that?" he asked.

The clone was walking ahead of them. She stopped at the question, turning around and looking at Zoelle.

"You may respond to any questions the Heil'bek has," Zoelle said.

"Yes, Dahm Zoelle. Heil'bek, can you please be more specific?"

"The mother on the table," Gabriel said.

The clone retreated to him and looked through the transparency.

"We are studying the effect of the crossed programming on the biology of the capsule," she said.

"I don't understand."

"If I may, Gabriel," Zoelle said. "The mothers that Gr'el produced were given the precognitive implantation of the soldier clone." She paused. "I should start closer to the beginning. My apologies. All bek'hai clones are preloaded with a standard set of instructions. How to walk, how to speak the bek'hai language, how to read. Then each subset of clones is provided more specific instructions. For the mothers, it is based on our research on human reproduction and companionship. For the soldiers, it is how to use our weapons, how to work as a team, and other combat related skills. The clones genetics are engineered precisely to optimize these instruction sets, not unlike a computer. By placing the instructions for one type into another, you are introducing mental instability and the potential for disaster. Here, we are examining the physiological effects of the soldier programming on the mother."

"And who gave you that order?" Gabriel asked. "These clones were killed during our takeover of your ship."

He worded the statement deliberately, to see how she would react. She smiled in response, not giving anything away.

"I gave the order," Theodore said. "Based on your mom's recommendation."

Gabriel tensed his jaw. He hated to hear his father speak like that for so many reasons.

"What is the ultimate goal of this research?" he asked. "What's the point?"

"Strategy," she replied. "I will explain in more detail as we continue the tour. Is that okay?"

Gabriel nodded. There was no point to being contrary just for the sake of it.

"Shielle, please continue," Zoelle said.

"Yes, Dahm," the clone replied.

She moved back to the front of the group, guiding them further into the factory. They paused a short while later, reaching another room filled with alien terminals.

"This is where the-" the clone paused, trying to think of the English word, "instructions, are managed. As Dahm Zoelle said, we have a standard set of instructions, but they can also be modified here, as needed to adjust to changing variables."

"For example," Zoelle said. "If we create a new weapon, or need to alter our programming so that the clone has a new piece of knowledge on emergence from the maturation chamber."

"One second there, darlin'," Theodore said. "Why don't you just give them everything you know up front, if it's as easy as writing a line of code into a computer?"

Zoelle gave him a warm smile. "It isn't as easy as that. And, like a machine, our modified human brains have a limit to the amount of information they can store. Experimentation revealed that too much data causes the clone to freeze, unable to make any decisions. Of course, we knew this was an outcome based on the bek'hai brain, but the human mind is able to hold almost four hundred percent more information."

"But we're the primitive ones?" Gabriel said.

"There is a difference between holding information, and utilizing it," she replied. "While the human brain has more capacity, the bek'hai brain is more efficient. That is why we have conquered advanced interstellar travel, while you are struggling to reach beyond your system."

"Whose side are you on again?"

Zoelle's face flushed as she realized she was speaking for the enemy. "My apologies, Gabriel. I've become accustomed to referring to the bek'hai as part of my own. I've only recently been reunited with you and your father, after all. Please forgive me."

Gabriel glanced at Theodore, whose face remained static. He needed to be careful how he handled the situation. "I understand."

She smiled. "Thank you. As I was saying, we have to be very cautious what instructions we give to the clones. There is a great amount of experimentation that happens in creation of another type. Shielle, continue."

"Yes, Dahm," the clone replied.

She brought them down a longer corridor. Gabriel began to hear the sound of flowing liquid as they approached. It was the only noise he had heard inside the facility since they arrived. In fact, he realized almost as if by accident that the Dread fortress, in general, was deathly quiet. He wondered if that would change once they managed to get it underway.

They reached a solid wall of lek'shah at the end of the passage. Shielle brought them to a stop in front of it, turning to face them.

"What's the problem?" Theodore asked.

Shielle looked at Zoelle, hesitant. Gabriel didn't like it. He glanced over at Tea'va, who seemed unconcerned.

"It is not typical for anyone other than the caretakers to enter the maturation hall," Zoelle said. "Most bek'hai do not like to be reminded of where they come from."

"Well, I didn't come from there," Theodore said. "And I want to see it."

"Me, too," Gabriel said. "You brought us down here for a reason."

"Open the door," Zoelle said to Shielle. "Tea'va, you may remain outside, if you wish."

The way she said it made it clear to Gabriel that she was challenging the warrior. He laughed in reply.

"I know where I come from," he replied. "I have no fear of it."

"Suit yourself."

Zoelle nodded, and Shielle put her hand on the wall.

The door slid open.

[9]

Gabriel could almost believe what he was seeing, but only because Zoelle's earlier statements had given him hints of what was to come. The maturation hall, as Shielle had named it, was a massive space toward the center of the facility. It was lined with row after row of capsules, three meters square, filled with a fluid of some kind, with tubes running in and out of machinery placed at the top. The fluid was in a constant state of motion, swirling toward the center, draining and being reintroduced.

In the center of each capsule was a human child. It floated freely in the goop, eyes open, head and limbs moving, seemingly aware of itself. Some were touching the transparency in front of them, trying to navigate their way in the fluid. Others were touching themselves, feeling their flesh, trying to make sense of who and what they were. All of them were male, identical in size and shape. All looked to be around ten years old.

It was difficult to tell how many capsules there were. They stretched ahead and to either side of them as they entered the space, moving down a short ramp and onto the floor. Gabriel noticed it was cooler in here than the other rooms, and he felt a sudden shiver as his body adjusted. He looked to Theodore, noting his father's disgusted expression, and then to Tea'va, whose normally pale face had somehow paled even further. The bek'hai looked as though he wanted to retch.

A clone approached Shielle from the left. A male, short and bald, wearing a simple gori'shah robe. He was flanked by two identical clones, who surprised Gabriel by being armed.

The clone said something to Shielle in bek'hai. Shielle responded, and then pointed to Theodore. The clone argued, she raised her voice, Zoelle got involved, and finally the clones retreated.

"The caretakers are very protective of the capsules," she explained once they were gone. "They are the only non-soldiers generally permitted to carry weapons."

Theodore grunted, and rolled his chair forward to the first capsule. The boy inside seemed to notice him, and he flailed his arms to position himself facing the General.

"They're alive in there," Theodore said.

"Yes."

"Is that why seeing the chamber is so traumatic? Do they remember?"

"No, Theodore. Their minds are erased when they reach maturation. The new instructions are implanted after the bodies are released. They wake up with no memory of their time being cultivated."

Gabriel flinched at the word. He noticed Theodore did as well. "How old are the children in there?" he asked.

"They aren't children," Zoelle said. "We need to be clear about that. These clones have been the chamber for seven days, their bodies aging ten years in that time. In seven more days, they will be ready for programming."

The clone in the capsule jerked and fell away from the transparency, its eyes rolling back in its head.

"Is it okay?" Theodore asked.

A caretaker rushed over, reviewing alien text that appeared on the glass.

"It is fine," Zoelle said. "It is part of the process. The enhanced maturation rate can be painful to the embryos, but they will never remember that it occurred."

"How many are there?" Gabriel asked.

"Four hundred," Zoelle replied.

"Soldiers?"

"Yes."

Theodore looked back at Gabriel, one eyebrow going up. Gabriel shook his head slightly. He didn't want his father to think he agreed with any of this.

"I know it is shocking for you to see, and can be difficult to accept," Zoelle said. She returned to Theodore's side, putting her hand on his as she knelt beside him. "Consider that I am only here because of this technology. I should have died long ago, Theodore. I was going to die. One of the pur'dahm, Tuhrik, brought me to a capsule and placed me inside." She stood and looked back at Gabriel again. "Like the bek'hai regeneration chambers heal the bek'hai, the maturation capsules have the ability to heal human frailties. To reverse the aging process." She glanced down at Theodore. "To return the ability to walk."

Theodore's face changed then. His disgust faded, and Gabriel could picture him running through the scenarios in his mind. He could have his legs back. He could be young again, with a young bride. He could have the second chance with Juliet that he had always wished for.

"The technologies are the same," Zoelle continued. "The fluid is filled with nutrients vital to the human genome. For the bek'hai, this fluid is mixed during delivery with a second plasma that contains all the drumhr need to be restored."

"How is it made?" Gabriel asked.

"It is produced from human and bek'hai stem cells. Our technology teases out the appropriate permutation to restore optimal health."

"Where did you get the stem cells?"

Zoelle's eyes turned sharp for an instant, her frustration over the question obvious to Gabriel. That frustration vanished a moment later as she removed herself from whatever she had been thinking.

"It took time to develop the cells," Zoelle said. "The original fluid was derived from the humans we collected when we took the Earth."

"People?" Theodore said. "That stuff is made from people?"

"Not anymore, as that would be untenable in the long-term. Though it is possible the Ishur is still utilizing some percentage of origin resources."

The disgust returned to Theodore's face. Zoelle noticed and knelt beside him again.

"Theodore, consider what this technology can do for you. For everyone on this ship."

"I'm not about to piss on the dead by using their life fluid like some kind of damn vampire," Theodore said. "Not for anything in this world." He looked at her. "You would never have agreed to anything like that either, would you? Ain't a God I know that sees anything right with that."

Zoelle was silent for a moment. "I did what I had to do, Theodore. To survive, but more than that. To return to you, but more than that. The freedom of all of humankind is at stake. I had an opportunity to make their deaths mean something. God delivered me to the bek'hai so that I could do something."

Tea'va tapped Gabriel on the shoulder, shaking his head at Zoelle's emotional outpouring. It was clear the bek'hai didn't believe it was real. Gabriel wasn't so sure. What would she have to gain by healing his father?

Theodore stared a Zoelle for a long moment. "I have to think about it," he said.

Zoelle nodded. "Very well. These clones will be mature in seven days. You have the option to continue the process or to terminate them now."

"Terminate? No. Ain't a God I know sees anything right with that, either. This batch is already underway; then we'll live with the hand we're being dealt. When they're done, I want this place shut down. No more clones."

"Theodore," Zoelle said, preparing to argue.

He put up his hand. "No more clones. If you did what you did to save us, that's one thing. You saved Gabriel; you helped us get this ship. If time changed you a bit, that's another thing, and I can live with it because I can't imagine what you had to live with, darlin'. I ain't about to make the same damn mistakes as the bek'hai. You become reliant on clones, on damn near slaves, soon enough you can't do a thing for yourself."

"How many soldiers do the humans have, Theodore?" Zoelle asked. "How many to fight against the bek'hai?"

"Hopefully, enough," he replied. "Now tell me this: you can make humans on this here ship. Can you make weapons, too? Armor? That kind of thing?"

"The clones, Theo-"

"I said no," Theodore said, his voice staying soft, treating her with a gentleness Gabriel knew he would never impart to anyone else. "And I mean no. I'm still a General of the New Earth Alliance Army, and apparently the Dahm of this here, what do you call it? Domo'shah. I always reserve the right to change my mind, but right now it ain't on the table."

Gabriel smiled at the response. Maybe he should have a little more faith in his father?

"Weapons? Armor?" Theodore repeated.

"Every Domo'shah is designed to be self-sufficient," Zoelle replied. "We have full manufacturing capabilities on board."

"Good," Theodore said, smiling. "Because we did a number on Maggie getting in here, and I have a feeling we're going to need her again before this is over. If you've got a program to make some of these clones into engineers, I'd sure appreciate it."

"We'll be crossing the programming," Shielle said.

"Violent to non-violent," Theodore said. "I imagine that isn't as bad as the opposite?"

"It should be less volatile," Zoelle replied. "But it is likely they won't be as performant as the clones specifically programmed for such tasks."

"As long as they can follow orders, it'll have to do. I hate to be so flippant with the brains of these things, but like I said, we'll work with the hand we've been dealt."

"It will be so, Dahm St. Martin," Shielle said.

"I appreciate it, Shielle." He rolled his chair to face Tea'va. "I want you to keep an eye on the soldiers when they come out, get them organized under Colonel Graham and the others."

"Yes, Dahm St. Martin," Tea'va replied.

"Theodore," Zoelle said. "What about yourself?"

"What about myself, darlin'?"

"The maturation capsule. When the clones are mature, will you be using one to restore your health?"

Theodore shook his head. "You know, I'm feeling pretty damn fine right now, and to be honest, I've gotten used to the alternate means of transportation. Maybe once the war is done, if I can get some of that synthetic juice, I'll give it a second thought. Until then, I'll be fine with what I've got. Now, let's head on back up to the bridge. We need to collect sitreps from the rest of the officers and see if we can figure out when we can get our asses back into this thing."

[10]

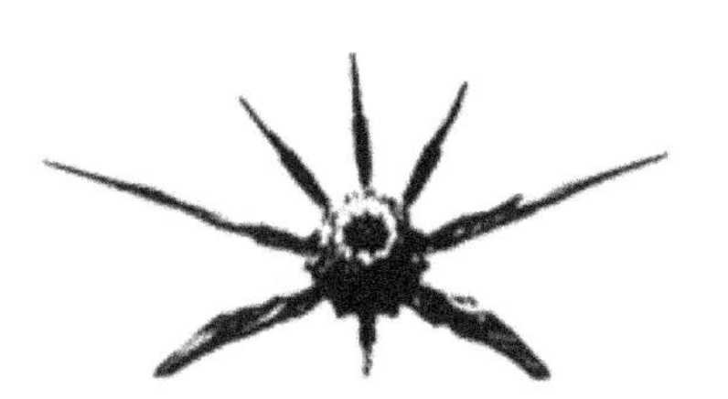

"General on deck," Colonel Choi announced as Theodore rolled onto the bridge of the alien starship.

The bridge crew was small, the members of it almost lost amidst the many stations afforded to the original bek'hai contingent, but they all stood and came to attention as their leader rejoined them.

"At ease," Theodore said, rolling past the command dais to the front of the space, as Gabriel moved to his position in the first bank of terminals, with Tea'va following to sit beside him. Zoelle remained at the back of the room.

Gabriel turned his head to look back toward the dais. Miranda was sitting in the first row ahead of the raised platform, and she smiled when she saw him looking her way. He smiled back before returning his attention to his father.

"Mr. Mokri, Mr. Larone, are you present?" Theodore asked, seeking the two engineers among the glow of the terminals.

"I'm here, General," Reza said, moving out from beneath one of the stations and raising his hand. "Guy and Sarah are with Lieutenant O'Dea, going over the damage to the Magellan."

"What are you doing down there, son?" Theodore asked.

"Trying to figure out the interface," he replied. "I'm monitoring the impulses along the organic wiring, and tracing them to the precise outputs in an effort to translate them into something we can use. Or interrupt and control, as the case may be."

"Any luck so far?"

"Limited. I think I can turn on the ship wide communication systems through my tablet. It isn't much, but it's a start."

"Still a job well done, Mr. Mokri. Do you have an ETA on shields and weapons systems?"

"Not yet, General. Although the weapons systems seem to be individually controlled, not networked. We can fire the main plasma cannon from the bridge, but using the smaller systems means having a crew stationed directly at the battery."

"Tea'va, how many batteries are on this thing again?" Theodore asked.

"Two hundred, Dahm St. Martin," Tea'va replied. "We only have enough soldiers to operate fifty-three."

"What he means, Mr. Mokri, is let's see if we can get them networked."

"Yes, sir."

"Seems to me your advanced tech isn't always all that advanced," Theodore said.

"There has never been a need to link the systems to one another," Tea'va said. "And it makes the whole vulnerable to a single point of failure."

"He has a point," Reza said.

"Yes, he does," Theodore agreed. "See what you can do, but don't make it a top priority." He paused. "What about flight control?"

"It's going to take a while, General," Reza said. "It's a lot more complicated than communications."

"Define a while for me, will you Mr. Mokri?"

"Two weeks, General. Maybe more."

"That isn't awhile, son, that's forever. We need to do better than that."

"I'm doing the best I can, General. I haven't slept in almost thirty-nine hours."

"I know. You're doing a bang-up job, Mr. Mokri. Don't ever let my impatience suggest that you aren't. But, and it's a big but, not only are we sitting ducks out here, but we've got friends on Earth waiting for our help."

"Dahm St. Martin," Tea'va said, standing and bowing. "I have offered my assistance in flying the Ishur before. Perhaps you have reconsidered?"

Theodore looked at Tea'va. "I'd prefer if Gabriel could take the stick while you observe. No offense because you've done good things for us, but you can understand why I'm hesitant to give you that much control."

"Of course, Dahm St. Martin. I would do the same in your position under most circumstances. However, this is not most circumstances. Pur'dahm Gr'el deposed me by the will of the Domo'dahm. This may not have a lot of meaning to you, General, but what it tells me is that he was reporting back to the Domo'dahm with regularity. There is a very strong possibility that reinforcements have been sent to this system."

"It took you more than two days to get here," Gabriel said. "I imagine it will take those reinforcements a similar amount of time?"

"That is true," Zoelle said from the back. "My team calculated the most optimal course."

"Even so, Dahm St. Martin," Tea'va said. "We currently cannot defend ourselves from an attack by another domo'shah. We will be torn apart."

"I hear you, Tea'va," Theodore said. "I'm open to ideas."

"General," Colonel Choi said. "What if we focused our efforts on getting the shields operational? If we can update them to use Reza and Guy's new modulation, we should be able to defend ourselves from any incoming attacks. Even if we only have the main plasma cannon, it should be enough at that point."

"I can't interface with the systems," Reza said. "Not until I finish the translation. I can probably get the shields online sooner if I concentrate my effort there. Five days, maybe? I really need to get a little sleep, though, I'm fuzzy as it is."

"Five days is still a long time, General," Choi said.

"We should have that much time," Gabriel said. "Assuming Zoelle is correct in her assumption about her slipstream path."

"I am," Zoelle insisted. "But if you don't believe me, I can still help you update the Ishur's shields. I do have some knowledge on their function, and I can integrate our systems directly. You don't have to spend the time on the translation right now."

"No offense, Zoelle," Choi said. "But we don't know you all that well yet."

"You do know me, Theodore," Zoelle said, stepping forward. "You know me better than anyone. You know who I really am."

Theodore smiled at her. Gabriel glanced to Colonel Choi, who made eye contact with him. He could tell she didn't like it either. The enhancements Reza and Guy had made to the phase modulation of the Dread technology was their secret weapon; their one means to level the playing field in a war where they were vastly outnumbered. Passing that information through Zoelle meant giving it to a former enemy, and if Tea'va was right about her, it could be a disaster.

"The lives of everyone on this ship are at stake," Zoelle said. "Please, let me help you, my love."

"Mr. Mokri, show Juliet what we've got," Theodore said. "Protecting the crew should be our number one priority right now. We've got too many people depending on us to take chances."

"Yes, General," Reza replied.

"Thank you, Theodore," Zoelle said.

"Do we have any other scientists on this boat, darlin'?"

"Three of my original cell remain," Zoelle replied.

"Get them working on coordinates for a slip. Tea'va, I'm doubling down here. Do what you need to do to get us going. Make sure you tell Gabriel every move you're making."

"Yes, Dahm St. Martin," Tea'va replied, showing his own version of a smile.

Gabriel expected his father to make eye contact with him, and when he did, he made a point to hold it. He hated the idea of giving so much of their control over to the former residents of the Dread starship, regardless of whose side they said they were on. He hoped his eyes could express as much to Theodore.

"Gabriel, come and see me in my quarters," Theodore said, holding his gaze with confidence. "The rest of you, if you have a specific job to do, get back to doing it."

[11]

"WHAT DID YOU WANT TO TALK ABOUT?" GABRIEL SAID, AS SOON as the door to Theodore's quarters had slid closed.

It was the space that had previously belonged to Gr'el. It was simple and spartan, with no visible effects to speak of, and no furniture save for a soft, flat surface that served as a bed. There was a regeneration chamber in the center of the room, but Theodore must have gotten Reza to disconnect it because it was powered down.

Theodore spun his chair around, reversing as he did.

"Your mother," Theodore said.

Gabriel tensed. He had been waiting for this. "My real mother? The one who died on Earth? Or the clone that thinks she's the real deal?"

Theodore's eyes looked angry, but he surprised Gabriel by not yelling. "You don't know she isn't your mother, Gabe."

"You don't know she is."

"Yes, I do, son. Oh, sure, my heart pretty much burst out of my chest when I saw her for the first time. And sure, I know it would be easy, real easy to believe it's her even when it isn't just because I want it so bad. Don't disgrace me by thinking because I'm old that I'm that daft. You've only seen what you've seen, and you haven't seen everything."

"I just saw you give her access to our only edge against the Dread. What if she's spying for the Domo'dahm, Dad?"

"She isn't a spy," Theodore said. "I'd bet my life on it."

"Based on what? She looks like Mom because she's a genetic duplicate. Even if the maturation capsule can reverse the aging process as she claims, there's no way that can be her. Of all of the Dread starships, in all of the Dread communities, and we end up with the one carrying the real Juliet St. Martin? I met another clone on Earth. You know that. How do we know she isn't the real thing?"

"It has to be her, Gabe. You never met your Mom. Oh, I wish you had. I've always felt guilty for bringing you into this world without her. But you didn't know her, and not like I do. That woman, Zoelle? She's your mom."

"I understand that you think that. I understand you want it to be true. I can't imagine what it's like for you to see her come back from the dead, young and healthy like you were never parted. But the Dread have been cloning people for years, and cloning themselves for thousands of years before that. You don't think they can make a convincing copy?"

"No. She knows things, son. Intimate things. Things I've never told another soul."

"Like what?"

"Heh. I'm not about to tell you. That's personal. The point is she told me about them. I didn't ask. She just knew. How would she know if she weren't your mother?"

"They can program brains. Maybe they reverse-engineered Mom's to get that information."

"To what end? Do you think there's any chance in the world the Dread thought we'd be capturing one of their ships? Do you think they ever expected they would come in contact with us? With me? So what would be the benefit?"

Gabriel knew he had a point. He shrugged. "Maybe it's a side effect of the programming? Maybe it comes along for the ride? Or maybe Mom did manage to alter her clones somehow? They have a special name for them, you know. Un'hai. They're different than the other clones."

"And all the others might be clones. Zoelle is Juliet."

"How do you know if we had the other clone from Earth on this ship, that she wouldn't say the same things? Know the same things? Let's say Mom did something to her clones and made them sympathetic to humans somehow. That still doesn't make her Juliet, no matter how much she knows. I'm sorry, Dad, but there are too many questions around it, and I think that by trusting her you're putting all of us at risk."

Theodore stared at Gabriel. When he spoke again, it was still at a normal volume, surprising Gabriel again. "Let's put our difference of opinion aside, son. It don't matter how much I want you to believe, because you're your own man, and I respect that. The fact is, I'm putting us at risk by not trusting her. What am I supposed to do? If the Dread are sending more ships out this way, we have to be able to defend ourselves. We have to. And we can, thanks to Reza and Guy. Damn fine work, that. We can take care of our people, we can get back to Calawan, and we can take care of our own there, too. We can rally the troops, and we can go back to Earth and duke it out with this Domo'dahm. Maybe we can even win. But none of that happens if we don't get the time we need."

"Tea'va can get us out of here. We can catch a stream and start heading home, long before any reinforcements can make it to us. You didn't need to give our secrets to her."

"It's funny to me that you question your mom's loyalty, and yet you trust that one so explicitly. Now, I know he saved our lives, but he wasn't the only one, and he's still a Dread, not a clone of a human. He's further from identifying with us than anyone. Anyway, didn't you hear me give him permission to get us out? I'm not taking any chances on this one, Gabe. We have to rely on every resource we have to get through this. Every resource, no matter where it originated. I know you can understand that."

"That doesn't mean I have to like it."

"Nope, it don't. And again, I'm not asking you to. But I could do without you making dirt face at me whenever I say something you don't like. I'd rather not dress you down in public, but I'm still your commanding officer, and you damn well better respect me."

Gabriel felt the heat run to his face. He had been overstepping his position in the last couple of days. "I'm sorry, Dad."

"I forgive you. We're gonna get through this, Gabe."

"I know. So, are you and Zoelle sharing these quarters?"

"I'm an Old Gator, son. And she might be Juliet, but she's been through more than her share these last fifty years. You saw for yourself; sometimes it's hard for her to separate herself from them."

"Do you think you'll do it? Use the maturation capsule to get your legs back? Heck, I think you'd come out younger than me."

Theodore laughed. "Wouldn't that be something? No, not so long as there's any chance one of ours gave their life in exchange. That isn't what God's about. It isn't what I'm about either. I haven't had these things for a long time, and I conquered that demon not very long ago. I've come to terms with the place I'm at."

"I'm glad to hear it."

"I bet you are. In all seriousness, Gabe, try to give your mom a chance. I know it's hard to believe, and hard to accept. Just try to look at her with a little less biased eyes."

"I'll try," Gabriel said.

"Thanks. And while you're at it, pay closer attention to Tea'va, too. I know you like him, but there's something about that one that I don't. He's got a politician's smile, and I always get the feeling when he talks to me he'd rather be sinking a knife into my chest."

"To be honest, I hate depending on either one of them."

"To be honest, I'd rather not lean on your mom, if only because I don't want her to have to be involved in this. Yeah, I get what you're saying, and overall, I agree. We just have to do the best we can."

"I will, Dad."

"I know." Theodore smiled. "I'm going to get a little shut-eye. Wake me if anything interesting happens."

"Then I'll hope I won't have a reason to wake you."

"Me, too."

[12]

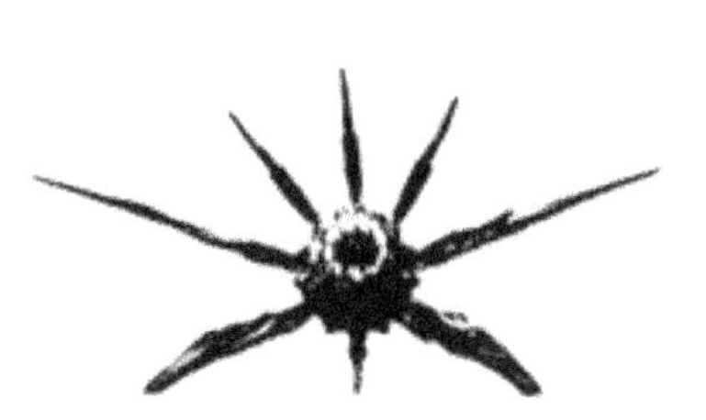

"Here she comes," Soon said.

Donovan turned the mech's torso, rotating it until Ehri came into view in front of him. She had been gone almost two hours, and he had considered going to look for her more than once, forcing himself to resist the temptation. He told her he trusted her. He had to prove it.

She walked calmly through the rubble-strewn streets, not moving in any particular hurry, despite her earlier concern that there might be more Dread units nearby. It would have bothered him, except their sensors had stayed clear the entire time, and he had a feeling pur'dahm Fior'el would prefer to delay his embarrassment for as long as possible.

He opened his cockpit as she neared, evacuating the mech and climbing down to meet her. She smiled at the sight of him, raising her hand in greeting.

"Major," she said.

"Did you find him?" Donovan asked.

"Yes. He will not be troubling us any longer."

Donovan raised an eyebrow at the statement, feeling chilled by the way she said it. "You killed him, didn't you?"

"Yes. He was unwilling to listen to reason."

"You said he was likely a highly skilled Hunter. You don't have a scratch on you."

"I was fortunate. He was tired from chasing us all of this time. He confirmed for me that there are no other forces nearby."

"I figured as much, but it's good to have it confirmed."

"Are you nearly finished with the salvage?"

"Yeah. We packed as much in as we could. I think we're all pretty anxious to get moving again."

"I'm sorry for my delay, Major. It took some time for me to find him."

"If it gets the monkey off our back, I'm not sorry at all."

"Hey, Major," Kroeger said, exiting the ped'ek with two Dread rifles in his arms. "This is the last of the weapons. I figure I'll carry them since they're not going to fit inside the big men." He looked at Ehri. "You're back."

"I am."

"Well, hell, did you kill the bastard?"

"Yes."

"Good work, then." He turned toward Mendez. "You owe me."

"Screw you, Kroeger. I wasn't serious."

"Damn right. I was."

"Forget it."

Kroeger laughed. "Good women are hard to find out here. Thompson, get off your tail and let's move it out."

The other remaining foot soldier was crouched nearby, watching the perimeter. He stood and moved over to them, joining them without a word.

"Would it kill you to burp out a yes, sir once in awhile?" he asked the soldier.

Thompson shrugged.

"I'm surrounded by crazies," Kroeger said. "Military company excluded." He laughed again.

"Let's get going," Donovan said. "I want to be in Austin within forty-eight hours."

"Yes, sir," Kroeger said. "You heard the man. Thompson, Mendez, we're on the move."

Donovan retreated to his mech, climbing into the cockpit and sliding it closed. He followed Ehri as she gained her ride, bringing the bipedal armor to life a moment later.

They were underway minutes later, with Donovan leading them through the remainder of the city. It was slow going, even after the soldiers climbed onto the back of the mechs. They couldn't move too quickly without the risk of knocking them off.

"It's like Jack and the Beanstalk," Kroeger said, finding a perch on the undamaged shoulder of Donovan's mech.

"How do you figure that?" Donovan asked through the mech's external speakers. He had heard the fairy tale a couple of times from his grandfather when he was young. He didn't see any connection to their current circumstances.

"You're the giant, and I'm Jack," Kroeger said. "My father's name was Jack. Did you know that? He was a car salesman. Can you imagine? A damn car salesman. Talk about a dying trade."

"I always thought your father was a soldier."

"Why?"

"You have a soft spot for the military. I assumed either your father, someone in your family or you were enlisted at some point."

"You know what they say about assumptions and assholes, don't you Major?" He laughed. "No. Nobody in my family was military. I had a sister who was a cop. That's as close as I ever got to organized violence." He laughed again. "I've always had an appreciation for those who risk their necks for others. A lot of respect."

"That didn't stop you from trying to rob us."

"Should it have? Besides, I thought we were over that? It's old news, Major. We're on the same side now. Anyway, I always loved military stuff. The jets. The tanks. The female officers. Let me tell you, Major; military women are the best kind of women. Tough. Strong. Confident. I know Ehri's a clone, but she's like that."

"She is," Donovan agreed.

"So, you do it with her yet?"

Donovan almost choked on the statement. He had kissed Ehri once, back in Mexico, and there was a definite attraction there for him, at least. But Diaz's death and the constant threat to their lives had stolen away any thoughts of romantic anything, and besides, Ehri seemed have cooled on him in the days since. He didn't blame her for that. He appreciated that she was as focused on their mission as the rest of them.

Kroeger knew he had hit a nerve, and he laughed raucously at his reaction.

"I can dump you off this thing," Donovan said.

"I'm just screwing with you, Major. It's what I do. When you've seen what I've seen, done what I've done, you need levity to stay as sane as you can. When I say I'm surrounded by crazies, I mean me, too."

"You've said that before. What have you done that's so horrible?"

Kroeger was quiet for a few seconds. "I don't know what I'm going to tell you this. I haven't told a soul since it happened." He paused again, hesitating. "Okay. I used to run with these jackals up in what used to be Phoenix, Arizona. They called themselves the Way. Seriously. The Way. It's like a bad band name or something. Some emo boy band or some shit like that. Anyhow, their leader was this messed up prick who called himself Itchy. I kid you not."

Kroeger paused again.

"Sorry major, I can't do it. I thought I could. Some things need to stay buried, you know? Long story short, they had an initiation. I was starving. Desperate. Half mad. I killed a girl. That was the easy part. There was more. That's all I'm going to say. Whatever you infer from that, whatever you think it is I did, I can almost guarantee the truth is worse than that."

Donovan looked over at the soldier. Kroeger was leaning on the mech, his head in his hands. Donovan looked back to the road ahead. A long silence passed.

"Anyway," Kroeger said. "This reminds me of Jack and the Beanstalk. Only in this version, the Giant and Jack are working together, trying to right all of the wrongs in the world. Right now, that's a damn shot better than the truth."

"What is the truth?" Donovan asked.

"You don't want me to tell you."

"Go ahead."

"The truth, Major? We're going to die. All of us. But at least we can die like heroes."

[13]

DONOVAN WAS ALMOST READY TO BELIEVE IN KROEGER'S prophecy by the time they neared Austin.

The area around the former city was as bad as he had ever seen, apparently owing to the larger flock of people who had come to the area to find refuge near the rebel base there. They started coming across the bodies from twenty-five kilometers out, finding random groups of corpses scattered along the one-time highways. Some had been gunned down by clone soldiers, their bodies burned with two or three plasma bolts each. Others had been torn apart by the Dread's armors, the heavy projectiles they carried chewing human flesh and bone into little more than a mist that settled on the area around them. A few had been hit by the enemy fighters, their remains surrounded by craters from the attacks.

He lost count of the dead within the first few kilometers. It was over four hundred, and that was only adjacent to the road. He was sure there had to be more scattered throughout the surrounding countryside, forever lost amidst the trees.

It got worse as they moved closer, the dead becoming more frequent, more concentrated, and more recently killed. By the time they were fifteen kilometers out, the blood on the ground was still wet, the carrion being picked over by circling vultures and other animals. The smell of death began to reach into the cockpit where Donovan was sitting, and a growing sense of foreboding started eating into his thoughts.

At ten kilometers, they began to hear the echoes of gunfire in the city ahead, still partially obscured by rolling hills.

At five kilometers, as they gained a vantage point to the decaying metropolis, they found that the battle for Austin wasn't quite over yet.

In fact, it appeared to Donovan as though it might have only been beginning. Not because there was a lot of opposition to the Dread units they could spot from their position, but because the Dread were still organized as though they suspected they might be effectively attacked.

"What do you think?" Donovan asked, opening a channel to Soon and Ehri.

"I believe they attempted to accelerate their assault and destroy the rebel assets here before we could arrive," Ehri replied.

"I concur," Soon said.

"What took them so long to get here in the first place?" Donovan asked. "We weren't exactly covering a ton of ground, and look." He pointed to the outskirts of the city, where he could see the edge of a transport. "They flew in. At least some of them. They should have been done with this place days ago, if not longer."

"I'm not sure, Major," Ehri said. "It is curious."

"Are we going to just stand here and watch them kill our people or are we going to go kick some ass?" Kroeger said.

Donovan scanned the Dread forces, trying to estimate their size. A few hundred foot soldiers, at least six mechs, and a handful of the tanks as well. The lack of fighters suggested the fighting was too spread out for them to be of any use. Maybe his initial impression had been wrong. Maybe they were there to mop up.

"We can't take them head on," Donovan said. "We need to find the rebel forces and start handing out rifles."

"How do we find them?" Soon asked.

"Follow the noise," Kroeger suggested.

"Kroeger, join Thompson and Mendez on Soon's mech. Soon, I want you to bring up the rear and carry the others down into the city. Ehri, you and I will advance on the east side of the city, and try to get ahead of the Dread. We'll try to locate the rebels, clear out any targets in the area, and arm them as fast as we can."

"Yes, sir," Soon and the others said.

"Good hunting, Major," Kroeger said, before sliding down the side of the mech to the ground. He hurried over to Soon's armor, easily scaling the side of it.

"Ehri, let's go," Donovan said, putting his mech in motion. He moved it horizontally across the slope, angling it parallel to the city below.

Ehri followed him, her mech easily keeping pace with his. The top speed of the machines were limited to the full extent of the biomechanical muscles that powered them, but also dictated by the skill of the pilot. Donovan knew she could have easily outdistanced him if needed.

They went nearly one kilometer on the parallel and then adjusted course to take a gentle vector down the side of the slope and into Austin proper. The complexion of the battle wasn't changing much as they made their way toward it, and after a few minutes, Donovan began to wonder why the Dread weren't advancing further into the city at greater speed.

He had his answer a moment later when he witnessed a massive bolt of plasma launch away from the city center toward a mech that was trying to close in. It hit the armor square in the chest, knocking it backward as it tore a hole through it and into the cockpit.

"Whoa," Donovan said. "What the hell?"

The profile of the burst looked like it came from a Dread tank. How could the rebels have gotten hold of one?

"I've locked onto the source of the blast, Major," Ehri said. "That must be the rebel position."

"They have a Dread weapon," Donovan said.

"Clearly."

"How?"

"I do not know. We must be cautious. They won't recognize us as friendly."

"That's definitely a problem. Can we adjust the frequency of the communications equipment?"

"Not from inside, Major."

Damn.

"Soon, what's your ETA?" Donovan asked.

"Three minutes, Major," Soon replied.

"Okay. Hopefully, if they see you carrying human soldiers they won't shoot at you. Ehri and I will try to pick off the Dread blocking your path."

"Hopefully?" Soon said.

At least now he understood why the battle wasn't over. Somehow, the rebels had gotten a Dread tank into a highly defensible position and were blasting anything that got too close.

"Stay close, let's hit them together," Donovan said. "Full speed ahead."

[14]

Donovan glanced to his left, finding Ehri's mech right beside him, so close he flinched in fear they might collide before remembering who was piloting the machine. They were bearing down on the edge of the city, almost on top of the torn and broken skyscrapers that littered the area. The rebel tank hadn't fired again, but now that they had moved in closer they could see there were other rebel soldiers on the ground, armed with Dread plasma rifles and firing on the enemy clones.

Somehow, the Austin rebellion had gotten their hands on Dread technology, before Donovan even had a chance to bring it to them.

They skirted through the war-torn streets, moving in tight synchronicity across the urban battlefield. Donovan checked his sensors every few seconds, tracking Soon on his way down behind them. It was their job to give him breathing room.

He aimed the mech's cannons, launching a barrage of projectiles into a squad of clone soldiers taking cover behind an old car. It burst apart under the assault, leaving a trail of metal and smoke that disguised the death of the enemy behind it. He found another target and opened fire, a plasma bolt ripping into another group of enemy combatants.

Beside him, Ehri did the same, seeking targets and cutting them down, creating a swath of destruction as they advanced toward the city center. They had to be careful they didn't draw too close and risk getting hit by friendly fire.

"Rebel One, on your right," Ehri said.

Donovan rotated the mech. The remains of a once massive building blocked his view, but his sensors had tracked another mech heading their direction. He immediately stopped moving, taking a few steps back. The mechs weren't able to register one another as enemy targets, and the Dread pilots didn't know they were there yet.

"On three," Donovan said. "One. Two. Three."

He and Ehri both moved out into the open ahead of the mech. They fired simultaneously, their combined plasma bursts ripping right into the cockpit of the armor and killing the pilot before he had a chance to react.

"Looks like you didn't need me after all," Soon said. "You've got friendlies cheering at your back."

Donovan turned his head to look toward his rear. Three human soldiers were at the corner of a building, fists in the air at their victory.

"Get Kroeger over to meet them," Donovan said. "We need word passed to that tank that we're the good guys."

"Affirmative."

"Rebel One, it looks like the bek'hai commander has realized we are here."

Donovan glanced at his sensors. They were picking up the signal of seven remaining mechs. All of them had turned to head their way.

"Damn," he said. "Rebel Three, drop your cargo and form up. We've got a fan club."

"Yes, sir," Soon said.

Donovan headed down a wide street, before ducking the mech through a tighter alley, crunching over a layer of rubble and attracting plasma attacks from clones on the ground. He hit them back, cutting them down and shaking his head at the futility of their efforts. Why didn't the pur'dahm let them run? It was so pointless. Ehri tracked down a separate lane, staying close but split apart as they moved to intercept the incoming mechs.

"Cargo unloaded," Soon said. "I'm on my way. Leave a dance partner for me."

"I don't think that will be a problem, Rebel Three," Donovan said.

"Incoming," Ehri said.

Donovan's HUD was showing red marks coming toward them. He ducked his mech, pressing it against the side of a building as most of the projectiles slammed into the area beside him, sending shards of concrete and glass and rubble everywhere. He cursed as two of the missiles hit the already damaged arm, the impact shaking the mech and causing the appendage to fall off completely, leaving only a trail of exposed biomechanical muscle and wires behind.

"Son of a bitch," Donovan said. His mech wasn't carrying any missiles. In fact, he was pretty sure his cannon rounds were nearly depleted as well.

"Back up, Rebel One," Soon said. "Lead them in. I've got you covered."

"Roger," Donovan said, moving his feet to put the mech into reverse. It backed away, crossing three streets as the enemy mechs appeared ahead of him. He took a few potshots with his plasma cannons and then reached a wider thoroughfare.

"Sharp left, Rebel One," Soon said.

Donovan made the turn, still backing away. The Dread pilot had sped up to reach him, and as he finally turned the corner, he left his back exposed to a waiting Soon. It didn't take much to destroy the armor from behind, taking one of the mechs out of the fight.

"This is Rebel Two. I could use a little help over here."

"On our way," Donovan said, checking his HUD again. Ehri was mixing it up with three of the mechs. The other three were still circling them, trying to get a better attack vector.

"Like sharks," Soon said.

"How do you know about sharks?" Donovan asked.

"I saw it on an old vid. I'd love to see a real one."

"Then let's finish off these assholes."

"Affirmative."

They reached Ehri, breaking around the corners on opposite sides and catching one of her assailants in a crossfire. The mech shook as their plasma dug into it, and then toppled over.

"That's two," Soon said.

"Watch the outliers," Donovan warned, noticing the three circling mechs beginning to close in from behind. "We're getting cut off."

"Crap," Soon said. "There's too many of them."

"One at a time," Ehri said. "Let's take the one on the left."

"Good idea," Donovan said.

They adjusted their vectors, using the buildings as cover while they circled the lone mech. It left them open to attack from the others, but there was no way around that anyway. They needed to thin the numbers, to have fewer weapons able to target them.

"Rebel Three, break left," Donovan said. "Rebel Two, ease off. Let's meet him at the same time."

The other two mechs followed his commands, angling in and emerging on the target as one. They blasted it with their combined firepower, knocking it into a pile of rubble and taking it out of the fight.

"Three," Donovan said, checking for the next target.

His heart raced as he caught sight of his tail. Two of the Dread mechs were closing in behind him, about to clear the cover he had inadvertently positioned himself behind.

"I need backup," he said as they reached the open space.

He swung his mech, rotating it around to clear the delicate backside as they opened fire. Plasma bolts tore into the side of the armor, ripping into the remaining arm and one of the legs. More red symbols appeared on his HUD, and a warning beep began to sound.

"Rebel Two, what does the beeping mean?" he asked as he tried to back away from the onslaught, fighting to remain calm.

"Critical damage," Ehri said. "You need to get out of the mech now, Major."

Donovan looked ahead to the two mechs. Another plasma bolt crossed the distance, slamming into the torso directly below him.

He grabbed at the cockpit release, finding some relief when it responded, and the mech opened up to let him out. He didn't give much thought to climbing down. Instead, he grabbed one of the Dread rifles before sliding down a leg, feeling the heat of the damaged mech against the gori'shah he was wearing under his clothes. He heard the stomping of feet, and watched as Ehri cut in front of his downed mech, unleashing her ordnance on the two attackers. The strikes hit them in the legs, blistering through delicate joints and knocking them off-balance. One fell, hitting the other, and they both collapsed in a heap.

Donovan couldn't communicate with them now that he was out of the mech, and he was reduced to little more than a bystander. At least for a moment, until the Dread clones started shooting at him. He ducked behind his mech, and then ran down an alley, turning his head back every few seconds to try to keep track of his squad.

Soon's mech passed in front of him, crossing his path as it tangled with one of the Dread armors. It had taken some damage but appeared fully operational.

The remaining enemy mechs were closing in, and even from the ground he could see Soon was in trouble. Every instinct in him told him to run toward the fight, not away from it. He tried to resist. What was he going to do on the ground?

Soon was going to die if he did nothing. Ehri, too.

"Major."

He heard Kroeger's raspy shout over the din of the battle. He looked that direction, finding him surrounded by rebel soldiers, all of them already armed with Dread rifles. Mendez was with him.

"Where's Thompson?" he asked.

Kroeger shook his head. Damn.

"We need to help Soon and Ehri. They're about to get pummeled."

"I wouldn't worry too much about that, Major," Kroeger said. He put his arm around one of the soldiers. "Give it up to my man here, will you Corporal?"

The soldier, who couldn't have been more than fifteen, held out a small device that looked like a radio. "Put it up to your ear," he said.

Donovan took it and did.

"Mech One, make your way across 38th. Mech Two, keep them coming. You're doing great."

It was a woman's voice, older and slightly gruff. She fed the orders like she had been doing it her entire life.

"Roger," he heard soon say. "Mech Two bringing them home."

Donovan glanced over at Kroeger, who was laughing like the whole thing was a massive joke.

"Seems we're late to the party, Major," he said. "It looks like our efforts back in good ole Mehico paid off big-time."

"Follow me," the Corporal said, leading them back down a smaller alley.

They moved parallel to the action, toward the city center. Donovan kept the radio to his ear, wondering how the rebels had managed to establish a connection with Ehri and Soon. The whole thing had taken him completely by surprise. They weren't supposed to be so well-equipped, or so able to fight back. Not that he was complaining.

"Mechs One and Two, we're ready for crossover. When you pass in front of one another, get as low as possible."

"Roger," Ehri said.

"Roger," Soon said.

Donovan had no idea what was going to happen, but it seemed the rebel commander had a plan.

The Corporal brought them to another intersection, already filled with smoke from smoldering wreckage. Then he turned to Donovan and smiled, his teeth a sharp contrast to his grime covered face. "We made it just in time for the fireworks," he said.

Donovan looked down the street as Soon and Ehri's mechs crossed one another a few streets apart. They were backing up, taking fire from the enemy as they retreated. He felt a wave of discomfort at seeing them on the defensive, and it only doubled when four of the Dread mechs moved into the same avenue.

"Fire," he heard the rebel commander say.

He lowered the device. He could feel the charge in the air even before the plasma beam reached them, washing past in a streak of heat and fury.

It tore into the Dread mechs, burning them into slag in an instant, cutting them apart like a sword. Within seconds, the four enemy targets were reduced to legs carrying misshapen carapace above them.

"What the hell was that?" Soon said.

He was feeling the same way. That blast was bigger than anything he had ever seen, including the Dread tanks.

"Four targets, four kills," he heard the woman say. "Nice work."

"It looks like the Dread are bugging out," the Corporal said beside him.

Donovan looked down the street. A Dread transport had risen in the distance and was moving away from Austin. Another followed a moment later.

"We won?" Donovan said in disbelief.

"Yes, sir," the Corporal said, laughing. "Welcome to Texas, Major."

[15]

The Corporal, whose name Donovan soon learned was James Wilkins, led him, Kroeger, and Mendez down the same street where the plasma beam had fired, covering nearly a kilometer before reaching the entrance to the rebel stronghold.

It was the entrance to a loop station, a small outbuilding only a few meters across and a few meters wide, resting on a corner and shielded from most sides by the remains of taller buildings. It was immediately obvious to Donovan why the Dread hadn't been able to bombard it from the sky. What wasn't clear was how they had managed to defend it from all sides or where that massive plasma beam had really come from.

"I'm confused, Corporal," he said as they neared the entrance, where three more squads of soldiers were standing guard, already armed with enemy rifles. "I thought we were the only ones fighting back against the Dread and hurting them."

"You were a few weeks ago," Wilkins replied. "I'll let the Colonel fill you in. She'll be pissed if I ruin it for her."

"What about my people outside? The mech pilots?"

"We've got a place they can store their equipment. We might

even be able to put the armor back together if we can grab some more salvage. Anyway, don't worry about them."

They entered the station, descending one hundred meters to the waiting area. There were tunnels on either side of it, and a few free-standing shops lining the center. Most of them still had their wares inside, forgotten after the initial Dread invasion.

"You have power," Donovan said.

"Yes, sir. We have even more power now."

"Where's the weapon that fired the plasma beam?"

"On its way home. It did its job."

"Home?"

Donovan was confused until he heard a soft whoosh from one of the tunnels. A loop car appeared a moment later, coming to rest beside the platform.

"The station is operational?" he said, barely able to believe it.

"It is now," Wilkins said. "And it sure beats the hell out of walking." He led them to the car. "Get in."

Donovan glanced over at Kroeger, whose face was stuck in shocked amusement. The smile hadn't faded since he had joined him outside.

"I never thought I'd see the day," Kroeger said.

"Me neither," Donovan agreed. He climbed into the car and sat. The textile seats were cracked and worn, but they felt like heaven compared to the Dread mech. He watched as the top of the car closed above him and then smiled like he was a kid again when it began to move.

The ride was short, the car passing underground, traveling thirty seconds to the next destination. The top swung open to release them, and then Donovan stood and marveled.

This station was four times bigger than the last, with eight tunnels leading away from it, two in each direction. The center island was huge and dotted with nylon tents, piles of equipment, cans of food, and everything else a rebel base required.

"We call it Fort Neverdie," Wilkins said.

Donovan kept turning his head, taking in the sight. He paused when his eyes landed on a large contraption in the corner. It looked like the Dread reactor he had seen inside the transport, hooked up to what resembled the turret of one of their tanks, nestled in a package that could be deployed anywhere in the city if they threw it into a loop car.

"That's-"

"Big Bertha," Wilkins replied. "Our magic plasma cannon."

"How?"

"Let me introduce you to the Colonel, Major."

"Good idea."

Wilkins brought them across the platform, weaving around the multitude of tents. They were all empty right now, the soldiers who occupied them out on the streets for the battle. Unlike Mexico, there were no non-fighting women or children to be seen. Were they somewhere else? Or were they not allowed to find refuge here?

At least now he understood why so many had been trying to reach the city before the Dread arrived.

Wilkins brought them to a stop outside of a small space stacked high with so many electronics that they created a room of sorts. Most of the pieces had been opened up and reconfigured in some way, with connections crisscrossing one another and joining other connections, creating a web of colored lines that seemed impossible to decipher. Dozens of wires snaked away from the mess, down the side of the platform and vanishing into one of the tunnels.

A dark-skinned woman was standing in the center of it all; her head turned toward one of a dozen monitors mounted to the other equipment. She had a device similar to the one the Corporal was carrying near her face, and she was barking orders to the teams outside.

"Colonel Knight," Wilkins said, getting her attention.

She glanced their way, her eyes narrowing.

"Corporal. Where's Captain Rami?"

"He didn't make it, ma'am," Wilkins replied.

Donovan could see the pain on her face. Judging by the wrinkles, it was an expression she had made far too often.

"Colonel Knight," Donovan said, getting her attention by saluting. "My name is Major Donovan Peters. I'm-"

"I know who you are, Major," she said, putting up her hand and giving him a small smile. "I'm very eager to speak to you, but right now I have to manage my crew."

"Understood, Colonel. Is there anything I can do to help?"

She hesitated for a moment, and then nodded. "Yes. Actually, there is. Come on in here."

Donovan entered the space. He quickly took in the different displays. It seemed they had gotten cameras hooked up at various places in the city.

"Keep an eye on the screens. You seen any Dread, you holler. Okay?"

"Yes, ma'am."

Donovan watched the screens while Colonel Knight returned to sending orders out to the troops. He noticed the volume inside the base grow as more and more of the soldiers returned home. Two hours later, and without another sign of Dread activity, the Colonel finally put down the comm device and looked at him once more.

"You showed up at a good time, Major," she said. "Your squad turned the tide in a hurry. We've been at a standoff for the last three days."

"I'm happy we could help, ma'am," Donovan replied. "Although it seems you're pretty well organized without us."

"We've done okay lately, but we weren't able to capture any heavy equipment. We only have one person who knows how to drive it."

"You have someone who knows how to pilot a Dread mech?"

"Yes. I'll introduce you to her as soon as I can."

Donovan raised his eyebrow. Her? It couldn't be. Could it?

"Where did you get the rifles? And the cannon?"

"I'll answer all of your questions, but let me give you the quick briefing first. Deal?"

"Yes, ma'am. My apologies."

"Major Donovan Peters, you are the biggest war hero this planet has right now. You don't have to apologize to me for anything."

Donovan felt a chill at the words. Him? "I'm just doing my duty, ma'am."

She laughed. "That's what all good heroes say. Come on over to the command tent, I'll give you the quick rundown." She led him out of the area. "You've already gotten the two-cent visual tour, I take it?"

"I looked around a little, yes, ma'am."

"Good. I'll show you more later. This way."

She brought him back into the sea of tents, leading him to a larger one near the corner. There was no way he would have guessed it was the command tent without having it labeled.

They went inside. There was another soldier already there, and he saluted as she entered. "Colonel."

"At ease, Captain," she said. "Captain Omar, this is Major Donovan Peters."

Omar looked at him and then smiled. "It's an honor, Major."

"Thank you," Donovan said, feeling uncomfortable with the greeting.

"Captain, can you go find Juliet and bring her here?"

"Of course, Colonel."

Donovan's heart jumped. "Juliet?"

"Our secret weapon," Colonel Knight said. "She was a Dread slave, but she managed to get free. It's a pretty incredible story, really."

"And her name is Juliet? As in, Juliet St. Martin?"

Colonel Knight furrowed her brow. "Yes. How did you know?"

Donovan felt numb.

"Lucky guess?" he said weakly.

[16]

"WELL, IT SEEMS WE BOTH MIGHT HAVE STORIES TO TELL, Major," Colonel Knight said. "I'll go first, and then you can fill me in on what you know about Juliet St. Martin. Unless I need to be concerned about her?"

Donovan overcame his shock, shaking his head. "No, I don't think you need to be concerned. I doubt she's a Dread spy or anything, especially if she's the reason you've managed to get your hands on Dread technology."

"Good enough. So yes, she is the reason we've managed to staunch the bleeding, so to speak. I've been running things down here since this base was established seventeen years ago. Four weeks ago, we were barely eeking out an existence, trying to keep up with the communications from the teams across the globe, and of course especially interested in your work down in Mexico. The transmissions to the space forces have been our lifeline to hope for a long time."

"They were for us as well."

"Then we caught wind of a message your General Rodriguez sent up to General Parker in New York. A transmission about the space forces, and your involvement in not only getting inside a Dread fortress but escaping with one of their weapons. Major, we were on the edge of our seats waiting to hear what had happened to you after that last transmission. Did you make the transfer? Didn't you? I even stood outside and tried to watch the sky, to see if I could get any clues."

"You saw the Magellan?"

"Yeah. I saw it. I damn near cried." She smiled. "Unbelievable. Anyway, two days later, one of our squads is out on routine patrol when this woman shows up. She snuck up on Delta, came up right behind them and they never knew she was there. She was wearing this black cloth." Colonel Knight paused, looking at Donovan. His uniform had been torn during his escape from the mech. "Like that one."

"It's called a gori'shah," Donovan said.

"Yeah, she told us. Anyway, she said her name was Juliet St. Martin, the wife of the General in charge of the space forces. She asked to be brought to see me, so she was. She then proceeded to tell me the craziest story I'd ever heard, about being made into a clone, about reversing her aging, and then about finally escaping from the Dread. She said they had been keeping her in their main research facility in Honduras, and that she stole a transport and headed here because she had heard the message from her husband and knew you would need her help. Of course, we didn't believe her at first, until she showed us the transport, and started handing out the weapons inside."

Donovan nodded. Things were starting to make a little bit of sense, anyway. Juliet St. Martin alive? She had said it, and he could still barely believe it.

"A few days after that, the Dread started sweeping the area. They came over in their fighters at first, but they couldn't do much to us from there. These tunnels are too deep, and there are too many stations to hit them all. By the time they close one up, we manage to dig out two more. They had to start sending in foot soldiers, except they didn't know right away that we had been armed.

"Juliet helped us salvage the power source from the transport, along with some of the communication equipment. We hooked it up down here. For the first time in years, we weren't relying on hand-made candles and the remains of fifty-year-old batteries that we scavenged from around the city. Even better, it turned out that the loop was still operational. All it needed was a little juice. Before that, we had to walk the tunnels everywhere."

"I get where the rifles came from, and how you've managed to move your resources quickly enough to shore up weak spots in the defenses," Donovan said. "What about the gun? The one Wilkins called Big Bertha?"

"Yeah. So, we had power. We had Dread rifles. Juliet said it wouldn't be enough. They would send mechs to dig us out. They would send clones to come down into the tunnels. We needed more firepower. I couldn't argue with that. We got a broadcast from someplace called Hell; they said that you were on your way to assault a Dread military outpost, and I thought, well hell, if he can do it, why can't we?" She laughed. "There was an outpost fifty klicks east of here. It isn't there anymore."

"You attacked the Dread?"

"And won. They aren't so tough when they aren't invincible. You proved that. We had to leave the mechs, but we did get our hands on one of those tank things, along with a whole bunch of small arms, enough for every soldier in the base, and then some. Anyway, we couldn't fit the tank down here, so we got to work on pulling the cannon off it."

"The one that vaporized those mechs?"

"Yes."

"That was more powerful than any Dread weapon I've seen."

Her smile grew bigger. "Yes. Juliet's quite handy with the Dread weaponry. She replaced some of the conduits with copper wiring instead of that stuff they use, and she was able to triple the strength and duration of the plasma. Boom. Big Bertha was born. What you saw was the first time we fired it at full strength. We didn't want to give anything away if we didn't have to."

"I would say it was a successful test."

"I would say that, too, Major."

"Does General Parker know about all of this?"

"Yes. In fact, he's on his way here."

Donovan leaned forward. "What?"

"He's on his way here. Two thousand rebels are doing everything they can to get to Austin alive. He left a week ago."

Donovan sat there in silence for a few moments, considering.

"You want to attack Mexico," he said.

"No, Major. We're going to attack Mexico. It's a given. The only question is when. General Parker isn't the only one on the move. We reached out to as many bases as we could. We told them to come to Austin. I don't know how many troops are incoming. Whatever we have, we'll use. One last push to get the Dread off our planet."

"What about the space forces?"

"I don't know. You made the exchange, but we haven't heard from them since. Did they survive? Are they coming back? We hope so, but we can't pin all of our hope on it. We need to make our own move. If we can coordinate something, we will. Otherwise, we're going in anyway. This is our moment. Our one chance. We can't let it slip away."

Donovan froze again. He couldn't believe it. He had expected to find a half-beaten army here, and instead, he had landed at the center of the rebellion. He felt a new energy flow into him, and the greatest sense of hope he had ever felt in his life.

"You need mechs. And mech pilots."

"Yes, we do," she agreed.

"Do we still have access to the ones you left behind?"

"I don't know for sure. Without pilots, what was the point? Now that you're here, we may need to reconsider."

"I'll go," Donovan said.

"I know. Hold that thought for now. At the moment, I want to hear your story. I want to fill in the gaps between the signals we've been receiving."

Donovan's heart and mind were racing. He could barely calm down. After all, he had been through, all he had lost. They were going to fight back. They were going to hit the Dread city and avenge Renata, Matteo, General Rodriguez, his mother, and all of the others.

He had just opened his mouth to speak when he was interrupted by a sudden commotion from outside.

"What's going on out there?" Colonel Knight said, getting to her feet and heading for the door to the tent.

Donovan followed her, exiting the tent at her back. He saw the cause of the uproar immediately.

Ehri was standing to his left. Juliet St. Martin was opposite her, on his right.

They looked like they were ready to kill one another.

[17]

"Ehri?" Donovan said.

She looked over at him, making sure to keep her head tilted to watch her twin out of the corner of her eye. "Yes, Major?"

"What are you doing?"

"Do not trust this thing, Major. It is false."

"What are you talking about?" Juliet said. "You're the one that's false."

"Both of you, calm down," Colonel Knight said. She looked at Donovan. "I have to admit, Major. I'm a little confused."

"Permission to handle this, Colonel?" Donovan said.

"Granted."

Donovan stepped between them, facing away from Ehri.

"Colonel Knight tells me that you're Juliet St. Martin," he said.

"Yes. That's correct."

"Juliet St. Martin would be almost eighty years old."

"Yes." She smiled. "Lord knows, I understand your doubt, Major Peters, is it?"

"Yes, ma'am."

"I understand your doubt, Major Peters. I can assure you that I am Juliet St. Martin. If Theodore were here, he would be able to confirm as much."

"Excuse me, Major," Ehri said.

Donovan turned around. "Yes?"

"The age of Juliet St. Martin is not in question."

"It isn't?"

"No. Only the identity of this clone is in question."

"I'm not a clone," Juliet said. "You are the clone. One of many produced by the bek'hai."

"Wait a second. Ehri, there has never been a question of whether or not you're a clone. Has there?"

She hesitated for a moment. "Not previously, Major."

"What do you mean, not previously?"

"It is a long story. I have not been completely honest with you."

Donovan froze. "What? I asked you, after we gave the weapon to Captain St. Martin, if you had any other secrets. You said no."

She looked at the ground. "I know. I am sorry. I had to. You would never have believed the truth, and you would never have trusted in me."

Donovan cringed to ask the question, because he was afraid of the answer. He had to put it forward regardless. "And what is the truth?"

She looked up at him. "I am Juliet St. Martin."

Donovan stared at her. Then he looked at the other Juliet. Then he looked back at her. "No. You aren't."

"Yes, I am."

"Major?" Colonel Knight said. "What is going on here?"

"I'm not sure yet," he replied. "Ehri, don't you think it's a little odd that there's another clone of you here that is helping the rebellion, and thinks they're Juliet St. Martin?" He looked at Juliet. "Don't you?"

"Not at all," Juliet said. "Some of my clones have been programmed to believe they're me. To activate when they come in contact with humans. It isn't a mistake. It was intended to help the rebellion fight the Dread."

"I would have said the same thing, had you asked me, Major," Ehri said.

"You would not," Juliet replied.

"Yes, I would."

Donovan wasn't about to accept the idea that either one of them was the real Juliet St. Martin. Even so, the tension between the two clones was obvious.

"Hold on," he said. "Both of you. If that's the case, how do either of you know you're the real thing?"

"I have memories of my time with Theodore," they both replied in unison.

Ehri paused, her face flushing. She looked at her twin.

"Name one," she said.

"I still remember the day we met," they both said.

Ehri froze again. So did Juliet.

"Major," she said. "I believe there has been some mistake."

"It can't be," Juliet said.

"Major?" Colonel Knight asked.

"I'm sorry," Donovan said. "Without definitive proof, the fact that you are both clones is the only thing that makes sense."

Ehri nodded. "I know I am Juliet St. Martin. I feel it in my soul. Down to the deepest core of me."

"So do I," Juliet said.

Ehri paused for the third time. Then she looked at Donovan, her expression frightened and sad. "I need to consider this."

She fled the scene, making her way around the tents and heading toward a dark corner of the platform. Juliet stood her ground, watching her go with them.

"We can't have the same memories," she said. "They don't copy memories."

"Can they?" Donovan asked.

"Yes. But they don't."

"What if they did?"

"Then any clone with the memories would believe they were Juliet St. Martin. They would believe it with everything in them."

Donovan stared at Juliet.

"It can't be me. I can't be a copy."

"Why?"

A tear trailed from her eye. "I just can't. I remember seeing the Magellan over the planet. I remember the moment when I realized who I am. It isn't my imagination. It can't be."

"What if it is?"

"I don't know."

She stood there, silent. What else was there to say?

"Major, you're suggesting there are two Juliet St. Martins?" Colonel Knight asked.

"At least two," he replied. "And probably more. Something is going on here. Something we don't completely understand yet."

"All I need to know is if these clones are on our side or not."

"They are, Colonel," Donovan said. "At least, I believe they are, and I've never had a reason to think otherwise."

"Then that's good enough for me. We're preparing to go to war, Major. We can't worry about a pair of Dread clones who think they're the same human."

"Maybe not, ma'am," Donovan said. "But we need them to be part of this. We need them to fill the roles they were made to fill."

"What do you propose?"

"I don't know. I'll go and talk to Ehri. We can't afford to lose our best pilot. Not when we have so few."

"Agreed." Colonel Knight walked over to Juliet. "Juliet, maybe you want to take a little break, clear your head?"

Juliet's eyes shifted to her, and she nodded meekly. "Perhaps that's best. I will be in my tent if you need anything, Colonel."

Donovan watched her go. Then he looked back in the direction Ehri had gone. He could think of a lot worse things than having multiple copies of Juliet St. Martin on their side. Now they just had to convince the copies of that.

[18]

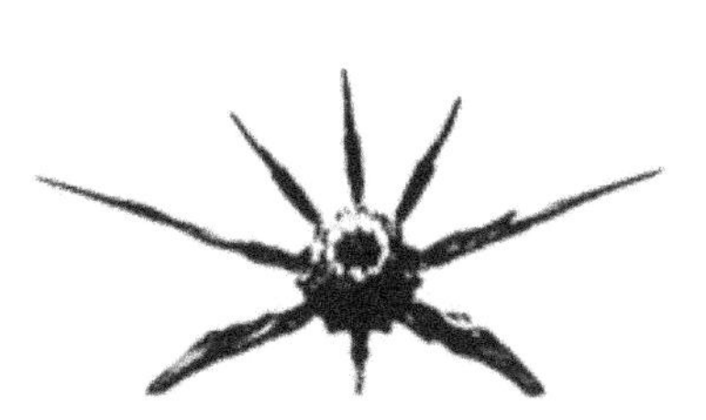

DONOVAN DIDN'T HURRY RIGHT OVER TO WHERE HE HAD SEEN Ehri disappear. He needed a few minutes to himself, to consider what was happening, and to figure out what he wanted to say.

He thought about what he knew of her. First, that she and her once pur'dahm superior, Tuhrik, had concocted a plan to bring a human into the Dread capital, ostensibly so that she could study them. It was a plan that the Domo'dahm had known about and approved, with the understanding that Ehri would return to the fold within a few weeks, after gathering information about how the rebels lived, and perhaps tactical details that he could use to finish his eradication. Tuhrik had expected to die in the process, or at least had known there was a risk to it, but he was nearing his time for retirement regardless and really, had nothing to lose.

She had joined them as a clone scientist, aware of her source genetics but otherwise ambivalent to them. At least, that was what she had said. Looking back at the way she had integrated into their society, such as taking care of the children with his mother or showing a level of compassion she said the Dread rarely felt, he could sense that there must have been some part of her that was relating to what he knew of General St. Martin's wife.

It was an understandable part considering they shared the same DNA, and she had never said anything about actually being Juliet St. Martin. Of course, if she had turned around and made the same claims as the Austin Juliet, would General Rodriguez, who had known the original Juliet personally, have believed her? Or would she have been putting the security of the base in jeopardy at a time when they most needed to be able to trust her, with the Dread closing in on their position and the entire war teetering on the edge, their future to be determined by a single alien rifle that could penetrate impenetrable shields?

If she had believed she was Juliet St. Martin then, would there have been a benefit for her to tell them? Would any of them have really believed, when they knew so little about the Dread in the first place? Would he?

He didn't think he would have, and it made it easier for him to accept the omission. In hindsight, he believed she had done the right thing.

He made his way past the tents, over to the corner of the platform. The rebels had stashed a large portion of their edibles there, in the form of thousands of handmade cans stuffed and sealed with whatever vegetables they had been able to scavenge, along with a large, functional refrigerator that he imagined was stocked with game. Ehri was sitting on one of the crates filled with cans, her back to him, her head in her hands.

"Ehri," he said.

"Please, Major," she said. "I'd like to be alone."

"I understand that, and given other circumstances, I'd be happy to comply. In this case, I can't. We're gearing up for the biggest battle in fifty years, and I need to know where you stand."

She lifted her head but didn't look at him. "Where I stand, Major? How am I supposed to answer that? I don't even know who, or what, I am."

"You've always been Ehri dur Tuhrik."

"I don't want to be Ehri dur Tuhrik. I don't feel Ehri dur Tuhrik. That was a disguise. A mask that Tuhrik placed on me to hide me from the Domo'dahm. At least, that is what my memories tell me." She paused. "Apparently, I can't trust my memories."

"When did the mask come off?" Donovan asked.

"When I heard his voice," Ehri said. "Theodore's voice. When I heard him speak. I wanted to help you before that. I always felt it within me. But when I heard him I knew who I really was. Or who I thought I was."

"Juliet St. Martin couldn't fight like you do."

"I had training, as Ehri dur Tuhrik."

"You know what I mean."

She turned to face him then. Her eyes were red and moist. She looked tired and miserable. "My enhanced abilities. Yes. In here, they come from the maturation capsule." She tapped the side of her head. "But to consider it scientifically, Tuhrik may have altered the cloning process in some way to make me stronger and faster."

"I didn't get the impression the other Juliet has those traits."

"Perhaps not. The weapon, Big Bertha, that is a technology the Dread do not possess. Not at that scale. Maybe she is smarter."

"Different clones with different strengths?" Donovan suggested. It made sense, although he had no idea how the bek'hai scientist could have done it.

"Or the personality helps determine the strengths. But to accept that is to accept that I am a clone, and that is very difficult for me to do. I feel like Juliet St. Martin. I feel the love of God. The love of my husband. And Gabriel." She looked down again, shaking her head. "I almost told him, when we met him on the mountain. I almost gave myself away. I wanted to touch him, to hold him. How can that not be real?"

"Nobody is saying it isn't real. Whatever is causing your emotions, they're completely real. Whatever is motivating you, that's real, too. Who you are is real. The truth is additive to that. There isn't one of you fighting for us. There's a multitude. Who knows how many? Think of what you could accomplish if you all worked together, instead of being at odds because you believe there can be only one."

Ehri was silent for a moment. "I understand what you are suggesting, Major. And logically, it makes complete sense. Emotionally? I desire to be unique. To be the one Juliet St. Martin. I don't want to share Theodore and Gabriel with the others."

"But do you want them to survive? Do you want them to have the opportunity to return to Earth?"

"Yes."

"Are you willing to sacrifice your ability to be with them to give them that?"

"I would sacrifice my life to give them that."

"Then what's the problem?"

Ehri looked up at him for the first time, meeting his eyes with hers. He could sense the immediate change in her, the sudden resolve. He was right, and she knew it.

Loving someone wasn't about being loved. It was about sacrificing anything and everything you had for them, without resentment, without remorse, without regret.

He hoped Diaz had felt that way before she died.

"I cannot argue your point, Major," Ehri said, getting to her feet. "Thank you for giving me some perspective. I won't say the truth isn't painful, but at least I have something to fight for."

"You're welcome. Let's go see what we can do to help."

[19]

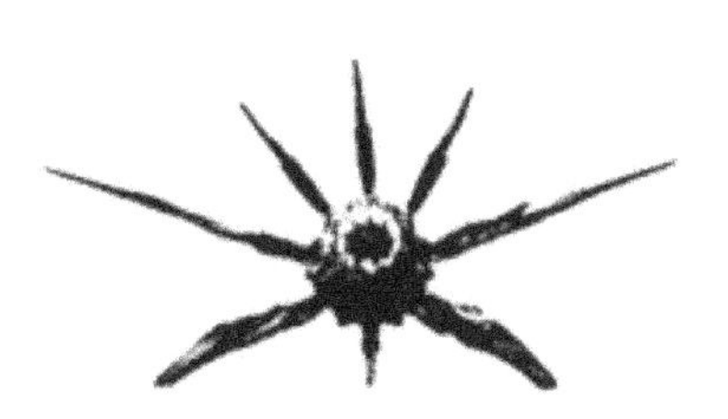

Gabriel retreated from his father's quarters, intending to return to the bridge. He was interrupted when Miranda appeared at the end of the corridor, heading toward him.

"Gabriel," she said, smiling as he neared.

"Hey, Randa," he replied. "Colonel Choi let you off the bridge for a while?"

"She dismissed almost everyone. There isn't much we can do up there until Reza gets some of the systems online. A skeleton crew is good enough to sit here."

Gabriel glanced out one of the transparencies that speckled the outer hull. There was nothing to see but stars floating on a sea of black.

"Where were you headed?"

"I was going to check on Wallace for you, and then make my way to the Magellan."

"Do you mind if I join you?"

"Never."

She flinched then. Gabriel wasn't sure why until he noticed the dark shape near the corner. It crossed the corridor and vanished into an access tunnel.

"I'm not used to them yet," she said about the cleaner.

"I'm not used to any of this," Gabriel replied.

"Like Zoelle?"

"Especially Zoelle. I just finished talking to my father. He said she told him about things nobody else would know. I don't know how that's possible, but it's sure got him convinced."

"What if she really is your mother?"

"Don't tell me you believe that."

"You're so sure she isn't. I'm just worried you might be missing a chance to get to know her. I mean, even if she isn't, she knows things about her that you'll never know any other way."

The statement reminded Gabriel of all of the time he had spent avoiding his father back on Alpha. He regretted that loss now, even while he was thankful to have the real Theodore St. Martin back.

"Maybe you're right. And what's that old saying again? Keep your friends close, and your enemies closer?"

"She's not our enemy. You told me she saved your life."

"Yeah. Maybe. Do you think I'm being stubborn?"

"Probably a little. It seems to run in the family."

"I think I'm going to take a pass on our walk if that's okay with you?"

"You're going to find Zoelle?"

"Yes. I want to see what Reza's up to, anyway."

Miranda nodded and leaned forward, kissing him on the cheek. "I'll see you later then, Major St. Martin."

"As you will, Spaceman Locke," Gabriel replied, smiling. "By the way, thanks for looking out for Wallace for me."

"It's no trouble at all."

He watched her walk down the corridor for a few seconds before heading on to the bridge. When he entered, he found the entire thing nearly deserted, save for a few of the Magellan's crew scattered around the terminals, and Colonel Choi sitting slouched on the command dais. She looked exhausted, too, but she straightened herself quickly as he approached.

"Colonel Choi," he said, saluting.

"At ease, Major. What can I do for you?"

"I'm looking for Reza and Zoelle. Do you know where they went?"

"Reza said something about the phase modulator, and Zoelle suggested that they get the schematics into the ship's replicators so they could try to match it."

"Replicator?"

"I'm assuming it is what it sounds like."

"Do you know where it is?"

"No. Zoelle said she would show him. I sent Diallo with them, just in case. She didn't seem thrilled with the idea, but too damn bad."

"Okay. I could stand a little exercise anyway. I might as well get it exploring this place a little bit."

"I don't know if that's the best idea. We can't be sure all of the mothers and the drumhr loyal to Gr'el are taken care of. Besides, you might get lost."

"I can take care of myself," he replied. "I'll grab a rifle before I go too far, and Tea'va showed me how to use the communications systems. I'll be able to call for help if I get into any trouble."

"Be careful."

"I will. You should get in touch with Colonel Graham and have him take over for you. You look like you're ready to collapse."

"I would, but Colonel Graham is busy with the repairs to the Magellan, and I don't want to interrupt him. I'll give your father six hours, and then he's coming back up here whether he likes it or not."

"Are you going to be the one to tell him that?"

She laughed. "At that point, I might be overtired enough to do it."

Gabriel left the bridge, heading down another corridor to the space where they had stashed their collection of Dread weaponry. Spaceman Ewing was standing in front of it.

"Major," he said, saluting as Gabriel approached.

"Spaceman Ewing. At ease. I need to borrow a rifle from the armory. I'm heading below decks, and I'm not completely sure what I might find down there."

"Are you sure that's a good idea, sir?" Ewing asked, moving aside and pressing the wall so the room would open.

"I'm sure it's not a completely bad idea," Gabriel replied.

He entered the armory. It was as simple and bare as any other in the Dread starship, save for the neatly assembled rows of plasma rifles they had collected from their defeated enemy. Rifles they would use to invade Earth with the entirety of the New Earth Alliance military, once they finally returned home.

He picked one of them up, checked the energy level, and carried it from the room.

"Good hunting, Major," Spaceman Ewing said as he headed toward one of the transport beams.

"Thanks," Gabriel replied.

He reached the beam a minute later, taking a deep breath as he prepared himself to enter it. He still found the technology a little frightening, probably because he didn't understand how it worked. He stepped in, lowering his hands for a moment and then coming to a stop at the bottom of the fortress, on the same level as the cloning factory. If the replicator was a similar thing, only for inanimate objects, then this was probably where it would be found. If he happened across anyone else, he would be sure to ask them.

As he moved into the dim corridors alone, he began to wonder if, like Colonel Choi, he was overtired enough to be doing something stupid.

[20]

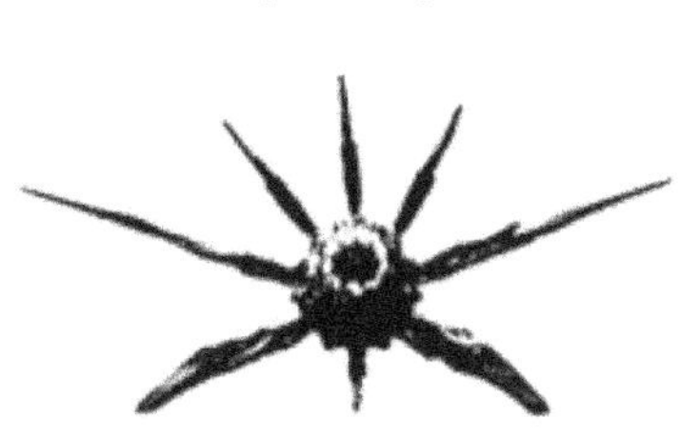

The fear of the unknown began to wear off as Gabriel navigated through the Dread ship, spending most of his time alone until he finally made his way out into the open space where the clone factory was found. He smiled, impressed with himself for finding his way to it, and from a different entrance. Then he scanned the area beyond the factory. There were three more corridors branching off from it, heading further into the fortress. He was sure he was going to follow one of them, but which one?

He decided on the middle and started crossing the open area beside the cloning facility to reach it. He had only gone a few steps when he noticed movement in the corner of his eye. He paused, turning to see what it was, growing curious when he saw Tea'va moving from an adjoining hallway toward the factory.

He was going to head over to meet him, but decided against it, choosing to observe instead. Tea'va took long strides to the facility's entrance, his head remaining straight, his posture was much more rigid and proud than Gabriel was used to. The bek'hai didn't look around as he walked, and didn't seem to notice him standing there.

What would he be doing, going into the factory by himself when he was supposed to be healing? And why had he told Theodore he would need to rest if he didn't?

Gabriel took a few steps toward the factory before stopping. What was he going to do? Confront the Dread warrior? He had seen Tea'va fight. If he were doing something subversive and was caught in the act, he could kill Gabriel with little effort.

He decided not to follow. Whatever it was, he could have Zoelle look into it later. Not that he could necessarily trust anything she said about it, but if one or both of them was playing games with their new human companions, it was only fair that the humans played them back. Either way, he didn't like secrets, and he could feel his trust in the bek'hai beginning to wane.

He pushed the thought aside, returning to his original plan. He crossed the open space to the center corridor, heading through it without hesitation. He began traveling down another long, glowing black hallway, his rifle resting on his shoulder.

As he walked, he found his mind wandering, thinking about Miranda. They had always been friends, but lately, he was starting to feel so much more for her. An attachment that hadn't been there before. Something had changed between them, and he liked it.

He also felt guilty about it. But how long was he supposed to mourn? How long was he supposed to be alone? Jessica would have wanted him to be happy, and she had been friends with Miranda, too. Wasn't it a good match?

He reached an intersection in the corridor, still distracted by his thoughts.

He almost walked right into a plasma bolt.

It hit the wall beside him, only centimeters from his face, so close he felt the burn of it as it was absorbed by the lek'shah plating. He caught himself, stumbling back the way he had come, getting under cover around the corner and dropping his rifle into his arms.

What the hell?

Another bolt sizzled past, smacking the wall again. Close. Too close. He looked back the way he had come. He had gotten too distracted, and hadn't been paying attention. He knew he had stayed in this corridor the whole time, but he could see there were other intersections branching off from it.

He retreated, running from the threat. He didn't know who was shooting at him yet, or why. If it was a pur'dahm, he was sure he was going to die.

He fired back as he went, his bolts wild. Someone turned the corner behind him. A mother. Two more followed. They traded fire with him, and he ducked around another corner.

He hadn't expected them to be this close to the cloning facility. Why hadn't Graham's team sniffed these out? He growled under his breath as the plasma bolts flowed past, slapping harmlessly into the walls. He couldn't make it back down the corridor. He needed to reach a functional space where there might be a static comm link and call in for help.

He started running again, down the adjacent corridor, trying to keep track of his movements in his head as he fled. Left, left, right, straight three intersections, left, right. He kept going, the mothers staying behind him, keeping up the chase. He was faster than them, allowing him to stay ahead of their attacks, but he couldn't keep going forever.

He had been right. He was stupid for coming down here alone.

He finally reached the end of the hallway, running out into another large, open space, similar to the one where the cloning facility rested. His eyes shifted nervously as he sought another corridor to run down or for a place to hide.

He froze as a strange smell reached into his nostrils, making his nose feel as though it were burning. Next, he noticed a dark pile near the far end of the space, and then that the ground was littered with rough, black rocks.

What was this place?

He ran out of time to think about it. He heard the mothers coming. He had to get away from them.

He hurried into the space, reaching one of the rocks and

crouching down behind it. The mothers appeared a moment later, entering the massive chamber before coming to a stop.

Gabriel stood, aiming his rifle and ready to shoot them.

They dropped their weapons. They weren't even looking at him.

He followed their gaze to the back of the space, where an inky darkness replaced the dim glow of the luminescent moss. He felt a chill run down his arms when he thought he saw something move. He ducked back behind the rock, something in him telling him to be very afraid.

It moved from the darkness like an extension of it, though the corners of the scales that covered its body seemed to catch a small portion of the light and throw it back, bending it at an odd angle as it did. It was fast, terrifyingly fast, as it slithered across the open space, ignoring every obstacle in a direct line toward the mothers.

They cried out as it approached them, raising their rifles and firing. Gabriel watched the plasma bolts smack harmlessly against the creature's scaly carapace. Then he watched as a short arm reached from the front of the creature, grabbing one of the mothers and squeezing. He felt sick as he watched her compress beneath the thing's claws, and he ducked back to his hiding place.

How had he managed to go from bad to worse?

And why did the Dread have a literal monster moving freely inside of a starship?

The remaining mothers managed to get moving. One of them made it back out of the room, far enough into the adjoining corridor that the large creature wouldn't be able to reach her. The second wasn't as lucky, and she cried out as it stabbed her with its claw, running her through, lifting her from the ground and tossing the carcass aside.

Gabriel looked around, trying to find a way out as the creature slowed and came to a stop, blocking the way he had come. He got a look at its face now, bony and angled, ridged and rough and covered in smaller scales. It looked vaguely familiar to him, but much more threatening. It opened its mouth, revealing a row of long teeth. A low groan sounded from it. Its nostrils flared, and a large tongue flicked out.

It knew he was there, and it was looking for him.

He swallowed hard, his heart racing. There was no way past it, no way to outrun it. He could only hope that it wouldn't be able to find him. He tried to duck even lower, but couldn't without shifting too much and risking being seen or heard.

The creature began to slither forward, slowly moving in his general direction, its head bobbing as it tried to get a bead on him. Gabriel cradled his rifle, trying to decide if he should shoot at it. He had seen the plasma strike harmlessly against the scales.

He froze for a second time as he realized what he was looking at.

Reza had said that a large portion of the Dread technology had an organic component. The walls, the wiring, everything. His father had even made a joke that there had to be a farm somewhere in the ship to provide replacement parts.

Except it wasn't a joke. He had accidentally stumbled onto the farm, and now he was about to be killed by one of the cows.

How did the Dread manage to keep this thing under control?

He held his breath as the monster came closer, still hoping it wouldn't notice him and would go away. The burning smell was stronger now, and his nose felt like it was on fire. He wanted to rub it, to hold it, to do something, but couldn't. His eyes began to water.

Without warning, the creature darted forward, rising up on its serpentine rear, pressing forward and looming over him. He brought the rifle up, as useless as it would be, his finger moving to the trigger.

"Kel'esh! Dukur hurulim bek."

A gravelly voice echoed across the large space, reverberating and repeating itself. Something approached Gabriel from behind, even as the monster in front of him suddenly became still.

He felt sharp fingers on his shoulder a moment later. He turned, coming face-to-face with what almost looked like a miniaturized version of the creature, blended with something else entirely. It was dark and demonic looking, reptilian and raw, and at the same time intelligent. Its eyes regarded him with curiosity, interest, and humor.

"You do not belong in here, Heil'bek," it said in rough English.

It knew who he was? How?

"I am lek'hai It'kek," it said. "A keeper of the lori'shah." It pointed at the creature.

"You're a bek'hai," Gabriel said, making the connection. "Not a human clone."

"A keeper is a clone, but not human," It'kek agreed. "Only the original bek'hai can commune with our forebears. Our visage is outlawed among our people. Our place in society secret and sacred."

"Why didn't you let it attack me?"

"We are keepers, not killers, and while the drumhr know better than to enter our place, the humans do not."

"But you let it attack the mothers?"

"They are lor'hai. Replaceable. You are not."

"That may be true, but we're supposed to be enemies."

"Are we? Your kind had something our kind required. The Domo'dahm chose to take it, instead of asking. You have done me no wrong. You are not my enemy unless you choose to be." It let out a soft hiss that Gabriel took for a laugh or a sigh. "You are within your rights to do so."

"You saved my life. I guess we're even?"

The keeper hissed again. "You remind me of your mother, Heil'bek."

Gabriel had calmed some once he knew he wasn't going to die. His heart began to thump again. "How do you know my mother?"

"We can smell her in you. We knew her. All of the keepers did. The Domo'dahm's pet human. His keepsake. She was like you. She was curious. She came to us. We spoke. She touched many within the bek'hai, with her words of kindness and compassion for all things. We weren't always like the drumhr, Heil'bek. We weren't always like the pur'dahm. Only in the beginning. And perhaps, in the end."

"There's a clone on this ship, Zoelle. Do you know her?"

"We see and hear everything that happens within the domo'shah."

"Is she really my mother?"

"We don't know. She has never come to us."

He couldn't hold that against her if she had only just remembered who she was, as she claimed.

"If I bring her to you, would you know the difference between her and a clone?"

"Unless the copy is identical, yes. We would know."

"Thank you for helping me. I was looking for the replicators when the mothers attacked me. Do you know how to get there?"

"We will show you our way, Heil'bek. Once you have left this chamber, do not return to it. Now that you know to stay away, we will not stop the lori'shah from attacking you again."

"What if I need to talk to you?"

"We will show you where to come. Where it is safe. Do not come this way."

"I understand. What I don't get is why you are helping me?"

"For your mother. For peace. As we said, this war is not our war. We do not agree with the Domo'dahm."

"Why didn't you stop him?"

"We are powerless to stop him. We are only keepers."

"But you control the lori'shah. The key to their survival."

"The lori'shah are prisoners on the domo'shah. As are the keepers. As are the lor'hai. As are the humans. The Domo'dahm takes many prisoners. The benefit of the few to the distress of the many. Remember that, Heil'bek. That is the truth of the bek'hai. Most of the bek'hai."

It'kek turned and began walking. Gabriel was nervous about turning his back on the lori'shah, but it hadn't moved at all since the keeper had yelled at it. He backed away from the creature, trailing behind It'kek. He would have never expected what he had found down here. It wasn't only a piece of the secret behind the Dread's technology. It was a truth he was sure most didn't know about.

"It'kek," he said as they neared another corridor that had been hidden in the darkness at the rear of the chamber. "If the domo'shah is made of lori'shah scales, if all of the Dread technology is made from these things, there must have been a lot of them on your home world before it was destroyed."

"Millions, Heil'bek," It'kek replied. "Until the hunters nearly made them extinct. Only then did the bek'hai learn to care for the lori'shah. Only once we realized how much we needed them to survive."

[21]

The keeper brought Gabriel to a transport beam hidden in one of the access tunnels, normally used only to travel to the assemblers for the tools and supplies they needed to do their work in the belly of the fortress. Once there, It'kek gave him detailed directions to navigate the area, as well as a suggestion on where to find Reza and Zoelle. Gabriel tried to get the keeper to come with him, to smell the clone and determine if she was telling the truth, but he refused to leave the lori'shah after its interaction with him had made it upset.

Gabriel would have laughed at that statement if It'kek hadn't said it with such serious reverence.

The transport beam brought Gabriel to the assemblers, which were almost what he and Colonel Choi had originally believed them to be. Machines that were able to create nearly anything from nothing by reconstituting them from their original atomic structure using base resources culled from other matter. The facility itself was composed of row after row of storage tanks which contained the fuel for the assemblers, which ranged in size from a few meters to large enough to produce an entire mechanized armor.

Looking at the technology, it was clear the Dread weren't limited by how quickly they could produce the things they needed. Instead, they were limited in specific raw materials to convert. He imagined there was another facility for that process somewhere nearby, but it wasn't obvious from his current position.

It didn't take him long to find Zoelle and Reza, once he was certain he was in the right place. He found the scientist and the clone where It'kek had suggested, in the control space where the molecular breakdown of new materials to copy was recorded. They were alone in the room, standing on opposite sides of a flat counter where a blue light was shining down on the rifle Reza had modified to create the darkspace shield. Reza looked somewhat bored with the process, but Zoelle was following it with intense interest, studying the updated design.

They both looked up when he walked in. Reza smiled when he saw Gabriel. Zoelle gained a look of concern.

"Gabriel? What happened to you?" she asked.

He hadn't thought about how he must look after being shot at and almost crushed by a lori'shah. "I was looking for you, but I took a wrong turn somewhere and wound up on the farm."

"Farm?" Zoelle said, before understanding set in. "You ran into a lori'shah den?"

"It was an accident. A keeper kept it from eating me."

"Lori'shah don't eat meat," Zoelle said. "It would have killed you for invading its territory. You're lucky there was a keeper nearby."

"Why didn't you tell us the Dread are keeping those things on board?"

"Would it make a difference?"

Gabriel paused. "No, probably not. It'kek told me that there used to be millions of them on the bek'hai home world."

"Yes. Many of them were slaughtered during the bek'hai civil wars, the need to produce more and more weaponry, overriding all sense. Now, they can keep only a few on each ship. It is the reason the bek'hai can't build more domo'shah, and can only expand so far. It is fortunate for us."

"You should come down to see the keepers with me," Gabriel said. "I was told you used to visit with them quite often."

Zoelle stared at him for a few seconds and then nodded. "I did. I remember now. So many things are still vague to me. So many things I still can't recall. Did your father send you down here?"

"No. I came on my own. Miranda suggested I should try to get to know you better."

"Miranda?"

"Spaceman Locke. She sits near the command dais."

"The woman with the brown hair?"

"That's her."

She smiled. "Your father told me you have an attraction to her."

How did he know? "You could say that. Anyway, don't let me interfere. I just thought I would observe whatever it is you're doing."

"What we're doing," Reza said, "is converting the tech in this rifle to something we can reproduce. Zoelle has been giving me a quick education in basic bek'hai technology at the same time. It's fascinating stuff."

"You looked bored before I came in."

"We were taking a break while it builds a prototype."

"Your engineer is a genius, Gabriel," Zoelle said. "His approach to the problem is unlike anything I've seen before. Now I understand how you were able to get onto the ship and absorb the attack from the main plasma cannon. You should be very proud of yourself, Reza."

Reza's face flushed, and he lowered his head. "Thank you," he replied.

"This system isn't networked, right?" Gabriel asked. "We aren't broadcasting how to make upgraded phase modulators to the entire bek'hai command?"

Zoelle laughed. "Of course not."

"I was able to update some of the sequences to make more efficient use of the organic compounds in the Dread tech. There is still going to be one limitation."

"What's that?"

"We can only push the modulation to a limited surface area at any given time."

"Which means what?"

"The shields will be cascading," Reza said. "Parts of the ship will be vulnerable as the modulation fields move around the hull."

"That doesn't sound good, Reza," Gabriel said.

"I know. The problem is that if we feed too much power into too much of the hull at one time, the lek'shah will break down and lose integrity."

"That sounds worse."

"Yes."

"You figured all of this out in two hours?"

"I have a good partner."

Gabriel glanced at Zoelle. "I thought you were more of an astrophysicist?"

"I've had fifty years to learn as much as I could," she replied. "I'm not anything special, Gabriel. Just a younger model of an older woman, who committed herself to saving not just humankind, but all of the innocents caught in this war and the wars that preceded it."

"Do you mean that?" he asked, wanting so much to believe it, but finding himself still skeptical. As it should be.

"Yes."

Something flashed behind them. Zoelle turned toward it immediately, approaching one of the smaller assemblers. The front of it slid down, revealing a small, cylindrical device. She picked it up, holding it out to Reza.

"We will scan it for a match," she said as he took it.

He nodded, removing the rifle from the table and placing the cylinder down on it. The blue light turned back on, sweeping across the device. It repeated the motion a dozen times, and then a holographic reading appeared above the cylinder.

"An accurate reproduction," Zoelle announced.

"Yes," Reza exclaimed. "Where can we bring it to test it out?"

"Engineering. The main links to the conduits sending impulses through the hull are there. It will take some time to update the systems to utilize it. Much longer than it took to duplicate the design."

Reza looked disappointed. "I was hoping we could get this done today. Wouldn't that have been a treat for the General?"

"I thought you were running on fumes?" Gabriel asked.

"I was until I got involved with this. A good technical challenge is the best way to wake up there is."

"Why don't you go and get some rest, Reza," Zoelle said. "I will begin the work to integrate the modulator with our existing systems. You can check my work when you return."

"Uh, I don't know," Reza said.

"Go ahead," Gabriel said. "I'll stay here with her. We need you at full brain capacity."

"Okay," Reza said. "Don't do anything exciting without me, deal?"

"Deal."

[22]

"So, I talked to my father," Gabriel said, as he followed Zoelle through the starship to wherever engineering was located.

He had dismissed Diallo from her guard duty, sending her back to Colonel Choi. They would need to assemble another team to search for more mothers hiding in the shadows before anyone else got killed by them.

"What about?" Zoelle asked.

"Why he thinks you're my mother."

"I am your mother, Gabriel."

"Yeah, that's what he said. You can't blame me for being a little less accepting."

"I don't. It is perfectly understandable."

"Good. I want you to tell me what happened. How you came to be here, on this ship, and fifty years younger than you should be. I want to know who you are, but I also want to know who you were before." He almost told her that Tea'va thought she was full of it, but he held that part back.

"Before?"

"Before you remembered that you're Juliet St. Martin, not Zoelle dur Tuhrik."

She paused for a moment, her expression dimming. "I'm not proud of who I was."

"Why?"

"I feel as though Tuhrik programmed me to be the opposite of who I really am."

"Programmed you? I think you need to go back a little more. What happened?"

"The Dread captured me. They brought me to one of their facilities and gave me the genetic test to see if I would make a good clone. When I passed, they sent me to the Dread capitol, the Domo'dahm's ship. He saw me there and was intrigued because I was calmly defiant. The others they had taken, they cried and screamed, or were silent and distant. I looked him in the eye. I stared at him while he stared at me. I prayed to God to have mercy on him. He thought I was interesting, and took me as his own."

She pointed at a transport beam ahead, taking his hand as they entered since he didn't know where they were going. Her skin was warm and tingling. She squeezed his hand as they exited the beam, smiling at him.

"I never had to try very hard. Only be me. The Domo'dahm, Rorn'el, grew affectionate toward me. Not in a sexual way. The Dread barely understand sexuality. He gave me more and more freedom. In time, I met Tuhrik, and he began to teach me the ways of the Dread. Meanwhile, they were working to clone me. I became more involved in the process as it continued, giving input to the programming. The Domo'dahm wanted my duplicates to be special, so he would have me throughout his life. Tuhrik and I became close. We spent many hours discussing the future of humankind and the bek'hai. We knew Rorn'el was wrong to kill off humanity."

They reached a larger door. It slid open at her approach, revealing a sea of glowing crystals surrounding some sort of dark machine.

"Our power source, and energy stores," she explained.

"Where are the technicians to maintain all of this?"

"There were none assigned to the Ishur. This technology is thousands of years old, and incredibly reliable. My team was able to handle potential minor problems."

She circled the engines, moving to a separate door that opened when she neared.

"It was Tuhrik who helped me, but his goal was to help everyone. The Domo'dahm, the pur'dahm, they have lost their way over the years. They are setting themselves up, either to be forced to seek another life form or to go extinct. It is a cycle that cannot be allowed to repeat."

"I can't argue with that. So what did he do?"

"He saved me after I died."

"What do you mean, after you died?"

"My body was brought to be processed, broken down into raw materials. It sounds horrible, but it was an honor that no other human ever received. I was to be retired as a true bek'hai would be retired. Only Tuhrik arranged for me to be brought to his laboratory. He had a maturation capsule there, and he put me in it. He knew the healing power it had from his studies with the clones. It didn't only reverse my aging. It brought me back to life."

Gabriel stared at her, a part of him beginning to wonder if maybe she was telling the truth. He couldn't deny that he wanted it to be so.

"Why didn't he tell the Domo'dahm?"

"To what end? To continue the cycle of violence and destruction and genocide? No, he decided that I should wait and that we would work together to fuel the change the bek'hai need. Clearly, I couldn't be alive as myself, and so he subjected me to the programming sequencer, turning me into a clone of myself, as odd as that sounds. Seeing a human in person would trigger my nascent personality."

They crossed another corridor until they reached the second room. This one was filled with large conduits and wires, along with a holographic terminal. She put her free hand to it, manipulating the alien writing.

"But what about this clone of yourself? I don't really understand. Clones should all be the same, shouldn't they?"

"That isn't how it works. Even with perfect genetics and

programming, all clones are unique to some extent. The un'hai were always more unique than others. They have the closest thing to free will of any of the lor'hai. When the programming Tuhrik inserted interacted with the rest of me, it made me very cold, very calculating, very hungry for power and control, and willing to do anything I had to in order to get it. I'm not proud of that."

Gabriel felt his heart beating faster. Was she admitting everything Tea'va had said to him? Could it be that Theodore was right after all? "Tea'va told me you couldn't be trusted."

"He was right. Before I remembered who I really am, I couldn't."

"But the fighting. The killing. Juliet St. Martin believed in peace."

"I would never let anyone hurt you, Gabriel," she said, looking at him. "You or your father. I can kill for that, as many as I have to. I'll beg God's forgiveness later."

Gabriel reached under his shirt, taking hold of the crucifix there. He lifted it out so that Zoelle could see it. He was going to ask her if she remembered it, but by the tears that formed in her eyes, he knew she did.

"I'm happy he gave it to you," she said. "I'm happy you're here. That we're all here together."

Gabriel felt himself losing the battle not to believe her. If she were faking everything, she was doing a masterful job. And that was possible, too, wasn't it? The clones could be programmed to do anything. How much of her story was true? What should he believe?

He was more confused than he had been before. Was it better than doubting?

He looked at Zoelle, trying to find words to express what he was feeling. Only she wasn't crying anymore. She wasn't sad anymore. Her face was pale, her eyes panicked.

"Oh, Gabriel," she said. "Oh, no."

"What is it?" Gabriel asked.

"I'm sorry. Gabriel, I'm sorry."

He felt his own panic setting in. "What?"

"I lied. I didn't know it, but I lied. Talking about it, I only now remembered. When I told Theodore that I plotted the optimal course. That isn't true. I delayed the Ishur intentionally."

"Why?"

A voice suddenly echoed across the room, and throughout the Dread fortress. Colonel Choi's voice.

"Red alert. Red alert. All hands to stations. All hands to stations. This is not a drill. I repeat, this is not a drill."

Zoelle's voice was weak when she spoke again.

"I transmitted a message to the Domo'dahm to send reinforcements."

[23]

Gabriel's shock vanished, his instincts taking over as Colonel Choi repeated the red alert.

"We barely have control over the ship," he said.

"I know."

"Where is the comm?"

"Here." She put her hand to a blank side of the wall, and a light appeared.

"Bridge, this is Major St. Martin. Can you hear me?"

"I hear you, Gabriel," Colonel Choi said.

"What's going on?"

"Two Dread fortresses just appeared off the slipstream. They're heading our way."

"ETA?"

"Twenty-two minutes. Where are you?"

"Engineering, with my - Zoelle."

"Well, get your ass up here, Major."

"Yes, ma'am."

Gabriel turned to Zoelle. "Twenty-two minutes. How well can this ship hold up to attack from two others?"

"Without any interceptors and only the main plasma cannon? Not long."

"Damn it." He took a step toward the door. "What about that?" he said, pointing at the modulator in her hand. "Can you get it installed in that time?"

"I don't know. I'm not as familiar with these systems as some of the others."

"We have to try. How can I help?"

"Aren't you needed on the bridge?"

"Tea'va can handle the flying. I don't know what I'm doing yet, anyway. What can I do?"

She nodded, her hand working the terminal faster. She tossed the modulator to him as a small hatch slid open, revealing a power conduit.

"The hard part is going to be programming the systems to handle the modulation. I'm going to cut the power to the conduit. Do you see the capsule joining the wires?"

Gabriel looked inside the panel. The capsule was filled with some kind of gel, glowing a soft blue as the power passed through it. "Yes."

The blue glow faded.

"Pull it out, carefully. You don't want to damage it."

Gabriel reached in, putting one hand around the capsule and another on the bundle. He pulled, flinching as a tangle of wires and deep red fluid seeped from the bottom of it. He lowered the wire to the side of the panel, and then disconnected the capsule from the top and removed it.

"Good. Look at the modulator. It has connectors for the wires on both ends."

Gabriel looked at it, finding the connectors. "There are an awful lot of them."

"I know. You'll need to join them individually."

"In what order?"

"The order doesn't matter. The strands can only carry so much power each; that's why there are so many."

He wondered if he had made a mistake in offering to help as he lifted the bottom bundle and separated the finer threads at the end, and then began attaching them one by one.

"What are you doing?" he asked.

"I have to adjust the power output through that conduit so that it will modulate the phase appropriately." She reached up and tapped the comm. "Bridge, this is Juliet in engineering."

"Juliet," Theodore responded. "What are you up to down there?"

"Gabriel and I are working to integrate Reza's phase modulator into the bek'hai systems. Theo, if this works, you'll have cascading shield coverage across the bow of the domo'shah."

"Cascading? As in non-static?"

"Yes. You'll have to adjust course to try to keep the ship angled to deflect the Dread fortress' attacks. They'll try to flank you and get you in a crossfire. Don't let them."

"Affirmative," Theodore replied. "You got that, Tea'va?"

Gabriel didn't hear the bek'hai's response. He was sure the pur'-dahm understood. He focused his efforts on binding the wires to the modulator.

The time passed too quickly for Gabriel to keep track of. He was halfway through the top end of the modulator when Zoelle announced that they only had two minutes left to make something happen. The ship had already shaken once from a long-range strike that Tea'va hadn't managed to avoid.

"I'm going as fast as I can," Gabriel said, reaching for another of the small wires.

Zoelle moved in beside him. "Here, let me do it." She took the modulator from him, her fingers dancing across it as she laced the rest of the wires to it in less than thirty seconds.

"I think you should have done this yourself," he said.

"I've had a lot more practice. I used to knit your father sweaters. Did you know that?"

Gabriel couldn't help but smile. "No, I didn't." He hadn't gotten to take any of them off of Earth with him.

She finished the wiring, reaching into the panel and slipping the modulator into place.

"What do we do with this?" Gabriel asked, holding up the gel-filled capsule.

"Hope that we don't need it," she replied.

"Juliet, darlin', give me some good news," Theodore said over the comm. "We're twenty seconds from firing range, and the bastards are sending fighters at us."

"Tell Tea'va to get the ship angled and fire the plasma cannon at them," she said, her voice angry. "What is he doing up there?"

Theodore's laughter filled the room. "Tea'va, what in the hell are you doing over there? Mr. Mokri, did you get me my damn fire control?"

"Yes, General," Gabriel heard Reza said. "Take my tablet. Charge status is here; fire button is here."

"Like a damn video game," Theodore replied. "Nice work, Mr. Mokri."

"Thank you, sir."

"We're almost done," Zoelle said. "I'm about to power it up. Remember, we can't control the cascade. It's going to cycle for now, and the Dahms on those ships are going to figure out what's happening pretty quickly. We need to hit them back as hard and fast as we can."

"I hear you, darlin'," Theodore said. "Nothing to do now but pray."

"Amen," Zoelle said, her hands a blur on the terminal.

A moment later, Gabriel could feel the charge of the energy as it began running through the conduit once more. The modulator began to whine softly, and two of the connectors on top sparked and smoked.

"I don't think it's working," he said, his stomach sinking.

"Come on," Zoelle said, her hands still working the terminal. "It can't handle the power. We need to reduce it. The surface area is going to be smaller than we planned."

"How small?" Gabriel asked.

"It will be just large enough to stop the main plasma cannon if it catches it square in the center."

"With rolling coverage? No pilot in the universe can keep the shields centered like that. What if we keep the power levels up?"

"It will destroy the modulator."

"How quickly?"

"I don't know."

"We don't have a choice," Gabriel said. "Do it."

"Okay. God be with us and have mercy on our souls. Theodore, the shields should be active, but they can't handle the strain for long. Remember, hard and fast."

"Affirmative. Tea'va, bring us in."

[24]

THEODORE DIDN'T LIKE THE DREAD'S COMMAND DAIS, EVEN though it wasn't much different than the raised platform on the Magellan. The seat was uncomfortable, designed for a taller, leaner shape, and certainly not adjustable for an old man with no legs. More than that, it was obvious when sitting on it that it was designed to make the rest of the bridge crew feel submissive and small, and he hated that. Each and every soul on the bridge was invaluable to him, even if they were limited in their helpfulness during their first taste of combat aboard the alien vessel.

They had held themselves well in the last two battles. At least this time they had a weapon to fire back at the enemy.

A weapon that could actually hurt them.

And now, Mr. Mokri had pulled a rabbit out of his hat one more time, and along with Juliet and Gabriel had given them some semblance of shields. He knew it was true because, despite the original blackness of the lek'shah armor, it had given way to an even deeper, darker black that he identified immediately as dark-space. It curled and rolled around the hull of the bow like a typhoon, as though they had somehow released a storm on top of the ship. He had been expecting it to be more evenly distributed and as such easier to adjust to, but they would take what they could get.

"Keep us heading in the right direction, Mr. Tea'va," Theodore said. "Full ahead."

"Yes, Dahm St. Martin," Tea'va replied.

The two Dread fortresses had come from nowhere, retreating from slipspace and making a direct line toward them, firing on them without any attempts to communicate. Theodore found that strange, considering they were supposed to be friendly and there was no way they could have heard about their takeover of the ship already. It meant that the incoming ships probably thought they were shooting at one of their own, and they were doing it intentionally and without any quarter.

It was a chilling thought.

"Hard to port, Tea'va," Theodore said as he watched the position of the fortresses ahead of them.

They were doing exactly as Juliet had said, trying to split apart and get to both sides of the ship. It was a standard but effective maneuver, especially considering their shield situation. They couldn't cover both at once, which meant they needed to take one out, and fast.

He held his finger over Reza's tablet, where a big red 'FIRE" button rested on the screen. There was a wire snaking from the tablet to one of the forward terminals, giving him interpolated access to the Ishur's main cannon. He didn't have a targeting computer to help him line the shot, which meant he had to do it by eye across the vastness of space.

No pressure.

He clenched his teeth as the two Dread fortresses fired their plasma cannons simultaneously. Tea'va rolled the Ishur slightly as the bolts approached, and Theodore couldn't help but pump his fist when he saw the first go beneath the ship, and the other hit the swirling maelstrom of darkspace. The ship shuddered from the impact, but the strike didn't leave any lasting damage.

"My turn," Theodore said, tapping the button.

The front of the fortress began to glow with bright blue energy which arced away a moment later, spewing toward the target on their port side. Theodore refused to blink as he watched it approach the ship, and as the ship tried to evade the strike. It managed to shift slightly, turning broadside and moving the impact further toward the rear. It still took the hit, leaving him satisfied as layers of lek'shah were burned away, and debris began to vent from the side of the vessel.

"That's one for the good guys," he said.

"Dahm St. Martin," Tea'va said. "The starboard target will be aligning their secondary batteries. We don't have coverage to stop them."

"Can we take the hit?"

"For a few minutes, Dahm."

Damn. They needed to be faster. He looked at the charge on the plasma cannon. Fifty percent.

"Juliet, you with me, darlin'?" he said, opening a channel.

"I'm here, Theodore. What do you need?"

"More power to the main plasma," he said. "Recharge time is slower than a gator in a mudhole."

"I will see what I can do."

Theodore shifted his attention to the starboard fortress. It was bathed in light as its secondary batteries began firing at them, dozens of positions belching plasma across a thousand kilometers, too close for comfort in space. Tea'va started to shift the bow toward them, to catch the attack with the shields.

"Stay on the port target, Mr. Tea'va," Theodore said.

"Dahm, I do not think-"

"I think, you steer," Theodore snapped. "Stay on the port target."

"Yes, Dahm St. Martin."

The ship shuddered slightly as the plasma attack began battering into it.

"Do we have damage reports showing anywhere?" Theodore asked.

"It isn't integrated yet, sir," Reza replied.

"Damn it. Get me a clone or something up here, someone that can read the alien symbols. Juliet?"

"I will contact Shielle. One moment."

The charge on the plasma cannon completed.

"Mr. Tea'va, give me four degrees port."

"Yes, Dahm."

The ship began to turn, the bow coming out slightly ahead of the enemy ship. Theodore slapped the fire button again and then watched as the bolt slammed into the front of the enemy ship. More debris exploded from the impact point, and it began to turn away from them.

"Was it just me, or did our cannon recharge faster than theirs?" Theodore asked.

"I rerouted the power from the batteries we can't use," Zoelle said. "Theodore, you must hurry, the modulator will not hold out much longer."

"Dahm St. Martin, the starboard target is turning to fire its main cannon."

Theodore stared at the fortress to their port side, trying to determine if it was out of the fight. It had turned its nose away from them and was still leaking debris. At the same time, secondary batteries were lighting up and beginning to fire out of sync.

"It is damaged," Tea'va said as if reading his mind. "If the Dahm of the ship is courageous, he will continue the fight until he is destroyed, but he is less of a concern. We should engage the other target, Dahm St. Martin."

"Agreed. Do it, Mr. Tea'va."

Theodore didn't know what the Dread did, but the ship began to shiver and moan, the forward velocity terminating abruptly as it shifted on its axis, the bow rotating toward the second domo'shah. It was already alight in the blue glow of the plasma cannon, and Theodore couldn't stop himself from flinching as it fired at relatively close range.

The Ishur shuddered again as it began to reverse, turning again, Tea'va working to move the shields to deflect the attack. It was as impressive a piece of flying as Theodore had ever seen, and he howled as the bolt smacked against it.

"Yes," he shouted, looking down at the status of their own cannon. It was almost ready.

He quickly checked on the first target, which was staying back further and firing the weaker secondary batteries at them. The bolts were striking the hull and digging into the lek'shah, but not nearly with enough focus to cause immediate critical damage.

A new figure arrived on deck, running across the bridge. Shielle, the clone of Juliet. He noticed that she glanced at Tea'va as she passed him by, and then took a position behind one of the terminals.

"Damage report," Theodore said.

"Hull breach on three decks, all sealed, Dahm St. Martin," she replied. "Damage is minimal."

"That's what I want to hear. Mr. Tea'va, get us lined up. Six degrees starboard, bring the bow up eight degrees."

"Yes, Dahm St. Martin."

The fortress began to turn again, maneuvering well considering the size. The enemy ship was turning as well, having realized the Ishur's shields were superior. It was trying to broadside them again, to stay out of their main cannon range and pepper them with secondary fire until they gave in.

"Dahm St. Martin, we have a breach on forty-six," Shielle said. "Emergency seals are closing."

The port side fortress was having some success with their own small arms.

"We need to end this now," Theodore said. "Give me some lead, Mr. Tea'va."

"Yes, Dahm."

The Ishur's bow kept turning, making it ahead of the starboard enemy.

"All ahead, Mr. Tea'va," Theodore said.

He didn't feel the acceleration, but he could see it in the rate at which the enemy fortress grew in front of them. They were bearing down on the ship, racing toward it, the shields on the bow absorbing most of its firepower. Their main plasma was charged, and they were getting so close he couldn't miss.

He pressed down on the trigger, and watched the blue bolt streak away from the Ishur, slamming into the side of the fortress, digging into the hull and through, vanishing on the inside.

"A good hit," Tea'va said. "That will reach the engines."

"Get us away from it," Theodore said.

"Yes, Dahm," Tea'va replied.

They accelerated, vectoring beneath the fortress as gouts of flame began to escape from it. The first fortress didn't follow, unwilling to risk getting caught in the second's death throes, and understanding that they had lost this fight.

Theodore kept an eye on the ships as they continued accelerating away from them. The first continued to vent fire for a couple of minutes before finally falling still and silent, the glow of the interior lights through the hull transparencies fading away and leaving it nearly invisible in the darkness of space. The other fortress retreated, heading in the opposite direction from the Ishur.

"Ha!" Theodore cried, pushing himself up on his hands. "Take that, you damn couillon bastards."

He smiled as the other crew members cheered along with him.

In front of him, Tea'va shifted in his seat, looking over at Shielle. She looked back at him, nodding slightly.

Then they both smiled.

[25]

Tea'va entered his quarters, his chest pulsing, his muscles pumping with adrenaline. It had been a good fight, and unlike anything he had ever experienced before. He had participated in a number of gi'shah competitions over the years and had done well enough to still be alive. This? This was something completely different. A record for his History that deserved to be kept. When was the last time a domo'shah had engaged another? It could only have been during the civil wars, over ten thousand years earlier.

He was honored to be the pilot who had maneuvered the Ishur, keeping the humans' incredible shield technology positioned to absorb the attacks of the opposing fortresses and lining up the main plasma cannon to fire direct, decisive hits. Not the Heil'bek. Him. He had proven his superiority to Theodore St. Martin, and to all of the others who saw how he had managed the massive starship. He had proven his superiority to himself.

His face twisted as he smiled once more. His plans were coming together well, much better than he could have hoped for at the moment when he decided to use the rebels to help him achieve his ends. Not only would he have his ship back, but he would have new defenses that none of the other domo'shah could match. Defenses that would allow him to bombard the capital from space and force the Domo'dahm to rise to meet him or face destruction on the ground. He would have the opportunity to force Rorn'el's hand, and in the end, destroy him and seize control of the bek'hai.

It was hard for him to be patient, but he knew he had no choice. The clones wouldn't be mature for another six days, and there was no way he could retake the Ishur without them.

Or without Shielle.

In the hours following the humans' capture of the Ishur, he had thought he would need to kill the un'hai, expecting that like Zoelle she would find some kind of regressed awareness of Juliet St. Martin buried within her subconscious. Not only had that not been true, but she was as sneaky and conniving as Zoelle. She had been the one working with Gr'el to alter the mothers, to shift the balance of power on the ship and assist the late pur'dahm in gaining control. She had been the one to come to him, to confide in him how much she hated the humans, and to find out where his loyalties truly were. It was a risky decision on her part. If he had been a subject of their new masters, he would have been wise to turn her in or kill her where she stood.

He had done neither. Instead, he chose to take a risk of his own and confide in her. He hated the humans as well and had only allowed himself to be submissive to them in order to gain their trust. It was a difficult thing to do, to bow and scrape before them. To call Theodore "Dahm St. Martin," and agree with his every command when he wanted only to stab him with a lek'sai and rest his corpse at the foot of the command dais.

It was almost made worse by the fact that he respected the human and his son. They were both skilled warriors, intelligent and brave. The Heil'bek was almost reverent of him, identifying his superiority and commending him for it. The Domo'dahm had never recognized what an achievement Tea'va was, or how skilled he was. Why did it take a human to recognize the evolution that he represented, and the step forward he could be for the good of the bek'hai?

Why did he have to fight to make them see he was better? The

Domo'dahm should have raised him to the top of the cells on his evolution alone.

He moved to his terminal in the back of the room, leaning over it and activating it. Should he have confided in her? It was a question he had asked himself over and over again. Trusting in others had been his downfall in the first place. At the same time, he couldn't do everything alone. He was a single bek'hai. He needed allies. Or at least, one ally. Especially one like Shielle. She had access to the cloning facilities, and neither Zoelle or the humans suspected her of being anything more than a standard clone. She was able to operate beneath their notice, while he was sure every member of the human crew was keeping a close eye on him.

He opened his History. How would he explain this to any that came after? How would he describe his allegiance to the humans?

"Today, the army of Tea'va dur Orin'ek encountered the forces of the incompetent Rorn'el -"

He paused, deleting the entry. That wouldn't do. He backed away from the terminal to give it more thought. Was he a fool for trusting Shielle? What else could he have done? He had considered killing Theodore St. Martin and his son and ordering the current clone soldiers to attack the humans. He had gone as far as to strategically organize them around the human crews to give them the best chance to overwhelm them. The problem was that there weren't enough remaining. One soldier for each human and they had all been disarmed. The element of surprise would help, but a victory wasn't guaranteed. If he were going to take chances anyway, he preferred to move his risk to a single point of failure. If Shielle did turn on him, he would have the opportunity to deny any accusations she made and start again. The Heil'bek would believe him. The Heil'bek trusted him. More than that, the Heil'bek actually liked him.

He nodded to himself, deciding once more that it was risky to trust her, but riskier not to. He returned to his terminal, considering the entry he wanted to add to his History again.

"Today, I alone directed the domo'shah Ishur in a direct confrontation with two domo'shah of the regime of Domo'dahm

Rorn'el, as he sought to put an end to the evolution of our people that would ensure our survival. I alone engaged the domo'shah, and with the power of my new technology and my command expertise, I was able to destroy the domo'shah, and preserve our future."

He paused the History. That was a better introduction. Embellished, but not too much. History was written by the victorious, after all.

He stood again, pacing. He had six days until the clones were ready. He had to make his move before the humans returned to their settlement and collected reinforcements. Otherwise, he would be left waiting again. At the same time, who knew what enhancements they would make in that time? They were an inferior species to be sure, but their resourcefulness was something to commend them on. Could they make the Ishur even more powerful than it already was?

He was about to return to his terminal when a heavy pounding sounded from the other side of the door. Tea'va almost laughed at the humans' continued struggle to utilize interspace communications and their reliance on physical presence and force to get one another's personal attention. He flattened his expression and walked over to the hatch to open it.

The Heil'bek stood in front of him.

"Can I help you, Gabriel St. Martin?" Tea'va asked, a mixture of hate and admiration crossing through him.

"The General asked me to collect you," Gabriel said.

Tea'va felt a moment of discomfort. Had Shielle said something? Did they know? "Is there a problem?"

"Zoelle's team has finished the calculations. General St. Martin has called a meeting of senior officers to debrief before we make the slip. He wants you to be there."

"He does?" Tea'va said, surprised. He had been part of the meetings on the bridge before, but not the human's more confidential discussions.

"You impressed the hell out of him, and me, with your flying. You've earned his respect, which isn't always an easy thing to do. You've also earned a little more of his trust."

"I don't see why he would trust me more. By defending the Ishur, I was preserving my own life as well." Tea'va smiled. The best way to invite more trust was to point out why it shouldn't be given.

Gabriel's eyes shifted back into the room, as though he were looking for something. Then he shrugged. "Be that as it may, you've proven yourself to be a valuable ally. Personally, I think you've earned it."

Tea'va studied Gabriel's face, trying to determine if he was going to be walking into a trap. There was no obvious attempt at deception there. In fact, was that pride? "Why do you look at me that way, Heil'bek?"

"When we met, you told me the Domo'dahm wanted to kill you because you're different. Because you're too human. Today, you helped prove that being more human is a benefit, not a malfunction. Now, come on. You don't want to keep the General waiting."

Gabriel turned away from him, taking a few steps down the corridor. Tea'va remained still. Being more human was the benefit? He made himself swallow the sudden fury he felt at the words. Being more human only made his body healthier, so that his bek'hai strengths did not deteriorate beneath him. He was better than the humans, better than the other bek'hai because of that. The thought that there was anything else in the human genome that had improved him was a disgusting one.

"Well?" Gabriel asked, noticing he wasn't following and looking back.

It took all of Tea'va's will to force himself to smile. "Yes. I am coming," he said, clenching his teeth once he was done, and at the same time feeling a crack beginning to form in his resolve. He had to forget about the fact that the Heil'bek was proud of him. He couldn't let that in. Wouldn't let that in.

Six days. He had to be patient for six more days. Then he would be in control of the Ishur once more. Then he would be the one returning to Earth to destroy the Domo'dahm.

Not the humans.

Him.

[26]

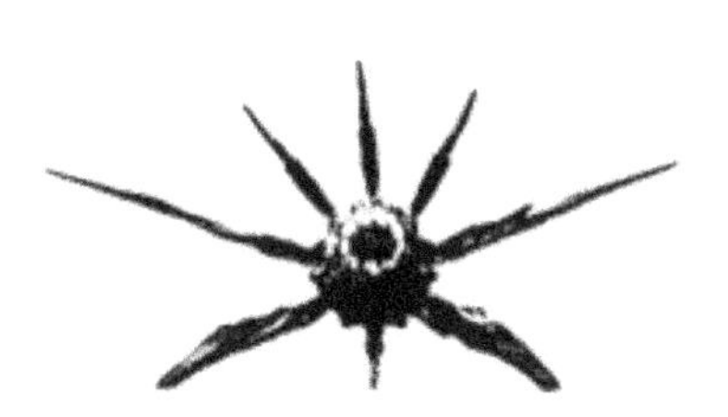

"Do you have any advice for me on how best to present myself, Heil'bek?" Tea'va asked.

Gabriel glanced over at the bek'hai and shook his head. "Be yourself," he replied. "If you have an opinion, don't keep it to yourself. The General doesn't bring his officers together to kowtow to his ideas."

"Kowtow?"

"Be subservient. Kiss his ass."

Tea'va considered for a moment and then nodded tersely. "Yes, I understand."

Gabriel smiled. He was happy his father had asked him to retrieve Te'ava and to make him part of the briefing. The Dread had proven himself more than capable in the thick of battle, and his experience in real combat would be invaluable to them as they tried to figure out how to proceed, now that they would have some time in slipspace to prepare for whatever came next.

He glanced over at the bek'hai again, opening his mouth to speak before putting his head forward once more. He had already made three weak efforts to tell Tea'va he had seen him going into the cloning facility and to ask him why he had been there. He had stopped himself every time. There was something about the Dread that gave him pause. Something in his body language that made him uncomfortable. He couldn't quite put his finger on it yet, but for as pleased as he was his father had invited the Dread to sit in on their meeting, he was also feeling hesitant about it.

He liked Tea'va, more than he had expected he would be able to like one of the enemy. Maybe it was because they were both pilots, and respected one another for the times they had met as enemies in orbit above Earth. Maybe it was because they shared a mistrust in Zoelle, though Gabriel was finding his fading after recent events.

He wanted to have complete faith in him.

He didn't, and so he didn't speak up. He didn't want Tea'va to know what he had seen. Not yet. He needed time to speak with Zoelle first, to ask her to check in on the cloning factory. He would go with her, and with Sergeant Diallo, to make sure everything was as it should be. What other choice did he have? None of their crew knew anything about the factory to be able to spot any inconsistencies.

They reached the hangar, the small personnel hatch sliding open. Gabriel smiled when he saw the Magellan resting there, beaten but not broken. The ramp leading into her was down, with crates resting on either side. Some were old parts to be removed; others were replacement parts to be installed. Soon, they would bring both to the assemblers and be able to put Maggie back together again.

"You are meeting in your starship?" Tea'va asked, surprised.

"It was the General's idea," he replied. "To remind us what we're fighting for, and what we started with."

"I am interested to see the interior."

"I thought you would be."

Tea'va made the low hissing sound Gabriel identified with laughter.

They climbed the ramp into the ship. Gabriel breathed deeply once he was on her, appreciating the smell of grease and alloy, a scent that was missing from the Ishur. The debris had all been removed from the corridors, as had the body of Spaceman Dix, the soldier who hadn't secured himself in time and had been killed by the impact of the crash. Everything had also been scrubbed down, their reduced water supply replenished by the ample volume stored on the Ishur. She looked as good as she was going to get before they could get the new parts installed.

The rest of the officers were already present when Gabriel arrived. Theodore, Colonel Choi, Colonel Graham, Second Lieutenant Bale, and two enlisted, Sergeant Diallo and Sergeant Abdullah, along with Zoelle, Guy Larone, and Reza Mokri. He was surprised to see that Sarah Larone wasn't there as well.

"Major Gabriel St. Martin and pur'dahm Tea'va reporting, sir," Gabriel said, coming to attention.

"At ease, Major," Theodore said. "Mr. Tea'va, thank you for joining us."

"It is my honor, Dahm St. Martin," Tea'va said, bowing low.

"Why don't you and Gabriel take a seat over there," Theodore said, pointing to two empty chairs near the rear of the table. "Then we can get started."

Gabriel led Tea'va to their seats. He stifled his laughter at how awkward the bek'hai was trying to sit in them. He was too tall for their basic chairs and looked uncomfortable when positioned.

"Now you know how I feel trying to sit on that command chair, Mr. Tea'va," Theodore said, laughing.

"Indeed, Dahm St. Martin," Tea'va replied, returning the laugh.

"In all seriousness. The reason I brought you all here is because, one, we just kicked the Dread hard enough in the ass to send them packing, and two, we need to be ready to do it again after we pick up the boys and girls back home. We're just about prepared to head into slipspace for, how long was it again, darlin'?"

"Twelve days," Zoelle replied. "Two slips."

"You're sure that is the fastest path?" Tea'va asked.

Gabriel looked over at him. Did he know something about that, or was he truly curious?

"Yes," Zoelle replied, not bothering to look at him. "The first slip will bring us out within fifteen AU of Earth."

"Close enough to send a quick message to our friends on the ground," Theodore said.

"The second will bring us to Calawan," Zoelle finished.

"Any idea how long to get back to Earth after that?" Gabriel asked.

"I ran some estimates," Reza said. He looked a little better, having gotten a couple of hours to sleep. "Another eight days."

"So, twenty days total," Colonel Graham said. "A day or two to get our soldiers organized and boarded. Depending on how you look at it, either that isn't a lot of time, or it's an eternity."

"I'm sure Major Peters would prefer us back yesterday," Gabriel said.

"Twenty-two days," Theodore said. "Let's start with the basics. When we come out of the first slip, we need to get a message down to Earth to tell the rebels we're going to load up and come on back for them. Does our new ride have the capacity to do that at long range? Remember, we need to hit their antenna hard to be heard. That question is for you, Mr. Tea'va, or you, Juliet."

"I believe our array does have the capability you desire, Dahm St. Martin," Tea'va said. "However, does such a message not pose a risk if the Domo'dahm intercepts it? You will lose the element of surprise."

"Yeah, I've been thinking about that. The trouble is, if the ground forces don't know we're on our way, how can we organize an offensive? We don't have enough firepower up here, even with reinforcements, to hit the central Dread capital hard enough to destroy it."

"There is truth to your words, Dahm St. Martin. However, I question the capability of the ground forces. They have failed to organize efficiently up until now and with the Domo'dahm intensifying his efforts to destroy them, I fear you may leave such a message and find there is no one remaining to hear it save the Domo'dahm himself. In which case, the element of surprise grows even more valuable."

"So you think the rebels on the ground are going to lose?" Colonel Graham asked. "Not that I'm surprised, all things considered."

"Colonel," Theodore barked. "Mind yourself."

"I am not offended," Tea'va said, though Gabriel doubted that was true. "I speak only from experience. The rebels have had some success of late, but they are still greatly outnumbered and possess an extremely limited arsenal. Dahm St. Martin, I would caution against letting your emotions interfere with your tactical mind."

"Ha!" Theodore said. "You have a point there, Mr. Tea'va. Nobody here can argue your logic."

"Thank you, Dahm."

"At the same time, we're in this together. All of us. Sometimes, emotions have to win out. We live or die as one. Up here. Down there. I know that isn't tactically right, but it is right."

Gabriel noticed Tea'va's face tighten at the statement. He wasn't surprised the bek'hai didn't agree. Even so, Tea'va held his tongue.

"So we can send a message out," Theodore said. "Maybe our people can get in position in time, maybe they can't, but at least we can try."

"Agreed," Colonel Graham said.

"Next question. What can we do to get ourselves ready? By that I mean, for one, can we get the Magellan flying again?"

"She's pretty beat up, General," Guy said. "I've examined her systems. Most importantly, we need to replace the reactors, because they're completely spent. After that, we need to do something about the armor, the life support, pretty much every critical system. Some of it is minor, some of it not as much."

"That wasn't what I asked, Mr. Larone," Theodore said. "I know she's beat up, but I have a feeling the big bird is going to be staying in orbit, taking on some of the other big birds in the air. That means we need a smaller bird to drop our soldiers. Can we get her good enough to use as a ferry?"

"I think I can get her ready enough to make a drop planetside," Guy said. "Other than that, I don't know."

"Mr. Mokri, Zoelle, tell me more about these assemblers. You made a copy of the phase modulator in what? An hour?"

"Yes, General," Reza said.

"The duplicate was insufficient," Zoelle said. "It failed to handle the power requirements and will need further refinement."

"I understand, and you'll have time to work on that. What I need to know is what all we can produce in twenty-two days. Parts for the Magellan? A new power supply? More guns for the troops? That sort of thing."

"All of those, Dahm St. Martin," Tea'va said. "There are twenty-six assemblers on the Ishur. The items you are requesting are all minor as long as we have the resources available, and there is no reason to believe we do not. The scrap from the gi'shah you destroyed can also be used as raw material, along with other surplus material."

"I like where it sounds as though you're going with this, Mr. Tea'va. What else are you suggesting?"

"We have two assemblers on board that are capable of building ships, Dahm St. Martin, both gi'shah, and ek'shah. They will need modification to utilize human pilots, but we should have materials and time to construct a few. We can also repair your damaged starships, including the Heil'bek's." Tea'va looked at Gabriel. "It would be my honor to soar with you."

"And mine," Gabriel said in return.

"That's what I want to hear," Theodore said. "Juliet, do you agree with Mr. Tea'va's assessment?"

"I will need to review the logs, but in general, yes."

"Excellent. Next question. Mr. Mokri, Mr. Larone, what about those modulation upgrades? The cascading shields are something, but I would prefer full coverage."

"I don't think that will be possible, sir," Reza said. "It's a limitation of the design. We might be able to give you a little more control over it, though. To at least try to direct the coverage."

"I'll take whatever you can give me."

"I'll work on it, sir."

"Good man."

"Sir," Colonel Choi said, speaking up for the first time. "With regard to our return to Calawan."

"What about it?"

"General Cave wasn't very happy with us when we left."

"Heh. No, he wasn't. I think coming back in a bigger, better starship might change his mind."

"You don't think he'll court-martial us?"

"Him and what army? No. Alan will fall in line. He lost, we won. He isn't too old or too dumb to see that. Let's move on down to the nitty-gritty. Colonel Graham, I expect you to organize the ground forces that we'll be dropping in the Magellan. Let's get our ducks in a row there. I don't want any question regarding our plan of attack. Mr. Tea'va, I'm going to need your expertise here. You know how the Dread capital is organized better than any of us."

"Of course, Dahm St. Martin," Tea'va said.

"Okay then," Theodore replied, bringing up a map of Earth on the table. The dark splotch that was the main Dread city was visible from space. "We collected this data on our pass through. Let's come up with a plan. Nobody leaves this room until we do. Understood?"

"Yes, sir."

[27]

"We're nearing the exodus, sir," Gabriel said, watching the terminal in front of him. He was getting the hang of recognizing the different shapes and symbols that made up the bek'hai language, deciphering them more quickly by the day.

"Great news," Theodore said, rolling his chair to the front of the bridge and rotating to look out the viewport. There was nothing in front of them but the blankness of slipspace.

Four days had passed since the Ishur had made the first of two slips, this one intended to carry her from the outer system the Dread called Pol'tek to the system near Ursae Majoris that they called home. For Gabriel, they had passed in an almost literal blur. As one of the highest ranking officers on the ship, he had been assigned the task of keeping an eye on the work being done to prepare for war. That included everything from check-ins on the status of the Magellan, to trips down to the assemblers to ensure everything was set up and coming along according to their designs. It had meant no time to do much of anything else, including his intended conversation with Zoelle about Tea'va's activity in down below.

Time had made that conversation seem less important, as Tea'va had been nothing but a model soldier over the past days. He had offered endless help to Gabriel, Theodore, Abdullah, and the others regarding the operational systems of the Ishur, and had even been able to assist Reza in nearing completion on the integration between interfaces. They had already managed to network half of the secondary weapons batteries on the fortress, and given another week they expected to have them all ready to go. Even better, Reza was making amazing progress on cooking up a solution to give them better control over the phase modulation, though he continued to be stumped by the mathematics surrounding full shield coverage.

"You're getting quite skilled, Heil'bek," Tea'va said. "We'll make a pur'dahm of you, yet."

The Dread was sitting behind Gabriel, allowing him to control the Ishur through an assembled duplicate of Reza's tablet. It allowed him to use his fingers to manage vectors and thrust, instead of needing to place his hands in a vat of goop to transfer electrical impulses through the organic subsystems.

"I'll pass," Gabriel replied. "Maybe we can make a human of you, instead?"

Tea'va hissed softly. "Perhaps."

The pur'dahm was more than a model soldier. Gabriel was beginning to think of him as a friend.

"Disembarking in twenty seconds," Gabriel said, watching the symbols. Eventually, the tablet would be able to convert it all to alphanumerics, but Reza hadn't gotten that far yet.

"Spaceman Locke, are we ready to transmit?" Theodore asked.

"Yes, sir," Miranda replied. "The message is loaded into the system. Transmitters are online and at full-power. From what Sarah told me, there's no way the rebels can miss this."

"Not unless every listening device on the planet is dead," Theodore replied. "I only wish the Dread weren't going to hear it, too."

"They'll be getting a nice earful, at least," Gabriel said.

"That they will."

"T-minus Five seconds," Gabriel announced. "Four. Three. Two. One. Disengaging phase generators."

He slid his finger on the tablet and tapped a button. The ship responded immediately, vibrating softly as the spiked nacelles that surrounded the main structure began to fold back. He closed his eyes, feeling the shift in his body as they were gently released from the stream and back into realspace, the blankness ahead convalescing into a sea of stars.

"Status?" Theodore said.

"We're right on target, sir," Gabriel replied.

"Good. Get us headed for the next insertion point and prepare for the next slip. Spaceman Locke, trigger the transmission."

"Yes, sir," Miranda said. "Transmitting... now."

Of course, there was no visible evidence of the transmission. Even so, they had just released a recorded message from Theodore St. Martin to the United Earth Rebellion, as he was calling it, giving them a time and place to be in eighteen days. Knowing the Dread would be listening in, he had also added a second message, in their language, just for them.

"Transmission sent, General," Miranda said.

"ETA to stream insertion?"

"Seven minutes, General," Gabriel said.

"How's our radar?"

"We're free and clear, sir," Gabriel said.

"And too far out for the Domo'dahm to waste his energy trying to catch us," Tea'va said. "Especially now that he knows when you'll be coming back."

"I know you don't agree with this one, Mr. Tea'va," Theodore said. "We have to trust in our people to get their jobs done. If they do, it won't matter what your leader throws back at us. We'll be just as indestructible as they were when they took the planet from us."

"He is not my leader," Tea'va said sharply.

Theodore smiled. "My apologies, Mr. Tea'va. No, he isn't."

"Five minutes to slip," Gabriel said.

"Sir," Miranda said. "Something just came up on my terminal here, but I don't know how to read it."

"Mr. Tea'va, would you mind?" Theodore said.

"Of course, Dahm St. Martin."

Tea'va stood and circled to the back, where Miranda was sitting. Gabriel lifted his head to watch him, curious about what Miranda had seen. When Tea'va reached her terminal, he glanced at the message, and then his eyes darted to Theodore and back again, almost too quickly to notice.

"It is nothing, General," he said. "A confirmation that the transmission has completed. Would you like to repeat it?"

"No. Once is enough. Thank you, Mr. Tea'va."

"My honor, Dahm St. Martin."

Tea'va returned to his position behind Gabriel as the countdown to the next slip continued.

"You're sure it was nothing?" Gabriel asked.

"Yes, Heil'bek. I am certain. A standard status message. That is all."

Gabriel nodded and returned his eyes to his terminal. He forced himself to concentrate, but something was eating at the corner of his thoughts. He had spent enough time with Tea'va to become familiar with his body language, and as much as he wanted to believe what he had seen was nothing, he didn't.

As he triggered the Ishur to re-engage its phase generators and return to the slipstream, he resolved himself to have that conversation with Zoelle after all.

And soon.

[28]

"WHAT DO YOU HAVE, SERGEANT?" DONOVAN ASKED. HE WAS crouched behind a small outcropping of stone, ten klicks east of downtown Austin and the rebel base.

"Call me Sarge if you have to use a rank," Kroeger said, lowering the pair of binoculars he was carrying. "I'm still not used to this enlisted shit."

"It makes organizing units easier to not have vigilantes roaming around. It's a matter of convenience as much as anything."

"Yeah, whatever. Anyway, to answer your question, it looks like we waited a little too long on this little scavenger hunt." He passed the equipment to Donovan. "Damn jackals are all over the place, even if they don't have a clue what they're doing."

Donovan raised the binoculars, looking at the Dread outpost two kilometers distant. It was the same one the Austin rebellion had hit earlier when they had captured the rifles and the tank but left the mechs behind. As he swept his eyes across it, he noticed the movement of people outside of the open entrances. They were dirty and disheveled and carrying old human rifles. They didn't look like much of a threat.

"The mechs should be to the eastern side," Orli said.

Donovan glanced over at the clone. He was glad Ehri had convinced her to see his way of thinking, and to start using her original name to prevent confusion.

"Where?"

She pointed to a larger bulb to the left of the hub. "In there."

"That's what we came for," he said.

"It's a good thing you picked the Dread guns out before they showed up," Kroeger said. "It'll make things a lot easier."

"Bullets can still hurt us," Soon said. "And I've been shot at enough recently."

"Those are humans down there," Donovan said. "I'm not too keen on killing them."

"You're suggesting we go talk to them?" Ehri asked.

"Yeah. We don't want the property, just the mechs. They certainly can't use them. They probably don't even know how to open them up."

"Major, how much experience do you have with jackals?" Kroeger said.

"You're the only one I've encountered before," Donovan replied.

Kroeger smiled at that. "Trust me. I'm reasonable compared to most of those assholes."

"You don't think they'll hear us out?"

"I'll tell you what I think is going to happen. We're going to go down there. You're going to ask to speak to the man in charge. Someone will go in and talk to him, and maybe they'll lead you back, or he'll come out. You'll tell him you came for the mechs, and he'll say, what'll you give me for them. You'll politely explain that they aren't his, he'll respond that they most certainly are. You'll ask him what he wants, and he'll point to her." He pointed at Ehri. "Or her." He shifted his finger to Orli. "Or, maybe even him." He pointed at Soon. "Just depends on which way the wind blows for him. Of course, you'll say no, and before you know it, we'll be shooting at one another at point blank range. They'll die, we'll die, and the whole thing will be net zero because all of our pilots will be dead."

"You can't be serious," Soon said.

"I'm dead serious. How did we meet again?"

"Point made."

"You think we should just take what we want?" Donovan asked.

"Yup. It's us or them, Major, and these assholes gave up civility a long time ago."

"That doesn't mean we need to come down to their level."

"It damn well does if you want to come and go in one piece."

Donovan leaned back, eyeing his team. Kroeger, Ehri, Orli, Soon, Corporal Wilkins, and another of Colonel Knight's men, Corporal Hicks.

"Civil or not, they're still human," he said, trying to rally support. "If we get rid of the Domo'dahm, restore some sense of community, they could come back in line."

"No, they can't," Kroeger said.

"Why not? You did."

Kroeger laughed. "I'm good at faking it; that's all."

"Bullshit."

"Think what you want, Major."

"I agree with you, Major," Ehri said. "We are all God's children, and we have no right to kill one another without just cause."

"Agreed," Orli said.

Soon shrugged. "I don't think it's up for debate. You're in charge, sir. You tell me what to do, and I do it."

Donovan hesitated, a part of him wondering if he was about to make a mistake.

"Okay, we'll go down and talk to them. Kroeger, I want you to stay here."

"What?"

"You're a crack shot. If things start to look bad, I want you dropping them before they can drop us."

"Yes, sir."

"The rest of you, let's go."

Donovan stood. So did all of the others, save Kroeger. He adjusted his Dread rifle, putting it on the ground beside him and swapping it out for an older human rifle that he had taken from the rebel's armory. Donovan had thought it odd he had brought the piece at the time, but it seemed the newly minted Sergeant had expected a problem like this.

"This thing'll drop a bear at half a kilometer," Kroeger said, catching him looking at it. "It'll pulp heads if that's what it comes to."

Donovan hoped it wouldn't come to that as he led his squad down the side of the incline and toward the outpost. They were still a ways out when the guards spotted them, yelling to one another and calling for reinforcements. Within seconds, the size of the jackal army had expanded from a handful to nearly fifty. Against six? He started to think he should have listened to Kroeger after all.

"Just stay right there," one of the guards said. A heavyset woman in a pair of torn pants, her head shaved. "Not another step, or we'll kill every last one of you."

Donovan stopped moving. His squad halted behind him.

"My name is Major Donovan Peters," he said. "Earth Rebellion."

"Major? You think you're some kind of soldier?" one of the other jackals said.

"Yes," Donovan replied. "I am a soldier. We're trying to get the Dread off our planet."

"Ha," the woman said. "That's a good one. How do you think you're going to manage that, pretty boy? You can't hurt the Dread. Everyone knows it."

"Really? Then where did all the Dread who ran this base go?"

"They left, I suppose. All the better for us."

"They left?" Donovan said. "What about the bodies? The clones?"

"Didn't' see them."

Donovan didn't know if the woman was being intentionally obtuse, or if she was outright lying. He didn't care. They couldn't afford to waste time here.

"There are some Dread mechs in that part of the base over there," he said, pointing toward the bulb. "The rebellion cleared this base. You're welcome to it, but we want those machines."

"We're welcome to it?" the other jackal said. "Who the hell do you think you are? You don't get to decide for us what is and isn't ours." He approached Donovan, looking angry and making Donovan wonder if Kroeger might get twitchy.

"You're right," Donovan said, putting up his hands. "My apologies. Look, the rebellion is planning to move against the Dread capital in Mexico. We know how to pilot the machines in there, and we want to use them against the Dread. That's the only thing we came for."

"Well, Major," the woman said. "This is our home now. It was empty when we got here, so we have every right to it. You want something from our home, there's only one way to get it."

"Which is?"

She rubbed her fingers together in a timeless suggestion. Donovan stared at her for a moment. This was going down exactly how Kroeger had said. He should have listened.

"I'll bargain," Donovan said. "But only with whoever's in charge."

The woman smiled. She was missing half her teeth, and the other half didn't look very good. "I thought you might say that. Frank, go get the boss."

The man closest to the doors retreated into them, vanishing a moment later.

They stood facing one another in tense silence until Frank returned, moving ahead of who Donovan assumed was their leader. He was a lanky man with a thick mustache and wiry muscle, wearing a leather jacket over his bare chest and a pair of jeans.

"This better be important," he muttered as he left the safety of the compound. "I've got a lot more important shit to deal with than another one of those so-called rebellion armies. Poor saps. You'd think they'd be tired of dying for nothing by now."

He saw Donovan, stopped moving, and smiled. "My man Frank over there tells me that you have an interest in the contents of this here-"

He stopped talking when his head exploded, splashing the woman beside him with blood and bone.

Three more of the jackals were down before Donovan heard the first report of Kroeger's rifle.

What the hell?

He raised his weapon, barely getting a bolt off and into the jackal immediately ahead of him before they fired back. Then he was moving, rushing toward the enemy. If they were trapped at close range, it was better to make them risk hitting one another. He had to trust that Kroeger wouldn't hit him.

The night echoed with pops as the jackals overcame their shock and started shooting for real. Three more fell to Kroeger's sniper rifle, but Donovan barely had time to see it. He dove into the melee, firing the Dread rifle directly into the flesh, filling the air around him with the smell of cooking meat and blood.

Screams followed the echo of gunfire as everything turned to chaos. Donovan didn't have time to think or time to plan. He simply reacted, letting his instincts to survive take over as he waded into the enemy, smashing one in the face with the rifle, bringing it back and shooting, grabbing one of the jackals from behind and throwing him just in time to let him take a bullet. He dropped the body, aiming and firing. He saw Kroeger take out two more.

He saw Soon ahead of him. There was blood on his hand, and he had dropped his weapon. He looked confused and frightened. He put his hands up as Donovan rushed toward him, trying to reach him. He shook his head, afraid. Donovan saw the jackal aiming his weapon at Soon. He watched that man's head vanish as well when Kroeger finally got him in his sights. Soon didn't drop his hands, though. He stood there, frozen, despite the fact that he was clear.

Donovan reached him, tackling him, pulling him down. He rolled over, quickly scanning the field. Where was Ehri? There. Orli? There. Wilkins? He didn't see Wilkins. There. On the ground. Was he dead?

Two more shots rang out. Then everything was silent.

Donovan counted five breaths before he moved, pulling himself to his feet. There were bodies all around him, half of which had been cut down by Kroeger. Ehri was up and moving, too. So were Orli and Hicks.

Kroeger was running down the slope toward them.

Donovan turned around, leaning down and putting out his hand to help Soon. Soon didn't take it.

He didn't move at all.

"Major," Kroeger said, his voice raspy and out of breath as he reached them. "Major. Shit. I'm sorry. I had to. I had to do it."

Donovan spun around, acting without thinking. His fist connected with Kroeger's jaw, hitting him hard enough that the older man fell back on his ass.

"What the hell was that?" Donovan shouted. "He didn't even have a chance to ask for anything."

Kroeger stayed down. "Major. I know you're pissed."

"You have no idea," Donovan said. He was shaking with anger. "Did you see him make a threatening move?"

"No, Major. But-"

"Soon is dead, damn it. So is Wilkins, and it's your damn fault."

"Major, wait," Kroeger said.

"We had four pilots. Now we have three, you asshole. I said-"

"Hold on there a minute," Kroeger shouted. "With all due respect Major, you don't know shit about shit. I've been out here. I do. That mustached asshole I killed? I know him. Shit, I thought that bastard was dead. He would have killed you. No matter what you said, no matter what he agreed to, he would have killed each and every one of you, and not quickly, and not in a good way. Go inside, Major. Step in and see. I bet the evidence is just waiting in there."

Donovan clenched his jaw. His head was pounding, his entire body numb. Kroeger's words beat through it, giving him pause.

"Who was he?" he asked.

"His name was Myles Sarkova. He used to be part of another group called the Innocents. We ran together for two years. Major, I never said I was a good man, but that guy made me look like a damn cherub. Last time I saw him he was dead in a ditch. At least, I thought he was." Kroeger spit on the ground. "Shit. If I had known it was him, I would have never let you go down to parlay."

Donovan stood in silence for a moment, feeling a sudden wave of guilt crash over him.

"It was my fault," he said, and he believed it. "I should have listened to you in the first place."

"Yeah, you should've," Kroeger said. "But I get why you didn't. I felt the way you do once, before I learned better. If we win this war, if we free the Earth from the grip of the Dread, that doesn't mean everything goes back to being just like before. Not right away. It may seem crazy, but it will get harder before it gets easier. I guarantee it."

Donovan might not have agreed five minutes ago. Now he simply nodded before glancing over at Soon one last time, using all of his strength to keep himself together.

"We have three pilots," he said, a chill running through him in response to the words. "We can take three mechs."

Then he started walking, certain he was as big of a piece of shit as he felt like, but not knowing what else to do.

[29]

DONOVAN CHECKED HIS SENSORS, KEEPING AN EYE OUT FOR THE familiar and at the same time unwanted display of more than their three targets on the HUD, happy to find that it remained clear.

His mind wandered as he steered the mech back toward Austin, leading Ehri and Orli as they returned to the rebel base with the added weaponry, bringing the count of functional armors to five. It didn't sound like much, and after what had happened it didn't feel like much, but Donovan would take what he could get.

At least Soon hadn't died for nothing.

Had he?

Donovan had dealt with the loss of soldiers before. He had dealt with the loss of loved ones as well. His mother. Diaz. Matteo. He was used to people dying around him. That was the world he was born into. The world he had grown up in. Even so, Soon's death was lingering, weighing on him like the mech he was riding in.

It was his fault the man was dead. His fault his wife would never have a chance to see him again. His fault they would never have the child they had wanted. He should have listened to Kroeger and killed the jackals before the jackals killed Soon. But how could he have done that in good conscience? How could he have just assumed the humans were bad when they were all supposed to be fighting on the same side?

He didn't know, but he still felt like he had made the wrong call. There was no going back in life, only forward, and so he was doing his best to shake it off and stay focused. It was just too new. Too raw. It was a struggle.

"Austin Actual, this is Rebel One. Do you copy, over?" Donovan said. They were getting close enough to the base their shorter range signal should have made it through to the loop station.

"This is Austin Actual," Colonel Knight replied. "I hear you, Major. What's your status?"

Donovan opened his mouth, closed it, thought for a second, and then spoke. "We had a run in with a jackal pack," he said. "Some group Kroeger said was called the Innocents. We have three mechs, but we took a pair of casualties."

He could hear the quiver in the Colonel's voice when she answered. "Acknowledged, Major. I'll expect a full debriefing when you return."

"Of course, ma'am."

There was silence for a moment, and then Colonel Knight came back on. "Who did we lose?"

"Corporal Wilkins, and Captain Kim," Donovan choked out.

"Oh. Donovan, I'm sorry," Colonel Knight replied. "Damn it."

"My sentiments exactly."

"What's your ETA to Checkpoint Alpha?"

"Fifteen minutes," Donovan replied. "I'll." He paused as his sensors picked something up to the north. "Actual, hold that thought. I'm getting something on my sensors." He looked at the HUD. A single small symbol had appeared there. "Rebel Two, do you know what that is?"

"Negative, Rebel One," Ehri replied. "But it's multiplying."

"Actual, have the scouts reported signs of a new Dread assault group assembling?"

"No, Major, they haven't. If you're picking up something new, we need to know what it is."

"Affirmative. Rebel Four, take Sergeant Kroeger and Corporal Hicks back home. Rebel Two, you're with me. Let's go see what we're dealing with."

"Roger," Ehri replied.

"Actual, I'm going to take Rebel Two and scout out the situation."

"Affirmative, Rebel One. You're going to be back out of short wave communications range. Do not engage. I repeat, do not engage. Find out what your sensors are picking up and get back in range to report. Understood?"

"Yes, ma'am," Donovan said, bringing his mech to a stop and turning it to the north. Orli continued toward Austin, while Ehri fell in beside him.

They headed out at a fast walk, the mech shuddering slightly each time a heavy foot landed on the ground. The targets on the HUD were still multiplying, growing from a single mark to a dozen, from a dozen to a hundred, and from a hundred to still more. The sensors weren't giving much indication of what was out there. While the Dread mechs would paint as friendlies, clones registered as unknowns. Even so, the size of the force suggested the Dread had landed another army somewhere else, and they were making their way south to the city.

"Soon died fighting," Ehri said. "It was an honorable death."

He felt a sudden tension fill him at the words. She always seemed to know what he was thinking. "I got him killed."

"You led him into battle. That's what commanders do."

"I made the wrong decision."

"And yet he believed in you and supported that decision. Give him the same option again, and he would have done the same."

"Do you really believe that?"

"Yes. You're a soldier, too, Major. Wouldn't you do the same?"

He sighed audibly. "Yes. I would. Without hesitation."

"Then why are you blaming yourself?"

"To be honest, I don't know. Maybe I feel like I should. Maybe because he survived all of that time in space, he survived our rescue; he made it all the way here." He paused. "I'm so sick of the violence. The death. The war."

"That is natural. It is also not a reason for guilt."

Donovan considered it. "I know you're right, logically. Emotionally? I'm struggling with that."

"Also natural. Just try to remember that he trusted you and he believed in you and the decision you made."

"Okay. I'll try." He checked the HUD again. "Looks like our targets are just beyond this incline. Let's go in low and slow and try not to give ourselves away. We aren't picking up any large assets, but you never know."

"Roger."

They slowed to a walk, crouching their mechs and lifting the feet only a foot off the ground before more tenderly bringing them down. It took a few extra minutes to near the crest of the incline this way, but it also prevented the shapes on the sensors to react to their approach.

Donovan eased his mech forward, taking a few more steps up the hill. As he did, he began to clear the obstruction, starting to gain visual on the area ahead.

He saw the rear of the column first. A few lines of soldiers, marching forward at a light jog. He stared at them for a moment before taking another step forward, gathering more height and becoming able to look further down the line. He felt his heart jump as he adjusted his view, zooming in on the scene below.

The uniforms were all wrong for Dread clones. These were olive green, drab and simple. Their wearers weren't identical either. They were male and female, dark and light, old and young. They were all on foot, each and every one of them, marching double-time in a column that had to be nearly four thousand strong.

At the front of the line was an older man with a chiseled face, marching along with the rest of the troops. The only reason he stood out at all was because he was carrying a metal pole. Affixed to the end of it was a shred of cloth, a field of stars amongst a series of red and white stripes printed on it.

"Rebel Two, run back to comm range," Donovan said, barely able to control his sudden elation. "Tell Colonel Knight that General Parker and his rebels have arrived."

[30]

Donovan was waiting for General Parker as the front of the army started climbing the hill. He left the confines of the mech, opening the cockpit and climbing out to stand on the foot of the machine, his hand raised in greeting.

The General lowered his flag as he neared, a big smile piercing his otherwise rough face as he stared up at the Dread armor. He said something to the woman next to him, and the army continued onward, flowing around Donovan and continuing on, the soldiers closest to him waving and saluting but otherwise remaining quiet. It was obvious they had a lot of experience avoiding notice.

"General Parker," Donovan said, jumping down from the foot and greeting the man with a salute. He had never actually seen the General before, but the hardware on the jacket he was wearing made it clear who he was.

"And you are, soldier?" Parker asked, returning the salute.

"Major Donovan Peters, sir. Mexico."

Somehow, the General's smile grew even larger. "Major Peters," he said. "The man who started the Dread downfall. It's an absolute honor."

"I'm just doing my part, sir. You've been at this for much longer than me. The honor is mine."

"Humble, too. I like it. We can share in the honor then, Major." He looked up at the mech behind Donovan. "That yours?"

"It's the rebellion's, yes, sir."

He moved forward and put his hand on it. "I've been running from these things for most of my life," he said softly, the smile vanishing. "I never thought I'd get to touch one. I never thought we'd capture one."

"We lost some good people getting our hands on them," Donovan said.

"I'm sure you did, Major. We've lost too many good people. Too damn many."

"I sent my second back to Austin to inform Colonel Knight of your arrival. I expect things to get a little interesting once all of yours start pouring in."

"Not enough space?"

"More than enough space, sir. We've got the city locked up tight. The Dread have failed to break it twice already. What I mean is that we'll have a big enough army to launch an offensive."

"That's the idea, Major."

Donovan pointed up to the shoulder of the mech. "Can I give you a ride? It's not the most comfortable perch, but it'll make a statement."

The grin returned to the General's face. "I like the way you think, Major," he said, holding up the flag again.

They climbed the mech. Donovan slipped back into the cockpit, while General Parker moved to the shoulder of the machine. When he got there, he raised the flag high. Then Donovan put the armor in motion, turning it around and bringing it back down the hill, careful not to hit any of the soldiers as he carried the General toward the front of the line.

It was a surreal experience. He could see the rebels around him. He could see the way their faces changed as they passed, carrying the flag through the line and toward the front. He could sense their excitement and their enthusiasm, even as they did all they could to keep a low profile.

They reached the front of the line, continuing on. Donovan could see Ehri's mech in the distance now, facing him and waiting. He could see Austin behind her, its mangled skyline taking on a new beauty in the dim light of the night sky.

He kept going, a new sense of hope filling him. He imagined it would infect all of them soon, as the General's forces began to mingle with theirs, and the plans for an assault were arranged. For fifty years they had been trampled on or used, taken or murdered, left so broken that all vestiges of civilization had been lost.

Not anymore.

Donovan reached Ehri. She reversed course, turning back toward Austin, syncing her mech's motion to his and helping him lead the troops home.

"Austin Actual, this is Rebel One," Donovan said. "We're on our way in."

"Roger, Rebel One," Colonel Knight said. "I've already given the orders to get a welcoming party going. Fresh uniforms and Dread for as many as we can equip."

"I'm sure the General will appreciate it, ma'am. ETA-"

Donovan was interrupted by a sudden burst of static over the comm, followed by a whine that registered loudly enough it hurt his ears.

"What the hell?" he said, wincing as the internal speakers squealed again. A new symbol appeared on his HUD, and then the noise normalized.

"Earth Rebellion," a voice said through the comm. "This is General Theodore St. Martin, New Earth Alliance. Heh. New Earth. Forget that. Earth Alliance."

Donovan felt his heart skip. General St. Martin? He was still alive. More importantly, he was close enough to send them a message. He reacted without thinking, leaning forward and hitting a switch to activate the external speakers so General Parker and the others could hear it.

"This message is being broadcast with all the juice this here starship can muster, which I've been told is quite a lot. We're taking a risk to send it because we're hitting the entire spectrum, which means the Dread are going to be hearing this, too. You know what? I don't give a damn, and you shouldn't either. Let them hear. Let them know.

"This message is being transmitted from a starship called the Ishur. You think that's a funny name? That's because it used to belong to the Dread. It was one of their fortresses. Now it's ours."

General St. Martin paused, as though he had known how they would react to the statement. More than one soldier on the field was close enough to Donovan's mech to hear the message, and they forgot themselves when they did, whooping and cheering at the news.

"We're on our way back to our home system to pick up the rest of our people. To pick up our soldiers. To arm them and get them ready. Then we'll be on our way back here to you. Back to Earth to reclaim what's ours. To challenge the Domo'dahm of the bek'hai for the right to this planet. If you can hear this, you need to get ready. You need to be prepared. Whoever you are, wherever you are, if you can get to Mexico, get there. Fifteen days from now, the Ishur will be back in Earth's orbit, and the battle for our freedom will begin. Fifteen days from now, the Dread occupation will end.

"You want to be part of it? Get to Mexico. Fight with everything you have. Fight with your bare hands if you have to. Show these alien coullions that we never gave up. We never lost hope. Show them that they'll never be rid of us. Never be free of us. Never have this planet to themselves. This is our home. Our Earth. You hear that, Rorn'el? Our planet. I'm coming, you son of a whore. You've got fifteen days to enjoy my planet, and then I'm tossing you and yours out on your ass. If you're with me, be in Mexico and be ready.

"General St. Martin, out."

[31]

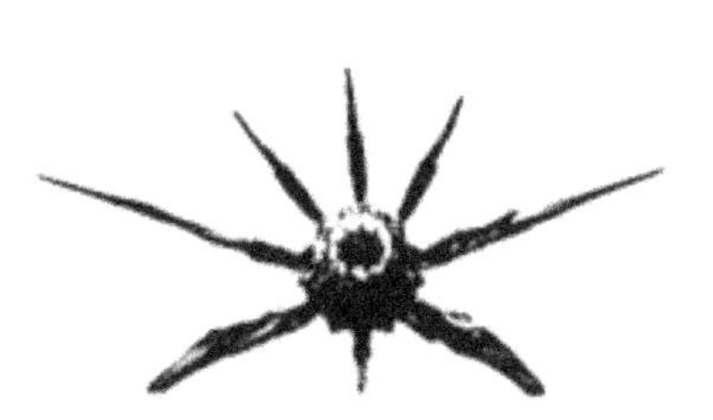

Domo'dahm Rorn'el shook with anger, his entire body quivering as he clutched the sides of his throne, holding them so tightly that his fingers scraped along the lek'shah. He had sent two domo'shah to confront Gr'el or Tea'va and the Ishur.

Gr'el or Tea'va.

Not a human.

Not Theodore St. Martin.

"What of the domo'shah?" he said softly.

"Domo'dahm?" Orish'ek said. "I did not hear."

"What of the domo'shah?" he shouted. "The two ships I sent to destroy the Ishur. What of them?"

"They have not returned, Domo'dahm."

"I am aware of that, Orish'ek. Were they destroyed?"

"I do not know, Domo'dahm. We have had no word from them. If the humans have taken the Ishur, we should assume that they were."

"How?" Rorn'el said. "How does this happen? Their ship had no weapons. No shields. How did they survive? How did they capture the Ishur? It defies all logic."

He hissed softly, trying to release his frustration. He knew how. There was only one reasonable explanation. Zoelle. The un'hai. It had to be. The clones had always been willful, but lately, they had started becoming more and more troublesome. First, there had been Ehri, who had tricked him into allowing her freedom to study the humans. Then there was Orli, a Dahm of a research team who had stolen one of the few clone pilotable gori'shah they had and taken it to the rebel base in Austin and ultimately helped them attack one of their bases and claim the resources there.

He forced himself to release his hands as they began to hurt from the pressure. He hissed louder, trying to deal with his anger. Zoelle. It had to be. Both Ehri and Orli were connected to Tuhrik at one time, as was she. His splice brother had done something to them. He had altered them somehow.

He reached up and clutched at Juliet's rosary. She and Tuhrik had been close. Maybe too close. They had both begged him to change the course of the bek'hai, to integrate more completely with humankind. He had insisted it was the only way they would survive in the centuries to come. He knew Tuhrik never agreed with his desire to exterminate the humans, but he never believed it would come to this.

"How could you?" he whispered.

Tuhrik had betrayed him. Juliet had betrayed him. She had taken the freedom he offered and used it against him. She had claimed to want peace while preparing her people for war.

"Domo'dahm, what are your orders?" Orish'ek said. "How should we respond to this declaration?"

"Respond? How else will we respond? If the humans are coming here to fight, then we will prepare to meet them."

"Domo'dahm, they took the Ishur. For all we know, they destroyed the other two domo'shah. We can't sit idle and wait for them to come. If they have developed a new weapon, we will be unprepared for it."

"You heard the human, General Theodore St. Martin," Rorn'el said. "You heard how he threatened me. How he challenged me. I will not back down. I will not respond with fear. You heard that he is returning to his home system? Pit'ek will be there ahead of him. He will find his home in ruin. He will find his people dead. The first victory will be mine, as will the last."

"Yes, Domo'dahm," Orish'ek said.

"That does not mean we won't prepare for war. Send messages out to our forces. Tell the Dahms of the precepts to bring their domo'shah into orbit to wait. Order the consolidation of our ground forces back to the capital. The rebels in Austin have been difficult to dig out, but now we will not have to. They will come to us, and they will die."

"Yes, Domo'dahm. It will be done."

"Have Sor'ek dur Kan'ek brought before me. I require him to trace all of the un'hai who have been produced so that we can identify those who may have been tainted by Tuhrik."

"Domo'dahm?"

"He changed them, druk'shur. He gave his loyalty to her over me."

"Who, Domo'dahm?"

Rorn'el hissed loudly. "Juliet St. Martin, and by extension the humans. He was a traitor. A legri'shah laying in wait."

"Then, would it not be wise to exterminate all of the un'hai?" Orish'ek asked. "If they are working against you, then they should not be permitted to exist."

The Domo'dahm squeezed the rosary. For as angry as he was, there was still a part of him that hesitated to let go. To destroy all of the un'hai would mean losing her forever.

"No. Only those with ties to Tuhrik. The others have shown no inclination toward deceit."

The doors at the end of the antechamber slid open. A drumhr hurried in, crossing the distance to the throne.

"Domo'dahm," he said, falling to his knees at the base of it.

"You were not requested, drumhr," Orish'ek said.

"I have important news, Domo'dahm."

"Rise and present it," Rorn'el said.

The bek'hai stood, keeping his head bowed as he spoke. "We have received an encrypted message from the Ishur," he said.

"What kind of message? Who sent it?"

"It is a data file, attached to the humans' signal but transmitted separately. It was not signed, Domo'dahm, but it was decrypted using current keys."

"And the contents?"

"It appears to be schematics pulled from the Ishur's assemblers. A device of some kind that the humans call a Darkspace Phase Modulator. It was saved to the databanks by Zoelle dur Tuhrik."

"A Darkspace Phase Modulator? Do we know what it does?"

"Not yet, Domo'dahm, as our science team has just started examining it. They believed it was important enough to tell you right away, as the human name suggests it may be a shield of some kind."

Rorn'el felt his anger begin to fade. A shield? That would explain how they had survived this long. But how had they taken the Ishur? At the moment, it didn't matter. At least someone on the ship was still loyal to him and had managed to feed him valuable information, perhaps at risk of their own life. If he ever discovered who they were, he would be sure to honor them.

"Orish'ek, send a message to Pit'ek, along with the schematics. Perhaps he can find a use for this device as well."

"It will be done, Domo'dahm."

"Drumhr, you are dismissed."

The bek'hai stood, still keeping his eyes on the floor. "Yes, Domo'dahm," he said as he retreated from the room.

Rorn'el leaned back in his seat, feeling his tension release a little. Perhaps there were a few traitors in their midst, but he was the Domo'dahm, and he was still in control. It would take more than a few un'hai to change that.

He lifted the rosary, holding it up in front of his face. This was the betrayal that stung the most. He knew she wanted him to spare her people, but he had never believed she would turn to violence to achieve it. Was her God not a peaceful being?

He closed his hand around the crucifix at the end of the beads and pulled forward, yanking it from his neck. The rope snapped, the wooden balls rolling from it, clattering to the ground and scattering on the floor. The other pur'dahm in the room were startled by the sudden noise and the appearance of the baubles, but they did not remark.

He squeezed the crucifix harder, pressing down on it until it finally cracked and splintered, breaking in half and dropping it to the floor.

"You cannot destroy me, Juliet St. Martin," he said quietly to the remains of the rosary. "This is my Earth. Not your mate's. Not your people's. Mine."

[32]

"Hey, Miranda, hold up."

Gabriel jogged up as she turned around, smiling when she saw him.

"Gabriel. Is everything okay?"

"To be honest, I'm not sure yet."

"Oh?"

"I've been trying to catch up to you since we went back into slip-space yesterday. It's been hard to find a few minutes to grab you in person."

"In person? What for?"

Gabriel put his hand on her arm, guiding her down the corridor, positioning himself close to keep his voice low.

"Yesterday, on the bridge. The symbol that came up that you couldn't read. Do you remember what it looked like?"

"Hmmm. I'm not sure. Why?" She paused to think, and then her expression changed. "Do you think Tea'va was lying about it?"

"I don't know. I hope not. I caught him looking over at my father before he said it was nothing. There was something in his eyes that I didn't like. Also, when I went down to look for Reza and Zoelle a few days ago, I saw him heading into the cloning facility when he was supposed to be in his quarters."

"Maybe he had a good reason?"

"Maybe. I don't want to think he can't be trusted. I like him. But I also can't ignore what I see. He was willing to turn on his own kind, how can we know for sure he won't turn on us? Anyway, I was going to take the symbol to Zoelle and get her opinion on it."

"How do you know you can trust her? She and Tea'va don't like one another."

"I know. Maybe I can't. I mean, I want to trust her, because like you said, whether she is really my mother or not she's still a conduit to her, and I'm eager for a chance to talk to her about her, instead of about phase modulators and assemblers. That doesn't mean that she might tell me it means something it doesn't and I wouldn't know the difference." He laughed. "It's hard to work all of this stuff out when the people you depend on the most are the ones you trust the least. Anyway, if we have enough time I can try to have Reza verify, but the clones are due to mature tomorrow, and if he did something to them-"

"It would be too late."

"Yes."

"Maybe I should come with you and try to describe it to Zoelle?"

"Do you have time right now?"

"Yes."

"Good. She should be down with the assemblers, working on the modulators. From what I hear, we've managed to produce three of them so far that can hold up to the power flow."

"How many do we need to cover the ship?"

"Three hundred. This is a big ship."

She laughed. "You can say that again. It's weird having so much space. It almost feels too big sometimes."

"You should have seen the legri'shah."

"Legri'shah?"

Gabriel realized he had never had time to talk to her about his adventure in the belly of the Ishur. "Let's walk. I'll tell you the story on the way."

They headed down the corridor, heading for one of the transport beams. Gabriel started to tell her about how the mothers had ambushed him, and how he had wound up in the legri'shah's den. They had nearly reached the edge of the hub leading to the beam when Tea'va emerged from it.

"Ah, much honor, Heil'bek," Tea'va said, seeing them. "And to you, Spaceman Locke." He dipped his head slightly.

'Tea'va," Gabriel said, wondering where the bek'hai was coming from. He couldn't think of a way to ask that didn't seem suspicious. "Have you seen Wallace around?"

"Wallace?"

"My dog. He's been sniffing his way around the ship lately, trying to find something edible, I guess."

It was a lie. A simple one. Wallace had been quarantined to quarters since he had panicked at the sight of the transport beam and led Daphne on an extended chase across the ship.

"No. I haven't seen your creature, Heil'bek. Would you like me to help you search for it?"

"That's okay. I'm sure you have better things to do. I was just asking."

"Of course. My regrets that I have not seen him."

"I'll see you later, Tea'va," Gabriel said.

"As you say, Gabriel," Tea'va replied, bowing again before continuing on his way.

"I don't know if it's just the power of suggestion or what, but that interaction gave me the chills," Miranda said.

"All the more reason to keep going forward with this," Gabriel said. "I trust your instincts."

"I wish you didn't have to. I don't like this at all."

"Me neither, but it is what it is."

They took the transport beam down to the lower decks and then made the long walk to the assemblers using the secondary passage that It'kek had shown him. Unlike the last time he had been there, the assemblers were all in use now, each of them humming and groaning as they collected the raw materials and recombined them into something else. A few of the Magellan's crew were there to monitor the progress, including Sergeants Abdullah and Hafizi, along with a contingent of the clone soldiers they had captured in the initial attack.

"Major St. Martin," Abdullah said as Gabriel and Miranda approached him, coming to attention. "What brings you down this way, sir?"

"Relax, Sergeant," Gabriel replied. "I'm looking for Zoelle."

"Assembler number twelve, sir," Abdullah replied.

"Thank you."

They made their way down the line, to the same assembler Gabriel had found her in the last time he had come down. She was leaned over a terminal, an updated version of the phase modulator resting on the table behind her.

"Zoelle," Gabriel said, getting her attention.

She smiled warmly. "Gabriel. It's good to see you." Gabriel returned the smile. He felt it from the way she said it. "What can I help you with?"

"I need a bek'hai symbol translated," he said.

"You came all the way down here for that? Why didn't you ask Tea'va to do it?" Her face changed as she made the connection. "What's going on?"

"Maybe nothing. Maybe I'm paranoid."

"It isn't like a St. Martin to be paranoid," she said. "If you think it's something, it probably is."

"Miranda, can you describe the symbol for her?"

"It came up on the bridge communications terminal," Miranda said. "It didn't have a translation, so I didn't know what it meant. It was something like 2 parallel lines with a circle in the middle, and then two circles, a line, and two more circles."

"Interesting," Zoelle said. "What did Tea'va say about it?"

"He said it meant the transmission was complete."

"He was not lying."

Gabriel could feel his entire body relax at the statement. He hadn't realized how tense he was about the whole thing. "I'm happy to hear it."

She lowered her voice, glancing around the small chamber as she did. "He was also not telling you the entire truth," she added. "What color was the text?"

"Orange," Miranda said.

"An encrypted message," Zoelle said.

"The message we sent wasn't encrypted," Gabriel said, feeling the tension begin rushing back.

"Yes, I know."

"That son of a-"

"Gabriel, wait," Zoelle said, her voice remaining quiet. "Just because he didn't tell you someone sent a second message doesn't mean he is responsible for sending it."

"What are you saying?"

"Why would Tea'va send a message to the Domo'dahm?" Zoelle said. "The Domo'dahm wanted him dead before he helped you."

Gabriel considered it. There was no good reason for Tea'va to do something like that.

But if he didn't, then who did?

[33]

Tea'va hurried through the back passages of the Ishur, his mind racing as he worked to adjust his strategy.

"Druk'shur, Shielle," he muttered to himself, angry. Trust. Risk. Why did he always wind up on the wrong end of it?

He had been trying to find an excuse to sneak back down to the cloning facility for hours, desperate to confront the un'hai clone and find out what exactly she had been thinking, sending an encrypted message to the Domo'dahm on the back of the humans' message to their brethren.

She had betrayed him; that much was clear. She had chosen the Domo'dahm over him. What he didn't understand was why?

He had offered her everything, just as he had offered it to Zoelle. Power. Control. A standing in the bek'hai ranks that was beyond what any lor'hai had achieved. There had to be some kind of malfunction with the un'hai. Bad programming that made them do things which defied logic. He couldn't comprehend her reasons, and he didn't care.

He would find out what she had sent to the Domo'dahm, and then he would kill her.

He had lied to the humans, telling them it was nothing. He

thought he had gotten away with it until he ran into Gabriel and the female, Miranda, in the corridor. He saw the way she was looking at him. Suspicious. Uncomfortable. He had worked so hard to earn the Heil'bek's trust, and Shielle had forced him to break it.

It was discouraging, but not the end of the world. He could recover from that lie. He was sure of it. They would ask questions, and he would answer them. He had always been ready for Shielle to double-cross him, only not this soon, and not in this way. It was infuriating.

He had to reach her before they did. If they questioned her first, she would have the opportunity to implicate him, to blame him for her actions. Perhaps they wouldn't believe her, but it would further any doubt they already held in their minds. And with only one more day until the clones matured, he couldn't afford for them to be watching him closely or limiting his movements out of their mistrust.

He slipped across a corridor and into another back passage, nearly colliding with a drek'er on the way by. He shoved the small clone aside, knocking him into the wall with a grunt. He was practically running now, racing to reach her before they did.

Gabriel would ask Zoelle what the symbols meant. She would tell them, and then they would suspect. Not him, at least. Zoelle was smart enough to know he wouldn't go crawling back to the Domo'dahm. No, they would guess it was her. She was an un'hai, the highest ranking clone on board after Zoelle herself. When they did, they would confront her, as he aimed to do now.

The race was on.

He came out of the passage right beside the transport beam, stepping in and heading down, coming out and skipping back into the hidden maintenance corridors. He didn't want her to see him coming. He didn't want anyone else to see him either. The only reason he was rushing now was because the human, Reza Mokri, had cornered him and asked him for help with more of the translations, tying him up for hours. It was work for a regular drumhr, not a pur'dahm, but he had forced himself to remain patient to avoid question. What other choice did he have?

He moved gracefully through the darkness, bypassing two more of the drek'er on his way. He reached the access hatch nearest to the front of the cloning facility, crouching as it slid open. He scanned the area, making sure it was clear, before sprinting across the distance and into the front.

He didn't slow as he went deeper inside, navigating the layout and heading for the sleeping quarters near the back. He was certain she was in hers. Where else would she go? She had no allies on the ship.

He entered the corridor, slowing his pace as he did so that he could approach more quietly. He eased himself through the hall, bypassing the other empty rooms in a direct line to hers. He had been here before, when he first decided he would need her to get what he wanted.

He reached her quarters, pressing himself against the entrance and trying to listen through to the other side. He didn't hear anything. He put his hand on the control surface to see if it would open for him. He was surprised when it did.

He leaned over, peering inside. The sparse room was vacant.

Where was she?

He paused, looking back over his shoulder, and then returning his attention to her room. He needed to know what she had sent. Could he retrieve it from her terminal? He stood there for a few seconds, considering, and then finally deciding against it. He had to catch up to her first, to ensure her silence. He could worry about the details later.

He retreated from the area, rushing back to the main facility. He made his way through it in search of her, checking each of the functional spaces in turn and growing more frustrated by her disappearance. Was it possible Gabriel had caught up to her ahead of him? Was he too late? He felt a wave of panic at the thought but forced it aside. The humans weren't that intelligent.

He made his way into the maturation hall. The caretakers were there, moving from chamber to chamber, checking on the contents. The clones had grown substantially since the last time he had been there. They were fully adult, nearly ready to emerge. They no longer thrashed and writhed in the nutrient bath. Instead, they sat quietly, their eyes closed.

Tea'va felt a new wave of panic. That was wrong. What was happening here?

"You," he said, grabbing the shoulder of one of the caretakers. "Why are they still?"

The clone pulled himself away but didn't speak.

"What did you do, Shielle?" Tea'va said, moving to one of the capsules and peering in. He touched the transparency, bringing up the readings. They were normal. How? Nothing about this was normal.

A caretaker approached him, weapon in hand. Tea'va almost laughed. They would always try to protect the clones. He backed away from the chamber, and the caretaker lowered the weapon.

"They're dead," Tea'va said to him. "Can't you see that? She faked the readings so that she could kill them."

The caretaker didn't react. He went to the capsule and put his hand to it, checking the same data before moving away.

Dead. Shielle had terminated them all to keep them out of the hands of the humans. No. Out of his hands. If he had any question she was sided with the Domo'dahm before; he was certain now.

"When I find you, I'll kill you," he hissed.

"Not if I kill you first," Shielle replied.

[34]

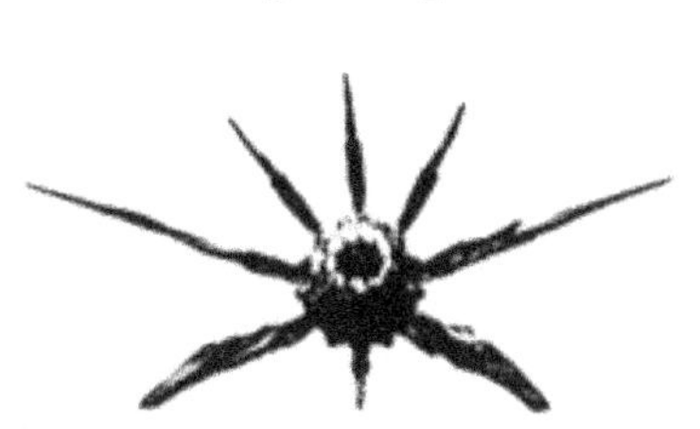

SHE APPEARED FROM BEHIND ONE OF THE CAPSULES, A caretaker's weapon in her hand.

"Why?" Tea'va said. "I trusted you."

"You are a fool, Tea'va. You have always been a fool. You think that you fail over and over again because of circumstance. It isn't the universe that is wrong. It is you. I am a loyal subject to the Domo'-dahm, and I will not let you challenge him, either alone or with the humans."

"Fool? I'm not the fool. I am superior. The future of the bek'hai."

"You are too human to be the future of the bek'hai."

"Oh? And what of you, Shielle? You are an un'hai. Why do you not care for the humans like Zoelle does?"

"Her programming is wrong. I don't know how it happened. Someone altered her, and who knows how many others of our type."

"She believes she is the real Juliet St. Martin."

"She believes it, but it cannot be true. The pur'hai is long deceased."

"How do you know?"

"You don't know enough about clones, pur'dahm. You can not make a clone without destroying the source."

"Maybe that isn't true. Surely Zoelle would know this."

"It is always true. She should know it but has forgotten. It is in her programming. I am sure of it."

Tea'va considered it. How many un'hai were there that believed they were the real Juliet St. Martin? How and why did they believe it?

Did it even matter in the end?

"I think you are the fool," Tea'va said, his eyes monitoring the area between him and Shielle. "You should have killed me first, and then spoken to my corpse."

She shot at him then. He was too quick for her, and he dove aside as the bolt struck the ground behind where he had been standing.

"You are no warrior," he said, rolling to his feet and charging toward her. "You are no bek'hai."

She adjusted her aim, firing again. The bolt hit him in the thigh, some of the impact reduced by his gori'shah. He grunted in pain as it began to burn, but didn't slow. She had ruined his plans to take over the Ishur. She had fooled him with her falsehood. He was angry. Furious. How could it be that the humans were the only ones who were honest?

She shot him again as he slammed into her, knocking her backward, throwing her to the floor. The weapon tumbled from her hand as they landed on the ground together. Tea'va could feel the burning in his chest, a close-range strike that was sure to have done damage. He knew by instinct that it wasn't fatal.

"What did you send to the Domo'dahm?" he asked, putting his hand to her throat and squeezing.

She writhed beneath him, trying to push him off. She didn't have close to enough strength to do it.

"What does it matter to you?" she said softly. "You are as dead as I am."

"Your bolts will not kill me," he replied.

"Perhaps you will wish they had."

He didn't know what she meant. He didn't care. He squeezed again. "What did you send? What did you tell him? That druk

Theodore already told him when he would be coming. I've never experienced such tactical stupidity before."

"You'll never know. More importantly, the humans will never know. I am loyal to the Domo'dahm, and to the bek'hai. We aren't all traitors, Tea'va."

"I'm not a traitor. I seek to rule the bek'hai so that our kind can flourish. The Domo'dahm wants to keep us as we are. He doesn't want us to evolve as we must, even as he says he does. That is incompatible with our future. I thought you understood that."

"The humans would allow you to evolve, Tea'va. To become like them, if that is what you want."

His face twisted in anger and pain. "That is not what I want. The humans are inferior. Pathetic."

"They have survived this long."

"Because I allowed it," he said, raising his voice. "Me. I let them onto this ship. I killed Gr'el for them and led them to victory so that I could claim victory for all of the bek'hai. And you destroyed it. You killed my clones. You ruined our chances. We will perish, Shielle. All of the bek'hai will perish for what you have done." He squeezed harder, holding her too tightly for her to be able to speak. "You and the Domo'dahm would see us all dead because you cannot admit the need to change. Because you are repulsed by me, instead of accepting, instead of thankful for my evolution."

He caught himself then, realizing what he was doing in his anger. He let go of her throat, sitting over her, his entire body shaking.

It didn't matter.

She was already dead.

Even in that, he had failed. She had tricked him into anger, tricked him into killing her before he found out what she knew.

"Tea'va," a voice said from behind him.

He closed his eyes, trying to calm himself. Gabriel. How much had he heard?

"Move slowly, Tea'va," Gabriel said.

He glanced over his shoulder. Gabriel was there with Miranda,

Zoelle, and the one called Sergeant Hafizi. The Sergeant had a rifle trained on his back.

"I wanted only to save the bek'hai," he said.

"You wanted power," Zoelle said. "Don't delude yourself with more excuses."

Tea'va felt his anger flare again. He struggled to keep himself still.

"Did you hear what Shielle said, Heil'bek? About the clones?"

"Yes."

Tea'va smiled. At least Gabriel knew the truth about Zoelle now.

"She may not be my mother, but she thinks that she is. That makes her loyal. That makes her trustworthy. Unlike you."

"What will you do with me?"

"I don't know. I'll let the General decide."

"Will you allow me to retire?"

"An honorable death? For you?" Zoelle said.

"Humans don't kill for retribution," Gabriel said. "You'll probably be confined to your quarters, imprisoned, until we can think of something else. Your knowledge is still useful to us."

Tea'va's shoulders slumped. "She sent the Domo'dahm a message. I do not know what it contained."

"I know. I saw you come down here once before. You didn't see me. Even if she hadn't, we would have figured out what you were planning."

He lowered his head further. He hadn't known about that. It seemed he was always destined to fail. Perhaps Shielle had been right? Perhaps he was the real fool?

"Get to your feet," Hafizi said. "Slowly."

Tea'va didn't move. His body hurt where Shielle had shot him. He could survive it, but then what? He could see the truth for what it was, now. He had never been superior. The Domo'dahm was right. He was defective. In all ways that mattered. It had taken this for him to realize.

"Tea'va, please, stand up," Gabriel said.

Tea'va opened his eyes. He noticed the caretaker's plasma gun at the tip of Shielle's fingers. She had been reaching for it when she died. No wonder they were concerned about him. He breathed in. He would have time for one shot. As far as he knew, only Sergeant Hafizi was armed.

"Tea'va. Now," Gabriel said.

He wasn't going to let them imprison him. His life was forfeit. He had failed. He didn't want to know how it was all going to end. All he had to do now was choose a target. If he shot Hafizi, he might be able to kill the others, but there was no guarantee. If he shot Gabriel, he would finally have his victory against the Heil'bek. If he shot Zoelle, he would have his revenge for her betrayal. There was no value in killing Miranda.

He breathed in again, tensing slightly as he made his decision.

"Tea'va."

He reached for the gun, grabbing it and turning as the Sergeant fired his rifle. The bolt hit him in the side, digging deep into him and causing a wave of immense pain. He didn't let it stop him, continuing to turn, bringing the weapon to bear on its target.

He fired, falling over as he watched the bolt streak toward Gabriel. If he had killed the Heil'bek back on Earth, none of this would have ever happened. He would have been a hero before he ever had to leave the planet. It was only fair.

He landed on his chest, his head up so he could see Gabriel die.

As his own life faded, he watched as Zoelle moved, faster than any human could, throwing herself in front of the plasma, taking the hit and falling to the ground.

Tea'va hissed softly, a final hiss of despair.

Then he died.

[35]

GABRIEL FELL TO HIS KNEES BESIDE ZOELLE. THE PLASMA HAD hit her square in the side of her face, tearing through her eye and into her skull, burning a hole right through to her brain. She was dead already, he knew, but it didn't stop him from leaning over her, feeling for a pulse and hoping beyond hope.

Maybe she wasn't the real Juliet St. Martin, but she was the closest thing he would ever have.

Now she was gone.

"Gabriel," Miranda said, coming to kneel next to him. He felt her arm over his shoulders. "Oh, my. I'm so sorry."

He didn't react. He stared at the mess the bolt had made of Zoelle's face. Then he looked to the traitorous bek'hai who had caused it. Tea'va had fired his weapon at him. The shot was meant for his face. He could barely believe it after he had come to think that at the very least they held a mutual respect for one another.

He could barely believe any of it.

"Hafizi, find a comm station and report in to Colonel Choi," he said, his voice weak. "Tell her what happened. Do not tell the General. Do you understand?"

"Yes, sir," Hafizi said.

Gabriel reached under his shirt, pulling out his crucifix. He squeezed it tightly as he made the sign of the cross over Zoelle's body and forced back his tears. He wasn't sure why he did it. It just seemed appropriate. She had never asked to be brought into the world as a clone. None of them did. It wasn't their fault for being what they were.

Then he made himself stand up. He looked over at Tea'va again, face down on the floor, his blood spilling out around him. The other Juliet clone, Shielle, was behind him, her neck purple, her eyes bulging. She had sent something to the Dread on Earth. She had exhibited more free will than any of them expected. It seemed at least some portion of the Juliet clones were capable.

He clenched his teeth, realizing that he had lost more than the best connection to his mother he would ever have, and more than a friend. They had lost their translators as well. Their guides through the Dread technology. Had they learned enough to use it on their own?

"Hafizi," Gabriel shouted, catching the Sergeant near the room's exit.

"Yes, sir?"

"Tell Colonel Choi to bring Reza and Guy with her."

"Yes, sir."

"We need to know what she told them," Gabriel said.

"Whatever it was, it's going to hurt us," Miranda replied.

"Yes."

"Your father-"

"I know."

"You have to tell him she wasn't really his wife."

"I know. I'll try. I tried before. I don't know if he'll believe me. Maybe if he had heard Shielle himself? I don't know."

He paused, his emotions in turmoil. His real mother had been dead for years. From the moment they had cloned her. He had always known she was gone, but Zoelle had brought her back to life somewhat. Now she was gone again.

"I'm sorry," Miranda said again, embracing him.

He held her back, letting the tears come. It wasn't just pain for himself. He knew what his father would go through. Even twenty years after he had left Earth, Theodore's wounds had been raw.

He gave himself sixty seconds. Then he broke away from Miranda, wiped his eyes, and straightened up. He would let her see him like that. Nobody else. He was still an officer, and he still had a job to do.

He walked over to one of the maturation chambers, looking in at the still form. She had destroyed all of the clones, as well. As much as he was against creating people this way, they had been looking forward to adding to their small numbers. They had been especially eager for the new engineers, who could help them accelerate their uptake of the Dread technology. That was lost as well.

Should he have seen this coming? He wasn't sure. Tea'va had been so convincing in his desire to help them, and in his anger at the Domo'dahm for his initial betrayal. And Shielle? She had responded as any subservient clone would. The only way to know for sure that they were secure would have been to lock up or kill every single clone, and they didn't have enough crew of their own to run a ship like the Ishur that way. For better or worse, they needed the clones. They were forced to trust them.

One of the caretakers came over as he stood in the chamber. It eyed him suspiciously, holding its weapon toward him. He backed away, and it went about its business. Some of the clones were so simple. So basic. Like the caretakers, or the cleaners. Others, like the keepers, or the Juliets, were so much more. None of them were the enemy. Not really.

He heard Colonel Choi coming, her boots clacking stiffly against the floor in an even cadence. He retreated back to where Zoelle was resting, Miranda joining him at his side. He felt a growing sense of dread as the echoes grew louder. The pace of her walk was familiar, and not in a good way.

His stomach dropped as she entered, with Theodore at her side and Reza, Guy, Hafizi and Diallo behind them. He could see the relief on his father's face when Theodore saw that he was unharmed.

He also saw the immediate agony when Theodore's eyes landed on Zoelle behind him.

"General," Gabriel said.

Theodore stopped moving. His face turned white. His eyes darted away from the body, back to it, and away again. His jaw clenched tight. His hands tore at the edges of the chair.

Gabriel felt it too. His father's pain. He headed for him, to do what he could to comfort him. To tell him that she wasn't the real Juliet, for all the good it would do.

"Dad," he said, breaking formality. "She-"

That was all he managed to get out. His father wheeled his chair around, retreating from the scene as quickly as he could.

"Dad," he said again, ready to give chase.

"Let him go," Colonel Choi said. "Major, let him go."

"I told you not to tell him," Gabriel shouted at Hafizi.

"He tried," Choi said. "Your father wandered onto the bridge while he was briefing me."

"Damn it. This disaster is getting worse by the second." He looked over Choi's shoulder. His father's back vanished ahead of him.

"What happened down here?" she asked.

Gabriel closed his eyes tight, pushing at the emotion. It killed him to see his father like that, but Choi was right. They didn't have time for that right now.

"We discovered that the clone, Shielle, sent an encrypted message to the Domo'dahm when we passed Earth."

"What kind of message?"

"We don't know. That's why I asked you to bring Reza and Guy. We need to figure it out."

"How are we going to do that?" Guy asked, his face paled by the violence. He looked like he was going to be sick. "I see our translators are all dead."

"Reza, how much of the language have you translated?" Gabriel asked, ignoring Guy. He had never been one for tact.

"I'm not completely sure. I don't think I know all of the symbols yet. Based on what I've done so far, maybe fifty percent."

"Do you think you can get a copy of the message that was sent, and break the encryption?"

"Uh. I don't know, Gabriel. With everything else you have me working on?"

"Guy, what about you?"

"I am willing to try, but I have other duties as well, Major. I'm to ensure the Magellan's systems are ready for the drop to Earth."

The pain of the loss kept growing. Did Tea'va have any idea of what he had done before he died?

"Colonel?" Gabriel said.

"The message has already been sent," she said. "We're struggling for hands as it is, and this is going to make it harder for us. Reza, Guy, find Shielle's quarters and see if there is anything you can do within the next hour. If not, we'll have to drop it for now. If we manage to get everything else ready ahead of time, we can come back to it, but what's done is done. We'll have to do our best to anticipate what the Dread could know that we don't want them to."

Gabriel didn't like it, but he knew she was right. "Yes, ma'am."

"Spaceman Locke, you're dismissed. You have three hours until your next shift."

"Yes, ma'am."

"Major St. Martin, you'll need to increase your familiarity with the flight controls. You won't have a co-pilot to guide you going forward."

"Yes, ma'am," Gabriel said. He paused. "Permission to speak to General St. Martin first?"

Choi nodded. "Granted."

"I'll need a little time, Colonel," Gabriel said. "Can we leave the bodies here for now?"

"You aren't going to bring him back down here, are you?"

"No, ma'am. I am going to bring someone to examine the body, though. His name is It'kek."

She eyed him curiously. "I don't know what you're thinking, Major, but I trust you. Make sure you alert Sergeant Hafizi when we can send in a team to clean up this mess."

"Yes, ma'am," Gabriel replied.

He wasn't quite sure what he was thinking either, but step one was confirming once and for all that the dead woman on the floor wasn't the real Juliet St. Martin. Shielle might have said she couldn't be, but all it took was one lie to put everything else into question.

Step two was to convince his father of that fact. It wouldn't ease all of his pain, but it would help, and he needed to get him through this as quickly as possible.

Too many people depended on them.

[36]

Gabriel went to the assemblers first, and then traced his path backward to where It'kek had shown him the keepers could be reached. The deepest corridors of the Ishur were faintly lit with the luminescent moss that seemed to hang from everything in the lower decks, and as he walked he began to feel the familiar sting of the legri'shah scent in his nose. It was a difficult feeling to ignore, and he wondered if that was part of the reason so few had ever met the keepers. He also wondered if it might be intentional, a defense to keep others away. The creatures were almost extinct, so rare that they were kept hidden in starships, far from freedom.

He cringed a little as he realized they had likely killed at least one of the beasts when they had destroyed the Dread fortress, along with the keepers who were raising them. He wished there was another way.

He rounded a bend in the corridor, reaching the larger common area of the keeper's community. It was a compact space surrounded by even more compact cells where the keepers slept, near the center of the pens where the legri'shah were kept. He had tried to count the clones' numbers when he had been through the first time, and had guessed that there were at most twelve of them on board, for two or three of the mature creatures and a growing number of younger ones.

He had been surprised to learn that the gori'shah the Dread wore were actually colonies of legri'shah larvae, microscopic creatures that fed on a silk-like substance spun by the second phase of the creature's growth. The entire life-cycle of the legri'shah was too complicated for him to fully grasp, but he appreciated how self-sustaining it was. When he had more time, he wanted nothing more than to learn all he could about them.

Two of the keepers were sitting on the floor in the common area when he arrived. They looked perpetually tired, and they smelled almost as strongly as the legri'shah themselves.

"It'kek?" Gabriel said, unable to tell any of the clones apart.

"He is with legri'shah," one of them said. "Can I help you, Son of Juliet?"

He was still surprised that the keepers knew who he was without ever having met him. "I don't know. I need one of you to come up to the cloning factory. Zoelle is dead."

"Yes. We heard your Sergeant Hafizi send a message to the bridge. If she is dead, why do you need us? We do not keep the dead."

"It'kek told me he would know if she were the real Juliet, or a clone. I'm pretty sure she's a clone, but I need to know for certain."

"We do not go that high," the keeper said.

"I know you don't usually, but this is very important. Please."

The two clones looked at one another. "Did It'kek agree to do this, if you ever asked?"

Gabriel considered lying. He didn't. There had been enough deceit already. "No. I never asked."

"We are not permitted to be seen by any drumhr. Our form is outlawed among the bek'hai."

"You don't have to worry about that. There are no drumhr remaining on the Ishur."

"None?"

"Tea'va was the only one who survived the attack and Gr'el's betrayal. He's dead, too."

The clones smiled. "Can we both go?"

Gabriel nodded. "You can all come, if you want."

"The others must stay to watch the legri'shah, but we will come now. They will come later. It has been many years since a keeper was able to visit the upper decks of a domo'shah."

The two keepers stood and followed Gabriel as he made his way back to the cloning facility once more. Sergeant Hafizi was standing watch over the area when he arrived, and he drew back slightly at the sight of the keepers.

"Major?" he said, unsure.

"It's okay, Sergeant. They're with me."

"Things have changed," one of the keepers said to the other.

"Yes. Many things."

"How old are you?" Gabriel asked.

"I am three thousand Earth years old, give or take," one of them said.

"I am two-thousand, seven hundred and twelve," the other said.

"And you used to be able to roam around the ship?"

"Yes. Before we were banned, back when the bek'hai left their home world. Back then, even the legri'shah were allowed some measure of freedom. They did not fear their masters then." He smiled. "It is good to roam once more."

"Where is the un'hai, Zoelle?" the other keeper asked.

"This way," Hafizi said, leading them into the maturation hall.

"I smell blood," one of them said.

"Too much blood," the other agreed.

"She's there," Gabriel said, trying to direct them without looking at her.

The keepers walked over to where Zoelle's corpse was resting. One of them leaned down and touched her face. Then he stood and looked back at Gabriel.

Gabriel felt his throat constrict, a sudden fear washing over him that he might say the words he least expected, and least wanted to hear.

"She is a clone," the keeper said, allowing him to breathe once more. "It is certain."

"Thank you," Gabriel said. "Shielle said that clones can't be made without killing the source."

"That was true many years ago. Is it still true? It seems we should have overcome that limitation by now."

"Yes, we should have," the other keeper agreed.

"It doesn't matter," Gabriel said. "This isn't my mother."

"No, it isn't."

"Can you come with me?"

"Where now, Son of Juliet?"

"Please, call me Gabriel. I want you to tell my father she's a copy. He thinks he saw his wife dead on the floor."

"We will tell him, Gabriel. You have given us what freedom you can. We will help you however we can."

"Thank you," Gabriel said. Then he turned to Hafizi. "Have the bodies taken to storage somewhere. Make sure to keep Zoelle separate from those two. I know the Dread have some kind of recycling system for corpses, but I don't know where it is in here or how it works."

"I will show you," one of the keepers said.

"And I will go with you, Gabriel."

"Thank you again," Gabriel said, impressed with their kindness.

If these keepers were the closest thing to the original bek'hai, what the hell had happened to their race?

[37]

GABRIEL KNEW HIS FATHER WOULD BE IN HIS QUARTERS. WHERE else could the General go to be left alone, after all?

He wasn't surprised when Theodore wouldn't answer his knocks. The most traumatic thing his father had ever done was leave his mother behind on Earth, even if it had saved thousands of people from death and enslavement. Was that easier than seeing a duplicate of her dead? At least then he was able to hope, and gradually become accustomed to the idea that she couldn't have survived. To have her come to life again? He would never say he knew how Theodore felt.

He knew how he felt, just to think for a moment, even a little bit, that she had been his mother.

He knew how he felt to find a certain closeness to her memory, and then have it taken away by a plasma bolt meant for him.

He was sure he would have time to fall into his own emotional upset later. But not now. Not when they were trying to prepare for all-out war. Not when every human in the universe was counting on them. He knew he could convince his father of the same thing, especially with the help of the keeper, who said his name was Pil'kek.

"Come on, Dad," he said, knocking one more time. "We need to talk about this. I know you're hurting, but hiding away isn't going to help anything."

He waited. Theodore didn't answer.

"Human emotions are intriguing," Pil'kek said. "We, too, used to feel loss. It seems like so long ago. When creating life becomes as simple as a switch on a machine, it loses its value. It is unfortunate."

"It's turned your kind into monsters," Gabriel said. "Some of them, anyway."

"They used to think the legri'shah were monsters to be destroyed until they realized the value of the lek'shah." He shook his head. "Then they became resources to control. It should not be that a human holds them in higher esteem than the ones they saved."

"No, it shouldn't." Gabriel prepared to knock on Theodore's door again. As much as he respected his father, he didn't have time or energy to be polite. "Damn it, Dad. You're making a mockery of her death. You might as well have died fifty years ago if you're going to give up now."

He figured that would bring Theodore out. He was right.

The door slid open, an angry Theodore in his chair behind it. His eyes were red, his face flushed, his uniform wrinkled, shirt untucked.

"What the hell do you know about anything, boy?" Theodore shouted. "Mockery? If I had my legs, I'd run you down and beat some damn sense between those ears of yours. I've given my whole life for this cause. This war. Everything I got. What the hell does it mean? What the hell is it for? She stayed alive for me. She did everything she could to come back to me. She brought me back to life. Now she's gone again."

The tears welled in his eyes. Gabriel felt guilty for what he had said, but there had been no other choice.

"She wasn't Juliet, Dad," he said. "She wasn't. A clone. A copy. Sure, she believed she was, but it wasn't true."

"Yeah, you keep telling me that, son. I've heard it over and over. You don't trust her. She ain't real. You trusted Tea'va, that son of a whore. You believed in him. How'd that work out?"

Gabriel felt the blow in his gut. He took it in stride. That was his fault, at least in part. But Theodore couldn't have argued that at the time, they needed the Dread. They would have never made it onto the Ishur without him.

"I'm not just saying she wasn't really Mom." Gabriel looked over at Pil'kek, who seemed uncomfortable with the whole exchange. "Pil'kek is a keeper. He knew Mom personally."

Theodore's eyes swept over to the keeper. He didn't react at all to the bek'hai's more reptilian appearance. "You knew Juliet? How?"

"She visited the keepers, Dahm St. Martin," Pil'kek said. "She spent time with us when all others were forbidden. She appreciated the legri'shah, as well as our nature, in comparison with the other bek'hai."

"Legri'shah?" Theodore said.

"The source of the Dread armor," Gabriel said. "Creatures, as big as a dinosaur. Kind of like a dragon. There are a few on board."

"And I didn't know this, why?"

"I only discovered them recently," Gabriel said. "Besides, it wasn't that important. The keepers are peaceful. Their concern are the legri'shah."

"What does this all have to do with Juliet?"

"We knew Juliet St. Martin well, Dahm St. Martin," Pil'kek said. "She was much loved among all of the keepers. Your son wanted me to come to tell you, and I mean this with all honesty, the clone known as Zoelle was only that. A clone. Not the real Juliet St. Martin. I am sad to say; she died many years ago. The bek'hai cannot finish the cloning process without killing the pur'hai. The source."

Theodore froze. He didn't move at all. Not for a minute or more. Gabriel could tell his mind was going, trying to make sense of it all. Trying to come to some kind of resolution on how he should feel.

"She knew things," he said. "Personal things."

"It is not recommended for the memories to be stored and transferred during the cloning process, as it makes the clone unstable for their intended use. It is also not impossible."

"But... that can't be. Shielle, she was a clone. She looked like Juliet. She betrayed us."

"The keepers listen to all communications sent from above, Dahm St. Martin. It is clear to me that there are some clones of Juliet who are, what is a good word? Enhanced. And some who are not. It is wrong to think that clones are all the same. They are not. Even for the bek'hai, biology is so complex that it cannot be fully controlled."

"You're saying that someone muddied the waters? Made a Juliet that was more like my Juliet?"

"That is what I believe."

Theodore grinned. "She always was good at making people see things her way. You think she convinced one of the other ones not to be such an asshole?"

"I'm not sure what you mean, Dahm St. Martin."

"How many of the bek'hai want war?" Theodore asked. "How many agreed with the Domo'dahm's invasion?"

"Many. Not all."

Theodore nodded. "Ah, my darlin'. Heh. The Domo'dahm doesn't know what he's done, does he?"

"Dad?" Gabriel asked.

"We're going to win this war, Gabriel," Theodore said. "Your mother's already seen to it. We just need to do our part."

"Which is?"

"Stay the course, for now. You said Major Peters had a clone of your mom with him?"

"Yes."

"I'm willing to bet she's one of the special ones. I'm also willing to bet there are more of them out there. I hope she's still alive. It'll make things easier."

Gabriel was happy to see his father's despair shrinking, but he still didn't know what he was talking about.

"I'm confused," he said.

"Heh. Don't worry about it, son. I'm gonna be okay, thanks to you, and to you." He looked at Pil'kek. "I'm not saying it don't hurt because it does. I never wanted to see my darlin' like that. But you're right. She didn't go through all of this to have me fail on her. I'm gonna get cleaned up, and then I'll be back on the bridge. We've got a lot of work to do. More now, without Zoelle."

Gabriel nodded. He was glad his father used the clone's name, instead of his mother's.

"The keepers can help us translate," Gabriel said.

"We do have one request," Pil'kek said.

"What's that?" Theodore asked.

"We must try to save as many of the legri'shah as we can. There are so few remaining."

"I'll do my best, Mr. Pil'kek."

"Thank you, Dahm St. Martin."

Theodore smiled. "No. Thank you."

[38]

General Alan Cave stared out of the small window of his quarters on Alpha Settlement, looking up at Station Delta in the distance. The military installation seemed so small from here. So unimportant.

Little had seemed important in these last few weeks, for him and for many others in the settlements. Not since Theodore St. Martin had taken away their only hope of ever escaping the nightmare they had been trapped in for the last fifty years, leaving them to wonder just how much longer the equipment that sustained them would last. They had always known the answer wasn't forever, and that they would need to leave Calawan. While they had always hoped it would be to return to their home planet, he had finally gotten many of them to accept that it wasn't meant to be and that drastic measures would be needed to preserve what was left of humankind.

It hadn't been easy to do, either. So many of the council members had been loyal to Theodore at first. Hell, even he had started out loyal to the Old Gator and his delusions. But the years had shown that nothing was going to change. The missions to Earth had only resulted in pilots dying and irreplaceable resources being lost, and the overload of work for their engineers was proof that the temporary facilities they had brought with them would only last for so long.

He had taken the hard road, the unpopular road. He had even gone so far as to drug the man he had once respected more than anything in order to keep him quiet while the important decisions were made. Doing it had made him sick. Lying about it had made him sicker. He had done it for the good of the many. For the future of their entire species, not because he wanted people to die. Not because he wanted to leave anyone behind.

Not that any of that mattered now.

The great General St. Martin had come roaring back to life on the news that the Dread armor wasn't completely impenetrable. He had used his reputation to break every law the New Earth Alliance had composed, and in one fell swoop had effectively killed every single one of them.

He had stolen the Magellan.

He wasn't coming back.

That was the truth General Cave was forced to live with. That they had all been forced to live with. He had sensed the change in the spirit of the people immediately after the Magellan had slipped away. He could still feel their resignation, their loss of hope, and their distress every time he made the journey from his quarters to his office. He could see the way they looked at him, their eyes pleading for a miracle he knew he couldn't produce. They didn't have the resources to build another ship. They didn't have another way out.

He turned from the viewport, picking up his jacket and slipping it on. He straightened himself and then headed out into the community. It had become more important than ever for him to appear to be in control. To stay strong, to look strong, and to act with a confidence he didn't feel. Sometimes, as he walked across the common area toward the loop, it seemed as though it might be the only thing holding any of them together.

He said hello to a few people he passed on his way to the station. The laughter of the children was such a stark contrast to the moroseness of the adults. They were young and innocent. They didn't understand the reality of their future. It was difficult to listen to sometimes, knowing that it was going to end badly for them. It was another thought he had to fight against on a daily basis. Another truth he didn't want to accept.

There was a pod waiting at the station when he arrived, and he stepped into it and sat down, finding himself beside Councilwoman Rouse.

"Angela," he said, nodding to her.

"General," she replied.

"What's on the docket for today?" he asked as the pod's lid sealed and it began to move.

"We're still working on the plans for the personnel reduction. The baby lotteries have been put on hold, and we've been forced to abort a few of the early-stage pregnancies."

"You're aborting people who are already expecting?"

"At their request, Alan," she replied defensively. "People don't want to have children knowing they're going to grow up here." She paused. "And die here."

"How far along is the planning process for contraction?"

"We have a plan to move Beta settlement over and recapture the resources for necessities. It should buy us at least twenty years. Once that's done, we're going to look into disassembling Delta."

"You should have started with Delta."

"I know, but that motion was blocked by the Believers."

"Is that what they're calling themselves?"

"Yes. They still think Theodore is going to come back and lead them to salvation."

"I guess it's as good a belief as any. People need something to pin their hopes on."

"I'd rather they help us be pragmatic and work out the logistics so that we can maybe find a way to ride this thing out."

"Ride it out? Like there's an end in sight?"

"The science teams are shifting focus to finding other potential ways to get us out of this system. We still have the coordinates to the New Earth; we just need a ship that can take us there. It may be that we have to do a generation style vessel, but it beats the hell out of waiting to die here. That's why we aren't dismantling Delta yet. Rachel Dawes in engineering thinks we might be able to fabricate a solar sail and hook it up to the station. It would take us a few hundred years to get to the New Earth, but we would get there."

"Pie in the sky," General Cave said. "The printers can't do anything that thin and light."

"Not now, but if they can improve them-"

"That's a big if."

"What the hell do you want us to do?" Angela cursed. "Accept that we're going to die?"

General Cave froze. "Damn it. I'm sorry, Angela. I woke up in a lousy mood today."

"I wake up like that every day recently. But we need to pull together. We aren't dead yet, and that's a start."

"Right."

The pod slowed as it reached the central hub. Councilwoman Rouse and General Cave got out together, heading for the administrative offices. They were halfway to the elevators when the doors to them opened, and Spaceman Owens came limping out.

"Sir," he said, seeing the General but forgetting to salute. "I've been trying to contact you. You need to get to the CIC immediately."

"The CIC? What's happening?"

"We just got a comm from Delta. Their long-range sensors are picking up two unidentified objects that just appeared in system and are headed this way."

"Two?" General Cave said. "That can't be Theodore."

"No, sir," Spaceman Owens agreed. "But whoever or whatever they are, sir, Major Looper said they're huge."

[39]

"Get me a visual," General Cave said as the doors to the elevator opened, and he stepped out into the CIC.

The settlement's emergency command center was located at the bottom of the central hub, buried four hundred meters deep. It was a claustrophobic space, small and dark and crowded with monitors and communications equipment. Five soldiers worked in rotating shifts within it, manning the stations in case of a red alert. For years, those shifts had changed from one to another without incident or interruption. For years, the entire ready room had been ready but never utilized.

Until today.

"And patch me in with Major Looper on Delta while you're at it," he added as he took a seat behind the main control unit.

The monitor in front of him changed, showing him the large blobs outlined by their sensors. They were massive. Easily bigger than any of the settlements, and even dwarfing Delta Station by order of magnitude.

"General," Major Looper said, his face appearing on the corner of the monitor.

"Major. I'm looking at your sensor images. What can you tell me?"

"Nothing good, sir," Looper replied. "They're big. Damn big. They came out of nowhere, just showed up on our sensors about ten minutes ago. And they're coming this way."

"Just showed up, as in traveled in from a slipstream?"

"We still have astronomy looking at the vector data to confirm, but my gut feeling says yes."

General Cave looked at the screen again. There was only one thing he knew of that was that big and could travel through slipspace. Just the thought of it sent a wave a panic rushing through him and prickling his skin.

"Major, scramble the fighters," he said, forcing himself to stay calm. "Prepare whatever BIS you have and get as many personnel clear of Delta Station as you can."

"Sir?" Major Looper said. "What is it?"

"I hope I'm wrong about this Major; I really hope I am. I think the Dread have found us."

The silence at the other end was all the confirmation General Cave needed that Looper understood the gravity of the situation.

"Looper, are you still there?"

"Yes, sir," the Major replied, his voice weak. "Sir, am I clear that you want me to send the starfighters to attack the Dread?"

General Cave drew back in surprise of his own. The Major was only thirty-three years old and had never seen the Dread before. He didn't understand what he was suggesting. "Attack them? Absolutely not. Our ships can't do anything against those things. No. I want you to evacuate Delta Station. Get as many troops to Alpha as possible, and get them down into the shelters. Do you understand, Major?"

"Yes, sir," Looper replied. "Affirmative."

"Good. Cave, out."

General Cave glanced at the soldiers manning the CIC. They all looked terrified at what he had said.

"Sound the general alarm," he said. "Red alert, across all settlements. All civilians are to report to their designated attack shelters."

"Yes. Yes, sir," the soldiers replied.

A moment later, a red strobe light began to flash above the hatch behind him, signaling the red alert. A similar strobe would be going off everywhere around Alpha, Beta, and Gamma settlements, along with announcements directing people to the underground bombardment shelters.

Not that it would make a difference if the Dread really had found them and were coming to finish the job they started all of those years ago. The shelters were deep underground, but they had also been bored into stone that would turn to slag under the heat of a massive plasma attack. A single crevice venting their limited atmosphere was all it would take to kill them.

"Now what, sir?" one of the soldiers asked.

"Now we pray," General Cave replied. "That's all we can do."

The soldier nodded, turning back to his monitors. General Cave shifted his attention to the monitors in front of his station. He switched the view, cycling through the cameras positioned around Alpha settlement, both interior and exterior. The contrast was stark and frightening. Inside, the base was a flurry of activity, as everyone within it was on the move, headed for the underground shelters. Outside there was near calm, save for a squadron of starfighters streaking away from Delta Station toward him.

"ETA to visual?" he asked, watching the monitor for signs of the enemy ships.

"One minute," one of the soldiers replied.

They were coming in so fast

He pulled in a deep breath, trying to steady suddenly shaking limbs. He was scared. Hell, they were all scared.

"Major Looper," he said, opening the comm to Delta again. "I don't see any BIS out there."

"Sir," Looper said. "We're still loading them."

"Loading them with what?" he asked.

"They were half-filled with supplies. We had to discard them to get more people on."

"There's no time left, Major. Get as many people on them as you can and get them away from the station."

"Yes, sir." He paused. "Sir?"

"Yes, Major."

"We only have space for five hundred on the transports."

General Cave closed his eyes. That was one-third of the people currently on the station. How were they even deciding who stayed and who went?

"I'm sorry, Major," he said.

"I should have gone with General St. Martin," Looper replied. "When I had the chance. I should have gone with him. Oh, God. I don't want to die."

"Get those transports launched Major. Don't think about anything else."

"Yes, sir."

General Cave felt his heart thumping in his chest. Everything was happening so fast. Fifty years and it was all going to be over within minutes.

He had been drowning in hopelessness for the last few weeks. Now that the end was near, he found he had held onto more hope than was probably reasonable. Maybe they had been down, but the scientists were working on the problem, and given a chance they might have even solved it.

He saw the first Dread fortress appear a moment later, coming out from behind Ursa Major, a dark spot against the light of the star. The second appeared seconds after that, trailing slightly behind the first, both headed right toward them.

A blue dot appeared on the front of the first fortress. General Cave cringed at the sight of it, knowing what it meant. Major Looper's voice echoed in his ears, his cries of "I don't want to die" causing him to lean forward for balance as the Dread starship unleashed the bolt from its main plasma cannon.

The blue streak arced across the distance between the Dread fortress and Delta Station, a flash of lightning that ended with the space station being torn to pieces, dark and silent as it disintegrated beneath the onslaught, literally vanishing in front of his eyes.

"No," he said, slamming his fist on the monitor and cracking the screen. "Damn it. No."

He stopped himself, wiping at the tears that had come to his eyes as he returned his attention to the Dread ships. They were spreading apart, one of them headed toward Alpha, the other breaking for Delta. He could only hope the other settlements had gotten underground in time.

The seconds passed like an eternity, the Dread ships slowing as they drew nearer. The tip of the second one began to glow, and General Cave closed his eyes as it unleashed its fury, sending a plasma bolt into Delta Settlement. Would the shelter protect the people there? He had no idea. He could only hope.

"We're going to die," one of the soldiers said, watching the same approach on his own monitor.

"We might," he replied. "And if we do, let us die with courage and dignity, not filled with fear."

"Yes, sir," the soldier said.

"Sir," one of the others said. "Sir, look."

"What is it, Spaceman?" General Cave said, looking at his screen. He didn't see anything. Then again, his view was obscured by the crack he made.

"There. Behind the Dread ships."

General Cave hurried to the soldier's position, leaning down beside him to look at his monitor. He squinted his eyes to make out the shape in the distance, positioned behind the Dread fortresses

"It looks like-"

"Another Dread ship," he said, identifying it. His heart might have sunk further, had there been anywhere else for it to go. "We have no weapons; we can't touch them, and yet they sent three ships to find and destroy us. Why?"

[40]

THEODORE GRITTED HIS TEETH AS THE ISHUR TRACKED BEHIND the Dread fortress while vectoring away from the slipspace exodus point. They had arrived only seconds earlier, just in time to see the the lead starship fire its plasma cannon on Delta Station and blow it into little more than debris.

Just in time to watch their people die.

"Mr. Mokri, divert power to the main plasma cannon," Theodore shouted, his eyes glued to the scene ahead of them. "Gabriel, get us on target to intercept the port ship before it can fire again."

"Yes, sir," Gabriel replied, manipulating the makeshift controls Reza had created to allow him to fly the fortress and turning the Ishur toward the enemy ship.

The domo'shah had already blasted the surface once, burning into the exposed part of Gamma Settlement and leaving little more than a crater behind.

It was possible the residents had made it into the shelters.

It was possible the blast hadn't dug quite deep enough to reach them.

Then again, it was possible they were all dead.

"Let's show them sons of bitches what happens when they screw with the Earth Alliance," he said, looking down at the status screen of his tablet. The button at the bottom of it turned red as the main plasma cannon finished charging. "Gabriel, give me five degrees starboard."

"Yes, sir."

The ship began to adjust again, shifting slowly as it crossed the space. The Dread fortresses were slowing down, beginning to make their own turns to come about and face them. Given a choice, he would rather hit them both before they finished the maneuver.

"Firing," he said. He squinted as the bolt of blue energy launched from the bow ahead of them, a streak of light that crossed thousands of kilometers in seconds, heading for the exposed side of the Dread ship.

Theodore tracked it intently, leaning forward in his seat, smiling at the very thought of the energy blast piercing the heart of the enemy. He may have promised the keepers he would try to spare the legri'shah, but he hadn't sworn to put the lives of the creatures over the lives of their people.

The bolt slammed into the side of the fortress, creating a flash of light as it struck. Then the light faded away, the bolt absorbed by a sudden ripple of pitch black that formed against the hull.

"What the hell?" he heard Miranda say in front of him.

"That looks like our shields," Gabriel said.

"Mr. Mokri?" Theodore said, asking for confirmation.

Reza was looking at his tablet and shaking his head. "Confirmed, sir. It has the same modulation signature as our Darkspace Defense System."

"In other words, they're using our tech against us?"

"Yes, sir."

"What?" Colonel Choi said. "How can that be?"

"Shielle," Theodore replied. "It has to be. We never had time to figure out what she sent. Well, now we know, damn that woman."

"General, if they have our shields," Colonel Choi said.

"We're on even footing offensively," Theodore said. "But also outnumbered."

He watched as the first Dread ship finished reversing course, getting the bow pointed back at them. They were heading directly toward one another on a terrifying collision course.

"Mr. Mokri, is the DDS ready for action?" Theodore said.

"Uh. General, I'm not-"

"That was a rhetorical, Mr. Mokri. It damn well better be, or we're all about to die."

"Yes, sir," Reza said. "But we haven't tried this yet. I'm not sure the modulators will hold up to the stress."

"Nothing like beta testing on the job. Turn the damn thing on."

"Yes, sir. Activating the DDS."

Reza tapped on his control pad. There was no immediate visual or audible change in anything, and for a moment Theodore wondered if there was nothing happening down in engineering but a shower of sparks and a nice big electrical fire.

"Forward DDS, online," Lieutenant Bale said from her station.

"Port side DDS, online," Miranda said.

"Starboard side DDS, online," Colonel Choi said.

"Rear DDS, online," Sergeant Hafizi said.

"Fantastic," Theodore replied to the news. "I know this is new for you ladies and gents, so do your best to stay calm and focused. Prioritize the mains over the secondaries. We can't afford to let that bad boy through."

"Yes, sir," the soldiers replied.

"Gabriel, don't let us get caught between them," Theodore said.

"Yes, sir."

The Ishur began to rise, vectoring up and away from the oncoming Dread ships.

"Picking up an energy spike from the starboard fortress," Miranda said.

"Colonel, that's yours," Theodore replied.

Colonel Choi stared intently at the hologram in front of her. It was a generated depiction of the side of the Ishur, matched to a line from the side that was piercing the lower portion of the hull, along with a red dot that was placed to the left of it. She put her finger to the red dot, dragging it toward the line.

The darkness lessened as the enemy domo'shah fired, sending a return volley back at them. It appeared as a tapering yellow line that was lining up almost perfectly with the line on Colonel Choi's terminal, and she held her finger steady while the heaviest part of the line slammed into the dot.

The ship vibrated softly under the impact.

"Damage report, Sergeant?" Theodore said.

"No damage reported," Sergeant Abdullah replied. "It looks like the DDS is working."

"Sir, energy spike from the port ship," Miranda said.

"Got it," Bale said, repeating the same motion as Colonel Choi.

The plasma blast filled their viewport, crossing the chasm of space and hitting the front of the ship. Again there was a soft vibration, but no evidence of harm.

"Hell, yes, Mr. Mokri," Theodore said in response to the success of the system. "Let's try part two. Gabriel, bring us in on that port side bastard. I want to broadside him and see how well they've integrated our technology."

"Yes, sir," Gabriel replied.

The Ishur began to shift and accelerate, heading toward the fortress while the other released another plasma blast. Colonel Choi shifted her hand, moving the dot to the impact point. The ship shook a little more violently this time but came out of it unscathed.

Theodore flicked the screen on the tablet, changing from the main plasma cannon to the freshly networked secondary batteries. With the push of a button the batteries opened up on the port side, over one hundred lighter plasma cannons creating a ripple of energy along the Ishur. The enemy ship followed suit, giving them the first true test of their makeshift system.

Miranda needed both hands to try to deflect the attack, raising them and placing them on the threat display, dragging the red dot across the visual and through a series of white lines. She kept the shield modulation on the move, sweeping it from the closest attack and across, catching a series of bolts with the DDS.

Meanwhile, the Ishur's guns pounded the side of the enemy fortress. Not only did the Dread's modulated darkspace shields hold up to the attack, but they didn't seem to have the same coverage limitations as the Ishur did.

"Damn it," Theodore said. "Mr. Mokri, how is your work on the weapons modifications coming along?"

"It isn't, General," Reza said. "I've hit nothing but dead ends so far."

"We need to think of something, son," Theodore said. "Gabriel, watch your starboard side. Duck and cover."

The Ishur shuddered as Gabriel manipulated the thrusters, bringing them downward in a sharp maneuver that wasn't quite exact. The second Dread starship opened fire on them again, the heavy plasma crossing the decreasing distance in a matter of seconds.

It didn't leave Colonel Choi much time to react, and she was a split-second late in dragging the red dot to the line on her display. The Ishur rocked more violently, taking a measure of damage from the plasma before recovering.

"Hull breaches on Decks thirty-four to forty," Abdullah said.

"Casualties?"

"No, sir. The decks are isolated. Emergency bulkheads are sealing."

"Sorry, General," Choi said.

"We're still alive," Theodore replied.

He eyed the two Dread fortresses. They were trying to maneuver around the front corners of the Ishur and get their main cannons in line. In fact, as Theodore watched them turn, it appeared to him that they were trying to target the same area of the ship, perhaps in the hope that a combined blast would penetrate their defenses.

If that was true, it was something they could use.

"Mr. Mokri, how much more power can we send to the plasma cannon?"

"I'm not sure, sir. Why?"

"I want to concentrate a steady stream on a single point. Can we do that?"

"Uh. I'm not sure, sir."

"That isn't a no. What do we have to do?"

"I'll need to make some adjustments to the parameters."

Theodore looked at the two Dread ships outside the viewport. They were getting dangerously close.

"You'd better do it fast, then, Mr. Mokri."

"Already on it," Reza replied, his fingers a blur on his tablet. "Sir," he added a moment later.

"Gabriel, head right for the port side ship. Full thrust. At five hundred klicks, bounce up and rotate the ass end to get us pointed down towards that couillon. Got it?"

"Yes, sir," Gabriel replied.

"Starboard ship is firing again, sir," Miranda said.

Theodore felt the soft shudder that signaled the attack had been deflected.

"I think I have it, sir," Reza said. "Hold down the trigger to keep firing a steady stream. You should know, it might fry the systems and leave us without the main cannon."

"A risk we have to take, I think," Theodore replied. "Gabriel, a little more rotation on the bow."

"Yes, sir."

The Ishur spun and rolled in space in a breaching maneuver that left them tilted over the top side of one of the Dread ships. "Keep us over it," he said. "Help me steady the shot."

"Yes, sir," Gabriel replied, working his own translated controls. The Ishur responded to them, the bow shifting in sync with the Dread ship's forward momentum.

Theodore pressed down on the firing button.

The blue bolt of plasma burst from the main cannon, hitting the Dread ship almost immediately. The darkspace flared beneath the attack, absorbing the energy. Theodore held the attack, and the flow of plasma continued, forming a near stream that bombarded the enemy ship.

One second passed. Two. Five. The beam remained solid, digging into the spot on the Dread fortress. The starboard ship fired again, its blow deflected by Colonel Choi.

"Come on, you bastard," Theodore said, watching the darkspace continue to absorb the attack. "I know you want to fail. Come on, damn you."

Seven seconds. Eight seconds. Nine seconds. Theodore could barely believe the cannon was still functional after all that time.

"Sir, DDS is offline," Lieutenant Bale said.

"We don't have the power," Reza replied. "General, half the ship is shutting down."

"We're already committed, son. We may not get another chance."

He kept his finger on the trigger.

Twelve seconds. Thirteen seconds.

He was about to give up, to try to think of something else, when the miracle he was waiting for finally happened, and in a way that was more fantastic than he could have ever expected.

One second, the darkspace shield was absorbing the energy of the plasma cannon. The next, it was collapsing inward, the pitch of the alternate continuum appearing to flip and fold backward and into the Dread fortress' hull, sinking through the lek'shah and eating away at the structure like a plague.

Theodore lifted his finger, the main cannon disengaging. The ship rocked from solid strikes by the second Dread starship's secondary batteries. A moment later, the DDS came back online, and his defense crew returned to work blocking the attack.

Small gouts of flame vented from the growing disintegration within the first vessel, the darkspace modulation almost seeming to implode and destroying everything in its path through the ship. It started to tilt a few seconds after that, and by the time the Ishur had swept past the side of the Dread starship it had fallen dead, drifting away from the human settlements.

"That's one," Theodore said, more than satisfied with the outcome. "Even if I don't know exactly what all just happened."

He refocused his attention on the other Dread ship. It had used their time in a relatively static position to improve its attack vector, sneaking in toward the rear of the Ishur and peppering it with secondary batteries. Both Colonel Choi and Sergeant Hafizi were working feverishly to keep their DDS points centered on the brunt of the force, absorbing the incoming attacks before they could burn into the lek'shah hide of the ship.

"Come about, Gabriel," Theodore said. "As hard and fast as you can."

"Yes, sir," Gabriel replied. "Coming about."

The Ishur was silent, the power to the thrusters cut. They floated freely for a few seconds, gaining proximity to the Settlements while Gabriel adjusted their vectors. The domo'shah behind them fired its main plasma cannon again, but this time Gabriel managed to steer them out of its path.

Theodore watched his son work with a measure of pride. Gabriel had blamed himself for the damage the Magellan had taken, but it seemed to him that the boy had used the situation to learn and improve. He was flying the huge fortress almost as well as Tea'va had done it and with much less experience, pushing it to extremes and getting the results.

The Ishur's bow swung forward, coming to rest in a nearly direct line with the enemy fortress.

Theodore pressed down on the trigger again.

He held it once more, counting the seconds as the beam tore into the leading edge of the opposing ship, somewhere within a few hundred meters of the bridge. He wondered what the pur'dahm in charge of the ship might be thinking after he had just watched his partner succumb to the same attack.

He found out a moment later. The second domo'shah accelerated toward them before altering course and ducking below, vectoring around in an effort to run.

"Oh no you don't," Theodore said, "Not after what you did to Delta. Stay on that bastard. We aren't letting this one run away."

"Yes, sir," Gabriel said, aligning the Ishur to give chase.

"She's heading for a slipstream," Reza reported.

"We're at max thrust, sir," Gabriel said. "We can't catch up to them."

"Damn it," Theodore cursed.

His finger hovered over the fire button while he considered whether or not to take the shot. It would be more for show than anything. The fortress was gaining range too fast for the weapon to be effective.

He hesitated for another second before pulling his hand away. "Pack it in, Gabriel," he said. "There's no point in risking the cannon, and we'll get another crack at him when we get to Earth."

Theodore could tell Gabriel didn't want to give up the chase, but he followed the order without hesitation, using the tablet to slow the Ishur once more.

"Lieutenant Bale, take over for the Major and bring us back toward the Settlements. Gabriel, Mr. Mokri, you're with me. Colonel Choi, you have the bridge."

"Where are we going, sir?" Reza asked.

Theodore lifted himself on his arms and shifted himself over, coming down in his chair. He began rolling toward the exit.

"To the hangar," he replied. "We aren't about to land this thing down there."

"What about General Cave?" Gabriel asked.

"Alan? What about him?"

"He's going to blame us for leading the Dread here."

"We've got a war to win, son. He can either get on board, or he can get the hell out of the way."

[41]

Gabriel eased the BIS away from its position on the floor of the Ishur's hangar. The Magellan loomed beside him, a definitive work in progress as it underwent the transformation from starship to dropship.

The remaining nacelle had been removed, the damaged side also picked apart and reduced to a stub. The plasma damage along the hull was in the process of being repaired, with random bits of lek'shah affixed over the original armor where the cuts were too deep to heal.

Also new to the ship were a handful of ion cannons. They were smaller than even the smallest of the secondary batteries on the Ishur, rebuilt from as much human material as they had been able to salvage. They wouldn't do much against a domo'shah or even the smaller ek'shah, but they would be effective against Dread starfighters and ground based weapons.

"Guy is installing the Dread zero-point reactors today," Reza said, a hint of pride in his voice. The two men had become unexpected friends after the whole ordeal with Guy's wife, Sarah, bonding over their shared desire to figure out and control the enemy tech.

"That means she'll be ready to fly soon," Theodore said.

"Yes, sir," Reza replied.

"The work your people have done is impressive, Dahm St. Martin," It'kek said from behind Gabriel.

"We couldn't have done it without you, Mr. It'kek," Theodore said.

Gabriel glanced back at the keeper. He had been hesitant to bring the reptilian bek'hai with them, but Theodore was insistent. According to him, it was important that the rest of the colonists understood what he had come to understand over the last few days.

That the bek'hai, the real bek'hai, weren't their enemies.

Instead, their enemy was the remnant of a once proud race, a descendent that had come about almost by accident, and who had been hugely responsible for destroying their world. It had started with the Hunters, who had learned to kill the legri'shah with abandon for the value of their scales, their muscles, and their meat. It had ended with the loss of genetic diversity and the need to turn to the same creatures to save them. Millions of the animals had died in the civil conflict that had engulfed the bek'hai and transformed them into a more violent race. Hundreds more were still being slaughtered every cycle in order to provide resources to build more war machines, to repair the domo'shah, and to satiate the Hunters desire to prove themselves against the creatures.

It'kek had told Gabriel about the competitions. The Circle of Honor was one thing. The legri'shah ring was another.

"This is Major Gabriel St. Martin," Gabriel said, opening a channel to Alpha Control. "Requesting permission to land."

There was a pause on the other side of the link. A woman replied a moment later.

"Roger, Major St. Martin. You have clearance for Bay C. General Cave has requested that you remain on board until he has arrived with a security detail."

"Ha," Theodore said. "Security detail? Who the hell does he think we are?"

"Traitors?" Reza said. "Deserters?"

"Bullshit. We didn't desert them. We're saving them."

"Affirmative Control," Gabriel said. "Entering approach to Bay C."

He guided the BIS deftly toward the small opening in the structure outside of the central hub, noting how much easier and more responsive the box in space was compared to the Ishur. While Reza had done a fantastic job getting it to interface with a human control system at all, the delays involved in the translation were still less than ideal.

"How does it feel to be home, son?" Theodore asked.

"Not like home," Gabriel replied. "I've seen Earth up close, remember?"

"We all have," Theodore said. "A little too up close."

He was referring to almost crashing the Magellan into the Pacific Ocean. At least they could laugh about it now.

"By the by, Mr. Mokri," Theodore said. "Any idea what happened with that Dread fortress up there?"

He pointed back into the deep black, where the dead domo'shah was still floating. They had already discussed sending a team to search it and look for salvage and survivors, especially among the keepers and legri'shah, but it was a secondary concern to getting the ball rolling with their own people.

"Not really," Reza replied. "Sir."

"Take a wild guess."

"Hmm. If I had to guess? I would say the energy in the plasma cannon destabilized the phase modulation enough that we created a wormhole of sorts, which wound up spinning out of control and through the enemy ship."

"A wormhole spinning out of control?" Gabriel said. "That doesn't sound good."

"It isn't if you happen to be in its path," Reza said. "Fortunately, space is a big place, and it isn't going in Earth's direction."

Gabriel tried to wrap his mind around the idea of a rogue piece of matter crushing darkspace as he steered the BIS into Alpha Settlement's main landing bay. He guided the ship to Bay C and brought it down.

"I have to admit, General," Reza said. "I'd rather not have to do that again. The plasma cannon was at critical heat levels, and an overload would have had a high likelihood of cooking everyone inside the Ishur ."

"Duly noted," Theodore replied. "Figure out the modulator for the plasma, and we won't have to do that again."

"Yes, sir."

"Your architecture is very interesting, Dahm St. Martin," It'kek said. His head had been turning back and forth during the entire trip, taking in the sights of the human base. "Very simplistic, yet functional."

"Well, thank you, I guess," Theodore replied. "It isn't much, but it does the job."

"Or did," Gabriel said. "Delta Station was destroyed. How many people do you think were on it?"

"Judging by the number of ships in here, hopefully not to many," Theodore said.

Gabriel nodded. Bay C was one of the only landing bays available, the rest filled with starfighters and BIS that he knew were usually assigned to the station.

"That's our cue," Theodore said, as soon as the light in the cockpit turned green, indicating the bay was pressurized.

"General Cave ordered us to wait," Reza replied.

"Mr. Mokri, do you work for him or for me?"

"For you, sir."

"Then I repeat. That's our queue."

"Yes, sir."

They moved to the rear of the BIS and down the opening rear doors to the floor of the hangar. It felt weird to Gabriel to be back where he had started, back to the confines of the place he had once called home. After spending the last two weeks on the Ishur, it felt small and primitive and dirty. After having landed on Earth, it felt downright unacceptable.

They reached the bay door. Theodore tapped the control to open it.

General Cave was standing in front of it, flanked by four armed guards. Councilwoman Rouse was waiting a few meters away, her hands folded against her chest.

"Ah, Alan," Theodore said. "I guess you knew I wasn't going to listen to anything you said."

General Cave stared at Theodore for a moment, his expression grim. Then he glanced over at Gabriel, and then at Reza, and finally at It'kek. He couldn't hold back his surprise at the sight of the bek'hai.

"Ha. That one caught you off-guard, didn't it?" Theodore said in response.

General Cave returned his attention to Theodore, who raised his hand.

"Hold up, Alan. Before you say anything, I think you should know; we're winning this here war."

It was General Cave's turn to surprise them. His stern expression melted away, and he started to laugh.

"The Old Gator," he said through his smile. "You've always had a flair for the dramatic, haven't you?" He stepped forward, leaning down to put his arms around Theodore. "I thought it was over for us."

"General Cave," Rouse said, sounding unhappy with his reaction. "Excuse me, General."

Cave ignored her, releasing Theodore and approaching Gabriel. "Gabe. I'm sorry for doubting you. I'm sorry for doubting any of you."

"General Cave," Rouse repeated, joining them. "These people are traitors."

Cave ignored her again. "They hit Delta Station, Teddy. They killed eight hundred of our people."

"We'll avenge them," Theodore replied. "That's why we came back. To gather the troops and take them home."

"You aren't taking anyone, anywhere," Rouse said. "General, I thought we came to meet them to arrest them?"

"Are you mental, woman?" Theodore said. "We just saved your life."

"You put us in danger in the first place. You stole our only means to travel away from this place, our only chance of finding a new home. You left the people here frightened and struggling to cope. You-"

"If I do remember correctly, Councilwoman, you were planning on sacrificing half the people in this colony so that you could head out to the stars in hopes of finding your new home. By my count, my way has only cost us approximately seven percent. I know that sounds harsh, but you can't argue the numbers. Furthermore, we came back. Oh, and if that weren't good enough for you, we brought you a big fat spaceship that can take every last resident of this here colony to their new home back on Earth as soon as we finish retaking it."

Theodore stared at Rouse, who tightened her hands against her chest, sighed, and moved back a few meters to her original position.

"I'm sorry for every soul we lost," Theodore said. "And I'm sorry I took Maggie. But it had to be done, Alan. You were wrong."

"Maybe I was. It doesn't matter now. I'm certainly not going to arrest you. What good would that do? You say we're winning this war? Then I say, what can I do to help?"

[42]

"AND THAT'S HOW IT ALL HAPPENED, IN A NUTSHELL," GABRIEL said.

General Cave leaned back in his chair, a look of focused interest replaced by something more contemplative. Gabriel had spent the last two hours debriefing the General and his immediate staff on the situation back on Earth, and on their pressing need to rally the New Earth Alliance military to join the fight.

"And you are one of the, what did you call them again, Major? Bek'hai?"

The question was posed by Major Janet Ames, who had taken over Colonel Choi's position after she had left with Theodore. She was looking pointedly at It'kek, a hint of disgust mixing with fascination, mixing with anger.

"That is correct," It'kek replied. "We are some of the few original bek'hai that remains."

"Interesting. What I'm not clear about is why you're helping us, instead of your own kind?"

"We are helping our own kind, Major. The Domo'dahm does not understand that his path of resistance to complete genetic splicing with the humans will continue the extinction vector our kind has been on for many generations. He will not accept that the only way we survive as a species is to work with the humans, not fight against them. These bek'hai are not what we once were, or what we have the potential to be. But the keepers and the legri'shah are few in number. We are powerless to stop them, or we would have already."

"But you are betraying your people."

"Is it a betrayal to sacrifice what you must to save them? For us, it is not about helping the humans defeat the bek'hai. It is about helping the humans and the bek'hai to coexist."

"And why would we want to coexist with you?" one of General Cave's other staffers, Captain Huang asked. "You took our planet. You killed billions."

"Because that is the only way either of us ever knows peace. Your kind on Earth have resisted bek'hai rule for fifty of your years. If you depose the Domo'shah, do you suppose there will be immediate peace? Do you think the remaining bek'hai will simply accept the loss of the planet and the death of their kind?"

"General," Huang said. "We can't seriously be considering trying to make peace with the Dread. Especially now, when we have the means to fight back." He looked at Theodore. "General St. Martin, surely you can't be in favor of this."

Theodore shook his head. "In favor of requesting an audience with the Domo'dahm? It'll be a cold day in hell. But here's the rub, Captain. There are thousands and thousands of prisoners living among the rest of the Dread. A lot of them are clones of one kind of another, each with a job that they're programmed to do. They're slaves of a fashion, locked into what they have always known, but they have individual personalities as well, and some of them can be influenced. Then there are the keepers like It'kek here. They want to change course for their people, but don't have the power to do it on their own." He smiled. "And then we have the un'hai."

"Un'hai?" General Cave said. "Oh, right, the clones of Juliet."

"We don't know how many there are, but they're already embedded deep inside the Dread system. Some of them, when they hear my name, it trips something in their minds, and they get access to Juliet's memories. They begin to think that they're her, and they start to act on those beliefs."

"Like spies?" Major Ames asked.

"Better than spies," Theodore replied. "Juliets. Heh. For all we know, there are drumhr in the Domo'dahm's circle that are opposed to what he's doing as well. The un'hai creator, Tuhrik, was one of them. Good old Juliet. She got to them all. She showed them the light of forgiveness and peace. I know it."

"That's all well and good, Teddy," General Cave said. "How do we use this to our advantage?"

"We're gonna have to fight on the ground. We're gonna have to fight in space. There're no two ways about it. And, even with our crews mixed with the rebels on the ground, we're still going to be heavily outnumbered and outgunned. But, if we can get through to these other groups behind the scenes? We may just have ourselves a chance."

"It seems like quite a longshot," Captain Huang said. "General Cave, we have other options, and I think we should at least discuss them."

"Like?" Gabriel said. He had a feeling he knew what the Captain was going to say.

"The Dread fortress, the domo'shah, is capable of slipstream travel. It's also larger than all of our settlements combined and built for longevity. We can take it to the New Earth. We can settle there. Let the bek'hai keep the old Earth. Let them run themselves into the ground. We shouldn't risk our chance at freedom on a fight whose odds are so against us."

Gabriel sighed. It was the same old argument as before, framed and updated to match current events. Nevermind the sacrifices people had made to get them here. Nevermind the people on the ground who were going to die. Earth wasn't home to billions anymore, but there were still a few million people under the Domo'-dahm's thumb.

"Alan," Theodore said calmly. "Would you like to court-martial this coward, or do you want me to do it?" He glanced at Captain Huang. "By the by, you aren't related to Councilwoman Rouse, are you?"

Huang opened his mouth to speak. General Cave put up a hand to silence him. "Hold on. Both of you. Teddy, I appreciate your decision to stay relatively calm. It's not like you. I want to make this clear to everyone gathered here right now, and to the entire colony once we leave this room. Under no circumstances are we abandoning Earth or the people on it. Just like the bek'hai nearly destroyed themselves with their own ignorance, if we run away now we'll be doing the same thing, and probably to the same result. Maybe we'll lose. Maybe we'll die. If we go out there and try to forget about what happened here? It will change who we are for the worse, forever."

"With all due respect, sir," Captain Huang said. "You used to be in favor of leaving Earth behind."

"You're right. I was. And I would have allowed the death of half this colony to make it happen. I'm embarrassed to admit that now. I'm embarrassed to know I never would have been embarrassed if Theodore hadn't come back and saved my life, and all of our lives. I thought running was the answer and the only option. I hurt a lot of people because of that. I regret those decisions."

Captain Huang stood up. He didn't look happy. "You don't need to court-martial me, sir. Either one of you. I resign." He pulled his rank insignia from his chest, dropping it on the table and storming toward the door.

Theodore cut him off, rolling his chair in front of him.

"Get out of my way," Huang said.

"No I will not get out of your way," Theodore said. "You listen to me, boy. For starters, you're in the military. You don't get to resign. For another, you're an officer in that same military, which makes you too valuable just to walk away. Third, I'd sooner kill you with my bare hands than let you disrespect me, General Cave, Major St. Martin, or even Mr. It'kek over there. What do you think we've been doing these last few weeks, twiddling our thumbs? Or maybe sticking them up our asses? Good men and women have been dying, down there on Earth, on my ship, and right here in our backyard. Those are our people, Captain. Not some other alien race that's no concern of ours. Now, why don't you go sit down? Take a minute to think about something other than yourself. We win through unity. We die with division."

Captain Huang stood in front of Theodore, glaring down at him. Theodore met his gaze, his expression so condescending that Gabriel expected Huang to punch him.

Instead, he retreated, taking a few steps back and then returning to his seat.

"That's better," Theodore said. "Alan, I promised the rebels back on Earth that we'd be in Mexico in eight days. That leaves us forty-eight to get as organized as possible. My thinking was to load up all of our troops and consolidate the civvies to Alpha. Once this thing is done, we can come back for them."

"I think that can work," Cave replied. "Although forty-eight hours isn't a lot of time."

"Excuse me," Captain Huang said.

Theodore shot a nasty look over at him.

"Yes, Captain," General Cave said.

"If the soldiers all leave and the civilians stay behind, there's a chance they could get stranded here."

"Only if we were to lose," Gabriel said.

"That's beside the point. I think we should give everyone the option to return to Earth. Some will choose to stay behind, but some won't."

Theodore's face softened. "Well, we do have the space. I don't see any harm in it."

"Neither do I," General Cave said.

"Then we'll do that. Damn. I should have brought Lieutenant O'Dea down to help us with the logistics. I'll ship her over on the next boat. For now, I think we should start moving troops by company. That way we can get them properly armed and outfitted on their way in. Parallel to that, we can begin moving whatever resources we can spare. I'm sure we can convert them into something we can use. Captain, does your statement mean you've reconsidered?"

Huang had picked his insignia back up and reaffixed it to his uniform. "Yes, General," he replied.

"Then don't worry too much about your little outburst. It won't leave this room, and I forgive you."

"Thank you, sir."

"I want you to be our liaison to the Council. General Cave is going to be too busy helping me organize to deal with Rouse and the others. Tell them what we're doing, make sure they know that part of it isn't optional, but coming along for the ride is. Can you do that, son?"

"Yes, sir."

"Good man."

"What about me, General?" Major Ames asked.

"You used to a be a pilot, didn't you? Before you got the arthritis?"

"I made three runs past Earth, yes, sir. I'd still be doing it if I could."

"Well, the Ishur is a bit of a different animal. I don't think your disability would affect your ability to serve on the bridge, and I have other plans for Major St. Martin." Theodore turned to Gabriel. "Would you mind giving Major Ames a few lessons on flying the fortress?"

"Not at all, sir," Gabriel replied.

"Good. Mr. Mokri, I want you to take a shuttle over to Gamma. Help the science teams figure out what they can salvage there, and what we can use. Thank God the bastards only got one shot off."

"Yes, sir," Reza replied.

"Mr. It'kek, you're with Alan and me. You and yours have been invaluable so far, but we need to pick your brain a little more to put together a complete plan."

"Of course, Dahm St. Martin," It'kek said.

"General Cave and I will be reaching out to all of you again over the next two days. If any of you were expecting to sleep, cancel those plans. You can catch up when we go into slipspace."

"Yes, sir," the others said.

"Alan, is there anything you want to add?"

General Cave smiled. "No. I think you covered it all."

"In that case, you're all dismissed. Let's get to work."

[43]

"I never got a chance to meet Captain Kim," General Alan Parker said. "I wish I had. I've spent a lot of years dreaming of the day when I would meet someone from the space forces. When I would get to sit with them, embrace them, and thank them for never giving up. For never leaving us behind. And while I didn't know Captain Kim, that's what he represents to me. Hope. Hope for a better future. A future without the Dread."

The assembled rebels clapped as General Parker finished his eulogy, putting his hand on the simple casket that had been made to lay the fallen soldier to rest. It was more than a lot of the dead received, but Donovan understood why the General was placing Soon front and center as a symbol of the war. They had all heard General St. Martin's message. They all knew the storm was coming. It was right to be afraid. It was natural. Having something to cling to and to rally around could be the difference between victory and defeat.

It had been two days since the General had arrived, riding into Austin on the shoulder of Donovan's mech, his American flag waving in the breeze. It was an arrival that had kicked the gears of war into full motion, an arrival that had set the already focused rebels into a greater sense of purpose and motivation.

Not only because of General Parker, but also because of General St. Martin.

Donovan could still barely believe the man General Rodriguez had called the Old Gator had managed to survive. It was even harder for him to believe that he had somehow captured one of the enemy fortresses for the rebellion. To think that only a short time earlier they had still believed the Dread to be untouchable. Unbeatable. Now it seemed as if victory, or at least the chance for victory, was imminent.

He watched the General finish the ceremony, and then joined Ehri and Colonel Knight at the front of the assembly. They lifted Soon's casket together, carrying it to the corner of the loop station, where a grave had already been dug. They lowered it in, and then General Parker handed Donovan a makeshift shovel.

"Thank you, sir," Donovan said. He used the shovel to return a scoop of the earth to its place and then passed it on to Ehri. She did the same, and the process was repeated, the shovel passed along to a line of soldiers that formed behind them. Most of them had never had a chance to get to know Soon, but they respected him for what he had done, and for what he represented.

After two days, the rebel army was almost ready to move out. Donovan had barely slept the entire time, getting involved with the effort to organize and coordinate the influx of new fighters, and to help Colonel Knight and General Parker put together a plan for when they reached the Dread capital. He and Ehri had the most experience with both the layout and military capabilities of the linked Dread fortresses, and so their input had been essential to the strategy.

Not that there was anything fancy about their plan. The intent was to use the same tactics that had gotten them this far, only on a larger scale and with a little more firepower behind it. That meant trying to stay out of the Dread's sensor range, to keep silent and cool as they made their approach. The mechs would hang back, aiming to cover the ground teams as they came under pressure, and to offer a distraction to pull the Dread heavy units away. The goal, they had decided, was to infiltrate the Dread fortresses, to get soldiers inside where they would have better success fighting the enemy army in close quarters. For Donovan, that meant he was going to see the worst of the fighting from within the cockpit of a Dread mech.

It also meant he was one of the soldiers who was most likely to be killed.

While the infantry would be sneaking through the streets of Mexico City, he would be looking to intercept both Dread mechanized armors and starfighters as they swept over the field, laying down cover fire and trying to pull the birds from the sky. The mech alone was going to make him a huge target, but that would make him impossible to ignore, and that was the idea.

He wasn't afraid of dying. He had seen too many of his friends fall to the Dread to fear being killed in battle. His real fear came from the thought of failure. Of being shot down before he accomplished his mission and gave the infantry enough time to reach the enemy's gates. He was comforted a little to know that Ehri would be covering his left side, but standing in front of Soon's grave only reminded him that someone else would be to his right, someone he would have to learn to trust in a hurry.

He wasn't sure who would receive the assignment just yet. They had returned with three mechs to add to the two they already controlled, and a salvage team had brought back his damaged armor to try to repair under Orli's supervision. That meant there were four seats for nearly a dozen people who had made the cut of initial volunteers and who had been training to drive the machines. He knew that Lieutenant Bastion and Corporal Knowles were currently at the top of the leaderboards they had devised to track progress. Would it be one of them?

Not that it mattered in the end. They were all in this together.

Donovan began moving away from the grave, clearing space for others to offer their respects. Kroeger was near the front of the line, and the soldier tossed a pile of dirt onto the casket before hurrying to catch up with him.

"Major," Kroeger said, keeping pace as they walked. "I hear we're moving out tonight."

"That's right," Donovan said.

Kroeger stopped and put out his hand. "Major, if we don't see one another again, I just wanted to thank you."

"Thank me?"

"I spent years out there in a world where hope was hard to come by, and civilization even harder. It changed me, in good ways and bad, but more in bad, I think. I was trying to do something good with Hell, and I think I did okay at it. But since signing up with you, I feel pride I thought I had lost. A sense of purpose that I thought was long gone. So yeah, thank you for that, Major. Even if we don't always see eye to eye." He paused, looking back at Soon's grave. "Even if you should have listened to me."

He gave Donovan a half-smirk and headed off, returning to the ground unit where he had been assigned.

"Asshole," Donovan said softly to his back. He still wasn't sure if he liked Kroeger or not, but he couldn't deny the man was a survivor.

"Excuse me, Major?" General Parker said, having overheard him.

Donovan turned to face the General, saluting as he did. "Sir. Not you, sir. Sergeant Kroeger."

"An interesting character for sure," General Parker replied. "I've seen a lot of people like him out in the human wasteland."

"Those are the people we're fighting to save?"

"Yes. We can't discriminate, even if sometimes we wish we could."

"Yes, sir."

Donovan kept his eyes on the General, waiting for him to announce his intentions. He had learned over the last two days that it was one of the General's strongest, most subliminal traits. He had a confident, commanding presence about him, one that made soldiers want to be still and listen or wait to be addressed. He was a leader. A true leader, who had taken over the Austin operation on his arrival and within eighteen hours had everyone in it following his command without question. Donovan admired the quality.

He also admired the man. Stories about General Parker had started circulating when his army from New York had arrived. Stories about his bravery and sacrifice, about his strategic genius and his fatherly demeanor. He had not only held things together as the situation had gotten worse in the northeast, but he had also overcome it, adding to their numbers even while they couldn't put a scratch on the Dread.

"I was going to talk to you about this later at the officer's meeting, but I thought it might lift your spirits a little bit to hear it from me right now. I want you to lead not only the mech unit but also the entire diversionary force, including the Bertha Brigade, as they've taken to calling themselves." He smiled. "I'm also going to shift two companies over to your command to help with the external defenses. Both J and K Companies will fall under your flag."

K Company was Kroeger's unit. It seemed they wouldn't be parting ways just yet.

"Major is a low rank to have that much responsibility," General Parker continued. "It won't affect your pay grade, but I'm promoting you to Colonel. Congratulations."

Donovan looked at the General's face, and then at his hand. Colonel?

"Yes, sir," he replied, taking the hand. "Thank you, sir." He knew his mother would have been proud of him for this.

"I also thought you might want to meet your new squad mate."

"You, sir?" Donovan said.

General Parker laughed. "I'd be honored, Colonel, but no. I need to help run the overall attack." He motioned back to Colonel Knight. "Colonel Knight has been taking lessons from Ehri in private. From what I hear, she might be a better pilot than you."

Colonel Knight approached at the mention of her name. "I thought we were going to cover this later, sir?" she said.

"Now seemed as good of a time as any."

"Colonel," Donovan said, saluting her.

"Colonel," Colonel Knight replied, returning the salute. "Looks like I'm taking orders from you now, sir."

"I guess you are," Donovan said, feeling a little uncomfortable with the role reversal.

"We're all professionals here," General Parker said. "And we all want the same thing. There's no need to feel strange about it."

"Yes, sir," Donovan said.

"Good. I recommend that you try to enjoy your last few hours of calm. It might be the last few we have for a while."

[44]

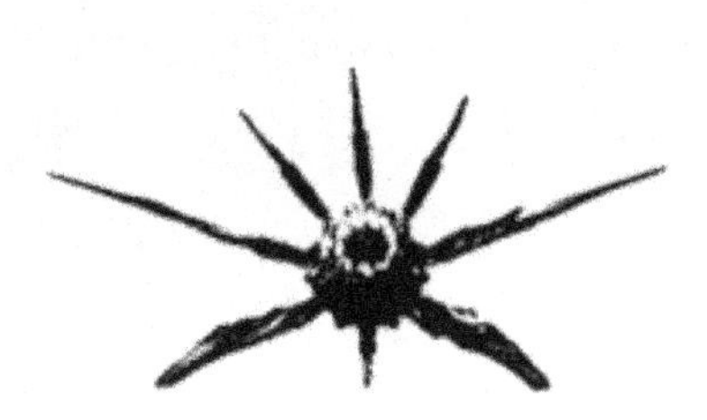

"Domo'dahm," Orish'ek said as he entered Rorn'el's private chamber beside the throne room.

Rorn'el turned at the approach, shifting his back toward the pur'-dahm to avoid being seen. It was improper for Orish'ek to look on him directly, and he would be forced to retire if he caught more than a glimpse. For as embarrassing as the human form was, the legri'hai shape was even more of a failure, and one that he hoped they could one day forget.

"Have you forgotten your place, Orish'ek?" he snapped. "Or do you intend to defy me as well?"

He hissed softly at the idea of it. Too many of his subjects were proving to be less than trustworthy.

"My apologies, Domo'dahm," Orish'ek said. "I thought you would want to know that Pit'ek has returned. I have already ordered him to appear before you."

Pit'ek was back from his hunt for the human settlement? Did that mean the technology that had been delivered to them from the Ishur had worked? That was news worth being intruded upon for.

"Excellent. I will prepare myself for the audience. What of our efforts to root out the un'hai?"

"Sor'ek has assembled a complete roster of all of the active un'hai as you commanded, Domo'dahm. The report is within your data store."

"Have you seen it?"

"Yes, Domo'dahm."

"What are your thoughts?"

Orish'ek was hesitant to respond. Rorn'el turned slightly, glancing back at him from the corner of his eye.

"What is the problem?" he asked.

"Domo'dahm," Orish'ek said. "Tuhrik was directly responsible for the creation of the un'hai, at your request."

"Yes. And?"

Orish'ek froze.

"And?" Rorn'el repeated with a hiss.

"Domo'dahm, the un'hai compose nearly ninety percent of our science and technology focused lor'hai. This includes our splicing research, the assemblers, astronomy, and many other vital roles. Further, it was the un'hai Kehri's work with the human technology that allowed Pit'ek to integrate the systems into the lek'shah."

"What are you suggesting?"

"Two things, Domo'dahm. First, there are very few, if any, un'hai that Tuhrik did not have any opportunity to manipulate. Second, it is clear from the actions of at least one of the un'hai that they are not all disloyal."

Rorn'el considered it. In his initial anger at Zoelle's betrayal, he had been of a mind to destroy all of the Juliet clones and replace them with something more reliable. Now it was clear that not only was that not feasible; it also might not be necessary. Only some of the un'hai seemed to be infected with whatever damage Tuhrik had introduced to them.

"Do we have any way to determine which of the un'hai might be traitorous?" he asked.

"No, Domo'dahm. Sor'ek has tested the brain function of a random sample and has uncovered no discernible differences. An autopsy has also failed to reveal any obvious patterns to identify these copies."

"But it is possible his sample was too small?" Rorn'el said.

"Yes, Domo'dahm. However, if there are only a limited number of tainted clones, it would be inefficient to continue destroying them in the hopes of discovering one."

"Of course. There is no reason to continue to focus on this. If there are more un'hai like Ehri hiding in our midst, they will reveal themselves sooner or later, and then they will die. As long as Sor'ek is certain this is not a widespread problem?"

"He is certain, Domo'dahm. His estimate places one to three of these un'hai on each domo'shah, along with another thirty scattered among our outposts."

"Less than one hundred? Surely our pur'dahm can handle them if the need arises."

"Yes, Domo'dahm."

"Go now, Orish'ek. I must prepare myself for audience."

"Yes, Domo'dahm."

Rorn'el turned around again once the pur'dahm had left. He used the arms of his chair to lift himself to a stand, shifting slightly as he did. His legs cracked at the motion, and he hissed in pain.

Old. He was getting old. He had taken Kesh'ek's place nearly forty cycles ago, himself already fifty cycles in age. While his natural lifespan was hundreds of years longer, his days in the legri'shah ring had taken their toll, and given him reason to look forward to his retirement. Not now, though. Not while the humans were still trying to take the planet back from him. He would see every last one of them destroyed before that day came.

He moved to the corner of the room, opening a small chamber there and removing a lek'shah mask from it. He lifted it out, lowered the hood of his gori'shah, and placed it over his scaled face. Then he raised the hood again, tilting himself downward to reduce his profile. He hobbled over to a second compartment, opened it, and looked down at the splintered cross he had recovered. It was no longer a symbol of peace of him, but one of anger and clarity. He had been too soft on the humans because of her. It was her fault he was in this position now.

He closed the compartment and then headed out into the hallway between his throne and his quarters. He looked at both ends of the corridor, finding it empty, before crossing the short distance to the other side and entering the antechamber. Once inside he climbed into the darkened cage that was his throne and removed the mask. Then he activated his console, using it to move the throne into position.

Orish'ek was already sitting in his proper place beside the throne as it moved into place. The pur'dahm did not look at him on his arrival. Neither did the others who were already present.

"Bring him in," he said a moment later, shifting his body to get more comfortable in his seat. The hatch at the end of the room slid open, and pur'dahm Pit'ek entered.

The commander of the Ishrem bowed at the rear of the room, and then made the long, lonely walk to the front. He bowed again when he reached Rorn'el, sweeping his head so low that the patches of black hair on the sides of his head hit the floor.

"Domo'dahm," Pit'ek said nervously.

Rorn'el stared at the pur'dahm. He could tell that something was wrong.

"Did you locate the human settlement?" Rorn'el asked, feeling a growing sense of unease and anger in his gut.

"Yes, Domo'dahm. We found the settlement. It was broken into five separate locations. We destroyed two of them."

"Two? Why not five?"

"With your honor, Domo'dahm." Pit'ek began to look more uncomfortable. "There were complications."

"Complications?" he replied, forcing himself to stay calm for now.

"The Ishur arrived just as we were commencing the attack on the humans. They attacked us."

"And the shields?"

"The shields were effective, Domo'dahm."

"What about the Ishur? Did they also have these shields?"

"Yes, Domo'dahm, only their defenses were not the same. The modulation of their hull seemed very unstable. I would claim that our technology is superior."

"Then the Ishur was destroyed? This General St. Martin was destroyed?"

Pit'ek kept his head low. "No, Domo'dahm."

"But you are not destroyed."

"No, Domo'dahm."

"Explain yourself, Pit'ek."

"With your honor, Domo'dahm. The Ishrek was destroyed, and the Ishur was deflecting all of our attacks."

"You just said their defenses were inferior," Orish'ek said.

"Yes, Si'Dahm," Pit'ek said. "Perhaps they weren't as inferior as we believed. They moved around the ship as though they were being controlled from the bridge. It was an interesting solution to the problems the scientists discovered."

"If the shields are effective, how was the Ishrek destroyed?"

"They converted the plasma cannon to a solid plasma stream, Domo'dahm. I believe this was possible because they are using only a small portion of the resources available on the domo'shah. They are not supporting thousands, and they are not utilizing the factories. The stream held for many ticks, many more than we could possibly achieve. It is possible that they have upgraded the systems similar to the shields. I do not know, Domo'dahm. I am unsure. The stream appeared to overwhelm the lek'shah modulation and invert, creating a small wormhole which traveled through the Ishrem and disabled it."

Rorn'el felt his hands clenching into fists as he listened to the story. They had the perfect opportunity to destroy the human settlement, to destroy the Ishur, and to leave the rebels on the ground exposed when their expected reinforcements never arrived. Instead, not only had Pit'ek failed in his mission, but he had failed to die with honor.

If entire wars hinged on single battles, this one would continue because of that failure.

"I do not understand," he said. "I told you that if you returned with the humans still alive your life would be forfeit, Pit'ek. And yet you returned."

"Domo'dahm," Pit'ek said, bowing low once more. "We could not match the Ishur in offensive capability, and I believed that this information was more valuable than my sacrifice."

Rorn'el smiled, shifting his head so that light would catch enough of it that Pit'ek would see his sharp teeth. The pur'dahm drew back slightly at the sight.

"You have done well to return this information to me."

"Thank you, Domo'dahm."

"Now that it is delivered, I expect you to fulfill the orders you were given."

"Orders, Domo'dahm?"

"Yes. I ordered you not to return to me without having destroyed the human settlement, or to be prepared for your retirement."

The pur'dahm lifted his head slightly, ready to argue, before lowering it again. "Yes, Domo'dahm."

"Be glad I do not disgrace you by killing you myself."

"Yes, Domo'dahm."

"You are dismissed."

"Yes, Domo'dahm."

Rorn'el sat in silence while Pit'ek fled the room. He had no doubt the drumhr would fulfill his obligation to retire.

"So, the humans continue to outmaneuver us," Orish'ek said.

"It appears that way. A plasma stream? It may have been effective against only two ships, but it will not be enough to save them." He paused. "Order all of the domo'shah not attached to the capital to take up position in orbit and bolster the defensive net. Once there, they are to deploy their full complement of ek'shah and to have the gi'shah on standby for deployment."

"Domo'dahm?" Orish'ek said. "All of the domo'shah?"

"You believe this is the wrong decision?" Rorn'el asked.

"If the ground forces break through, it will make it all the easier for them to reach us."

"The rebel forces are not the problem here. They have a secure position underground, but once they emerge they will be decimated by the gi'shah before they can even get close. No. The Ishur is the real danger. They possess the firepower of a domo'shah, and the ingenuity to survive. It is a shame I will have to destroy General St. Martin. He would have made a fine splice." Rorn'el looked at Orish'ek. "Why are you still here? Send out my orders."

Orish'ek hesitated for a moment as if he wanted to say something else, and then bowed and left the room.

Domo'dahm Rorn'el leaned back in his throne and closed his eyes.

He would see the humans destroyed before his time came to retire.

It was his legacy.

It was his destiny.

[45]

"PREPARING TO JOIN THE SLIPSTREAM IN FIVE, FOUR, THREE, two, one, now," Gabriel said, counting down as the Ishur accelerated toward the subspace wave, her large quantum phased fins stretched out around her.

They shimmered and began to vanish to the alternate thread of time and space, pulling the main body of the fortress along with them. A few seconds later, the stars collapsed, leaving them in a place of infinite black.

"Slipstream joined," he said, turning to look back at his father.

"And we're on our way," Theodore said with a smile. "ETA to arrival, Mr. Mokri?"

"Five days, nine hours, sir," Reza replied.

"Three hours ahead of schedule. I hope the rebels don't mind that we're early."

"I hope they weren't planning on cutting things that close," General Cave said. He was sitting in the station right in front of the command dais, two seats from Miranda.

As expected, the two days at the colony had passed in a blur, finding everyone involved with the war effort under increasing pressure to get everything organized and prepared. While General Cave and Theodore, along with Colonels Choi and Graham had gotten to work organizing a definitive strategy, Gabriel had been tasked with both training Major Ames on how to fly the Dread starship, and in keeping abreast of the status of the many other projects underway. It had meant a lot of shuttling back and forth between the Ishur and Alpha Station, a lot of walking through the corridors of both, and absolutely no sleep.

He was tired, but he would never show it. He had wanted nothing more than to be the one to bring the Ishur into slipspace, and now that it was done he felt the sudden weight of his exhaustion.

He didn't realize he was yawning until his father called him on it.

"Major St. Martin," Theodore said, using his rank. "Are we boring you?"

"Sorry, sir," Gabriel said, feeling his face flush. "It's been a long couple of days."

"Long? It went by like a dream to me. Give me a quick sitrep on our preparations and then head on to your quarters. I can't afford to have my top pilot going into the shit with eyes half-open."

"Yes, sir," Gabriel said, trying to remember all of the reports he had received in the hours before the Ishur had departed. "The Ishur's current population is eight-thousand forty-four souls, including two thousand six hundred and forty civilians, one hundred and three clone soldiers, twelve keepers, three mature legri'shah, and an unknown number of cleaners. We also have five thousand two hundred and seven trained soldiers from the colony on board, who have been armed with three thousand seventy-two Dread rifles. It is expected that the assemblers will complete almost one hundred percent of the inventory needed for the infantry before we arrive."

"I am seriously impressed with your memory, son," Theodore said.

"I'm just getting started, sir," Gabriel replied. "The assemblers have also completed four gi'shah capable of being piloted by humans, and two of the larger ek'shah, which require at least a dozen souls to operate. They have also used recovered salvage to repair or produce sixteen of our own starfighters, with upgrades to the ion cannons for standard phase modulation. The bad news is that we currently only have ten qualified pilots and eight academy trainees who are advanced enough to put in the cockpit."

"Too many ships. We have six days to find soldiers we can train."

"Yes, sir. It is expected the assemblers will produce two more starfighters during the trip."

"What about Maggie?"

"According to Guy, the Magellan is as fit to fly as she'll ever be. They'll be adding plasma cannon mounts during the trip. Unfortunately, we only have enough resources for five of them."

"Not ideal, but I'll take what I can get."

"Yes, sir. The civilians have all been assigned berths on decks three to nineteen. Its one level above the cloning facilities and the legri'shah pens. We've done our best to teach them how to use the transport beams and to warn them about wandered randomly, but we don't have the manpower to babysit."

"I told Councilwoman Rouse to do what she could to keep them in line," Theodore said. "Damn that woman for being good at what she does; once she put her mind to being part of the solution instead of part of the problem."

"Yes, sir. There are still two thousand or so civilians remaining on Alpha Station that we'll need to pick up after we win. With the reduced population, they should have the capacity to stay alive for years."

"In case we don't come back? Heh. The ones who stayed behind are idiots."

"Yes, sir. We have enough food and water to last for months and enough space that everyone on the ship is pretty happy with the living situation. Although, they might change their minds once the fighting starts."

"You can say that again. I think half of them think we're going for a stroll and we'll just land somewhere and let them out."

"Yes, sir."

"Anything else, Major?"

Gabriel thought about it for a few seconds. "Just that I'm proud to be part of this offensive, sir." And proud to be your son. He didn't say it, but he felt it.

"I'm proud to have you," Theodore replied. "If you're done with your report, you're dismissed."

"Yes, sir. Thank you, sir."

Gabriel stood to leave.

"Spaceman Locke," Theodore said. "When was the last time you had some bunk time?"

Gabriel found Miranda, who looked surprised at the question. She looked spent, too. "Uh. I lost track, sir."

"You're dismissed as well. I'll get one of the new recruits up to take your place. We aren't running a skeleton crew anymore."

"Yes, sir."

Gabriel felt himself blush. He knew what his father was doing. He probably thought he was a sly old gator.

Gabriel headed off the bridge, with Miranda right behind him. They stopped together a short distance away.

"The General seems to think that there's a benefit to us being off duty at the same time," she said, a smile creeping across her face.

"He does, doesn't he? He wasn't exactly subtle about it."

The smile turned to a laugh. "Do you think he knows something we don't?"

"No. I think he knows something we know."

"Gabriel-"

"Miranda. Wait. Come on."

Gabriel reached out and took her hand. She followed him as he led her through the ship and to his quarters.

"Do you want to come in?" he asked. "Wallace is going to pee when he sees us."

She laughed again. "Of course."

Gabriel opened the hatch. Wallace came charging out, yipping and wagging his tail, circling both of them and leaving a little urine on the deck, just like Gabriel had guessed he would.

"Who's my good man?" Miranda asked, petting him while he licked her face.

Gabriel watched her, feeling his pulse quickening. Theodore had given them this time for a reason, and he wasn't going to waste it.

"Miranda," he said.

She looked up at him and stood, keeping her hand on Wallace's back. "Gabriel, I-"

"I love you," Gabriel said, spitting it out before he could reconsider.

"I love you," she said at almost the same time.

They both laughed.

"I've wanted to say that for a while," she said. "Years, actually. I never wanted to push or pressure you after Jessica."

"I didn't know that I did until recently, to be honest. But I do. You've brought me more joy than I thought I would feel again. You're my best friend." He paused and looked down at Wallace. "After him, obviously."

She laughed again. "I love that you're honest, Gabriel. I love your courage and your strength and your loyalty."

"I love the same things about you," he said, looking in her eyes. "I know this is a little awkward, but I didn't want anything to happen before I got to say it, even though I've been so busy I haven't had the chance."

"Are you sure you're not just overtired?" she asked.

He stepped toward her, reaching out. She moved into him, accepting his embrace. "Absolutely."

They kissed. It was a simple kiss. Soft and short, an expression of an emotion born of admiration and respect. Then they held one another. Gabriel enjoyed running his hands through her hair and feeling the weight of her head on his shoulder.

"Will you marry me?" Gabriel asked. "After this is over?"

"Yes." She picked her head up. "Why not before? Your father can do it. Or General Cave."

"Motivation," he said. "If I have that to look forward to, there will be nothing the Dread can do to stop me from making it back."

She reached up and put her hand on his face. "I believe you when you say that."

"Good, because I mean it." He looked over at his bed. "Now if you don't mind, I'm going to crash and burn here before I crash and burn out there."

"I think you might be on to something. I'm about ready to fall over myself."

"I'll see you on the bridge?"

"Affirmative."

He pulled her close and kissed her again. "Goodnight, Miranda."

"Goodnight, Gabriel."

They kissed one last time, and then she left his room, headed for her own quarters. He retreated to his bed, falling onto it and descending quickly into the best sleep he had ever had.

[46]

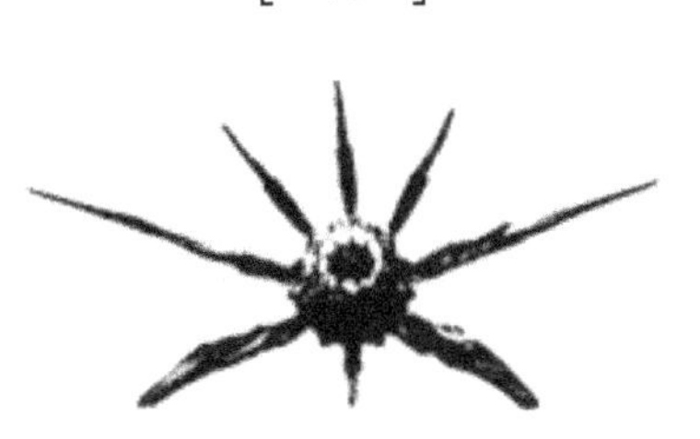

Donovan brought his mech to a stop as they reached the outskirts of San Luis Potosi. He felt a chill at the sight of the city, remembering the battle that had happened there, and the person who had died there.

Diaz. His eyes shifted to the area of the city where he had burned her body, knowing the ashes would still be there. It had only been three weeks since they had left. It felt strange to be back again so soon.

It felt even stranger to be at the head of an army almost twelve-thousand people strong.

It was more than they had started with. It was more than they had ever expected. Men, women, and even children had been streaming in from the world around them, every day since they had marched from Austin at a breakneck pace. They were rebels from other camps, they were jackals, they were scavengers, they were anyone and everyone who had been near any kind of transmitter and had heard Theodore St. Martin's message. They were people who had found their humanity, who had been inspired, and who were ready to fight back.

"Are you well, Colonel?" Ehri asked.

"Yeah. We aren't coming back with our tail between our legs."

"No, sir."

"What do you think the Domo'dahm is waiting for?" he asked.

They hadn't seen a single Dread fighter, a single Dread mech, or even a single Dread soldier since they had left Austin. The route was as clear as any of them had ever seen, trouble and conflict free, as though the aliens had never existed at all.

"General St. Martin issued him a challenge. He will be dishonored not to meet it. Do not let this lull fool you. You will find his forces in Mexico."

"I'm looking forward to it."

"Yes."

"Colonel Peters," General Parker said, his voice coming in over the makeshift receiver mounted to the front of the mech's cockpit. "Take Ehri and Colonel Knight down into the city and make sure it's clear. We'll hang back and wait for your report."

"Yes, sir," Donovan replied, putting his mech in motion once more. "Come on."

The three mechs moved into the decimated city, crossing through the main thoroughfare and winding through the side streets. As expected, Donovan came across the place where Diaz had been put to rest. He bowed the mech's head there out of respect before contacting the General again.

"We're all clear, General."

"Good. We'll rest here for three hours, and then we have to be on the move again. We're running behind as it is."

"The stragglers are slowing us down, sir," Donovan said. That was the downside to the civilians that had been joining them. They were threatening to get the army there late.

"I know, Colonel. We have to make a decision whether or not to leave them behind."

"It doesn't seem like much of a decision to me, sir. We can't ask General St. Martin to manage this war on his own."

"You're absolutely right, and I was thinking the same thing. We'll pass the word down the line to them. They need to keep up or get left behind."

"Yes, sir."

"Split your squad into two shifts, Colonel. I want your sensors on the surroundings, just in case the Dread try something sneaky."

"Yes, sir. Bastion, Knowles, Knight, you're on first shift. Move into position to maximize sensor coverage. I don't want anything getting near this city without us knowing about it."

"Yes, sir," the pilots replied.

Donovan moved his mech back toward the oncoming army. J and K Companies moved in first, two hundred soldiers strong. They swept through the area, taking up defensive positions on rubble piles and broken rooftops. Donovan spotted Kroeger among them, finding a good place to roost with his sniper rifle.

"The rest of you, try to get a little shut-eye," Donovan said. "Ninety minutes and then we switch."

Donovan settled back in the cockpit, closing his eyes and trying to relax. He was nervous. Impatient. They couldn't get to Mexico City soon enough.

He was halfway through his ninety minutes when the sudden sound of deep rumbling and a beeping from the mech's terminal caused him to wake. His eyes snapped open, and he looked around outside. The buildings were shivering, throwing up a cloud of disturbed dust, and the rumbling was getting louder.

"What the-" he started to say. The sound was familiar. He had heard it before, but it was so much louder now.

"More domo'shah are launching," Ehri said. "Judging by the vibrations, a lot more."

Donovan turned his mech to the south. There was a building in his field of view, so he walked the armor over to clear his sightline. He could see the light in the distance, illuminating the entire sky. The rumbling was getting louder, the ground shaking even more. The soldiers resting around him were all up and standing, searching for the source of the distress.

"There," Ehri said, using her mech to point into the distance.

The first of the domo'shah was rising, reaching a point where they could see it climbing into the night sky, a bright red and blue flare of energy behind it. Another appeared a moment later. Then another.

"How many of them does he have?" Donovan said.

Another appeared, and then another, creating a train of the massive starships climbing toward the atmosphere. The ground shook, the air around them rippling and heating up from the energy being used to bring them all into orbit.

"Seven, not including the capital ship, which is nearly twice the size of the others," Ehri said.

Donovan watched them rise, counting them.

"Seven," he said. "He's sending all of them to intercept General St. Martin and his forces."

"It is a good sign," she replied. "It means he is worried about the General. Seven ships to defeat one?"

"Eight," Donovan said. They had seen the other fortress appear a few hours earlier, coming to rest in geosynchronous orbit. "Eight against one. They're going to be slaughtered."

"Then the weight of this war has shifted back to us," Ehri said.

General Parker seemed to understand that instinctively. His voice carried over the receiver a moment later.

"All units, break time is over. This is a red alert. I repeat, this is a red alert. I know you're tired. I know you're stretched to the limit. But that there is a sign that the enemy is afraid. It's also the opportunity we've been waiting for. We need to dig deep and take whatever strength we have left, and we need to use it now. We have to get to the Dread capital before the Ishur arrives. We have to use the chance we're being given. General St. Martin is depending on us. All of humankind is depending on us. Gather your things and let's move. I want to be on the Domo'dahm's doorstep ASAP. Are you with me?"

"Yes, sir," the soldiers replied as one, a shout that almost reached through the din of the rising fortresses.

"I said are you with me?" Parker repeated.

"Yes, sir," they replied.

"Let's beat those bastards this time. Are. You. With. Me?"

"Yes, sir," they shouted, the sound of it overcoming the rumble and echoing through the night.

It was immediately followed by a flood of humankind as it continued its journey toward what would prove to either be a new beginning or a final end.

[47]

Gabriel stood at the front of the open space next to the dark cloning facility. The lights within the factory had been put out, the doors sealed shut. The caretakers who had worked within had been relocated to another area of the ship, where two of the New Earth Alliance's social workers were both trying to comfort them over the loss of their singular programmed task, and determine whether or not Dread clones could be rehabilitated. He had heard that early results indicated it was not only possible but that the programming was easily overcome with the right mental stimulation.

He looked over to his left, at the line of officers standing at attention beside him. Colonel Graham, Colonel Choi, Major Ames, and of course Generals Cave and St. Martin. The New Earth Alliance council members who were making the trip were also present, headed by Councilwoman Rouse. They were at the head of an all-hands assembly his father had called, causing the large open floor of the deck to be crowded with both military and civilians.

They were still nearly a day out from Earth, still traveling through slipspace toward their final destination. They would spend the next series of hours in active preparation for the battle to come, checking their equipment, moving assets into place, making sure they were as ready and organized as they could be. This would be their last chance to see one another before it happened. One last motivational push. One last opportunity to say whatever needed to be said.

Gabriel shifted his attention to the crowd in front of them, finding Miranda near the front. She was already looking at him, and he smiled and tapped his chest. She returned the knowing gesture. Everything had been better since he had declared himself to her. He had only realized in hindsight that he had loved her long before they had stolen the Magellan, he had just never let those emotions in.

"I think we're ready to start," he heard General Cave say to his father.

Gabriel kept scanning the crowd. He found Daphne in the corner, surrounded by a contingent of Dread clone soldiers who had served under Tea'va and Gr'el. The former had ordered them to follow her commands, and they continued to do so with precision even after his death, becoming invaluable to the logistical preparations. For her part, Daphne had continued to be strong, confident that Soon was down there with the rebels, and that she would see him again. He didn't blame her for that. He believed the same thing.

"Angela, if you will," Theodore said to the Councilwoman.

She nodded, sticking her fingers in her mouth and whistling. The sound of it echoed across the chamber, and they were all surprised when a soft rumble responded to it from deeper within the bowels of the Ishur. Gabriel glanced over at It'kek, who had an amused expression on his face. It appeared the legri'shah enjoyed the sound.

"Ladies and gentleman, and esteemed allies," Councilwoman Rouse said, looking over that keepers when she said the last part. "Thank you all for coming. I know these last few days have been stressful for everyone, and for different reasons. I think you should all be proud of yourselves for being here, and for the strength and courage you've exhibited so far. I'm going to turn this meeting over to General Theodore St. Martin. You all know him, and what he has meant to the New Earth Alliance, and while the General and I have not always seen eye-to-eye, I can honestly say that there are few people whose words I respect more."

She turned to Theodore, who rolled over to her position, shaking her hand when she offered it.

"Thank you, Angela," he said.

He looked out at the gathering, unable to see past the first row because of his diminished height in the chair.

"Men and women of the Earth Alliance," he said, his voice booming through the space. "You'll notice I left off the 'New.' That's because there is no New Earth. There's only our Earth. The one we evolved on. The one we lived on for the last few thousand years. The one that was taken from us, without justification and without cause by an alien race known by us as the Dread, known by themselves as the bek'hai. Some of you may have already met the keepers. It'kek and the others. Some of you know the real story of the bek'hai. You see, those coullions that took our Earth, they're like the bastard sons of a race that was once intelligent and peaceful. A race that I think at times made us look like bloodthirsty monsters. You might wonder why I'm telling you this. Why I'm leading with this. I want you to look around this room. I know it's hard to see past your neighbor but take a look around. Make eye contact with every face you see. Some of them will be different than ours, but everyone in this room is an ally and a friend."

He paused, turning his chair to follow his instructions. Gabriel nodded to him as he did, and he nodded back before returning forward.

"Did you take a good look? You might be thinking; this is it? We're going to get our planet back with this? Hell, I know I am. Except this isn't it. We've got good people on the ground on Earth, making their way to the Dread capital to put the pressure on their leader. It's an army whose size we can't even estimate because we can't put a limit on how big it might be. It's an army with the same strength and courage y'all are showing by being here, especially the civilians among you who didn't need to come. Even so, you think that's the only army we got?" He shook his head. "It isn't. You see, we have ourselves a secret weapon. A weapon forged fifty years ago when those bastard Dread decided they wanted my Juliet. That she was a good match to make copies of and program as scientists and researchers. For those of you were left Earth with me, who knew Juliet, you can imagine what a mistake they made by letting her in. Even the most brutal bastard sons couldn't ignore the peaceful, devout beauty of that woman."

He paused again, wiping at his face at the memory of her. His father had accepted the truth about Zoelle, and he wore a strong face in public, but Gabriel knew that he was still hurting over the revelation, and over knowing that his wife was truly lost to him.

"We don't know how strong our weapon is until we try to use it, but we're going to find out. We've got a plan to turn the Dread infrastructure into chaos, and if it works? Hoo-boy, if it works, our victory is all but assured. Even if it doesn't, I believe in the people I see in front of me. I believe in every man and woman on this ship. I believe in your strength, in your courage, in your energy and enthusiasm. I believe in your heart and your spirit and your love. I believe in humankind, in humanity, and in the truth that we're going to give every last ounce of ourselves to see this thing through, to reclaim our planet, and to send them sons of bitches home. And I only have one question for all of you here: do you believe?"

"Yes," Gabriel said, along with a handful of others.

"That was pathetic," Theodore said. "Am I wrong about all of you? Tell me, do you believe?"

"Yes," a large contingent said, the sound of it echoing through the chamber.

"Really? Then why are you here? Do you believe?"

"Yes," most of the people shouted.

"Do you believe?" Theodore repeated one last time.

"Yes!"

The sound of it was so loud the room vibrated. Once more, the legri'shah answered the call, a massive roar sounding from deeper behind them, echoing out from the tunnels. It almost seemed to energize the crowd, and they cheered and hollered, leading to a greater response from the creatures. Gabriel's heart pounded, his body and spirit energized by the crowd. He put his hand on the crucifix below his shirt, holding it tight. Whatever happened, he would remember this moment.

"Gabe," Theodore said, rolling over to him.

"Dad. Good pep talk."

"Thank you, son."

"I'm not completely clear what you meant about our secret weapon, though. Do you know something I don't?"

"I do. But not for long. Kneel down next to me so we can talk for a minute."

Gabriel did, coming close so he could hear his father over the continuing sound of people cheering and talking, using the time they had as a group.

Theodore put his hand on Gabriel's arm. "I've discussed this with General Cave, and with It'kek. I would have brought you in on it, but I needed you rested." He paused. "By the by, congratulations on your engagement. I'm sorry I didn't get to hear about it from you. She's a good woman, and she'll take good care of you."

Gabriel glanced over to Miranda, who was talking to one of the soldiers beside her. "I know."

"We think that there are clones of your mother implanted on all of the Dread ships, at least one or two, but they don't know it yet. You remember how Zoelle changed when she heard your voice, and she heard you talk about your mom and me? Well, we think that if we can get a broadcast across their network, we can turn them all on. Even better? We think that the Juliets can get more of the clones, and the keepers, to pitch in."

"Why do you think that?"

"Juliet got real close with the keepers. She used to come and see them all the time. They bonded over their beliefs. Now, the keepers don't want to fight, but they know it might be their only shot at breaking free of the prisons they've been stuffed into, and of not only saving the legri'shah but also increasing their population. There's a lot of history there that we still don't know, and won't for some time, but it's important to them and could make a huge difference for us."

"So why are you telling me this?" Gabriel asked.

"According to Mr. Mokri, we can't force the Dread to output our signal across their ships. While we're pretty sure the Domo'dahm listened to our broadcast, it didn't make it everywhere. We need to get a message out to all of the ships in the Dread fleet, emitted over their internal PA systems. Now, you would think we'd maybe have the ability to do that from here, but we don't. Sure, we can open a channel from one bridge to another, but we can't make them push the signal ship-wide. Do you get what I'm saying?"

Gabriel nodded. "I understand. So how do we get the word out?"

Theodore looked at him, hesitant. He bit his lip. It was as uncomfortable as Gabriel had ever seen him.

"Dad?"

"You know I love you, don't you, son?"

"Of course. I love you, too."

"It isn't that I don't believe in you because I do with all my heart. I just think it isn't right a man should have to ask his son to do this sort of thing."

"What do you need me to do? Whatever it is, I'll do it."

Theodore smiled. "I know you will. You're a St. Martin." He paused again. "Okay. Here's what we need you to do."

Gabriel listened while his father explained the mission they had in store for him. It was nothing he would have expected. It was as close to impossible as he could have ever imagined. More than likely, it was going to get him killed, and if he failed it could mean the rest of them might die as well.

When the time came to accept the assignment, he was honored to do it.

[48]

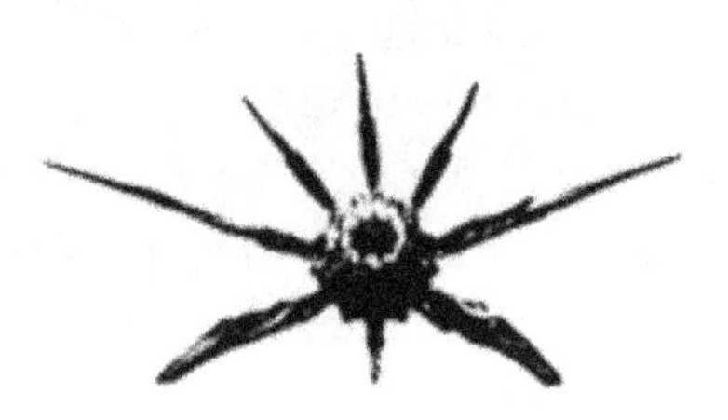

They could see the dark black carapace of the Dread capital long before they got close to it. It rose through the haze of the morning, blurry and frightening, a black splotch against clear blue. It resembled a wart, or a bruise, or a disease.

To Donovan, it was fitting. The Dread were an infection that needed to be cured. A wound that had to be cauterized. Perhaps not all of them, not the clones like Ehri, if there were any more of them, at least. But the Domo'dahm and the pur'dahm for sure. They were the ones with the power. They were the ones with the weapons.

They were prepared to use them.

The rebels had been on the move for forty out of the last forty-four hours, finally nearing the massive fortress and the hubs that had once connected it to the other ships. They were still visible in the daylight sky, smaller bruises spread across the aqua, waiting for General St. Martin and his forces, whatever they might look like, to arrive. When? Today, sometime. In hours, minutes, or seconds? There was no way to know.

They were all tired. The energy of General Parker's rallying cries had been draining a little more with each passing minute, each heavy step, each slow blink of tired eyes. Somehow, the man had kept at it without pause. He was there when they stopped to rest; he was there when they moved again. He was there all of the time, pushing them, urging them on, proving why he had survived as long as he had, and giving them hope that they would survive as well.

As the CO of the D Battalion, it was Donovan's role to take the lead as they neared the fortress, ready to intercept any heavy mechanized resources and try to get them caught up in an extended firefight, or otherwise attempt to distract them from the ten battalions that trailed behind them, with their eyes on reaching the fortress and getting inside. It was no small task. They had no idea what was waiting for them up ahead, but judging by how eerily quiet everything felt, he knew it couldn't be anything good.

"This is Delta Battalion," Donovan said across the open channel. "We're four klicks out of Mexico City. Sensors are clean. No sign of activity up ahead."

"Roger, Delta," General Parker replied. "I don't expect it to stay that way for very long. You're practically on top of them."

"Affirmative, Actual. If the Dread had any history of ambushes, I'd think we're walking right into one."

"Roger that. Take your team further south and sweep back. I want you to have a clear line to retreat away from the city itself. The cover will help us close in on the fortress under fire."

"Affirmative, Actual." Donovan switched channels to the Battalion frequency. "You heard the General. We'll keep moving south and come in from the rear. Remember, our mission is to harass the enemy as much as possible. Mech One, out."

Donovan rotated the mech's torso toward Mexico City on his right. A waterfall of memories erupted from the sight of it, even though he had only been gone a few weeks. The missile silo, his mother, Matteo, and Diaz. General Rodriguez. The missions into the city to raise the transmission needle and connect with their brethren in space. His mind even wandered to his experience beneath the city, swimming through the sewers and winding up inside the fortress they were preparing to attack. Killing Tuhrik. Meeting Ehri. It all seemed so distant, and so close at the same time.

Humankind had been waiting fifty years for this moment.

Would they win the day?

"Mech One, this is Bertha Actual, I've got visual at three o'clock."

The CO of the second of the two infantry companies was steady as he reported the position. Lieutenant Colonel Dickerson, if Donovan remembered correctly. There had been so little time; it had been difficult to learn everyone's name.

"Roger, Bertha Actual," Donovan replied, checking his sensors. Whatever the man had seen, it was sitting beyond his range. He switched to the mech's networked communication system, opening a channel to the rest of the armors. "Mech Two, this is Mech One. Make a right turn and head toward the visual, see if you can get them on the HUD."

"Roger, Mech One," Ehri said, her mech turning immediately and heading toward the city.

Donovan tracked it on his HUD, watching the spot move away from their group. He put his eyes on the edge of the city, to the broken buildings that spotted the outskirts, and then to the more densely packed destruction beyond. He still wasn't seeing-

His mind switched gears when he caught sight of the movement and a flash of sunlight vanishing against the dark armor of a Dread mech.

"Mech Two, hold position," he said, bringing Ehri to a stop. "Actual, we have positive ID on the enemy. At least one mechanized armor, but I'm willing to bet there are more."

"Copy that, Delta. See if you can pull them out."

"Affirmative." Donovan switched systems again. "Able, Bertha, spread out and find cover. Bertha One Two, get Bravo Bravo online and in position."

"Roger, Delta Actual," the units replied.

Donovan steered his mech to the right, approaching Ehri. The Dread mech hadn't moved or revealed itself. It was stationary, shrouded by the remains of the skyscraper it was resting next to.

"They aren't attacking," Donovan said, opening a direct channel to Ehri's mech.

"No."

"Even though we're getting into a better position?"

"The Domo'dahm has decided to allow us to attack first. It is not required of a challenge, but he is acting confident."

"Should he be?"

"The domo'shah in orbit carried close to fifty mechanized armors and nearly fifteen thousand clone soldiers. I imagine they have left most of the armors behind, and a large contingent of the infantry. There is little reason to think that he is concerned about our assault. Clearly, his focus is on General St. Martin."

Donovan had known they were going to be outnumbered. It wasn't even the first time Ehri had outlined what they were up against. How the hell were they supposed to win, again?

He forced the sudden wave of panic down. He wondered how many of the other rebels out there were feeling the same way? It didn't help to think about what they were up against, or how impossible it seemed. If they didn't fight today, they were going to die tomorrow anyway. At least they were giving themselves a chance.

"Delta Actual, this is Bertha One Two. Bravo Bravo is online and in position."

"Roger, Bertha One Two," Donovan replied. "Prepare to fire on my mark."

"Affirmative."

"They will attack as soon as we fire, Colonel," Ehri said.

Donovan stared at the outline of the city in front of him. He turned the mech slightly, looking north to the remainder of the rebel army. They were still a few klicks behind, hanging back while Delta Battalion did its job.

"Actual, this is Delta," Donovan said. "We are in position to commence the attack. Bravo Bravo is prepared to fire. Waiting on your mark, sir."

"Roger, Delta," General Parker replied. "Hold tight."

There was a long pause. Donovan imagined the General was passing orders to the other battalions, getting them into position to make their runs. They didn't expect everyone to get through. They didn't need to all get in. The inside of the domo'shah would be lightly defended, or at least they hoped it would.

"Delta, this is Actual. All battalions are in position. Bertha One Two, fire on my mark."

Donovan's heart began to thump at the words. He quickly checked his renovated mech's weapons systems, confirming a full payload of projectile ammunition and a ready state on the plasma cannons.

"Delta Actual, this is Bertha One Two. If you could, please take two steps to the left."

Donovan swallowed, surprised by the statement. This was no time to lose it. "Roger, Bertha One Two," he replied, moving his mech to the side.

"Bertha One Two," General Parker's voice said. "Fire."

[49]

The beam from Big Bertha passed right beside Donovan, so close that the mech began bleating warnings into his ears. He took another involuntary step to the side, squinting his eyes in reaction to the brightness of the bolt as it streaked past.

Less than two seconds later, it speared its target, the dark shape of the mech Donovan had spotted vanishing against the point of light, vaporized by the power of the augmented weapon. The bolt continued through, into the city, blasting into a building and bringing the remains of it down into a heavier pile before fading away.

"So it begins," Donovan said to himself before connecting with the squad channel. "All units, move in." He shifted to the human radio mounted in front of him. "Able, Bravo, hold steady, we'll try to bring them to you. Prepare Bravo Bravo for another volley."

"Roger," the company COs replied.

The six mechs moved in toward the city limits, in the direction the plasma bolt had traveled. It would take another minute or two for the charge to rebuild in the cannon and allow it to fire with such devastating force again. They were on their own in the meantime.

Donovan had only made it a dozen steps before the plasma bolts began to pour from the city. They were well-aimed blasts that slammed into the mechs, catching them square and sending more warnings into his ears. One bolt wouldn't be nearly enough to drop the armor, but it was a bad omen of things to come. He slipped his armor to the side, tracking the source of the attack to locate the attackers. They were still hidden from his sensors, and he knew they shouldn't be.

It seemed the Domo'dahm hadn't just been sitting back and waiting.

"Actual, this is Delta. I'm not sure how, but it looks like the enemy is invisible to our sensors. Repeat, we're blind beyond line of sight."

The pause before General Parker's response was long enough Donovan knew he was trying to work out a new approach on the fly. Without sensor readings, they had no idea what their main force was stepping into.

"Roger, Delta." Another pause. "It's too late to turn back now. Get us a path if you can."

"Roger," Donovan said, shifting his mech as a plasma bolt streaked past. He checked the location in the HUD and fired back, quieting the enemy attack for a moment. He shifted to the mech comm. "Okay people, we're going in. Head for the front lines, we'll try to engage and start pulling them south. Bertha One Two, hold position. Bertha One Three, Bertha One Four, stay with Bertha One Two and provide fire support. Mech Six, hang back with Bertha One Two, we can't afford to let them hit Bravo Bravo."

He looked up as the units affirmed his instructions. Luckily, the air was still clear of gi'shah. A few good strafing runs would whittle their numbers down in a hurry, but it seemed the Domo'dahm was holding those resources in wait for the space force.

Donovan brought his mech ahead at full charge, running across the open space toward the cover of the outlying buildings. Of course, Ehri was tracking ahead of him, while Colonel Knight was hanging close to his side. Orli was in Mech Six, and she backed away toward Big Bertha while the others advanced.

Plasma bolts were joined by projectiles as they drew nearer to the city, and Donovan diverted to find cover behind a blown out building. Colonel Knight joined him there, while Ehri, Bastion, and Knowles found cover further south.

"This is Bertha One Two. Bravo Bravo is charged and ready. Fire in the hole."

A second massive plasma bolt streaked between the mech unit, blasting forward and striking its target. Donovan rose from cover behind it, just in time to see the remains of two mechs topple to the ground with a soft thud. He opened fire into the space around the blast, pouring projectiles and plasma into a third mech that had been forced into the open. It rocked from the attack, falling back as Colonel Knight added her firepower to his. It fell over a moment later and didn't move again.

"Mech One, this is Able Three One. We've got movement from the south. A whole lot of movement."

The commander of Third Platoon sounded frightened. Donovan turned south, his view blocked by a building. He sidestepped around it, searching for line of sight, nearly caught off-guard by an enemy mech that popped out from a nearby alley. A line of projectiles tore into his left arm, leaving a large, open wound before he could back away from it, getting himself under cover.

"I've got him, Mech One," Colonel Knight said, crossing his path and moving in on the mech. She was joined there by Bastion, catching the mech in the crossfire and mowing it down.

"Bertha One Two," Donovan said. "Get Bravo Bravo turned to the south and find a target. Fire when ready."

"Roger, Mech One."

"Mech One, this is Bravo Five One," Kroeger said, sounding angry. "We have incoming from the west. Transports, Colonel, just about ready to drop an entire army on our asses."

Donovan spun his mech to the west, looking back past their positions. He saw the transports dotting the sky behind them, two dozen at least. Damn.

"Nobody said this was going to be easy," he replied. "Actual, we have incoming from the south and rear."

"Roger, Delta," Parker replied, sounding a little overwhelmed. "Keep pushing forward, clear a lane. We'll handle the rear as best we can."

"Roger."

Donovan got his mech moving again, running parallel to the city in an effort to get a visual on the forces moving up from the south. He nearly shouted as a powerful plasma beam struck the building a few meters in front of him, sending chunks of slagged concrete rattling against his mech.

He rounded the debris and froze, making eye contact with two columns of Dread tanks, approaching almost leisurely from the south, a dozen mechs and a few hundred clones soldiers in support.

He bit down on his lip, preventing himself from saying out loud what he was thinking at that moment.

They were all going to die.

[50]

RORN'EL WATCHED THE BATTLE UNFOLD FROM THE DISCOMFORT of his throne, a projection of the battlefield being delivered to him from a gi'shah monitoring the fight from far above it. As he had suspected, the ground forces the humans had sent against him were far too little and far too weak to be of much concern, even with the large number of bek'hai assets they had taken. While the plasma cannon that had given his units so much trouble on the streets of Austin continued to inflict heavy damage, it wasn't as easy to move its position out here, and it would only be a matter of time before his forces got close enough to destroy it.

"Domo'dahm, shall we order the gi'shah to join the attack?" Orish'ek asked, observing the battle from his usual position. He spoke softly, as if he were already bored with the humans' efforts.

"No. We will follow the plan and keep the gi'shah in reserve for the Ishur."

"Domo'dahm, with all honor, we have an opportunity to make a quick end of the ground forces before they can reach the cover of the city. Should we not seize on it?"

Rorn'el considered it for a moment. He had expected the battle against the rebels to go smoothly, as long as they launched their attack before the Ishur arrived. His pur'dahm were not disappointing him, their forces circling the enemy and slowly boxing them in. In time, there would be nowhere for the humans to go. They would be surrounded on all sides, defeated whether they knew it then or not. How could the humans have believed they could possibly win this fight? Were they so desperate they had abandoned all reason? It certainly seemed so.

"Am I not the Domo'dahm?" Rorn'el hissed.

"Yes, Domo'dahm," Orish'ek replied, lowering his head.

"We do not need the gi'shah to win this battle." He pointed to the projection. "Look at how they are moving. Already, their formations are breaking down as they seek shelter from our soldiers. These are not warriors, Orish'ek. Their courage lasts only as long as they are away from our plasma."

"What about the mechanized armors?" Orish'ek asked, pointing to them on the display. "They are inflicting heavy damage on our units. We have lost ten mechs to their one already. That is more than we have ever lost in a single day since we arrived here."

"We won't need the mechs anymore, once this battle is over. What does it matter if we lose ten, or twenty, or even fifty? When we have defeated the Ishur, the humans will be broken. We can continue the extermination without distraction."

"The Ishur has yet to arrive."

"All the more reason to remain patient. Believe me, Orish'ek. The humans will either crumble when they see their last hope destroyed, or we will have crushed them long before that. Look. Look."

He pointed to where the humans had placed their plasma cannon. A single gur'shah was defending it, and while the pilot was fairly skilled they were about to be overcome. Three gur'shah were closing in on the position, along with an entire cycle of gel'shah and a hundred soldiers. The humans were putting up a solid fight, but they simply didn't have the numbers.

One of the gur'shah vanished as the plasma cannon fired for the last time, catching it head on and reducing it to slag. A few of the clones died with the hit, caught in the radius of the blast. Immediately after, five human soldiers lifted the cannon to their shoulders, attempting to change locations with it. He had seen them move it back a few times already while it recharged, but now there were more enemies at their back, closing in, sweeping through the rebels.

The gel'shah fired on the position, the entire cycle at once sending a mass of plasma into the area. The lone rebel gi'shah managed to avoid the bolts, but the cannon was not so fortunate. It exploded at the impact, sending shrapnel out and into the humans around it and killing dozens of them.

"That will be a strong hit on their will to fight," Rorn'el said. "I do not expect this battle to continue. The Ishur will come, but they will be fighting alone."

"Only if that one goes down," Orish'ek said, bringing Rorn'el's attention to another part of the battle. One of the rebel mechs was moving through the city, trailing a sizeable force behind it as they tried to destroy it. It moved unlike the others, with a smoothness and grace that was beyond human.

"Ehri dur Tuhrik," Rorn'el said. "There is none other that it could be. Their cannon is destroyed. Redeploy the gel'shah toward her location. I want her destroyed."

"Yes, Domo'dahm," Orish'ek said, shifting to his terminal. He spoke into it, and a moment later the gel'shah began moving back south in pursuit of the un'hai.

Rorn'el leaned back on his throne, his eyes drifting to the different parts of the projection, watching the humans scatter and break beneath the onslaught of his military. They had learned of the loss of their cannon, and even from above the effect on them was obvious. Whatever morale they had possessed when the fight began, it was quickly evaporating.

And where was the Ishur? His domo'shah were in position, ready to blow it to dust the moment it appeared from slipspace should General St. Martin be foolish enough to drop too close to the planet.

He was even prepared for it to come out of slipspace below their defensive web again, with over one hundred gi'shah and ek'shah ready to deploy at a moment's notice.

The General was a fool to challenge him. Any who might think to oppose him were fools for the idea. At the same time, in a way he was thankful for all that had happened since Ehri dur Tuhrik had allowed the humans to escape with their technology. After all, the human rebellion had continued for fifty cycles, and now they would be able to put an end to it, to all of it, within a single rotation.

He had sworn that he would see the humans extinct before his retirement, and he was glad it was a promise he would be able to keep.

He reached into his gori'shah robes, taking out the splintered crucifix from Juliet's rosary. He had always admired her desire for peace, her desire for understanding between the bek'hai and the humans, and her efforts to introduce them to her all-powerful God. But there was a great divide between admiration and agreement. Like the legri'shah, the humans were tools to be used. So it was for the strongest of the bek'hai, and so it would always be.

"Domo'dahm," Orish'ek said excitedly. "We have a report from the Ishkrem. A domo'shah has just appeared on our sensors. It is undoubtedly the Ishur, Domo'dahm."

"Undoubtedly," Rorn'el replied, his lips parting, his tongue flicking out between sharp teeth. "What is their position?"

"They are positioned behind the moon, Domo'shah, using it as a shield against a potential attack."

"General St. Martin was wise to be cautious, but it will not save him. Order the domo'shah to intercept the Ishur. Do not give it an avenue to escape."

"Yes, Domo'dahm."

Rorn'el turned his attention back to the earthbound battle. The General had arrived too late to prevent their defeat. Much too late. The truth of it gave him pause.

Why was the General so cautious, after all of his past maneuvers had been so bold?

There was something about it that he didn't trust, but he couldn't quite grasp what it was. Not that it mattered. The battle was already over, the war already won.

The humans just didn't know it yet.

[51]

GABRIEL BREATHED SLOWLY, FORCING HIMSELF TO REMAIN calm as the domo'shah's phase generators powered down, dropping the Ishur from slipspace back into reality. He felt a sudden wave of nausea at the change, his body affected by the number of times they had slipped in the last two weeks, and he swallowed and tried to focus beyond it.

"Status," he said, looking down at the skeleton crew helping him run the Magellan.

"The Ishur is out of slipspace," Miranda said, looking back at him. "Comm systems are online."

""Weapons systems are online," Colonel Choi said, staring at her tablet.

"Power levels are at one hundred percent," Sarah Larone said. Phase modulators are stable."

"The Dread zero-point reactor is purring like a kitten," Guy Larone said.

Gabriel nodded, his hand running across the controls of the starship from the command station. Everything was running the way it was supposed to, which meant it was all up to him now.

"Attention all hands, attention all hands," he said, opening a ship wide channel. "Prepare for ingress. I repeat, prepare for ingress. This is not a drill."

He couldn't see it, but he could picture the thousands of soldiers filling the belly of the repaired starship doing their best to buckle themselves in, preparing for the drop.

Gabriel had expected that Theodore would be the one making this run, piloting the ship with the same deft hand that had gotten it away from the Dread twice in the past. When his father had approached him during the all-hands and asked him to take the controls, he was both surprised and honored. The argument for the position was manifold. One, his father was a valuable symbol of the war, a figurehead that the rest of the forces both above and below the thermosphere could rally around. Second, he needed to stay around to help guide the Ishur during what promised to be a grueling fight against a superior defensive force. Third, while he had been successful navigating the Magellan inside of the planetary defenses, it was Gabriel who had the most experience dealing with approaching Earth from beyond them. He was the more seasoned pilot and as such more fitting for the job.

Finally, he had a secondary mission he was tasked to accomplish, one that required reaching Earth's surface. One that might mean the difference between victory and defeat.

"Magellan, this is Ishur Actual," Theodore said, his voice mixing with a small amount of static from their makeshift integrated systems. "We're nearly in position."

"Roger, Ishur Actual," Gabriel replied. "We're ready and waiting. Guy, can you do anything with that static?"

The Guy Larone who had once been a whiney, privileged ass had vanished right after the Magellan had landed on the Ishur. Since then, the scientist had been one of the most valuable cogs in their machine, helping to put Maggie back into fighting shape in record time. That he had volunteered for this mission was a testament to his change of heart.

"I'll see what I can do, sir," he said.

"Excellent. Spaceman Locke, is the DSS ready?"

"Yes, sir," Miranda replied.

While the DSS on the Ishur used a holographic projection to handle manipulation of the darkspace shields, the Magellan's system was more primitive, offering only a three-dimensional schematic of the ship on a table touchscreen, which could be manipulated and tapped to direct the phase modulation along the ship. More importantly, they had only one control unit to cover the ship, versus four on the Ishur. At least Maggie was a much smaller animal.

Gabriel checked the Magellan's sensors. He could see the domo'shah on the longer range array. Seven of them, already moving in their direction.

Time to thread the needle.

"On your mark, General," Gabriel said.

"Prepare for launch in five. Four. Three. Two. One. Go."

Gabriel tapped the control pad, quickly increasing the Magellan's forward vectoring thrusters, pushing the ship backward through the open hangar bay where they had landed. It took a good thirty seconds to get the ship clear of the Ishur, leaving them floating face-forward, drifting upward to the Dread fortress' bridge, giving him one last glimpse of the crew there as he manipulated the other thrusters, pushing the Magellan out and away.

"Magellan is away," Gabriel said. "I'll see you when it's over, Dad."

"Roger. Godspeed, and good hunting," Theodore replied, his voice slightly choked. "Give them hell."

"You, too."

Gabriel got Maggie facing toward the moon, and then hit the main thrusters, almost feeling the acceleration as the Dread reactor provided more than enough power to the ion generators. The ship burst forward, and he adjusted course as they neared the moon, using its gravity to slingshot them toward Earth.

They cleared the dark side within minutes, finding themselves nearly face-to-face with one of the incoming Dread domo'shah.

"Maggie, how long until the Dread starships reach the Ishur?" Gabriel asked at the same time he vectored to get around the fortress.

"At current velocity, twelve minutes and seventeen seconds," the computer replied.

"How long until we reach Earth's surface?"

"Eight minutes and four seconds."

Gabriel tensed for a moment. He had been hoping they could keep the Ishur back and away from the line of fire long enough for him to finish his secondary mission. It was an incredible long shot to begin with, but now he knew it would be impossible.

"We've got incoming fire," Miranda said, as the domo'shah ahead of them began firing its secondary batteries.

Her hand moved across the tablet, guiding the DSS to the impact points, blocking as many of the bolts as she could. The thick armor handled the rest, taking the hit from the smaller plasma cannons without serious damage.

"Taking evasive maneuvers," Gabriel said, firing top thrusters to drop the Magellan from its current plane. He reversed course as the bolts began sweeping down, crossing over them and rising above while the gunners on the Dread ship tried to adjust.

"Enemy starfighters incoming," Miranda said, helping him keep track of the threat display, impressing him with her ability to multi-task with the DSS.

"There's nothing we can do about them," he replied. "Their weapons won't do much against us."

Blue flashes passed all around them as they neared the domo'shah, and a second started releasing volleys in their direction. The Dread starfighters maneuvered around the two fortress' attacks, mixing in and making strafing runs across the Magellan's bow. The power flickered on the bridge, the terminals blanking out for a second before returning.

"We may have lost a conduit," Guy said. "Good thing we added backups. Rerouting."

Gabriel shook his head. He had to do more. He adjusted the vectoring thrusters, throwing the Magellan into a wild rotation.

Plasma bolts streamed past them, only a few passing the combination of his maneuvers and the DSS.

"Are the enemy ships following?" he asked as they slipped past the fortresses.

"The starships are maintaining course for the Ishur," Miranda replied. "The fighters have split up, though. We've got a tail."

Gabriel could see the smaller ships on the Magellan's display. They were trying to gain velocity to keep up with the larger ship, but it was unclear if they would succeed. It didn't matter. A new threat had appeared ahead of them in the form of the smaller Dread starships. They were on an intercept course, on their way to take them out.

"Targets incoming," Miranda said, too late.

Gabriel adjusted the vectoring thrusters again, leveling the ship and turning it to run perpendicular to the Earth. The Dread ships began firing their plasma weapons, creating another barrage of fire for him to avoid.

"I wish we could use our guns," he said. He and Theodore had decided not to risk them on the way down, in fear of revealing their existence and having them destroyed before the Magellan reached the surface. A few plasma cannons weren't going to be the difference between success and failure on this part of the mission.

He cursed as the lights flickered on the bridge again, and the gravity control momentarily shut down, leaving him rising against his restraints. He shot a look over at Guy, who was tapping furiously on his tablet. They had forgone any non-essential crew, leaving nobody down in engineering to speak to their damage. If Maggie couldn't report it, it didn't exist.

"We're taking a lot of fire, sir," Miranda said, doing her best to keep the DSS moving, blocking the attacks. "I can't keep up."

"I know," Gabriel replied. "You're doing great. Maggie, ETA to the atmosphere?"

"Three minutes, six seconds," the computer replied.

Too long. Much too long. His forward throttle was maxed out, the ship gaining velocity as quickly as it could. The smaller Dread ships were closing in and smelling blood, and a second contingent of starfighters had been sent in.

They weren't going to make it.

He gritted his teeth, his hands moving over the flight controls as quickly as they could, adjusting thrust, changing direction, trying to throw the enemy ships off their tail. They continued to take fire, the ship vibrating as plasma bolts burned into the hull, some of the attacks avoiding the DSS.

He had survived too many runs just like this one to die now.

He changed course, pointing the Magellan toward the nearest starship.

"This worked the last time," he said. "Put the DSS on the bow, Spaceman Locke."

"Roger," Miranda replied without hesitation.

He could see the dark point shift the front of the Magellan, and he looked ahead of it to the quickly approaching starship. The shields captured the incoming volley of plasma, bringing them closer and closer to the ship.

At the last second, the Dread commander blinked. The ship began vectoring away, trying to avoid the bow of the Magellan before it speared them. Instead of a direct hit, Gabriel scored a glancing blow, one that tore a gash in the bottom of the enemy ship on their way by. It vented atmosphere, its attack fading as it sought to stabilize.

The Magellan continued its descent toward the planet, the automatic Dread defense systems drawing near. They began to activate, directional thrusters aligning them toward Maggie as she approached. The good news was that they were simple machines, and they didn't understand the idea of the darkspace shields. They focused their attack on the same point against the Magellan's bow, allowing Miranda to place the shields and leave them, absorbing the firepower of the defensive net as they neared.

More Dread ships were closing in, firing with a fury that lit up the darkness of space. Gabriel skirted the Magellan around most of it, and Miranda caught a large portion of the rest. They were taking fire, but it was a light rain shower instead of a potential deluge.

"Hull breach on deck nine," Sarah said a moment later. "Bulkheads are sealing, but. Oh, Colonel, we had people down there."

Gabriel winced. They needed to get inside the thermosphere and headed for Mexico City. He adjusted thrust again, diving toward the nearest defense pods. The systems peppered the Magellan with fire right up until the starship slammed into them, the darkspace shields throwing them violently out of the way or smashing them completely.

Then they were through, dropping ever downward toward the planet.

"Maggie, enter coordinates for Mexico City and give me a guideline," Gabriel said.

"Setting coordinates," Maggie replied. "Guideline activated."

A flight path appeared on his command screen, giving him the optimal route to the city even as the ship began to shake, hitting the thermosphere and working to break through. Heat flared ahead of them while the ship made its second approach to Earth in a month, the Dread starfighters remaining behind it, still shooting at them as they crossed into the upper atmosphere.

"We're in," Miranda announced.

"Activate all batteries," Gabriel said, watching the ground growing beneath them as they swept toward the surface. "Fire at will."

The new weapons systems were separate from the pre-existing controls, and Colonel Choi took control of them without hesitation, tapping the commands to rotate them on their turrets. They didn't have a complete field of fire, but there was one battery that could reach behind them, and she didn't waste any time triggering the system. The plasma cannon sent bolt after bolt at the fighters behind them, forcing them to evade.

"Almost there," Gabriel said, the dark spot of the Dread capital becoming visible on the ground ahead of them. "Miranda, activate our comm system, let's see if we can get the ground forces on the line."

"Roger." She abandoned the DSS for a moment, leading to the ship shaking as it took another hit. She tapped the console ahead of her, activating the radio. "Comm online. Channel open."

"Earth Rebellion. This is Major Gabriel St. Martin in the starship Magellan. Do you copy? Over."

A flow of static greeted him from the open channel.

"Guy, are we getting anything?" he asked, jerking the ship to the left as Colonel Choi's defenses hit one of the Dread fighters. "Nice shooting, Colonel."

"Working on it," Guy said, tapping his controls. "Try again, please, sir."

"Earth Rebellion. This is Major Gabriel St. Martin in the starship Magellan. Do you copy? Over."

"Major St. Martin, this is General Alan Parker. Damn, you showed up just in time. We're getting our asses kicked down here."

He had a feeling the Ishur wasn't doing much better above him. "I'm looking for Major Donovan Peters, is he with you?"

He held his breath waiting for the reply. Their plan would be easier to follow if the Major and the clone were still alive.

"Colonel Peters is commanding the mech unit," General Parker replied.

"Is the clone with him?"

"Clone? You mean Ehri or Orli?"

There were two Juliet clones down there? "I don't know, sir. I never learned her name."

"He's not responding to my requests," Parker said. "It could be that his comm is offline. The mech unit is taking a pounding. We all are."

"Understood, General. We'll see what we can do to help."

"Whatever you're going to do, do it fast, son."

Gabriel's eyes tracked over the landscape in front of the ship. The city was getting close, and he reversed throttle in response, slowing the starship down. She wasn't intended for atmospheric flight, and the anti-gravity systems would only do so much.

It was going to be a rough landing any way he tried it, but as his eyes landed on a pair of mechs squaring off against a second, almost identical pair backed by a line of lek'shah carapaced vehicles that resembled tanks, he was satisfied to at least have an idea of where to land.

"Don't worry, General," he replied. "I intend to."

[52]

DONOVAN BACKED AWAY, HIS EYES SWEEPING THE LANDSCAPE ahead of him in search of even the barest of cover.

It had been nearly an hour since the battle against the Dread had started. An hour of running and shooting, ducking, and hiding, pausing and issuing commands to a quickly diminishing battalion.

They had lost Big Bertha nearly thirty minutes ago to a heavy assault by the Dread mechs and tanks, an assault that had also claimed Orli as she tried to take on six heavy armors at one time. They had lost Bastion and Knowles at some point, too, their mechs blasted to slag by the deadly gel'shah that seemed to be in endless supply. Half of Able and two-thirds of Bertha were also down, and their mission to pull the enemy away from the Dread capital was a total and complete failure.

Donovan had long given up the idea of winning this fight. Instead, he had decided that he would press on, keep attacking, and take as many of the bastards with him as he could. His mech was beaten but not quite broken, pitted and scarred across most of the surface, out of projectile ammunition and overheating from the constant use of the plasma cannons. He was coated in sweat and soaking wet, the gori'shah unable to wick the moisture away quick enough. His legs were tired, too, tired of maneuvering the mech away from the enemy, of trying to keep pace with Ehri as she tore apart all comers. She was a machine. He was only a man.

Where was General St. Martin, he wondered, as he sidestepped another bolt fired from a gel'shah, ducking down behind a pile of rubble and raising his right arm over it to fire his plasma cannon. Ehri was circling behind him, using the same cover, silent in her focus. The General was supposed to be here today. Donovan hadn't realized what a wide block of time that was until now. An hour was all it would take for the rebel army to fall apart, to be decimated and sent to early graves. General Parker had even given up on sending orders through the comm, leaving him to himself as he did his best to wreak havoc before he too was destroyed.

The enemy mech ahead of him paused, waiting while the three gel'shah behind it fired on the rubble, blasting it away, sending shrapnel thunking off his lek'shah shell and leaving him in the open. He forced his legs to move again, pushing the mech away from the scene, hoping Ehri would see and follow. She didn't. Instead, she broke the other direction, laying down suppressing fire and drawing the attention away from him. The mechs stayed on her, launching another barrage, blasting her mech in the leg and torso. He saw something break, a loud pop, and the mech fell to one knee.

She wouldn't survive another shot like that. He reversed course, sending his mech to block them, trying to get in front of her before they could fire once more. The enemy mechs were closing in, and there was no way he was going to reach her in time.

The thought caused him to stumble, his mech nearly toppling over from the motion of his exhaustion. Only backup systems kept it upright, though it slowed considerably at the miss. He cursed, pushing harder, while two of the gel'shah brought her mech into their sights.

He checked his HUD. His sensors were dead, the array long destroyed. It suddenly occurred to him that maybe that's why everything was so quiet. Had his comm system been destroyed as well?

"This is Delta Actual. Can anyone hear me?" he said over the human channels. He switched to the networked mechs. "Ehri, do you read me? Over."

There was no reply.

He kept moving, trying to reach her but knowing he couldn't. One of the gel'shah fired, and somehow she managed to tip her mech sideways, bringing it over to avoid the blast. It crumpled onto its side and then rolled onto its back, giving the enemy a smaller profile. He thought it was odd when she didn't move right away.

Then he looked up.

He had barely noticed the din of the starship approaching; he had become so numb to the noise of battle. When he saw the long bow of the Magellan dropping toward him, he didn't know whether to laugh, cry, or wet himself. When a series of plasma bolts traced from the sides of the ship and into the enemy position nearby and destroyed the gel'shah and one of the mechs, he almost did all three.

"Oh, shit," he cried. "Wooooo!"

He limped his mech toward Ehri, still trying to reach her and block her from the remaining enemy. More plasma bolts rained down from the Magellan, the growl of the incoming ship growing louder with each second. More of the Dread armor vanished beneath the assault, mounds of dirt spraying aside and crystallizing as each powerful blast slammed into the ground.

The earth began to shake as the Magellan neared, the roar so loud that it drowned out everything around it. Donovan saw the fighters now, the Dread gi'shah peppering the ship with fire and trying to avoid its return volleys. It was coming in fast, so fast, its forward and hull thrusters at full burn to break the velocity. He could feel the pressure from them, the heat, and he tucked over Ehri as it buffeted against him. The Dread mechs weren't quick enough, and the force of the displaced air knocked them down and pushed them back.

It was as though God had dropped a steel wall from the sky. The Magellan seemed to float a dozen meters in the air beside him before tumbling straight down, countless kilograms of mass dropping onto four heavy landing gear that extended from the hull just in time. The ground shook harder as they hit the surface and began to sink, hydraulics flexing to catch the rest of the bulk. He knew the ship had anti-gravity technology within it that would make it lighter, but it was still a heavy beast.

The ship dipped slightly and then rose again, coming to rest on the gear with a satisfied thunk. The plasma cannons on the starship continued to move and fire, tracing airborne targets and continuing to slam the ground forces now blockaded by the Magellan's sizable bulk.

Then the next part of the miracle came. Three ramps dropped from the side of the ship, extending to the ground below. Soldiers poured out from them, men and women in neat gray uniforms charging down the ramp and into the battle. They avoided the heavy armors but swept across and back toward the city, where the embattled infantry was making its stand. They moved with a uniformity that Donovan had never seen from the rebels, a clear contrast to the two different types of training they had received.

Donovan shifted his mech away from Ehri's, looking down as he did. Her cockpit slid open, and she climbed out, looking up at him. She pointed at herself and then at the Magellan. She was going to it.

He decided to follow.

[53]

"Status," Gabriel shouted, getting to his feet as the Magellan came to rest.

"We're down," Miranda replied. "No luck getting through to Major Peters, though."

"Colonel Graham is deploying the units to the ground," Colonel Choi said. "Hopefully they'll remember to follow their training, instead of marveling over the fresh air."

"It doesn't look that fresh," Gabriel said. "It probably smells like burned flesh out there. We went over it all with them a dozen times on the way over. They'll do their jobs. Colonel Choi, you have the bridge."

"Where are you going?" Choi asked, not breaking her concentration from operating the plasma cannons.

"I have to find Major Peters and the clone," he said.

"Why?"

"My father didn't tell you?"

"No." She dared a glance at him. "What are you two up to?"

"Trying to save the world," Gabriel replied. "Give me three minutes to get off this boat, and then get her back in the sky. We can offer wider fire support hovering over the site than sitting down here."

"Who's the Colonel here?" Choi said.

"If you will, ma'am," Gabriel added.

"I'll take care of it."

Gabriel broke for the exit before pausing. "Miranda," he shouted. She looked up from the DSS display. "I love you."

"I love you too," she replied, but he was already out the door.

He ran down the corridor, his boots clanking along the metal flooring as he headed for the nearest exit. He paused at the nearest armory; a single Dread rifle left intentionally for him to claim. He grabbed the weapon before continuing on, spilling out into the wide hangar where light from outside was filtering in from the open ramp.

He hurried toward it, his heart racing, hoping beyond hope that the mechs they had saved were being piloted by the Major and the Juliet clone. So much had gone right so far, why not that?

He was halfway across the hangar when two figures appeared at the top of the ramp, silhouetted by the light. At first, Gabriel raised the rifle, unsure of their intentions. Then he caught a glimpse of the long red hair and cherubic face of his mother, dirty as it was.

"Captain St. Martin?" Major Peters said.

"Major Peters," Gabriel replied, unable to hold back his smile. "Thank God."

"We got your father's message," the Major said. "Where is he? Where's the Ishur?"

"In trouble," Gabriel said. "We need to go."

"Go? What do you mean?"

"You," he said, pointing at the clone. "What's your name?"

"Juli... Ehri," she said, catching herself.

"Major, we need to get into the Dread capital asap. It doesn't matter how, but we have to find a way. My father is a hell of a pilot and a hell of a commander, but there are seven Dread fortresses up there trying to blow him into space dust."

"Captain, I appreciate your enthusiasm," Major Peters said. "We're nearly four kilometers away from the domo'shah, and there's a battlefield separating us."

"I don't care," Gabriel said. "In four minutes, those ships are going to reach the Ishur's position and start firing. Do you know what happens then?"

Major Peters' face turned pale, and he nodded. "Okay. How are we going to get there before that happens?"

Gabriel pointed to the corner of the hangar. There was something low and long sitting in the shadows there. An excavator they had brought in from Alpha Settlement. "It doesn't look like much, but it's as heavily armored as anything else we have. Let's go."

The three of them ran to the machine. It had a drill mounted to the front of it, and a mechanical arm with a second drill attached to the rear. Gabriel led them onto the top of it, and then down into a manual hatch.

"Close that up for me, will you?" Gabriel asked as he moved to the front of the narrow internal confines and fell into the driver's seat.

Ehri paused, grabbing the hatch and pulling it closed.

Gabriel pressed the ignition, bringing the machine to life with a soft hum. The battery was only good for a hundred kilometers or so, but they didn't need to go anywhere near that far.

"Here we go," he said, pushing the control yoke forward.

The excavator shuddered and jerked as it built up power, and then kicked ahead toward the ramp and onto it, heading down and building speed. Donovan grabbed for the side of the machine as it slammed into the ground, bouncing back up and shaking from side to side before leveling out.

"Sorry," Gabriel said. "Major, we had a pilot crash land after our first meeting. Captain Soon Kim. I don't suppose you know what happened to him?"

Gabriel turned his head, his heart sinking when he saw Donovan's expression.

"I'm sorry, Captain. We rescued him after the crash, and he was with us for a while. He was killed in action back in Texas."

Daphne was going to be heartbroken. He felt his own sense of loss at the news. There would be time for mourning later. "I understand. Thank you, Major."

"He was a good man. A hell of a mech pilot, too."

"He was." Gabriel paused, pushing those emotions aside. "Major, there's a standard radio over there. You should be able to tune into your people's frequency through it."

Donovan dropped into a small seat beside a series of analog switches. "Please, call me Donovan. How do I use it?"

"Donovan, the dial tunes the frequency. Press down on the button to speak. It's old tech, but it works. By the way, my name is Gabriel."

"I know," Donovan replied. "You St. Martins have quite a reputation."

Gabriel felt the ground shake as the Magellan fired her bottom thrusters, beginning to process to regain altitude. It would have put an impossible strain on her original power supply to stay inside gravity for any length of time. With the Dread reactor, she could remain almost indefinitely.

"We can't see if anything is attacking us in here," Ehri said, finally making her way to the front.

Gabriel scanned the world outside through a narrow window. He could see the Magellan's troops ahead of him, working their way toward the city. "The armor is meant to withstand mountains falling on top of it. We can take a pretty solid beating."

"I think I've got it," Donovan said from the co-pilot seat. "Actual, this is Delta, do you read me? Over. Actual, this is Delta. Over."

"Colonel, is that you?" Kroeger said after Donovan repeated himself a few times.

"Kroeger," Donovan replied. "What's your sitrep?"

"I've got three guys from my unit with me, holed up in a building near the front lines. We've been sniping any of the clone bastards that show their faces and trying to help the rest of the units through to the fortress, but they've got a serious barricade in the way. Mechs and tanks, and they ain't moving."

Gabriel looked back at Donovan. "Colonel Choi will spot the defenses and start hitting them. We need to be ready to move in."

"Roger that," Donovan said. "Kroeger, did you see the starship that landed behind you?"

"Yes, sir."

"She's one of ours, and she's ticked off. See if you can organize a team to make a break for the fortress when she starts clearing the field. We'll be right behind you in a big ugly thing with a pointed front."

"Hell yes, sir," Kroeger replied. "Sir, it looks like she's got a lot of mosquitos biting at her neck."

Gabriel didn't like the sound of that.

"Oh, there goes one," Kroeger said a moment later. "Ouch. That had to hurt. Who's shooting on that thing?"

Gabriel smiled, keeping the excavator on track.

"The tide is turning, Donovan," he said. "I can feel it."

"You and me both, Gabriel. You and me both."

[54]

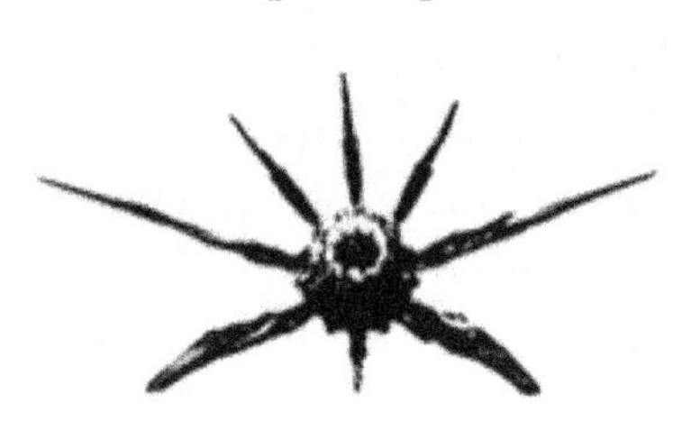

Theodore kept his eyes glued to the Magellan from the time it backed out of the Ishur's hangar until it vanished around the dark side of the moon. He felt a heavy mixture of fear and pride at the sight of it, knowing it was his boy out there instead of him, running the gauntlet on a mission that was as impossible as anything they had ever tried.

A mission as impossible as getting a starship away from Earth during an alien invasion.

Once the Magellan had vanished from sight, he settled back into the Dread command chair, shifting a few times to get comfortable. Alan was sitting at the station directly in front of him, and he glanced back knowingly. The two men had their past differences, but the shared goal had brought back the friendship they had once shared. Grudges were pointless, especially when lives were at stake.

"Alan, how long do we have?" he asked.

"About twelve minutes," General Cave replied.

Theodore shifted in his seat again. He picked up the tablet that was spliced into the terminal in front of him and checked the threat display for himself. Seven ships. Seven! He smiled. The Domo'dahm wasn't taking any chances with them.

"The question now is, how do we stay alive long enough for Gabriel to do what he needs to do?"

He said it out loud, posing it to his bridge crew. He was down some of his most trusted people after they volunteered to go with Gabriel. James, Vivian, Miranda, Guy and Sarah Larone. Had he made a mistake letting Spaceman Locke go with Gabriel? Would she have accepted his decision if he had said no? He doubted it.

"We can slip away and come back," Reza said, offering up a suggestion.

"And leave our people behind? No. Never again."

"Then what if we reverse course? Back away? We can gain about six minutes."

"And be that much further away from Earth," Theodore replied. "Let's split the difference. Colonel Ames, reverse at half."

"Yes, sir," Colonel Ames replied.

"Any other ideas?"

There was silence on the bridge.

"Mr. Mokri, can you give me an estimate of how long we'll last against seven Dread fortresses based on our shield accuracy from that tangle with the last two coullions?"

"Yes, sir. One minute."

Reza began working on his tablet while the precious seconds ticked away. Theodore didn't waste them, considering their other options.

"What if we charge one of the flanks?" General Cave asked. "Get in close. It will make it harder for them to all target us at once."

"Not a bad thought, but close range makes the DSS less effective. We need to find the right balance."

"Do we have time to slip past them, and get them all gathered on one side? That will lower our profile and make it easier to cover the area with the shields."

"Except it won't. The modulation only covers a small area at any given time. Multiple angles of attack give us four points to try to defend ourselves with instead of one. Again, it's a balance."

Another minute of silence followed.

"I have the calculation, sir," Reza said. "At optimal DSS positioning, we can gain another eight minutes."

"Giving Gabriel about twenty," Theodore said. "That's not enough time."

Two more minutes of silence had passed when the edge of the first fortress appeared around the corner of the moon, dark and imposing.

"They're launching fighters, sir," General Cave said a moment later.

Small ships would be hard-pressed to take down the Ishur alone, but they could get in close and weaken it.

"ETA?"

"Four minutes, seven seconds."

"Scramble the defenses," Theodore said. "Get our units out there."

"Yes, sir."

General Cave reached out to Lieutenant Bale, who got the squadron launched. Sixteen fighters, a mix of human and Dread configurations, along with the two ek'shah, moved out ahead of the backing up fortress, shooting ahead toward the oncoming swarm of enemy ships. If they were lucky, the Dread either hadn't figured out how to shrink the modulation to cover their fighters or didn't care enough about them to bother. It had taken some time for the assemblers to make the phase paint, but it was the one advantage they held.

"Ishur Actual, this is Red One," Lieutenant Bale said, her channel patched into the bridge. "We are in position."

"Roger, Red One," Theodore said. "Don't dilly-dally on my account. You see a snake; you choke it."

"Roger," she replied. "You heard the General. Let's give them hell."

The smaller ships burst forward on flares of thrusters, splitting apart as they approached the oncoming enemy mass. Plasma bolts began littering the space between them seconds later as the battle was truly joined.

Theodore watched from the bridge, his eyes darting across the swarm of ships as they circled and danced around one another. He saw an enemy fighter get the drop on one of their fighters, firing plasma into its rear. He smiled when a flare of darkspace appeared, swallowing the bolt.

"Thank God for that," he said, as the same enemy starfighter was hit by one of Lieutenant Bale's bolts and stopped maneuvering, drifting away from the battle.

He was quickly snapped out of his reverie when a flare of light near the moon caught his attention. The first Dread fortress had completed its circuit and taken a long-range pot shot at them.

"We're under fire," General Cave said. "Sergeant Abdullah, that one's yours."

"Yes, sir. I have it, sir," Abdullah replied, manipulating the DSS. The bolt flared as it hit the darkspace shield and then vanished.

"What are those couillons thinking?" Theodore said. "They should know they can't slip one by from that range."

"There's no harm in trying," General Cave replied.

"No, I suppose not."

Theodore checked on the fighter groups. They were holding their own, making quick work of the Dread forces with the help of their superior shields. The ships were small enough that the modulation offered full coverage from enemy attacks.

"Another shot incoming from the port side," General Cave said, monitoring the domo'shah.

A second fortress had cleared the moon and fired. Three more were almost clear enough to join the attack.

"Here it comes," Theodore said.

Except there was no plan that gave them more than twenty minutes. Not without a miracle.

He closed his eyes, his thoughts drifting to Juliet.

"I know you're out there," he said softly. "Somewhere better than this. Somewhere peaceful and free. I know you've done your best to get us this far, and I know it isn't fair to ask, but I don't suppose you have one more blessing to pass on? It isn't for me. It's for the people on board. The civilians. The ones who trust in me to keep them safe. They're counting on me. They believe in me like I believe in you."

"Three more bolts incoming," General Cave said. "More fighters are heading this way."

Theodore kept his eyes closed in silent prayer, hoping that something would come to him. Some way of keeping them alive. The seconds passed. The Ishur shuddered as the first of the Dread bolts slipped past their defenses.

"Damn," Sergeant Abdullah said. "They're spacing out their shots, but firing at the same time. I can't cover them all."

The Ishur shuddered again.

"Theodore, we need to do something," General Cave said. "We're out of time." He turned back toward Theodore. "Teddy? Don't quit on us now. We need you."

Theodore opened his eyes. Juliet hadn't answered him, and that was okay. He knew what it meant.

"Quit? Oh no, I'm not about to quit. Just thinking is all. Hoping for a miracle, too. If God isn't going to give us one, we'll have to make it for ourselves. Colonel Ames, reverse course, full ahead."

"Yes, sir," Colonel Ames replied.

"What are you thinking?" General Cave asked.

"Stay alive, as long as we can, any way we can. Estimates are just estimates. It's our will to fight, our will to live that's going to decide our fate. Tell Red One we're on the move, and to either pack it in and hitch a ride or keep fighting. It's her call."

"Yes, sir."

Theodore surveyed the field ahead as General Cave made the call. He never expected the fighters to disengage and come home, and he wasn't surprised when they didn't.

He located each of the domo'shah. All seven had cleared the moon now, and the change in direction was bringing them in faster and faster. As Abdullah had said, they were synchronizing their attacks, firing all seven heavy plasma cannons at once, clustered but not joined. It was an impossible task for the Sergeant to continue to block them all.

"Colonel, evasive maneuvers, do your best to keep them guessing."

"Yes, sir."

The Ishur shook again, another plasma beam striking one of the long slipspace fins. It sparked and vented oxygen as it was torn from the fortress.

"Too close," Theodore said.

"General, shouldn't we attack them?" Reza asked.

"What good will that do, Mr. Mokri? We can't afford to sit still and pour energy into their shields, and we certainly don't want a wandering wormhole sucking up our planet."

Reza's face paled. "Yes, sir."

"Colonel, see if you can get us in close to that one over there. Alan's idea isn't perfect, but it's the best we've got. We'll try to bounce around it and hope we can slow their attack. Mr. Mokri, head down to engineering. When things get bad, I intend to spike the shields, and I need you to do your best to keep the modulators from exploding."

"Uh. Yes, sir."

Reza stood and ran from the room, heading for the inner bowels of the ship.

"When things get bad?" General Cave said. "I think we're already there, Teddy."

"Heh. You ain't seen nothing yet."

"You're putting a lot of faith in your son."

"I gotta put it somewhere, Alan. He'll come through. I know he will."

[55]

"There she goes," Gabriel said, pointing through the small viewport of the excavator.

Donovan could feel the pressure from above, the Magellan's anti-gravity systems pushing down on the planet and on them. He could hear the harsh hissing of the thrusters, and he opened his mouth to pop his ears one more time.

He looked forward through the viewport, at the line of enemy targets ahead. They had abandoned the ground forces as the starship had moved in position over them, sending everything they had up into the belly of the ship and causing black splotches to spread across the painted hull, splotches that seemed to be absorbing at least a portion of the damage the Dread were inflicting.

Their attacks were countered by the plasma cannon mounted to the bottom of the ship. They slammed into the Dread mechs, cutting them down one by one in a fight that seemed less than fair. The Domo'dahm had made a huge mistake by sending all of his fortresses out to attack General St. Martin and leaving the Magellan and the space forces free to seize control of the ground battle.

They had already driven through the city, where the soldiers in the gray uniforms were making short work of the enemy clones, and even the few pur'dahm he had spotted in their battle armor. The Dread warriors were fast and strong, but the soldiers had them outnumbered, and their aim was steady and true, so much more so than a good portion of the rebels. These were people who had spent their lives preparing for war, not focusing on survival from one day to the next. All they had ever needed was an opportunity and a weapon that could hurt the enemy, and now they had both.

"Kroeger, we're almost at your position," Donovan said. "What have you got for us?"

"The remnants of a dozen units," Kroeger replied. "Including part of General Parker's company. The General's dead."

Donovan winced at the news. No wonder he hadn't been able to raise him on the comm. "We're almost at your position. Do we have an opening?"

"You will in a minute, Major. That ship is cutting through them assholes like they're made of paper."

"Donovan, switch to channel seventy-two," Gabriel said from the driver's seat.

Donovan turned the dial, watching the numbers climb. He stopped at seventy-two.

"Do you want to broadcast?" he asked.

Gabriel nodded, and he pressed the transmit button down.

"Alpha Actual, this is Major St. Martin. Colonel Graham, can you hear me?"

"Major, this is Alpha Actual. I hear you. Was that you in the excavator?"

"Yes, sir. Radio the others, switch to channel-" Gabriel paused.

"Twenty-six," Donovan said for him.

"Channel twenty-six. We're preparing to move on the capital."

"Roger. Switching now."

Donovan moved the dial back to its original channel.

"This is Alpha Actual, Colonel James Graham of the Earth Alliance."

"We hear you, Colonel," Donovan said. "What's your position?"

"We're about halfway through the city. It's getting harder to find targets out here."

"Good. How quickly can you reach the western side of the city?"

"Where the fortress is parked? I can get a battalion there in ten minutes."

"Too slow," Gabriel said. "He'll have to bring up the rear."

"Roger, Colonel. Major St. Martin suggests you bring up the rear. We're heading for the ship."

"What's the hurry, Gabriel?" Colonel Graham replied.

"We may be winning down here right now, but once the Ishur is destroyed those ships will be coming back. When they do, you can bet they'll hit both the Magellan and this city from space. We have to stop the Ishur from being destroyed."

"How are we going to do that from down here?"

"My father had a plan."

"He's playing it close to the chest, then. He didn't tell me anything about it."

"No, sir."

"Are you going to tell me?"

"No, sir."

Donovan reached out to steady himself as the excavator rounded a corner, slamming into a pile of rubble and pushing it out of the way. He could see the Dread capital rising up directly ahead of them, a kilometer away and backed by deep craters where the other domo'shah had been resting. The line of mechs and tanks had taken a pounding from the Magellan, and there was a clear opening between them.

"Kroeger," Donovan said. "Get your people on the move. Double-time. We're coming in."

"Yes, sir," Kroeger replied.

The soldiers poured out of every dark crack and crevice ahead of them, nearly two hundred people strong. They ran ahead toward the break in the defenses while the excavator gained from behind.

The Magellan loomed above them, firing down at the defenses and up at the circling Dread starfighters. There was more activity from the domo'shah now, a mass of airborne reinforcements bursting from the top of it as the Domo'dahm decided to up the ante.

"Gabriel," Donovan said, pointing toward the new targets.

"I see them," he replied. "We have to keep moving."

The pilot of the Magellan seemed to see them too, because the ship began shifting forward, moving over the ground forces as they raced across the broken terrain toward the capital. Plasma bolts tore into the top of the ship, and Donovan could hear the return fire and the explosions when the Magellan's cannons hit the gi'shah.

They kept going, the excavator overtaking the soldiers. Donovan recognized Kroeger as they moved up on him, and the former jackal smiled at the sight of the machine, slowing down and leaping onto it as it passed. A few of the others saw his maneuver and did the same, climbing onto the vehicle as it churned toward the Dread ship.

They covered half a kilometer, bringing the capital so close it became a black wall in front of them and bringing the Magellan within the angle of the secondary batteries. They began firing, heavy plasma heating the air above them and slamming the starship with volley after volley. Donovan could hear loud pops and cracks above them, and he knew the ship was taking a beating, risking itself to protect them as they ran.

A shift in the pressure from above told him when the Magellan had suffered one critical strike too many. He looked at Gabriel, whose face was tight with concern. He leaned up and over the control yoke, trying to get a look at the Magellan, shaking his head.

"She's going to crash," he said, his voice cracking. "Damn it."

They couldn't see it happen from their protective cocoon, but they heard it a minute later and felt it when the ground shuddered beneath the impact. Had the pilot managed to avoid hitting any of their own? The ship was so big; it seemed impossible.

Plasma bolts began to land around them from all sides, the gi'shah from the air joining the gur'shah and gel'shah on the ground. Donovan heard a scream from outside as someone was hit, and he felt the heat of the plasma burning into the armor above them. Maybe they weren't doing as well as he had thought.

He shifted his position to see through the small viewport, surprised to find that they were nearly on top of the fortress and racing toward a cavernous opening ahead. Gabriel didn't seem concerned that there were only the three of them and the few other soldiers who had managed to cling to the excavator to wage their war inside the ship. He was focused on getting there. And then what? He said he had a plan of some kind that involved him and Ehri.

Whatever it was, he hoped it was good.

[56]

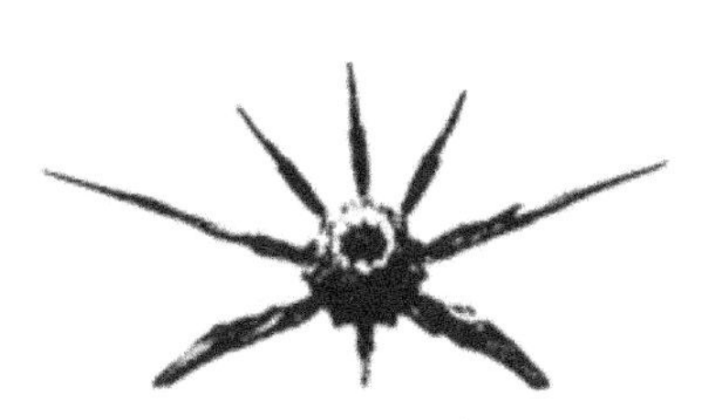

THE EXCAVATOR SLIPPED INTO THE OPEN MOUTH OF THE domo'shah's hangar, still moving at a good clip toward the rear wall. The massive bay had already been emptied of mechs and starfighters, but a handful of transports and a pair of larger ek'shah were still organized around them, along with a number of clone soldiers.

They traded rifle fire with the rebels who had survived their entrance clinging to the top and sides of the excavator, flashes of blue reaching back and forth across the space. Gabriel had a vague idea of where he wanted to go, and where it would be if this ship was at all similar to the Ishur, but he turned his head toward Ehri regardless.

"The keepers," he said. "Do you know the quickest way to reach them."

"The keepers?" she asked. "What do you want with them?"

"Reinforcements," he said, nearing the far wall.

"I'm not sure I understand," Ehri said.

"You will. Quickest way?"

"I will lead you."

Gabriel hit the brakes, bringing the excavator to a stop. Ehri was the first out of the hatch, with Donovan close behind. Gabriel joined them a moment later, surprised to find that most of the already present clones had already been dealt with.

"Sergeant Kroeger," Donovan said to an older man who was standing beside the hatch, shooting at anything that moved.

"Colonel," Kroeger replied. "Who's the new guy?"

"Major Gabriel St. Martin," Donovan replied.

Kroeger smiled. "You're St. Martin? It's a pleasure."

"We don't have any time to waste," Gabriel said.

He tried to ignore the burn marks, craters, and blood while taking stock of their forces. Eight soldiers in total, including himself.

"Ehri, lead the way."

She jumped down from the vehicle and the others followed. The cleared the excavator only seconds before a large plasma bolt slammed into the back of it, pushing it forward and into the wall. A second bolt hit it, and then a third. A Dread mech reached the edge of the hangar, shifting to target them.

"In here," Ehri said, opening a hatch ahead of them.

They ducked inside, making it to safety only moments before an unphased plasma bolt struck harmlessly against the lek'shah.

"This way."

Ehri guided them through the corridor, pausing at each intersection.

"I can't believe we made it," Kroeger said quietly. "I should have been dead a dozen times already."

"You and me, both," Donovan said.

"In here," Ehri said, bringing them into one of the domo'shah's many smaller maintenance passages.

"You're familiar with the keepers?" Gabriel asked her.

"Yes. I used to talk to them all the time. They have always abhorred violence, and reject what the Domo'dahms have done."

"Just like you."

Ehri looked back at him, smiling sadly. "Like Juliet St. Martin. I understand that I am not her, Gabriel."

"You do?"

"Yes. I am no peacemaker. I was trained to fight. I was modified to fight. But I do agree with your mother. The path of the pur'dahm is a path to an end to both humans and bek'hai. This way."

They hurried through the rear passages until they reached a dead end. Ehri put her hand on the wall, and a hidden hatch opened, bringing them out right beside a transport beam.

"Most drumhr do not know how to reach the keepers," she said. "They don't know the secret ways. Your mother spent years exploring this ship. She knew them all, and so do I."

They hurried toward the transport beam. A shout at the end of the corridor alerted them that they had been spotted only seconds before the bek'hai at the end of the hallway started shooting, cutting down two of their number before they could react.

It was Ehri who ended the threat, moving with a speed that Gabriel had only seen from Tea'va. She lunged out to the front of the group, shooting at the pur'dahm while moving toward him, rolling to the side, leaping from the side of the wall, and ultimately coming down only a meter away, ready to strike him with the rifle.

She didn't need to. He fell backward, dead.

She scanned the corridor, and then rushed back to them.

"There are two squads of clones headed this way. We must hurry. Take the beam to the bottom."

Gabriel was the first in, lowering his hands and traveling in the beam, stepping out into a nearly identical corridor. Ehri came through a moment later and led them into another hidden passage. They ran along it for four hundred meters or so, and then came out into yet another hallway. This one was dim and damp, and the familiar, biting smell of the legri'shah greeted his eyes

Ehri continued ahead, leading them closer and closer to the creatures. Finally, they reached a round room that was nearly identical to the one on the Ishur. Nine of the keepers were resting there, sitting on the floor, their cloaks hiding their faces. They stirred at the rebels' approach, shifting and looking at them.

"My name is Gabriel St. Martin," Gabriel said. "I carry a message from It'kek." He paused, taking a deep breath. The entire future of both races hinged on what the keeper had told him to say.

"The time has come," Ehri said before he had the chance to. "The walls are crumbling, the cycle completing, the rebellion at hand. Fight, my brothers. Fight, this one time, for the future of our people, the future of the bek'hai. Fight for justice and equality, for the sake of all things that deserve to live. Fight for the legri'shah, but more importantly, let the legri'shah fight for themselves."

Gabriel looked at Ehri, who seemed as surprised as he was at the words. They both turned their attention to the keepers, who were all coming to their feet. One of them lowered his hood, revealing his reptilian face, the splicing of the original bek'hai with the creatures that saved them. The creatures they repaid by slaughtering and imprisoning, just as they had with humankind.

"The keepers of the Ishur are free," Gabriel said. "And the legri'shah will be released as soon as it returns to Earth. But they won't make it without your help."

The keeper continued staring at him. Then he nodded.

All nine of the keepers left the room, headed down separate corridors.

"Well, that was interesting," Kroeger said.

Gabriel looked at the soldier. For a few seconds, nobody moved. Then a loud roar burst from the tunnels, followed by nearly a dozen more.

"I think it's about to get a lot more interesting," Donovan said.

[57]

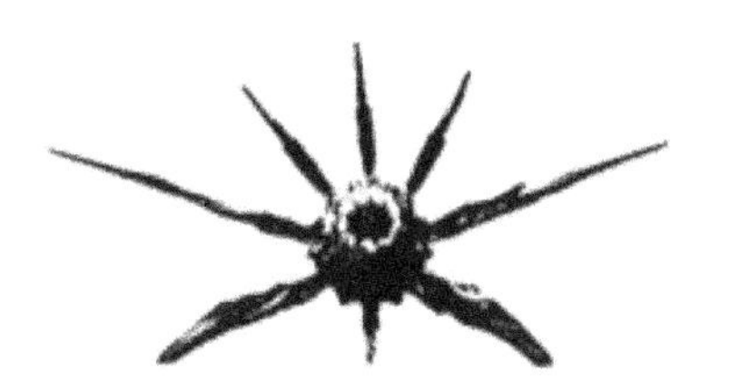

"Hull breach on decks eleven to twenty," General Cave said, his attention split between two tablets. "Inner hatches are sealing, but we lost a little more atmosphere."

Theodore looked to the right of the Ishur, to where small bits of debris were drifting from the latest in a series of wounds inflicted by the Dread fortresses.

"We're running out of time, son," he said under his breath.

They had done their best to stay close to the fortresses, to position themselves away from the main line of domo'shah and present as small a profile as possible. They were still trading smaller battery fire with the enemy ship alongside them, beating at each other with little effect, save for a few lost guns. It had given them a few minutes more than Reza's best projections, but even those few minutes were spent.

Theodore could barely believe the Ishur was still functional. If he could look at the fortress from the enemy's perspective, he would have seen gash after gash, deep holes, torn fins, and a battered warship that had no right to still have power or air.

"They're firing again," Cave said.

O'Dea had replaced Abdullah at the main DSS, giving him a rest from the stress of trying to defend the ship on his own. For a logistics officer, she was a fine shield controller, and she slid her hand deftly across the projection, bringing the power to the proper place on the hull and causing it to phase and pull in a whorl of darkspace. The first enemy plasma bolt struck it. She whipped her hand over, moving the system, cursing as she only caught part of the second beam. The Ishur shook one more time.

"One of the oxygenation modules just went offline," General Cave reported.

"Open a channel to engineering," he said. It was time.

"Done," Cave replied.

"Mr. Mokri, shift all of the power to the modulators. Full shields."

"We'll only have a few minutes like this, sir."

"I'm aware of that, Mr. Mokri. We only have one more shot in us if we don't."

"Yes, sir. It will take me a minute to adjust the settings."

"Then stop talking and get to it, son."

"Yes, sir."

Theodore looked out the viewport again. He could see four of the Dread fortresses to his left, floating almost stationary in space, firing their plasma cannons as soon as they were charged. He looked further out, to where the starfighter dogfights had shifted. He knew why Lieutenant Bale was staying out there, but he didn't know why the Dread were still bothering with them, especially when that side of the fight was still going in the rebel's favor. They could pack it in, head home, and wait for the bigger ships to finish the Ishur off. The glory of the fight, he supposed.

"Theodore, I'm receiving a transmission," General Cave said, his voice surprised. "If I'm reading this thing right, it's coming from Earth."

"Gabriel?" Theodore said. He hadn't given up hope, but the thought of it boosted it to the next level.

"It doesn't look like it." General Cave was staring at the tablet. "Even the translation is gibberish to me."

The Ishur shook again. The projections and terminals on the

bridge all flashed and flickered, and something internal to the ship stopped making noise. Everything returned to normal a moment later.

"Sir," Reza said over the comm. "One of the reactors just went offline. We won't have enough power to hold the shields for long, even if the modulators are stable."

"Damn it," Theodore said. "Alan, pass the transmission to Mr. Mokri. Mr. Mokri, we just received this from Earth, and we have no idea what it is. Can you read it?"

"Sending it to the engineering terminal," General Cave said.

"I've got it, sir," Reza said. "One second. General, where did you get this?"

"It just arrived from Earth. I don't know the source. Why?"

Reza was laughing in the comm. "I don't believe this."

"What is it, Mr. Mokri?"

"Uh. If I have to guess, I think it's the algorithm the Dread ships are using for their improved darkspace shields, but scanning through it. Oh. Wow. Why didn't I think of that?"

"Don't leave me hanging, Mr. Mokri."

"Hold on, General. I'm patching the system with this."

"General, the DSS just went offline," Daphne said.

"Sorry," Reza said. "It has to reinitialize the system."

"The enemy is firing," General Cave said.

Theodore looked up and out at the fortresses. He could see the blue spears at the tips of their design, preparing to lance out at the Ishur, all at once, in one final effort to bring the starship down.

"DSS is still offline," Daphne said.

"Mr. Mokri," Theodore said.

The bolts streaked towards the Ishur, growing brighter as they neared. Reza didn't answer.

"Mr. Mokri," Theodore shouted.

The light from the plasma bolt was blinding, as it was aimed directly at the bridge. Theodore closed his eyes in anticipation, all sense of time and space fading, replacing with a field of white nothingness that he could have easily mistaken for the afterlife. It was all calm and peaceful and silent. Maybe Juliet was here?

It ended as quickly as it had come. The sound of breathing, of shouting, of beeping and pulsing and throbbing came back in a rush of sound. He opened his eyes.

They were still alive.

"You wanted a miracle, General?" Reza said. "I think you have it. Oh. Uh. Hmm. It looks like there's more in this transmission than shield upgrades."

[58]

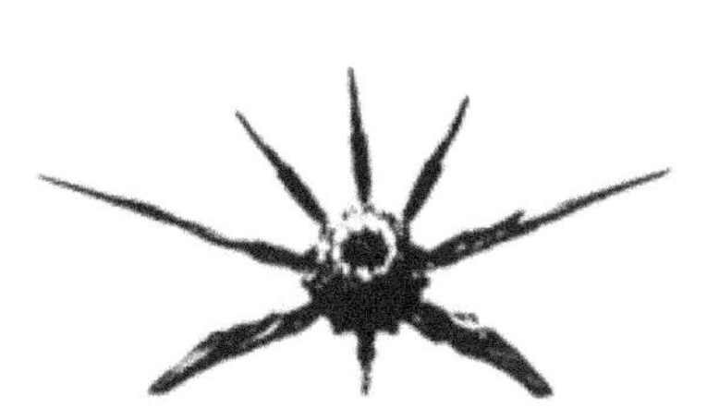

THE CORRIDORS OF THE DREAD CAPITAL SHIP TURNED TO CHAOS within minutes, as after hundreds of years of captivity, the legri'shah were set free.

Gabriel couldn't see the creatures from his place within the maintenance passages, but he could hear them, a constant barrage of roars and chirps that echoed across the decks. He didn't understand at first how the large animals could move from their pens to the other decks since the transports beams were too small to carry them. El'kek, the keeper who had risen first, explained while they made their way toward the bridge.

"The domo'shah were not always prisons to the legri'shah," he said. "There are tunnels for them, tunnels that can take them almost anywhere in the ship. Tunnels that haven't been used for hundreds of cycles. You and I can't travel them; they are too steep and smooth and narrow. But the legri'shah can."

"Why were the legri'shah imprisoned?" he asked.

"To hide them away from the new drumhr. Domo'dahm Pir'el decided long ago that we should forget our past to create a new future."

Gabriel couldn't keep himself from snorting. "Huh. Our human leaders were trying to do the same thing."

"Be grateful they did not."

"Are we there yet?" Kroeger said. He was bringing up the rear and growing impatient.

"We are almost there," Ehri replied. "Are you prepared?"

"Locked and loaded."

She led them out of the maintenance hatch once more, coming out near a transport beam. "Up sixty-one decks," she said to them before stepping in.

Gabriel trailed close behind her, with Donovan, Kroeger, El'kek, and the two soldiers whose names he didn't know bringing up the rear. He raised his hands to go up, subconsciously counting decks, and then stepped out of the beam.

Ehri was standing in front of him, two dead clones at her feet.

"This deck is heavily defended," she said.

"Will the Domo'dahm be on the bridge?" Gabriel asked.

"It is not likely. He will remain in his quarters below."

"It is difficult for him to travel through the ship," El'kek said. "He is an original bek'hai. His visage is also banished from sight."

"What?" Kroeger said. "The leader of your race can't go out in public?"

"Yes."

"Because of his ugly mug?" He laughed.

"Keep it quiet, Sergeant," Donovan said.

Kroeger stopped laughing. They moved the corner of the hallway and checked the intersection.

"I don't hear any of the legri'shah," Gabriel said.

"They will find their way out," El'kek replied. "My brothers will keep them from attacking your brethren."

They headed down the corridor, reaching one of the many circular hubs that composed the layout of the decks. A squad of clone soldiers was moving through it, headed for the transport beam in a hurry, and as a result coming right toward them.

"Take them out," Donovan said, raising his rifle.

The clones reacted with surprise, bringing their weapons up. Gabriel brought his Dread rifle to bear and fired, adding to the sudden barrage from his unit. The clones were overwhelmed, and they stepped over them to continue on.

"That's what I'm talking about," Kroeger said.

Gabriel glanced over at the man, disgusted. He was enjoying the violence way too much. Kroeger either didn't notice the look or ignored it.

They kept going, making a quarter-circle in the hub before heading down another corridor. They turned one more corner and entered an area that was familiar to Gabriel. The layout seemed to be identical to the Ishur, and he knew exactly where he was.

They were almost there.

He had expected the resistance to get heavier the closer they came to the bridge. Instead, the opposite soon became true, as all of the soldiers on the deck were abandoning the control center of the ship and heading to the lower decks in an effort to defend against the rampaging legri'shah.

Ehri brought them to a pause a few hundred meters from the bridge, motioning for them to draw near.

"This is a trap," she said. "Designed to cause us to lower our guard. Do not be fooled."

"How do you know?" Gabriel asked.

"I understand Rorn'el, and how he thinks," she replied. "Your mother knew him very well. He wants you to believe the bridge is undefended. This is false."

"What kind of shit are we about to step in?" Kroeger asked.

"Hunters of the Third and Fourth Cell," Ehri replied. "High-ranking pur'dahm warriors. Four of them at least, although it is hard to say how many Rorn'el may have called to his side to protect him. This type of chaos may give other pur'dahm ideas on removing him from power."

"They would turn on one another in the middle of a battle?" Gabriel asked.

"If they believed it would benefit them, yes."

"The madness of our kind," El'kek said.

"They will be fast," Ehri said. "As fast as I can be. Stay together, cover one another. I will do my best to stop them."

"Wait a second," Gabriel said. "I need you alive."

"Then I will have to stay alive. There is no other choice, Gabriel."

Gabriel nodded. "Okay. I'm ready. Let's stick together, keep a clear line of fire. El'kek, you may want to stay back."

"No," the keeper replied.

Gabriel didn't argue. "Let's go."

They made their way across the distance to the bridge, pausing to peer inside. The capital ship's command center was larger than the Ishur's, with more stations circling a much higher central dais. The dais was unoccupied. The rest of the bridge appeared to be the same.

"Are you sure about this?" Gabriel whispered.

"Yes," Ehri replied. "I will go in first. Cover me."

Gabriel opened his mouth to argue, but Ehri was already running toward the bridge.

"Shit," he said, getting his rifle up and pointed at her back. The others did the same.

She dove as she passed the threshold, coming in low, somersaulting and getting to her feet. Two plasma bolts burst past where she should have been from either side, hitting nothing but air.

Gabriel caught sight of a dark shape heading for her and fired, sending a bolt toward it. The Dread Hunter shifted slightly, letting the bolt go by, barely breaking his stride. Two more of the Hunters revealed themselves, facing Gabriel and the others, rifles in hand.

Plasma bolts filled the corridor, forcing the Hunters to duck back. Gabriel caught a glimpse of Ehri in the center of it all, ducking beneath an attack by one of the bek'hai, who was using some kind of blade to strike at her. She lashed out with a foot, catching him in the back of the knee and bringing him off-balance. Instead of following up the attack, she skipped away, narrowly avoiding another of the weapons.

"What are we doing out here?" Kroeger said, starting to advance on the room.

They kept a steady stream of plasma targeting the two Hunters near the entrance, while also keeping an eye on the two attacking Ehri. She was holding her own, keeping them away, but for how long?

They took a few more steps forward. The Hunters near the entrance rolled across the hallway, firing as they passed. Gabriel heard a shout and saw one of the soldiers fall. He heard Donovan curse as well, and saw a burn mark and blood spreading from his shoulder.

"Druk'dahm," El'kek said, grabbing his robe and shedding it. He was nude beneath, muscular, and at the same time lacking in genitalia. A short stub of a tail protruded from the small of his back.

He bared his teeth and rushed toward the bridge. One of the Hunters emerged to shoot at him, but he batted the rifle away and barreled into the pur'dahm, knocking him back.

Gabriel kept advancing, keeping his focus on the Dread attacking Ehri. She avoided a strike from one of the Hunters and then shouted in pain as the blade of the second caught her arm. She threw herself away from them, gaining a little distance.

The Hunter still near the entrance took advantage of the opportunity, leaping at her from behind. He was fast, so fast. Gabriel shifted his rifle almost without thinking, squeezing the trigger and sending three bolts at Dread. The first two went wide, but the third hit him square in the side and cost him his momentum. He stumbled instead of striking, and Ehri bounced out of the way of his corpse as he fell to the floor.

"Nice shot," Kroeger said, reaching Gabriel. He crossed the corridor, taking aim at the Hunter engaged with El'kek. "That's it. Keep him steady. No sudden moves."

Gabriel realized just in time what the man intended. He lunged forward, bringing his rifle down on top of Kroeger's and disrupting his aim. Kroeger's bolt went wide, hitting the wall instead of blasting through the back of El'kek's head and into the Dread Hunter.

"What the hell are you doing?" Gabriel said. "He's on our side."

"Are you kidding me?" Kroeger shouted back, pulling himself

free. "I've got a shot to kill that bastard I'm taking it, even if I have to kill that other dragon man son of a bitch with him."

"You're out of your damn mind."

"Yeah, right. Maybe I'm the only one who's sane."

Kroeger shoved Gabriel aside, bringing his rifle up again.

"Sergeant," Donovan shouted. His arm was dark with blood, and he looked pale.

Kroeger looked at him, his eyes wild. "Sorry, Major. I guess I'm the real giant now."

He looked back at El'kek and the Dread, ready to pull the trigger once more.

A sharp blade sank into his arm, cutting it off at the elbow, causing the rifle to fall from his grip and clatter to the floor. Kroeger shouted in pain, his cry cut off as the blade came back around and through his neck, removing his head.

The Hunter scowled at them before rushing toward Gabriel. He tried to get his weapon up to defend himself, but there was no time. He shifted his grip, barely getting it positioned to block the Hunter's blade, leaving their faces only centimeters apart.

Then he felt a rush of heat, heard a soft thud, and saw the Dread's expression change. A second thud followed. Then a third. The pressure against him vanished as the pur'dahm collapsed.

Donovan could barely lift the rifle with his one good hand, and he let it fall as he leaned against the wall to keep himself upright.

Gabriel stepped over the Dread, taking the last few steps onto the bridge. Ehri was leaning against one of the terminals, her arm bleeding, but no longer under attack. El'kek was standing over the final Hunter, breathing raggedly, looking down at his victim with an expression of sadness unlike anything Gabriel had ever seen.

"It's over then?" Donovan asked.

Gabriel turned back to the soldier, getting himself under his good arm and helping him up. "How are you feeling?"

"I don't know yet. It's numb, and I'm cold."

That didn't sound good.

"Ehri, we need to send a message fleet-wide. Can you do that?"

"Yes," she replied, moving across the bridge to another terminal.

Gabriel took two steps toward her when he heard footsteps coming up from behind them. He tried to turn, but holding Donovan was limiting his movement.

El'kek broke from his mourning, whipping around and positioning himself in front of the bridge. By the time Gabriel could see, the keeper had come up short and was staring at another Juliet clone.

"Colonel Peters," she said.

"Orli?" Donovan replied. "It's okay; she's with us."

El'kek moved aside.

"What are you doing here? I thought you were dead?"

"No. I escaped the destruction of my mech. I snuck behind the bek'hai infantry line and stole a transport and brought it here. Colonel, we have to go. The Domo'dahm is on his way here with too many Hunters for us to fight."

"Can you help keep Colonel Peters upright?" Gabriel asked, handing him over to Orli. "Ehri, do you have it?"

"One moment, Gabriel."

"Gabriel?" Orli said, her expression changing. Gabriel would have been taken back by it, but he had seen it before in Zoelle.

"I know," he replied. "Not now. I don't know how much longer the Ishur will last."

"The Ishur?" Orli said. "Oh. Don't worry, Gabriel. Your father should be safe for now. I've already taken care of that."

[59]

"HOW ARE WE DOING, MR. MOKRI?" THEODORE ASKED.

"Uh. Shields are holding, sir. Modulators are stable. Power is going to be a problem though, sir, if we have to take much more of this. With one of the reactors down, we can't take this pounding forever."

Theodore smiled, looking out at the Dread fortresses arranged ahead of them. The reaction from the enemy ships had been almost comical when they realized the humans had miraculously managed to provide a vast upgrade to their defenses.

As Reza had explained in the first minute following the shift, it all came down to math.

"How much longer do we have?" Theodore asked.

"I'm shutting down some non-essential systems. Five minutes?"

"Not a lot of time. What about our other upgrade."

"Almost done, sir."

Theodore's comfort faded. Where was Gabriel anyway? They had managed to outlast their predicted demise by nearly thirty minutes, but there was no word from him. Had he failed in his mission? Had the Magellan even made it to the ground?

If Gabriel was dead, there was only one thing left to do.

"I'm sorry, Mr. It'kek," Theodore said, looking over at the keeper on the bridge. "We can't afford to wait any longer."

The keeper's expression was dour, but he nodded. "I understand."

"Mr. Mokri, tell me as soon as the update is complete."

"Oh. Uh. We just finished replacing the last of the conduits, sir."

Theodore looked down at his tablet, switching the screen to the plasma cannon fire control.

"Colonel Ames, bring us toward the fortress furthest to port."

"Yes, sir," Ames replied.

"Uh, sir," Reza said. "We'll only have enough power for five shots, and the shields will go down for a few seconds after you fire. I thought you might want to know that."

"Duly noted, Mr. Mokri."

The Ishur began to vibrate, the damage it had taken causing it to shudder from the thrust. The Dread ships in front of them stood their ground, still unsure of what he was up to. They fired their plasma cannons again, sending heavy bolts into the darkspace shields where they were absorbed.

"Firing," Theodore announced, pressing down on his tablet. The Ishur shuddered even more as power was diverted to the main plasma cannon.

"Thrusters are offline," General Cave said. "Life support offline. Anti-gravity offline on half the decks. I don't know what this one means. I think it's the transport beams? It's down, too."

The plasma cannon was sucking all of their power in. A moment later, it spit that power back out.

A stream of blue plasma lanced across space, pouring into the center of the fortress opposite them. For an instant, a black whorl of darkspace blocked the stream, but it was too small to collect the entire blast. It shattered as the plasma burned the area around it, sinking through the lek'shah, passing into the domo'shah, continuing onward until it appeared out the other side, like a giant azure lance.

It vanished a moment later. The Dread ship was still at first, and then slowly began to break apart, the debris spreading from the center.

"Direct hit," General Cave said.

"Get us on the next one, Colonel," Theodore said.

They would only get one surprise attack, and the Dread ships were already breaking formation, spreading out to avoid another bolt. They returned fire with secondary batteries, which dug into the sides of the Ishur while the reactor was still recovering.

"Thrusters online. Life support online. Anti-gravity still down."

"We don't need gravity," Theodore said. "Colonel Ames, get us a better angle."

"Yes, sir."

The Ishur started moving again, changing direction to get a better vector on the Dread ships. They were still firing their secondary batteries, but the attack was being absorbed once more.

"They're decimating our power supply, General," Reza said over the comm. "You need to back away."

Theodore didn't give it much thought. "No. This is our last stand. Let's make it count. Red One, you still out there?"

"I'm here, sir," Lieutenant Bale replied.

"Take what you have left and harass those batteries. Get them shooting at something else."

"Yes, sir."

Theodore could see the remaining fighters break off from their diminished dogfights and race toward the Dread fortresses. At the same time, he kept an eye on his terminal, and on the ship ahead of them.

"Three degrees starboard, lift the nose four degrees, Colonel."

"Yes, sir."

The Ishur shifted in space, getting into position to fire. Theodore held his finger over the trigger.

A soft wash of static burst over the comm, followed by a sharp, shrill tone.

"Bek'hai cruhr dur heil," a familiar voice said. "Un'hai. Lor'hai.

Legri'hai." It paused a moment, and a new voice echoed across the bridge.

"The time has come," Gabriel said. "The end of the pur'dahm is here. My name is Gabriel St. Martin. My father is Theodore St. Martin. My mother was Juliet St. Martin. We are here, and we're fighting to be free. The keepers, the un'hai, the legri'shah, and the humans. The drumhr are leading you to the end. Join us, and help us bring a new beginning. Soldiers, scientists, cleaners, caretakers. You knew Juliet St. Martin. You knew what she believed in. You have the power to see that happen, right now. Preserve the true bek'hai, preserve your identity, save your future. Fight back against the pur'dahm, as the keepers are fighting back. Set the legri'shah free. Set yourselves free."

The comm fell silent again. Theodore's heart was racing, his eyes tearing from the well of pride and thankfulness that Gabriel was still alive.

"My name is El'kek," a new voice said. "I am a keeper on the Domo'dahm's domo'shah. Our legri'shah are free. We are free."

Theodore looked over at It'kek, whose teeth were bared in a smile. He returned his attention to the Dread fortress ahead of them. He kept his finger over the trigger of the plasma cannon while it continued to fire at them. Had they been right about the Juliet clones? Would this really work? He couldn't wait forever to shoot.

They drew within a thousand kilometers. The fortress continued to shoot, but Theodore noticed that the volume was lessening, the batteries falling silent one by one. Something was happening out there, wasn't it?

"There is no reason for war between the bek'hai and the humans," he heard Gabriel saying. "Except that the Domo'dahm wishes it. Why choose violence over peace?"

"Ishur, this is Dahm Pirelle of the domo'shah Ishkore," a voice said, cutting in over Gabriel. "General St. Martin, please respond."

Theodore was surprised by the interruption. Another Juliet? "Alan, patch us in."

"On it, Teddy," General Cave replied. "Go ahead."

"This is General St. Martin. We hear you, Ishkore. What is your status?"

"Theodore, the uprising has begun. We are in control of the bridge, and the entire ship will be ours soon."

"Roger, Ishkore," Theodore replied. "Do you know about the others?"

"Yes. They too are rebelling. They too desire peace. All of the lor'hai desire peace. It is within their nature. It is the gift I gave to them. The gift that was always meant to undo them, though the Domo'dahm never understood it well enough to realize."

It took Theodore a moment to remember that this clone also believed she was Juliet St. Martin. It was tough for him to keep being reminded of her, and at the same time, he was proud of what she had done for them.

"Well, Teddy," General Cave said, turning back to look at him. "It looks like we might just win this thing after all. I'm sorry I ever doubted you."

"Apology accepted," Theodore replied.

He was just happy he never stopped believing.

[60]

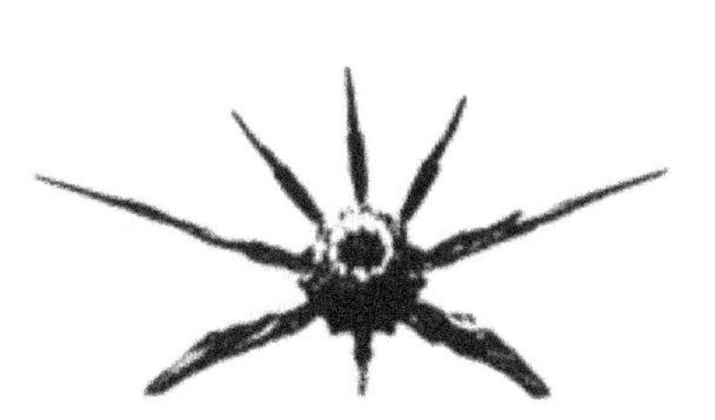

DOMO'DAHM RORN'EL GRABBED HIS MASK, SLIDING IT OVER HIS face and hissing at the discomfort. It was one thing to wear the apparatus to pass from his private chambers to the throne room. It was another to have to travel the halls of the Dahm'shah in it.

As if he had a choice.

It was all falling apart. Everything he had worked to build since he had become Domo'dahm was coming undone. The humans had made it into the ship. They had somehow freed the legri'shah, and now the creatures were running amok within, killing every bek'hai they saw who wasn't a keeper.

It was Juliet St. Martin who had done it. His Juliet, who he had so adored. A woman of peace and God, who had betrayed his trust by befriending those who were beneath him. He had spent so much time and energy deflecting attacks from his pur'dahm; he had never seen or suspected she would be capable of such a thing.

He opened the door to his chamber, stepping out into the hallway. He could hear the cries of the legri'shah echoing throughout the ship, and it made him want to weep. He was trying to preserve their race. Their purity. Their history. As best he could with the limited resources he was given. Humans were inferior and so unsuitable as splices, yet he had done what he could to make it work. It wasn't fair for it to end like this.

"Domo'dahm," Orish'ek said, approaching him.

He was wearing full battle armor, carrying both a rifle and a lek'-sai. Ten members of the Second Cell were with him, ready to protect their leader.

"Orish'ek. We go to the bridge. We can destroy the rebellion from orbit."

"Yes, Domo'dahm."

He led them from his chamber, making sure to keep himself postured so they would never guess what he looked like beneath his robes.

They were near the transport beam when a sharp roar brought them to a stop. One of the legri'shah turned the corner a moment later, pausing for a moment as it spied them. Then it hissed and charged, half-running, half-slithering along the corridor toward them, its bulk filling the space. Rorn'el looked at the beam up ahead, knowing it was too far to run.

The Hunters didn't flinch. They dropped their rifles, raising their lek'sai and charging back at the creature, shouting in challenging response to its growls. All except Orish'ek.

"This way, Domo'dahm," he said.

Rorn'el hesitated, watching as the Hunters were attacked. The legri'shah's head dipped down, mouth open, teeth reaching for one of them. He stepped aside, swinging his lek'sai, cutting into the legri'shah's face. The creature hissed and snapped, catching the Hunter's leg and biting it off, its teeth passing easily through the lek'shah.

"Domo'dahm, we must hurry," Orish'ek said.

Rorn'el nodded and followed. He could hear the Hunter's screams as they battled the creature. Right before he stepped into the beam, he heard the legri'shah cry out in a high-pitched wail of defeat.

Then he was into the beam. He came out in the hub nearest the bridge, with Orish'ek ahead of him. There were no soldiers left here. No legri'shah either. He took two steps, and then paused as a voice surrounded him. Ehri dur Tuhrik, followed by a human voice.

He hissed as the human spoke of freedom as if he were some manner of tyrant. He hissed as the human used the words he had heard Tuhrik speak before he had abandoned the pur'dahm cells.

"They must be on the bridge," Orish'ek said. "Transmitting to the other domo'shah."

"I will kill them myself," Rorn'el replied.

"No, Domo'dahm," Orish'ek said. "I will take care of it." The pur'dahm lifted his rifle in Rorn'el's direction. "You have failed us."

Rorn'el eyed the weapon, tensing. "And you also will betray me, Orish'ek?"

"I have done my duty, and watched you drive us to ruin. I will save the pur'dahm."

"You will not."

Orish'ek pulled the trigger. Rorn'el slipped to the side, the plasma bolt going wide. The shocked pur'dahm tried to back away, to shoot again. Rorn'el tore off his mask and dropped his robes, revealing his bek'hai form.

"You have seen me Orish'ek," he said. "Now you have to die."

Orish'ek dropped the rifle and pulled his lek'sai, barely getting it up in time to block Rorn'el's claws.

"I am Domo'dahm for a reason Orish'ek. Not because I am soft. Because I am strong."

He stayed on the traitor, striking at Orish'ek's face, at his chest, at his shoulders. The pur'dahm didn't try to block every attack, thinking the lek'shah would protect him.

Thinking wrong.

Rorn'el's nails sank through the material. He was spliced from the legri'shah, and his claws bore the same properties as the creatures'. They were in phase with the armor, and they dug into it without resistance, sinking into Orish'ek's flesh, cutting deep enough to force him to drop his weapon.

"Domo'dahm, please," Orish'ek said, standing unarmed in front of him.

"You beg?" Rorn'el said. "You are no pur'dahm. You are barely a drumhr. More like a druk'shur."

Rorn'el kicked him, the claws of his feet sinking deeply into his chest. He held him for a moment with powerful legs before throwing him back into the transport beam.

He hissed one last time, leaving his robes and mask behind while he continued on to the bridge.

It was empty when he arrived, and while the sight of the dead humans pleased him, the dead Hunters angered him more. They had failed him, as all of his pur'dahm were failing him.

He entered the bridge, closing and locking the hatch behind him. The humans were gone, likely trying to escape before he arrived, with Ehri dur Tuhrik leading them through the ship. It was well. They wouldn't be able to clear the area before he bombarded it from space.

He climbed the command dais, sitting and activating the terminal, feeling powerful in his freedom. He had spent too long covered from head to toe.

He used sharp, blood-crusted claws to activate the reactors, running quickly through the launch sequence. It was challenging to fly a domo'shah without help, but he was up to the task. What else could he do?

Three minutes later, the massive fortress began to rise. It shook the ground beneath it, knocking down loose structures, and dislodging tons of earth that had shifted over the ship through the years. He rotated the ship as it climbed so that he was able to look down on the battlefield. There was smoke and fire everywhere. The wreckage of gur'sha and gel'shah, and plenty of corpses. And there was the human starship, its outer shell in ruins, dead and silent nearby.

That would be his target. While all the land around it would burn regardless, he would get such satisfaction, such pleasure from finally destroying the one ship that got away. The one ship that allowed all of this to happen. It wasn't too late to start again. There were outposts scattered across the planet, where the clones and the drumhr wouldn't know what was happening here. The legri'shah might be lost, but they wouldn't need them anymore.

The Dahm'shah continued to climb, rising quickly, reaching the atmosphere and then punching through. He noticed his sensors now, and the domo'shah returning to the planet. Were they still his?

A symbol appeared on his terminal. A hail from one of his ships, probably seeking orders.

"Speak," he said, answering it.

"Hello. My name is General Theodore St. Martin. I'd like to speak to a Domo'dahm Rorn'el?"

Rorn'el shuddered at the human voice, tempted to close the channel immediately. He hissed softly and then replied.

"I am Domo'dahm Rorn'el," he said, as confidently as he could.

"I'd say it's a pleasure, Rorn'el, but it isn't," Theodore said. "You took my planet, and I've never appreciated that much. My wife Juliet was a peaceful, gentle soul. I believe you knew her? I want to spread your ashes across the universe, but she would want me to give you a chance to live. So, that's what I'm gonna do. One chance, Rorn'el. What do you say?"

Rorn'el could barely contain his anger.

It was gone. All gone. The bek'hai race would die, and he would be forgotten. Or, if he were remembered, it would be as the Domo'-dahm who killed them.

All because of Juliet St. Martin.

He wasn't going to die without destroying the one that got away. He owed himself that honor at least.

He checked his terminal, noting his position. He found the human starship sitting on the planet below and moved into the weapons systems. He shifted his claws, activating the main plasma cannon.

"I'll take that as a no," Theodore said.

Rorn'el looked up and out the viewport. Six domo'shah were arranged ahead of him, dropping into his field of view. The tips of each were glowing blue, indicating that their plasma cannons were about to fire.

He checked his own. It was still charging. Would there be enough time?

The domo'shah fired, six beams converging on one point near the center of the ship, where the reactors sat. He had never upgraded his shields with the human technology. He had never thought he would need it, and didn't want to soil his systems with their designs.

The beams hit the ship, causing it to shudder.

The terminal indicated the cannon was ready to fire.

His claw never came down on it.

The bridge shook violently, knocking him to the ground. He tried to get back up, but it continued shaking as the energy of the plasma drove through the structure. The viewport cracked and splintered, the entire frame breaking apart. Oxygen began to spill out, and the temperature dropped.

"That was for the human race, you bastard," he heard Theodore St. Martin say.

Then the bridge vanished around him, the pieces blowing out and into space.

Then he died.

[61]

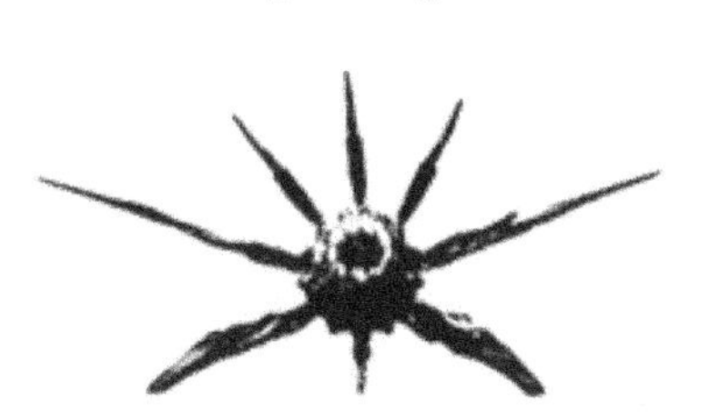

THE DREAD TRANSPORT LANDED BESIDE THE MAGELLAN, AND Gabriel jumped out of it as soon as the hatch finished opening. He turned and looked up at the sky, ignoring Ehri, Orli, El'kek, and Donovan as they joined him.

The Dread fortresses were all visible in the space above the city, but none were more visible than the Dahm'shah. Or at least, what was left of it.

Chunks of material sank into the atmosphere. The lek'shah, no longer given an electrical current, burned the same as any other part, all of it creating a spectacle of light in the sky that reminded him of streams he had seen, where parties on Earth ended in fireworks. He felt the moisture in his eyes at the sight.

"Gabriel."

He turned, smiling as Miranda ran toward him. He opened his arms for her, catching her in a solid embrace, his eyes landing on the others trailing behind her. Colonel Choi, Guy and Sarah Larone, and Wallace, who barked and circled them, tail wagging.

"We did it," Miranda said. "I can't believe we did it."

"Me neither," he replied, eyes streaming with tears. "I always believed, but I never thought it would actually happen."

"Look," Guy said, pointing up.

A few smaller shapes had broken through the atmosphere, past the burning debris. They dove toward the city, leveling out and streaking across the sky. Starfighters of both human and bek'hai design. Gabriel raised his hand to them, waving at them as they passed overhead and circled back.

A sharp hiss caused them all to freeze. A shape formed to their left, obscured by the smoldering wreckage of a Dread mech. A large, reptilian head appeared a moment later, followed by a huge body.

The legri'shah approached them slowly, while Wallace ran to the front of the group, barking at it.

"Wallace," Gabriel said, reaching for the dog.

"Do not fear," El'kek said, moving calmly to the dog's side.

He put a hand on Wallace's head, and he quieted immediately. Then he said something to the legri'shah in bek'hai, and the creature lowered itself until it was flat on the ground.

"There has been enough killing today. Enough for many lifetimes."

Gabriel couldn't argue with that. He took Miranda by the hand, leading her over to where Donovan was standing. His arm was dead at his side, but he would survive.

"Colonel Peters," Gabriel said.

"Major St. Martin," Donovan replied, smiling.

Gabriel moved forward, embracing him for a moment before backing away. "This is my fiancee, Miranda."

"A pleasure," Donovan said. "A real pleasure, just to have something so normal after all of this."

Miranda hugged him, careful of his arm. "It's an honor, Colonel."

"So," Guy said. "What happens now?"

"Peace," Ehri replied. "Between the humans and the bek'hai, at least."

"It will take some time to restore order," Donovan said. "Some of us have been living in chaos for too long just to give it up."

"It will take time," Gabriel agreed. "But we have time, now. We have all the time in the world." He looked over at Ehri, and then at Orli. "What will you do?"

The two Juliet clones glanced at one another.

"I believe Juliet St. Martin would have wanted us to spread the news of peace," Orli said.

"I agree," Ehri said. "We will help return order to this world, as emissaries for both the Earth Alliance and the bek'hai."

"You'll do her proud," Gabriel said. "Her and Theodore."

He moved away from them, back to Colonel Choi, giving her a hug before first embracing Sarah, and then shaking hands with Guy.

"You both did a fine job," he said. "I'm even starting to like you."

Guy laughed. "Likewise."

Gabriel looked back at the sky. The domo'shah were growing larger above them. The one in the lead was in bad shape. Half its fins were missing, the profile battered and ragged.

"The Ishur," Ehri said. "Your father."

"He'll be happy to see the Magellan's still in one piece," Miranda said.

"He'll be happier to see Gabriel's still in one piece," Donovan said, laughing.

"He always said he refused to die until we had our planet back," Gabriel said. "But I hope he' ll stick around a little bit longer."

"He will," Miranda replied. "He won't want to miss the party."

They watched as the Ishur descended, coming to rest in the crater the Dahm'shah had left only minutes earlier. As it settled to the Earth, a new sound began to echo across the landscape. It was like a rumble, but higher in pitch.

"What is that?" Donovan asked.

Ehri titled her head, listening, and then turned toward them. "Cheering," she said with a smile. "The soldiers in the city are cheering. Humans and clones."

"It's the best sound I've ever heard," Donovan said.

"Me, too," Gabriel agreed.

He closed his eyes, his hand falling to the crucifix around his neck. He clutched it tightly, turning his thoughts to his mother.

"Thank you," he said softly. "Thank you."

THE END.

THANK YOU FOR READING REBELLION!

Thank you so much for reading Rebellion.

If you enjoyed this series and want to help support these books, please, please, please consider leaving a review and letting me and others know how much you enjoyed it. A star rating and a sentence is all it takes.

Think I'm an author worth following? I have a mailing list. New releases, sales, the occasional giveaway, and a free, exclusive short story for signing up. No spam guarantee. You can join here at mrforbes.com/mailinglist.

Looking for more highly-rated sci-fi? If you liked Rebellion, you might like War Eternal (mrforbes.com/starshipeternal) or Forgotten Colony (mrforbes.com/deliverance). Or you can check out my complete backlist at mrforbes.com/books or flip to the next section for a smaller sampling.

Whatever path you choose, there's a good chance you'll find something else in there to enjoy.

Thank you again!

Cheers,

Michael.

OTHER BOOKS BY M.R FORBES

Browse my backlist:
mrforbes.com/books

Deliverance (Forgotten Colony)
mrforbes.com/deliverance

The war is over. Earth is lost. Running is the only option.

It may already be too late.

Caleb is a former Marine Raider and commander of the Vultures, a search and rescue team that's spent the last two years pulling high-value targets out of alien-ravaged cities and shipping them off-world.

When his new orders call for him to join forty-thousand survivors aboard the last starship out, he thinks his days of fighting are over. The Deliverance represents a fresh start and a chance to leave the war behind for good.

Except the war won't be as easy to escape as he thought.

And the colony will need a man like Caleb more than he ever imagined...

Forgotten (The Forgotten)

mrforbes.com/forgotten

Some things are better off FORGOTTEN.

Sheriff Hayden Duke was born on the Pilgrim, and he expects to die on the Pilgrim, like his father, and his father before him.

That's the way things are on a generation starship centuries from home. He's never questioned it. Never thought about it. And why bother? Access points to the ship's controls are sealed, the systems that guide her automated and out of reach. It isn't perfect, but he has all he needs to be content.

Until a malfunction forces his Engineer wife to the edge of the habitable zone to inspect the damage.

Until she contacts him, breathless and terrified, to tell him she found a body, and it doesn't belong to anyone on board.

Until he arrives at the scene and discovers both his wife and the body are gone.

The only clue? A bloody handprint beneath a hatch that hasn't opened in hundreds of years.

Until now.

Starship Eternal (War Eternal)

mrforbes.com/starshipeternal

They are coming. Find the Goliath or humankind will be destroyed.

Those chilling words are the first thing Space Marine starfighter pilot Mitchell "Ares" Williams hears, waking in a hospital after an ambush nearly ends his life. He tries to ignore them, convincing himself the voice in his head is a side-effect of his injuries.

It isn't.

The warning is only the beginning. A glimpse into a struggle against an enemy older than time.

An enemy that's very real and much closer than he ever imagined.

An enemy that will do whatever it takes to keep him from finding humankind's first starship, lost during its inaugural voyage and long believed destroyed. A starship that may be the key to defeating them once and for all.

Narrowly escaping capture, Mitchell lands in the company of the Riggers: a ragtag crew of black-ops commandos who patrol the outer reaches of the galaxy. Guided by a captain with a reputation for murder, they're dangerous, immoral, and possibly insane.

They may also be humanity's last hope for survival in a war that has raged beyond eternity.

Hell's Rejects (Chaos of the Covenant)

mrforbes.com/hellsrejects

The most powerful starships ever constructed are gone. Thousands are dead. A fleet is in ruins. The attackers are unknown. The orders are clear: *Recover the ships. Bury the bastards who stole them.*

Lieutenant Abigail Cage never expected to find herself in Hell. As a Highly Specialized Operational Combatant, she was one of the most respected soldiers in the military. Now she's doing hard labor on the most miserable planet in the universe.

Not for long.

The Earth Republic is looking for the most dangerous individuals it can control. The best of the worst, and Abbey happens to be one of them. The deal is simple: *Bring back the starships, earn your freedom. Try to run, you die.* It's a suicide mission, but she has nothing to lose.

The only problem? There's a new threat in the galaxy. One with a power unlike anything anyone has ever seen. One that's been waiting for this moment for a very, very, long time. And they want Abbey, too.

Be careful what you wish for.

They say Hell hath no fury like a woman scorned. They have no idea.

ABOUT THE AUTHOR

M.R. Forbes is the creator of a growing catalog of science fiction and fantasy titles. He lives in the pacific northwest with his family, including a cat who thinks she's a dog, and a dog who thinks she's a cat. He eats too many donuts, and he's always happy to hear from readers.

To learn more about M.R. Forbes or just say hello:

Visit my website:
mrforbes.com

Send me an e-mail:
michael@mrforbes.com

Check out my Facebook page:
facebook.com/mrforbes.author

Chat with me on Facebook Messenger:
https://m.me/mrforbes.author

CPSIA information can be obtained
at www.ICGtesting.com
Printed in the USA
LVHW090409020920
664817LV00011B/272